D1577132

Ruth Rendell

INSPECTOR WEXFORD

Ruth Rendell

INSPECTOR WEXFORD

The Speaker of Mandarin

An Unkindness of Ravens

The Veiled One

CRESSET EDITIONS

This edition first published by Cresset Editions in 1995
an imprint of the Random House Group
20 Vauxhall Bridge Road
London SW1V 2SA

Copyright © Kingsmarkham Enterprises Ltd 1995

The right of Ruth Rendell to be identified as the author of this
book has been asserted by her in accordance with the Copyright,
Designs and Patents Act 1988.

All rights reserved. No part of the publication may be
reproduced, stored in a retrieval system or transmitted in any
form or by any means, electronic, mechanical, photocopying,
recording or otherwise, without the prior permission of the
copyright owner.

The Speaker of Mandarin copyright © Kingsmarkham Enterprises Ltd 1983
An Unkindness of Ravens copyright © Kingsmarkham Enterprises Ltd 1985
The Veiled One copyright © Kingsmarkham Enterprises 1988

First published by Hutchinson Ltd

ISBN 07126 866 57

Papers used by Random House UK Ltd are natural, recyclable
products made from wood grown in sustainable forests. The
manufacturing processes conform to the environmental regulations
of the country of origin.

Jacket illustration by Tony Nutley

Printed and bound in Great Britain by
Mackays of Chatham PLC, Chatham, Kent

CONTENTS

The Speaker of
Mandarin

For Don

Author's Note

For the transcribing of Chinese words and Chinese proper names into English I have used both the Wade-Giles and the Pinyin systems. While Pinyin is the officially endorsed system in the People's Republic, Wade-Giles, which was evolved in the nineteenth century, remains more familiar to Western readers. So I have used each where I felt it to be more appropriate and acceptable; e.g. the modern Pinyin for Lu Xing She, the Chinese International Travel Service, but Ching rather than Xing for the name of the last Imperial Dynasty, and I have used Mao Tse Tung in preference to the Pinyin Mao Zedong.

Acknowledgement

The poem quoted on p. 448, 'To Wang Lun' by Li Po, the poem quoted on pp. 484 and 493-94, 'Drinking Song' by Shen Hsun, and the two lines on p. 557 from the 'Song of a Chaste Wife' by Chang Chi, are all from the *Penguin Book of Chinese Verse'*, translated by Robert Kotewall and Norman L. Smith, translation © Norman L. Smith and Robert Kotewall, 1962, and are reprinted here by permission of Penguin Books Ltd.

Part One

Part One

1

The perfectly preserved body of the woman they call the Marquise of Tai lay, sheathed in glass, some feet below them on the lower level. Two thousand odd years ago when she died she had been about fifty. A white shift covered her thin seventy-five-pound body from neck to thighs. Her legs were a fish-like pinkish-white much marked with striations, her right arm, on account of a mended fracture, was rather shorter than her left. Her face was white, puffy, the bridge of the nose encaved, the mouth open and the tongue protruding, the whole face bearing an expression of extreme agony as if she had died from strangulation.

This, however, was not the case. According to the museum's brochure and Mr Sung, the Marquise had suffered from tuberculosis and a diseased gall bladder. Just before she died of some kind of heart attack she had consumed a hundred and twenty water melon seeds.

'She have myocardial infarction, you know,' said Mr Sung, quoting from memory out of the brochure, a habit of his. 'Very sick, you know, bad heart, bad insides. Let's go.'

They moved along to look down through a second aperture at the Marquise's internal organs and *dura mater* preserved in bottles of formaldehyde. Mr Sung looked inquiringly into the face of his companion, hoping perhaps to see there signs of nausea or dismay. But the other man's expression was as inscrutable as his own. Mr Sung gave a little sigh.

'Let's go.'

'I wish you wouldn't keep saying that,' said Wexford irritably. 'If I may suggest it, you should say, "Shall we go?" or "Are you ready?"'

Mr Sung said earnestly, 'You may suggest. Thank you. I am anxious to speak good. Shall we go? Are you leady?'

'Oh, yes, certainly.'

'Don't reply, please. I practise. Shall we go? Are you leady? Good, I have got it. Come, let's go. Are you leady to go to the site? Reply now, please.'

They got back into the taxi. Between the air-conditioned building and the air-conditioned car the temperature seemed that of a moderate oven, set for the slow cooking of a casserole. The driver took them across the city to the excavation where archaeologists had found the bodies of the Marquise, her husband and her son, clay figures of servants, provisions, artefacts to accompany them on their journey beyond the grave. The other bodies had been skeletons, their clothing fallen to dust. Only the Marquise, hideous, grotesque, staring from sightless empty eyes, had retained the waxen lineaments of life, wrapped in her painted gown, her twenty layers of silk robes.

Wexford and Mr Sung looked through the wooden grille at the great deep rectangular burial shaft and Mr Sung quoted almost verbatim a considerable chunk from *Fodor's Guide to the People's Republic of China*. He had a retentive memory and seemed to believe that Wexford, because he couldn't decipher ideographs, was unable to read his own language. It was even Wexford's *Fodor's* he was quoting from, artlessly borrowed the night before. Wexford didn't listen. He would have given a good deal to have been rid of baby-faced pink-cheeked slant-eyed Mr Sung. In any other country on earth a bribe equivalent to a month's wages – and here that would easily have been within Wexford's means – would have freed him for good of his guide-interpreter. Not in China, where even tipping was banned. Mr Sung was incorruptible. In spite of his youth, he was already a party member. A fanatical light came into his eyes and his flabby muscles tautened when he spoke of the great statesmen, Mao Tse Tung included, his own native place of Hunan Province had produced. Wexford sometimes wondered if the day would

10

come, twenty years hence perhaps, when if he still lived he would open his *Times* and read that the new Chairman of the Chinese Communist Party was one Sung Lao Zhong, aged forty-seven, from Chang-sha. It was more than possible. Mr Sung came to the end of his memorized paragraph, sighed at the call of duty but refused to shirk it.

'Light,' he said. 'Shall we go? We visit now porcelain factory and before evening meal teacher training college.'

'No, we don't,' said Wexford. A mosquito bit him just above the ankle bone. The heat was enormous. Like the imagined casserole, he was slowly cooking, a gravy-like viscous sweat trickling stickily all over his body. It was the humidity as much as the ninety-eight degree temperature that did it. 'No, we don't. We go to the hotel and have a shower and a siesta.'

'There will be no other time for porcelain factory.'

'I can't help that.'

'It is most necessary to see college attended by Chairman Mao.'

'Not today,' said Wexford. The ice-cold atmosphere in the car stimulated a gush rather than a trickle of sweat. He mopped his face.

'Velly well. I hope you not leglet,' said Mr Sung, indignation, as any emotion did, causing acute confusion in the pronunciation of liquids. 'I aflaid you be solly.' His voice was vaguely threatening. Much more rebellion on the part of this obstinate visitor, Wexford thought, and Mr Sung might even insist that no such omissions were open to him. If Lu Xing She, the Chinese Tourist Board, whose vicar on earth, so to speak, Mr Sung was, required Wexford to see factories, kindergartens, colleges and oil refineries, these institutions he would see and no doubt about it.

Mr Sung turned away and looked out of the window. His face seldom expressed anything but a ruthless affability. The top of his head came approximately to Wexford's shoulder, though for a Southern Chinese he wasn't particularly short. He wore a cotton shirt, white as driven snow, a pair of olive-green baggy cotton trousers and sandals of chestnut-brown moulded plastic. His father, he had told Wexford, was a party cadre, his mother a doctor, his sister and own wife doctors.

11

They all lived together in a two-roomed apartment in one of the city's grey barrack-like blocks with Mr Sung's baby son, Tsu Ken.

Hooting at pedestrians, at cyclists who carried on their bikes anything from a couple of live fat piglets and a chicken to a suite of furniture, the car made its way through drab streets to the Xiangjiang Hotel. There were very few buildings in Chang-sha that pre-dated the Revolution of 1949, only the Kuomintang general's house with green curly roofs just by the hotel and a ruined European church of grey stucco whose provenance no one seemed to know anything of. Mr Sung got out of the car and came into the lobby with him. There he shook hands. Any more casual mode of behaviour wouldn't have satisfied his sense of duty. It was all Wexford could do to prevent his accompanying him to the eighth floor in the lift. He would be ready, please, by seven, said Mr Sung, for an open-air showing of a film about the history of the Revolution.

'Oh, no, thank you,' said Wexford. 'Too many mosquitos.'

'You take anti-malaria pill evly Fliday, I hope?'

'I still don't like being bitten.' Wexford's anklebone felt twice its normal size. 'Mysteriously enough –' he caught sight in a rare mirror of his sweat-washed, sunburnt, never even adequately handsome face, ' – I am particularly attractive to *anopheles* but the passion isn't mutual.' Mr Sung looked at him with uncomprehending relentless amiability. 'And I won't sit in the open inviting them to vampirize me.'

'I see.. Light. You come to cinema in hotel and see *Shanghai Girl* and Charlie Chaplin in *Great Dictator*. *Shanghai Girl* very good Chinese film about construction workers. I sit next so you don't miss storly.'

'Wouldn't you rather be at home with your wife and your baby?'

Mr Sung gave an enigmatic smile. He shook Wexford's hand once more. 'I do my job, light?'

Wexford lay on his iron-hard bed on a thin quilt. The undersheet, for some quaint reason, was a blue and white checked tablecloth. Cold air blew unevenly over him from the Japanese air conditioner, while outside the window the general's house and the brown pantiled roofs of Chang-sha

12

lay baking in moist sizzling heat. He had made himself, with water from the thermos flask that was one of the amenities of his room, half a pint of green tea in a cherry-blossom painted cup with a lid. They made you eat dinner here at six (breakfast at seven, lunch, appallingly, at eleven-thirty) but there was still an hour and a half to go. He couldn't stomach the lemonade and strawberry pop and Cassia fizz you were expected to pour hourly into yourself to combat dehydration. He drank green tea all the time, making it himself and making it strong, or else he bought it from the street stalls for a single *fen*, something like a third of a penny, a glass.

Presently, after a second cup of tea, he dozed, but then it was time to shower and put on a fresh shirt for dinner. He would write to his wife later, there wasn't time now. Hong Kong, where she was staying, waiting for him, seemed infinitely far away. He went down to the dining room where he would eat at a table by himself with his own private fan, discreetly half-concealed from the only other foreign contingent, Italians sitting at the next broad round table by a bamboo screen. He sat down and asked the girl for a bottle of beer.

The Italians came in and said hallo to him. The girl turned their fan on, tucked their screen round them and began bringing Wexford's platters. Chicken and bamboo shoots im ginger sauce tonight, peanuts fried in oil, bright green nearly raw spinach, fried pumpkin and fried fish. Setting off with his nephew Howard and those other police officers who all ranked so much higher than he, he had brought a spoon and fork in his suitcase because he was afraid the Peking Hotel might not have Western cutlery. How green he had been, as green as the tea! The Peking Hotel was like an austere Ritz with arctic air conditioning and a huge shopping arcade and curtains that drew and undrew electrically. But somehow none of them had ever bothered with the silver that was offered them but had eaten from the first as the Chinese eat, and now he was as proficient with chopsticks as might have been any dignitary in the Forbidden City. He could even, he now discovered, pick up a slippery oil-coated peanut with chopsticks, so skilful had he become.

13

The girl brought him a bowl of rice and the big green bottle of Tsing-tao beer.

A feeling of tremendous well-being invaded him as he began to eat. He could still hardly believe after two weeks in China that he, Reg Wexford, a country policeman, was here in Tartary, in Cathay, had walked on the Great Wall, set foot on the Stone Boat in the Summer Palace, touched the scarlet columns in the Temple of Heaven, and was now touring southwards, seeing as many marvels and experiencing as many delights as Lu Xing She would permit.

When Chief Superintendent Howard Fortune of Scotland Yard, who was Wexford's dead sister's son, had first told a family gathering he was going to China in the summer of 1980, his uncle had felt something he wasn't usually a prey to – envy. Howard would spend a good deal of time, of course, over the conference table. The particular branch of the Chinese Government who were his hosts wanted advice on crime prevention and crime detection and they would no doubt want to indulge in that favourite communist pastime of showing off national institutions – in this case, probably, police stations, courts, prisons. But Howard and his team would still have leisure to see the Imperial Palaces, Coal Hill and the Marco Polo Bridge. All his life Wexford had wanted to see the Forbidden City and been pretty sure he never would. But he had said nothing of this and had jollied Howard along and told him, as everyone else did, to be sure to buy jade and silk and to bring back a fragment of the Great Wall as a souvenir.

A week after that Howard had rung up to say he had to go to Brighton and would call in on his uncle in Kingsmarkham on the way back. He walked in at about six on a Saturday night, a cadaverous giant of a man who, though perfectly healthy, had always contrived to look twenty years older than he actually was. His parents-in-law lived in Hong Kong. After the China trip he would be joining his wife in Hong Kong. What would his aunt Dora think of joining Denise out there for two or three weeks?

'Reg too?' Dora had said quickly. She was used to being

14

left for long hours, days, by him. But she would never go off and leave *him* of her own accord.

'Can't be done,' Howard said, shaking his head. 'He'll be occupied elsewhere.'

Wexford thought he meant Kingsmarkham. He cocked an eyebrow at his nephew, though, at this curious choice of words.

'I shall need him in Peking,' said Howard.

There was a silence. Wexford said, 'You have to be serious, don't you, Howard?'

'Of course I'm serious. I've got *carte blanche* to pick my own team and I'm picking you as about the best detection expert I know, bar none. And I'm giving you plenty of notice so that you can get your own visa. These group visas are such a bore if you want to go wandering off on your own round China, which I'm sure you will.'

And that was what he was doing now while Howard, the amateur antiquarian, prowled about the yellow-roofed pavilions of Peking at his ecstatic leisure, and the other team members, nursing incipient coronaries, hastened back over the skies of Asia to British worries and British crime. It was two weeks of his own annual holiday Wexford was taking now. He had flown down from Peking three days before and been met at Chang-sha airport by Mr Sung. He would never forget that flight, the stewardess bringing a strange meal of hard-boiled eggs and sponge cake and dried plums wrapped up like toffees, and the passengers – he had been the only Caucasian – the boys and girls in blue cotton, the high-ranking Korean army officers, military and correct in khaki-green uniforms, yet fanning themselves with fans of black silk trimmed with gold.

Wexford was disturbed in his reverie by a discreet cough. Mr Sung was standing over him, waiting no doubt to take him to the cinema. Wexford asked him to sit down and have a beer but Mr Sung wouldn't do that, he was a teetotaller. He did, however, sit down and began lecturing Wexford on higher education in China with particular reference to the Peking Institute of Foreign Languages which he referred to as his alma mater. Had Wexford visited the university while

15

there? No? That was strange, he would certainly regret it, he would be sorry. Wexford drank two cups of green tea, ate four lichees and a piece of water melon.

'Mind you not swallow seeds like two-thousand-year-old lady,' said Mr Sung, who had a sense of humour of a kind.

The Great Dictator was dubbed in Chinese. Wexford stuck it for ten minutes. It seemed to him that all the children in Chang-sha must be in the cinema, all laughing so much that they nearly fell off their mothers' laps. He excused himself to Mr Sung, saying with perfect if strange truth that he was cold. The air conditioning was blasting away over his left shoulder and down his neck. He strolled out into the street where the air had a warm furry dusty feel to it like the inside of a muff. Opposite was a shop where they sold tea. Wexford thought he would buy more tea there in the morning, he had almost exhausted the packet the hotel supplied.

He walked. He had a good sense of direction which was as well since the ideographs in which the street signs were written rendered him illiterate. The city was dimly lit, a warren, exotic and fantastic without the least pretension to beauty. In a broad intersecting highway people were playing cards on the pavement by the light of streetlamps. Remembering what the hotel's name meant, he headed back for the river. Crowds thronged the streets, friendly people too polite to stare, though their children looked and pointed and giggled at this blue-eyed giant. Ten o'clock is the middle of the night when you have to be up again at six. Wexford made himself a cup of tea, went to bed and to sleep and plunged soon after into the kind of dream he never had, or hadn't had for years.

A nightmare. He was in China but it was the China of his own youth, before the Communists came to power, long before the Cultural Revolution destroyed the temples of Taoists and Buddha and Confucius, when the cities were still walled-in clusters of pagodas. And he was a young man, Chinese perhaps. At any rate he knew he was on the run – from the Nationalist soldiers, it could have been, or the Communists or the Japanese. He was walking barefoot and with a pack on his back along a path to the north of the city, outside the city walls.

The stone door in the hillside stood a little open. He went inside as into a place to shelter for the night, finding himself in a cavernous passage that seemed to lead into the heart of the hill. It was cold in the passage and close with a dank, ancient kind of smell, the smell of the Han Dynasty perhaps. On and on he walked, not exactly afraid, no more than apprehensive. The passage was dark, yet he had no difficulty in finding his way into the big rectangular chamber, its walls shored up with wood, its dimness relieved by the light from a single small oil lamp of green bronze.

The lamp burned by the side of a wooden table or bench that looked to him like a bed provided for his own night's rest. He went over to it, lifted off the painted silk cloth which covered it and looked down upon the Marquise of Tai. It was a sarcophagus that he had uncovered, set in a burial chamber. The dead woman's face was convulsed in a grimace of agony, the cheeks puffed, the eyes black and protruding, the lips curled back from shrunken gums and sparse yellowed teeth and swollen tongue. He recoiled and started back, for there came from the misty, gloomy depths of the coffin a sweetish smell of putrefaction. But as he took hold of the silk to cover once more that hideous dead thing, a shudder seemed to pass along the striated limbs and the Marquise rose up and laid her icy arms about his neck.

Wexford fought his way out of the dream and awoke with a cry. He sat up and put the light on and came round to the roar of the air conditioner and the beating of his own heart. What a fool! Was it going to the cinema or eating fried fish spiced with ginger or the heat that had brought him a dream straight out of *Curse of the Mummy's Tomb*? It certainly wasn't as if he had never seen a woman's corpse before, and most of those he had seen had been a good deal less well-preserved than that of the Marquise. He drank some water and put out the light.

It was on the following day that he first saw the woman with the bound feet.

2

She wasn't the first woman of her kind he had seen since coming to China. The first had been in Peking on one of the marble bridges that cross the moat towards the Gate of Heavenly Peace. She was a tiny little old woman, very shrunken as the Chinese become with age, dressed in a black jacket and trousers, clasping a stick in one hand and with the other holding the arm of her daughter or daughter-in-law, for she could do no more than hobble. Her feet were like nothing so much as hooves, dainty hooves perhaps when she was young, shuffling club feet now in pinkish stockings and black slippers the size for a five-year-old.

Wexford had felt fascination, then a rush of revulsion. Foot-binding had come in about AD 500, hadn't it, and gone out with the Kuomintang? At first only aristocrats had practised it but the fashion had caught on even among peasants, so that you could scarcely have found a girl in China with normal unrestricted feet. He wondered how old the woman was who crossed the marble bridge on her daughter's arm. Perhaps no more than sixty. They used to begin the tight bandaging of feet, turning the toes under and up into the sole, when a girl was little more than a baby and the bones were pliable. Such was the power of fashion that no man would have wanted a wife with normal feet, a wife who could walk with ease. In the nineteen thirties the custom had been banned by law and feet that were not beyond remedy unbound. Fascination conquered revulsion, pity and distaste, and Wexford stared. After all, everyone stared at *him*.

How would that woman feel now? What would she feel? Self-pity, resentment, envy of her freer descendants and, worse, her liberated near-coevals? Wexford didn't think so. Human nature wasn't like that. For all the pain she had suffered, the curtailment of movement, the daily agony of dressing and cleansing and rebandaging, no doubt she looked with scorn on those girls who ran across the bridge on large whole healthy feet, and with a sniff of snobbish contempt shuffled the more proudly on her own tiny pointed deformities.

She was the first of several such women he had seen, maybe ten in all. They had caused him to look with curiosity at the shapely flexed feet of the Marquise of Tai, even though he knew she had been born centuries before the custom came into vogue. His dream seemed to him ridiculous when he reviewed it in the morning. He didn't have nightmares, never had, and had no intention of starting on them now. It must have been the food.

Breakfast was by far the least palatable meal he got and he viewed the spread before him with resignation. Fried bread rolls, sliced soda bread, rancid butter, plum jam, chocolate cream cake and coconut biscuits. Tea was brought in an aluminium kettle and he drank two cups of it. Mr Sung was hovering before he had finished.

He had a fresh pink shirt on – he was one of the cleanest-looking people Wexford had ever seen – and his black hair was still damp from its morning wash. How could you achieve that sort of thing when you shared a bathroom not only with four or five members of your family but with the other tenants on the same floor besides? It was wholly admirable. Wexford now recalled uneasily how it was said that Westerners smelt bad to the Chinese, owing to their consumption of dairy products. If this was true his own smell must lately be much improved, he thought, pushing away the nearly liquid greenish butter.

'You will not mind come on bus with party?'

'Not at all. Why should I?'

As if Wexford had protested rather than concurred, Mr Sung said in a repressive scolding way, 'It is not economic drive bus fifty kilometre for one man. This is very wasteful.

19

Much better you come with party, very nice Europe and American people. Light?'

The very nice European and American people were trooping off to the bus as he came out of the hotel. They looked weary and somewhat dishevelled and as if the last thing they wanted was to be driven out into the scorching Chinese countryside to the scenes of Mao Tse Tung's birth and infancy. However, they had little choice about that. Their guide, with whom his own was chatting in rapid Mandarin over a post-breakfast menthol cigarette, looked as relentless, determined, cheerful and clean as Mr Sung. He was a little taller, a little thinner, his English a little worse, and was introduced to Wexford as Mr Yu. They shook hands. It turned out he was a fellow alumnus of Mr Sung's from the alma mater of foreign languages.

Of all green growing things the greenest is rice. Wexford looked out of the window at rice seedlings, rice half-grown, rice near to harvest. This was the very quintessence of greenness, perhaps Aristotle's perfect green which all other greens must emulate and strive for. Men and women in the age-old Chinese blue cotton and conical straw hats worked in the fields with lumbering grey water buffalos. To distract Mr Sung and Mr Yu from their enthusiastic disquisitions on Mao's political career, Wexford asked what the crops were and was told peanuts, aubergines, castor oil plants, cassava, taro and soya beans. Sheets of water – ponds, lakes, canals – studded the neat landscape like jewels on patterned silk.

After a while Mr Yu got up and went to the front of the bus and began translating items from a newspaper into bad English for the benefit of the tourists. Wexford was trying to decide what was meant by a pirates' strike in Hungary and measles in Afghanistan when one of the men from the party came and sat in the seat next to him. He was a small man with a lined red face and a shock of sandy hair.

'Mind if I join you?'

What could he say but that he didn't mind?

'My name's Lewis Fanning. It was either coming to sit with you or jumping screaming off the bloody bus. You can't be worse than that lot and there's a chance you're better.'

20

'Thanks very much.' Wexford introduced himself and asked for an explanation of Mr Yu's news disclosures.

'He means pilots and missiles. If I'd known he was coming on this jaunt I wouldn't have myself. I'd have stayed in my room and got pissed. As it is I don't reckon I'll make it sane to Canton.'

Wexford asked him why he had come if he hated it so much.

'Dear God in heaven, I'm not on my hols. I'm *working*. I'm the tour leader. I brought this lot here by train. D'you wonder I'm going bananas?'

'On the train from where?'

'Calais,' said Fanning. He seemed cheered by Wexford's incredulity. 'Thirty-six days I've been in trains, the Trans-Siberian Railway among others. Ten lunatics to shepherd across Asia. I nearly lost one of them at the Berlin Wall. They uncoupled the carriage and she got left in the other bit. She jumped out yelling and came running up along the track, it's a miracle she's still here. There's another one an alcoholic and one who can't leave the men alone. To my certain knowledge she's had four in various wagons-lits en route.'

Wexford couldn't help laughing. 'Where's your destination?'

'Hong Kong. We leave tomorrow night on the train via Kweilin. I'm sharing sleeping quarters with two guys who haven't been on speaking terms since Irkutsk.'

Wexford too would be on that train, sharing his four-berth compartment, so far as he knew, only with Mr Sung. But he hesitated over inviting Lewis Fanning to join them and in the end he didn't. Instead he listened to a long account of the alcoholic tourist's propensities, how she had drunk a bottle of whisky a day and had had to be carried by four men back on to the train at Ulan Bator. This lasted until they reached Shao-shan and were drinking tea before climbing the hill to the Mao farmstead. The countryside here had that fresh sparkling look you occasionally see in England on a rare fine day after a long spell of rain. In front of the house the lotus reared its round sunshade leaves and pink lily flowers out of a shallow pond. The rice was the soft tender green of imperial jade. But for all that the heat was intense.

Thirty-nine degrees, said Mr Yu, which Wexford, multiplying by nine, dividing by five and adding thirty-two, made out to be a formidable hundred and two Fahrenheit. In the shade it became suddenly and shockingly cool, but they weren't in the shade much and when they walked back down the hill, their heads stuffed with Maoism, they still had the museum of Maoiana to inspect, before lunch in the hotel.

Wexford was one of those Englishmen who aver they find a hot drink more cooling and refreshing than a cold one. Once they were in the dining room of the hotel he drank about a pint of hot strong tea. Mr Sung sat with Mr Yu at a table with two local guides. The train party, for some inscrutable, Chinese, culinary reason, were placed behind a screen and once more Wexford found himself alone.

He was rather annoyed at being so affected by the heat. He misquoted to himself, 'My mother bore me in a northern clime'. Was that the reason for his feeling felled and bludgeoned in this temperature? Behind him a fan moved the warm heavy air about. Two girls brought a banquet in to him, no less than seven platters. Hard-boiled eggs, battered and fried, lotus buds, pork and pineapple, duck with beansprouts, mushrooms and bamboo shoots, prawns with peas and raw sliced tomatoes. He asked for more tea. From the moment he picked up the carved wooden chopsticks and began to eat the sweat rolled off him, wetting the back of his chair through his shirt.

Across the room the guides were eating fried bread rolls and hundred-year-old eggs and what Wexford thought might be snake.

'As long as it moves they'll eat it,' Lewis Fanning had muttered to him on entering the room. 'They'll eat mice if they can catch them.'

A murmur of soft giggling voices came from the girls. It was like the twittering of birds at sundown. The men's voices rose and fell in the strange purity of ancient Mandarin. Wexford wondered how it had come about that Europeans called the Chinese yellow. The skins of those four were a clear translucent ivory, a red flush on their cheeks, their hands thin and brown. He turned away, compelling himself not to stare, and looking instead into the shadowy part of the room from which the waitresses emerged where he saw an old woman standing by the doorway.

She was looking at him intently. Her face was pale and pouchy, her eyes black as raisins. Chinese hair scarcely ever turns white, remains black indeed long into middle age, and hers, though her age seemed great, was only just touched with grey. She wore a grey jacket over black trousers and her bound feet were tiny and wedge-shaped in their grey stockings and black child's slippers. She stood erect enough but nevertheless supported herself on a cane.

The mother of the proprietor or the cook, Wexford supposed. Her stare was almost disconcerting. It was as if she wanted to speak to him, was girding herself up to find the courage to speak to him. But that was absurd. The overwhelming probability was that she spoke nothing but Chinese. Their eyes met once more. Wexford put down his chopsticks, wiped his mouth and got up. He would go to Mr Sung and ask him to interpret for them, so evident was it that she wished to communicate something.

But before he reached Mr Sung's table the woman was gone. He looked back to where she had stood and there was no longer anyone there. No doubt he had imagined her need. He wasn't in Kingsmarkham now, he reminded himself, where he was so often consulted, grumbled at, even pleaded with.

Lunch over, they went once again into the relentless sunshine to visit the school Mao had attended and the pond where he had swum. On the way back to the bus Wexford looked again for the old woman. He peered into the dim lobby of the hotel on the chance she might be there, but there was no sign of her. Very likely she had gazed so intently at him only from the same motive as the children's – because his height and size, his clothes, ruddy skin and scanty fair hair were as remarkable here as a unicorn galloping down the street.

'Now,' said Mr Sung, 'we go to Number One Normal School, Chairman Mao's house, Clear Water Pond.' He jumped on to the bus with buoyant step.

Wexford's last day in Chang-sha was spent at Orange Island and in the museum where artefacts from the tombs at Mawangdui were on show. There, reproduced in wax this time, lay the Marquise of Tai, still protected by glass but available for a closer scrutiny. Wexford drank a pint of green tea in the museum shop, bought some jade for Dora, a fan for his younger daughter made of buffalo bone that looked like ivory – Sheila the conservationist wouldn't have approved of ivory – and a painting of bamboo stems and grasshoppers with the painter's seal in red and his signature in black calligraphy.

There was an English air about the old houses on the island with their walled gardens, their flowers and vegetables, the river flowing by. Their walls were of wattle and daub like cottages in Sewingbury. But the air was scented with ginger and the canna lilies burned brick red in the hazy heat. Off the point where Mao had once swum, boys and girls were bathing in the river. Mr Sung took the opportunity to give Wexford a lecture on Chinese political structure to which he didn't listen. In order to get his visa he had had to put down on the application form his religion and politics. He had selected, not without humour, the most stolid options: Conservative, Church of England. Sometimes he wondered if these reactionary entries had been made known by a form of red grapevine to his guide. He sat down in the shade and gazed appreciatively at the arch with its green pointed roof, delicate and jewel-like against a silvery blue sky.

Through the arch, supported this time on a walking stick with a carved buffalo-bone handle, came the old woman with bound feet he had seen at the hotel in Shao-shan. Wexford gave an exclamation. Mr Sung stopped talking and said sharply, 'Something is wrong?'

'No. It just seems extraordinary. That woman over there, I saw her in Shao-san yesterday. Small world.'

'Small?' said Mr Sung. 'China is very big country. Why lady from Shao-shan not come Chang-sha? She come, go, just as she like, all Chinese people liberated, all Chinese people flee. Light? I see no lady. Where she go?'

The sun was in Wexford's eyes, making him blink. 'Over by the gate. A little woman in black with bound feet.'

Mr Sung shook his head vehemently. 'Very bad feudal custom, very few now have, all dead.' He added, with a ruthless disregard for truth, 'Cannot walk, all stay home.'

The woman had gone. Back through the arch? Down one of the paved walks between the canna lily beds? Wexford decided to take the initiative.

'If you're ready, shall we go?'

Astonishment spread over Mr Sung's bland face. Wexford surmised that no other tourist had ever dared anything but submit meekly to him.

'O.K., light. Now we go to Yunlu Palace.'

Leaving the island, they met the train party under the leadership of Mr Yu. Lewis Fanning was nowhere to be seen, and walking alongside Mr Yu, in earnest conversation with him, was the younger and better-looking of the two men who had quarrelled on the Trans-Siberian Railway. His enemy, a tall man with a Humpty-Dumpty-ish shape, brought up the rear of the party and gazed about him with a nervous unhappy air. The women's clothes had suffered irremediably from those thirty-six days in a train. They were either bleached and worn from too frequent washing or dirty and creased from not having been washed at all.

Already, and without difficulty, Wexford had decided which was the nymphomaniac and which the alcoholic: a highly-coloured woman and a drab one respectively. Apart from these four apparently single people, the party consisted of another lone, and much older, woman, and two elderly married couples, one set of whom were accompanied by their middle-aged daughter. On the whole, Wexford reflected, it would seem that the young and the beautiful couldn't afford five-week long tours across Asia.

That evening the screens were drawn closely around their table and he had no further sight of the party until he and they were boarding the bus for Zhuzhou where they would pick up the Shanghai to Kweilin train.

3

It would have been easier and quicker to fly. Fanning's party, of course, had to make every leg of their journey by train but Wexford would happily have gone on by air. It wasn't a matter of his will, though, but the will of Lu Xing She and Mr Sung.

He had a double seat to himself on the bus. Silently he observed his fellow passengers. A couple of days in the hotel at Chang-sha had gone a long way towards reviving them and they looked less as if they had been pulled through a hedge backwards.

Each of the enemies had also secured a double seat, one of them behind the driver, the other on the opposite side of the aisle to Wexford. Out of the corner of his eye Wexford read the label tied to the older man's handcase. A. H. Purbank, and an address somewhere in Essex. Purbank was perhaps forty-five, unhealthy-looking, thin, dressed in baggy jeans and an open-necked pale green shirt. His sprucer, dark-haired adversary was also in jeans, but a snugly fitting pair of denims which looked smart and suitable with a 'friendship' tee-shirt. He had swivelled round in his seat and was talking to the woman in the seat behind him. This was the daughter of one of the elderly couples and after a little while Wexford saw her get up and sit in the empty place beside him. Wexford, with another glance at Purbank, thought how uncomfortable it must have been travelling all those miles from Irkutsk away up there on Lake Baikal with a man with whom you weren't on speaking terms. What quarrel had sprung up between these inoffensive-seeming travellers? Both were English, both middle-class, prosperous presumably, adventurously inclined surely, having a fair bit in common, yet they had fallen out so bitterly as purposely not to have exchanged a word across all those vast stretches of eastern Asia. At table in the hotels they must have sat, if not together, near enough to each other, perhaps have been allotted adjoining rooms. Now they were to share a sleeping space some eight feet by five and lie breathing the same warm air in the rattling darkness for eight or nine hours. It was grotesque.

Was one of them or perhaps each of them among the four men with whom Fanning alleged that pretty, painted, ageing creature in the spotted blouse and white pants had engaged in sexual relations during the trip? Fanning, of course, exaggerated wildly. Certainly he couldn't have been indicating as among her partners the fair woman's father, asleep now with his white cotton hat drooped over his eyes, or the austere silver-haired man with the ugly wife. Of course, Wexford reflected, he hadn't exactly specified members of the party and presumably there had been plenty of other men in the Trans-Siberian train.

The bright sky had clouded over and a little warm rain had begun to fall. It was still raining lightly when they came on to the station platform. By each door of the train stood a girl attendant in grey uniform and with the red star of the People's Republic on her cap. Wexford was shown to the carriage that was to be his for the night. Though clean and with comfortable-looking berths it was insufferably hot, the thermometer on the wall telling him the temperature was two degrees short of a hundred. Once the train started, he opened the window and switched on the fan. A very slightly cooler air blew in through the fly screen.

As soon as they were off Mr Sung came in. Wexford, who had discovered a thermos flask and was busy with the Silver Leaf he had bought in Chang-sha, offered him a cup of tea but Mr Sung refused. Here, as elsewhere, he contrived to give the impression of always being busy and involved. The restaurant car would open at eight, he said, and drinks would be available: beer, red and white wine, Maotai, maybe Japanese whisky.

27

Wexford drank tea and read his *Fodor's*. It was dusk now, growing dark, and was no longer unpleasantly hot, though smuts came in through the fine mesh of the screen. Hunan Province, blanketed in darkness, fled past as the train reached a steady speed. After a while he went out into the corridor to establish the whereabouts of lavatory and bathroom.

Next to the bathroom, in the first compartment of the carriage, four Hong-Kong Chinese in Palm Beach shirts and white trousers sat playing cards. The door of the next one was opened as Wexford passed it and a voice said, 'Oh, excuse me. I wonder if we could possibly trouble you a moment?'

Wexford went in, not entirely reluctantly. He had been curious enough about these two women to want to make a closer personal estimate. The one he had privately styled the alcoholic was lying in one of the lower berths, her shoes tumbled on the floor and her swollen feet raised up on two pillows. She gave him a wan smile.

'It's so awful constantly trying to make oneself understood to these Chinese,' said the other, 'and that beastly Yu has disappeared again. He always disappears when you want him. I suppose he thinks playing hard to get makes him more desirable, do you think? Oh, by the way, I'm Lois Knox and this is Hilda Avory – I already know your name, I *spied* on your luggage – and now, please, please, do you think you could be awfully sweet and make our fan work?'

The attendant who had shown Wexford to his carriage had worked his fan for him, so he had no difficulty in finding the switch which was rather cunningly hidden under the back of the table.

Lois Knox clasped her hands together girlishly.

'And since you're so clever, could you be even more of an angel and find out how to suppress that bloody radio?'

The martial music which had greeted him on entering the compartment – interrupted now for what was presumably a political harangue – Wexford had supposed to be on at the desire of the occupants.

'Oh, no, we hate it, don't we, Hilda? There should be a knob under there but it's broken and it won't move. How shall we ever get a wink of sleep?' Her eyes were a brilliant sea-blue, large beautiful eyes which she fixed intensely on his face. The muscles of her face sagged rather and her jawline was no longer firm but she had something of a youthful look as the gyrating fan fluttered her black hair about. It was dyed hair, greyish-brown at the roots after five weeks away from a hairdresser.

'You're all by yourself, aren't you?' She didn't wait for confirmation. 'We're on that beastly train tour but never again, so help us God. How we should love an aircraft or even a humble bus for a change, shouldn't we, Hilda?'

Hilda Avory made no reply. She put out a hand for her teacup and drank from it with a shudder. She had a damp look, skin glistening, tendrils of hair clinging to her forehead, portions of her dress adhering to thin flesh, as if she had been out in the rain or had sweated profusely.

Wexford set about hunting for the controls of the radio. 'I could fix it for you if I had a pair of pliers.'

'Imagine trying to explain pliers to that inscrutable little Yu! Do have a cup of tea, won't you? Or some *laoshan?*'

'That's Chinese for mineral water,' said Hilda Avory, speaking for the first time. She had a gravelly voice, unexpectedly deep.

'I'm terribly afraid we haven't anything stronger but the fact is Hilda is drying out, aren't you, darling? And she doesn't feel it's very wise to have spirits about, such an awful temptation, you know.'

There seemed no answer to make to this. He accepted a cup of tea. The music burst forth once more in a kind of Chinese version of 'Washington Post'.

'What shall we do?' cried Lois Knox. She brought her hands together appealingly. The red nails were as long as a Manchu's. 'We shall be found stark raving mad in the morning.'

'How about cutting the wires?' said Wexford.

The deep voice from the other berth said, 'Not a good idea. I heard of someone who did that in China and they had to pay to have the whole train rewired. It cost them thousands of *yuan.*'

'I'll see what I can do,' said Wexford. He drank up his tea and went off down the corridor to find an attendant.

29

The only one he came upon, a very young boy, had nodded off to sleep, his head against the hard wall, in a little
cubby-hole next to the bathroom. Wexford went on over
the intersection into the next carriage, the sweat gathering
on his body now and breaking out on his forehead and
upper lip. Away from the fans the heat was as great as ever.
There was nothing but dense blackness to be seen outside
now and, dimly through the upper part of the windows, a
few faint stars. In a compartment with Mr Yu and another
young Chinese sat Mr Sung, the three of them poring over
a map of the Li River spread out on the table.

'Restaurant will open eight o'clock,' said Mr Sung as soon
as he saw him. All the guides seemed to think that visitors
from the west needed to eat and drink all day long in order
to maintain equilibrium, and that any requests they received
from tourists must necessarily be for food or tea or beer. 'I
come fetch you when restaurant open.'

'I want a pair of pliers,' said Wexford.

Mr Sung, Mr Yu and the other man looked at him in blank
inquiry. Wexford recalled how, in Peking, he had asked an
interpreter where he could buy a packet of aspirin and had
been directed to an ice-cream shop.

'Players,' said Mr Sung at last.

'You want cigarettes?' said Mr Yu. 'You get plenty cigarettes when restaurant open.'

'I don't want cigarettes, I want pliers.' Wexford made
pinching movements with his fingers, he mimed pulling a
nail out of the wall. Mr Sung stared amiably at him. Mr
Yu stared and then laughed. The other man handed him a
large shabby book which turned out to be an English-Chinese
dictionary. Wexford indicated 'pliers' and its ideograph with
his fingertip. Everyone smiled and nodded, Mr Sung went off
down the corridor and came back with a girl train attendant
who handed Wexford a pair of eyebrow tweezers.

Wexford gave up. It was a quarter to eight and he began
to look forward to a beer. In the intersection he met the little
elderly woman who was travelling in what he had mentally
dubbed – though it certainly was not – a *ménage à trois*.
She was carrying a packet of teabags.

'Oh, good evening,' she said. 'This is quite an adventure,

isn't it?' Wexford wasn't sure if she spoke with seriousness or irony, still less so when she went on to say, her head a little on one side, 'We English must stick together, is what I always say.'

He knew at once then, he intuited, he hardly knew how, that she was getting at him. It was neither witty nor particularly clever, though she intended it to be both, and she was referring to his brief association with Lois Knox which she had perhaps observed from the corridor. Her expression was dry, her mouth quirked a little. She was as small and thin as a Chinese and the dark blue trouser suit she wore unsexed her. What was she to the man Fanning had told him was a retired barrister? Sister? Sister-in-law? Wife's confidante or best friend's widow? As she went on her way into the next compartment he observed that her left hand was ringless.

In the cubby-hole next to the bathroom the boy was still asleep with his head against the wall. Wexford saw what he hadn't noticed before, a cloth toolbag lying beside the boy's legs on the floor. He went in, opened the toolbag and helped himself to a pair of pliers.

Outside the windows a few feeble clusters of light showed. They were passing a village or small town. For a moment the outline of a mountain could be seen and then the darkness closed in once more as the train gathered speed. Wexford stood in the doorway of Lois Knox's compartment. The radio was still on, playing a selection from *Swan Lake*. Hilda Avory still lay in the lower berth and on the end of it, beside her feet, sat Purbank. He seemed to be addressing them on the very subject which had been the reason for Wexford's visit to China in the first place, crime prevention. Lois's face wore the expression of a woman who has been taught from childhood that men must at all costs be flattered. Hilda's eyes were closed and slightly screwed up.

'These Communists make a lot of high-flown claims about how they've got rid of crime. Now that's all very well but we know in practice it just isn't true. I mean, where did I have my watch pinched and my Diners Club card and all that currency? Not in Europe, oh, no. In the Union of Soviet Socialist Republics. And that, mark you, was in a train. Now why should it be any different here? Same lack of material

31

possessions – worse, if anything – so you can bet your life they can't wait to get their hot little hands on rich capitalists' property – and that means yours. So don't leave it in the compartment, carry it with you, and when you . . .'

Wexford coughed. Lois saw him and jumped up, clasping her hands. In his absence she had put on more lipstick and eyeshadow and had changed into a low-necked dress of thin yellow material with a black pattern on it.

'Oh, what a fright you gave me! Tony has been scaring us out of our wits with tales of robbery and murder.'

Purbank gave a very *macho*, reassuring-the-little-woman haw-haw of a laugh. 'When did I mention murder now? I never said a word about murder. I merely counselled the inadvisability of leaving valuables around.'

'Quite right too,' said Wexford.

He groped under the table, got a grip on the broken knob with the pliers and wrenched it anticlockwise. The music stopped.

'Oh, you wonderful, wonderful man!' cried Lois. 'Listen to the blessed silence. Peace at last! Don't you adore the masterful way he *strode* into the compartment? You couldn't do that, Tony. All you could do was say we'd have to put up with it all night and get robbed as well.'

'Give the man a cup of tea,' muttered Hilda into her pillow.

'I'll give him anything he wants!' She extended the teacup to Wexford, holding it in both hands and bowing over it in what she perhaps thought was the manner of an emperor's concubine. 'Oh, if only you hadn't drunk up all the Scotch, Hilda!'

But at that moment Mr Yu appeared in the doorway, announced that the restaurant was open and please to follow him. Mindful perhaps of Purbank's warning, Lois gathered up purse, handbag, hand case and what looked like a jewel box. Wexford gulped down the by now lukewarm tea, realizing he was about to be trapped into a foursome with the two women and Purbank. This being China, though, the restaurant would hardly be open for long. Everywhere he had been so far what night life there was came to a halt at about ten. But was there much chance of sleep in this stuffy train?

He felt himself being overtaken by those sensations which result from an insufficiency of sleep, not so much tiredness as a lightness in the head and a feeling of unreality.

They walked down the corridor, Wexford at the rear with Lois immediately in front of him. The boy was still asleep, his head having slid down the wall and come to rest on the table. Wexford slipped in to replace the pliers in the toolbag. Lois hadn't noticed his absence and had gone on in the wake of the others. Wexford stood a moment by the window, trying to make out some indication of the terrain in the darkness that rushed past. He heard a footstep not far from him, the way they had come, turned round and saw approaching him, though still some yards away, the old woman with the bound feet.

This time she was without her stick. Had she followed him on to the train? He closed his eyes, opened them again and she was gone. Had she turned aside into one of the compartments? A hand, red-taloned, was laid on his arm, he smelt Lois Knox's perfume.

'Reg? Do come along, darling, we thought we'd lost you.'

He followed her down the corridor to the restaurant car.

Blue velvet curtains, lace curtains, and on the seats those dun-coloured cotton covers with pleated valances that cover the chairs all over China in waiting rooms and trains and airports and even aircraft. Lois patted the chair next to hers and he had no choice but to sit there. On the table were a plate of wrapped sweets, a plate of wedges of sponge cake, a wine bottle which contained, according to Purbank, spirit and a spirit bottle containing wine. Both liquids were the colour of a Riesling. Wexford asked the waiter for a bottle of beer. Purbank, lighting a cigar, began to talk about the frequent incidence of burglaries in metropolitan Essex.

The restaurant car was full. Chinese passengers sat eating noodles and vegetables out of earthenware bowls. The guides were drinking tea, whispering softly together in Pu Tong Hua. Behind Wexford the two married couples shared a table and the older of the men, in the high-pitched, jovially insensitive voice common to many surgeons, was instructing

33

his companions in the ancient art of foot-binding. A gasp of revulsion came from the barrister's wife as he described toes atrophying.

The beer arrived. It was warm and sweetish. Wexford made a face and signalled to the waiter who was walking round with a tea kettle. Under the tablecloth Lois's knee touched his. 'Excuse me,' Wexford said and he got up and walked over to Mr Sung's table. 'Let me know when you're ready for bed. I don't want to keep you up.'

One of those complex misunderstandings now arose. Why did Wexford want him, Mr Sung, to go to bed? He was not ill. It was (in Mr Sung's words) only twenty-one hundred hours. The dictionary was again produced. Mr Yu smiled benignly, smoking a cigarette. At length it transpired that Mr Sung was not sharing Wexford's compartment for the night, had never intended to share his compartment, would instead be sharing with Mr Yu and the other man whom he introduced as Mr Wong. Because the train wasn't crowded Wexford had his accommodation to himself. He went over to Lewis Fanning and offered him one of the spare berths in his compartment.

But Fanning rejoined in a fashion very interesting to those who are students of character.

'Good God in heaven, I couldn't leave those two alone together! They'd be at each other's throats in two shakes of a turkey's tail. They'd tear each other to pieces. No, I'm frightfully grateful and all that but it'd be more than my life's worth.'

From which Wexford gathered that Fanning was by no means dreading the night ahead and looked forward to extracting from it the maximum of dramatic value for the delectation of those willing to listen to him. Mr Sung, Mr Yu and Mr Wong had begun to play cards. The surgeon was drawing diagrams of the metatarsals, before and after binding, on a table napkin. Wexford sat down again. His teacup had been refilled. Having apparently postponed her drying out, Hilda Avory was drinking steadily from a tumbler filled out of the wine bottle Purbank said held the Chinese spirit Maotai, while Purbank himself told anecdotes of thefts and break-ins he had known. Lois Knox's knee came back against Wexford's and he felt her bare toes nudge his ankle, her sandal having been kicked off under the table. The train ran on through impenetrable darkness, through a dark that showed no demarcation between land and sky and which was punctured by not a single light.

The little woman in the blue trouser suit came into the restaurant car and hesitated for a moment before making for the table where the two married couples sat. The barrister jumped up and pulled out a chair for her. And then Wexford understood it was she he had seen. It was she who had been coming down the corridor when he turned away from the window, she who, while his eyes were closed, had vanished into her own compartment. She too was a small slight creature, she too was dressed in a dark-coloured pair of trousers and a jacket, and though her feet had certainly never been subjected to binding, they were not much bigger than a child's and they too were encased in the black Chinese slippers on sale everywhere. He laughed inwardly at himself. He must be very weary and light-headed if he really believed that the Chinese woman he had seen in Shao-shan and then on Orange Island was following him by train to Kweilin. He drank his tea, accepted a glass of Maotai. Who knew? It might help him to sleep.

Hilda Avory got unsteadily to her feet. She said in a shaky tone, 'I think I could get a little sleep if I try now. Please don't be long, Lois. You'll wake me up if you come bursting in at midnight.'

'Darling, I never burst,' said Lois. She edged a little closer to Wexford. 'Be an angel and give her a hand, Tony, this awful awful train does jerk so.'

Purbank hesitated, torn between being a gentleman and ordering another bottle of laurel flower wine before the bar closed. Fanning, alerted, had half-risen from his seat. 'Allow me,' said Wexford, seizing his opportunity. Lois made a petulant little sound. He smiled at her, rather as one might at a difficult child who, after all, is not one's own and whom one may never meet again, and taking Hilda's arm, shepherded her away between the tables and out into the corridor.

She was sweating profusely, deodorized, French-perfumed sweat, that trickled down her arm and soaked through his own shirt sleeve. Outside the window a box of a building, studded all over with points of light, flashed out of the darkness and receded as the train passed. Wexford slid open the door of the compartment next to his own and helped her in. It was silent in there now. The fan had been switched off so that the air was heavy and thick and densely hot with a faint smell of soot. The thermometer read ninety-five degrees or thirty-five Celsius. He switched the fan on again. Hilda fell on to the left-hand berth and lay face-downwards. Wexford stood there for a few moments, looking at her, wondering if there was anything more he could do and deciding there wasn't, moistening his lips, passing his tongue over the dry roof of his mouth. The Maotai had set up a fresh thirst. He closed the door on Hilda and went into his own compartment.

The fan was off there too. Wexford switched it on and turned back the sheet on the lower left-hand berth. His thermos had been refilled and there were two teabags on the table. He had never cared for teabags. He put a big helping of Silver Leaf into the cup and poured on the near-boiling water. A pungent aromatic perfume came off the liquid, as unlike supermarket packet tea at home as could be. For a moment or two, drinking his tea, he peered into the shining, starless darkness that streamed past the window and then he pulled down the blind.

Lois Knox and Purbank were coming along the corridor together now. He could hear their voices but not what they said. Then Purbank spoke more loudly, 'Good night to you, ladies.' His footsteps pattered away.

Wexford waited for the corridor to empty. He made his way to the bathroom. The lavatory was vacant, the bathroom engaged, the barrister having stolen a march on him and got there first. In the lavatory it was hot and there was a nauseous smell of ammonia. The train rattled and sang. Wexford waited in the corridor, looking out of the window at nothing, saying goodnight to the doctor and his wife who passed him, waiting for the barrister to come out of the bathroom and leave it free. Purbank's enemy and the doctor's daughter, he reflected, hadn't been with the rest in the restaurant car. A holiday romance? The bathroom door opened, the barrister came out, said rather curtly, 'Good night to you,' and walked off, carrying his dark brown towel and tartan sponge bag.

Wexford washed his hands and face and cleaned his teeth, trying not to swallow any of the water. Of course he should have brought some of the water from the thermos flask with him.

All the compartment doors were shut. The light that burned in the corridor wasn't very powerful. Wexford wondered, not for the first time, if there were such a thing as a hundred-watt bulb in the whole of China. He slid open the door to his compartment.

In the right-hand berth, on her back, her striated pinkish-white legs splaying from under the white shift, her face white and puffy, the bridge of the nose encaved, the mouth open and the tongue protruding, lay the Marquise of Tai.

4

He didn't cry out or even gasp. He closed his eyes and held his fists tightly clenched. Without looking again at the dead thing, the mummified, two-thousand-year-old thing, he turned swiftly and went out into the corridor. He didn't know whether he shut the door behind him or not.

He walked down the corridor. The bathroom window was open and he went in, inhaling the cooler air. He put his head out of the window into the rushing darkness. None knew better than he that this was an unwise thing to do. Years ago, when he was young, he had been to an inquest on a man who put his head out of a train window and was decapitated as the train entered a tunnel. He breathed deeply, closed his eyes again. Any attempts at thinking were impossible. He would have to go back there and *do something*.

The bathroom door opened and someone said, 'Oh, sorry.' It was the old doctor.

'I'm just going,' said Wexford.

He wondered if his face was as white as it felt. The doctor didn't seem to notice anything. Humming to himself, he began to wash his hands. Wexford walked swiftly back down the corridor the way he had come, blindly as well as fast, for he almost collided with Lois Knox who was sliding open the door to her own compartment. She wore a short, white, crumpled negligee of broderie anglaise and her face had the stripped look women's faces have that are usually coated with make-up.

He apologized. She said nothing but drew the door across

38

with a slam. Drawing breath, tensing himself, he opened his own door and looked at the berth. It was empty.

Wexford sat down. He closed his eyes and opened them and looked at the berth and saw it was still empty. He would dearly have liked a stiff whisky or even a glass of Maotai, but he was pretty sure he wouldn't get either at this hour – it was after eleven – even if he knew how to summon an attendant, which he didn't. He scattered Silver Leaf into a clean cup and poured hot, no longer boiling, water on to it.

There was no doubt of what he had seen. The corpse had been lying there. And what he had seen had been precisely what he had seen when he had looked down through the cavity in the museum floor at the glass sarcophagus below. It had been the same even to the shortened right arm, the flexed feet, the yawning tongue-filled mouth. *He knew he had seen it.* And now, gingerly, then more firmly, touching the opposite berth, he saw that something had indeed lain there. There was a distinct indentation in the pillow and a creasing of the upper sheet. Something had lain there, been put there, and in his absence had been removed.

He found there was no way of locking his door, but it was possible by stuffing the side into which the door slid with the Peking *Blue News*, to prevent anyone's opening it from the outside. He drank his tea. The fan had gone off for the night and, in spite of the open window, a close heavy warmth filled the compartment. A nasty thought came to Wexford as he undressed. By means of the metal step which let down out of the wall, he climbed up and checked there was nothing in either of the upper berths. He had just recalled a particularly unpleasant story by F. Marion Crawford in which a traveller at sea finds a drowned corpse, or the ghost of a drowned corpse, in the upper berth of his cabin.

When he had had a second cup of tea he put out the light. After several hours of tossing and turning he got about an hour's sleep but no more. It was still only three when he awoke and he knew he wouldn't get any more sleep that night.

He sat up, switched the light on and asked himself a question. Was it possible that what he had seen lying in that berth was Lois Knox?

39

Wexford was a modest man with a humble idea of his own attractions insofar as he ever thought about them. To his own wife he seemed to be unfailingly attractive after thirty years of marriage, but this was something to be thankful for and dismissed rather than speculated about. His life hadn't been devoid of feminine admiration; he had taken none of it very seriously. He hadn't taken Lois Knox seriously at all, yet now he came to think of it . . . if what Fanning said was true, or even partly true, this holiday was for her a kind of sex tour. Wexford knew very well that a woman of this sort need not even find her selected partner attractive; it would be enough that he were a man and accessible, someone to boost her drooping ego, for an evening or an hour, someone to quell her panic, push old age and death an inch or two further away.

Foolishly, he had smiled at her on leaving the restaurant car. Had she taken this smile for an invitation? She had been in the corridor when he came back from the bathroom. She had been wearing a short white shift or at any rate a short white dressing gown, and she had seemed offended with him, in high dudgeon. Had it been she, then, lying in that berth, waiting for him? What must she have felt when he recoiled, closed his eyes in horror and stumbled out without a word?

Wexford was aware that a good many people would have found this funny. After all, the woman, no longer young, no longer attractive, but as forward and brazen as any young beauty, had only got what she deserved. At least, thank God, she didn't know he had mistaken her for a two-thousand-year-old, diseased, disembowelled corpse. But had he? Again, closing his eyes in the dim warm jogging compartment, he saw what he had seen. The Marquise of Tai. The face wasn't Lois's face – God preserve him! And that shortened right arm? Those thighs, scored with deep striations?

Perhaps he needed glasses for daily wear, not just for reading. Perhaps he was going mad. Presumably if you developed schizophrenia – which was quite possible, there was such a thing as spontaneous schizophrenia coming on in middle age – presumably then you had hallucinations and didn't know they were hallucinations and behaved, in short, just as he had. Don't be a fool, he told himself. Get some sleep. No wonder you see visions when you never get any sleep. Towards morning he dozed, until the sunrise came in and the fan came on again.

Things always seem different in the morning. We reiterate this truism always with wonder perhaps because it is such a remarkable truth. It is invariably so. The fearful, the anxious, the monstrous, the macabre, all are washed away in the cool practical morning light. The light which filled Wexford's compartment wasn't particularly cool but it performed the same cleansing function. He wasn't mad, he could see perfectly, and no doubt he shouldn't have drunk that big glass of Maotai on the previous evening.

Events quickly confirmed that it had been Lois Knox in the lower berth. In the restaurant car she and Hilda Avory were sharing their table with the barrister, his wife and the wife's friend, and all but Lois looked up to say good morning to him. Lois, who had been reading aloud from her guide to Kweilin, paused, stared out of the window, and once he had passed on, continued in a gushing voice.

Wexford took a seat opposite Fanning.

'How was your night? I see they haven't killed each other.'

'Mr Purbank and I slept soundly, thank you. Mr Vinald didn't honour us with his presence, thank God. As far as I can gather, and I can't say the subject fascinates me, he had the vacant berth in Dr Baumann's compartment.'

'Unconventional,' said Wexford.

'There's nothing like a few days on the Trans-Siberian Railway to make you forget all the dearest tenets of your upbringing. Not that there'd be anything like that with the Baumanns and Mr Vinald. Daddy and Gordon up top, Mummy and Margery down below.'

Wexford glanced at the plump fair-haired woman who now sat next to her father and opposite Gordon Vinald, eating the Chinese version of a Spanish omelette which always appeared under the sweeping generic title of 'eggs' and which was served up without fail each breakfast time wherever he had been. She was pleasant-looking with a serene face and she hadn't made the mistake which Lois had of cramming an hour-glass shape into trousers and tee-shirt. His glance now fell upon Lois herself. Her hair was carefully dressed, her face painted to a passable imitation of youth. She bore not the least resemblance to the Marquise of Tai and it would have been a cruel libel to suggest it. Her eyes met his and she looked away in calculated disdain.

'Mrs Knox given you the old heave-ho yet?' asked Fanning innocently.

'Good God, no,' said Wexford.

'I only wondered.'

Mr Sung, Mr Yu and Mr Wong were eating with chopsticks from bowls of noodles with rice and vegetables. Purbank came in and Wong immediately got up to speak to him. Whatever it was he said, it brought an expression of edginess to Purbank's face, for a moment he looked almost panicky. He walked away from the Chinese and sat at a table by himself.

Wexford felt relieved. He was noticing people's behaviour again, he was himself again, he had cleansed his thoughts of what hadn't, after all, been a corpse in the berth. He held out his cup as the waiter came by with the tea kettle.

Another grey barrack of a hotel, its design so uninspired that Wexford felt sure no true architect had had a hand in its building. But when he crossed his room and looked out of the window the view was enough to dispel any speculations about man-made things. The mountains that formed the skyline, and in front of the skyline a long ridge, were so fantastic in shape as to resemble almost anything but the karst formations the guidebook said they were. These mountains were shaped like cones, like cypress trees, like toadstools. They rose, tree-studded, vertically out of the plain, their sides straight and their peaks rounded curves. They were the mountains of Chinese paintings that Wexford had until now believed to be artists' stylizations. While you gazed at them you could forget the grey blocks, very like this hotel, that had sprung up too frequently all over the town, and see only those curvy cone mountains and the little red-brown roofs and the water everywhere in ponds and lakes and the Li River twining silver amongst it all.

It was unusual in China for one's guide to accompany one on a train journey. Generally, Mr Sung would have parted from him at Chang-sha station and would have been met by a fresh guide at Kweilin. It appeared, though, that Mr Sung was a native of Kweilin and hadn't been above fiddling this trip for reasons of his own. Mr Yu, in company with Mr Wong, had disappeared at Kweilin station and Fanning's party were now in the charge of a cadaverous man, exceptionally tall for a Chinese, called T'chung. This new guide had relentlessly organized his tourists into an excursion to caves.

They had only two days here. No doubt they had to make the most of it. Wexford eluded Mr Sung and took himself for a quiet walk about the town, under the cassia trees. You could get knocked down by the bicycles which thronged the streets here just as you could in Peking. Men with bowed shoulders and straining muscles pulled carts laden with concrete blocks while women, wearing the yoke pole with a loaded basket at each end of it, jogged by with their curious coolie trot. Among the cassia leaves flew green and black butterflies. Wexford paid a few *fen* to look at an exhibition of paintings and brush calligraphy and to walk in a bonsai garden. He went into one of the dark spice-scented grocery stores, stacked with sweet jars, and bought more green tea. In there he lingered, examining the wares, dried seaweed in bundles and barrels of rice, pickled fish, root ginger, casks of soya sauce, *tofu* in tanks of water. When he turned round to look at the cakes and pastries displayed under glass, he saw across the shop, leaning on her stick, peering as he had just been doing into a drum of rice, the old woman with the bound feet.

It was no more than a split second before he realized that this wasn't the same woman. She straightened and turned her head and he saw a face like a brown nut, scored with a hundred wrinkles, spectacles on her tiny snub nose. Her eyes passed indifferently over him, or at least there was no more in them than a spark of natural curiosity, and then she began speaking in a rapid sing-song to the assistant she had called over to her. The shops here were like they had been in England forty years ago, Wexford thought. This was the way they had been in his early youth. Assistants were polite to you, served you patiently, took trouble, made you into the customer who was always right. How times had changed! The old woman bought her rice, her two pastries, her bag of roasted soya beans, and set off at the clumping pony trot which is how you have to walk if you have no toes and your instep is bowed like a U.

At dinner he was glad they continued the discreet custom of giving him a fan and a carefully screened table to himself. On the other side of the screen he could hear Purbank and Lois Knox grumbling about the miles they had been expected to walk in those caves, and on top of that train journey too. The waitress brought him fried carp, pork and aubergines in ginger sauce, glass noodles with mushrooms, slices of duck, boiled eggs dipped in batter and fried. They made the tea very strong here and aromatic. When he had finished he went up on to the roof to the new bar the hotel seemed so proud of.

It was evident that its creators had never seen any sort of bar in the west. Perhaps they had read of bars or seen old films. The effect was of a mixture of a bunfight in an English village hall and a one-horse town saloon in a Western movie of the thirties. On the concrete of the roof with its concrete parapet, large bare trestle tables had been set out and folding wooden chairs. Light came from bare bulbs and the moon. At the counter you could buy fireworks and on a distant unlit part of the roof a group of Chinese were setting off firecrackers.

Whatever amenities the rooftop bar lacked was made up for by the view. The sky glowed with moonlight and above the river's thread the mountains floated like black stormclouds. As Wexford, a glass of cassia wine beside him on the parapet, leaned over to gaze at the town and the mountains, music burst forth from a record player set up on a card table. It was an LP of Christmas music they were playing. The syrupy voices of an angel choir began with 'Silent Night', went on to 'Santa Claus is Coming' and then Bing Crosby started his soft crooning of 'White Christmas'. It was hotter here than in Chang-sha, stickily humid, the treetops rich with foliage, a bright June moon illuminating it all. As the

44

record went relentlessly on, the Americans at the next table to Wexford's began laughing. The neat smiling Chinese boy who supervised the player and had put the record on beamed at them with gratification. He had made the foreign tourists happy, he would make them even happier by starting it all over again.

As 'Silent Night', with all its evocations of bitter cold, of church bells, of the star of Bethlehem, crept for the second time over the still, hot air, Lois Knox came up the stairs from the floor below. She came from under the concrete canopy which sheltered the bar out on to the roof and she was accompanied by a large paunchy Australian with whom Wexford had gone down to dinner in the lift. Lois's make-up was fresh, she had at some time contrived to visit the hotel hairdresser, and she was wearing a newly pressed blue linen dress and high-heeled blue shoes. She was looking better than he had ever seen her and the Australian seemed smitten already. Wexford understood that he was forgiven, she could afford to forgive him now. She waved, calling out, 'We won't intrude on your reverie!' The Australian took her arm and led her away to a part of the roof where neither the moon nor the lights penetrated.

He sat down at a table alone. After last night it might be wise not to drink too much. Besides, the cassia wine was sweet to the point of cloyingness. Presently Gordon Vinald and Margery Baumann came up on to the roof together. He talked to them for a while and then he went off to green tea and bed.

Going out of the hotel in the morning was a little like walking into a cloud of steam. Already, at a quarter to eight, the temperature was soaring into the eighties. To Wexford it seemed absurd to board a bus for a three- or four-hundred-yard journey to the landing stage. He walked, attempting to shake off the light-headed unreal feeling that was still with him. The roar of his air conditioner had awakened him at two, and when he turned it off the oven temperature returned, closing in like a thick soft blanket. Moreover, the bed was the hardest he had ever attempted to sleep on, a wooden cot with a thin layer of cotton wadding over it. He had lain there, reading, shifting his aching limbs about. Having already got through most of what he had brought with him, *Vanity Fair* (a third reading), the poetry of Lu Yu (because he was coming to China) and last year's Booker winner, he had started on a weighty anthology called *Masterpieces of the Supernatural*. The first story in the collection was 'The Upper Berth' and he was glad he hadn't tried to read it in the train.

Gradually coming round, shaking off the miseries of the night, he walked along the avenue of cassia trees. The boat was in and the American party and the Australian businessmen were already going on board. As Wexford started to follow them the minibus drew up and Mr Sung came bounding out, cross and pompous.

'This is very bad. Must not go alone. Why not wait bus like I say? Cannot board ship without tickets.'

He thrust a piece of coloured cardboard at Wexford. Mr T'chung gathered up the train party by waving his arms like one making semaphore signals. Wexford took the ticket stub that was handed back to him. It had a map of the Li River on it and their route down to Yang-shuo marked, a number of ideographs in pink ink and the somewhat pretentious words printed: Ship's papers. But the boat itself was nice enough, a typical river boat, with a saloon and a big upper deck with deckchairs.

'Good scenery begin ten-thirty,' said Mr Sung.

'Isn't this good scenery?' Wexford asked as the gangway went up and they cast off. The Li River, broad and bronze-coloured, wound out of the town between green cone mountains.

'Ten-thirty,' said Mr Sung. 'Then you take photographs.'

Wexford was tired of explaining to him that he didn't have a camera. Impossible to make Mr Sung understand that to be without a camera was to be free. Gordon Vinald, the barrister's wife and her friend were already up on deck, grumbling, changing films, struggling with telescopic lenses. Wexford sat at a table in the saloon with Margery Baumann, drinking tea that was just being served. Sometimes it is possible for a middle-aged woman to look as fresh as a girl and that was how Margery Baumann, in blue and white checked cotton and with her fair hair

46

newly washed, looked at eight-thirty in the morning on the Li River.

'I'm looking forward to this trip,' she said. 'It's going to be wonderful. And after that – well, we can't get home soon enough for me.'

'I don't imagine you're doing the homeward trip by train as well?'

'Oh, no, thank goodness.' She had a nice light laugh and laughed a good deal but not, Wexford thought, from any sort of nervousness. 'Train to Canton, train out of China to Hong Kong, then the flight home with dear old comfy Swissair.'

'You haven't enjoyed your holiday?'

'In some ways tremendously.' For a moment her eyes had a dreamy look as of delightful, perhaps romantic, things remembered. She became practical. 'But I've had enough, six weeks is too much really. And then I'm needed at home. I'm beginning to feel guilty.'

'What job do you have, Miss Baumann?'

'I'm a GP.' He didn't know why he was so surprised. The children of doctors are often doctors themselves. But she looked so much more the sort of woman who had devoted a gentle life to her old parents. 'I hadn't taken a holiday, not more than a long weekend, in three years. So I got a locum and took the lot owing to me in one – well, not fell, but super swoop!' She laughed.

'The practice is in London?' He really mustn't ask so many questions. It was the habit of an investigating officer. She didn't seem to mind.

'No, Guildford.'

'Really? I'm not far away in Kingsmarkham.'

'Then the Knightons are even nearer to you. They come from a place called Sewingbury.'

'The Knightons?'

'Those people,' she said, as the barrister and his wife walked past the windows. Lois Knox came into the saloon with her Australian. She introduced him as Bruce. Wexford, keeping a straight face, shook hands. Bruce began to talk loudly and vituperatively about Chinese double-think, the way everything was the people's – the people's money,

47

the people's hotel, the people's school – while the people themselves had nothing. He buttonholed Mr T'chung who was peaceably drinking tea with Mr Sung.

'You say it was slave labour built the Ming Tombs, right? It's wrong to force men to build a grandiose tomb for some lousy emperor?'

'Of course,' said Mr T'chung.

'But it's O.K. to make men build a damn great tomb for Mao Tse Tung in Tienanmen Square, is it? What's the difference?'

Mr T'chung looked at him calmly. 'That is a question,' he said in his little clipped voice, 'no one can answer.'

Bruce threw up his hands and gave a bark of laughter.

'Don't let's talk dreary dreary politics,' said Lois.

Wexford went up on deck. The Knightons' friend and Hilda Avory were sitting in deckchairs, drinking tea and Maotai respectively. Hilda said in her gravelly voice with its dying fall, 'Some people who did the trip yesterday told me the boat broke down in mid-stream and they were three hours repairing it.'

'Then the odds are against its breaking down today.'

'It's not a matter of odds, it's a question of efficiency. My only comfort is this place isn't quite so bad as Russia.'

There were boys swimming in the river on one side and water buffalo on the other. High up on the cliffside, against the limestone, wheeled a pair of birds that might have been eagles. Wexford sat in silence, watching the life of the river go by, a village in which was a little curved bridge over an inlet, a temple with a blue roof that the Cultural Revolution had managed to miss, men fishing with cormorants . . .

He stayed up there in the sun for as long as he could stand the heat. Mrs Knighton came up on deck and indefatigably took pictures of everything she saw, water buffalo, cormorants, peasant farmers in the fields, boats with square orange sails, even a utilitarian building Wexford suspected might be a sewage works. By the time it was ten-thirty he had gone below, scorched off the deck. But it was true what Mr Sung had predicted. The scenery suddenly became spectacular, the mountains looping like fantastic clouds, the water clear as glass but with a fierce current running.

Lunch was served at the favourite Chinese time of eleven-thirty and it was the worst meal Wexford had so far eaten, the main course being mainly those organs and entrails which in the west are not eaten by human beings. It amused him to consider how Chinese food, which is usually thought of in Rupert Street or at Poon's as crisp and delicate, may have its slime and lights side too.

It was during lunch that, looking round, Wexford saw the man who had been introduced to him in the train as Mr Wong. He was very surprised. But perhaps it wasn't Mr Wong, perhaps he was confusing him with someone else. But he didn't think so. To say that all Chinese look alike to Europeans was as great a fallacy as that all Chinese had yellow skins. Ah, well, there must be some reason for his being there, not mysterious at all probably to Lu Xing She.

There was just room to wedge a chair into one of the shady companionways. He sat there sleepily while the boat chugged along from Kao Ping to Hua Shan through the deep water, past the drifting boats on which whole families lived, past the cormorant fishermen, between the domed mountains on which trees grew like moss on boulders. When he didn't want to sleep, he couldn't keep awake . . .

A commotion awoke him to an immediate awareness that the boat was no longer moving. Normally, his was a quick rousing from sleep, but after so many white nights and in the slumbrous steamy heat he came to gradually and slowly. His first thought was that Hilda Avory had been right and the boat had broken down. But the engine room was just behind where he was sitting and, turning round, he saw it was deserted.

Then he saw the heads bobbing on the water. He got up and tried to go forward but after a few yards his passage was blocked by the press of people. The saloon was empty, twenty or thirty people were in the bows. Wexford turned back and made his way up on to the upper deck. Here too was a similar craning crowd but the river could be seen. He could see Mr Sung swimming, fully clothed, and what seemed like the entire crew of the boat in the water. And not only the crew – Margery Baumann, Gordon Vinald, Tony Purbank,

49

all swimming or treading water, searching for something, someone . . .

Mrs Knighton, holding her camera in thick red hands, said to him, 'A man went overboard. He couldn't swim, they can't find him.'

'Who is it?'

She began to take pictures, and said with indifference, 'Not one of us. A Chinese.'

5

It was an hour before they gave up trying. Before that they had put one of the crew ashore and he had set off to walk, a distance of four or five miles, to the nearest place where there would be a telephone. Wexford watched the little figure in the blue shirt walking along between the river bank and the rice fields until it was swallowed up by the richer blue and the green.

Margery Baumann was the first of the would-be rescuers to reboard the boat. She was in a one-piece black swimsuit. Wexford thought she was exactly the sort of woman who would never take this sort of trip without wearing a bathing costume under her clothes. She said nothing, went down to the bathroom to get dried and dressed. Purbank came next, shivering in spite of the heat. The crew member who had stayed on board – young, though older than the others, who all looked to Wexford about eighteen – seemed to be the captain. He helped haul Purbank aboard, tried to say something to him in very halting English, failed, and shrugged, holding up his hands.

Gordon Vinald was still swimming among the reefs which reached in places almost to the surface of the water. But as, one by one, the Chinese gave up the search, he too swam reluctantly towards the boat in a slow crawl and allowed himself to be hauled in. Now the search had been abandoned, almost everyone had either gone up on deck or retreated into the saloon. The river was empty, a shining sheet of turquoise under a pale blue sky, the mountains behind making a horizon of misted blue loops. Such a beautiful, gently smiling river! A river artists had been painting for two thousand years and would paint, no doubt, for a thousand more. Under its silken rippling surface, trapped in the teeth of one of those reefs, hung a drowned corpse, small, thin, white as a root.

'What happened?' Wexford said to Purbank. 'I was asleep.'

Purbank, in blue underpants, the sun drying him, pushed his fingers through his wet hair. 'Nobody knows really. It's always like that, isn't it, when someone goes overboard? This chap was up here in the bows where we are now. He must have been alone and he was sitting on his haunches, I reckon, the way they all do, and somehow or other he toppled in. Couldn't swim, of course. Captain Ma got everyone who could swim to go in after him but he'd gone before I was even in the water.'

'Who was it?'

'Who was what?'

'The man who was drowned. Who was he?'

'God knows. To tell you the truth I never asked. I mean, we wouldn't know anyway, would we? He was Chinese.'

'Not one of the crew?'

'I wouldn't know. Anyone would think you were a policeman, the questions you ask. I daresay we shall get enough of that from the Chinese cops when we get to what's it called, Yang Shuo.'

But Captain Ma, apparently, had no intention of continuing the journey to Yang Shuo. They were within a bend of the river of a village with a landing stage and it was to there, Mr Sung told Wexford, that they were now heading. The engines started up and the boat began to move. A bus would come and pick them up. It was best, there was nothing to worry about, the incident was unfortunate, that was all.

'Who was the drowned man?' Wexford asked. 'One of the crew?'

Mr Sung hesitated. He seemed to be considering and he looked far from happy. Wexford, from long practice in studying the reactions of men, thought that what he saw in Mr Sung's face was not so much sorrow at the death of a fellow human being as fear for his own skin. Eventually he said with reluctance, 'His name Wong T'ien Shui.'

52

'Mr Wong?'

Mr Sung nodded. He stood looking over the side at the reefs, one of which the boat's bottom had slightly scraped. 'Impossible navigate here at all January, February,' he said brightly.

Wexford shrugged. He went into the saloon and helped himself to one, then a second, cup of green tea. The pungent tea revived him with almost the stimulus of alcohol. The passengers were gathering up their belongings – bags, carriers, raincoats, umbrellas, maps – preparatory to landing.

'What the hell was that Wong doing on this trip anyway?' grumbled Fanning to Wexford. 'I thought he was supposed to be a student? I thought he was supposed to be at university in Chang-sha? Chinese can't just run about the country like that, going where they please. They're not *free*. I bet you fifty *yuan* there's going to be hell to pay. Heads will roll over this. Thank God I'm whizzing my little lot off to Canton tomorrow.'

They went ashore. On a little beach sat an old man with a sparse beard and two strands of moustache. Three small children played about him in the sand. The beach was also populated by a hundred or so chickens and ducks and two white goats. The old man looked at the people from the West with a kind of impassive polite curiosity. He put a few words to Captain Ma and nodded his head.

The village lay above them, at the top of a sloping lane. It was the hottest part of the day. Wexford had never before experienced the sun as an enemy, something to retreat from, to fear. The party wound its way up the street where mirages danced ahead of them in the light. The ground was thick with reddish-brown dust which rose in spirals at their tread. Dust coated everything, the hovels that lined the lane, the walls, the grass, even the legs and arms and faces of the children who came out of their houses, chewing on handfuls of glutinous rice, to stare at the visitors.

At the top of the hill half a dozen men and a girl were building an apartment block. The smell of the river and the dust gave place to a pleasanter one of sandalwood. There was a shop next door into which the entire party, with the exception of Wexford and Fanning, immediately disappeared, and at the end of the village a big house with a walled-in court

53

which had perhaps once been the home of the local warlord. Fanning squatted, oriental fashion, on the broad veranda of the shop and lit a cigarette.

'I make call Yang Shuo,' said Mr Sung. 'Bus come very soon.'

'*I* make call,' Mr T'chung corrected him in a very admonitory voice. He began lecturing the other guide in a hectoring sing-song, wagging his finger. Wexford began to think that if it were to be a question of finding a new Chairman from this part of the world, T'chung Bei Ling might stand a better chance than Sung Lao Zhong.

It was too hot to explore the village, though Wexford walked down one or two narrow little lanes. Children followed him in a giggling huddle. As he returned once more to the square or market place where the shop was he saw an old woman standing in the deep shadow of an overhanging roof. He stood still and looked at her, from her black hair laced with grey, her white puffy face – the Marquise of Tai's face – down to her tiny wedge-shaped feet in child's slippers. He approached till he was no more than a yard from her.

'You want to speak to me?' he said, enunciating clearly.

She made no answer. He repeated what he had said. She seemed to shrink, from shyness or fear. From the other side of the square Mr T'chung began calling, 'Bus has come. Please come quick down hill to bus. Come along, bus has come.'

When Wexford turned from the voice and looked where the old woman had been she was gone. Into the house? It was impossible she should keep vanishing into the abodes of strangers. He went up to the dark doorway and looked inside. It was a dirty hovel in which a child sat eating rice on the floor and a small pig rooted in the far corner. No old woman and no other exit for her to have departed through. If for one moment he were prepared to entertain the idea of the supernatural . . .

Talking excitedly about their purchases, the drowned Wong for the time being forgotten, the train party and the Australians made their way down the hill to where the bus waited. It was parked by the beach and beside it was what was very evidently a police car. Police were on the boat, talking to Captain Ma. An officer came up to Mr T'chung and fired a string of questions at him.

'People's police will come to hotel this evening,' said Mr T'chung.

All this would normally have interested Wexford very much. The reason it didn't was that he had been aware, all the way down the hill, of the old woman with the bound feet following him at a distance. He turned round once or twice, like Shelley's traveller, he told himself, and saw not exactly a frightful fiend but this old creature, hobbling on her stick, who was becoming fiendish enough to him. Now about to enter the bus, the heat thick and gleaming, radiated off the still blue water in a dazzling glare, he made himself turn round and face behind him boldly. She was gone. There was nowhere for her to disappear to but she was gone.

For the rest of the passengers the bus ride back was as rewarding as the boat trip had been on account of the scenery through which the route passed. They drove along lush valleys, green with young rice. Wexford thought about the old woman whom he had now seen three, or possibly four, times. Was she real? Was she a real woman who, incredible as it might be, was for some reason following him across China? Or was she a hallucination such as he supposed schizophrenics might have?

He was sitting next to Tony Purbank who was as silent as he. Purbank was also a fair-skinned person who reacted badly to the sun and his face hadn't been protected as Wexford's had. Moreover, he had a big bald patch on top of his head. His forehead and his bald pate began to glow a fiery red as soon as he was in the air-conditioned shelter of the bus. He spoke not a word, he looked as if he were suffering from a mild degree of heatstroke. Mr Sung too made the return journey in total silence. From the back seats, where Lois Knox sat with Bruce and the Knightons, Wexford could hear a continuous hum of speculation as to how Mr Wong had come to fall overboard.

Wexford expected to see the old woman get off the bus after him but she didn't. It was an absurd relief. He went straight off upstairs and made himself a cup of Silver Leaf.

He lay on the bed, thinking about schizophrenia, wondering what he was going to do if she moved in with him, if she came into his room in the night and lay down in the other bed. Presumably, the truth was that she had never existed at all. He thought back. At Chang-sha he had heard the tap of her stick, her voice as she spoke to her companion. Besides, if his mind was going to produce figments to haunt him, why produce *her*? Out of what recesses of experience, unconscious processes, even trauma, was his mind conjuring an old Chinese woman?

The tea, as always, made him feel better. Could he convince himself it was a mirage he had seen in that river village, a trick of the heat and light?

'People's police say no need talk with you,' said Mr Sung, coming up to his table as dinner was being served. 'No need ask questions any tourists, ship's crew only.' He paused, said, carefully choosing his words, 'They have find dead body Wong T'ien Shui.'

'Poor chap,' said Wexford. 'He can't have been more than twenty or so.'

'Age I don't know,' said Mr Sung. 'Very young, yes. Body cut and – what you say? – brushed very bad by rocks.'

'Bruised?'

'Bruised, yes. Thank you. Many bad rocks there under river so body all cut and bad bruise.'

There was as usual a screen between Wexford and the table at which the train party sat. From beyond it he could only hear a general buzz of conversation. The girl came round with the tea kettle and he had two cups, strangely disturbed now by the death of Wong T'ien Shui. It was still only seven and the sun was just setting. He walked out of the hotel, crossed the road and took the little causeway to the island in the middle of the lake. Somehow – sentimentally, no doubt – he couldn't help imagining Wong as he must have been when a little boy, not so long ago, attending the kindergarten, being met by his mother with her hair in two braids, having a doughnut bought for him in a dark scented grocer's shop, flying a kite shaped like a butterfly or a dragon, going home to loving grandparents. It was a very young life to have been cut short like that.

It should have been pleasant out on the island but because of the weighty thickening humidity, it wasn't. The undulations of mountains looked blue now, veiled in mist, and the air hung full of sluggishly moving mosquitos. After being bitten for the second time he went back to the hotel. Malaria and dengue fever might now be avoidable, but you could still have a leg or an arm swell up like a balloon.

Up on the roof it was too high for the mosquitos. He knew he shouldn't drink, because of his blood pressure and an ever threatening weight problem, but he had to get some sleep somehow. He bought a smallish bottle of cassia wine. The Baumanns, the Knightons and Gordon Vinald called him over to the table they were sharing, only a second before he was similarly summoned to the other – necessarily a few yards away because of the Purbank-Vinald feud – shared by Lois Knox, Hilda Avory and Purbank. There was no sign of the Australians, Fanning or Mrs Knighton's friend. Lois looked sour and Hilda ill, and it was a relief to Wexford to follow the rule of first come, first served.

The people at the table he joined were indulging in the favourite tourist pastime of showing off to each other the souvenirs they had bought that day. As Gordon Vinald began talking, Mrs Baumann whispered to Wexford that he was an antique dealer.

'Jade is always cold to the touch,' he was saying. 'That's one of the best ways for the amateur to tell if it's jade or not. If it stays cold in a hot room or against the skin the chances are it's jade.'

He told them of various jade frauds. How the unscrupulous dealers of Hong Kong would arrange a display with five items of plastic to one of jade, five items of plastic to one of ivory. China was safe, though. The Chinese were either too high-principled to deceive or too innocent to understand the mechanics of deception. But if, of course, the jade they were selling had been imported into China they might themselves have been deceived . . . Wexford thought of the little pieces he had bought for Dora and Denise and his daughters. Were they cold to the touch? He couldn't remember. He put a tentative question about it to Vinald.

'You're in the room next to mine, aren't you?' Vinald

replied. 'No doubt we'll be keeping our usual nursery hours, so why don't you bring them in at the witching hour of nine-thirty and show me?'

Margery Baumann laughed. She took a tissue-wrapped parcel out of her handbag and out of it tumbled half a dozen little cups, medallions, a ring and a pendant in the shape of a turtle. She put the ring on to her finger. Vinald examined all the pieces and pronounced them to be jade, one indeed very close in colour to the imperial jade beloved by the emperors. Then suddenly, as if no one else was there, he lifted her hand in his and brought it up against his cheek. Ostensibly, he was testing the temperature of her ring on his own skin, yet the gesture had a very lover-like air to it. Wexford saw Mrs Baumann smile with pleasure and Margery blush.

Vinald released her hand. 'That's your true nephrite. You've done well, Margery. If you hadn't a worthier profession already I'd say you've a flair for my business.'

She said nothing, only laughed again. And yet the remark, delivered in such a tone and after such a gesture, could almost have been leading up to a proposal of marriage. Wexford thought he wouldn't be surprised if an announcement were made to the party on the following day.

He offered his wine round the table. The beer drinkers refused but Mrs Baumann and Mrs Knighton each took a glass. His bottle wasn't going to last long at that rate. He went off to the bar to get another as 'Silent Night' came crooning out of the record player.

Standing at the bar, in the company of an older woman, was the best-looking girl he had seen since he came to China.

The best-looking Caucasian, that is. Of Chinese beauties there had been plenty but it had seemed to him that women with the looks of his daughter Sheila or his niece Denise weren't interested in visiting the People's Republic.

This girl, though, would have compelled glances in the most sophisticated milieu. She and the older woman were standing by the counter, talking to the three Australian businessmen about the topic which commanded the attention of the whole hotel, and probably the whole city of Kweilin, the drowning of Wong T'ien Shui. Wexford heard her say, 'There's always something with that boat. If I believed in things like that I'd say that boat had bad joss. Maybe the place they built it was on a dragon's eye or something.'

She laughed. The Australians laughed uproariously. Her accent, he thought, was that of New Zealand. The older woman – her mother? – spoke to her.

'Are you having that red wine again, Pandora, or the Japanese whisky stuff?'

Pandora pondered. She was tall and extravagantly slender, somewhere in her early twenties. Her hair was as black as Lois Knox's raven dye, but Pandora's was natural and it fell as straight to her shoulders as if it were wet. There was no make-up on the dazzling white skin but for a stroke of emerald green on her eyelids. Her eyes were hazel green and the lashes as thick and sooty as a black kitten's. She had on a bright green dress with a pink and black cummerbund and pink sandals. Deciding on the whisky, she turned away and walked out on to the roof. Bruce took a tray and piled bottles and glasses on to it.

Wexford bought his wine and went back. For a moment he thought he saw the old woman with the bound feet standing up against the parapet, but when he looked again he saw only a Chinese boy with a firecracker in his hand. Back at the table they were once more on the topic of Wong's death. Dr Baumann couldn't understand how anyone could have drowned where there were so many reefs to provide footholds. Margery wondered if he had struck his head on one of those reefs as he fell. Mrs Knighton, with an unpleasant little laugh, said be that as it might it had ruined what had promised to be an interesting day out. And then Wexford's attention was caught by the action of Lois Knox who, seeing her Australian come out on to the roof with a woman and two other men, seeing him home in on the table where Pandora had sat down, got up, muttered 'excuse me' to her companions and walked swiftly away towards the stairs. Purbank said something inaudible but Hilda Avory's reply carried on the night air.

'Of course it makes her unhappy. What does she expect if she goes on like that at her age?'

Knighton was staring ahead of him. He had contributed little to the conversation but now he had extracted himself from it entirely. Gazing across the roof like that, he looked as if he had had some transcending vision or had just seen a ghost. Abruptly he jerked his head aside and Wexford was astonished to see his enraptured expression. What had produced that?

His wife was showing family snapshots to Mrs Baumann. 'We've four children, three sons and a daughter, and four simply adorable grandchildren with another on the way.'

Mrs Baumann was beginning an appropriate comment when Knighton spoke. He seemed to be addressing no one in particular. He looked at the view, at the stars, and said:

'"I had gone aboard and was minded to depart,
When I heard from the shore your song with tap of foot.
The pool of peach blossom is a thousand feet deep
But not so deep as the love in your farewell to me." '

The Baumanns looked extremely embarrassed. A sheepish smile lingered on Vinald's face. Mrs Knighton looked at her friend and her friend looked at her and Mrs Knighton very slightly cast up her eyes.

'The work of Li Po,' said Knighton in his more usual cold and dry tone. 'The famous eighth-century Chinese poet.'

'I don't know about you, Irene,' said Mrs Knighton, 'but I feel like going up to my room.'

'Down,' said her friend.

'I mean down. Don't be late,' she said to her husband. 'You've had a long day.' She achieved, like someone doing facial exercises, a broad smile and said briskly, 'Good night, everyone.'

Knighton got to his feet with the air of someone following a weary old rule of politeness. But when the women had gone and the elder Baumanns had gathered up their things and started to follow them, instead of sitting down again, he walked away from the table to a distant part of the roof, leaned over the parapet and gazed at the moonlit landscape.

Wexford was left to play gooseberry to the lovers. He said

good night to Margery, went down to his room and made himself a cup of tea. The old woman with the bound feet had departed to wherever such materializations go when off-duty. Settled down with Poe's 'The Tell-tale Heart', he waited for Vinald's footfall in the corridor – unless, of course, he should forget his appointment and his footfall sound tonight in the corridor below, where Margery's room was.

But no more than half an hour had passed before he heard Vinald's light switch go on. Wexford collected his pieces of jade and knocked at the antique dealer's door.

6

Treasures set about the austere Chinese hotel bedroom had transformed it into something resembling a corner of a museum in the Forbidden City. There were dishes of *famille jaune*, pieces of blue and white ware, a magnificent tall pearl-coloured vase with a design on it of birds and ripe peaches on a peach tree, lacquer trays, boxes of chops in jade and carnelian and soapstone, three or four plain pale bowls of exquisite shape, a pair of carved jade vases with lids, and everywhere a scattering of tiny pieces of carved jade, of snuff bottles, seals and metal scent bottles.

'I confess to liking the gorgeous stuff best,' said Wexford. 'Does that prove me ignorant and undiscriminating?'

Vinald laughed. 'Not really. That vase is a lovely piece. I'm lucky to have found it. There are a pair just like it that were made for the Dowager Empress.'

'It's not so very old then?' Wexford knew that much.

'Under a hundred years.' Vinald handed his purchases back to him. 'Your jade's O.K. Frankly, I'd be surprised if it wasn't. Can I offer you a cup of tea?' When it was poured he began tidying the room. 'We're off again tomorrow, a ghastly round-about journey since there's no direct route from Kweilin to Canton. It seems that the mountains get in the way.' He was thrusting items from the desk into a hand case, a ball-point pen, a stick of red sealing wax, a note book, the hotel writing paper out of the blotter. Wexford was amused. How people loved acquiring something for nothing, even the wealthiest! Here was this evidently rich man pinching three sheets of writing paper when there was little doubt he could have bought up all the notepaper stocks in Kweilin and given it back again without much noticing the loss.

Vinald took a drink of tea. 'I didn't exactly come to China to buy antiquities,' he said. 'I was in need of a holiday, I was literally dying on my feet for a holiday. But I had every intention of buying antiquities when I got here. I knew what a hoard China has, you see.'

Wexford raised his eyebrows enquiringly.

'Oh, yes. You can imagine the stuff that got pinched at the time of what they call Liberation, can't you? Not to mention the Cultural Revolution. They claim it has all passed through Government hands but the fact is they simply stole it from its rightful owners, and murdered them too if the truth were known.'

'The truth never really is known about China,' said Wexford. 'And that's not new, it's always been so.'

Vinald passed over the interruption with a slight impatient wave of his hand. 'I can tell you that if China chose to let loose what she's got on the world the bottom would fall slap bang out of the antiques market.'

'Which would hardly suit you, I suppose.'

'You're right there. I've helped myself to a few unconsidered trifles.' Vinald pulled tissue paper out of a drawer and started wrapping things up, packing them into boxes, some of which were padded with straw. 'Tell me,' he said, speaking rather abruptly, 'do you think it's wrong to buy something for fifty *yuan* – say fifteen pounds – when you know perfectly well its real worth would be five hundred pounds?'

'If by wrong you mean illegal, I shouldn't think that's illegal anywhere in the world. No doubt it's unethical, some would say it's taking advantage of innocence. Why? Have you done much of that sort of thing?'

'A bit,' said Vinald. 'They're so ignorant they don't know what they're offering you half the time. It might be unethical in some places, I don't think it is here. You can't think of yourself as taking an unfair advantage of the Chinese Government, can you? It's not as if it were some individual trying to make a living.'

'How about a nation trying to make a living?' Vinald

looked uncomprehending so Wexford turned aslant of the subject. 'I don't envy you carrying that lot home.'

'Most of it'll go in my suitcase.' Vinald packed the blue and white dishes, an ikon, a gleaming white bowl. 'I brought the minimum of clothes because I knew I'd want to fill up this end.'

'You don't anticipate trouble with the Customs?'

'I shan't fall foul of them. As long as you don't take anything out of China that's more than a hundred and twenty years old you're O.K.'

Wexford thanked him for his opinion and his tea and left him wrapping up and packing a blue, crimson and gold ikon. In his own room, standing in the corner by the air conditioner, was the old woman with the bound feet. He stared and she changed into the wooden coat stand over which he had hung his jacket.

Her shadow flitted across the window blind. He knew she wasn't real now and because of something that had happened to his eyes or his mind he was imagining her. In the book of supernatural stories he was reading was one by Somerset Maugham called 'The End of the Flight', which had nothing to do with aircraft but was about a man in the Far East who had done some sort of injury to an Achinese and thereafter, no matter where he fled to, was haunted by this Achinese or his spirit or ghost. He, Wexford, had of course never done any sort of injury to an old Chinese woman.

The room was empty again, not a trace of her. The air conditioning made it rather too cool. He went to bed, pulling the quilt up over his head. It was impossible to sleep, so in the middle of the night he got up again and made tea. There was no sign of the old woman but still he couldn't sleep, and to keep sleep still further at bay, at about four in the morning the drone of the air conditioner was augmented by a rushing roaring sound. It was raining.

When it began to get light he got out of bed and looked at the rain. He could see the rain crashing against the windows and that was about all he could see, the lake, the city roofs, the mountains were all blotted out by dense white fog.

It was absurd to attempt to go out unless one had to. The

64

train party had to. They were embarking on a journey to Canton that was only about two hundred miles as the crow flies but which would take two days in a train. Their luggage was piled in the hotel lobby. In twos and threes they came down in the lift to await Mr T'chung and the bus.

Wexford sat in a rattan chair, reading Maugham's story about the ghost of the Achinese. The Knightons came first with their friend, who was wearing her dark blue trouser suit but not looking much like the old woman with the bound feet. The bus had drawn up outside. Lois Knox came out of the lift with Hilda Avory behind her.

'I suppose we must say goodbye,' Lois said with a meaning look as if she and he had been on intimate terms.

Wexford shook hands with her, then with Hilda and Vinald. 'Have a good journey.'

'And you,' said Vinald. 'Flying off in a nice little Fokker Friendship aren't you? We should be so lucky.'

The Baumanns and Margery waved to him. Fanning got out of the lift with Mr T'chung. 'So help me God,' whispered Fanning to Wexford, 'but once I get home the furthest bloody abroad I'm going ever again will be the Isle of Wight.'

Under umbrellas held up by their guides they filed out to the bus, joined at the last moment by the two women from New Zealand. The beautiful Pandora was in tight yellow trousers and a yellow tee-shirt and Wexford saw Lois give her a glare of dislike.

The rain swallowed the bus as it went splashing off towards the railway station. Wexford drank some tea, tried to sleep, read a story by M.R. James about a man dogged by the ghost of a Swedish nobleman whom he had inadvertently released from a tomb. He didn't finish it. He had seen the old woman with the bound feet cross the lobby just after the bus had left and now he could see her most of the time hovering on the edge of his sight. When he stared hard she would disappear and then, as he looked away, he would be dimly aware of her waiting, so to speak, in the wings of his vision.

It was useless to worry about it. When he got home he would get Dr Crocker to send him to an oculist or specialist in allergies or maybe, if it had to be, a psychiatrist. Instead of worrying, or instead of worrying more than he could help, he began to wonder if he ought to go and call on the local police. After all, he had originally come to China because he was a policeman, he had come at the express invitation of the Ministry of Internal Affairs. Having actually been on the boat at the time of Wong's fatal accident, should he not go and inform them of this fact? Rather glumly he thought about it. With his lack of Chinese and their undoubted lack of English? With Mr Sung as his interpreter? And what help could he be? He had been asleep at the time.

No, he wouldn't go. Such an action would smack of 'putting himself forward', of showing off his greater sophistication and that of the nation he came from. Besides, he could do nothing, tell them nothing, beyond revealing himself as possibly the least effective witness on the boat.

It rained all day. But twenty-four hours later, when he was starting to think his flight would be cancelled because of the bad weather, the sky cleared, the sun came back and the looped mountains stood out so sharply against the translucent blue that it seemed one could pick out every tree on their slopes. Mr Sung escorted him to the airport in a taxi.

'I like to say,' said Mr Sung, 'the very great pleasure it has been to me to be your guide and I wish you good journey and pleasant stay in Guangzhou.'

This, Wexford knew, was what the Chinese called Canton, or perhaps it would be more correct to say that in trying to pronounce Guangzhou, Canton was the best those European merchants who had come there had been able to do.

'You will please convey best wishes to your friends and relations in UK and say they are welcome to China. All friends are welcome to China.'

The aircraft had no air conditioning. Once they were airborne steam poured across the non-pressurized interior and the passengers fanned themselves with fans painted with the Kweilin mountains which the stewardess provided. Wexford was the only European on board. He knew that the stewardess walking up and down the aisle with fans and sweets on a tray was a young girl in her early twenties but for a moment he had seen her as an old woman with bound feet.

Would he see her in Canton? In Hong Kong? Would he –
like Maugham's man with the Achinese – would he see her
in *England*?

At Canton he was met by his new guide, Lo Nan Chiao. Mr
Lo shook hands and said he was welcome to Guangzhou and
if he was agreeable, while his luggage went on to the hotel,
they would proceed straight to Martyrs' Mausoleum.

The old woman with the bound feet was there waiting for
him. He closed his eyes and opened them and she had changed
back into the uniformed attendant. She emerged from the
doors of the Sun Yat-sen Monument and came across the
bridge from Sha Mian to meet him. By that time he would
have been convinced of his own madness if Mr Lo hadn't
gone up to speak to her, remarking afterwards to Wexford
that she was an acquaintance of his mother's.

Wexford sweated. She wasn't *always* an acquaintance of
Mr Lo's mother. It was even hotter here and the humidity
was intense. When he tried to make tea he found the water
in his thermos flask was only lukewarm and repeated requests
to the hotel staff failed to produce boiling water. But at dinner
he discovered a new brand of Lao Shan, the coldest and
best mineral water he had so far tasted, and he bought a
dozen bottles to the amazement of the waitress to whom
such extravagance perhaps represented a week's wages. The
food was good too and the coffee was drinkable.

He dozed in his bedroom and this time it might have been
a dream and not a vision he had. He never knew. But he
took the traditional action honoured in ghost stories. He
threw something. Almost anywhere else in the world a holy
book would have been provided in an hotel bedroom, the
Bible or the Koran or the Gita, but here he had to make
do with *Masterpieces of the Supernatural*. The old woman
disappeared. Wexford felt worn out. He was sure he wouldn't
sleep and he prepared for another white night, only to fall
into a heavy dreamless slumber he didn't come out of until
six when the phone rang.

'Good morning. Time to get up,' said a chirpy voice,
habituated to the rhythms of Cantonese.

Wexford felt much better. The sun was shining on the
green wooded mountains that he could see from his window.

Breakfast and then off to the porcelain factory with Mr Lo, to the factory at Fu-shan where all the great Chinese porcelain of the past was made and from where it had been exported to Europe, where the peach-blossom vase acquired by Gordon Vinald certainly had been shaped and painted and glazed.

It was while he was having dinner back once more at the Bai-yun Hotel that he realized he hadn't seen the old woman once she had scuttled out of sight at the factory behind a group of girls modelling figurines. She didn't appear in his room that evening nor next day in Tung Shan Park nor was she anywhere around to spoil the beauty of the orchid garden.

Mr Lo came with Wexford's exit visa and a packed lunch to eat on the train to Kowloon. They went to the station and the old woman wasn't there. She wasn't waiting for him in his carriage either. The train had dun-coloured cotton covers with pleated valances on the seats and net curtains and pale blue velvet curtains at the windows. There was closed-circuit television on which sometimes a girl announcer appeared and sometimes acrobats gyrated. Wexford couldn't yet believe the old woman had gone and he even tried to catch glimpses of her round the edges of his vision but he achieved nothing by this beyond a headache.

He was leaving China. Quietly, without pause or frontier fuss, the train crossed the border into the Hong Kong New Territories at Sum-chun. By now Wexford had a feeling of complete certainty he would never again see the old woman with the bound feet. Ghost or hallucination, for some reason she had come to him in Shao-shan and, equally inexplicably, left him in Canton. He felt tired, shaky, with relief. The cool airy train raced pleasantly along towards the Crown Colony, back to luxury, ordinariness, a 'too high' standard of living, soft beds, capitalism.

Dora was there to meet him on the platform at Kowloon Station. She had missed her husband and guessed he had missed her but they had been married, after all, for more than thirty years and so she was a little surprised by the ardour of his embrace.

Part Two

Part Two

7

Thatto Hall Farm stands about a mile outside the small town of Sewingbury in pleasant hilly wooded country. The Hall itself was pulled down many years ago and the smaller house, which was bought by a London couple in 1965 and converted for use as a weekend residence, is now the only dwelling in Thatto Vale. Paunceley is the nearest village, a collection of cottages and a small council estate linked to Sewingbury by a B-class road and a system of footpaths that run close by the farmhouse.

It is a long low brick house, about a hundred and sixty years old, comprising six rooms, two bathrooms, a small washroom and a kitchen. The gardens have been well kept and the house has acquired a tended, even luxurious appearance. In October the Virginia Creeper which covers half the front of the house turns to a blaze of crimson and the two circular flowerbeds in the two front lawns are filled with dwarf Michaelmas daisies in shades of purple, rose and deep blue.

It was on a morning in October that Mrs Renie Thompson, the cleaner at Thatto Hall Farm, arrived at nine to find her employer lying dead on the dining-room floor.

Wexford got to work half an hour later and that was the first thing they told him. The name rang a bell and so did the address.

'*Who* is it that's dead?' he said to Detective Sergeant Martin.

'A Mrs Knighton, sir. A Mrs Adela Knighton. The woman who found her said she'd been shot.'

'And Inspector Burden's gone over there, has he, with the doctor and Murdoch? I think we'll go too.'

It was a fine sunny day, a little morning mist still lingering. The leaves had not yet begun to fall. Where the footpath met the road, just before the farmhouse, a man came over the stile, carrying a shotgun and with two dead rabbits slung over his shoulder. Thatto Hall Farm lay in a misty golden haze. On its well-trimmed dewy lawns lay a scattering of red and yellow fruit from crab apple trees. The front door was open and Wexford walked in.

Murdoch, the Scene-of-Crimes Officer, was in the dining room with Dr Crocker and the body. Naughton, the fingerprint man, was busy in the hall. At the kitchen table with Burden opposite her, drinking strong tea, sat Renie Thompson. She was much the same age as her dead employer had been, somewhere in the middle sixties, a big gaunt woman with dyed brown hair in a hairnet and wearing a skirt and jumper covered by a mauve flowered overall.

'Where is Mr Knighton?' Wexford asked.

'Don't ask me.' Mrs Thompson kept up a bold and truculent manner even while in shock. 'I always come in nine sharp Mondays, Wednesdays and Fridays and this is the first time I've known him not be here as well as her. I went upstairs and looked. I mean he might have been dead and laying up there too for all I knew. They had twin beds and his wasn't slept in. I've never known that before, not all the time I've worked here and that's donkey's years.'

Wexford went upstairs. The staircase was of polished oak, uncarpeted, and, though the bedrooms were carpeted, the spacious upper hall had a polished floor on which lay blue and silvery grey rugs. The principal bedroom, with its made bed and its unmade bed, was done in shades of rose, the other three in blue, green and gold respectively. Victorian furniture, chintz curtains pinch-pleated or on rings, Arthur Rackham drawings in narrow silver-coloured frames, on a console table a bunch of everlasting flowers in a Bing and Grondahl bowl, and in every bedroom a jar of pot-pourri. All very correct and tasteful. Wexford looked in all the cupboards, he even

72

looked under the beds. He went downstairs and looked in the large, similarly conventionally furnished living room. Having looked in the bathrooms, he looked in the washroom where he noticed a pane of glass was missing from the window. Knighton, alive or dead, wasn't in the house.

Dr Crocker came out of the dining room and said, 'Old Tremlett's on his way. I managed to get him at home before he left for the infirmary.'

'Is it true she was shot?'

'Through the back of the head. He must have brought the barrel of the gun right up against the occipital itself. All her back hair was singed.'

'He shot her through the *back* of the head? Put the gun against the back of her head and shot her? The mind boggles a bit. What do you think, Sergeant, she heard a sound, came down to see what it was, he crept up behind her and shot her?'

'She might have heard glass breaking, sir. There's a piece of glass missing from the window in there.'

'Except that it was cut out. You can get together with Mrs Thompson and find out what sort of valuables they've got or had in this house.'

Wexford knelt down and looked at the body. It was cold and heavy to the touch and rigor was already established. What he had seen of Adela Knighton in China he hadn't cared for but he forgot that in a rush of pity. She was a sad sight and there was no dignity in her death. While alive and in health she had been a plain, stocky, rather aggressive, no-nonsense sort of woman. Now in death she lay as a flabby heap, her face having a look of half-melted wax, her grizzled sandy hair burned black at the nape of her neck and around the red, charred-edged hole the bullet had drilled there. She wore an expensive-looking nightgown of some thick, shiny, peach-coloured silky material with lace borders and lace insertions and over it a dressing gown of dark blue velour. On her feet were flat-heeled slippers of quilted black velvet. Her wedding ring, a chased platinum band worn down to the thinness of wire, was on her left hand.

'It doesn't look as if anything very alarming fetched her

down,' said Wexford. 'There's a phone extension by her bed and the wires haven't been cut.'

A black Daimler drew up on the gravel drive. Sir Hilary Tremlett, the pathologist, had arrived. Wexford went into the washroom off the hall. It contained a lavatory pan with low flush cistern, a vanity table with bowl insert, a small round mirror on the wall above the bowl. The window was the sash kind divided into four panes, each about fifteen inches square, and from one of these the glass had been cut. Wexford decided there was no way he himself could have squeezed through the aperture thus obtained but he was a large man with a big frame. Most women could have got through there and any average-sized man.

Directly below the window outside was a small narrow flowerbed in which pink sedum was blooming. Wexford knew there wouldn't be any footprints. He went out to look and there weren't, though someone had plainly kicked over the remains of what footprints there had been.

Mrs Thompson was telling Martin that the Knightons had never kept money in the house as far as she knew. Mrs Knighton, like a lot of well-off people, Renie Thompson implied, was always short of cash and as often as not would pay her with a cheque. No ornaments were missing, no attempt had been made to remove heavy equipment, television, record player or any kitchen machinery.

'Presumably she had some jewellery.'

'Must have done,' said Martin in a way that indicated he wouldn't have thought of it if his chief hadn't reminded him. 'How about jewellery, Mrs Thompson?'

'I only saw her in the mornings, didn't I? It's no good asking me what rings and whatnot she had.'

Wexford remembered, from China, a platinum watch and an engagement ring with, he thought, a square-cut stone. He mentioned those items to Mrs Thompson.

'If you say so. Don't ask me where she kept them.'

'Very well, we won't ask you,' said Wexford, irritated by her truculent huffy manner. 'We'll look. There are a limited number of places. She didn't keep them in the fridge or up a chimney.'

Sir Hilary had finished his preliminary examination and

they were about to take the body away. Murdoch was still meticulously at work on table surfaces, banisters, door jambs. The doctor, about to leave, said to Wexford, 'Did she live here alone?'

'There's a husband,' said Wexford.

'Where is he then?'

'I wish I knew.'

Martin came downstairs. 'There's no jewellery or jewel case in her room or any of the bedrooms, sir.'

'Right.' He said to Mrs Thompson, remembering a table on a hotel roof, a yellow envelope of snapshots, 'She had children. Where do they live?'

'The daughter in Sewingbury, that I do know. Don't ask me where you'll find the sons, all off abroad somewhere, I daresay. There might be numbers in that book.'

A leather-bound directory lay on a table by the telephone. Wexford himself held his daughters' phone numbers in his head. He was justly and secretly proud of his memory, knowing it to be exceptional.

'What's the daughter's married name?'

'Her *surname*? That I wouldn't know. I'd no reason ever to be told that, had I? Jennifer, they call her. Mr Knighton could tell you.'

'Yes, I've no doubt he knows his own daughter's name,' said Wexford. 'You can go home now, Mrs Thompson, if you like. I expect we'll want to see you again. We'll let you know.'

'Don't I get a lift home then?'

'I beg your pardon?'

'I should think the least you could do is one of you run me home. I reported finding her, didn't I? I've helped you with your enquiries. It's usual to arrange for transport under the circumstances.'

Wexford was amused. 'Not in this neck of the sticks it isn't. Maybe in Y Division or Los Angeles. You've been watching too many crime serials.'

Renie Thompson stuck her chin in the air and flounced out. Wexford laughed.

'She only lives in Paunceley,' said Burden. 'You don't think she could have done it?'

'Come on. She couldn't tell a Beretta from a bottle opener. Have you finished, Murdoch? Better get back then. Martin, I want Knighton's daughter found – she lives somewhere in Sewingbury – and the sons too if possible. I want a house-to-house between here and Sewingbury and the other side of Thatto Vale through Paunceley. Luckily, or maybe unluckily, there aren't that many houses.'

'What are we looking for, sir?'

'Any suspicious happenings during the night, any strange cars seen, strangers on foot yesterday or in the night. Oh, and we're looking for Knighton. Very keenly are we looking for Knighton.'

When they had gone Wexford began telling Burden about China. Not about the trip in general – with restraint he had done that weeks before – but everything he could recall of Adam and Adela Knighton. It wasn't much. By a curious irony he had paid more attention to the other members of the train party than he had to the Knightons and their friend. Perhaps it was because the others had been rather thrust upon him and when, belatedly, he had made the Knightons' acquaintance it was at a time when he was being most bedevilled, haunted, plagued by that fantasy or hallucination or whatever you liked to call it. To the women he had hardly spoken a word, to Knighton . . . What could he remember of him? A tall, thin, silver-haired man in his sixties who had looked for a moment as if he had seen a vision and who had recited, for no apparent reason, a strange little piece of Chinese poetry. To Burden, now that he told all this – leaving out only the bit about his own visions – and delved in that excellent memory of his, he was able to reproduce, accurately, he was sure, every sentence he had heard Adam and Adela Knighton utter.

'It may be useful,' said Burden not very encouragingly.

Wexford retorted rather obscurely, though Burden understood, 'Well, it wasn't a burglar, was it? She didn't get up and go down for a burglar. A burglar didn't come up behind her and stick a gun in the back of her head. It wasn't like that. And where the hell is Knighton?'

'Murdered his wife and run off with her friend. No, but seriously, it looks as if he might have. Not run off with the friend, I don't mean that. Not at their ages. But had a row with her in the night and shot her and then got the hell out. Why not? It's the most likely thing. He could be out of the country by now, probably is. People in his position always have wealthy and influential friends.'

'You don't need wealthy and influential friends,' snapped Wexford. 'You just need to buy a plane ticket. On American Express. It's all made so damned easy these days. O.K., I agree it's quite likely, though I'd have expected them to be upstairs having their row if she was in her nightdress, and I certainly wouldn't have expected an English gentleman like Knighton to shoot anyone, let alone his wife, through the *back* of the head.'

'That's going to bother you a lot, isn't it?'

'Of course.'

They were in the living room. Once three or four small rooms, now made into one, it was about thirty feet long with French windows at the back and casements giving on to the front lawns and the drive. A grandfather clock began chiming eleven with rich sonorous notes. Wexford heard another sound. He moved to one of the windows and looked out. A car was coming up the drive, a large dark blue Ford.

'That's one of the Kingsmarkham station taxis,' said Burden.

'Yes.'

The car drew up. A man got out of the back of it, paid the driver and picked up a black leather suitcase of overnight bag size which he had set down on the gravel for a moment, and walked towards the front door where he was lost to their view.

'Knighton,' said Wexford.

His key turned in the lock. The two policemen stood absolutely still, waiting. The front door opened and closed, footsteps sounded across the hall and Knighton's voice called, 'Adela!

8

It was time to declare themselves. Wexford coughed but perhaps Knighton didn't hear, for when he saw the two men emerge from his living room he gave a violent start.

'What on earth . . . !'

'Good morning, Mr Knighton,' Wexford said. 'Yes, we've met before. In China. I see you recognize me as I do you. Chief Inspector Wexford of Kingsmarkham CID. This is Inspector Burden.'

'Mr Wexford, yes. I do remember you, though I had no idea . . . What are you doing in my house? Has there been some sort of robbery or what . . . ?'

'That we don't yet know. However, something very serious has taken place. You must be prepared for . . .'

'Where's my wife?'

Wexford told him. All the colour went out of Knighton's face. He walked into the living room and sat down in an armchair.

'Shot?' he said. 'Adela – shot?'

'I'm afraid it's true, sir.'

'Shot by some intruder? She's dead?'

'Yes, it appears she was shot by someone who forced an entry to this house during the night.'

Knighton passed a hand across his face. 'And you – you're a policeman in Kingsmarkham? You came in here and found my wife dead?'

'I among others. Your cleaner notified us.'

'Good God. Good God in heaven!'

Burden had sat down and now Wexford sat down too. Knighton's face was still paper-white, his eyes glassy with shock. Wexford could have sworn it had been a shock. He noticed something that hadn't really struck him while they were in China – his wretched preoccupation with the old woman with bound feet, no doubt, had distracted him – he noticed how extraordinarily good-looking Knighton was. He was still good-looking now, though he looked ill with shock. What must he have been like when young? He still had a boy's figure, a young man's lithe carriage, and his features were of the classical sort, grown somewhat marble-like with age. His golden locks time had to silver turned. Adela Knighton, on the other hand, had been very plain, ugly even. And hers was the kind of ugliness not created by time but bred in the bone.

All that, of course, might be quite irrelevant. Wexford asked the classic requisite question that always made him feel like a character in a detective story.

'Where were you last night, sir?'

'Where was I? Staying with a friend in London. Why do you ask?'

'Routine.'

'Good God.' A sort of horrified understanding twisted Knighton's mouth. 'I thought you said a burglar . . . '

'If you could just tell us where you were last night, sir, the name of your friend and so on, we should be able to get through this painful business a good deal faster.'

'Oh, very well.' Knighton hesitated a fraction. 'An old friend of mine, Henry Lacey,' he said, 'was giving a dinner party at a club to which both he and I belong. The Palimpsest in St James's. It was to celebrate his fifty years at the bar, what it would be the fashion to call a Golden Jubilee, I suppose. I was invited. On such occasions I stay in London as I have never cared to fetch my wife out with the car at one o'clock in the morning. And the station taxi service is not available at that hour, as you doubtless know.'

'You stayed at the club?'

'No, with a friend who has a flat in Hyde Park Gardens.'

The phone rang. Knighton gave another violent start.

Wexford was rather surprised that he glanced at him for the go-ahead before answering it. He nodded.

Knighton gave the number in a steady low voice. Whoever was at the other end, unless exceptionally insensitive, would have recognized it as the voice of one recently bereaved. A cruel estimate, Wexford thought, but just. Knighton was shocked but he was not unhappy – perhaps unhappiness would come hereafter.

'Oh, Jennifer . . . ' It was the daughter. 'The police have told you? Have you talked to Rod? Yes, please do come . . .' He put the phone down, again touched his forehead with his hand. 'My son is coming and my daughter and son-in-law.'

'I understand you have four children?'

'A daughter and three sons. One is in America and one in Turkey.'

'While we're waiting for your son and Mr and Mrs . . . ?'

'Norris. My son-in-law is a solicitor with Symonds, O'Brien and Ames in Kingsmarkham.'

'While we're waiting for them, perhaps you'll give me the name of your friend in Hyde Park Gardens and the address of Mr Henry Lacey.'

Jennifer and Angus Norris got there first. She was a plain young woman, dumpy and freckled, who resembled her mother. She was also about seven months pregnant and Wexford remembered Adela Knighton speaking of another grandchild 'on the way'.

Her brother Roderick turned up soon afterwards in a yellow Triumph TR7, having driven very fast from London. He was handsome and tall like his father, though anxious-looking and a good deal older than his sister. A barrister also, Wexford gathered. The law was well represented in the Knighton family to whom this lawless thing had happened. The spry little son-in-law, no taller than his wife and with a shock of dark curly hair surrounding a bald spot, he had sometimes seen in the Magistrates' and Crown Courts.

Young Mrs Norris had a manner Wexford had met before in women of the upper middle class who have led indulged lives. She called her parents Mummy and Daddy and spoke of her family and its immediate circle as of an élite.

'It's so awful, I feel it just can't be happening to us. Daddy was at the criminal bar, you know, and I remember Mummy saying how that really brought home to one what a horrendous lot of murders there actually are. And Daddy used to say she needn't worry because only a fraction of those murders happened to people like us, they were nearly all confined to the lower classes. And now poor Mummy . . . I mean, it seems so unfair. You lead a decent life and try to keep up some sort of standard and then an appalling thing like this has to happen.'

No doubt she would have found the murder more comprehensible if Renie Thompson had been the victim. But for those remarks of hers Wexford might not have asked where she and her husband had been on the previous night.

'What sort of time had you in mind?' said Norris. 'What does "night" mean?' He spoke in the style he used when cross-examining nervous witnesses. 'What time did all this take place?'

'Let's just stick to "night" for the moment, Mr Norris.'

'I asked because it so happens I took my wife out for a while during the evening.'

Jennifer Norris made a sound which in the circumstances couldn't have been laughter but which came very near it, an unamused grim laugh. Her brother turned cold magisterial eyes on her.

'Yes, but really, Angus, *you* took *me* out! What he means, Rod, is that we walked down to the river and back and had a drink at the Millers', the usual extent of our wining and dining these days . . .'

Wexford coughed.

'Yes, well, Chief Inspector,' began Norris who had gone rather pink, 'we went to bed early, we . . .'

'Oh, Angus, let me tell him. My doctor gives me a mild sedative and the result is I sleep like a log. And lately we've been taking the phone off the hook, so if poor Mummy had tried to get through . . .' It was plain to Wexford that she couldn't for a moment imagine she or her husband might come under suspicion. This was murder in the course of robbery. This was a 'lower class' crime. 'We live in Springhill

81

Lane, actually,' she volunteered. 'In one of the *old* houses.' This was a facet of local snobbism Wexford had encountered once or twice before. People living in this prestigious district of Sewingbury had an edge on their neighbours if they possessed one of the original seventeenth-century houses. There were perhaps half a dozen of these, around and among which new building had taken place during the past twenty years.

'Mummy can't have heard that glass breaking. She had a phone by her bed and even if she couldn't get through to us she'd have tried to phone the police. I mean, how could she have hoped to deal with some rough type like that?'

'He forced an entry by breaking a window?' said Norris.

'Not exactly, Mr Norris. Rather let's say a pane of glass was cut out from a window. And what were your movements last night, Mr Knighton?'

Roderick Knighton had a breezy manner. He glanced frequently at his watch. Already he had made several phone calls, declaring during the intervals between them that he didn't know what use he could be here but if there was anything he could do his father, sister and the Chief Inspector had only to ask. He yawned, looked once more at his watch and replied to Wexford that he had hardly slept a wink on the previous night, he and his wife and the au pair having been up for most of it with the youngest child who was ill.

'Mumps, actually,' he said. 'Poor little scrap.'

Jennifer Norris had put her feet up. Her husband was standing by one of the windows, looking thoughtful. He seemed worried or puzzled, perhaps only concerned that a man in his position – as he would doubtless refer to himself – could suddenly find himself involved in so unsavoury a business. And Wexford's next remark made him turn slowly round to exchange with his wife a glance of dismay or possibly incredulity.

'I'd like to see what we can do by way of making an inventory of Mrs Knighton's missing jewellery.'

For Knighton this was a hopeless task. He now seemed stunned or bemused by what had happened and his face was drained of all colour and animation. He sat limply in an armchair, gazing at a fixed point and occasionally shaking himself out of his reverie with a shiver. Wexford's suggestion fetched from him a vague shake of the head. Roderick was on the phone again, whispering discreetly, sometimes cupping his hand round the mouthpiece.

'Is any jewellery actually missing?' said Norris in his court-room drawl.

'One would suppose so. There's none in the house.' Wexford said dryly, 'I'm assuming Mrs Knighton possessed jewellery apart from her wedding ring.'

'Of course she did,' said Jennifer very sharply. Wexford wondered how much of that steel-trap snapping Norris had to put up with. 'There was a gold bracelet that had been my grandmother's,' she said, and added with a resounding lack of discretion, 'that she always said would be mine one day.' Norris closed his eyes and winced. 'And her pearls, of course. A few rings and brooches, a couple of watches. We aren't the sort of people who decorate ourselves like Christmas trees. Mummy thought it dreadfully vulgar to have your ears pierced.'

'I'd like you to do your best to make a list, Mrs Norris. No doubt your father gave her presents of jewellery over the years?'

Knighton said nothing. Wexford suddenly noticed the large, square-cut diamond on the daughter's small red left hand. 'I don't actually think he did much,' she said.

Dr Moss, who was Crocker's partner and Adam Knighton's GP, arrived at one and offered Knighton sleeping pills, tranquillizers and restrained sympathy. Roderick said he would be off but if there was anything he could do they had only to ring him. He left a string of phone numbers. Jennifer Norris remarked to her husband that they could phone her brother in Washington now, it would be eight in the morning in Washington. To her brother in Ankara she had sent a cable.

Wexford went back to the police station.

The house-to-house had produced nothing. Wexford hadn't thought it would. Thatto Hall Farm was too isolated. Pending Sir Hilary Tremlett's report, Crocker had volunteered that death had taken place approximately between two and four a.m. It would be at least tomorrow before they knew more:

the type of gun used, the precise cause of death, other injuries, if any, to the body.

'It wasn't a burglary, was it?' said Burden. 'It was a clumsy half-hearted attempt to make it look like a burglary.'

Wexford nodded. 'Possibly not even what Jennifer Norris calls a "rough type".'

'Knighton,' said Burden cautiously, 'is not what anyone would call a rough type.'

Wexford's eyebrows went up.

Burden sat down in the only other seat apart from Wexford's swivel one that might remotely be called an armchair. 'He's fixed himself up a wonderful alibi for an innocent man. Going up to London, dining in St James's, staying in Hyde Park Gardens. He hardly ever spends a night away from home but the very night he does his wife gets murdered. Would you have reckoned when you met him in China that he was – well, fond of his wife? I mean, was it a happy marriage?'

'Marriage is a funny old carry-on altogether, isn't it? Hard to say. I couldn't say.'

'Helpful. I really came to say do you feel like a spot of lunch? The Pearl of Africa? Oh, God, I can see it in your face, you want to go Chinese again. The day is coming when I shan't be able to face another crispy noodle.'

'I can't resist impressing people with my dazzling virtuosity with the chopsticks,' said Wexford as they walked down Queen Street towards the Many-Splendoured Dragon. 'D'you know, Mike, I wish I'd paid more attention to the Knightons in China. I've a feeling it would have been profitable. But all I can really remember is Knighton sitting at a table and suddenly looking as if he'd seen a ghost. Or maybe not a ghost.' He paused thoughtfully. 'Maybe the Holy Grail or the City of God or, if he were Dante, Beatrice.'

9

Lodged in the dead woman's skull, egress stopped by the frontal bone, was a bullet from a Walther PPK 9 mm automatic. She had been shot at the closest possible range, the barrel of the gun having been in contact with the back of her head.

Sir Hilary Tremlett's more precise assessment narrowed down the time of death to between 2.15 and 3.45 a.m. Adela Knighton had been a normal healthy woman of about sixty-five, somewhat overweight, who had borne several children and at several times in her life had undergone surgery. For mastoid, for varicose veins, appendicitis and, within the past four or five years, a hysterectomy. There was a mild degree of bruising on the upper left arm.

The fingerprints in Thatto Hall Farm proved to be those of the dead woman herself, Adam Knighton, Renie Thompson, Jennifer Norris and Angus Norris. On the evening of the day of her mother's death, Mrs Norris had provided Wexford with a list of all the jewellery she believed her mother had possessed. But by that time Wexford's officers, combing the grounds of Thatto Hall Farm, had found a green leather jewel case under the hedge by the front gates. Items from it also came to light, scattered haphazardly with no apparent attempt at concealment, in flowerbeds, under the same hedge, on the bank that bordered the road. Two watches, a gold bracelet, a string of pearls, two diamond and ruby rings in old-fashioned settings. Mrs Norris identified it all as having belonged to her mother and told Wexford that nothing was missing.

He saw clearly what had happened. This was no burglar who had come into Thatto Hall Farm during the small hours. Whoever it was had taken the jewel case, having at the time the intention of making the intrusion look like robbery. Later, abandoning this idea as likely to deceive no one and not wishing to be encumbered with some not very valuable jewellery, he had thrown it away, item by item, as he fled from the house.

He had known the house, he had known about that window. He had known Mrs Knighton would be alone. He had cut out that pane of glass and rested the cut-out pieces neatly up against the wall, entered silently, gone upstairs and awakened the sleeping woman. She had been forced to get up and walk downstairs ahead of him at gunpoint. The gun had been pressed against the back of her skull and she had been gripped by the upper arm. There, in the dining room – because she had refused to show him something, tell him something, lead him somewhere, promise, betray, give? – he had pressed the trigger and she had fallen forward, dead on the floor.

That was what he thought had happened. It would do as a working hypothesis.

'Knighton,' said Wexford, 'says he left home at three on Tuesday afternoon, having phoned for a car to take him to Kingsmarkham station, and caught the three-twenty-seven train. He has a car, a Volvo estate, but he says his wife wanted to use it and if he had let her drive him to Kingsmarkham it would have delayed her.'

'Where was she going?' Burden asked. They were in the car, being driven to London.

'Shopping in Myringham. A regular Tuesday afternoon exercise, apparently. Knighton got to Victoria at four-fifteen and from there he went by tube to Lancaster Gate and walked the short distance to the flat of a friend of his called Adrian Dobson-Flint in Hyde Park Gardens, Dobson-Flint having arrived home a little earlier than usual to let him in.

'This dinner at the Palimpsest Club was at seven for

seven-thirty. He and Dobson-Flint left Hyde Park Gardens in a cab at ten to seven, remained at the club having their dinner and generally merry-making until eleven-thirty, at which time they left and walked home. There they had something to drink and went to bed at about half-past midnight. Dobson-Flint had to be in the Old Bailey by ten in the morning, so they were both up by eight. Dobson-Flint left soon after nine and Knighton about nine-twenty, catching the nine-forty train to Kingsmarkham from Victoria.'

'You suspect him,' said Burden.

'Not really. Only I don't know who else to suspect. Early days, I daresay. She left a will, by the way. Angus Norris told me all about it without waiting to be asked. His firm were her solicitors. Adela Knighton had quite a bit of money of her own, a few thousand inherited from an aunt, another few from an uncle, parents' property, as like as not some share in a family trust. Anyway, there was two hundred thousand and she left it equally between her four kids.

'Julian, the son in Washington, is married to an American woman whose father is some sort of millionaire. Roderick has a thriving law practice and his wife's got her own employment agency. Colum, the youngest – he's thirty – is an attaché at the British Embassy in Ankara and whether or not he was looking to his inheritance there's no doubt he was in Turkey at three on Wednesday morning.

'I jib a bit at the idea of a woman seven months pregnant killing her own mother. On the other hand, she wouldn't have had to get in the window. She, apart from Knighton himself and Mrs Thompson, was the only person to have a key to the house. She would certainly have known her father was going to be away for the night and her mother would be alone. But where's her motive? The fifty grand she would inherit? Norris is only an assistant solicitor but he's obviously no fool and likely to be a partner one day. They live in Springhill Lane which is hardly a milieu for people short of the ready. We can put them on one side for the moment. Julian and his wife were in Washington, Colum, as I said, in Ankara and Roderick is alibi'd – if he needs an alibi – by his wife, his au pair, his unfortunate GP and

87

no doubt would be by his mumps-stricken daughter if we asked her.'

The chambers of which Adrian Dobson-Flint was a member were those to which Adam Knighton had formerly belonged. It was the death, and such a death, of Knighton's wife which was presumably responsible for the expression of discreet woe on the face of the Clerk to Chambers, a man called Brownrigg, who showed Wexford and Burden into Dobson-Flint's room.

Adam Knighton's friend was some seven or eight years younger than he, a man who must have been improved by his barrister's wig, for he was almost totally hairless. Since his face was unlined, pink and youthful-looking, this gave him something of the appearance of a skinhead. His room too was untypical, neither dusty and dark nor a litter of books, but a coolly, creamily painted office with fawn carpet and mahogany furniture, a view of a little enclosed garden and a window that let in sunlight.

'In what way can I be of assistance to you gentlemen?'

The skinhead image was quickly dispelled by Dobson-Flint's gracious, modulated voice. It too held the requisite, muted note of sorrow. The baby face contorted into a twist of petulant distress.

'I must say this is really the most shocking and appalling thing I ever heard.'

Which, if it were true, would give a very curious slant to the man's courtroom activities over the past quarter of a century or so. Wexford asked him for an account of Tuesday evening. In discussing alibis, times, reasons why persons should be in such and such a place rather than in another, Dobson-Flint was very much at home. And in spite of having heard his voice raised in public almost every day for many years, he was still fond of the sound of it. He discoursed lucidly, mellifluously, on the dinner party, the date some weeks previously on which invitations to it had been received, the time of Knighton's arrival at his flat, the time of their departure for and arrival at the Palimpsest. There was a note of faint amusement, such as would have been present had he been playing with a witness like a fly fisherman tickling a salmon. Underlying it seemed to be the unspoken question:

Are you so obtuse that you can even remotely consider my old friend Adam Knighton under suspicion of murder?

His distress at the death of his friend's wife, if he had ever felt it, now seemed forgotten. His pale blue eyes twinkled. He sat back in his chair with his legs crossed at the knees, one arm resting negligently on the arm of the chair, the other hand supporting his chin.

'It being a fine clear night,' he said, 'we resolved not to indulge ourselves with a cab but instead, in short, to walk it. We arrived on my doorstep at precisely two minutes to midnight. And now, Chief Inspector, you will ask me in time-honoured fashion how I can be so sure of the time, will you not? And my answer will be to you that as I raised my hand to insert my latchkey in the lock Mr Knighton informed me of the time, remarking that twenty-eight minutes from St James's to the Bayswater Road was not bad for two men no longer in their first or indeed second youth.'

With people of Dobson-Flint's kind Wexford generally allowed his own manner to become dull and dead-sounding, and it was in a leaden voice that he asked, 'You live alone, sir?'

'Oh, yes, and have done these twenty years since my wife and I reached an amicable agreement to part.'

Wexford made no comment on this marital revelation. Dobson-Flint said, 'Shall I proceed? Mr Knighton and I each took a glass of Chivas Regal whisky and retired to our beds at approximately twenty-past twelve. I say "approximately", because this time Mr Knighton did not happen to make any remark upon the time. At seven forty-five or thereabouts in the morning I rose up, took my bath, girded my loins and was about to enter Mr Knighton's room with a cup of China tea when he appeared, fully-dressed, and announcing his kind intention of taking breakfast with me. At nine-ten, as is my wont, I departed to win my bread, leaving Mr Knighton to go on his way rejoicing, though in point of fact it was rather to a weeping, a wailing and a gnashing of teeth.'

'Yes, sir. Did Mr Knighton often stay with you?'

'Often is an imprecise adverb,' said Dobson-Flint in his best Central Criminal Court manner. 'A man might say "I often go abroad", implying he leaves the country three or four times a year, but he may equally aver, "I often visit a cinema", meaning in this case that he attends a picture palace twice a week.' He smiled.

'And which would be true of Mr Knighton's overnight stays with you?'

'Neither!' said Dobson-Flint triumphantly. 'It would probably be true to say that, in the three years since his retirement and removal to the country, he has stayed with me on an average one and a half times per year.'

Wexford got up. 'I expect you'll be having a lunchtime break now, sir?'

'If you will excuse me, Chief Inspector.'

'I didn't quite mean that, Mr Dobson-Flint. I meant that since you'll no doubt be free for the next hour or so, we might use the time in having a look at this flat of yours. '

'Oh, come, is that necessary?'

In the same deadening voice Wexford said, 'It's essential. I have a car. You won't be much inconvenienced.'

Hyde Park Gardens, the mid-nineteenth-century terrace which faces the Bayswater Road and Hyde Park at the Lancaster Gate, is divided by Brook Street into two sections. The eastern part is older, larger and rather grander. Here the Sri Lankans have their embassy, and from a house once owned by the mysterious Duke of Portland (who went about always in a black veil) legend has it a secret passage runs underground to Baker Street. However, it was in the western terrace of Hyde Park Gardens that Adrian Dobson-Flint had his flat. Wexford had been into the block once before, years ago, and then had gone in through the front entrance, up the steps, through double doors, past the porters' office and up the wide curving staircase. He expected to do so again but Dobson-Flint directed the taxi into Stanhope Place which runs along the back of Hyde Park Gardens and led them up to the front door of a flat which though on the ground floor at the back would have to be designated 'basement' or 'lower ground floor' at the front. It took Wexford no more than a few seconds to realize that it was only from these flats which had access to Stanhope Place that occupants of Hyde Park Gardens could come and go without passing through the front entrance or chancing an encounter with porters.

On the doorstep Wexford said, 'What time did Mr Knighton get here on Tuesday afternoon?'

'I was back here by five,' said Dobson-Flint. 'Shall we say ten past? Yes, I should say about ten past.'

They went inside. There were two bedrooms, the spare one being the nearer to the front door. Dobson-Flint had dropped his keys into a shallow pewter dish which stood on a console table and which already contained another bunch of keys and car keys attached to a fob.

'Are you a heavy sleeper, Mr Dobson-Flint?' Burden asked.

'I succeed in sleeping through some of the worst traffic noise in London, so I should say yes, I am.'

There was nothing else of interest to see. Wexford said, 'I suppose Mr and Mrs Knighton were a happy couple?'

He didn't expect a frank answer but he wanted to see just what sort of answer he would get. Dobson-Flint replied with a kind of forced impatient enthusiasm.

'Oh, absolutely devoted. They simply adored each other. The Knightons were what is generally called a very united family. Until this fearful tragedy struck them Mr and Mrs Knighton lived for each other. I can't imagine either of them ever having had eyes for anyone else!'

He refused Wexford's offer of a lift back and departed in a taxi, leaving them in the street outside his front door.

Wexford said thoughtfully, 'He doth protest too much.'

'About the Knightons' mutual devotion, do you mean?' asked Burden.

'That was a strange remark. "I can't imagine either of them ever having had eyes for anyone else." It's not the sort of thing that would come to mind at all when considering the domestic happiness or otherwise of people in their sixties. Why did he mention it? It's a funny thing, Mike, but I keep having this feeling that what's happened in this case, and maybe is happening, ought to be to people thirty years younger than the Knightons. I've got a feeling this was a crime of passion, yet any less likely candidate for passion than Mrs Knighton I've yet to see.'

'And that bald-headed stuffed shirt feels it too?'

'Harsh words, Mike. But maybe, yes, I think he does.

91

Knighton could have gone back to Sussex during the night, shot his wife and returned here hours before Dobson-Flint started fiddling about with his Lapsang-Souchong.'

'How? There's no train between the twelve fifty-five and the six-forty.'

'It doesn't have to be by train. In fact, train would have been no use to him since he couldn't have got from Kingsmarkham to Sewingbury at the other end. But he could have done it by car.'

'We know he didn't. His car was in the garage at Thatto Hall Farm.'

'Listen, Mike. What was he doing between getting to Victoria at four-fifteen and arriving at Hyde Park Gardens at ten-past five? Fifty-five minutes to get from Victoria to Lancaster Gate? There's something he could have been doing. He could have been in a local car hire place, renting a car, and returning it next morning.

'All he had to do was book himself a car by phone and turn up to collect it at four forty-five, drive it here and leave it on a meter. It looks to me as if the whole of this area is metered, I noticed as we were coming along. Metering ends at six-thirty so he'd only have to put his money in for an hour and a half. After Dobson-Flint's gone to bed he leaves the flat, helping himself to a key out of that pewter plate thing, retrieves his hired car and drives to Sewingbury – an hour's drive at that time of night. He lets himself in by the front door, awakens Adela and shoots her, takes her jewel case. Then he cuts the pane out of the loo window. On his way back to the road where he has left the car parked on the verge he discards the jewellery and the case. An hour later he's back in Hyde Park Gardens and it's still only three-thirty. How about that?'

'He was taking a hell of a risk,' said Burden. 'Suppose Dobson-Flint had gone into his room?'

'Never! Can you imagine it? Not those sort of people, they never would. Their sons might, yes, but never those two. Dobson-Flint would have gone in there only if Knighton had cried out and even then he'd have hesitated.'

'By the way,' said Burden as they got back into the car, 'his son lives in London. Why couldn't he stay with him?'

'Roderick Knighton and his wife live in Mill Hill, quite a

92

way out. Too far out if you're depending on public transport and taxis. Or I think that's what Knighton would say. The truth may of course be that if he was planning a small hours murder trip the Bayswater Road is a good deal nearer to Sussex.'

Men were searching for the weapon in the grass verges, the hedges, the fields, the footpaths, even wading in the Kingsbrook itself where it flowed through Thatto Vale. Wexford asked himself if the gun had belonged to Knighton. A retired counsel who had been at the criminal bar might well know where to acquire an automatic. The little gun, it had been discovered from a hairline scratch on the bullet that had killed Adela Knighton, had a tiny pinhead-sized protuberance, a minute wart-like flaw, on the inside of its barrel.

It was a damp chilly day, rather colder than usual for the time of year and darker than usual for the time of day. The surrounding hills and woodland were blanketed in grey mist. The gun might be hidden anywhere in there, a tiny metal tube in innumerable tons of earth, leaf mould and water. Or it might be cleaned and polished, folded in a soft cloth, put away in a drawer. He went up the drive to Thatto Hall Farm.

Julian Knighton with his wife Barbara had arrived that morning from America. Julian was shortish, thick-set like his mother, moon-faced like his mother, perhaps forty years old. The Knightons had evidently belonged in that category of couples who, like the Queen, had had two families. The first pair, the two older sons, must surely have been about ten and eight years old before Jennifer was born, and then they had had another son two or three years later, the still absent Colum.

Adam Knighton looked ill, stricken with suffering. His face was drawn in under the cheekbones. Wexford remembered how astounded he had been, how disbelieving, when first told of his wife's death. Only a brilliant actor could have feigned that. He looked at the chief inspector with sunken haunted eyes. The pregnant Mrs Norris reclined in an armchair with her feet up. Barbara Knighton was drinking something from a glass that might have been iced tea or heavily diluted whisky. Her husband presented Wexford with a theory.

'It strikes me as being highly probable he expected to find a safe, Chief Inspector. My father did in fact have a safe in this house at one time but when break-ins became so frequent in Sewingbury he had it taken out. Its presence did seem to advertise that one had rather special things to protect.'

'It was while we were still using this house as a weekend retreat,' said his father. 'On a Sunday night before we left to go back to Hampstead I used to put our few valuables in the safe. Could he have been looking for that? Is that at all feasible? Do you think it conceivable my wife was shot by accident? That this man threatened her with the gun if she refused to reveal the whereabouts of the safe to him and when she did refuse the gun went off by accident? Is that at all a useful theory?'

The man had been a distinguished, even brilliant, counsel. It was hard to believe it in the face of this nonsense. Wexford remembered reading of him in the newspapers, 'Mr Adam Knighton, defending . . .' 'Mr Adam Knighton's masterly presentation of the prosecution's case . . .' Something soft and weak had come into the hard aquiline face. When they were in China it had been like the face of some noble bird of prey but now it was as if those features had been made of wax and a warm hand had passed, smudging, across them. There had been a pathetic loosening of the muscles around the mouth. The uncomfortable thought came to Wexford, became a conviction, that when he was alone, when he went to his bedroom and shut the door on all those sympathizing considerate children, he wept. His face was the face of a man who has soaked it with tears.

'Have you ever possessed a gun, sir?' The question was addressed to Julian Knighton who exclaimed, 'Good God, no! Certainly not!'

Wexford's eyes rested on Adam Knighton.

'When I first came here and fancied myself a week-end country gentleman I had a shotgun. I sold it five years ago.'

Jennifer Norris whispered something to her sister-in-law. They both looked truculently at Wexford.

'I should like to have another look over the house, if I may,' he said.

'I thought my brother made it plain the safe isn't here any more,' said Jennifer Norris in the tone of a nineteenth-century chatelaine addressing a bailiff.

'Quite plain, thank you.' Wexford looked at Adam Knighton.

'You must do as you please, Chief Inspector.'

Wexford closed the living-room door after him and went upstairs to the bedroom where Adela Knighton had slept alone that Tuesday night and from where she had been peremptorily and terrifyingly summoned. Since his last visit the bed had been made. There was nothing to be learned from a perusal of Mrs Knighton's clothes. Their pockets, as were her handbags, were empty. On the windowsill, between looped-up rose-printed curtains, stood a china candlestick, a pomander and book ends encompassing the reading matter of someone who stopped reading when she was in her teens: two or three Jeffery Farnols, *Precious Bane*, *The Story of an African Farm*, C.S. Lewis's *Mere Christianity*, Mrs Gaskell's *Cranford*. Wexford was looking for something he hadn't been consciously looking for when, two days before, he had searched the desk downstairs.

The dressing table had only one drawer. He opened it. Handkerchiefs, a box of tissues, a card of hairclips, two unused face flannels, a cardboard carton of cotton wool. Mahogany bedside cabinets supported pink porcelain lamps with pink tulle shades. Each cabinet had a drawer. In Mrs Knighton's were a bottle of aspirin, two more handkerchiefs, an old-fashioned silver-handled manicure set, nasal drops, a pair of glasses in a case; in Knighton's a pair of glasses in a case, two ballpoint pens, a scribbling pad, a tube of throat pastilles and a battery shaver in a leather case. Each cabinet had a cupboard under its drawer. Mrs Knighton's held a pair of black corded velvet bedroom slippers and a brown leather photograph album, Knighton's a stack of books, evidently his reading-in-bed for some weeks or months past, for the present and possibly the immediate future. They were, to Wexford, an unexpected collection.

Han Suyin's *A Mortal Flower* and a book of linguistics

called *About Chinese*. Understandable inclusions, those two. The man had recently been in China. *Anna Karenina*, *The Return of the Native*, Elizabeth Barrett's *Sonnets from the Portuguese* and *The Browning Love Letters*. Wexford looked at them, intrigued. 'Romantic' was the word that had come into his mind. With the exception of that linguistics book they were all voluptuously romantic. They seemed highly unlikely reading matter for that white-haired, dried-up, unhappy old lawyer downstairs. Yet they must be there because he had read them, was reading them now or had at any rate intended to read them.

He opened *Sonnets from the Portuguese* where the place ('If thou must love me, let it be for naught Except for love's sake only . . .') was kept by a marker. The marker was a scrap of paper torn from the scribbling pad and on it, in Knighton's stylized 'ronde' handwriting, were written a few lines of verse. Not Elizabeth Barrett, nor the piece Knighton had quoted leaning over the parapet in Kweilin, but a fragment that was also, unmistakably, Chinese poetry:

> Shoot not the wild geese from the south;
> Let them northward fly.
> When you do shoot, shoot the pair of them,
> So that the two may not be put asunder.

Very curious indeed. Of course it might be assumed that Knighton had written that down after his wife's death, after someone had in fact shot her and put the two of them asunder. Somehow Wexford didn't think so. Those words hadn't been written since Tuesday. The paper was creased from many usings, many insertions into that volume of sonnets. And when he went out on to the landing again and looked through the open doorway of the 'green' bedroom opposite, he saw the bedcover turned down and a brown plaid dressing gown lying over a chair. Temporarily, the widower had removed himself from the room he had shared with his wife.

They were still in the living room, all four of them. Jennifer Norris still reclined with her feet up. She and her father were drinking tea. Barbara Knighton was arranging the last roses

96

of summer in a copper bowl, October blooms from a second or third flowering. They were a little pale and worn, those roses, with a papery look.

'Just one thing, Mr Knighton. What has become of the photographs you and Mrs Knighton took while you were on holiday?'

'Photographs?'

'They aren't in the album I found in Mrs Knighton's bedside table, though pictures from your previous holidays are.'

'Probably you didn't take any this time, did you, Father?'

Knighton hesitated. Wexford guessed he might clutch at the straw Julian offered him and to prevent this said firmly, 'I don't think there's much doubt that both you and Mrs Knighton took photographs, do you?'

Their eyes met. Wexford wondered if he was reading the other man's expression accurately. Or was he imagining the reaction that nothing could have been less fortunate than that he and this policeman had happened to encounter each other on that Chinese holiday? 'We did take a few snaps, yes,' he said languidly. 'If they came out, if they were ever developed, no doubt they're somewhere about the house.'

But they were not.

Wexford said no more about it. He pondered on Adam Knighton, his wistful predilection for romance, his listless, sometimes hag-ridden or haunted look, the possibility that he who loved poetry and the great love stories, had held a gun to his wife's scalp and sent a bullet into her brain.

The inquest was on Monday morning, the funeral the following day at All Saints, Sewingbury. By that time it had been established that no car hire company within a three-mile radius of Adrian Dobson-Flint's home had hired a car to a man answering Adam Knighton's description. By then the search for the gun in the vicinity of Thatto Vale had been called off.

Sewingbury has about four thousand inhabitants, a golf course, a convent and girls' school, a disused mill on the Kingsbrook and a huge market square, usually packed tight with parked cars. The church is half-way down the hill that leads to the river and the new 'weir'. Wexford's driver took the route along Springhill Lane, over the newly built bridge, along the river bank past where the footpath from Thatto Vale comes out and up River Street.

All the Knighton family were assembled, Adam, lean, gaunt, bareheaded, wearing a waisted black overcoat, Roderick in a dark suit with a black tie and Roderick's wife Caroline in a tight black suit and high-heeled black patent shoes. Julian and his wife were in light colours, grey and green respectively, but wore the most doleful expressions, perhaps to compensate. The fair young man with the beaky nose and the thin dark Greek-looking girl Wexford decided must be Colum and his wife. Only Jennifer was absent, though represented by her husband who arrived late and on foot.

Leaving the church when it was all over, after the family had filed out, Wexford, who had been sitting in the very back row, happened to look over his shoulder along the aisle. The small elderly woman he remembered from China as Adela Knighton's friend was walking towards him from where she had been sitting in one of the front pews. He had forgotten all about her until now.

He could tell she was astounded at seeing him. She looked at him as he must have looked when he saw his persecutor with the bound feet. And then her eyes turned sharply away.

Wexford went out and waited for her in the porch.

10

'My name is Irene Bell. I don't believe we were ever introduced in China.'

'Chief Inspector Wexford of Kingsmarkham CID. How do
you do, Miss Bell?'

'So you're a policeman and living here. How very odd!
That must have been quite a shock for poor Adam on top
of everything else. He's very cut up, isn't he? Well, we all
are. Adela and I were at school together, we'd known each
other nearly all our lives. I suppose we'd been friends for
something like half a century.'

'It's a long time,' said Wexford. 'Can you and I have a
talk, Miss Bell?'

'Now, d'you mean? I suppose so. I wouldn't go back to the
house anyway. I don't care for all this eating and drinking at
funerals. People don't mean to be irreverent but somehow
they forget what they're there for, someone starts laughing
and before you know where you are it's turned into a party.
I call that very bad taste.'

Wexford nodded in agreement. She seemed a woman
of character. 'I'll see you get to Kingsmarkham station
afterwards. You wouldn't think a cup of tea irreverent,
would you?'

'I could do with a cup of good hot tea,' said Miss Bell.

She was short and sturdily built, though not fat, with a
round sharp-featured face and dark hair that still hadn't
much grey in it and was crisply permed. The blue trouser
suit would have been unsuitable for today and in any case

99

too light in weight, for the previous night had seen the first frost of the winter and a little white frost still lay in shady places. She had on a dark grey tweed suit, beige silk blouse and black court shoes that were nevertheless 'sensible' ones. Up until three years before, she told Wexford, she had been the manager of a travel agency at Swiss Cottage near where she lived. In fact it was this agency that had arranged the trans-Asia trip for her and the Knightons. It wasn't the first time the three of them had been away together. She had gone with them to Egypt as well as on various European holidays. It was company for Adela, she said, which Wexford thought an interesting remark.

Back in Kingsmarkham Wexford took her into the Willow Pattern, a café in the High Street, and ordered tea for two. Irene Bell refused food, perhaps once again on the grounds of the unsuitability of eating just after one has buried one's best friend. For this was what Mrs Knighton had evidently been, a devoted dear friend, as close as a sister, and when Miss Bell referred to her in this way a look of heavy bitter sadness came into her sharp face. She was, she said, godmother to Jennifer, 'Aunt Irene' to all the young Knightons, as nearly a member of the family as one could be who was not allied by blood. Wexford let her talk for a while about her long friendship with the dead woman, noting that though she referred to all Mrs Knighton's children by name and spoke of their children, Adam Knighton was never mentioned. He interrupted her by reverting to what she had said in the car.

'You said you were company for Mrs Knighton. Wasn't her husband company enough for her?'

She lifted her shoulders and gave a half-smile.

'Was it a happy marriage, Miss Bell?'

'Someone said the state of marriage is unhappy only insofar as life itself is unhappy.'

'Samuel Johnson said it. What do you say?'

'In general, Mr Wexford, I don't think much of it. It goes on too long. If it could be for five years, say, I think it would be an excellent institution. Who can stand the same person morning, noon and night for forty years? People think a single woman of my age hasn't married because she hasn't had the chance. That's not so of course.' Irene Bell chuckled. It was

100

a grim chuckle that hadn't much to do with amusement or pleasure. 'I'm not much to look at and never have been but neither are most of the married women you see around you. If folks only got married because they were pretty or charming it'd be a world of singles. No, I never fancied marriage myself. I don't much like sharing. I don't like cooking or housework or babies or sex. Oh, yes, I've tried sex. I tried it three times forty years ago and those three times were enough for a lifetime in my opinion.

'But those are my views. That's marriage in general. In particular, which is what you're asking, I daresay the Knightons were as happy as most people. She was very fond of *him*, poor Adela. She made her choice and she stuck to it and she was a good wife, no one could have had a better wife.'

You don't like him, Wexford thought to himself. Or is it more complex than that? Is it that once you liked him too much?

'They never had much to say to each other. That's partly what I mean when I say I don't think much of marriage. How else do we communicate but in words when all's said and done? You hear a lot of nonsense about the language of the eyes, the language of love, silent communion, all that kind of thing. There wasn't anything of that sort with Adela and Adam, I can tell you. Adela wasn't that sort of woman anyway. Adam – well, it always seems a funny thing to me, a man who reads poetry.'

'Most of it was written by men.'

'That's different,' said Miss Bell. 'Don't confuse me. I mean it's not very robust, it's affected, if you ask me, a man reading – what d'you call 'em? – sonnets.'

Wexford said abruptly, 'Was he unfaithful to her? Did he have love affairs with other women?'

She was taken aback. She had been raising her teacup to her lips. The motion was arrested in mid-air then slowly she restored the cup to the saucer. 'Good God, no. What an extraordinary idea! He was sixty-three.'

'He wasn't always sixty-three. In any case he's a very handsome man, with what I'd call an attractive presence.' Wexford paused. How intimate they had become, how frank, in ten minutes over the teacups! It seemed at that moment as

101

if there were nothing they couldn't have said to each other. It was a pity she hadn't more to say. 'There's many a man of sixty-three,' he said, 'would be horrified at a suggestion his emotional life was over.'

She gave a short, rather harsh, cackle. 'See the day looming yourself, can you? No, there was nothing like that with Adam, you can forget that. Who would he carry on with? Never saw a woman but the vicar's wife. If you're thinking he shot poor Adela to take up with someone else, you're cold like they say in "hunt the thimble", you're stone cold. Adam wouldn't point a gun at anyone, let alone fire it. He gave up shooting pigeons because he said it wasn't ethical. I once saw him get stung by a wasp trying to put it out of the window because he wouldn't kill it.' She laughed again, then set down her cup with a rattle. 'I knew it!' she said. 'This is turning into a party, a beanfeast, and I'm not having it. I call it very bad taste. It was good of you to give me tea but now you'll take me to the station, please.'

Wexford pleaded, 'Five more minutes, Miss Bell, and I promise I will. I want to ask you something about China. Do you remember when we were all sitting in that bar on the hotel roof in Kweilin?'

She was putting on her gloves. 'The temperature was ninety and they were playing "White Christmas". Of course I remember.'

'Mr Knighton had a shock. He went white. He saw something or someone and he was absolutely astounded by what he saw. Did you notice that?'

'I can't say I did.'

'A minute or two later Mrs Knighton said she thought she would go to bed and you and she got up to leave.'

'Maybe, but I don't remember.'

'And the next day he didn't mention it to you? Or to Mrs Knighton in your presence? I mean, he didn't say "Something I saw on the roof last night amazed me"?'

'No, he didn't. Why don't you ask *him*?'

'I will. You took a lot of photographs. So did Mrs Knighton. Did she show you the ones she took?'

'Weeks ago,' said Irene Bell. 'She came up to town. She

always had lunch with me when she did that. We had lunch and we looked at each other's snaps.'

'What did she do with hers?'

'Took them away, of course. She was going to put them in an album she'd got.'

Up in his office on the second floor of the police station he found Burden and Dr Crocker talking about guns. Burden even had a replica of a Walther PPK 9 mm, one which they had taken off a young tearaway who had threatened a visiting pop star with it and which, after the case was over, had unaccountably got into Wexford's desk drawer and remained there ever since.

'I feel more at home with a scalpel,' said the doctor. 'Had a nice funeral, Reg? It beats me why people who aren't religious have funerals. Boring, embarrassing, awkward affairs with no grace or beauty to them now the old prayer book's more or less gone.'

'You have to have a funeral, don't you?' said Burden.

'If you mean by law, certainly not. People have them because they think they've got to but they haven't. You can just get your undertaker to do a quiet little disposal when the crematorium's not busy. Nothing to it. Mind you, it'll cost you much the same. Five hundred quid give or take a little, that's what a funeral comes to these days.'

Wexford, who had been silent, sat down at his desk and, taking the replica gun, turned it slowly over and over in his hands, saying, 'He was sitting on that roof, drinking cassia wine, and suddenly he saw something that utterly astounded him. Not something unpleasant, mark you, rather the reverse. I could almost hazard a guess he saw something wonderful. But what did he see?'

'A pretty girl,' said the doctor.

'Oh, come on. You'd only look like that when you saw a pretty girl if you'd been shut up in solitary confinement for the past twenty years.'

'An old friend?' said Burden. 'Someone maybe he'd defended in court years ago and thought he'd never see again?'

'In that case why didn't he immediately get up and go and

speak to him? Why did he go and lean over the parapet and start muttering Chinese poetry?'

'You'd better ask him.'

'I will, but I'm sure he'll lie about it. One of the things we have to do is find out just who knew he was going to be away last Tuesday night. We haven't done much about that but it's on the cards a good many people did know. Everyone at that Golden Jubilee party at the Palimpsest Club for a start. Probably most of Mrs Knighton's acquaintances in Sewingbury. Friends or relations she may have written to or talked to on the phone.'

'You mean,' said the doctor, 'it's a bit fishy it happened that night. I mean here's a chap stays away from his home once a year and on the very night he's away his wife gets murdered.'

'At any rate it teaches us that it was planned. It may have been planned by one of those people who knew he'd be away or it may have been planned by Knighton himself in collusion with someone else or Knighton may have done it alone.'

'Everyone in Hyde Park Gardens,' said Burden, 'is being questioned as to the possibility of their having seen Knighton that night.' He hesitated, said in a rather embarrassed way, 'You may think this very far-fetched . . .'

Wexford countered, 'I'm the one that gets accused of that.'

'Maybe it's infectious. Maybe it's because I – well, I sort of read more than I used.' It was well-known that Burden's cultured wife was in the habit of recommending books to him, was one of those rare people who like being read to and had discovered in her husband an unexpected histrionic talent for reading aloud. Burden's face had become a little pink. 'Fiction, you know. I must admit to having read only novels lately.'

Wexford exploded into a quotation from Jane Austen.

'Only novels! Only some work in which the most thorough knowledge of human nature, the happiest delineation of its varieties, the liveliest effusions of wit and humour are conveyed to the world in the best chosen language!'

'O.K., let him tell us his idea,' said Crocker.

'It's just that – well, it sounds like somethimg out of Conan

104

Doyle really. On the other hand, you do read in the papers sometimes . . . ' Seeing Wexford's eyes sharpening with rage, Burden went on hurriedly, 'You hear of old lags, or any villains really, getting sent down by a judge and swearing to get back at him later. Right? And I'm pretty sure I've come across actual cases – attempts anyway. It did strike me it might be something like that which had happened here.'

'Knighton wasn't a judge.'

'No, but someone accused of a crime in a case where he was prosecuting might feel much the same towards him as towards the judge. He might easily feel that Knighton's presentation of the evidence against him had more effect on the jury than the judge's summing up. Say that because of what Knighton said for the prosecution some guy either got convicted when he expected to be acquitted or got sent down for twice as long as he anticipated, mightn't he then resolve to get back at Knighton when he came out? And I reckon Knighton's prosecuted in dozens of possible cases. His name was always in the papers.'

'You mean this chap shot Mrs Knighton to get revenge on her husband?' Wexford was interested. He didn't dislike the idea. 'It's a possibility, especially if as you say Knighton got him put away for ten years instead of four or five. Wouldn't he shoot Knighton, though?'

'There's many a married man,' said Burden, 'whose life wouldn't be worth living without his wife.' He gave the doctor an uneasy look as if he expected to be laughed at. 'I know I felt that way when Jean died and if it doesn't sound too ridiculous I'd feel it now about Jenny.' The others didn't laugh but Burden himself did in a high embarrassed sort of way.

'Knighton had been married a very long time too,' said Crocker. 'If you believed the funny postcards and the cartoons and whatever you'd think that made people less fond. But it doesn't. The long habit of the years, the shared things, the curious kind of oneness – my God! You haven't had a chance yet, young Mike. You don't know the half of it.'

And nor did Irene Bell, thought Wexford. He quoted:

'Shoot not the wild geese from the south;

105

Let them northward fly.
When you shoot, shoot the pair of them,
So that the two may not be put asunder.'

'Where did you get that from?'

Wexford told them. 'I got the library here to trace it for me. It's a Chinese poem from a collection of T'ang verse, ninth century. The poet was called Shen Hsun and a curious note to it is that he and his wife were murdered by a slave.

'We keep coming back to China, don't we? I've got a feeling, I've had it almost since the murder really, that the key to all this was in China.'

'You can't very well go back there,' said the doctor.

'No, but I can at least see the people Adela Knighton travelled across Asia with. I met them too, remember. There were some strange things . . . ' He told them about the two men who hadn't spoken to each other from Irkutsk to Kweilin, about Wong who had drowned. 'She and he took photographs in China, they were always making with the camera. What's happened to those photographs? Why aren't they in her album or sculling about the house in packets? No, I'm more and more sure it's to China and what happened there that we have to look. I just wish I'd taken more notice. I wasn't to know, of course, but usually I like watching people, seeing how they behave. I was too damned preoccupied with that woman with the bound feet.'

Crocker looked at him. 'What woman?'

Diffidently Wexford told him. He had often felt he should have told him long before but he never had. When the symptoms disappear who cares about the cause of the disease? Crocker, who hadn't even smiled at Burden's marital confidings, now burst out laughing.

'What had you been reading?'

'O.K., I know, something called *Masterpieces of the Supernatural* and I never finished it.'

'I wouldn't have your imagination for all the tea in China.'

'Sure, but all hallucinations are from the imagination. That doesn't make them any less real to the hallucinator. D'you think it was just that book and lack of sleep?'

106

'And getting dehydrated and drinking that filthy Maotai you brought home a bottle of.'

'Start getting worried,' said Burden, 'when you see the lady tottering over the Kingsbrook Bridge.'

Wexford gave him a bland look. 'We mustn't risk not investigating the possibilities of this revenge motive, so you can make it your business to inquire into the present circumstances of every villain Knighton prosecuted in, say, the fifteen years prior to his retirement. And for good measure into those of every villain he failed successfully to defend. That should keep you busy for a bit.

'As for me, I shall "fire a mine in China here with sympathetic gunpowder".'

11

Donaldson went off to find somewhere to park the car and Wexford crossed Kensington Church Street to the shop above whose window in gilt Times Roman was the single name 'Vinald'. In the window itself, in solitary splendour, stood a vase. Not one of those Vinald had collected in China, but a vessel as tall as a small man and of dully gleaming black porcelain with a design on it of a blood-red gilt-clawed dragon.

Inside, deep soft black carpet like cat's fur. The place was discreetly lit by wall lights in gilt rococo brackets and by a single spot that fell upon a spinet or harpsichord or some such thing. A few other *objets d'antiquité* were set about the long room, wax fruit under a glass bell, a china clock around whose face a Chelsea china Eros and Psyche sported, a tall slender glass jug, and on a console table a book of Audubon prints open at a picture of green and yellow birds.

Wexford introduced himself to the woman in charge and asked for Gordon Vinald. She was afraid Mr Vinald was at a sale and not expected back until late afternoon. Was it very important? Wexford said yes but he would come back.

'Would it help to see Mrs Vinald? I know she's in. She phoned just a couple of minutes ago.'

Surely he hadn't been married when Wexford had last seen him? 'I didn't know there was a Mrs Vinald.'

She smiled in the way people do who find something sweet or touching about matrimony in its early stages. 'Mr and Mrs Vinald have only been married a month. Shall I give

108

her a ring? Their house is just round the corner in Searle Villas.'

He realized what had happened. Hadn't he foreseen it? Vinald had married Margery Baumann.

'Mrs Vinald says if you'd like to go straight over, Mr Wexford, she'll be happy to see you.'

Searle Villas was indeed just round the corner. The garden of number sixteen must have backed on to the shop. It was a house in a Victorian terrace that no one would have looked at twice in Kingsmarkham but here was no doubt worth about half a million. He was admitted by a young black woman in jeans with a duster in her hand. She pushed a door open and said to him indifferently, 'She's in there.'

The room was a museum, seemingly furnished with over-flow from the shop. In the middle of the Chinese carpet sat a very large stout lushly-furred tabby cat which ceased washing itself to stare at him with glittering zircon eyes. Standing by the marble fireplace, one white arm extended along the mantel, was the beautiful black-haired Pandora.

She didn't recognize him. Probably she hadn't even noticed him on that previous occasion. While a man of Wexford's age will inevitably notice and remember such a woman, to her he may be invisible.

Her hair was longer, cut now with a fringe that curved symmetrically down into a page-boy, the Egyptian queen look. Her mouth was as red as cinnabar and her eyelids painted jade. Wexford felt that either he had seen her before – and he meant before the encounter on the hotel roof – or that she reminded him strikingly of some famous beauty. A film star from when he was young? Hedy Lamarr? Lupe Velez? She wore a clinging black silk jersey and a skirt of black and red printed velvet and her legs were the best he had ever seen, better even, he thought disloyally, than his daughter Sheila's.

'I think you've come to talk about the late Mrs Knighton. Am I right?'

He was surprised and his eyebrows went up.

'What else could it be?' Her twang brought her down to earth, made her less of a goddess. 'I travelled with her to

109

Hong Kong. Well, all the way to England, if you count being in the airplane. Don't you care to sit down?'

The cat leapt – gracefully for one of her girth – up on to the chair before he could sit in it.

'Oh, get out, Selima.' She picked it up and dumped it on to a chaise longue. 'She's called the Pensive Selima for some reason known to my husband, some poem.'

'Demurest of the tabby kind,' said Wexford.

'Maybe. I'm not poetical myself.' In a way she was, though. Any man would have wanted to write a poem to her or about her. But with a faint feeling of disappointment he saw what she meant. Despite her looks, the Hollywood profile, she was of the earth, earthy. 'So what can I do for you?'

'I don't know, Mrs Vinald, I'm a bit in the dark. You didn't travel on that train across Asia, did you?'

She shook her head. 'We met up with the train party in a place called Kweilin. I first met my husband in the hotel there. I was doing a kind of world tour. We'd come from Auckland to Jakarta, Jakarta to Singapore, Singapore to Peking. It was going to be Bombay after Hong Kong but – well, London suddenly seemed that much more attractive! But I have to tell you, I don't think I spoke one single word to that poor Mrs Knighton. I only know her name because Gordon said who she was after we saw in the papers about her getting murdered.'

Wexford thought it was time he explained that he too had been in China. She was astonished and then confused. Had he been there tailing Mrs Knighton, watching her or what? No, she couldn't follow it. He'd actually seen her, Pandora Vinald, before? It is always hard to understand that someone very beautiful, particularly someone with a sensitive face and a sweet expression, may be quite stupid. Pandora Vinald, he decided, was – to put it as kindly as possible – not very intelligent. Not a patch really – except in one vital way – on Margery Baumann.

'Have you seen any of the train party people since you came here?' he asked.

'No, we haven't. Gordon says holiday friendships are a dead loss, they never lead to anything.'

'Unlike holiday romances.'

110

It took her a moment to understand but when she did she broke into merry gratified laughter. The Pensive Selima sat up and began frantically washing her face in the way cats do, as if they have suddenly been warned by some inner voice of a disfiguring smut. Pandora Vinald said, 'We did have a photo sent us by a Mrs Knox. I mean Gordon did. We were in it, you see, and a lot of other people. You couldn't see us very well, it wasn't very good. Gordon said not to answer, it would only encourage her, but I didn't think that was very kind, I thought of how *she'd* feel, you see.' She smiled and said naively, 'So I wrote back and thanked her and said it was very nice, though it wasn't, and mentioned we were getting married.'

'Do you still have her address?'

The cat jumped off the chaise longue, stalked to the door and emitted a shrill impatient mew. Because the mew wasn't attended to she followed it up with a series of near-screams.

'Oh, Selima, you noisy beast. She's a terribly spoilt cat. Gordon's ex-wife let her do anything she wanted, scrape her claws down some practically priceless old pieces, just awful.' The door was opened and the cat went out with a slowness that was insolent. 'Address, did you say? I've got all their addresses, as a matter of fact. The tour company sent Gordon a list of the people going with their addresses before he went and it's right here in the top of the desk. Would that be of use to you?'

There they all were in alphabetical order:

Mrs H. Avory, 19 Oswestry Place, Rosia Bay, Gibraltar.
Dr and Mrs C. Baumann, Four Winds, Southwood Hill, Purley, Surrey.
Dr M. Baumann, 2 Crestleigh Drive, Guildford, Surrey.
Miss I.M. Bell, Flat 6, Meleager Court, Queen Charlotte Road, London NW3.
Mr L. Fanning (tour leader), 105a Kingsland House, New King's Road, London SW6.
Mr and Mrs A.D. Knighton, Thatto Hall Farm, Myringham Road, Sewingbury, Sussex.
Mrs L. Knox, 26 Redvers Lodge, Redvers Road, Rosia Bay, Gibraltar.

Mr A.H. Purbank, 10 Fairmead Farm Court, Disraeli Road, Buckhurst Hill, Essex.
Mr G.W.M. Vinald, 16 Searle Villas, London, W8.

He thanked Mrs Vinald and said goodbye to her. Outside, ornamenting the top of one of the columns that flanked the gate, sat Selima like a sphynx. Unwisely Wexford put out a hand to stroke her and got a scratch that made the blood run.

Only Lewis Fanning's wife was at home in the mansion flat down below the World's End, a stringy woman with grey roots showing in her henna'd hair. She was short with Wexford and indifferent. Her husband was away again, shepherding a party round the Aegean and wouldn't be back till the end of the month.

Purley, where the Baumanns lived, would be passed through on the homeward journey, it was on the route of the Brighton Road. Before that Wexford thought he might take a look at what had been the Knightons' home before their permanent removal to Sussex. He told Donaldson to take him up to Hampstead.

His knowledge of London was better than Burden's but it was still full of gaps. It was only seeing a sign to Swiss Cottage which reminded him that Irene Bell had said she lived there, though to him the postal address looked like Hampstead.

'See if you can find Queen Charlotte Road.'

But Donaldson who, long before he joined the force, had thought of being a London taxi driver and had gone so far as to ride round on a bicycle to acquire the 'knowledge', knew where it was without a map. Meleager Court was a block that seemed to be composed entirely of red brick balconies set among plane trees. Irene Bell looked more the way he remembered her today, in a grey trousered garment which, when he was young in the forties, had been called a 'siren suit'. She showed no great surprise at seeing him.

'I've just made a pot of our favourite poison, Chief Inspector. Come in. Mind the step. It takes a true-born Englishman to fancy tea at one pip emma, that's what I say. I've made a sandwich too or have you had lunch?'

'I was thinking of having it at my daughter's. She lives

112

up the hill in Keats Grove, only I've just remembered it's Thursday and she's got a matinee.'

'Sheila Wexford,' said Miss Bell. 'That's who you are, her father. I mean apart from what else you are. *Sluttish Time* still running, is it? Not my kind of play but I loved her in it, she's a joy to look at.'

Wexford felt that he really liked Irene Bell very much. He accepted tea and a ham sandwich. Perhaps she could tell him, he said, whereabouts in Hampstead the Knightons had lived. She told him, pouring a second cup for both of them.

'I should have been more forthcoming the other day,' she said. 'I was upset and it didn't seem right. But there's quite a bit more to say, though I don't know if it's the kind of thing you want to hear.'

'I want to hear everything.'

'Old stuff from years ago?' She frowned, thinking back. Then she said, 'I'd like you to find who killed Adela and I'd like him to get his just desserts. Not that that'll be much these days – five years inside doing an Open University degree, I daresay, and then let him out with a new suit and fifty quid out of the poor box.'

'Not quite that,' said Wexford who couldn't help smiling. She said abruptly, 'They had to get married, you know.'

'I beg your pardon?'

'Adam and Adela. You know what the expression means, I suppose? They used it in your young days as well as mine. Don't any more of course. Girls have babies or abortions and as often as not from what I hear it's the boys who beg the girls to marry *them*. Adela fell in love with Adam the first moment she saw him. His sister had been at school with us too and she asked us to be her bridesmaids and that's how we came to meet Adam. We were all twenty-four and Adam was twenty-one. He was up at Oxford. Well, I've never been much for men as I think I said the other day but Adam was something else again as the young folks say. He wasn't handsome, he was beautiful. You hear people talk about "tall, dark and handsome" but to my mind there's nothing to beat a really good-looking *fair* man. Sound soppy, don't I, but he was like a god in a painting.

'I was very fond of Adela, very. Anyway I think she'd

have been the first to agree with me she was never much to look at. Mind you, she came from a very good family. The Aylhursts, you know. They're a cadet branch of the Staffordshire Aylhursts, nothing wrong there.' She hesitated. Wexford hadn't guessed her a snob and was surprised to find such frank snobbery in her. But there, she had been Mrs Knighton's closest friend . . . 'Gerald Aylhurst was her father. He was the Recorder of Salop. I can't tell you how Adam came to be interested in her. I don't know. Perhaps he was flattered because she was older or something. I've heard men of my generation say they used to suffer from terrible sex frustration when they were young – far cry from these days, eh? – so maybe it was that. Adela didn't say no, though you'll no doubt recall that nice girls usually did say no in 1939. Anyway she got pregnant and of course there were no two ways about it, Adam had to marry her. I don't think he ever questioned that he had to marry her but he told his sister and his sister told me that when they sort of first made it clear to him he decided he'd rather die. He said he was in love with someone else and he'd kill himself before he married Adela.'

'Who was the someone else?'

'Don't ask me. You needn't look like that. It wasn't *me*. Come on, Adam Knighton wouldn't have looked twice at me. I don't know who it was, some girl at Oxford, and it can't matter now, not after forty years.'

Wexford agreed that it couldn't matter now. Irene Bell went on, 'He didn't kill himself as we know. The Aylhursts fixed up a big white wedding at their village church. Very bad taste, with Adela four months gone and showing it. Adam went back to Oxford and took his finals, and got himself a First incidentally, and in September Julian was born.

'They must have got on well enough because the next year, in the November, Adela had Roderick. That was 1941 and Adam had to go off with his regiment to the Far East somewhere, Burma, I think it was. He was away four years. When he came home he went back to reading for the bar and he was called and everything and he made quite a success for himself, as we all know. I used to see quite a bit of them. I was sharing a flat with another girl in Maitland Park and

114

they were living in one of those roads off Haverstock Hill near Belsize Park station. He had a funny way of treating her, sort of tolerant exasperated patience. I don't know if I make myself clear? These days they'd say he was always putting her down. I remember once – they'd just got their first TV set – he said he was going to watch *The Brothers Karamazov* and Adela said, "Is that from the London Palladium, darling?" Well, I happened to know it was a famous sort of Russian novel, though I'd never read it, but it was the kind of mistake anyone might make. It does sound like acrobats, doesn't it? Adam called the boys in and said, "Come and hear what your intellectual mama's just said," and then when that pansy phoned, that Dobson-Flint, he repeated it to him.

'Adela had the other two children. I think she did that to keep a hold on Adam. I don't know for sure but that's what I think.'

'You mean he was straying?'

'I don't know. It got so that he was never at home. Working, he used to say, and perhaps he was. He had to do a lot of entertaining too, he said, though Adela always entertained well at home for him. She was a good wife, like I said, she cared, she went to a lot of trouble. Anyway she had Jennifer and Colum but that didn't seem to have much effect on Adam. He slept at home, they'd moved to Fitzjohn's Avenue, and that's about all you can say. It'd be true that for – what? Five years? – anyway for years after Colum was born Adela had a husband insofar as there was a man sleeping in the other bed in her room.

'And then, suddenly, I remember it well, some time in the late fifties it must have been, he came back. He lived at home, he had his meals there, he started taking Adela out – the lot. It was as if he'd had a shock and come to his senses. It's my belief she threatened to leave him and take the children with her, take them away from him. He was fond of his kids all right. Anyway back he came and there he stayed. They were quite a model couple after that except that they never had anything to say to each other. All the old Adam had gone out of Adam, that's for sure. He was bored stiff but he was resigned. And poor old Adela, she went on beavering away at being a good loving wife, but she had to take me on holiday

115

with her, there are limits to how much you can stand of a man who doesn't say two words to you for hours on end.

'Good God,' said Irene Bell, 'do you wonder I don't think much of marriage when that was the marriage I saw at close quarters?'

A fine house of many rooms, rose madder brick, Edwardian probably, with the gables and diamond panes the Edwardians loved. It stood about half-way up the big hill to Hampstead on the right-hand side. Its garden was a shrubbery of rhododendrons, an ilex, in the oval lawn a monkey puzzle. As Wexford looked from the car at the house where the Knightons had lived in such sad contiguity, a hooknosed man in a burnous came out of the front door. Only an Arab could have afforded to buy the house and live there now.

'Marriage,' murmured Wexford, as if to himself, 'is a desperate thing. The frogs in Aesop were extreme wise. They had a great mind to some water but would not leap into the well because they could not get out again.'

Donaldson said nothing to this. But he remarked some time afterwards to Loring that life was full of surprises, he had always thought the Chief Inspector got on O.K. with Mrs Wexford.

'Purley now, sir?' he said after a minute or two.

'Purley it is and then Guildford.'

But from that particular journey across Surrey they were to be saved. Just as Wexford had been taken aback *not* to see Margery Baumann open Vinald's front door to him, so he was surprised to see her open this one. She recognized him at once and was herself as astonished as anyone would be to find a man she had encountered by chance in China three months before standing on her parents' front doorstep.

He explained who he was and why he had come. Margery Baumann understood more readily than Pandora Vinald had done. Since she had no late surgery on Fridays, she said, she always spent those evenings with her father and mother. By that time they had passed through the panelled hall of the Baumanns' rather opulent thirties house and entered a living room where the Baumanns were having a thirties tea. Cucumber sandwiches, bread and butter, strawberry jam, Victoria sponge and custard creams. Dr Baumann wore grey flannels, white shirt, college tie, sports jacket, his wife a flowered afternoon dress and pearls. She was in the act of pouring from a silver teapot. It looked exactly like a stage set for a piece from the vintage days of drawing-room comedy, and but for the autumnal state of the garden and the grey of the sky, one would have expected at any moment the entry from the French windows of a young man in flannels holding a tennis racquet.

All this Wexford remarked while Margery went through the business of explaining to her parents his status and the reason for his visit. They seemed very little less puzzled when she had finished than when she began.

'Now you're here, do sit down and have a cup of tea,' said Mrs Baumann rather faintly.

'I expect he would like a piece of your splendid cake, Lilian.' Dr Baumann got up. 'I shall go and fetch him a plate. I can't say it's at all clear to me why he's here but he's not the man I take him for if he won't enjoy Mother's excellent cake.'

'Milk *and* sugar, Mr Wexford?'

'No sugar, thank you.'

'What exactly did you want us to tell you then?' Margery asked.

'For a start, everything you can remember about the Knightons. Oh, thank you, very kind of you.' Dr Baumann had returned with a tea plate and a small napkin with lace round it. Wexford, who was always more or less on a diet, was obliged to accept a large slice of yellow sponge cake with jam filling. 'You travelled in the train with them. I'd like to know whatever you can recall about them.'

'Aha,' said Dr Baumann, 'so that's what he wants. Well, my dear? Well, Margery? He'll be surprised to find what an observant couple of girls I've got, I daresay.' He barked at Wexford, 'How d'you find the cake?' It was the first time he had addressed him directly. Wexford had been beginning to think the doctor had acquired his habit of speaking in the third person from constant reference for the benefit of students to bedbound patients.

117

'Very nice. Do you think you could give me your impressions of the Knightons, Mrs Baumann?'

He had utterly floored her. 'I didn't have any impressions. They were just – well, quite nice, ordinary people. That's what we said, wasn't it, Cyril? At the time, I mean, when we were talking about the other people in the party, you know the way one does. I said to my husband that the Knightons seemed quite nice and that Miss Bell they were with, she seemed quite nice. Mr Knighton had been a lawyer, I remembered seeing his name in the papers. He was a very well-informed man, I thought.'

Margery said suddenly, 'She was anti-Semitic.'

A shadow passed across Mrs Baumann's face and was gone. Her husband smiled, a little too widely and tolerantly. It hadn't occurred to Wexford before that they were Jewish, but of course they were.

'That sort of thing is very nasty,' Margery said. 'It was embarrassing. *I* didn't like hearing somebody or other called a "Jewboy" and her call her husband an old Jew when he didn't want to spend money on something. But my mother lost all her family in the Holocaust – did Mrs Knighton consider how she must have felt?'

'That wasn't the first time your mother and I have had to put up with that kind of thing and it won't be the last.' Baumann took his wife's hand. 'He doesn't want to hear about that. He wants to hear about threats and blackmail and murder attempts. About revolvers fired at the dead of night and arsenic in the chop suey.'

'I hardly think . . .'

'Oh, good heavens, no. There was nothing of that. But I know what you chaps like, something to get your teeth into. He doesn't think I've ever read a detective story, Margery.'

Wexford suppressed a sigh. A light rain was falling now and the dusk was coming down. Margery switched on a couple of wall lights and a table lamp with a galleon painted on its parchment shade. 'We really didn't notice anything out of the ordinary about the Knightons, Mr Wexford.'

'Then let me ask you something else. Do you remember when we were all sitting at a table on the roof of the hotel at Kweilin? The three of you, I, Mr Vinald, the Knightons and

118

Miss Bell. Knighton saw something that astonished him, he looked as if he had had a tremendous, though not unpleasant, shock. I want to know what it was he saw.'

Dr Baumann laughed at that and shook his head from side to side several times as if at some amusing idiosyncracy. The idiosyncracy, though, he seemed to make clear, was Wexford's and not Knighton's. What a question to ask! What kind of answer could he expect?

'I can't say I noticed that,' said Mrs Baumann complacently.

Her daughter looked at Wexford. 'It was that very good-looking girl of course, the one that got so friendly with Gordon Vinald on our way home. Pandora Something. A girl from New Zealand. She walked out on to the roof and all the men were looking at her.' Her voice when she mentioned Vinald had an edge of awkwardness but not perhaps pain. 'I did happen to notice the expression on Mr Knighton's face. He was just startled at suddenly seeing such a very striking – well, beautiful girl.'

'I didn't even see her,' said Dr Baumann in a triumphant way.

'Well, maybe not, Dad, you wouldn't. But I should think every other man on that roof did. I know exactly what Mr Wexford means, I saw it just as he did. I expect Mr Knighton is very sensitive to beauty and there hadn't been much in that line, had there? What struck me about those tour parties was that we were all as old as the hills.'

'Margery!' said her mother. 'A young woman like you! I'm sure I didn't see much to write home about in that Miss Pandora Whatever-it-was.'

'Mrs Vinald now,' said Wexford.

Mrs Baumann looked cross, her daughter wryly amused. 'I'm sure he's welcome,' said Mrs Baumann. 'I never liked the man, he wasn't a nice man at all. And I'm sure he wasn't honest, I don't believe antique dealers ever are quite honest.'

'Oh, Mother! He was very kind to us. You know how pleased you are with that little vase and you never would have bought it if Gordon hadn't said it was worth far more than the man was asking. And it was too. My father had it valued, Mr Wexford, and the valuer put it at three hundred pounds. Not bad when Mother gave twenty for it.'

She picked up from a coffee table a small blue and white jar and handed it to Wexford. It was inconceivable to him that anyone would give three hundred pounds for such a thing, a whitish mottled thick piece of pottery with a blue bird and some squiggles on it. On its base was a small red seal.

'You can't take anything out of China that's more than a hundred and twenty years old,' Margery said. 'They put the red seal on an antique piece to show you it's within the limit and therefore all right.'

Wexford handed it back. 'Do you happen to know what it was Mr Vinald and Mr Purbank quarrelled about so that they didn't speak to each other after the train left Irkutsk?'

Now it was Margery's turn to laugh. 'I know they didn't but I haven't the faintest idea why. Gordon just said he was a "nasty piece of work" and left it at that.'

He went home to another good, almost elderly, marriage – his own. Dora was watching an old British film on television, *The Snow Moth* with Trevor Howard and Milborough Lang.

'I wonder if people will see old films of Sheila's in thirty years time.'

'Considering she's never made any,' said Wexford, 'they don't stand much chance. You don't want her going off to Hollywood, do you?'

'I'd like her to make just one or two really good films as well as acting on the stage. There's that old TV series of hers, of course, I don't count that. I'd like to think of her – well, her beauty recorded for posterity. In a lovely setting, in a sensitive film like this one. After all, what do you suppose Milborough Lang looks like now? She must be fifty-five.'

Wexford always did his best to jolly his wife out of these alas-for-my-lost-looks moods of hers. To him, of course, she looked much the same as she had done when he first married her. As the credit titles came up he switched off the set.

'I wish to God you'd been with me in Kweilin. You'd have observed people. You'd have talked to people, you always do, you'd have got to know them. You wouldn't have been distracted like I was by – hallucinations.'

120

She looked a little worried. 'Reg, I wish we knew what those hallucinations of yours actually were.'

'Lack of sleep; Maotai.'

'Oh, come on. I doubt if you had more than a couple of sips of the stuff.'

Wexford shrugged. 'You might have been able to tell me why a man who sees a pretty girl walk across a roof looks more like he's seen the Virgin Mary.'

The phone rang. It was Burden.

'I'm getting more help than I expected from that chap Brownrigg who's the Clerk to Chambers where Knighton used to be. He's a meticulous old boy and he's got records of all the cases they've handled back for twenty years. But what I'm phoning for is because a fellow by the name of Vinald's been on the blower for you three times since midday. I'll give you his number.'

Wexford dialled it. Vinald himself answered. 'Oh, Chief Inspector, how super of you to phone. I've been trying to get in touch ever since my wife said you'd been here.' The voice was hearty, ingratiating. It was also very nervous. 'I really did want to know precisely what you wanted of me.'

'Any little bits of help you or your wife could give me on the background of Mr and the late Mrs Knighton, Mr Vinald, that's all.'

There was a short silence. Vinald cleared his throat. 'There's more to it than that, though, isn't there? I don't think it can be just that, eh?'

Wexford thought quickly. He would play along, though in the dark. 'I expect,' he said, 'you remember that last evening in Kweilin as well as I do.'

'Oh, certainly. And I realize a fuller explanation is actually called for here. I suppose I should begin at the point we all met up in that roof bar place . . .'

'Mr Vinald,' said Wexford heavily, 'I don't want to hear this on the phone. I'll come along and see you tomorrow. I'll see you in your shop at noon sharp.'

'Well, of course. I'll make a point of being there. I can assure you there's a perfectly simple and reasonable explanation for the whole thing . . .'

'Good night, Mr Vinald,' Wexford said firmly. Far better to

121

confront the man in the morning and hear it face to face. He rather enjoyed the feeling of suspense, of revelation deferred. Tomorrow, perhaps, indeed probably, Vinald was going to tell him what had so affected Knighton on the roof.

But that, though not in detail, Wexford thought he already knew. Knighton had seen Pandora Vinald. Of course it wasn't the sight of a pretty girl which had brought that look to his face. The people who had suggested that to him simply hadn't thought what they were saying. It was *this particular pretty girl*, and Knighton hadn't looked like that because he was seeing her for the first time but because he was seeing her again, perhaps after the passage of years.

A girl who had once meant a great deal to him – whom he had loved? – had walked out on to that roof and by the merest chance he had been there, had looked up and with joy and wonder and fear had seen her.

Part Three

12

Inspector Burden was a conventional conservative man who believed passionately in law and order. The slightest offence against those principles irked him and he loathed crime. That curious understanding of the criminal mind and its workings which some policemen have to such a degree that there is not much to choose between them and their morality and the criminals and theirs, was foreign to Burden, was distasteful to him. That perhaps was why he was a less successful policeman than he might have been. For between them and him a great gulf was fixed which grew wider and deeper as he grew older.

He was insensitive and he lacked sympathy. Supporting a cliché he didn't know to be one, he would often say he reserved his compassion for the mugger's victim, the beleaguered householder or even the Inland Revenue. He was a believer in retribution and was one of that majority of policemen – to which Wexford did not belong – who favoured the reintroduction of capital punishment. And this not solely for the taking of the lives of policemen. That the French, who had been sensible enough to keep the guillotine for so long, were now proposing to get rid of it, was beyond his comprehension.

More even than young rioters and muggers he disliked recidivists. This was a word his wife had taught him, he had always called them old lags himself, but it came to the same thing. It was just his luck, as he remarked to Jenny on leaving the house, that he should have to spend the day, maybe the next few days, hunting them out. And that without even the satisfaction of the housewife hunting cockroaches, in that there was nothing he could do to them when he found them.

He had taken an unprofessional dislike to Adam Knighton but he had to see him first. Renie Thompson opened the front door to him. She showed him into the living room where to his mild surprise he saw his chief already there, seated opposite Knighton and in the throes of an enquiry into the topic that was at present obsessing him. Knighton had grown gaunt in the past few days, his feet were in carpet slippers and a grey heavy knit cardigan was wrapped round his shoulders. He had become an old man, all that style and presence gone.

Wexford gave Burden a nod but the other man made a gesture of rising from his chair.

'Don't get up, Mr Knighton,' Wexford said. 'I'd like you to give a little more thought to what I've been asking, if you please.'

Knighton moved his shoulders. He was frowning. 'I told you, I remember very little about it. My memory has been affected by all this,' he said bitterly, as one recalling a tranquil time that can never return. 'It was all very beautiful, wasn't it? The most beautiful view I think I've ever seen. If I looked astonished up on that roof I suppose it was at the beauty of the sight.' A ghastly smile widened across his face and turned it into a death's-head.

With a shrug Wexford turned to Burden. He had tried his best. The man was lying, of course, or at least that last sentence of his was highly ambiguous. Burden suggested the possibility that the murder had been committed by someone out to 'get his own back' on the former prosecuting counsel. The smile shrivelled on Knighton's face, he looked almost faint. He took from Burden the lists Brownrigg had compiled.

It took him a few moments to collect himself. But he made the effort. He spoke in an almost normal conversational tone.

'I see Hayward's name is here. Gilbert or 'Gib' Hayward. He threatened me, actually threatened me in court. The jury

126

had returned a verdict of guilty and he was awaiting sentence. When the judge asked him if he had anything to say he began shouting threats at me. It was really rather alarming, though of course there was nothing he could actually do.

'I've had anonymous letters too but they won't be much use to you, will they, since they were anonymous?' Knighton was burbling on in this half-crazed way, Burden thought, for the sake of saying something, anything, rather than reveal his true feelings, his deep fears. 'Oh, and there was this other chap here, one Peter Kevin Smith. I was *defending* him. For some reason he thought I hadn't done a good enough job. He went to prison for five years and the next day his mother came in to see me, made her way into chambers, if you please, burst in threatening he'd shoot me when he came out.'

'When you look at these names, sir, does any one or more of them give you a feeling that, yes, here's someone who might have done more than threaten?'

Knighton gave the lists back as if he didn't like holding them, as if he didn't care for the feel of them on his hands. 'None of them ever did. I can't imagine anyone carrying out such a threat against my – my wife. And do men have such long memories?'

'Some do,' Wexford said rather enigmatically, and he added, 'It depends on how much they want to remember.'

Now how to act on the information in the lists?

Those people whom Knighton had successfully defended and those whom he had unsuccessfully prosecuted could be ignored. But this still left so many that Burden realized he was going to have to be ruthless, categorize them according to the circumstances of the case, perhaps decide to disregard all petty crime and go only for killers and perpetrators of manslaughter, robbery with violence and grievous bodily harm. Could he dare assume it wasn't a woman? For a start he thought he could. He just couldn't see a woman not personally antagonistic to Adela Knighton getting her out of bed and forcing her downstairs and shooting her in cold blood. A girlfriend of Knighton's who had had reason to hate or resent Adela, that would be a different thing. But Knighton had no girlfriend.

127

The murderer wasn't going to be in his dotage either. Knighton's own age was just about the oldest at which Burden could imagine anyone climbing up and squeezing through that window, and Knighton was a well-preserved thin sixty-three. The murderer was going to have to be thin, no more than middle-aged. He had started making his list and on it, prominently, were 'Gib' Hayward and Peter Kevin Smith, the former now fifty-two years old, the latter forty-six. They might be fat, though, they might even be dead.

Hayward had killed a man in a fight outside a West London pub and Peter Kevin Smith had hit an old woman im the stomach, rupturing her spleen, prior to breaking into the till in her tobacconist's shop. Narrowing down, rejecting women, people over sixty-five, forgers, con men, straight burglars, bank robbers – though he didn't know if he could afford to do this – he had ended up with a total of sixteen men. In fact there had been more clients in Brownrigg's records with reason to be grateful to Knighton than inimical towards him. Certainly he had been the kind of counsel newspapers and hardened villains adore, spectacular, unscrupulous, witty, savage and subtle.

He went up to London with Wexford where their ways diverged. Though he had set Martin on to 'Gib' Hayward in Brighton, he intended to see Peter Kevin Smith personally.

'He's still living with that loyal and supportive mother of his,' Burden said as they parted. Wexford kept the car and Burden got into the train for Mile End.

The Pensive Selima was sitting in the shop window this time. Not on the lofty vase's side but on the edge of the blue plush drapery that covered its plinth. She sat cosily folded up into roughly the shape of a fat tawny brown armchair. The woman in the big glasses wasn't there. If he hadn't been seeing him at the appointed time and in his natural habitat, Wexford might not have recognized Vinald. In China he had always worn jeans. He looked quite different in a suit of dark grey fine tweed, pure white shirt and grey tie with a silver zig-zag down it. He looked older, cleverer and much more suave.

'Chief Inspector, do sit down. It's good of you to come.'

Wexford thought this remark strange since it must have

been obvious to meaner intelligences that he had come out of duty rather than altruism. He chose a chair which, because he had once apprehended a man who had stolen half a dozen like it, he suspected of being by Hepplewhite. Vinald sat down opposite him on the yellow satin cushion of a love seat. He leant forward in an intimate fashion and, low-voiced, plunged into a – what? The answer to an unasked question? A lecture on iconoclasm? Or just a defence?

'Chief Inspector, China is an extremely long way away and pretty alien to us anyway, I'm sure you'll agree. And who knows how long the present regime will last? What's thirty years? Nothing in historical terms. The next lot to get into power would only do so by bloody revolution. And what's going to happen during any new insurrection? Much the same as happened during the Cultural Revolution. Anarchy. Armies of sixteen-year-old boys told by the highest authority to destroy anything old they could lay their hands on. Did you know that every village in China had its own temple, Taoist, Buddhist or Confucian, and many of them had all three? Where are they now? We know the answer to that. Destroyed. Razed to the ground and the very sites ploughed over as with ancient Carthage. When I hear sentimentalists groaning over our so-called thefts from China in, say, the Boxer Rebellion, I thank God for those – appropriations. Thank God we do have the Dowager Empress's throne in the British Museum. What do you suppose the Red Guards would have done with that?'

Wexford was not at all sure what Vinald was driving at but the man was evidently very very guilty over something. 'What indeed?' he said equably.

'Again only a romantic idealist would insist that the means are never justified by the end. The end here is to save priceless art treasures for the world. And these are not China's but indisputably the property of *all mankind*. They are our heritage, for in art all men are brothers. So therefore I maintain we should get our hands on what we can of it by fair means or foul – not that my means were foul, not at all.' Wexford's mystification, though veiled by experience, was now reaching him. 'And my scale is small enough,' he said more confidently. 'I would hardly have thought it worth anyone's while . . .'

'If we in the force decided that what you call things on a small scale weren't worth our while, Mr Vinald, I think we might very soon have anarchy in our own country.' He would get to the bottom of what Vinald was on about but not now. 'Since you're being so frank with me I'm sure you won't mind answering a couple of questions.' Vinald was looking very nervous indeed now. 'Like where you were on the night of October the first, for a start.'

It surprised him that Vinald didn't have to pause to think. Still, there were people with very good memories, people who in a flash could tell you exactly what they had been doing on any evening in the past fortnight. Wexford himself was one of them.

'I was at home with my wife. You know where I live, just round the corner in the Villas. My wife's mother brought a friend of hers round to meet us after dinner, a film cameraman or some such thing. They stayed till nearly midnight and after that my wife and I went to bed.'

Wexford asked him for his mother-in-law's address and was told she had a flat in Cadogan Avenue.

'I can't tell you where the guy she brought with her lives. His name's Phaidon, Denis Phaidon with a ph.'

As if to leave, Wexford got up and said with deceptive indifference, 'By the by, what *did* you and Mr Purbank quarrel about in the train on the way to Irkutsk?'

'*What?*'

Patiently Wexford repeated his question.

'What can that possibly have to do with it?'

'To do with what, Mr Vinald?'

'My buying antiques,' Vinald muttered, 'or the fact that this Mrs Knighton was murdered.'

'It's just one of those small things we think it worth our while to bother about,' said Wexford.

Vinald shrugged. 'I don't remember anyway. It was a long time ago and no doubt I did my best to forget it and forgotten it I have. The man was simply a very nasty piece of work.'

Cats never make a sound when they move. Wexford was aware that the Pensive Selima had left the window only when he felt the faintest sussuration against his trouser leg. She

130

stalked slowly into the back regions as if she owned the place and no one else was present.

The old woman herself came to the door, eyeing Burden with such contemptuous hatred that he knew it would be useless to place credence on any alibi she might produce for her son. But as it had happened no alibi of hers was needed. For one thing, Peter Kevin Smith had grown far too fat in the ten years since he had come out of prison to have got through that window. For another, his right hand was in plaster and he was a right-handed man. He had broken it falling in the street – drunk, Burden supposed – and to prove the break had occurred before 1 October, exhibited an appointments card from an orthopaedic hospital with appointments listed back to 18 September.

Next on the list was Sidney Maurice Wills of Southwark. He was more interesting than Smith, being thin and wiry and in fit condition. Also he was still in his early thirties, having been out of prison not more than a year. Knighton had been prosecuting counsel in a curious case in which Wills had been found guilty of being an accessory to murder and of concealing a body. He had undertaken to dispose of the corpse of a woman stabbed to death by an acquaintance of his and had subsequently buried it among roadworks.

'What you want to do instead of wasting your time on me is find out who that bastard Knighton paid to do it for him.'

'Oh, he paid someone?'

'Only natural, isn't it? He wouldn't do it himself, no more than he'd fix up his electric wiring or service his own Rolls-Royce motor car himself. He'd call in a professional. Like Chipstead, for instance. Used to be with Lee's mob, could be dead for all I know, I never mix with them sort of people these days, but he's just an example. Christ, do I have to teach you your job?'

Wills had an alibi nearly as good as Smith's, or would have once it was verified. He had been on a week's holiday in Minehead with a girl he called his fiancée, returning to London on 3 October.

There were eight more Londoners to see. The other men on the list lived in the north of England and would be seen by

131

their local police. Of the London eight, George Lake had been celebrating his Silver Wedding at a restaurant in his home suburb of Wandsworth until 1 a.m., Mojinder Singh, a Sikh from Southall, had been at home with his huge family of wife, parents-in-law, two brothers and six children, Norman Trimley and Brian Gage were far too fat, Henry Rossi was seventy-two and growing feeble, George Catchpole had been working a night shift, and Walter 'Silver' Perry . . .

'Silver do harm to Mr Knighton?' Mrs Perry screamed at him in the council flat on the top of the Bethnal Green tower. 'Silver worships the ground Mr Knighton treads on. Didn't he save his life?'

Burden nearly groaned aloud. He realized he had muddled the lists. That was what came of doing a task as distasteful to him as this was. Silver Perry had coshed and killed a night watchman and had done so some years before the abolition of capital punishment. Or it was generally believed by every newspaper reader in the country that this was what he had done, yet the skill of Adam Knighton had acquitted him. Burden vaguely remembered the man's story sold to the *News of the World* and, as he was recalling it, a scrapbook was thrust into his hands by Mrs Perry. There was the half page of cutting, the first instalment, yellowed by time. 'I firmly believe I owe Mr Knighton my sanity and indeed my very life . . .' These ghost writers! He was handing the scrapbook back when Perry himself walked in.

He was a tall man, getting on for sixty, with hair like that of an elderly woman who has just had a rinse, styling and 'set'. Silver's hair, however, was naturally metallic-looking and naturally wavy and had looked just the same, according to the *News of the World* photograph, when he was thirty-three. He gave Burden a parsonical look and said gravely, 'I would lay down my life for Mr Knighton.'

'Really? I don't know what use that would be to him.'

Silver went on as if Burden hadn't spoken. 'I was grieved to hear of his great loss, and him such a devoted husband by all accounts . . .'

Burden hadn't heard of Knighton as a devoted husband by any accounts. He left and when the lift didn't come walked down by the stairs, all the hundred and fifty feet.

132

There was one more man to see. Coney Newton, who also lived in the East End, had raped a girl and afterwards stabbed her, though not fatally. Nearly a year later, when the girl was at last recovered, Knighton had held her up to ridicule in the witness box, but the jury would have none of it and Newton had gone to prison for eight years. No one could say, except perhaps the paranoid Newton, that Knighton hadn't done his best for him.

'I don't bear a grudge, mind. I said to Silver, I don't bear a grudge and I don't hold you to blame . . .'

'Silver?' said Burden.

'Silver Perry. He's a mate of mine. It was on account of him, what he'd said in the papers like, that I was set on getting that Knighton to defend me. I said to them, I want a fella called Knighton and then I'll be O.K. I don't bear a grudge, mind, but I might have saved me breath. All that carry-on, that telling the jury the girl was asking for it, that wasn't to help me, that was just for show. Using a lot of long words and making her colour up and getting a laugh, that was for show. What he should have done, what I told him again and again, was just stick to it I wasn't *there*. That was the truth, I wasn't there. All I wanted was him to tell the true fact which was, I wasn't *there*.'

'I suppose that's what you'll say when I ask you where you were on the night of Tuesday, October the first?'

Coney Newton looked narrowly at Burden. He was a thin, gaunt, grey-headed man of perhaps fifty, with a rampart of prominent grey teeth. In every sense an ugly customer. 'I wasn't anywhere I shouldn't have been and that's for sure,' he said, and he went into an elaborate explanation of how on that evening he had been in a pub with someone called Rocky whose surname he didn't know, then at his sister's, then in a club round the back of Leicester Square with 'old Silver'.

'You were in a club with Silver Perry?'

'That's what I said.'

'Till when?'

'Maybe two,' said Newton and he gave Burden another narrow look.

It would have to be checked along with the alibis of Lake, Singh and Catchpole. The club, which Newton said was called the El Video, would very likely be closed at this hour, but Burden had time to kill before meeting Wexford. He got on a bus and went on to the upper deck, always his favourite way of jaunting around London.

Really he should have gone to see Newton first, then he could have checked that alibi with Perry. The last thing Perry would do, surely, was support the false story of someone intending harm to his hero. Still, the El Video first.

It was, as he had expected, closed. With the tightening up of the pornography law, the photographs in the narrow glass case beside the door had been softened to mere languishing close-ups of breast and buttock, succulent mouth and swelling flank. The door itself had a cardboard notice on it which said the club was strictly private and for members only and underneath that a poster advertising a rock concert. There were three bells and Burden rang the middle one.

After a while the door was opened by a young black woman in velvet knee breeches and a red tee-shirt. She looked at Burden, said there was nothing doing till six and then it was only by appointment, but then seemed to understand he meant the club. She giggled and said Moggy would be opening up at eight. Burden walked off up the Charing Cross Road, wondering how Wexford was getting on.

Purbank wouldn't tell him what the quarrel was about. He also said he had forgotten the reason for it, though being more restrained than Vinald, he didn't add that the other man was a nasty piece of work.

His flat, on the fringe of Epping Forest, was in an apartment block with huge picture windows which pictured panoramas of tree tops. Purbank turned out to be an accountant who operated from home, in a big room drably furnished in 'safe' shades of porridge, cardboard and mud. Like Vinald he was made highly nervous by Wexford's visit and, when asked if he had been in touch with any other members of the train party since their return, particularly if he had received photographs from any of them, he cried, 'No, no, no!' with the vehemence of someone pleading not to be assaulted.

134

But of the Knightons he seemed genuinely to know nothing. In the train it was the single people who had congregated, the married couples keeping a little apart, though the Knightons had always made a three with Irene Bell. On the hotel roof in Kweilin he disclaimed having noticed anything out of the way except what he called the 'silly' music and, remembering it, he gave a nervous bellowing laugh.

Wexford thought the chances of his having shot Adela Knighton were about as remote as they could be. But he was rather taken aback when Purbank was unable to account for his movements on the night of 1 October. He could only say that he had been at home alone, or so he supposed, he couldn't really recall, but he thought he had been at home alone and could recall no visitors or phone calls. He seemed a friendless man, not so much a recluse as one whose manner, both boring and blundering, had driven possible friends away.

His head full of China, remembering China and wondering where Adela Knighton's photographs of China had got to, Wexford walked across the lobby of the flats and came face to face with a Chinese man. In other circumstances, even in Kingsmarkham where there was at least a Chinese restaurant, he would scarcely have given him a second glance. But here, in spite of himself, he stared just as those Chinese in Chang-sha had stared at him.

The man spoke pleasantly in an English that was a little high-pitched. 'Good afternoon. Were you looking for someone?'

Wexford collected himself. 'No,' he said, 'thanks all the same.'

He was tall for a Chinese, about forty, professional-looking, in a dark suit and plum silk tie and carrying a dark red leather briefcase. His English was accented but absolutely fluent and idiomatic. 'Nasty day,' he said. 'It's getting very chilly out,' and with a smile walked away to the lift.

Wexford had a look at the names above the doorbells outside. Number 7: Y.S. and M. Hsia. That would be it. And Purbank lived at number 8. Of course there was no reason why Purbank shouldn't have a Chinese next-door

135

neighbour. There must be many thousands of immigrants from Hong Kong, Taiwan and Singapore in this country. They mostly lived in cities and city suburbs, just as well in a flat in Buckhurst Hill as elsewhere. And yet it *was* odd. It made him look on Purbank, whom he had almost dismissed as of nugatory interest, with new eyes.

He picked up Burden at the appointed place by London Bridge. By now it was raining hard and the inspector was standing under his umbrella.

'We'll have a look at Knighton's bank account,' said Wexford. 'See if any large sums have gone out since he got back from China.'

Burden said rather gloomily, 'Can you see that guy hiring an assassin?'

'The wine he drinks is made of grapes. Other men in his station and class of life have done murder. Whatever he may have said on the subject to his wife and children, murder is by no means confined to the working class. And, you know, Mike, it ill becomes him to have said so, it was a fault of character in him that he could say that and it makes me feel his guilt more likely. I don't agree with you, I feel it's more likely he'd have hired someone than done it with his own hand.'

'Well,' said Burden with unexpected shrewdness, 'that might account for why he's so ashamed, why he seems to *hate himself so much*.'

13

If he was more interested in the Vinald family than in other members of the train party this was because he was coming to believe that it was the sight of Pandora Vinald, then unmarried, which had occasioned that look of ecstatic shock on Knighton's face. Somewhere, somehow, Knighton had seen her before, and if that look was anything to go by, had done more than see her. The next step would be to call on Jennifer Norris in her 'old' house in Springhill Lane.

Today she looked more like her mother than ever. Her hair had received a recent perm and her face was as shiny as a new coin. He had expected to be admitted by a cleaner or the present-day equivalent of a maid and into opulent luxury. It was rather a surprise to find her alone and the room into which she took him sparsely furnished. She didn't ask him to sit down.

'Where did my parents go on previous holidays? Do you mean since Daddy retired?'

'Go back five years, would you, Mrs Norris?' How old was Pandora? Younger than Jennifer certainly. Perhaps no more than twenty-four.

She didn't immediately answer him. It was impossible for her to miss an opportunity of dilating on her family's prosperity and social advantages. 'Mummy had what she called her holiday fund, you know. It was her way of getting the best out of her own money. She wanted real travel, you see, not just the usual winter sports in January and some Mediterranean beach in the summer everyone has.' This last sentence nearly took Wexford's breath away. He said nothing. 'So Angus invested this fund for her and she drew on it whenever they wanted to go anywhere – well, really super, you know. Like China. Mummy adored travel.'

Wexford nodded. 'Where did they go the first time after this – er, fund was started?'

'Egypt, I think, or it might have been Thailand and Java. I think they went to Mexico some time but I can't be absolutely sure. And once they just went to Jugoslavia and Corfu.' The Balkans were dismissed and put on a level with Bognor Regis. 'But that was at least six years ago.'

Keeping his patience, Wexford asked if they had ever been to New Zealand.

'People don't go to New Zealand for holidays, do they?' She was a girl of limited horizons. 'We have some sort of remote cousin in Sydney or it may be Melbourne, some place down there, and they did go to him for a while, maybe a month.'

'They spent a month in Australia? When was that?'

'Oh, years and years ago, six or seven years.'

It was stretching things a bit. Wexford found it hard to imagine the fifty-six-year-old Knighton popping across from Sydney to Auckland and there falling in love with a girl of seventeen. And what was being suggested, after all? That the girl had still loved him after seven years, had been reunited with him in China and then shot the rival wife?

'Mummy wanted to go to India and Nepal next,' said Jennifer Norris. 'She wanted to go in February, poor Mummy.' For the first time he saw signs of real emotion in her face.

He noticed something on the walls of a kind of study as they passed back through the hall to the front door which set him inquiring of Sergeant Johnson of the uniformed branch as soon as he was back in the station. But Johnson knew all about it.

'He's got a gun licence all right, sir, had one for years. Had one long before he was married when he was living in a flat in the High Street here. We do inspect, check he keeps the lethal stuff under lock and key. What you saw on his wall is mostly old fowling pieces, flintlock stuff and so on. He does have modern weaponry. I've a list of what he's got kept up to date.'

'But no Walther PPK?'

Johnson shook his head. 'He was the first one I checked on when your directive went round at the start of the case.'

Of course.

Wexford walked into his office and found two parcels awaiting him with the rest of the post. One had come by post, the other, in a large brown envelope and unsealed, by hand. He looked into that one first. The envelope contained a secondhand copy of the collected short stories of that Victorian writer of the macabre, Sheridan Le Fanu, and a bit of paper torn from a prescription pad with *Len* scrawled across it. Wexford wondered what Dr Crocker could be up to but he had never read any Le Fanu and thought this would do very well for relaxation during the Saturday afternoon and Sunday which he intended to take off.

In the other package, the one that had come by post, there was no clue to the identity of its sender. Wexford removed from their brown paper wrapping eight cardboard folders, the kind that film processors use. The name 'Knighton' was written across the top of each of them. Undoubtedly, these were the snapshots the Knightons had taken during their holiday, sent to him from an unknown source. His name on the wrapping and the address of Kingsmarkham Police Station had been printed. The postmark was a London one, Chingford, E.4.

Carefully, he went through the photographs. But it didn't take much perspicacity to tell that some, three or four, were missing. The appropriate negatives had also gone, the strip of celluloid cut through. It wasn't then just a failure to 'come out' that accounted for their disappearance. But which ones weren't there?

The first six envelopes were all of Eastern Europe and Russia, including one of a Russian railway station which the authorities would certainly have pounced on had they known of its existence. It was from the photographs in the other two folders, the Chinese ones, that the shots were missing. He recognised Chang-sha, the Marquise of Tai's tomb at Mawangdui, the Mao birthplace at Shao-shan. There

139

were several shots of loop-shaped mountains in Kweilin, all apparently taken from the hotel roof. Then nothing till the Five Goats statue in Canton. What had become of the Li River excursion then, the most spectacular trip to be taken between Peking and Hong Kong? Had the Knightons left their camera behind? Wexford knew they hadn't. He could remember Adela Knighton taking shots on deck – of the cormorant fishers, the villages, the boats with their square orange sails. Someone, the sender of this parcel, had for a reason as yet unfathomable to Wexford, abstracted those pictures and doubtless destroyed them along with their negatives.

Knighton put up no opposition to the suggestion that his financial circumstances be examined. Without expression he handed Wexford his latest bank statements, of which he received one every month. When Wexford asked why he had statements so often he explained that this was because, a year ago, owing to a standing order for a direct debit he had forgotten about, he had been briefly overdrawn. Since then his bank had kept him up to date with frequent statements. Prior to his retirement he had had a private account but since then he and his wife had used only their joint account. It was for this account that the statements had been issued. Knighton telephoned his bank and asked the manager to tell Wexford the facts about the private account, that it had been closed for three years.

There was nothing in the statements for the past year to indicate that any large sum which couldn't be accounted for had been withdrawn. A substantial monthly sum was paid in which Wexford took to be from some pension or annuity of Knighton's, and there were injections of larger sums, presumably from interest on Knighton's or his wife's investments. Four thousand pounds had been paid into the account in April, very obviously from Mrs Knighton's holiday fund, and a similar amount withdrawn two weeks later to pay in advance for the train tour. It was evident that Knighton had parted with nothing in fee to an assassin.

Of course there was no way of knowing whether this particular account was the only one he had. But in his previous exploration of the house and its desk and drawers, Wexford had found no cheque book or paying-in book for any account apart from this one and the closed private account of which Knighton had kept his final cheque book.

'Mr Knighton, I'd like you to come down to the police station with me so that we can have a talk. I think it would be profitable for you to have a talk with me and my colleague, Inspector Burden.'

'I see no reason why you can't talk to me here.'

'Perhaps not but I do. It will be more straightforward for all of us at the police station.'

'You mean more intimidating for me? I am quite sufficiently intimidated, I assure you.' Knighton made a weary movement of his head. 'I don't know if it's fear or shock or what it is, but I seem to be suffering from some kind of amnesia, what a mad doctor would call a fugue.' Knighton used the quaint and old-fashioned expression for an alienist without awkwardness. 'I seem to live in a stupefied daze,' he said.

Wexford noted he hadn't included grief among the emotions which distressed him.

'If I am going to be interrogated, I think I should have legal advice.' It seemed a strange thing for such as he had been to say. 'My legal adviser should be present,' he said.

'That's entirely your privilege, sir,' said Wexford more blandly than he felt.

It was a curious interview. And this was because of Knighton's frankness in certain areas and obtuse caginess in others. However, no legal adviser was present. Perhaps he thought that with a lifetime of experience behind him he could advise himself.

They used one of the less cell-like interview rooms. It had a rug on the floor. The chairs had straight backs but padded seats. Knighton sat on one side of the table and Wexford and Burden faced him. He looked ill, his eyes were fast becoming dark holes in his face, some sort of remorse was piling years on him as cancer does. He looked as if he had reached the end of his tether or some eleventh hour. Yet he could make a pedantic lawyer's joke.

It was chilly in the room. The central heating was not due

141

to be started until 1 November. Wexford had a small electric heater brought in and apologized to Knighton for the cold and general mild discomfort.

'*De minimis non curat lex*,' said Knighton with his death's-head grin.

The law may take no account of trifles but lawyers do. In accordance with Wexford's expressed wish, Knighton went into long detailed theories of how a potential killer might have known he was to be away on the night of 1 October. Once again he named the people to whom he had spoken of his projected trip to London, his wife, his daughter, son-in-law, village cronies, his son Roderick, and his daughter Jennifer. His host naturally had known of it and Dobson-Flint. Whom those people had told he couldn't begin to guess. Suddenly he said, 'You've asked my children and Miss Bell and Adrian Dobson-Flint and a good many others too, I suspect, if my marriage was a happy one. You haven't asked me.'

'In the circumstances,' said Burden, 'we took it for granted you'd say it had been.'

'In a murder inquiry, Inspector, you shouldn't take anything for granted. It was not a happy marriage. It never was. For years it was common knowledge I didn't get on with my wife. My wife felt towards me as many women feel towards their husbands. I was her possession and her protector and she had a right to my continued presence in her life. I don't suppose she ever thought whether she cared for me or not. I disliked her. As the years went by I disliked her more and more.'

Temporarily this silenced Burden. It took more than that to nonplus Wexford.

'Perhaps you feel like making a new statement, Mr Knighton?'

'I'm not going to confess to anything if that's what you mean. I disliked my wife but I bitterly regret her death. I would give everything I have – ' he hesitated and Wexford thought he was going to say 'to bring her back' but he ended ' – to turn time back to before the first of October.'

Wexford said, 'You were an unwilling husband. Were you a faithful one?'

142

'For twenty-five years I was. Before that – there was someone I wished to marry but it was impossible and we parted. I had my children to think of.'

'And your career, I daresay,' said Wexford.

Knighton winced. He made a vague gesture in front of his face. 'And my career, yes. I was thinking of a judgeship. As it happened, it never came. Let me say that I knew it wouldn't come if I deserted my wife and children for a young actress.'

They talked to him for a further hour. Gates came in with coffee and a plate of ham and cheese sandwiches. Knighton took the coffee but refused to eat anything. Wexford asked him about his knowledge of guns. Knighton said he knew nothing about the Walther PPK beyond that in fiction it was the gun used in the later James Bond books and that in fact it was used by the Stockholm police force. As the afternoon wore on to five o'clock they let him go home.

Two things of significance happened on Monday morning. One was the collapse of Gordon Vinald's alibi. Mrs Ingram and Denis Phaidon had been sounded out and both agreed that they had been to visit the Vinalds for coffee and drinks but it had been on Wednesday, 2 October, not Tuesday, 1 October. And Phaidon, in all innocence, made matters rather worse for Vinald by saying that they had originally intended to go there on the Tuesday but had been put off until the next night because, according to Pandora, her husband had been called away on business to Birmingham.

Wexford was reading the report on this and thinking about it, when Detective Constable Archbold who, with Bennett and Loring, was still pursuing a house-to-house enquiry in Sewingbury, came in to tell him it seemed they had at last found a witness. Thomas Bingley, an old man, retired, a one-time agricultural labourer. He had been in the wood through which the footpath from Sewingbury to Thatto Vale ran . . .

'An old man?' Wexford interrupted. 'In a wood at half-past two in the morning? What the hell for?'

'Well, sir, for poaching. Pheasants, it would seem. That's why it's taken us so long to find him, he's been lying low. It

143

was his niece put us on to him, thought we ought to know uncle was often out on that path at night at this time of year. Apparently he sets running snares and goes to fetch his booty in the small hours.'

'And he was there on October the first, was he? I call that adding insult to injury, poaching a man's birds on the very first day shooting officially begins.'

'Cheeky,' Archbold agreed. 'The point is, sir, he says he saw a man on that path. It was a clear night and the moon was shining and he says he saw a tall thin man with grey or white hair walking rapidly along the path towards Sewingbury.'

'With a smoking automatic in his hand, I daresay,' said Wexford.

By chance, thanks to the anonymous parcel, Wexford had photographs of several possible suspects in his possession. In the single living room of Bingley's unsavoury cottage down by Sewingbury Mill he showed the old man a picture of Knighton. Bingley looked at it and scratched his head and said that could have been the man he saw, though he thought he wasn't so tall. Purbank, pictured on the Kweilin hotel parapet in conversation with Irene Bell, he looked at and seemed to consider as a possibility. Then he hesitated and pointed with his little finger, a dirty finger with a broken nail, at someone in the background of the photograph, a man whose hair was covered by a straw sun hat. It was Vinald.

'This feller I saw looked a lot like him.'

'You can't put any credence on anything a bloke like that says,' said Burden when they were outside by the river bank.

'It's a muddled effort to please us in case we do him for poaching. He's one of those who thinks we won't love him if he says he doesn't know.' Wexford surveyed the recently completed concrete embankments, already known locally as 'the weir', through which the Kingsbrook had now been made to pass. There had been considerable controversy over whether it should be done at all. The river which, three weeks before, had flowed between reedy (and often litter-strewn) banks, was trammelled into a symmetrical gorge with a paved sitting area, holes in the paving for

144

trees and a new brickwork arch to the bridge that carried Springhill Lane.

'It doesn't look all that bad now it's finished,' Wexford said. There came into his mind a vision of the Li River and its landscape of looped mountains, the porcelain blue sky, the rippling water – and Wong drowned. 'Purbank has grey hair,' he said.

'Oh, come *on*. Any port in a storm, that is.'

'Not a bit of it. Purbank has no alibi for that night. And he may have a motive.' They strolled over to the car that was waiting for them at the point where the footpath to Thatto Vale joined the road. 'Three or four photographs and their negatives are missing from this set of Knighton's. Suppose it was to Purbank that Adela Knighton sent her pictures? The postmark on the package returned to me was Chingford, and Chingford, according to my map of Greater London, is pretty well next door to Buckhurst Hill where Purbank lives. Suppose one or more of those snaps showed Purbank in a compromising situation, a situation which he would do a great deal to avoid having made public.'

'Like what?'

'That I don't know. I haven't seen them. But Purbank might conceivably have thought Adela Knighton sent them to him, not out of kindness or interest, but to inform him what she knew. *And perhaps she did.*'

'So what do we do about that?'

'Nothing, at the moment. First we're going to find out why Vinald lied and said he was at home having cosy little drinks parties when in fact he was in Birmingham. Or Herstmonceux or Mevagissey. There's no knowing with a liar of his calibre. The really interesting thing about that alibi of his, though, was that it alibi'd Pandora as well. And now it doesn't, nothing and no one does.'

In Birmingham, it appeared, Vinald had done no more than meet the agent of a South American collector of porcelain. He had taken with him certain of the pieces he had brought out of China and two vases more recently acquired. In saying that this had taken place on the evening of 2 October instead of the true date, 1 October, he had made a simple mistake.

Vinald brought all this out very glibly but he couldn't conceal a terrible underlying nervousness. He was afraid of something and his fear was mounting. Wexford and Burden saw him at home, not in the shop, and Pandora came into the room while they were talking. Was it for her that he was afraid?

She was in a dress of white knitted wool today, bronze belt and shoes, her black glossy hair in the current fashion of smooth top and the sides a Renaissance frizz. She looked calm, not at all nervous. Wexford was suddenly sure he had been quite wrong in connecting her with Knighton. It was most probable they had never even spoken to each other.

'So you and your wife were alone here on the Tuesday night?'

They both said yes to that rather quickly and in unison. Their haste made them break off and smile awkwardly at each other. Pandora shrugged, opening her eyes wide.

'I'm going to have to insist on your telling me the cause of your quarrel with Mr Purbank.'

Vinald waited a moment. He smiled stoically, making the best of things.

'If you must know, he persistently made remarks insinuating I was turning the trip into what he called a buying spree.'

'And if you were, how did that affect him?'

'He suggested that every time we went sight-seeing and had a choice of what to visit I opted for the places where there would be artefacts for sale rather than for museums or panoramic views or whatever.'

'That may have been irritating to you but it was hardly offensive, was it?'

'It was the way he said it. It was more in the implication than what was actually said.'

'Mr Purbank says he has forgotten the cause of your quarrel.'

There was no mistaking the satisfaction this afforded Vinald. He smiled gaily. He put his arm through his wife's. 'He's a very nasty piece of work. Frankly, when he said he'd tell our guide it was my object to turn other people's holidays into a commercial venture to feather my own nest, I'd had enough. I slapped him down and we – exchanged no further words.'

Wexford knew he was lying, or rather that he was telling a heavily diluted version of whatever the truth was. As they left going down the steps, Wexford paused to stroke the head of the Pensive Selima who was sitting among some dead lobelias in an urn. She suffered his attentions, shook herself distastefully, jumped out of the urn and skittered down into the area.

'Not all that tempts your wandering eyes,' said Wexford, 'and heedless hearts is lawful prize . . .'

'What's that?'

'The poem the cat gets her name from. Come on, we're going to the V and A.'

Once Burden wouldn't have been quite sure. His wife had altered all that. 'The Victoria and Albert Museum,' he said to that London expert, Donaldson, and to Wexford, 'What are we going there for?'

'China's gayest art,' said Wexford.

That night, tired but not particularly late home, he finished Le Fanu's novella of vampires, 'Carmilla', and went on to the next story in the collection, 'Green Tea'.

14

He didn't tell Burden. He didn't tell anyone but his wife. Sitting up in bed reading Le Fanu beside Dora reading Charlotte Brontë, he came wonderingly to the end of the story and started to laugh.

'You mean,' said Dora as he explained, 'that this man was writing a book and he got overtired and he kept himself going by drinking green tea? Tremendous quantities of it as a sort of stimulant?'

'You might say he chain-drank cups of green tea. And he was very much frightened by a monkey-like creature he began seeing in the corner of his room. Then he saw it in the street and it got on an omnibus with him. Well, I saw an old woman with bound feet.'

'I suppose it was Len Crocker sent you the book.'

'Of course it was. He realized I'd made myself hallucinate in the same way as the Reverend Mr Jennings did in Le Fanu's story. I chain-drank green tea too, you know. I must have been drinking a couple of gallons a day.'

He laughed, remembering. But thinking about it before he fell asleep, he wasn't entirely satisfied with the explanation. He was relieved, it took a niggling little load off his mind, it was obvious it had been the green tea that produced the visions – but was that really all there had been to it? Surely there had to be more, though he might never find out what.

It made him feel a little strange about drinking his breakfast cup of tea, though this was Twining's Assam and in no way green. After breakfast he looked among his books, found *Masterpieces of the Supernatural*, and saw as he suspected that the last story in the collection was 'Green Tea'. If only he had read on to the end he would have known the answer when his anxiety was at its height.

Now what to do about what the poacher saw? About Purbank and the photographs? Burden was busy with reports from Middlesbrough, Manchester and Newcastle, all of them clearing the remaining men whom Knighton had prosecuted, respectively, on charges of murder, arson and grievous bodily harm. Back in the cottage down by Sewingbury weir, Wexford struggled to get something more satisfactory out of Bingley. But the old man again picked Vinald out from the photograph, qualifying his selection by saying the man he had seen looked more like Vinald than anyone else there. All he was positive about was that he had seen a man walking along the footpath at three in the morning or thereabouts and that man had been walking *back* from Thatto Vale.

Wexford and Burden had lunch together im the Many-Splendoured Dragon. Spring rolls, beef and onions, bean-sprouts, water chestnuts, Chinese mushrooms. Burden had a pot of jasmine tea but with a restrained shudder Wexford stuck to Perrier. He had been back in his office five minutes when the switchboard told him there was a girl downstairs wanting to see him. A Miss Elf.

'A Miss what?'

'Elf, Mr Wexford. Like, you know, gnomes and fairies.'

He nearly said, 'Is she pale green?' but green for the moment was a dirty word with him. 'Get someone to bring her up.'

Loring brought her in and left at a nod from Wexford. She was a small fair girl, perhaps five feet tall, and she looked very young. Fourteen or fifteen was his first impression. Her face was babyish, innocent, with large soft blue eyes. She wore jeans, a red sweat shirt and a red and white track suit top, blue and white canvas and rubber running shoes and, carrying no handbag, came in with her hands in her pockets.

'Miss Elf?' Wexford said.

149

'That's right.' Her voice didn't quite match the appearance. 'What can I do for you?'

'It's more what I can do for you. O.K. if I sit down? I've got some info for you. A friend of mine – well, more a client – he said the police here were looking for this old guy hanging about H.P.G. in the night time on October the first. So I never let on to my client but I reckoned I'd better present myself to you seeing as I did. Did see him, I mean.'

It was all very unclear. Miss Elf had aged in his estimation about two years but he was still mystified. 'You live in Hyde Park Gardens or Stanhope place? Your parents live there?'

She broke into laughter. 'No, no. I'd better begin at the beginning, hadn't I? Tell you who I am and what I am and what I was doing there at that hour, right?'

'What are you?' Wexford said slowly.

'I'm a whore,' said Miss Elf.

Wexford had begun to guess it. He disliked people trying to shock him, he wondered when they would ever learn he couldn't be shocked and hadn't been shockable these thirty years.

'I suppose you mean you're a prostitute, a call girl?'

'Right.'

'You look very young for that.'

'Well, that's the point, isn't it? I mean, me looking young. That's what you might say got me into it, me looking so young always. I'd got a rare commodity to sell and it was a sellers' market. I'm twenty-four actually. But wanting to screw twelve-year-olds didn't go out with the Victorians, you know, and I looked twelve when I started. I'd pass for fifteen now, wouldn't you say?'

Wexford nodded. He couldn't resist asking, 'Is your name really Elf?'

Her laughter was loud and harsh, with a coarse note. 'Really and truly. I was born Elf, the only daughter of Mr and Mrs Elf. Piece of luck, wasn't it? But I don't insist on it, you can call me Sharon.'

Of this offer he resolved not to avail himself. He was thinking that most of her clients were probably men of his age and he knew enough of prostitutes to be aware that she

150

would look on him with the same eyes as she looked on them, believe him subject to the same desires and the same perverse needs that made them want little girls. He felt a bit angry and a bit sick over it all and then he told himself that at any rate what went on now was ten thousand times better than in the days when it was really little girls they had.

'So to the night of October the first,' he said coldly.

Sharon Elf fixed her large blue eyes on him. 'This client of mine in Stanhope Place, he's one of my regulars, reminds me a bit of you actually.' She didn't see Wexford wince, or if she did, didn't care. 'He gave me a buzz around eight that night and said would I come and see him at midnight. Half twelve would be better if I could make it on account of he'd got people for dinner and by twelve-thirty they were sure all to have gone.'

'Where exactly does this client of yours live?'

'One of those houses facing the back of H.P.G.'

'Hyde Park Gardens, yes, I see.'

'As it happened, I could make it very well. I'd got another client at eleven, that was up in St John's Wood, so I left there around twelve-twenty, twelve twenty-five and I got a cab and it got me round to Stanhope Place just before twenty to one. I know you're going to ask me how I can be so sure of the time. The fact was I didn't want to embarrass my client – you know, if his guests hadn't gone on the dot like he said. So I kept looking at my watch and it was just before twenty to one we got there.

'I took a look at my client's house and I saw the light on in the hall and the bedroom but not the lounge, so I knew that was O.K. Anyway, I was paying off the driver when this old fella came out of the back of H.P.G., one of the lower ground floor flats – well, basements really. He came across the road and took my taxi.'

'Did you hear where he asked the driver to go to?'

'Sorry. There I can't help you. I wasn't interested, you see, didn't know any reason why I should be. Not then.'

'How exactly do you know now?' Wexford asked.

She said simply, 'My client in Stanhope Place gave me a buzz last night and I went round around ten. He told me the fuzz had been asking questions. It was the first time I'd seen him for three weeks, you see, or I reckon he'd have told me before.'

Wexford could almost have blessed Purbank or whoever it was had sent him those photographs. They were coming in very handy. There was one of the whole train party together on the Kweilin hotel roof. Only Adela Knighton, who had taken the shot, was missing. Unhesitatingly Sharon Elf picked out Knighton.

'That's him.'

'You're quite sure that's the man you saw in Stanhope Place at twenty minutes to one on the night of October the first?'

'Positive,' she said cheerfully. 'I had a good look. You see, I rather fancied him.'

Wexford's brain reeled. Did it work both ways then? If tired old men were looking for girls too young to criticize or have standards, were the girls looking for surrogate grand-fathers? He was glad, though, to see the back of Miss Elf and feeling a fool, asking himself who was he to sit in judgement, nevertheless opened his window for a little while after she had gone. Perhaps it was only to blow away the smell of rubber soles and Palmolive soap.

He turned his thoughts to what she had told him. There was Bingley's evidence and now this. He pressed his buzzer and said, if Inspector Burden was about, would they ask him to come up? Burden came in carrying a report on the last man on his list, a certain Dudley Preston whom Knighton had defended on charges of manslaughter and drunk driving but had failed to save from three years in prison.

'Do you know your window's wide open? It's like an icebox in here.'

'You can shut it if you like.' Wexford told him about Sharon Elf and what she had seen.

Burden's mouth went down at the corners. But that, Wexford thought, was more on account of Miss Elf's profession than the destruction of Knighton's alibi.

'You believe her? A woman like that?'

'Sometimes you talk like a mid-Victorian beadle. I don't see why a call girl shouldn't be as truthful as anyone else. Look at it how you will, it's an honest trade, it parts with

152

what it's paid for. Enough of this rubbish anyway. She picked him out from a group photograph, so of course I have to believe her.'

Burden shrugged. 'If it's true, and I suppose it is, things look bad for Knighton. The presumption would be that immediately he and Dobson-Flint had retired to their rooms, he prepared to go out again. No doubt he hung about while Dobson-Flint used the bathroom, then he slipped out, taking with him one of the bunches of keys from the hall table. It was too late for a train, so he must have had the taxi take him to wherever he had a rented car waiting. Who knows? He might have rented a car somewhere near Victoria Station and left it parked and waiting for him. He'd have hired that when he got to London and put enough in the meter to last him till six-fifteen. With meter charges stopping at six-thirty he wouldn't have had to worry. I suppose that means checking on the car hire places round Victoria now.

'If he took the taxi at twenty to one he would have been in Victoria by ten to. I may be ignorant of London but even I know there wouldn't be much traffic at that time of night. By one at the latest he would have been in that car and starting his drive. It wouldn't take him more than an hour so we'll say he got there at two.'

'A quarter of an hour to cut out the pane of glass, maybe a few minutes to steel himself – yes, it just about works out.'

'He didn't have to get through the window, he had a key.'

'He still had to cut out the glass.'

'Of course he did,' said Burden. 'I'm a fool. Of course he did. And he wouldn't have done it *after* he'd killed her. There's one thing, though – can you imagine him hoicking her out of bed and bringing her downstairs and shooting her through the back of the head?'

'There are a lot of things I can't imagine human beings doing but still they do them, Mike.'

'Well, I can't swallow it. Not a woman you'd been married to for over forty years. Not your own *wife*. And Knighton's not one of these yobs I've been hob-nobbing with, is he? Wouldn't we, I mean wouldn't anyone, call him a *civilized* sort of man?'

'Look, there are a lot of things I don't like too. I don't like any of it much but this is evidence we've got, Mike. Sharon Elf saw him at twelve-forty slipping out of Dobson-Flint's flat. Bingley saw a man walking back to Sewingbury around three and it wasn't Vinald he saw. Adela Knighton died between two-fifteen and three-thirty. The timing works out very neatly. What was he doing, taking a taxi at twenty to one in the morning when his friend thought him in bed asleep if he wasn't going clandestinely back to Sussex? We have to see him, we have to get him down here again. We have to know where that gun is now.'

'I don't see any motive.'

'Motive sometimes has a way of showing itself rather late in the day. Anyway, someone said that every married man has a motive for murder.'

But as Wexford reached for the phone, it rang. The switchboard again, announcing a second visitor.

'There's a Mr Shah here, sir, asking to see you.' The voice went lower. 'A Chinese.'

'He doesn't sound Chinese.'

Sha? *Shah?* Did they mean Indian or maybe Tibetan? For a moment Wexford was mystified. Then a little tug of excitement caught at his throat. The name might be pronounced more or less Shah but in fact it was Hsia.

His visitor was Purbank's next-door neighbour in Fairmead Farm Court, Buckhurst Hill.

'I'd like you to stay,' he said to Burden.

The tall man in the dark suit that Wexford had encountered in the lobby of the flats came into the office. He was wearing a dark suit of a slightly different shade today and he still carried his briefcase. His black hair was so smooth and sleek it seemed to have been painted on his scalp. His eyes were mild, intelligent, his expression one of gentle impassivity. He held out to Wexford a narrow pale brown hand on which he wore a signet ring in obsidian and gold.

'My colleague, Inspector Burden,' said Wexford. 'Mr Hsia.'

Hsia sketched a slight bow. 'It's Chief Inspector Wexford, I believe? I hope I haven't come at an inconvenient time?'

'Not at all. Won't you sit down? I think we might all

154

have some tea, don't you?' Wexford put his finger on the buzzer.

Sitting down, Hsia kept his arms tensely along the arms of the chair, then, as if by some oriental relaxation technique, lifted them and laid his hands calmly in his lap.

'Chief Inspector, I have come here to tell you something my friend and neighbour Mr Purbank cannot bring himself to tell you. It may seem I am betraying a trust, you see, but while this secrecy goes on I fear very much he will become ill. He is very much frightened, you see, so for his relief I must speak the whole truth to you.' Hsia's face relaxed and he gave a sort of rueful chuckle. 'You may feel, you see, that I am the one who should need to keep the secret, for I am the criminal. May I begin now?'

Wexford nodded. The tea came in. It rather surprised Wexford to see Hsia take milk and two lumps of sugar.

'My name is Hsia Yu-seng,' he began. 'You know where it is I live. I work for the Kowloon and Fuchow Bank in London Wall.' He paused and Wexford thought that 'work for' was probably a modest understatement. 'Most people,' Hsia went on, 'suppose that I am originally from Hong Kong or Taiwan, you see, but this isn't so. I was born in Shao-shan in the People's Republic – in fact, you know, in the very birthplace of the late Chairman, Mao Tse Tung. I was born in that place ten years before what they call liberation.'

'How did you come to leave China?' Wexford asked.

Hsia raised his teacup to his lips and drank a little. 'May I?' he said, reaching the ringed hand out for a Garibaldi biscuit. 'I committed a crime,' he said. 'I was twenty-one. If I had been caught – and I should have been caught, there is no hiding such things in China, you see – I would have been executed.'

Wexford moistened his lips. Inescapably, he associated capital punishment with murder. 'What crime?'

'I raped someone,' said mild sleek Mr Hsia, and he turned up the corners of his mouth in an apologetic smile.

15

Burden made a choking sound over his tea. He wiped his mouth with a crisp white initialled handkerchief. 'Excuse me.'

'*You raped someone?*' Wexford said.

'I and three others. You don't know how it was, the life there, the deprivation, the oppression, the *re*pression. This girl, she asked us, you see, she teased us, it was an invitation with the eyes, the walk. And then, when it is happening first with my friend, then with me, she is frightened and later she tells her father who is Party cadre.' With the stress of telling, Hsia's English worsened, approaching pidgin. He recovered himself and loosened his clenched hands. 'For this in China there is execution. There was then and there is now. My uncle, my mother's brother, he was a truck driver, driving every week to Canton. He took me in the truck, hid me, and from Canton I got into the New Territories. I am cutting a long story short, you see, but that was how it was. I walked to the border, crossed into the New Territories and came to Hong Kong. English I could speak a little, I had studied it at the University of Chang-sha, so after a while I came to England with my wife that I had married in Hong Kong, you see, and whose father is director of the Kowloon and Fuchow Bank. And from then on all goes very well for me.' He smiled again and this time slightly inclined his head.

Wexford looked at him, the bland parchment-coloured face, the still features that have led to 'inscrutable' being the adjective invariably associated with the Chinese. Undreamt-of

156

adventures, terrors, privations, struggles, lay hidden between the lines of that long story cut short. A less likely rapist than Hsia Yu-seng, Wexford had never seen.

'This is all very interesting,' he said, 'but what has it to do with Mr Purbank?'

'I am coming to it,' Hsia said, nodding. 'I have said all goes well for me and this is true, you see, except in one respect. That is my mother. My father died, you see, in the fighting of 1949 and my mother is widow, living with my brother and his family. But I was her favourite and always I have been very sad that I cannot get news to her. Always I have been afraid for her sake, you see, to send a letter and it is out of question for me ever to set foot in People's Republic. Often I have been thinking of ways to get news but find nothing better than what my father-in-law already has done – send her message only that I am alive. Then one day my neighbour Mr Purbank says to my wife that he is going in a train to China.'

'I begin to see,' said Wexford. 'Mr Purbank's itinerary would take him to Shao-shan and you asked him to deliver a message to your mother.'

'I asked him if he would take a *letter* to my mother. I had heard through my father-in-law that my brother's wife is cook in Wu Jiang Hotel, you see, so I thought to myself, there can be no trouble for Mr Purbank, who will surely eat there when he visits Mao's birthplace, to ask for the cook in order to praise his meal. He was to ask her name and if she answers, 'Mrs Hsia,' to slip her my letter.

'But all this goes wrong, you see, for Mr Purbank lost my letter when some things were stolen from his bags in Russia. And this made him very nervous and anxious to do the right thing, but he didn't know how to do it, you see. So he asked the interpreter to say to the cook, 'Your brother's friend is here,' which he does and my sister-in-law, very excited, you see, sends home for my mother who is an old woman now, more than seventy years old.'

With bound feet, Wexford thought. And when he had seen her that first time, then, when he had seen her as he was lunching in the Wu Jiang Hotel, it was no green tea hallucination. It had been a real woman that time that he had seen standing by the screen and waiting for news of her son. 'Go on,' he said.

'Well, then it was that Mr Purbank became really frightened, for whatever he said he must say through this interpreter, this official guide and interpreter from Lu Xing She. He knew I had been criminal, you see, and feared that if this was known he and the party might be expelled from China, so to my mother and sister-in-law, through the interpreter, he says that he has made a mistake, there has been a misunderstanding.

'But with this my mother was not content. She guessed, I think, that Mr Purbank has much to say but was frightened to say it, so next day when my cousin, the son of my uncle who saved my life, when he drives to Chang-sha she goes with him to look for Mr Purbank . . .'

The second sighting, Wexford thought, on Orange Island.

' . . . and there she finds him but they cannot communicate, you see, except by signs and by then both are afraid, Mr Purbank and my poor mother. Then, as luck would have it, while Mr Purbank is walking in the street in Chang-sha a student called Wong comes to him and asks to practise his English.' Hsia had gone entirely into the present tense now and Wexford remembered reading somewhere that Mandarin has no tenses. 'Perhaps this happens often in present-day China?' Hsia asked.

'Yes, it does.'

'So Mr Purbank has bright idea, you see, of asking this Wong to be interpreter for him. My mother still sits, waiting, in lobby of Wu Jiang Hotel. Mr Purbank tells Wong all about me, how I live in England, work in Kowloon and Fuchow Bank, have wife, have two boys at boarding school, everything about me, and Wong tells my mother who is made very happy and goes off full of happiness when my cousin calls back for her. But this is not, you see, the end of the story for Mr Purbank.

'This Wong is himself perhaps a criminal element or perhaps it's true he wants only to escape from People's Republic. Again to cut the story short, he follows Mr Purbank on the train to Kweilin, pleading with him to get him out of China. Also, Mr Purbank says, he asks always for money, you see, as if to threaten Mr Purbank that he has done a wrong thing that will get him in trouble unless he gives money.'

'You mean this Wong was blackmailing Mr Purbank? Unless Mr Purbank agreed to help get him out of China and gave him money, he would make the whole story of your contact with your mother known?'

'Something of that kind, yes. Mr Purbank was very frightened by now, always to be followed everywhere by this Wong, and although it was dreadful thing to happen he wasn't so very distressed when there was accident on the Li River boat and Wong was drowned.' The still features widened into a reflective smile. 'Mr Purbank then thought his troubles at an end till when he got home, a good while after, this Mrs Knighton whom someone has shot sends him photographs of the Li River trip. In them he is talking with Wong and Mr Purbank is very afraid once more . . .'

'Did you see these photographs, Mr Hsia?'

'No, I didn't but I was told of them. Mrs Knighton's husband, you see, is in some way connected with the law and Mr Purbank thinks, suppose this whole story comes out and causes international incident, you see. So he burns the pictures and the negatives and sends the rest back to you and then he becomes nervous again in case you think he shot this Mrs Knighton . . .'

Wexford very nearly laughed. There was something he knew and Hsia very evidently didn't which stopped him laughing.

'It was wise of you to come to me,' he said.

'I thought it best. And now I shall tell you where Mr Purbank was on the night of October first till after midnight – with me and my wife in our flat.' Getting up to leave, extending his hand, Hsia added, 'I fear he thinks it safer to be suspected of Mrs Knighton's murder than have it known he associates with such politically dangerous people as ourselves.'

From the window Wexford watched him cross the police station forecourt and get into this year's registration dark blue BMW. Strange to reflect that this sleek capitalist was the son of that old woman with the hoof-like mincing feet, that forerunner and instigator of hallucinations.

159

'Can you believe that?' Burden said. 'Can you believe Purbank was actually afraid of high-level repercussions because photographs existed of himself in conversation with a dissident Chinese?'

'Hsia believes it.'

'Sure he does. He grew to manhood in a country with perhaps the most repressive political system on earth.'

'I'll tell you what I think for what it's worth,' said Wexford. 'I'll never be able to prove it, I've nothing to go on but my own feelings, but it's my belief Purbank pushed Wong overboard. He was harassed by Wong's persecution and when they were on the boat and he came up behind Wong squatting down in the bows, he gave him a shove and pushed him overboard. Not intending to kill, I daresay, intending to frighten, to show Wong in his muddled way that he wasn't going to be used and battened on in the way Wong hoped.

'Back home I expect he soon forgot about it. We all know the old postulation: if by raising your hand you could acquire a million pounds and kill a Chinaman, would you do it? It's generally believed that few would hesitate long. Maybe it seemed a little like that to Purbank. After Wong was drowned I asked Adela Knighton what had happened and she said indifferently that someone had been drowned – "not one of us" she said "a Chinese". Purbank had raised his hand and acquired peace if not money and it was all twelve thousand miles off and there are a lot of Chinese anyway . . . until the picture came with his hand reaching towards Wong's back.'

Burden nodded. It was likely enough. Suspects were being cleared, others implicated. Rape had reminded him of Coney Newton and what he had to tell Wexford of the El Video Club. Loring had been there the night before, making inquiries.

'It's managed by a man called Jimmy Moglander – 'Moggy' to his associates. Newton was in there all right. He and three or four other men he was with were there until they closed on the Wednesday morning. The lives these villains lead! Moglander and the barman both remember Newton being there. So that seems to clear each and every old lag that might have had a grudge against Knighton.'

'So how about Knighton?'

'He'll keep till the morning, I should think.'

'You're right.' Wexford thrust back his chair and got up. 'I'm going home, Mike. If I hang about here someone'll be bound to drop in and tell me how he saw an old woman with bound feet climbing in through Knighton's loo window. We'll leave Knighton till tomorrow.'

But for Adam Knighton tomorrow never came. It was like *déjà vu*, Wexford thought in the morning, or the rerun of a tape. It was like going to see a film and sitting through the whole programme to see the beginning again. Only you usually did that because you liked the film. He hadn't liked this one the first time round, and as for the second . . .

The same credit titles, the same opening. It started with Renie Thompson phoning the police station at nine, with Burden and the fingerprint man and the scene-of-crimes man and Dr Crocker all going up to Thatto Hall Farm. The sun was shining and there was dew on the grass, and if the Michaelmas daisies were a little more mature and frost had shrivelled the leaves of the dahlias, if the sun was a little higher because the clocks had gone back an hour, only a purist would have noticed. All things up until this point seemed the same. They found a divergence only when they were inside the house, for this time it was Knighton who lay dead and by his own hand.

'Two times in a month,' said Mrs Thompson. 'It makes you think twice about going into a person's house. I thought he must be having a lay-in but the bedroom door wasn't shut, it was like on the jar, so I just gave a tap and put my head round . . .'

Since Wexford's last visit, Knighton had moved back into the room he had shared with his wife and there, on the evening before, he had undressed, put on blue cotton pyjamas and a brown wool dressing gown, lain on his bed and surrendered himself to death. On the bedside table beside him was an almost empty brandy bottle, an empty wine, not brandy, glass, and a cylindrical plastic container that had once held fifty capsules of tuinal.

161

'His doctor prescribed that for insomnia, presumably.'

'Not me, thank God,' said Crocker. 'I'd have given him mogadon. The only way you can kill yourself with mogadon is stuff down so many you choke to death.'

He closed Knighton's pale blue staring eyes. On the dressing table were two sealed envelopes, both addressed in Knighton's bold and beautiful hand. One of them was to the coroner.

'Who's Mrs M. Ingram?' said Crocker.

'God knows.' Wexford read the address, Thain Court, Cadogan Avenue, London, SW1, and then he knew. 'It would seem she's the mother-in-law of an antique dealer I happen to know. I see he's provided a stamp but I think I'll deliver this by hand.' Outside, below the window, the gravel crunched. Wexford looked out. 'Angus and Jennifer,' he said and he stuffed the letters into his pocket.

Knighton's yellowish-white waxen face looked as long dead as the Marquise of Tai's. It looked as if it were made of porcelain but a porcelain they had forgotten to colour before the glaze went on.

'Poor devil,' Wexford said. 'There was no loophole left for him.'

'He did kill her then?'

'I didn't mean that. I've a feeling his predicament was a moral one, that it was his conscience he couldn't escape.' They left the room and closed the door. 'I never thanked you for the book.'

'I'm not sure if it would really happen.'

'Well, yes and no,' said Wexford cryptically.

Jennifer and her husband were in the hall. Her expression was as surly as ever. As he came down the stairs Wexford heard the tail end of what she was saying to Mrs Thompson, something about having no help in the house and a shock like this being enough to send her into premature labour. But Angus Norris looked as shocked and distressed as if Knighton had been his own father.

'This is a bad business, Mr Norris,' Wexford said. It was a phrase he used when he found himself in these or similar circumstances. Non-committal, it nevertheless expressed everything needful.

162

Norris took it *au pied de la lettre*. He spoke with a kind of tragic enthusiasm. 'A dreadful business, dreadful.' His face was rather pale and lined in a way some adolescents' faces are, though this ages them not at all. He looked round for his wife, to comfort her perhaps or be comforted, but Jennifer had gone into the living room and was lying in a chair with her feet up.

He said carefully, in a more controlled tone, 'Was there – a suicide note or anything of that sort?'

'Something of that sort,' said Wexford and he followed the doctor out through the front door.

Roderick Knighton's yellow TR7 had just joined the Norrises' worn-out Citroën on the gravel drive. The barrister got out of it and rushed into the house, closing the front door behind him with almost a slam.

The letters burned Wexford's pocket. He would have been justified in opening the envelope addressed to Mrs Ingram and reading the contents. A suicide has forfeited his right to privacy and this suicide was also a prime suspect in a murder case. Who *was* Mrs Ingram, apart from being Pandora Vinald's mother? What had she been to Adam Knighton that he had written her a letter from his deathbed?

He wouldn't open it without phoning her first. He picked up the phone to ask the switchboard to find her number for him, then put it down again. On the hotel roof in Kweilin there had been another woman with Pandora, a much older woman, white-haired. In all the thought he had given to the events of that evening at the rooftop bar, in all his recollections of the people involved, that woman had never figured. The beauty of Pandora had eclipsed her.

For him perhaps, for almost everyone who saw them together, but not for Knighton. Knighton, sitting at that table with his wife, had seen her as Dante saw Beatrice and in a moment his life and his hopes had been transformed. But unlike Dante he wasn't seeing her for the first time. Wexford was sure of that. There was a romantic side to his nature that had a weakness for the phenomena of passion, yet he couldn't admit of the possibility of a man of Knighton's age falling in love at first sight with a woman of Mrs Ingram's.

He must have known her before, perhaps years ago. When they had interrogated him he had said that his career would have been damaged if he had 'deserted my wife and children for a young actress'. Mrs Ingram would have been young then, when the Knightons lived in Hampstead during the week and Sussex at the weekends, when Jennifer and Colum were babies, when Knighton by his eloquence was saving at least one murderer from execution.

The interesting thing was that the first time he saw her in London Pandora had reminded him of some famous beauty of thirty years back. He had thought of Hedy Lamarr or Lupe Velez. Thou art thy mother's glass and she in thee calls back the lovely April of her prime . . . Mrs Ingram had friends in the film world. She had brought a film cameraman to meet her daughter and son-in-law.

'What do you suppose Milborough Lang looks like now?' Dora had said, watching *The Snow Moth*. 'She must be fifty-five.'

The letter to the coroner, Dr Neville Parkinson, Wexford delivered in person. Then he went off to meet Burden for lunch at the Many-Splendoured Dragon.

'It's unlike you not to be hungry,' said Burden.

Wexford was picking rather listlessly at his food. 'It's Setzuan here too,' he said. 'Nicer than the Hunan we mostly got served with.'

Burden looked impressed. 'Have you ever heard of a play called *The Good Woman of Setzuan* by a chap called Brecht? The drama society here is doing it at the end of the month. You ought to go.'

'I suppose your wife's playing the lead?' Wexford could tell from Burden's sheepish look that he had guessed right. He dipped in his chopsticks to catch a curl of okra while Burden, resigned to a spoon, watched him warily. Wexford dismissed the versatile Jenny Burden with a wry smile. 'Fishing for trouts in a peculiar river,' he said. 'Knighton was too old for that kind of thing. He was too old to have a mistress and too old to murder his wife.'

'What did Parkinson's letter say?'

'It was very short. I can probably quote it from memory.

164

"This is to inform you that on the morning of 2 October I killed my wife, Adela Knighton, by shooting her with a Walther PPK automatic pistol. As a consequence of that act I shall, by the time you read this, have taken my own life." And he signed it. That was all.'

Burden poured himself a glass of mineral water. 'I wonder where he got the gun and, come to that, what he did with it afterwards.'

'I wonder about a lot of things. Frankly, Mike, I think it's all these doubts I have that are making me – well, I won't say upset. Uneasy.'

'You don't mean you think it's a false confession?'

Wexford didn't answer him directly. 'He was devoured by guilt, wasn't he? You could tell that.' He pushed away his plate. For a moment he hesitated, then he asked the waiter to bring a pot of green tea. 'And certainly he wanted her dead. He left Dobson-Flint's and came back here that night. He must have killed her. Why say so if he hadn't? It's not your run-of-the-mill false confession. The man killed himself. The whole point of a false confession is to attract attention and the kind of hysteric who does that doesn't defeat his own object by committing suicide immediately afterwards.'

'Certainly not,' said Burden firmly.

'Let's go. I have to phone Mrs Ingram and then I have to see her.'

165

16

Fashion had come full circle and the clothes she wore were not unlike those she had been dressed in for her films, a little grey flannel suit with a straight skirt, a pearl-coloured silk blouse with a high pleated neckline, stockings with seams, high-heeled shoes. Her figure seemed unchanged. But that kind of black silk hair is perhaps of all shades the most vulnerable to time. It was whiter than her skin now and that skin itself webbed with lines.

She hadn't sounded surprised by his phone call. Why should she have been? For weeks now she must have been waiting for the police to come to her. *Why* he had come, that was something else again. She greeted him with a gentle, ever so slightly ironical, friendliness.

They went into a living room. The flat was in a small block of apartments for rent on short leases, smart, even luxurious, in one of the most highly desirable residential areas on earth. It lacked any particle of character. It was a suite of motel rooms, biscuit-coloured Wilton on the floors, chocolate-coloured linen at the windows and upholstering the furniture, here and there murals that were blends of Samuel Palmer and Rowland Hilder or montages of beaten tin cans and bits of bamboo. She had added pieces of her own, a pair of water colours, a red, blue and gold ikon, a vase or two that very likely came from Vinald, and flowers in abundance. She had filled vases and bowls with what October afforded in the way of dahlias and chrysanthemums and what October

166

couldn't afford but she evidently could, roses and gladioli and carnations.

She sat down on the sofa, her knees together, her body held a little to one side, her head up, a very Milborough Lang attitude. Suddenly Wexford's heart felt heavy. He was desperately sorry for her.

'I believe you knew Adam Knighton well?' he began.

She was immediately apprehensive. '"Knew"?' she said. 'What does "knew" mean? I know him, yes.'

This was how the man felt who drew Priam's curtain in the dead of night. And like Priam, she had begun to guess. 'Mrs Ingram, I used the word advisedly. I have bad news for you. I think it will be bad news.' She was very still, her eyes on him. 'You must prepare yourself for a shock. Mr Knighton is dead.'

Her lips parted. She brought her hands together.

'He was found dead this morning,' Wexford said.

'Do you mean – he killed himself?'

'I am afraid so.'

'How?' she asked softly.

'Brandy and an overdose of sleeping pills. He left a note for the coroner and a note for you. I have brought yours with me.'

On the third finger of the thin veined hand she put out to him was a diamond cluster as big as a grape. She wore a diamond watch and diamond earrings. From the neck up she had grown some ten years older since he had told her of Knighton's death.

'It was kind of you to come personally to tell me.' She started to get up. She was politely dismissing him.

'I'm sure you would like to read your letter in private,' he said, 'but after that I'm afraid I shall have to see it.'

She held it against her breast, her hands crossed over it in the traditional gesture of a girl keeping a love letter from father or husband. She was still an actress.

'I shall have to see it, Mrs Ingram. It may be of great relevance to Mrs Knighton's murder. I must see the letter and then you and I must have a talk.'

'If I don't show it to you, could you get an order or a warrant or something like that to force me to?'

167

He nodded. 'Something like that. But I'm sure you'll let me see it without that, won't you?'

'Yes.' She pushed her thumbnail under the flap of the envelope and began to open it. 'Excuse me if I go away to read it.'

He was taking a small risk but he hadn't the heart to refuse her. While she was absent, the door between the communicating rooms left ajar as if she guessed what he slightly feared, he thought of what Irene Bell had told him about Knighton's attitude towards his family in the past. 'For five years after Colum was born Adela had a husband insofar as there was a man sleeping in the other bed in her room.' Colum Knighton would be about thirty. It fitted. 'And then suddenly Adam came back. He lived at home, he had his meals there, he started taking Adela out – the lot.' What else had she said? 'It was as if he'd had a shock and come to his senses.' What in fact had happened was that after a five-year-long love affair Milborough Lang had left him and married someone else.

She came back and gave him the letter in a quick, almost disdainful gesture. A lamp was on but he took it to the window and read it by the dying daylight.

My darling, I shall be dead when you come to read this. I had dreamed of our being so happy together, I had longed for it and it really did seem within our grasp for a little while. I believed I could live with anything so long as you and I had each other at last, but I was wrong. The love I have for you is the strongest emotion I have ever felt for anyone, stronger than my feeling for my children. I have loved you for thirty years and kept the image of you always in my mind.

But remorse is stronger than love. When I killed Adela I did not know myself. Though I had spent a lifetime in association with evil, I did not know how insidious evil is, how it destroys the joy of everything, even the joy of love. I had never considered that this act which was designed to bring me happiness would instead show me a hell of shame and self-hatred, a hell that is with me night and day, every moment of every day.

That is not something I can live with or expect you to

168

share with me. Therefore I have resolved to put an end to it. Twenty-five years ago my children and my responsibilities and my own fear held me back. This time I think I shall have the courage. Not so much courage, perhaps, as the lack of it, lack of fortitude for a continuance of the life I am living now.

Do you remember how we read the Chinese poems together? Here are two lines from Chang Chi.

So I now return your shining pearls with a tear on each. Regretting that we did not meet while I was still unwed. Good night, my darling, and God bless you, Adam.

She hadn't cried when she read the letter but the sight of him reading it brought the tears. They fell silently, she hardly seemed aware of them.

'Please sit down, Mrs Ingram. Do you feel able to talk about this or would you rather wait a while?'

'It may as well be now.' She spoke the ungracious words graciously. She sat down. 'I should like my letter back, please.'

'Later. You shall have it before I go. Now I should like you to tell me the whole story.'

She made a movement of recoil, she shook her head. 'He didn't kill her, whatever he says. He *couldn't* have killed her.'

'I'm afraid you're going to have to accept that he could and did. Now you're going to tell me about yourself and him. It will be good for you as well as for me. Have you anyone else you can tell it to? Anyone at all who will care enough to listen?'

'No,' she whispered.

He had been thirty-two, she twenty-five. They had met at a dinner party given by that very Henry Lacey who had entertained Knighton on the eve of his wife's death. Adela had been there too. The young Milborough Lang had become famous overnight when her first film was shown, a curious and almost mystical story of a deaf girl called *The Snow Moth*, and she had followed this with a stage success as Petra in Ibsen's *An Enemy of the People.* Wexford remembered seeing *The Snow Moth* when it first came out. As was probably true of Garbo, it was the star's beauty and grace of movement and look of other-worldliness which had brought her fame rather than her acting ability. Milborough Lang had been wonderfully beautiful.

'We were a handsome couple,' she said, seeming to read his thoughts. 'Isak Dinesen says that life is but a process for turning frisky young puppies into mangy old dogs. Only we never were a couple really. Adam had Adela and he had four children. Colum had been born just three months before we met. He told me Adela had had his two younger children to ensure he stayed with her, and it worked, it did ensure that.

'We saw as much of each other as we could. Technically, he still lived with Adela, he slept under her roof. It was very cruel, it was a hateful way to behave to her, I know that. I think I felt more guilty than he did.' She paused and put her fingers to her cheeks to wipe away the drying tears. 'We paid for it, of course. We were punished. The times we had together were always a rush, always a race against the clock. He had to get back to work, to court, to Adela, and I had my career too. I got this Hollywood offer and I went to Hollywood and made that terrible *Mind Over Matter*, but I couldn't stay there without Adam.

'I was the one who made the break. We couldn't have gone on like that. It had been five years but Colum was still only five, and it would have meant another fifteen years maybe of rush and subterfuge and passion and mad muddle. Besides, it had never had the chance to become a real workaday relationship, it was a romance.

'I met Ryan Ingram. He wanted to marry me and take me away to New Zealand. I think he saw himself, poor dear Ryan, as a sort of new world Prince Rainier, transporting his beloved from the rat race of the screen into a life of wealth and peace. I seem to be predisposed to these romantic men, don't I? Anyway, I did marry him and I did go away with him and Adam and I didn't write to each other or see each other for twenty-five years – until I walked out on to the roof in that place in China.'

*

Ryan Ingram had died of a coronary three years before. Their daughter Pandora had made a mistaken marriage when nineteen. It was partly to distract her mind from this and from the subsequent divorce that she and her mother had come on the trip that had been intended to take them round the world but had ended, in each case because of a love affair, in London.

'Adam recognized me at once. It must be true that love is blind because I think I've altered more than most people do in twenty-five years. I recognized him, of course. It was an extraordinary sensation, seeing him sitting there, still with Adela.'

She got up and drew the curtains on the dark late afternoon. When the lamp underneath it went on the rich colours of the ikon, the gold in its border and the Virgin's crown, glowed in the light. Wexford suddenly recalled reading an illustrated article in a Sunday supplement about ikons that looked like that and which came from the neighbourhood of Lake Baikal . . . Milborough Ingram smiled, a little sadly, a little ruefully, and went on, 'Adela went to bed. He came over to our table and said – to be prudent, you know. Oh, that eternal prudence! – "Miss Lang, we met years ago at Henry Lacey's house in London. I don't suppose you remember." "I remember," I said. Pandora was talking to some Australians, I don't think she noticed Adam. The young don't notice, they aren't interested in us. Why should they be? He said – his voice was shaking – "May I buy you a drink?" I excused myself to the others and we went inside the hotel. I never had that drink – I think I'd like one now, though. Will you?'

Wexford nodded. She fetched ice and poured whisky on to it in big glasses.

'We found a sort of banqueting room, a great empty gloomy place, and we went in there and talked. You were in that hotel too, Adam said. Isn't that strange? I wonder where you were then.'

'Being shown his porcelain collection by your son-in-law.'

The delicate dark eyebrows went up. 'He's scared stiff of you because he thinks you're after him for selling something or other to an American. Are you?'

171

Wexford smiled. 'I think the Chinese would be after him if they knew. China's a long way away.'

'Yes.' Her voice grew grave again. 'China's a long way away. Adam once told me about the Chinese mandarin, how most people wouldn't think twice about killing a Chinese mandarin if they could get a million pounds by doing so. China is so far away, so remote, even today. If one just had to make a sign, he said . . .' She sat down again, looking at him. 'In China, that night, everything seemed simple. Adam could leave Adela. Time had sorted things out for us and we could be together.'

'You still wanted to? After a quarter of a century? After your marriage?'

She delayed answering, drank some of her drink. 'I will be honest,' she said at last. 'I didn't feel the same as I had. How could any ordinary realistic person feel the same? Adam wasn't an ordinary realistic person. I'm not flattering myself when I say he felt just the same, perhaps even more so.

'I wanted to make him happy. I would have liked to remarry and to be married to him. Oh, yes, I would have liked it.'

'So he went home and you and your daughter went to England all on the same plane. Did you speak to Adela Knighton?'

'No. She had seen me once, thirty years ago at a dinner party and naturally she had forgotten me. Adam and I didn't speak to each other again until we saw each other in London. Pandora and Gordon were instantly attracted to each other. That was why it was easy to get straight to London, Pandora wanted it, she would have gone without me if I'd objected. In London I took a lease of this flat and Adam came to see me here. He and Adela used to have days out in London, they'd come up together on the train and he'd go and look up various old cronies while she went shopping and called on some friend of hers in Primrose Hill. I replaced the old cronies.

'It was very much like it had been twenty-five years ago. Patterns repeat themselves, don't they? There was I with my flat and there was Adam living with his wife. We were ruled by the clock as we had been. Almost from the first I knew he

wasn't going to leave Adela. I tackled him about it and he –
he wept, he actually cried, poor Adam, it was dreadful. He
couldn't leave her, he said, not after forty years. He couldn't
face her and his children with a thing like that. That quarter
of a century might never have been. I'd married and had a
child and lived on the other side of the world and he'd become
a QC and retired and was a grandfather – but everything was
just the same, it was uncanny. And yet he did love me, he
loved me more than I loved him, poor Adam.

'And then I tried to break it off just as I had before. I said
it was hopeless going on in this way, simply history repeating
itself. I said I was too old for that kind of thing and when
the lease of this place was up I'd go home to my house in
Auckland.'

'You mean you held that over him as a threat?'

She lifted her shoulders and there came to her lips the
ghost of a Milborough Lang smile. 'He knew I'd go unless
things could be made more permanent, yes.'

The smile angered him. 'You might say then, Mrs Ingram,
that you share some of the responsibility for Adela Knighton's
murder and hence for Adam Knighton's own death.'

She jumped up, her serenity gone, and cried out to him,
'That's not true! Adam didn't kill her. Haven't I told you he
couldn't have killed her?'

'He's admitted it. Before his confession we were pretty certain – all the evidence, circumstantial and otherwise, pointed
to his having killed her. He had motive and opportunity and
he was there.'

'He was not there,' she said more calmly. 'He was here
with me.'

173

17

'It sounds ridiculous,' she said, 'a man of over sixty sneaking out of his friend's house and dashing across London in a taxi to be with the woman he loves – a woman of fifty-five. To spend the night with her and go back at dawn. A superannuated Romeo and Juliet. It really does happen, it did happen.'

He believed her. It was so evidently true. 'What time did he come?'

She replied at once. Had it been the only whole night they had spent together? 'A few minutes after one.'

Knighton wasn't the first man to confess to a murder he hadn't committed, Wexford thought. And yet . . .

'No doubt you saw him several times after that?'

'We talked a lot on the phone. I saw him – oh, three times? Four?'

'He never said anything to you to suggest he had killed his wife?'

'How could he have when I knew he was here with me at the time? I could tell he was unhappy, he seemed tormented. But his wife had been murdered and however he felt about her and me, she *was* his wife.' Milborough Ingram put her hand to her forehand and leaned her face forward on it. Her voice had taken on a faltering note. 'He never said any more about our marrying, about our being together. He was different, changed. I thought he was ill. I said he ought to have a holiday and I'd go with him. He just stared at me, he held my hand and stared at me.' She reached for her whisky. 'Oh, God, I mustn't have any more to drink. I'll get drunk and that won't help. Ever since I was eighteen I've had it dinned into me I mustn't drink because it'd spoil my figure and my face, and it dies hard, all that. What does it matter now?'

He got up to go. She was composing herself but hysteria trembled beneath the surface of her composure.

'Would you like me to get your daughter to come to you?'

'I'm better alone. Really.'

He turned his eyes away from that ravaged, once-beautiful face. They lighted on the ikon. He remembered where he had seen it before – in Vinald's bedroom in the Kweilin Hotel.

'I gave my son-in-law two hundred pounds for that.'

Wexford heard a rasp in her voice. 'I'm sure it's worth it,' he said politely.

'Oh, no doubt. Only Pandora told me afterwards he gave two pairs of jeans for it and one of those wasn't even his own.'

She had spoken in the bitterness of her heart. It was an anger with the injustice of the world she was venting on Gordon Vinald. Already she looked ashamed of her indiscretion.

'What does it matter now?' she said again.

Wexford made no reply. He said goodbye to her and went down to where Donaldson and the car waited.

Tabard Road, Kingsmarkham, the bungalow that was almost as familiar to Wexford as his own home over the other side of the town. Dora Wexford had dealt with the problem of being a policeman's wife by acceptance, by patience, but Jenny Burden solved it more positively, filling her evenings with learning – and teaching – at classes, with drama groups and string trios. She was out this evening, at a rehearsal, Burden said. He fetched two cans of beer from the fridge.

'Knighton wasn't mad,' Wexford said. 'It wasn't a matter of having some sort of delusion he'd done it. He knew he hadn't held the gun and squeezed the trigger and shot her. He meant he was morally responsible, he instructed someone else to do it.'

175

'Not someone he paid. We know he parted with no large sums.'

Wexford said thoughtfully, 'I don't think it was anything as direct as that. I think it was more a matter of nodding, of raising one's hand and killing the mandarin.'

'I don't follow you.' Burden had put on his obtuse look, the one he wore less and less since his second marriage. Once it had inspired Wexford to say he was reminded of Goering who said that whenever he heard the word culture he reached for his gun. Sometimes it came back to make the Inspector's normally intuitive face mulish. 'I haven't a clue what all that means,' he said.

'I can't enlighten you. I'm not being purposely obscure, I don't know any more yet. Let me tell you about Vinald and Purbank instead. I can tell you what they quarrelled about. Vinald pinched a pair of Purbank's jeans to pay for an ikon.'

'He did *what*?'

'I imagine he discovered this ikon in the possession of some peasant in the far east of Russia. Russians are crazy to get their hands on denim jeans, or so I've heard. Probably Vinald hadn't got very long there, wherever it was, or the ikon vendor wouldn't hang about, so Vinald went back to the train and fetched a pair of his own jeans. Because he hadn't any more of his own clean or didn't want to part with them or something he took Purbank's. No doubt he explained to Purbank afterwards and maybe offered to pay for them but Purbank was outraged and refused to have any more to do with him.'

Burden laughed. 'But why not tell us?'

'Vinald wouldn't because it makes him look such a crook. Purbank wouldn't because it makes him look a fool. What could be more undignified than someone nicking a pair of your trousers? It's a kind of vicarious debagging.'

'I suppose it is,' Burden said. 'Put that cat down if you don't want it.'

Jenny's Abyssinian, as lithe and sinuous as the Pensive Selima was stout, had sprung up delicately on to Wexford's lap. He drew his hand down the smooth slippery back.

'Is Vinald a crook, d'you think?'

'D'you remember when we went to the V and A I paid particular attention to the Sung ware? Celadon, they call it. White or pale grey or pale green, an attempt to imitate jade, around a thousand years old. While we were in Kweilin Vinald showed me the Celadon ware he'd bought, trusting, and rightly, to my ignorance. He said it was a hundred years old, Ching stuff, and of course I believed him. He had a whitish bowl, a dull plain thing, and I remember thinking to myself that Dora wouldn't have given it house room. You wouldn't reckon on anyone paying ten thousand pounds for a thing like that, would you?'

'Ten grand? For a white pot a hundred years old?'

'Well, not a hundred years old, Mike. That's rather the point. Say eight hundred? I saw the stick of red sealing wax in Vinald's hotel room and it meant nothing to me. I didn't know then that any antique you bring out of China has to have the government's red seal on it. Vinald was getting hold of priceless pieces from people who didn't know any better, paying virtually nothing for them, and then putting the red seal on himself. Especially that bowl – which he took up to Birmingham on October the first and sold to the agent of a South American purchaser for ten thousand pounds.'

'Can we do anything to him?'

'Like what? Extradite him to China? Do you know what he'd answer if we said to him what I've just said to you? That he gave a fair price for the bowl, believing it to be Ching. Of course it had the seal on it. What can we mean? It was only when he got it home and examined it carefully that he discovered he'd paid five quid for a piece of Sung.'

As Wexford stroked it the cat began emitting a harsh rumbling purr. Still shaking his head over man's chicanery, Burden fetched more beer. Wexford changed the subject. 'When you went hunting up those old lags – what you might call recidivisiting – you had two lists, didn't you? The men Knighton had helped send down and those that had got off or got off lightly because of his defence?'

'That's right.'

'What was the point of the alternative list?'

'You mean the ones he got off?'

177

'I mean, what was the point of listing people who have had no motive for revenge on him?'

'There wasn't a point really. Brownrigg and I simply made a note of every case Knighton had been involved in that we thought important enough. I put those friendly to Knighton in the right-hand column and those – well, possibly revengeful on the left. I got them muddled too, I . . .'

But Wexford didn't want to hear about that. 'You've still got the lists?'

'Of course I have.'

In the morning Wexford looked at them.

'This Coney Newton seems to be on both lists. What did he get sent down for?'

'Rape and attempted murder,' said Burden. 'He's on both lists because – well, I thought he might have reason to be grateful to Knighton for getting him off with only seven years or vindictive towards Knighton for not getting him off altogether. And funnily enough, he didn't seem vindictive, he just seemed to think Knighton hadn't made a very efficient job of his defence. Anyway, he's got a good alibi for that night and he alibi's Silver Perry.'

'That's fine for him then, isn't it, having his word backed up by a really exemplary citizen like that?'

'They were in a club together,' Burden said slightly offendedly. 'I went to the club. There's no question . . .'

'All right. Who's Henry Thomas Chipstead?'

'Once upon a time he was an East End of London gang-ster. Around twenty years ago he was up on a charge of grievous bodily harm and Knighton got him off. Wills – ' Burden indicated with his finger the name in the left-hand column. 'Wills suggested to me that Knighton might have called in "a professional like Chipstead". Those were his words, not mine. He said Chipstead had been with Lee's mob, might be dead now for all he knew. He's not dead, though, he's alive and living in Leytonstone. But he's over seventy now and in any case we know Knighton didn't pay anyone.'

'And what was this Wills's contribution to the disintegra-tion of society?'

Burden grinned wryly. 'Aiding and abetting. He didn't

178

actually kill this woman but he was an accessory. He concealed the body by night in roadworks on a motorway, only one of the workmen discovered it before they laid the road surface . . . What's the matter?'

'I know where he put that gun,' Wexford said slowly.

'Where who put it?'

'Ah, that's something else. I mean I know where whoever our perpretator is put the weapon. You just told me. What you said about this Wills and roadworks told me.'

'It did?'

'The weir, Mike, the weir at Sewingbury Mill.'

It was a long shot. Burden's opinion was that 'they' would never be got to demolish all that concrete and brickwork, embankment and paving, for the sake of finding a gun, it wasn't as if it was a body. And the chances, he said pessimistically, were that the gun wasn't there anyway.

'Once I've got a warrant,' said Wexford, 'they'd get on with the demolition if it was a pin they were looking for and Sewingbury Agricultural College they were demolishing.'

Colonel Charles Griswold, the Chief Constable of Mid-Sussex, was as uneasy about it as Burden. And perhaps Wexford would never have been allowed to swear out that warrant but for the clerk of works who had supervised the construction of the 'weir' for the county authority telling the chief constable that, when the workmen knocked off for the day at five on 1 October, only the paved area remained to be completed. At that time, on that afternoon, he said, the areas waiting to be paved had lain open and uncovered except for a foundation of 'hard core' spread on the soil.

'Suppose we say he left his car in the market square in Sewingbury,' Wexford said. 'He made his way by the footpath to Thatto Vale and got to Thatto Hall Farm at about two. There he either entered by the washroom window or let himself in with a key, having made it appear as if he entered by the window. He woke Mrs Knighton, brought her downstairs at gun-point, shot her, feebly faked a burglary and returned by the path where he was seen by Bingley at around three. At the Sewingbury end of the footpath he spotted the nearly completed paving work on the weir and it would have been the work of only a few moments to bury the gun in the soil under the hard core.'

It was a cold day with a bitter wind blowing. The Kingsbrook, swollen by recent rains, rushed and tumbled under the Springhill bridge and through the new channel constructed for it. The same contractors that had built the 'weir' came to knock part of it down again. As soon as they had the paving stones up Sergeant Martin and Archbold were to go along and grub about under the hard core for the gun. Wexford looked in for a few moments at the inquest on Adam Knighton. Angus Norris was there but otherwise the family was not represented.

Wexford knew there could be no possible outcome but that the inquest be adjourned. Dr Parkinson was reading aloud Knighton's confession and now and then quoting Wexford's own words that Knighton could not himself have been physically responsible for his wife's death. Wexford crept out of the court. At the far side of the quadrangle that divided the courts from the police station Donaldson was awaiting him at the wheel of his car, Burden already seated in the back. The wind struck him with a sharp gust and blew out his scarf like a flag.

'The river bank is no place to be this morning,' said Burden, rubbing his hands.

'You sound like Mole.'

'Who?'

'It doesn't matter. We're going up to the Smoke anyway. Or near enough. The Haze, we should maybe call it. Is Leytonstone the sort of place we can get lunch in, Donaldson?'

But the London expert, to his own evident chagrin, didn't know, he had never been there.

'Chipstead, I suppose,' Burden said.

'Henry Thomas Chipstead, fifty-two Dogshall Road, Leytonstone. He's seventy-three and doesn't seem to have been up to anything in the hit man line since Knighton got him off the hook when he was fifty. But he'll do for a start.'

'I wish you'd explain to me what you meant about that killing the mandarin.'

They were on the motorway now, heading for London.

The wind was so strong that gusts of it shifted and swayed the heavy car. Occasionally spatters of rain in large drops dashed against the windscreen.

'I think that years and years ago,' Wexford said, 'Knighton had reason to be in contact with some villain who was a professional assassin or hit man. Defended him, presumably. After the case he went to Knighton and said to him something on the lines of, if there's ever anything I can do for you, Mr Knighton sir, you've only to say the word, you know what I mean, nudge, nudge, anything you want done on the quiet, and Knighton, no doubt, got all upstage with moral indignation, but later on he got to thinking about it. Much later on and when it would really have suited him to have someone put out of the way.

'No money would have to pass, you see. That would be the beauty of it. He wasn't going to have to be specific with this old lag, wasn't going to have to give him three or four grand in used oncers or anything like that. Beforehand he might even be able to think he wasn't really the instigator. Suppose it was no more than a matter of making a phone call and saying something like, My wife's going to be alone on the night of October the first? Suppose it was even more subtle and slight than that?

'But afterwards the remorse and the guilt, to a man like Knighton, would be as great as if he had paid an assassin or pulled the trigger himself.'

'Well, he'd be just as guilty,' said Burden.

'Of course he would, but a good many men wouldn't *feel* just as guilty. That's the analogy with the mandarin. One of China's teeming thousand millions is just as much a human life as one's wife or child, but it doesn't feel like that because it's so remote, so far out of sight. And if one only has to raise one's hand . . . I think maybe Knighton only had to raise his hand, or do something as slight as that, to rid himself of his wife and have Milborough Ingram.'

They came into London through the Blackwall Tunnel. From its northern end it wasn't far to Leytonstone. Dead leaves from the fringe ends of Epping Forest whirled in the wind. Dogshall Road was a long straight street that passed with a hump over one suburban railway line and in a dip under another. The gutters were choked with leaves, the trees in the pavement, three times as tall as the little squat terraces of houses, were shedding leaves into the wind. There was a red brick church and a pre-fab church hall with an asbestos roof but nothing else to relieve the long monotony of Victorian terraces, the long double row of parked cars. Donaldson pulled into a gap a little way down from number seventeen.

'Moralizing would be out of place,' said Wexford, 'but this is a fine illustration of how crime *doesn't* pay, don't you think? Chipstead made his living for years, for most of his life, out of violent crime. I'm not saying it was in vain, it wasn't, it caused a lot of suffering, it damaged society, provoked fear, made work for the police, cost the taxpayer money. But it didn't profit Chipstead himself much, did it?'

The three men looked at what Chipstead had got out of it, a hundred-year-old brown brick box with six feet of concrete, on which stood a dustbin and a dead geranium in a tub, separating it from the street. There were only three windows at the front of the house and at all of them the curtains were drawn. Wexford got out of the car and Burden followed him.

The house had a dead empty look as if its occupants had closed it up and gone away, and Wexford, banging hard on the knocker, for there was no bell, had very little hope of an answer. But after a moment or two a woman's voice was heard saying something and then footsteps sounded on the stairs.

The door was opened to them by Renie Thompson.

182

18

'Henry was my brother,' she said.

They stood in the hall. There was a light on upstairs and women whispering.

'Was?' said Wexford.

'He's dead, isn't he? You mean you didn't know? Today's the funeral. To tell you the truth, when you knocked I thought it was the undertakers come.' She wore a grey coat and a black felt hat. She looked at them truculently, at their dubious suspicious faces. 'You'd like to make something out of it, wouldn't you? I know. There's nothing to make.'

'Give us the raw materials, Mrs Thompson, and we'll decide that.'

A woman had begun coming down the stairs, evidently a sister. She stood there, staring, listening, holding the banister.

'I'd worked for Mrs Knighton since nineteen sixty. Him and her, they was the best employers you'd find anywhere. Henry had to come up in court for something he never done and I said, you want Mr Knighton to speak up for you and he got Mr Knighton, Mr Knighton was on his side on account of knowing *me*, and he got Henry off, of course he did, considering Henry never done it.'

The woman on the stairs clicked her tongue.

'Henry thought the world of Mr Knighton.'

'So did you too, Renie,' said the woman on the stairs.

'You a Sewingbury family, are you?' Burden asked. They

183

both nodded, eyeing him warily. 'Had your brother been ill prior to his death?'

The third sister now came down, buttoning herself into a black astrakhan coat.

'In the hospital six months,' said Renie Thompson. 'He had it in his chest, you see, the lung, and then it went to his spine.'

The door knocker rattled. The woman in astrakhan went to the door and the wind blew a dead leaf in to cling to her coat. Two men in black stood outside, their hats in their hands.

'All right,' said Wexford, 'we won't trouble you any more at the moment.'

Among the other parked cars two black Daimlers now waited, one empty, one bearing the body of the former gangster in a coffin laden with flowers. Wexford and Burden went back to their car. Donaldson said a message had come through on the radio that the gun had been found under the paving stones at the 'weir'.

Wexford nodded. He was watching Chipstead's house. Until now it hadn't occurred to him that there had been others inside as well as the three sisters. These people, no doubt, had been sitting in silence behind the bay window with the drawn curtains, waiting to follow Chipstead's body to the grave or the fire. They came trooping down the path, an elderly man and woman arm-in-arm, a boy of eighteen in a borrowed black jacket and tie, a little man with red hair, a fat man with practically no hair, a tall man with silver hair.

'Silver Perry,' Burden said.

'Were they old pals or something?'

'Evidently. It wouldn't surprise me.'

The Daimler took the sisters and the old couple. The rest of the mourners got into an old dark blue Ford Popular.

'Where do you suppose they're going, Donaldson?' said Wexford.

'City of London Crematorium, Manor Park, sir,' Donaldson said promptly. 'Twenty minutes there, twenty minutes for a hymn and our-dear-brother-to-the-fire, twenty minutes back.'

'We may as well go and have lunch then.'

*

184

The wind had dropped and it became very dark, dark enough to have the light on in the front room at 52 Dogshall Road. The light shimmered through unlined green curtains. The boy was the first to leave, dressed in leathers now and carrying a crash helmet. He got on the Yamaha parked next to the Ford Popular and roared off in the direction of the bridge. A little while later the front door opened again and Silver Perry came out. Conventionally dressed in a dark suit and dark waisted overcoat, he had something of a look in the fading light of Adam Knighton, but of Knighton debased, vulgarized, roughened. He was a little less tall and lacked the presence of the man for whom he had said he would do anything, would lay down his life.

'He used those words?' Wexford said.

'Well, in a newspaper,' said Burden. 'I was going to tell you, I nearly did tell you only you interrupted me with your idea about the gun, they remember Coney Newton being in the El Video till three or whatever and Newton says he was there with Perry but no one in the club said a word to me about seeing Perry.'

On the doorstep Perry kissed Renie Thompson and then walked quickly away. Wexford thought he would get into the Ford but evidently it wasn't his, he had come on foot. And on foot he was departing through the thin grey drizzle that had now begun to fall steadily. The street lights had come on, lozenges of fruit drop orange among the stripped branches of the trees. Perry turned up the collar of his coat and trudged along, hands in pockets. He was heading, probably, for the tube station, a quarter of a mile up the hill past the hump in the road.

The car crawled after him, Donaldson driving very slowly. A van behind started hooting but Donaldson took no notice.

'He thinks he's going to cross here,' said Wexford. 'Pull round the corner.'

Donaldson turned sharply to the left just as Perry approached the edge of the pavement to cross the street. The side of the car presented itself in front of him like a wall. Silver Perry took a step back as the car door was thrown open and Wexford got out.

185

'Care for a lift, Silver?'

Wexford had his warrant card out but he need not have troubled. Perry belonged in that category of men who could pick out a policeman on a nude beach or at a fancy dress ball. It was child's play to him to detect three of them in a London suburb, in a car, in the rain. For all that, he looked for a split second as if he might try making a run for it. In that second his face showed the spark of hope, the flare of panic, the commonsense realization that quenched them. He shrugged and got into the car. Rain was running off the glossy white cap of hair.

'D'you know where Cyril Street, Bethnal Green is, Donaldson?' said Burden.

'I can find it, sir.'

'Off Globe Road,' said Perry.

'Or do we take him straight back with us? Your gun's been found, Perry. Shooters usually do turn up in the long run.'

'Shooter? What shooter?' said Perry.

'Cyril Street first, I think,' Wexford said, 'and then maybe we can think again. Enjoy yourself at the funeral, did you, Silver? By God, but you niff of Cyprus sherry.'

'I suppose you think you're funny. I didn't go to enjoy myself. Henry Chipstead was a lifelong friend.'

'And we all know how good you are to your friends. Laying down your life and so forth. Or laying down other people's lives.' Wexford looked into the man's pale blue eyes, watery eyes, narrower and shiftier than Knighton's. 'You've no alibi for the night of October the first. And you were seen near Thatto Hall Farm. You were seen walking along the footpath to Sewingbury from Thatto Vale at three in the morning.'

Silver Perry said nothing. The car wound its way along a one-way street system, through back doubles, from the eastern suburbs into the East End of London. It was raining hard now and the wipers were on at high speed.

'You left your car in the market square at Sewingbury,' said Burden. 'You must know the area well.'

Perry admitted nothing. In a low voice he said, 'Renie and me – like a hundred years ago I used to know Renie pretty well.'

'When you came back you saw the building works and

186

you buried the gun, knowing it would be concreted in next day.'

Perry tapped Donaldson's back. 'Second one on the left now, son.'

'I reckon Knighton must have given you something for your trouble,' said Burden. 'Reimbursed you for the shooter at any rate.'

Perry sighed. 'The wife's out, round at her sister's. I wouldn't want her brought in on this.'

The tall stalk of a tower, punctured all over now with squares of light, and its fellow stalks, vertical dormitories. There were several hundred cars now on the shiny black wet tarmac that was clean of shed leaves since there were no trees here to shed them. Wexford sent Donaldson off for a cup of tea in a Globe Road café. The lift took them up what felt like ten miles to Perry's eyrie and the kind of view that would once have made men gasp but now is a commonplace to air travellers and frequenters of revolving restaurants.

No one was at home. The place was dark. Perry put on a light or two and took them into the room that had nothing in common with the accepted notion of a penthouse except altitude. He said, 'I'll tell you about it. It's too late to worry about Mr Knighton now. There's nothing can harm him where he's gone.'

The cheap sentimentality of these people! Wexford thought. It was typical. Perry had once shot a man in cold blood, had since then done appalling violence, to say nothing of accepting Knighton's commission to kill his wife, yet he talked like some guiltless and gullible old woman.

'You, however,' said Wexford, 'aren't yet in that happy hereafter and there's plenty of harm can come to you.'

'You mean you're going to caution me?'

Wexford shook his head. 'Not yet. Tell us about when you first knew Mr Knighton.'

'It's twenty-five years. More. But for him they'd have hung me.' Silver looked at Burden. 'You know how it was. I wrote my story for the paper and I cut the piece out and sent it to Mr Knighton. He never answered, naturally he didn't, a man in his position. I waited for him in Lincoln's Inn one evening and we got talking.'

187

'Just like that?' Wexford tried to imagine it, this shifty tyke and Knighton meeting, getting 'talking'. Knighton would surely have frozen him with a stare and if he persisted, threatened him with the police.

'Not "just like that",' Silver said. 'I never pestered him, I never annoyed him. I just said I wanted to thank him properly, I said it quiet like. I told him there was nothing in the world I wouldn't do for him.'

And then Wexford did see. Knighton's integrity was already shaky, he was already becoming corrupted. For five years he had been Milborough Lang's lover but by then he knew they couldn't continue on that impermanent, uneasy basis. She would go and he would be left with Adela. Unless . . .

'By all this "anything in the world" claptrap you meant you'd get rid of his wife for him, didn't you?'

Silver winced at the plain speaking. 'He knew what I meant. I knew and he knew, there wasn't no need to put it into words. Help him get what he wanted, that's what I meant and he knew what I meant.'

'How did you know what he wanted?' asked Burden.

'I said I waited for him. It was a few times I did that and I followed him before I got him alone and we got talking. A couple of times I saw him meet this girl. Actress, she was, world-famous.'

'Still, Knighton didn't take you up on your generous offer?'

'He had a lot of scruples, had Mr Knighton,' said Silver with a kind of sage reverence. 'Well, you have to in his position. I said to him I'd never forget what he'd done for me and any time he wanted you know what, any time, he'd only to let me know. I wouldn't bother him, I said. I knew a man in his position don't want to be seen with the likes of me, I understood that. I was living in rooms in Cambridge Heath then. When the council put us in here I dropped him a line with my address and my phone. He never answered, naturally he didn't.' Silver looked up, straight into Wexford's eyes. 'It used to bother me, I used to think about it a lot, the fact that I'd never done a thing to repay him, I had it on my conscience.'

'Your *what*?'

'I know the meaning of gratitude, the same as other folks.'

'No, not the same as other folks, Silver,' said Wexford. 'The way you know it is pathological.' He shook his head reflectively. 'What was he supposed to do, give you a ring and say he'd changed his mind?'

'I told you we never put it into words. It was subtle like, we understood each other. He had to give me a ring, yes. I arranged it, I knew he wouldn't want to ask me outright.' Silver shifted in his seat. He had kept his black overcoat on but now he pulled himself out of it and threw the coat across the arm of a chair. Behind him the glittering view twinkled like a million fallen stars. 'I said to him, if ever you want you-know-what, you give me a tinkle. He never said a word. I looked him in the eye. You don't even have to say it, I said. You dial my number, I said, and when I answer you say one word. Any word you like, I said, so long as I know it.' There were beads of sweat on Silver's forehead now, up near the wig-like white hairline. 'He never answered me direct. He just looked at me and started telling some story about a Chinese mandarin, I don't recall the ins and outs of it now. That's it, I said, mandarin. You give me a call and when I answer you say "Mandarin" and I'll know. That was all of twenty-five years ago, nearer twenty-six. "Mandarin", I said, "any time, you say that one word and I'll know – and I'll do it".'

What had passed through Knighton's mind at the time? Had he conceived it as possible even in those days? Or had he merely been humouring Silver Perry, jollying him along, preparatory to getting rid of him for good? Wexford supposed they had been in a pub or even on a park bench somewhere. Just the one meeting, he was sure of that. Perry eager, grateful, gratified that this august man would condescend to converse with him, Knighton inexpressibly shocked, horrified, yet tempted. Raise the hand, say the word, do nothing more and she will die and you may have your heart's desire. What evil wicked nonsense! Better take one's own life in one's misery than countenance this, than even stay here listening to this. But 'Mandarin', one word . . .

189

'But one day, not long ago, he did ring you and he did say the word,' said Burden.

'Early in September it was. I picked up the phone and no one spoke for a bit, though you could hear breathing, and I was just thinking this was some joker when this voice says it. Stuttered a bit and spoke very low. The funny thing was, I'd *forgotten*. I mean I'd never seen Mr Knighton all that time, I'd never heard his voice. I'd had a bit of news via Renie over the years, but not for a long time, I never even knew he was retired, I never knew they lived in Sussex permanent like.

'The voice said this word. I could hear it started "man" and I thought what it said was "managing", but the receiver was put back before I could say anything. But I must have like recognized it in my subconscious or whatever on account of it kept haunting me all day. And suddenly it came to me. After all those years I could repay Mr Knighton at last, I could fulfil my promise.'

Wexford got up and turned his back. 'You make me sick.' He stood at the window, looking down on lurex-embroidered London, up at a homing aircraft laden with lights, breathing steadily to command his anger. 'Get on with it,' he said, 'and we can dispense with the noble sentiments.'

'You went ahead on that single word, a word you didn't even hear properly?' Burden put in.

'I *knew*,' said Silver. 'I hung about his chambers but he never come out and then I saw his name gone from the list at the door. I went up to Hampstead but I only had to take one look to see the place was full of bleeding Arabs. A couple of times I rung Thatto Hall Farm and he answered the first time and she answered the second but that didn't help me any.'

'Help you?'

'I had to know her movements, didn't I? I had to get her alone. Then one day I saw him. Coming out of Victoria Station it was, round about four in the afternoon, Wednesday, October the first. He was carrying this overnight bag, I knew he'd gone away for the night.'

'What were you doing at Victoria?'

'I have to work, don't I? I've got my living to earn. I was driving the mini-cab, I'd just dropped a fare. He was looking for a taxi, Mr Knighton was, and I thought to myself, why

190

don't I offer him a lift to wherever he's going? But I knew I was the last person he'd want to be seen with. Besides, I'd had a better idea. Seeing that overnight bag gave it to me. He'd come up to town for the night and she'd be alone. I reckoned on her being alone. I'd been to see poor old Henry in the hospital, you see, a couple of weeks before, and Renie was there and she said the daughter was married and expecting a kid and all. So I reckoned on the old woman being alone. I reckoned if I was going to do it I'd better get on with it, I'd better get it over with that night.'

Wexford thought he heard the front door click. There were sounds of movement in the hall and the woman who had screamed at Burden came in. Like her husband, she knew policemen by instinct and she gave Wexford a look others reserve for a thief or a vagrant. Wexford and Burden went out into the hall.

'Do we take him back with us and charge him?'

Wexford shrugged. 'Nothing to charge him with. I doubt if we could even make conspiracy stick.'

When they went back into the room the woman had disappeared and Silver Perry was drinking something that looked like whisky. It appeared to have been rationed out to him, as if for medicinal purposes.

'I was working till midnight. I got on to a pal of mine, never mind who, it don't matter now, I got on to him to say I'd been with him at the El Video if there was questions asked. Anyway, my last fare kept me a good half-hour over the odds and it was gone two, more like two-fifteen, two-twenty, before I got to Sewingbury. I left my vehicle in the market square and I walked. I came back by the footpath but I went by the road, not being too sure of my bearings if the moon was to go in.

'It was well after three when I got to Thatto Hall Farm. I got out my glass cutter and cut out that pane in the toilet window. Must have taken me ten minutes, maybe fifteen. The house wasn't that dark inside because of the moon shining in. I took my shoes off and went upstairs.

'All the bedroom doors was open and I went in the big front one, thinking to find her there. There was twin beds and one of them had the bedclothes turned back. I went back there later and took her jewel box and chucked some of her bits and pieces away to make it look like an outside job. He was an amateur, you see, he didn't know what's what. But first I looked in the other rooms and when I couldn't find her I went downstairs again. I was beginning to wonder what was up, I can tell you.'

Silver drank his drink and put the glass down heavily.

'I found her on the floor. She was dead, she'd been shot dead. I knew what it was right away, Mr Knighton had got there before me and done it himself.'

19

Wexford held the gun in his hands. Everything that could be deduced from an examination of it was in the report on the desk in front of him. It was a Walther PPK 9 mm automatic and approximately half-way along the barrel, on the underside, was a minute wart-like fault in the metal which would mark each bullet that passed through it with a fine hairline scratch. Burden, looking over his shoulder, said, 'What was Perry going to use? His bare hands?'

'I daresay. They're weapons you don't have to dispose of. A strange business, wasn't it? Perry was sure Knighton had killed her, not knowing she didn't die till some eleven hours after Knighton's departure for London. He thought Knighton had got tired of waiting for him to keep his promise and had killed her himself.' Wexford put the gun down on the desk. 'I've no time for a villain like that, Mike, but I believe him when he says he was ashamed of himself for having failed Knighton. Because he had shilly-shallied since the beginning of September, Knighton had been driven to do it himself. And because he thought Knighton hadn't done a sufficient job of faking a break-in and burglary, hadn't done any sort of job of that at all, he himself took the jewel box out of the house and having no great opinion of our acumen, scattered its contents about the front garden.'

According to Perry, in spite of his ploy with Mrs Knighton's pieces of jewellery, in spite of the evidence of break-in, he had expected Knighton to be arrested and charged with his wife's murder almost at once. He had cursed himself for

193

the delay which he saw as having led Knighton to commit the crime. When nothing had happened to Knighton he had simply put this down to police ineptitude. If he had ever doubted Knighton's guilt, that doubt had been dispelled by his suicide.

'And certainly Knighton believed Perry had killed her,' Wexford went on. 'From the moment he came home on October the second and I told him his wife had been shot he believed Perry had done it and done it on his instructions. That accounts for the feeling we always had of his being surprised yet not surprised, guilty yet innocent. That day he phoned Perry at the beginning of September – I wonder what impelled him to do that, what particular thing happened? We shall never know now. Had Adela found out about Milborough Ingram and threatened or ridiculed? Had Mrs Ingram begun to talk of going home? Or had Adela begun talking of another long holiday – we know she wanted to go to India and Nepal in February – which would take him away from Milborough again? Whatever it was, a temptation that was a quarter of a century old came back and this time he succumbed. But I can't think he really believed in it, Mike. It must have seemed like fantasy. With anyone but Silver Perry, who isn't, I think, quite sane, it would have been fantasy.

'You can imagine him leaving Milborough Ingram's flat late one afternoon, going off to meet Adela and travel home with her. Maybe it was on a street corner or in a station that he saw the empty call box and remembered the past, remembered "Mandarin".

'Of course it was all nonsense, it could never happen now. "Mandarin" was all he had to say and the murder would be done and his happiness secured. In fantasy, in dreams, not really. But he went into the phone box and he dialled and he said it. At any rate he said something like it and then he went off and met Adela and no doubt told himself what a fool he was.'

Burden came round the desk and sat down. He was frowning.

'He must have wondered if anything would happen.'

'Perhaps. Nothing did, though, did it? Three or four

weeks went by and nothing had happened. He must have thought Silver Perry had forgotten "Mandarin" or got old or reformed or had never really meant it in the first place. But as soon as Adela was killed he knew. But happiness wasn't secured. There was no freedom, no future, no joyful looking-forward. Not happiness, but remorse. For he believed Perry had done it on *his* word, though that word was a muttered whisper given after a gap of twenty-five years.'

'He killed himself in vain,' said Burden. 'He killed himself for an illusion. He might have been happy, he might have re-married. He'd done nothing and Perry had done nothing.'

'The intention was there, Mike,' Wexford said thoughtfully. 'And it was more than just a wish for his wife to die, wasn't it? However slight, it was an express instruction and he had delivered it to a dirty little crook and murderer he shouldn't have lowered himself to speak to. Even if we'd found someone for this job while he was alive he'd still have had that on his mind, wouldn't he? On his conscience, disgusting him with himself and, I suspect, pretty well poisoning the feelings he had for the great love of his life. Men like Knighton had better not commit crimes even vicariously, they had better not be involved im crimes they *imagine* they have committed vicariously.'

Burden looked at his watch. 'He should be in by now. It's just gone ten.' When Wexford didn't respond he said more sharply, 'The one that really committed it, I mean. You said you didn't want him fetched from home.'

'Not in the circumstances, no.' Wexford sighed. 'Not that it's going to make much difference, maybe a couple of hours. I'm not planning on talking to him much, we don't need a confession. It's all as clear as glass. I should have seen it from the start, only China intruded, China and what went on there confused me. Not that China didn't have a good deal to do with his motive, it did.'

'He bought the gun,' said Burden, 'quite openly from a very respectable gunsmith's, Warrington Weapons of London Wall. It was easy. And it makes our task easier.'

195

'The books he was keeping, or not keeping, are going to be pretty damning evidence too. We'll be spending the rest of the day looking into his financial juggling, Mike. Come on, then, let's go and take him.'

They had finished. There was nothing more to do until the special court in the morning. It had been dark for hours, the damp foggy dark of November. Wexford picked up his coat and slung it over him. 'I feel like a drink.'

'Come back to my place,' Burden said.

Wexford felt deeply tired, as tired as he had been after those white nights in China. His head floated, it seemed full of a crowding of figures and prevarications and lies. Yet there was nothing to think of or talk about except what they had done that day and he went on talking about it.

'But surely it was Perry that Bingley saw in the wood?' Burden had asked.

'How can it have been? Confused as Bingley was, he was sure the man he saw was walking back from Thatto Vale, not going towards it. Besides that, Perry went by the road and only came back by the footpath. Now if Perry didn't get to Thatto Hall Farm till three, took ten to fifteen minutes cutting out that glass and another ten going over the house and finding the body, it would have been more like ten to four before he passed the spot where Bingley was. Or had been, for by that time Bingley had certainly gone off home.'

They got into Wexford's car. Jenny had taken Burden's. Wexford drove slowly because he was tired.

'It was a grey-haired man he saw,' Burden insisted.

'But was it? He came to see us in the first place because his niece told him he ought to. He had seen a man walking that footpath back to Sewingbury at three in the morning of October the second. But he was nervous about coming to us because he'd been poaching. So to please us he makes his story as near to what he thinks we want as he can. Knighton is tall and has grey or silver hair. He either knows Knighton by sight or has seen his picture in the paper. Therefore he describes the man he saw as tall and with grey hair. But when I show him photographs that's a different matter. He is reminded then of what the man in the wood *really* looked

196

like. Of the figures in the pictures he's shown he doesn't pick out Knighton who resembles Silver Perry more than any of them. He picks out Gordon Vinald who doesn't resemble him at all but is youngish, dark, rather short and slightly built.'

Burden's porch light was on. The bungalow itself was in darkness. Wexford got out of the car and walked up the path towards the light and something soft and slinky came out of the shadows and rubbed itself against his trouser leg. He jumped because he was weary and it had been a long day. Burden unlocked the front door and Wexford followed him into the house, holding the cat in his arms.

'Bingley couldn't pick out the man who killed Adela Knighton from the photographs because he wasn't in them. So he picked out the man most nearly like him. He chose the only man in the group who was also young, dark, short and slight.'

The centre light in the living room came on but the bulb in the table lamp flashed, fizzled and went dark. The bright glare from the middle of the ceiling made Wexford wince and blink. Burden switched it off.

'I'll get another bulb. I'll just have to think where it is Jenny keeps them. And then what? Scotch?'

'I shouldn't,' said Wexford in much the same way Milborough Ingram had, though he was thinking more of his health than his face and figure. 'But I will.'

He sat in the dark, a little light coming in from the hall. The back door slammed as Burden went out to the garage. The cat began doing that uncanny things cats do, staring at nothing, following nothing round the room with its eyes. It slid off Wexford's lap and sat with its tail faintly moving, gazing towards the doorway and the light.

An old Chinese woman with bound feet, in dark trousers and a quilted jacket, walking with small mincing steps, came out of the light – out of nowhere, it seemed – and stood on the threshold. His heart simply stopped. It felt as if it had stopped and the restarting, the thuds of its beat, were almost painful.

'Why are you sitting in the dark?' Jenny Burden said. 'Where's Mike?'

He managed to speak in his normal voice. 'Gone to find a light bulb.'

197

She retreated into the kitchen, the high wooden-soled sandals she wore restricting her walk, and came back at once with a bulb. The table lamp came on and showed him Burden's wife, made up to look Chinese but not to look old, a black wig covering her fair hair. The cat rubbed itself against her, winding in and out between her ankles.

'The Good Woman of Setzuan, I presume?'

'It was our dress rehearsal. It was dark so I thought I might as well come home just as I was.' She kissed Burden who came in with their drinks. 'If you'll excuse me, I'll go and take all this lot off.'

'My God,' said Burden. 'I wonder you didn't think you were hallucinating again.'

Wexford said nothing. He took his whisky with a steady hand.

'So it *was* Angus Norris that Bingley saw?' Burden said.

'Of course. Having let himself' into Thatto Hall Farm with his wife's key, got his mother-in-law out of bed, brought her downstairs and shot her, he made his way home again along that footpath, thus enabling Bingley to see him at three o'clock.

'I suppose he told her,' said Burden, 'that his wife had been taken ill or gone into early labour or some such thing and they hadn't been able to get through on the phone. He shot her through the back of the head because, like the gentleman he is, he let a lady precede him into a room. And that wife of his is having a baby any minute . . .'

'I hope it may be a consolation to her,' Wexford said sombrely. 'Mother, father and now this. Norris was shattered by Knighton's suicide. Did you see his face? He hadn't expected that. I daresay he thought he was doing Knighton a favour, killing Adela. Mind you, I don't think he planned it, or not very far in advance. He didn't go up to London and Warrington Weapons and buy the gun with that in mind. He bought the gun because he collects firearms. Then – maybe not till the very day of October the first – his wife told him her father would be going to London for the night.

'Jennifer slept soundly because she was sedated. She would have been unaware of it if he was absent for an hour. I think

198

he was desperate. He had married someone who expected to be kept in the style of her mother, of her older brothers and their wives, but he couldn't make the grade. He had only what he earned as an assistant solicitor with Symonds, O'Brien and Ames. I'm guessing here but I hardly think it can be otherwise, that he bought that house on a mortgage far above what he could afford. The cost of living went on rising and mortgage interest rates edged up too. It's apparent the house isn't even adequately furnished. We've seen enough of his financial affairs today to know that he was substantially in debt. And now there was a baby on the way which probably meant Jennifer would demand some sort of living-in help.

'He was frantic with money worries. He took his gun and walked to Thatto Hall Farm and killed Jennifer's mother, believing it would be thought she had come down and admitted some stranger who had knocked at the door. Norris, you see, is tarred with the same brush as his wife's family – he thinks he belongs to an élite that is above suspicion of criminality.'

Burden said, 'His firm were Mrs Knighton's solicitors, they drew up her will for her, so he knew what was in it – fifty thousand pounds for his wife.'

'That was a contributory motive only. That was a bonus. His motive was Mrs Knighton's holiday fund.'

'We didn't find a single record of that, not a word referring to it.'

'I daresay Norris felt it was safer that way. I daresay he even had a bold dream that if ever it came to the crunch he could deny that his mother-in-law had entrusted him with a large sum to invest. But to do that would have meant cutting himself and his wife off from her family entirely and certainly losing that future inheritance. Anyway, he didn't have the nerve. He only had nerve enough to kill her.'

'I suppose he had drawn on the fund for his own use and was hoping against hope that by some means or other he could make up the deficit before Adela demanded a really large sum.'

Wexford nodded. 'After all, last April he had had to provide her with four thousand pounds to go to China, a substantial amount for one holiday.'

'But that was more than six months ago. Why kill her now?'

'Because she asked for more. She wanted to go to India and Nepal in February. What would that have cost for the two of them? At least as much as the China trip. Very likely he didn't even have that much remaining in the fund. With Jennifer's inheritance he could pay his debts. He could make good what he had helped himself to out of the fund and present the money intact as soon as Knighton or a brother-in-law started asking questions.'

'Strange, isn't it, that a man would rather do murder and thereby shut himself up for fifteen years, not to mention losing his wife and child – for I'm sure he will – he'd rather do that than stand up and confess to having lost a sum of money?'

Wexford shrugged. 'We're all cowards one way or another.' He looked up and smiled as Jenny came back dressed as herself.

An Unkindness
of Ravens

To Sonia and Jeff

1

She was a neighbour. She was an acquaintance of Dora's and they spoke if they met in the street. Only this time there had been more to it than passing the time of day.

'I said I'd tell you,' Dora said. 'I said I'd mention it. She had that strange look she sometimes has and, to tell you the truth, I was awfully embarrassed.'

'What did she say?' Wexford asked.

' "Rod's missing" or "Rod's disappeared" – something like that. And then she asked me if I'd tell you. Because of who you are, of course.'

Detective chief inspectors have better things to do with their time than waste it listening to the complaints of women whose husbands have run off with other women. Wexford hadn't been in the house five minutes before he decided that was what had happened. But she was a neighbour. She lived in the next street to his. He ought to be glad really, he thought, that it hadn't the makings of a case for him to investigate.

His house and this one had been built at the same time, in the mid–1930s when Kingsmarkham was growing out of being a village. And structurally they were much the same house, three bedrooms, two receptions, kitchen, bathroom and downstairs loo. But his was a home, comfortable and full of lovingly collected things and this was – what? A shelter to keep the rain off, a place where people could eat, sleep and watch television. Joy Williams took him into the front room that she called the lounge. There were no books. The carpet was a square surrounded by mustard yellow vinyl tiles and the furniture a three-piece suite covered in grainy mustard-coloured synthetic leather. The 1935 fireplace, which in his house had been replaced by one of York stone, accommodated an electric fire of complicated design, part Regency, part medieval, and with a portcullis effect at the front. Above it hung a mirror framed in segments of green and yellow frosted glass, a fine specimen of Art Deco if you liked that sort of thing. The only picture was a composition in coloured silver paper of two cats playing with a ball of wool.

'She's rather a colourless person,' Dora had said. 'Doesn't seem interested in anything and always seems depressed. I don't suppose living with Rodney Williams for twenty years has done much for her.'

Joy. Dora had said rather apologetically that it was a misnomer. She was a woman whose whole self had turned grey, not just her hair. Her features had once been good, were probably still good, only her awful complexion, lined, pitted, pinkish-grey, rough and worn, masked them. Apparently she was forty-five but she looked ten years more. Up until his arrival she had been watching television and the set was still on, though with the sound turned off. It was the biggest set Wexford had ever seen, at any rate in a domestic setting. He guessed she spent a fair proportion of her time watching it and perhaps felt uneasy when the screen was blank.

There was no seat in the room that did not face it. He sat on the end of the sofa at an angle, turning his back. Joy Williams's eyes flickered over the flashing figures of skaters taking part in some contest. She sat on the extreme edge of her chair.

'Did your wife tell you what I . . . ?'

'She said something.' He interrupted to save her the embarrassment he could see already mottling her nose and cheeks with dull red. 'Something about your husband being missing.'

Joy Williams laughed. It was a laugh he was to hear often and get to know, a harsh cackle. There was no humour in it, no gaiety, no amusement. She laughed to hide emotion or because she knew no other way of showing it. The hands in her lap stretched and clenched. She wore a very wide, heavily chased platinum or white-gold wedding ring with an even more ornate platinum or white-gold engagement ring containing amid the pits and pyramids a minuscule diamond.

'He went on a trip to Ipswich and I haven't seen him since.'

'Your husband's a sales representative, I think Dora said.'

'With Sevensmith Harding,' she said. 'The paint people.'

She need not have added that. Sevensmith Harding were probably the biggest suppliers to builders' merchants and home decorating retail stores in the south of England. Sevenstar matt and silk emulsion coated a million walls, he thought, between Dover and Land's End. He and Dora had just had their second bedroom done up in it, and if he wasn't much mistaken the paintwork in Mrs Williams's own hall was the newest shade in Sevenshine non-drip high gloss, Wholewheat.

'He covers Suffolk for them.' She began pushing the rings up and down.

'It was last Thursday he went – well, yesterday week. It's the twenty-third now, that must have been the fifteenth. He said he was going to Ipswich to stop the night and start first thing in the morning.'

'What time did he leave?'

'It was evening time. About six. He'd been home all afternoon.'

It was at this point that Wexford had his thought about the other woman. It would be a good three and a half hour run from Kingsmarkham to Ipswich even via the Dartford Tunnel. A salesman who was legitimately going to drive to Suffolk and could have started at four instead of six would surely have done so.

'Where did he stay in Ipswich? At a hotel presumably?'

'A motel. Outside Ipswich, I think.'

She spoke listlessly, as if she knew little about her husband's work and took no interest in it. The door opened and a girl came in. She stopped on the threshold and said, 'Oh, sorry.'

'Sara, what time did Dad go when he left?'

'Around six.'

Mrs Williams nodded. She said, 'This is my daughter Sara,' pronouncing the name so that the first syllable rhymed with 'car'.

205

'I believe you've a son too?'

'Kevin. He's twenty. He's away at university.'

The girl stood with her arms over the back of the yellow plastic armchair no one was sitting in, her eyes fixed on her mother in a more or less neutral way, though one that tended towards the hostile rather than the friendly. She was very slender, fair, with the face of a Renaissance painter's model, small-featured with a high forehead and a secretive look. Her hair was exceptionally long, reaching almost to her waist, and with the rippling appearance hair has which is usually done up in plaits. She wore jeans and a tee-shirt with a design on it of a raven and the letters ARRIA superimposed over it.

She picked up a photograph in a chrome frame off the only table in the room, a bamboo affair with a glass top almost hidden by the sofa back. Passing it to Wexford, she stuck her thumb at the head of the man sitting on a beach with a teenage boy and a girl who was herself five years before. The man was big, tall, but out of condition and running to fat around his middle. He had a huge domed forehead. His features, perhaps because they were dominated by this bare dome, looked insignificant and crowded together, the mouth a lipless slit stretched into a smile for the camera.

Wexford handed it back to her. She replaced it on the table, let her eyes linger on her mother for a moment, a curious, faintly contemptuous look, and walked out of the room. He heard her feet going upstairs.

'When did you expect your husband to come back?'

'The Sunday night, he said. I didn't think much about it when he didn't. I thought he'd stayed another night and he'd be back Monday, but he wasn't and he never phoned.'

'You didn't phone the motel yourself?'

She looked at him as if he had proposed to her some gargantuan and complex task quite beyond her capacity, writing a fifty-thousand-word thesis perhaps or devising a computer programme.

'I wouldn't do that. I mean, it's a long-distance call. I haven't got the number anyway.'

'Did you do anything?'

She laughed the dry humourless cackle. 'What could I do?

206

Kevin was home for the weekend but he went back to Keele on the Sunday.' She spoke as if action in such a matter could only be taken by a member of the male sex. 'I knew I'd have been let know if he'd had an accident. He's got his name on him, his bank card and his cheque book and ever so many things with his name on.'

'You didn't phone Sevensmith Harding, for instance?'

'What good would that have done? He never went in there for weeks on end.'

'And you haven't heard a word from him since? For – let's see – eight days, you've had no indication where he might be?'

'That's right. Well, five days. I expected him to be gone the first three.'

He would have to ask it. After all, she had called him in. As a neighbour to confide in certainly, but primarily as a policeman. Nothing he had heard so far made him feel even a preliminary inquiry into Rodney Williams's whereabouts was called for. Looking at Mrs Williams, the house, the daughter, the set-up, he could only wonder with an unkind-ness he would never openly have expressed even to Dora why the man had stayed so long. He had run off with another woman, or run off *to* another woman, and only cowardice was holding him back from writing the requisite letter or making the obligatory phone call.

'Forgive me, but is it possible your husband could be – ' he sought for a word and came out with a mealy-mouthed one he despised ' – friendly with some other woman? Could he have been seeing another woman?'

She gave him a long, cold, unshocked look. Whatever she might say, Wexford could tell his suggestion had already crossed her mind and done more than cross her mind. There was something in that look which told him she was the sort of woman who made a point, a principle almost, of avoiding admitting anything unpleasant. Push it away, suppress it, get out of the habit of thinking, don't wonder or think or specu-late, for that will make you unhappy. Don't think, don't wonder, turn on the telly and in mindless apathy stare at the screen until's it's time for bed and the doctor's little Mogadon that comes on a permanent prescription you pick up at recep-tion.

Of course, he might be doing her an injustice. All this was only in his imagination. 'It's just a possibility,' he said. 'I'm sorry I had to suggest it.'

'I don't know what he does when he's away days and nights on end, do I? All our married life he's been away selling as much as he's been home. I don't know what floozies he's had and I wouldn't ask.'

The old-fashioned word suited the room and Mrs Williams's grey, Crimplene-clad, scurfy respectability. For the first time he noticed the thick sprinkling of dandruff, like a fall of flour, on the shoulders of her blouse. He had given her a solution which to most women would be the least acceptable, but she, he thought, was relieved. Did she suspect her husband of having been up to something *illegal* so that something *immoral* would be seen as a happier alternative?

You suspect everyone and everything, he told himself. You policeman!

'Do you think we ought to do anything?'

'If you mean by that should you report him as a missing person and the police takes steps to find him, no, certainly not. The chances are you'll have word from him in the next few days. If you don't, I think your best course will be to see a solicitor or go to your Citizen's Advice Bureau. But don't do that before you've been on to Sevensmith Harding. The likelihood is you'll find him through them.'

She didn't thank him for coming. He hadn't even been home yet, he had called on her on his way home, but she didn't thank him or apologize for taking up his time. He looked back and saw her still standing on the doorstep holding the door, a very thin angular woman in fawn blouse and unfashionably cut dark green trousers with bell bottoms and a high waist. Her front garden was the only one in Alverbury Road with no spring bulbs out, not a narcissus to relieve the bit of lawn and the dark yew hedge.

It was a cloudy evening, bright as noonday still, April-cool. This little honeycomb of streets was like an orchard in springtime, puffs and clouds of pink and white blossom all over the gardens and drifts of petals already lying on the pavements. A great weeping cherry, pink as ice cream, had taken over his front lawn.

His wife was sitting in an armchair placed in much the

208

same position at the same angle to the fireplace as the chair Joy Williams had sat in, in a room of the same size and proportions to the one he had just left. But there the resemblance ended. A log fire was burning. It had been a cold winter and the spring was cold and protracted, frosts threatening nightly to nip that blossom. Dora was making patchwork, a bedspread in blues and reds, all shades of blues and reds in a multiplicity of patterns, and the finished part covered the long red velvet skirt of the housedress she had taken to wearing in the evenings because of the cold. Her hair was dark and plentiful. Wexford had told her she must be a gipsy to have hair still not grey at nearly sixty.

'Did you see Mike today?'

She meant Detective Inspector Burden. Wexford said no, he had been at court in Myringham.

'Jenny came in to tell me she'd had the results of the amniocentesis. The baby's all right and it's a girl.'

'What's amniocentesis?'

'They stick something through the abdominal wall into the womb and take out a sample of amniotic fluid. The fluid's got cells from the foetus in it and they grow them like a sort of culture, I think. Anyway, the cells divide and they can tell if Down's Syndrome is present and spina bifida too. And of course they can tell the sex by whether the chromosomes come out XY or XX.'

'What a lot you know! Where did you pick up all that?'

'Jenny told me.' She got up and transferred the patchwork to the seat of the chair. 'They can't do an amniocentesis till the sixteenth week of pregnancy and there's always a risk of losing the baby.'

He followed her out into the kitchen. He was more than usually aware this evening of the warmth and light in his own house. It occurred to him that Joy Williams had offered him nothing, not even a cup of tea. Dora had opened the oven door and was looking critically at a steak and kidney pie that was almost ready on the top shelf.

'Do you want a drink?'

'Why not?' she said. 'Celebrate Jenny and Mike's healthy baby.'

'I'm surprised she took any risk,' he said when she had

her sherry and he his Bell's and three parts water. 'She's very set on having this child. They've been trying for years.'

'She's forty-one, Reg. At that age there's also a much higher risk of having a mongoloid baby. Anyway, all's well.'

'Don't you want to hear about your Mrs Williams?'

'Poor Joy,' said Dora. 'She was rather pretty when I first knew her. Of course, that was eighteen years ago. I suppose he's gone off with some girl, has he?'

'If you knew that I don't know what you roped me in for.'

Dora laughed. She had a rich throaty giggle. Immediately she said she knew she shouldn't laugh. 'He's such an awful man. You never met him, did you? There's something so secretive and deceitful about him. I used to think no one could be so obviously like that if they really had something to hide.'

'But now you're not so sure.'

'I'll tell you something I was scared to tell you at the time. I thought you might do something violent.'

'Sure,' he said. 'I've always been so wild and free with my fists. What are you on about?'

'He made a pass at Sylvia.'

She said it defiantly. Standing there in the long red dress, holding the sherry glass, her eyes suddenly wide and wary, she looked astonishingly young.

'So?' His elder daughter was thirty, married twelve years, and the mother of two tall sons. 'She's an attractive woman. I daresay men do make passes at her and no doubt she can take care of herself.'

Dora gave him a sidelong look. 'I said I was scared to tell you. She was fifteen at the time.'

The violent feelings she had predicted were there to hand. After all those years. His fifteen-year-old daughter! He resisted the temptation to bellow. Nor did he stamp. He took a sip of his drink and spoke coolly. 'And, like a good little girl, she came to mother and told her?'

Dora said flippantly, 'Sweet of her, wasn't it? I was touched. I think the truth was, Reg, she was scared stiff.'

'Did you do anything?'

'Oh, yes. I went to him and told him what her father was. He didn't know. I don't think there was ever much communication between him and Joy. Anyway, it worked.

210

He made himself very scarce and Sylvia didn't baby-sit for them again. I didn't tell Joy but I think she knew and was disillusioned. Anyway, she didn't adore him any more the way she used to.'

'I was adored once,' Wexford quoted.

'And still are, darling. You know we all adore you. You haven't forfeited our respect, running after little girls. Can I have some more sherry?'

'You'll have to get it yourself,' said Wexford, opening the oven and taking out the pie. 'All this drinking and gossiping. I want my dinner.'

2

The firm of Sevensmith Harding had been founded in 1875 by Septimus Sevensmith who called himself a colourman. He sold artists' materials in a shop in the High Street in Myringham. Paints for exterior- and interior-decorating use came along later. After the First World War in fact, when Septimus's granddaughter married a Major John Harding who left a leg behind him at Passchendaele.

The first great house-building boom of the eighties and nineties were past and gone, the next due to begin. Major Harding got in on it. He began manufacturing in huge quantities the browns and greens dear to the hearts of builders creating the terraces and semidetacheds which were growing in branches and tentacles out of South London. And towards the end of the decade he brought out a daring shade of cream.

Already the company had been renamed Sevensmith Harding. It kept its offices in Myringham High Street, though the factory behind was soon to be moved to sites on distant industrial complexes. With the disappearance of its retail trade the shop as such also disappeared.

The world's paint industry enjoyed a steady growth during the 1960s and early 1970s. It is estimated that close on five hundred companies make paint in the United Kingdom but the bulk of the sales volume is handled by a few large manufacturers. Four of these manufacturers dominate the British Isles and one of them is Sevensmith Harding.

Today their paints, Sevenstar vinyl silk and Sevenstar vinyl matt emulsion, Sevenshine gloss and satin finish, are manufactured at Harlow in Essex, and their wallpapers, borders and coordinating tiles at Crawley in Sussex. The head offices in Myringham, in the centre of the High Street opposite the Old Flag Hotel, have more a look of solicitors' chambers or the establishment of a very refined antique dealer than the seat of paint makers. Indeed, there is scarcely anything to show that they are paint makers. The bow windows with their occasional pane of distorted glass that flank the front door contain, instead of cans of paint and display stands of delighted housewives with brushes in their hands, a *famille noire* vase of dried grasses on one side and a Hepplewhite chair on the other. But over the door, Georgian in style and of polished mahogany, are royal armorial bearings and the legend: 'By appointment to her Majesty Queen Elizabeth the Queen Mother, Colourists and Makers of Fine Pigments'.

The company chairman, Jeremy Harding-Grey, divided his time between his house in Monte Carlo and his house in Nassau, and the managing director, George Delahaye, though he lived in Sussex, was seldom seen in the vicinity of Myringham. But the deputy managing director was a humbler person and altogether more on the level of ordinary men. Wexford knew him. They had met at the home of Sylvia's father-in-law, an architect, and since then the Gardners had once been guests at a drinks party at the Wexfords' and the Wexfords guests at the Gardners'. But for all that Wexford would not have considered himself on the kind of terms with Miles Gardner to warrant dropping in at Sevensmith Harding when he found himself in Myringham at lunchtime to ask Miles out for a drink and a sandwich.

A fortnight had passed since his talk with Joy Williams and he had virtually forgotten about it. He had dismissed it from his mind before he went to bed that same night. And if he had thought about it at all since then it had only been to tell himself that by now Mrs Williams and her solicitor would be settling things to her satisfaction or that Williams had returned home, having found like many a man before him that domesticity is the better part of economics.

But even if Williams were still missing there was nothing to justify Wexford's making inquiries about him at Sevensmith Harding. Let Joy Williams do that. He wouldn't be missing as far as his employers were concerned. No matter how complex a man's love life he still has to go to work and earn

213

his bread. Williams earned it on too humble a level though, Wexford reflected, for it to be likely Miles Gardner had ever heard of him.

He and Burden had both been at Myringham Crown Court, witnesses in two separate cases, and the court had adjourned for lunch. Burden would have to go back to watch his case – a rather ticklish matter concerning the receiving of stolen goods – through to the bitter end, but Wexford's day, at least as far as appearing in court went, was over. As they walked towards the hotel Burden was silent and morose. He had been like this since they came out of court. If it had been anyone else Wexford would have supposed his mood due to the dressing down, indeed the scathing tongue-lashing, meted out to him by the alleged receiver's counsel. But Burden was impervious to such things. He had taken that sort of stick too many times to care. This was something else, something closer to home, Wexford thought. And now he came to think of it, this, whatever it was, had been growing on Burden for days now, weeks even, a morose surly misery that didn't seem to affect his work but militated badly against his relations with other people.

He looked the same as ever. There was no sign of anxiety or care in his appearance. He was thin but he had always been thin. Wexford didn't know if it was a new suit he was wearing or last year's cleaned and the trousers nightly pressed in the electric press his wife had given him for Christmas. ('Like those things you get in swish hotels,' Burden had said proudly.) It was a happy marriage, Burden's second, as happy as his first. But almost any marriage Burden made would be happy, he had a gift for marriage. He was uxorious without making himself ridiculous. There couldn't be anything in his marriage that was bugging him. His wife was pregnant with a longed-for child – longed for by her at any rate. Burden had a grown-up son and daughter by his first marriage. Wexford considered an idea that came to him and then dismissed it as absurd and out of character. Burden was the last man to dread the coming child just because he was now in his mid-forties. That he would take in his stride.

'What's wrong, Mike?' he asked as the silence became oppressive.

'Nothing.'

The classic answer. One of the cases in which a statement means the precise opposite of what it says, as when a man in doubt says he's absolutely certain.

Wexford didn't press it. He walked along, looking about him at the old market town which had changed so much since he had first known it. A huge shopping complex had been built, and since then an arts centre, incorporating theatre, cinema and concert hall. The university term was three weeks old and the place was thronged with blue-jeaned students. But up at this end of the town, where preservation orders proliferated and buildings were listed, things were much the same. Things were even rather better since the local authority had woken up to the fact that Myringham was beautiful and worth conserving and had therefore cleaned and tidied and painted and planted.

He looked into the bow windows of Sevensmith Harding, first at the Hepplewhite chair, then at the vase. Beyond the dried grasses he could see a young girl receptionist talking on the phone. Wexford and Burden crossed the road and went into the Old Flag.

Wexford had been there once or twice before. It was not a place ever to be crowded in the middle of the day. The busy lunch trade went to the cheaper brighter pubs and the wine bars. In the smaller of the lounge bars where food was being served several vacant tables remained. Wexford was making for one of them when he caught sight of Miles Gardner sitting alone.

'Won't you join me?'

'You look as if you're waiting for someone,' Wexford said.

'Any congenital company that offers itself.' He had a gracious warm manner of speaking that was in no way affected. Wexford recalled that this was what he had always liked about him. 'They do a nice prawn salad,' Miles Gardner said. 'And if you can get here before one they'll send up to the butcher for a fillet steak.'

'What happens at one?'

'The butcher closes. He opens at two and then the pub closes. There's Myringham for you.'

Wexford laughed. Burden didn't laugh but sat wearing the sort of stiff polite expression that indicates to even the most insensitive that one would be happier – or less miserable –

on one's own. Wexford made up his mind to ignore him. Gardner seemed delighted with their company and, having bought a round of drinks, began to talk in the easy rather elegant way he had about the new house he had just moved into which Sylvia's father-in-law had designed. It was a valuable gift, Wexford thought, to be able to talk to people, one whom you had only just met and the other a mere acquaintance, as if they were old friends whom you conversed with regularly.

Gardner was a small, undistinguished-looking man. His style was in his voice and manner. He had a much taller wife and two or three rather noisy daughters, Wexford remembered. From the new house and the time it had taken to get itself built, Gardner had moved on to talk of work, lack of work and unemployment, eliciting mild sparks of interest from Burden, at least to the extent of extracting monosyllables from him. Sevensmith Harding had battled against laying off workers at their Harlow factory and the battle had been won − allowing for the few redundancies which Gardner insisted had been acceptable to the men and women concerned.

'Yes,' said Burden. 'I daresay.'

Always reactionary, he had until a few years back threatened to become unbearably right wing and Blimpish, but Jenny had reversed the tide. Burden was far more of a moderate now. He did not, as he once would have, launch into a tirade against unemployment benefits, Social Security payments and general idleness. Or perhaps it was only this depression of his that made him forbear.

'The whole attitude towards work and employment and keeping one's job is changing, I find,' Gardner said. He began talking about what he thought gave rise to these new patterns and made it interesting enough. Or so Wexford thought. Burden, eating prawn salad rather too rapidly, kept looking at his watch. He had to be back in court by two. Wexford thought he would be glad to be rid of him for a while.

'Isn't what you're really saying,' he said to Gardner, 'that, in spite of the threat of unemployment and the inadequacy of unemployment benefits, men seem to have lost that craven fear of losing their jobs they had in the thirties?'

'Yes, and to a great extent, any rate among the middle

216

class, lost the feeling they used to have that they had to stick in a hated job or career for the rest of their lives just because it's the one they went into at twenty.'

'Then what's brought this change about?'

'I don't know. I've thought about it but the answers I come up with don't satisfy me. But I can tell you that just as the fear has gone, and the respect for employers because they were employers, so had pride in one's job and the old loyalty to a company. My marketing manager is a case in point. Time was when you could say a man in that position would also be a responsible person, someone you could trust not to let you down. He'd have been proud – and yes, I'll say it, *grateful* – to be where he was and he'd have had a real feeling for the firm's welfare too.'

'What's he done?' said Burden. 'Decided to change his career in midstream?'

It was said acidulously but Gardner gave no sign of having noticed the edge to Burden's voice and replied pleasantly.

'Not so far as I know. He simply walked out on me. He's on three months' notice, or supposed to be. First we get a phone call from his wife saying he's sick, then not a word until a letter of resignation comes, very clipped and curt, and a note at the bottom – ' Gardner looked almost apologetic – 'quite an *insolent* sort of note, saying he'd be in touch with our accounts department about his superannuation.'

'Had he been with you long?'

'All his working life, I gather, and five years as marketing manager.'

'At least you'll have no difficulty in finding a replacement in these hard times.'

'It's going to be a case of promotion for one of our best reps. That's always been Sevensmith Harding's policy. Promote rather than take in from outside. Only usually, of course, we're given a bit more time.'

Burden got up and said he must get back to court. He shook hands with Gardner and had the grace to mutter something about its having been good to meet him.

'Let me get you another beer,' said Wexford when Burden had left and been described (very much to his surprise) by Gardner as a 'nice chap'.

'Thanks so much. I don't suppose they'll sling us out before two-thirty, will they?'

The beer came, one of the 130 varieties of 'real ale' the Old Flag claimed to stock.

'It's not by any chance my neighbour Rodney Williams you'll be promoting, is it?'

Gardner looked at him, surprised.

'Rod Williams?'

'Yes. He lives in the next street to me.'

Gardner said in a patient tone, 'Rod Williams is our former marketing manager, the one I was telling you resigned.'

'Williams?'

'Yes, I thought I explained. Perhaps I didn't say the name.'

'Somebody,' said Wexford, 'is getting hold of the wrong end of the stick here.'

'It's you,' said Gardner, smiling.

'Yes, I expect it is. Somebody has given me the wrong end of the stick. Am I to take it then that Williams wasn't one of your reps and didn't cover the Suffolk area for you?'

'He was once. He did once. Up till five years ago. We kept to our customary policy and when our former marketing manager took early retirement due to a heart condition, we promoted Rod Williams.'

'As far as his wife knows he's still a rep. That is, he's still spending half his time selling up in Suffolk.'

Gardner's eyebrows went up. He gave a twisted grin. 'His private life is no affair of mine.'

'Nor mine.'

It was Gardner who changed the subject. He began talking about his eldest daughter who was getting married in the late summer. Wexford finally parted from him with a promise to be in touch, to 'get Dora to give Pam a ring and fix something up'. Driving home to Kingsmarkham, he thought for a while about Rodney Williams. There had been no room in his own marriage for alibis. He wondered what it would be like to have a marriage in which a permanent, on-going, five-year-long alibi existed as an integral part of life. Unthinkable. Unimaginable. He stopped trying to identify and thought about it with detachment.

What had happened perhaps was that five years ago Williams had met a girl with whom he wanted to spend time

218

without ending his marriage. Keeping his promotion a secret from his wife would have been a way of achieving this. Probably the girl lived in Myringham. While Joy Williams believed her husband was staying at a motel outside Ipswich he was in reality seeing this other girl, no doubt sharing her home and doing his nine-to-five job at Sevensmith Harding in Myringham.

It was the sort of situation some men chuckle over. Wexford wasn't one of them. And there was another aspect, one that few men would find funny. If Williams hadn't told his wife about his promotion he presumably also hadn't told her about the considerable increase in salary that went with it. Still, there was no more mystery. Williams had written to the company. Joy had phoned with excuses. Back in Alverbury Road Williams was still perhaps managing to shore up a few fragments of deceit against discovery.

It was nine at night and he was still in his office, going through for the tenth time the statements he had taken for the preparation of a case of fraud against one Francis Wingrave Adams. He still doubted whether they would constitute a watertight case and so did counsel representing the police, though both knew he was guilty. On the final stroke of nine – St Peter's clock had a dead sound too, like St Mary Woolnoth's – he put the papers away and set off to walk homewards.

Lately he had taken to walking to and from work. Dr Crocker recommended it, pointing out that it was less than half a mile.

'Hardly worth it then,' Wexford said.

'A couple of miles' walk a day could make a difference of ten years' life to you.'

'Does that mean that if I walked six miles a day I could prolong my life by thirty years?'

The doctor had refused to answer that one. Wexford, though feigning to scoff, had gone some way towards obeying him. Sometimes his walk took him down Tabard Road past Burden's bungalow, sometimes along Alverbury Road where the Williams family lived, and there was an occasional longer route along one of the meadow footpaths. Tonight he intended to drop in and see Burden for a final assessment of the Adams' business.

But now he began to feel that there was very little left to say about this man who had conned an elderly woman out of £20,000. He wouldn't talk about that. Instead he would try to get out of Burden what was happening in his life to account for his depression.

The Burdens still lived in the bungalow Burden had moved into soon after his first marriage where the garden after twenty years or more still had an immature look and the ivy which tried to climb up the house had been ruthlessly cut back with secateurs. Only the front door changed. It had been all colours – Burden was a relentless decorator – but Wexford had liked the rose pink best. Now it was a dark greenish blue – Sevenshine Oriental Peacock probably. Above the door, now dusk had come, the porch light was on, a lantern of leaded lights in the shape of a star.

Jenny came to let him in. She was halfway through her pregnancy now and 'showing', as the old wives say. Instead of a smock she wore a full-sleeved, square-necked dress with a high waist, like the one the woman is wearing in Vermeer's *The Letter*. She had let he golden-brown hair grow and it hung to her shoulders. But, for all that, Wexford was shocked by her appearance. She looked drawn and dispirited.

Burden, having years ago agreed to stop calling Wexford 'sir', now called him nothing at all. But Jenny called him Reg. She said, 'Mike's in the living room, Reg,' and added in a way quite unlike her usual self, 'I was just going to bed.'

He felt constrained to say he was sorry for calling so late, though it was only twenty past nine. She shrugged and said it didn't matter and she said it in a way which seemed to imply that nothing much mattered. He followed her into the room where Burden was.

On the middle cushion of the three-seater settee Burden sat reading *Police Review*. Wexford would have expected Jenny to have been sitting beside him but she hadn't been. Beside a chair at the far end of the room lay her book face downwards and a piece of white knitting that had a look about it of the knitter's having no enthusiasm for her task. In a glass vase on the windowsill dying wallflowers stood in three inches of water.

'Have a drink,' said Burden, laying down his magazine. 'There's beer. There is beer, isn't there, Jenny?'

'I don't know. I never touch the stuff.'

Burden said nothing. He left the room, went out to the kitchen and came back with two cans on a tray. Burden's first wife would have said, and Jenny once would have said, that they must have glasses to drink the beer out of. Jenny, languidly sitting down, picking up book and knitting but looking at neither, said, 'You can drink it out of the can, can't you?'

Wexford began to feel awkward. Some sort of powerful angry tension that existed between these two seemed to hang in the air like smoke, to get in his throat and give him a choky feeling. He snapped the top off his beer can. Jenny was holding the knitting needles in one clenched hand and staring at the wall. He had no intention of talking about Francis Wingrave Adams in her presence. On other occasions like this he and Burden would have gone into one of the other rooms. Burden sat on the settee, wearing his half-frown. He opened the beer can with a sharp, rough movement and a spurt of froth shot out across the carpet.

Three months before Wexford had seen Jenny soothing and practical when her husband had dropped, not a spoonful of beer, but a bowl of strawberry mousse on the paler newer carpet of the dining room. She had laughed and told him to leave the clearing up to her. Now she gave a cry of real distress and jumped up out of her chair.

'All right,' said Burden. 'All right. I'll do it. It's nothing anyway. I'll get a cloth.'

She burst into tears. She put one hand up to her face and ran out of the room. Burden followed her. That is, Wexford thought he had followed her but he came back almost immediately holding a floorcloth.

'Sorry about that,' he said on his hands and knees. 'Of course it's not the beer. It's just any little thing sets her off. Take no notice.' He lifted an angry face. 'I've made up my mind I'm simply not going to take any notice any more.'

'But if she's not well, Mike . . .'

'She is perfectly well.' Burden got up and dropped the cloth onto the tiled kerb of the fireplace. 'She is having an ideal trouble-free pregnancy. Why, she wasn't even sick.

When I remember what Jean went through . . .' Wexford could hardly believe his ears. For a husband – and such a husband as Burden – to make that comparison! Burden seemed to realize what he had said and a dull flush crept across his face. 'No, honestly, she's perfectly fit, she says so herself. It's simply neurotic behaviour.'

Wexford had sometimes thought in the past that if every instance diagnosed by Burden as neurotic were taken as sound, almost the entire population would have to be tranquillized, not to say confined in mental hospitals. He said, 'The amniocentesis was all right, wasn't it? They didn't tell her something to worry her?'

Burden hesitated. 'Well, as a matter of fact they did.' He gave an ugly humourless laugh. 'That's just what they did. They told her something to worry her. You've hit the nail bang on the head. It doesn't worry *me* and I'm the child's father. But it worries her like hell and I'm the one who has to bear the brunt of it.' He sat down and said very loudly, almost shouting, 'I don't want to talk about it anyway. I've said too much already and I've no intention of saying any more. I feel like learning a formula to explain my wife's conduct and repeating it to people when they first come in the door.'

Wexford said quietly, 'You can do it extempore for it is nothing but roaring.'

He got a glare for that. 'I came to talk about Adams. Or are you too preoccupied with your domestic fracas to care?'

'I told you, I'm simply not going to take any notice any more,' said Burden, and they talked about Adams not very profitably for the next half-hour.

Dora was in bed when he got home, sitting up reading. While he undressed he told her about the Burdens.

'They're too old to have babies,' was all she would say.

'Flying in the face of nature, would you call it?'

'You'd be surprised, my lad. I might. And by the way, Rod Williams hasn't come back. I saw Joy and she hasn't heard a word.'

'But I had the distinct impression she'd phoned Sevensmith Harding,' Wexford began.

'You told her to, you mean. You told her to phone them

222

and find out if they could tell her anything and she's going to.'

That wasn't what he had meant. He got into bed, sure now that he hadn't heard the last of the Williams affair.

3

For more than a couple of weeks now he had been keeping his eye on the dark blue Ford Granada parked outside his house in Arnold Road, Myringham. It had appeared there for the first time soon after Easter. Graham Gee couldn't see it from his front windows nor, because of the tall lonicera hedge, from his front garden. He saw it when he drove his own car out of the entrance to his garage each morning and when he drove it in each afternoon at 5.30.

At first (he told the police) he thought it might have something to do with the boy opposite, the teenage son of the people in the bungalow. But it was too respectable a car for that. Well, it was *then*. Dismissing that theory, he wondered if it belonged to some commuter who was using Arnold Road as a station car park. Arnold Road wasn't very near Myringham Southern Region Station, it was a good quarter of a mile away, but it was probably the nearest street to the station not clogged on both sides with commuters' cars.

Graham Gee began to see the presence of the Ford Granada outside his gate as the thin end of the wedge. Soon there would be a hundred rail travellers' cars parked in Arnold Road. He was not a commuter himself but a partner in a firm of accountants in Pomfret.

Arnold Road was known as a 'nice neighbourhood'. The houses were detached, standing in large gardens. There weren't any rough elements, there wasn't any trouble, except perhaps for the theft of dahlias from someone's front garden the previous autumn. So Graham Gee was surprised to notice one morning that the Granada's hub caps had gone. Perhaps they had always been gone though, he couldn't remember.

Still, he knew the wheels hadn't always been gone. The car hadn't always been propped up on bricks. Dirty now, streaked with rain, it sat on its brick supports, looking as if it might after all be the property of the teenager opposite.

He still did nothing about it, though he knew by now that it was there all the time. It wasn't driven there in the morning and taken away in the evening. For a week now it hadn't been drivable. It took the smashing of a rear window to get him to do something.

The rear window had been broken, the front doors opened and the interior stripped. The radio had been removed, the headrests taken off the front seats, and something dug out of the dashboard, a clock perhaps. Though the boot was open, the thieves hadn't thought it worth their while to help themselves to the snow shovel inside. Gee phoned the police.

There was no need for the police to go through the procedure of tracing the driver through the Vehicle Licensing Department in Swansea, for the vehicle registration document was in the Granada's glove compartment along with a road map of southern England, a ballpoint pen and a pair of sunglasses.

Vehicle registration documents have named on them the 'keeper' of the vehicle, not its owner, a fact which was also of assistance to the police. The one listed the keeper as Rodney John Williams of 31 Alverbury Road, Kingsmarkham.

Why had Williams dumped the car in Arnold Road when Sevensmith Harding's own car park was less than a quarter of a mile away behind the company's High Street offices? That car park was never locked. It had no gates, only an opening in the fence and on the fence a notice requesting 'unauthorized personnel' not to park there.

'I don't understand it,' Miles Gardner said. 'Frankly, we've been wondering what to do about recovering the car but we don't know where Williams is. He didn't mention the car in his letter of resignation. Apparently, wherever he was when he first left, he's no longer with his wife, otherwise we would have tackled her. He's disappeared into thin air. It's a bit much really, isn't it? I gather the car's in a state, not much more than a shell?'

'The engine's still there,' said Wexford.

Gardner made a face. They were in his rather gloomy though luxurious office, a room not so much panelled as lined with oak, the decor dating from those between-wars days when hardwood was plentiful. None of your Sevenstar matt emulsion here, Wexford thought to himself.

There were more framed photographs than in the average elderly couple's living room. On Gardner's desk, placed to catch his eye every time he looked up, was a big one of tall Mrs Gardner and her three girls, all affectionate nestling and entwined arms. The walls were reserved for various groups and gatherings of men at company functions or on sporting occasions. One was of a cricket match with a tall gangling man going in to bat. Rodney Williams. The high forehead, slight concavity of features that would no doubt show more clearly in profile, the thin mouth stretched in a grin, were unmistakable.

Gardner looked at it dolefully.

'He was a lot younger then,' he said. 'The company had a crack team in those days.' He made as if to take the photograph down, angered no doubt by the sight of the permanently grinning Williams, but seemed to change his mind. 'The whole thing's extraordinary. He was very keen on cars, you know, one of those car men. You don't think anything's happened to him, do you?'

The euphemism that always signified death . . .

'If you mean some sort of accident, I don't know but I don't think so. It's more what has he been up to, isn't it?'

Gardner looked mystified.

'It looks to me as if he may have been up to something he shouldn't have been, he's been on the fiddle. Either he decided he'd made enough out of it and was going to call it a day or else something happened to make him think discovery was imminent. Now, the most likely place for him to have been cooking the books is here. Do you have any thoughts on that one?'

'He wouldn't have had the opportunity. He never went near any books, so to speak. Do you want me to have our chief accountant up? I mean, as far as I can see, any fiddle

226

he was up to would have to be an expenses fiddle and Ken Risby would be the man to tell you about that.'

Gardner made a call on the internal phone. While they waited for Risby Wexford said, 'There is nothing small, portable but of considerable value he could have stolen? No cheque coming into his hands he could have falsified? No forgery he could have perpetrated?'

Gardner looked simply bewildered. 'I don't think so. I'm sure not. I mean, I should know by now. Good God, the man's been gone over three weeks.' He jumped up. 'Here's Ken now. He'll tell us.'

But Risby was not able to tell them much. He was a thin, fair man in his thirties, with a nervous manner, and he seemed as shocked by Wexford's suggestion as Gardner had been. You'd think the pair of them lived in a world where fraud had never been heard of, Wexford thought impatiently, and every businessman was a sea-green incorruptible.

'He was a mite heavy on his expenses sometimes but that's all, that's positively all. He never had the handling of the firm's money. What makes you think he's done something like that?'

'You think about it. Look at it for yourself. For five years the man's been lying to his wife about his position with this firm. What salary was he getting, by the way?'

'Twenty-five thousand,' said Gardner rather grudgingly.

More than Wexford had expected, £5000 more. 'And lying about that too. You can bet on it she thinks he was getting less than half that. One day he tells her he's going to Ipswich, a place he doubtless hasn't set foot in for five years, and off he goes, dumps his company car in the street, and disappears. Apart from getting the lady he's in cahoots with to phone here and say he's ill and apart from writing his resignation he's never heard from again. And you ask me why I think he's been up to something? Tell me about the man. If he's not a man who'd steal or forge, is there some other disgraceful thing he might have done?'

They looked at him. Having no imagination, they didn't know and couldn't hazard guesses. Wexford had plenty of imagination and very little knowledge of marketing.

'For instance, he couldn't have been selling this paint of

yours at prices over the odds and pocketing the difference? Something like that?'

Gardner, who had looked as if he would never smile again, burst out laughing.

'He never actually *sold* anything, Reg. It doesn't work like that. He never handled money. He never handled money in any shape or form.'

'You make him sound like royalty,' said Wexford. 'Anyway, will you, Mr Risby, have a good look at your books for me, please? Do a supplementary audit or whatever.'

'Really not necessary, I assure you, not necessary at all. I'd go into court at this moment and swear there's not a squeak of a discrepancy in my books.'

'I hope you'll never have to go into court on this matter, but don't count on it.' Risby's eyes opened wide at that one. 'And do as I ask and check the books, will you? And now,' Wexford said to Gardner, 'I'd like to see that letter of resignation Williams wrote to you.'

Gardner called his secretary in to find it. Wexford noticed he called her Susan, and what was less expected, she called him Miles. The letter was typed and by someone not accustomed to frequent use of a typewriter.

Dear Mr Gardner,
This is to give you notice of my resignation from Sevensmith Harding from today. I am afraid it is rather sudden but is due to circumstances beyond my control. I shall not be returning to the office and would prefer you not to attempt to get in touch with me.

Yours sincerely,
Rodney J. Williams
PS. I will contact the Accounts Dept. about my superannuation refund in due course.

Wexford said, 'Everyone in this office calls each other by their Christian names but Rodney Williams called you Mr Gardner? Is that right?'

'No, of course not. He called me Miles.'

'He doesn't in this letter.'

'I took that to be because he thought the occasion demanded something more formal.'

228

'It's a possibility. Don't you find it odd when a man on three months' notice gives you one day's? Wouldn't you have expected a more detailed explanation for common courtesy's sake than "circumstances beyond my control"?'

'Are you suggesting someone else might have written that letter?'

Wexford didn't answer directly. 'I'll take it with me if I may. Maybe have some experts look at that signature. Can you let me have a specimen of his signature? One we *know* is his?'

Nine separate sets of fingerprints have been found on and in the car. These would presumably include the prints of whoever had vandalized it. The others would be Williams's, Joy's, Sara's, Kevin's. Early days yet to ask these people to let him check their own prints against those in the car. A lot of hairs, fair and grey, had been on the upholstery. No blood, of course, nothing dramatic. There was one odd thing, though. On the floor of the boot, along with the shovel, were some crumbs of plaster the lab had identified as either Tetrion or Sevensmith Harding's Stopgap.

It took a few more days to get a verdict on the letter.

A manual portable machine, the Remington 315, had been used to type it. There was a chip out of the apex of the capital A on this machine, a similar flaw in the ascender of the lower-case t and a smudging of the head of the comma. As to the signature, it wasn't Wiliams's. The handwriting expert was far more categorial than such people are usually willing to be. He was almost scathing in his incredulity that anyone could for a moment have believed that the signature was made by Williams.

When Joy had told Dora of her intention to phone Sevensmith Harding she had followed this up with a request to 'send' Wexford round to her house once more. This time Dora had said in quite a sharp way that her husband wasn't a private detective and Wexford, of course, hadn't gone. But Williams's disappearance had stopped being a private matter. At any rate, he thought, he wouldn't be unwelcome at 31 Alverbury Road. The answer to a prayer, in fact. He walked round there in the evening, at about eight.

This time the girl Sara let him in. She spoke not a word but closed the front door after him, opened the living-room door, left him and went back upstairs.

Joy Williams was watching television. The programme was one of those contests in which teams of people go through ridiculous or humiliating ordeals. Men in dress suits and top hats were trying to walk a tightrope over what looked like a lake of mashed potato. Just before the door was opened he had heard her laughing. She didn't turn the set off, only the sound. He thought she looked anything but pleased to see him. Her expression had very quickly become sullen.

Yes, she admitted, they had a joint bank account. Rod was away so much they had had to. Wexford asked her if he might seen some recent bank statements.

She hunched herself, arms wrapping her thin body, right hand on left shoulder, left hand with the ugly showy rings on right. It was a habitual gesture with her which a psychiatrist might have said began as a way of protecting herself from assault. She had the green trousers on and a knitted jumper, its shoulders sprinkled with fallen hairs and dandruff.

'How often does your bank send you statements?'

'It's been once a month lately.' Her eyes strayed to the silent but tumultuous screen. A contestant had fallen into the mashed potato. 'They made a mistake over something and Rod complained, so they started sending statements once a month.'

Dr Crocker had told Wexford of a recent visit to one of his patients, a woman ill with bronchitis. The television had been on in her bedroom, all her six children sitting there watching it. When he tried to examine her she had protested angrily at his request that the set be turned off.

'I pull the plug out now without a by-your-leave,' said the doctor. 'If the TV's on or their video I don't ask any more, I pull out the plug.'

Wexford would have liked to do that. He would have done it if he had had just a fraction more evidence for disquiet over Rodney Williams. It was curious that Joy, who had come close to pestering Dora for his attention, was now making it plain she didn't want him here.

'Will you show me the statements?'

230

She turned her head reluctantly. 'OK, if you want.' He had put his request very politely as if she would be doing him a favour and she responded as if she was.

It didn't take her long to find the statements. She wasn't going to miss more of her programme than she had to. As he began to look at the statements she leaned across and summoned a little sound out of the television, so that shrieks, exclamations and commentary were just audible. He wondered what could possibly distract her, what real event or shock, and then he knew. The phone bell. Somewhere, elsewhere in the house, the phone began to ring.

She jumped up. 'That'll be my son. My son always phones me on Thursday nights.'

Wexford returned to the monthly bank statements. Each one showed the sum of £500 paid into the account more or less at the beginning of the month. A salary cheque apparently. Several objections to that one. Williams's salary had been £25,000 a year and there was no way £500 a month, even after all possible deductions, could amount to as much as that. Secondly, the sum would vary, not be a set round figure. Thirdly, it would be paid in on the same day of the month, give or take a day each way, not sometimes on the first and sometimes on the eighth.

It was evident what had been going on. Williams had another account somewhere into which his salary was paid. From that account he transferred £500 a month into the account he had jointly with his wife. If this was so, and it must be, it was going to be useless asking Joy, as he had intended, if her husband had drawn on their joint account since his disappearance.

Sevensmith Harding would make no bones about telling him where this other account was. The problem would be the intransigent bank manager refusing to disclose any information about a client's account. He looked at the April statement again. Five hundred pounds had been paid in on 2 April. No May statement had yet been sent to Mrs Williams as May was only half over.

She came back into the room, looking brighter and younger, her face more animated than he had ever seen it. She had been talking to her son, her favourite.

'I'd like you to give your bank a ring,' he said, 'and ask

231

them if the usual five hundred was paid into the account at the beginning of the month. Will you do that?'

She nodded. He asked her to tell him about the last afternoon and evening Williams had spent at home. Rod had mowed the lawn in the afternoon, she said, and then he'd taken her shopping to the Tesco discount. She couldn't drive.

'We came back and had a cup of tea. Rod had a sandwich. He didn't want more than that. He said he'd get something on his way to Ipswich. Then he went upstairs and packed a bag and left. He'd be back on Sunday, he said.' She gave one of her dull laughs. 'And that was the last of him. After twenty-two years.'

'What did you do for the rest of the evening?'

'Me?'

'Yes, what did you do? Did you stay at home? Go out? Did anyone come here?'

'I went over to my sister's. She lives in Pomfret. I went on the bus. I had something to eat and then I went to my sister's.'

'And Sara?'

'She was here. Up there.' Joy Williams pointed to the ceiling. 'Studying for her A-levels, I suppose.' She made it sound an unworthy, even slightly disgraceful thing for her daughter to have been doing.

There was something wrong with this description of how the evening had been passed, something incongruous, only Wexford couldn't put his finger on what.

'I'd like to talk to Sara,' he said.

'Do as you like.'

She twisted round in her chair and looked fully at him, the television for the moment forgotten.

'She'll be in her bedroom but you can go up. She won't object.' The awful laugh came. 'Rather the reverse if I know her.'

4

So young Sara, who looked like one of Botticelli's girls, a
Quattrocento virgin, had been caught in bed with a boyfriend. Or not in bed, most probably. On the yellow plastic
settee or in the back of a car. It was difficult with daughters.
You knew what your enlightened principles were but things
looked different when it was *your* daughter. Still, that hardly
justified Joy's snide insinuation. Wexford, going upstairs,
decided that as well as disliking what he knew of Williams,
he didn't care for Mrs Williams either. Not that it mattered
whether he liked them or not. It made no difference. Perhaps
the woman did have some justification. She was going
through a bad time; she, who was surely in the process of
losing her man, would feel bitter towards a daughter gaining
one. And the discovery of Sara and the boy might have been
made very recently.

He knew which bedroom it was because music was coming
from behind the door. Rock music of some kind, soft with
a monotonous drumbeat. She must have heard his feet on
the stairs by now. He had taken care to make a bit of noise,
not difficult on the linoleum covered with thin haircord. He
knocked on the door.

She didn't say, 'Come in!' She opened it herself. Wexford
had often noted reactions to a knock at the door. They
offered indications of character and motivation. The woman,
for example, who calls out 'Come in!' is more open, relaxed
and easy-going than she who opens the door herself. The
latter will be cagey and reserved. In the thirty seconds or so
before she opens the door, what has she put away in a drawer
or hidden under a magazine?

He could see that Sara had created the room herself. What attractiveness it had had nothing to do with the furniture, carpet and curtains provided by her parents. It was the smallest bedroom. Wexford had had an extension built on to his own house when the girls were little but this house remained as it had originally been. There would be a large front bedroom for the husband and wife, a slightly smaller back room – in this case for the son – and a tiny boxroom no more than nine feet by seven for the daughter. She had put posters all over the walls, one of a red horse galloping in the snow from the Yugoslav Naive school of painting, another of a thin naked black man playing a guitar. Between them hung a tennis racket, a corn dolly and a montage of Tarot cards. Perhaps the most striking poster was the one that faced the door. A harpy-like creature with the head and breasts of a woman and the body, wings and claws of a raven, clutched at an unfurling ribbon on which was painted the name – acronym? – ARRIA. Wexford remembered the tee-shirt Sara had been wearing when first they met. The raven woman had a face like Britannia or maybe Boadicea, one of those noble, handsome, courageous, fanatical faces, that made you feel like locking up the knives and reaching for the Valium.

Bookshelves that looked as if put up by Sara herself held a paperback *Life of Freud*, Phyllis Grosskurth's *Havelock Ellis*, Fromm, Laing, Freud on the *Wolf Man* and *Leonardo*, Erin Pizzey and Jeff Shapiro on incest and child abuse, but not a single work of fiction. With her tiny radio providing background music, she had been sitting at a dressing table that doubled as a desk, swotting for an exam. It was evidently chemistry. The textbook lay open at a page of formulae.

'We're trying to find your father, Sara. I wouldn't exactly say he's disappeared but he's making himself very hard to find.'

She had fixed him with her grave contained look. He noticed her skin, creamy and smooth like velvet, with a gold dusting of freckles on her small nose. When she opened the door to him she had been holding a green felt-tipped pen in her hand. On the back of the other hand she had drawn a green snake. Teenagers had always drawn on their hands, they had done so when he was in his teens and when his daughters were in their teens, but now some sort of specific fashion for it has sprung up. To have black and red and green drawings on your hands and arms and body was the 'in' thing. Sara had drawn with her green pen a spotted snake, not curled around itself but stretched out and slightly undulant, its forked tongue extended.

'Have you any thoughts about where he might be?'

She shook her head. She put the cap on the pen and laid it down.

'Would you like to tell me about the last time you were with your father? Were you here when he left?'

She hesitated, then gave a nod. 'It was the second day of term after the Easter holidays. I was late home because I went to the library. They'd got a book in for me, a new book I'd put my name down for and they'd sent me a card to say it was in.' She lifted two books off the stack and handed him one from underneath. She was out to impress and the book was a learned work: Stern's *Principles of Human Genetics*. He didn't take much notice of that but he did look at the date stamp in the back. 'I rang the library to renew it,' she said defensively. 'I couldn't read it in three weeks. It's very difficult.' She smiled at last and became at once a beauty. 'I'm not saying it's too difficult for me but genetics is an abstruse subject. I've got my A-levels and they have to take priority.'

'You're interested in this sort of thing?'

'I've been offered a place in medical school, St Biddulph's.' Crocker had trained there, Wexford recalled. 'I shall get it, of course, but in theory it depends on my A-level results.' Her tone was such as to show she was in no real doubt that these would meet the standard. 'I have to get at least three Bs but an A and two Bs would be better.'

She must be a bright girl. A year or two back statistics had been published showing an excess of medical students and that at this rate there would be a surplus of forty thousand doctors by the end of the century. Medical schools were being instructed to raise their standards and cut their intake. So if Sara Williams had been offered a place at the highly prestigious St Biddulph's . . .

'Your mother and father must be proud of you.'

The sweeping glance she gave him told him he had said something stupid or at least wide of the mark.

'I can see you don't know my parents.'

'They'd prefer something else for you?'

'I could be a shorthand typist, couldn't I? I could be a nurse. I'd get paid while I was being those things, wouldn't I?' Her voice was full of scorn and anger. 'I can't be stopped, though. I'll get a grant anyway. I don't know what I'd have done in olden times.'

By 'olden times' he supposed she meant the days of his own youth when your parents paid for your education or you borrowed the money or worked your way. Things were different now. A father couldn't put his foot down with the same effect. He could only persuade or dissuade.

'The last time you saw your father,' he reminded her.

Her anger had died. She was practical again, crisply reciting facts. But there was something derisive in the way she spoke of her father, as if he were a joke to her – or an organism under a microscope.

'I came in and he was just leaving. I heard him talking to Mum about the route he was going to take. The A26 for Tonbridge, then the Dartford Tunnel on to the M25 and the M25 to the A12 which would take him to Ipswich.'.

'Why was he telling her the route? Would she be interested? I mean, wasn't it the route he normally took?'

'I said you didn't know my father. I'd say for a start he wouldn't be much concerned about the other person's *interest*. Dad talks a lot about cars and driving, roads, that sort of thing. I'm not interested but he talks to me about it. The car's a person to him, a woman, and she's got a Christian name. He calls her Greta. Greta, the Granada, you see.'

'So your father left and your mother went to Pomfret and you stayed here on you own studying?'

Was he imagining that hesitation, that brief wary flare in her eyes?

'That's right. I don't go out in the evenings at the moment. I haven't time.' She smiled again, this time with great artificiality. 'I heard they'd found his car.'

'In the process of being dismembered for its wheels and its radio.'

'Cannibalized,' she said, and she laughed the way her mother did. 'Poor old Greta.'

236

Could he have a look round the rest of the house? Notably through William's papers and clothes? Joy put up no objection. The television clack-clacked through the floor and the pop music thumped and droned through the wall. In the book of rules of human behaviour he kept in his head one of the first laws was the one about who got which bedroom. The British middle class mostly lived in three-bedroomed houses, one big bedroom, one slightly smaller, one little. In a family of parents, son and daughter, the daughter invariably got the second bedroom and the son the tiny one, irrespective of seniority. It was one aspect of life (the women's movement might have said if they'd noticed it) in which the female had the advantage over the male. Presumably it came about because girls from the first were conditioned into being more at home, more centred on home things and being confined within walls. In which case the women's movement wouldn't like it so much. But it was the girl in this household who had the smallest bedroom, even though her brother was now away most of the time. Of course, it might be that she had chosen this arrangement, but somehow he didn't think so.

He opened the door of the second bedroom and looked inside. There was a newish pine bedroom suite, two bright Afghan rugs, a fringed bedcover that was recognizably one of Marks and Spencer's designs. It looked as if someone with not much taste or money had done her best to make a 'nice' room of it and the sole personal touch its occupant had contributed was to hang a map of the world on the wall opposite the bed.

The main bedroom was like his own in size and proportions. The walls were even painted in the same colour as his own, Sevenstar emulsion Orange Blossom. There the resemblance ended. The Williamses slept in twin beds, each narrower than the standard three feet, he thought. He could tell hers was the one nearest the window by the nightdress case on it, quilted peach satin in the shape of a scallop shell. The rest of the furniture consisted of a wardrobe, dressing table, dressing-table stool, chest of drawers and two bedside tables all in some dark reddish wood with a matt finish and with rather bright gold chrome handles. There was also a built-in cupboard.

237

Wexford looked first in the drawer of the bedside cabinet between Williams's bed and the door. He found a box that had once held cufflinks but was now empty, a comb, a tube of antiseptic skin cream, an unused toothbrush, a packet of tissues, a tube of throat pastilles, two safety pins, several plastic collar stiffeners, a half-full bottle of nasal drops and an empty pill bottle labelled 'Mandaret. One to be taken twice daily. Rodney Williams'.

In the cupboard part of the cabinet were two paperback novels of espionage, an unused writing pad, a current British passport in the name of Mr R. J. Williams, a clean handkerchief initialled 'R' and two electric shavers.

The wardrobe contained Joy's clothes, a collection that had an unwashed, unclean smell about it with a whiff of camphor and some kind of disinfectant. Rodney Williams's clothes were in the cupboard. An overcoat, a sheepskin jacket, a plastic mac, two hip-length showerproof jackets, a shabby sports jacket and a new one, four suits, two pairs of slacks. All the clothes were good, all of much better quality than Joy's. Not a large wardrobe, Wexford thought, looking into the linings of coats and feeling in pockets. In the side compartments were underwear, pyjamas, on the floor three pairs of shoes and a pair of sandals. Whatever Rodney Williams had spent his surplus money on it wasn't clothes. Unless he had taken more with him than Joy or Sara knew. Maybe he had secreted a couple of bulging suitcases in Greta's boot during the course of the day.

The dining room, you could see, they hardly ever used. A light-coloured polished table stood in the dead centre of it with four light-coloured wood chairs with moquette seats around it. A sideboard with an empty Capo di Monte bowl on it nearly filled one wall and opposite this was a mahogany roll-top desk, perhaps a hand-down from a parent and certainly the nicest piece of furniture in the house. French windows, at which hung curtains of mustard-coloured rep – a favourite shade with Joy Williams – gave onto the back garden, a quarter acre of grass surrounded by close-board fencing and relieved by two small apple trees on which the blossom glimmered palely in the dusk. It didn't look as if the grass, several inches long now, had been mown since Williams did it five weeks before.

The desk wasn't locked. Wexford rolled back the top. There wasn't much inside. Writing paper, not the headed kind, envelopes, a bottle of ink in a cardboard box from which it had never been removed and never would be, a box of drawing pins, a glass jar of gum, a roll of Scotch tape. In one of the drawers was nothing but old Christmas cards, in the other a receipted electricity bill, a pocket calculator and a broken ballpoint pen.

If Williams had meant to go away for good wouldn't he have taken his passport?

He looked through the pigeonholes but found no cheque books, used or in use. Joy probably kept hers in her handbag. He went back to her. She was still watching television and now the programme was the everlasting serial *Runway* in which his daughter Sheila played the stewardess heroine. Had, in fact, played her for the last time the previous week. But this was a secret known to no one but her own family as yet. No newspaper had so far got hold of the story that a major air disaster would in the autumn end the career of Stewardess Charlotte Riley for ever.

Joy Williams didn't know it. If she knew Sheila was his daughter – and surely she must – she gave no sign. He had the curious experience of standing beside her while they both watched his daughter attempting to placate an ill-tempered passenger. Then he did what Crocker recommended – or nearly so. If he didn't go so far as to pull out the plug he did switch off the set. She blinked at him.

'Does your husband possess a typewriter, Mrs Williams?'

'A typewriter? No.'

'Is he still taking Mandaret?'

She nodded, looking at the blank screen as if she expected it spontaneously and without benefit of electricity to spring into cinematic life.

'It's a form of methyldopa, isn't it? A drug for high blood pressure?'

'He's had blood pressure for two or three years.'

'I found an empty Mandaret container in his bedside cupboard. I suppose he took a supply with him?'

'He wouldn't forget them. He didn't like to miss a day on them. He always took one when he got up and one with his tea.'

'I take it he had a bag with him? A suitcase? Something to put his clothes in?'

Again she simply nodded.

'What was he dressed in?'

'Pardon?'

'What clothes was he wearing when he left here to drive to Ipswich?'

It was plain she couldn't remember. She looked blank – and she looked bored. Wexford understood in that moment that she didn't love Rodney Williams, hadn't perhaps loved him for years. His presence or absence as a life companion were matters of indifference to her but his financial support and the status he gave her were not. Or were her feelings more subtle and diffuse than that? Of course they were. Feelings always are. There is never a simple clear analysis of a woman's reaction to her husband or his to her.

He pressed the point he had made.

'Sort of fawn trousers,' she said, screwing up her face with the effort of it. 'Cavalry twill, they're called. A dark blue pullover. Is his raincoat upstairs?'

'A plastic mac?'

'No, he's got a good raincoat. It's nearly new. He must have taken that. I expect he had a jacket in his bag too. He's got a brown suede one.'

'Did he like a wet or dry shave?'

'Pardon?'

'Did he use a razor with shaving cream and water?'

'Oh, yes. He couldn't get on with those electrics. He'd tried but he couldn't get on with them.'

And that accounted for the Remington and the Phillips upstairs. She was staring miserably at the blank, grey, shiny screen. Wexford felt it was cruel to deprive her of her solace, like keeping a dumb hungry dog from its plate of Kennomeat. He asked her for her sister's name and address and then he switched the television on again. She looked at him as if she thought him completely mad but she said nothing and her eyes were compelled back to the screen and to Sheila, dressing now in a hotel bedroom for an evening out with the Boeing 747 captain in Hong Kong.

Wexford walked home, thinking about Williams and money. What had he done with all that money? Even after tax and other deductions, after the stingy allotment to his household of £500 a month, he would have been left with at least £12,000 a year. He'd had a company car. It didn't go on cars. The passport, which was seven years old, showed a single visit to Majorca. It didn't go on foreign holidays. Of course, he had to keep his son Kevin at Keele and pay for his keep. He wouldn't get much of a grant on his salary . . .

And then, suddenly, Wexford understood what had been bugging him for the past hour. It had been a Thursday evening when Williams had left. Kevin Williams always phoned home of Thursday evenings. And that Thursday was certainly the first since he had returned to university after the Easter vacation. Yet his mother, who plainly adored him, who waited excitedly for his call and spoke proudly of his devotion to duty in regularly phoning at that time, had gone out on that particular Thursday evening and for no more pressing or life-enhancing appointment than a visit to her sister.

If she had visited her sister.

And how about his clothes? Was she lying when she said he had taken only a jacket and a raincoat with him? Or didn't she know? Somehow he couldn't imagine Williams leaving his car in Arnold Road and then humping huge bulging suitcases the quarter of a mile to Myringham station. Why go to Myringham anyway when, if he wanted to catch a train to London, Kingsmarkham station was eight miles nearer?

The following week the clothes, or some to them, turned up.

5

A lonely country road links Kingsmarkham with Pomfret. Once Forest Road, Kingsmarkham, is past, the only houses to be seen are those few up on the hillsides crowned by Cheriton Forest. The forest is always rather dark and forbidding as coniferous forests are. On the horizon stands an obelisk, a needle of stone, placed there by some local magnate a hundred and fifty years ago.

Almost the last building in Kingsmarkham is the police station. On the other side of the High Street Cheriton Lane runs down to the buildings and courts of the Kingsmarkham Tennis Club, and half a dozen other narrow roads compose a small residential web. The gardens of houses in Forest Road back onto open fields, and fields traversed by a footpath lie between the club grounds and the town. The street lamps stop two hundred yards on the Pomfret side of the police station and after that there is an isolated one to light the bus stop.

Roughly halfway between the towns, at the point of no return, is the bus stop with bus shelter. The shelter was out there because there are no trees at this point to break the wind or provide cover from the rain. And on this night it was raining as it had been for many nights. The fine rain swept across the meadows in grey sheets.

The last bus from Pomfret to Kingsmarkham was due at 10.40. It came ten minutes late, rolling along not too fast through the rain, sending up fountains of spray onto the grass verges. The stop where the bus shelter was was a compulsory one, not a request, so the bus pulled in to make a token stop and prepared to pull out again, for there was no one waiting. A shout from a woman passenger sitting in a front nearside seat alerted the driver. He had already taken off the brake but he put it on again and the bus juddered to a halt.

'There's a person crawling on the pavement!'

Here, where the shelter was, the lay-by was bordered by a few yards of pavement. The driver got down. Two or three of the passengers, disobeying the driver – who was he to tell them? – got down. There was no conductor on those single deckers. The rain was coming down in torrents, needles of it pounding the surface of the lay-by, the kerb, and the sodden bundle that crawled and whimpered with blood coming from its chest.

At first the conductor thought it a wounded dog. But the passenger was right, it was a man. It crawled up to the conductor and rolled over at his feet.

Next day, on the other side of Kingsmarkham, the Forby side, a firm called Mid-Sussex Waterways began dragging a pond. Green Pond Hall had stood empty for years but at the end of the previous January a buyer had been found for it and the purchase was completed by April. The grounds contained a pond and a stream and the new owner intended to turn the estate into a trout farm.

If the proper definition of a lake is a sheet of water covering the minimum of one acre, Green Pond was just too small to fit the requirement. But as a pond it was very large. It wasn't stagnant, for the small fast stream flowed through the middle of it, disappearing into a pipe which passed under a path and gushing out through a spout on the other side to fall away down to the Kingsbrook. In spite of this the pond was shallow and coated with the thick green slime of blanket weed. The purpose of the dragging was to clean it, increase its depth and rid the water of the algae Mid-Sussex Waterways believed might be caused by an influx of the nitrates which had been applied as fertilizer to the nearby meadows.

In the net, after the dragging, were found a wire supermarket basket minus its handle, a quantity of glass bottles, jars and light bulbs, the silencer part of a car exhaust system, wood in the form of twigs and chopped lengths, stones among which were flints and chalk pebbles, a rubber boot, a Pyrex casserole dish, chipped and cracked, a metal door handle and lock, a pair of scissors and a dark burgundy-coloured travelling bag.

The bag was coated with green slime and thin, fine-grained black mud, but when the clasps were undone and the zip unfastened it was seen that only water had penetrated the seams of the bag, soaking but hardly discolouring the clothes inside, the topmost of which was a brown suede blouson.

It was a piece of luck, Wexford thought, that William Milvey, the boss of Mid-Sussex Waterways, had found money inside the bag, £50 in fivers rolled up and fastened with a rubber band. If it had contained nothing but clothes, and damaged clothes at that, it was probable he would have tossed it into the pit which had been dug out by a mechanical digger for the purpose of receiving the rubbish caught in the dragnet. Money, Wexford had often noticed, has this kind of electric effect on people. Many a man who thinks himself honest, on finding an object bought with money will keep the object but not the money itself. It is as if the adage 'Finders keepers' applies to things but never to money, which has its own aura of sacredness, of being absolutely the preserve of him who has earned it.

But even so, Wexford might never have heard of the existence of the bag were it not for a kidney donor card which was in the breast pocket of the blouson and which was signed R. J. Williams.

William Milvey knew who R. J. Williams was. He lived next door but one to him in Alverbury Road.

This fact it took Wexford some half-hour to find out. He questioned Milvey thoroughly about the bag. Had he seen it in the pond before he saw it in the net? Well, yes, he thought he had, now Wexford came to mention it. He fancied he had. At any rate he thought he could remember seeing a brownish-red lump of something up against the bank of the pond nearest to the path and the Kingsbrook. No, he hadn't touched it or attempted to pull it out. The dragnet had pulled it out.

Milvey was a shortish thick-set man with the heavy build

and big spread hands of someone who has done manual work for most of his life. He looked about fifty. The discovery of the bag seemed disproportionately to have excited him – or his excitement appeared disproportionate to Wexford at first.

'Fifty quid in it,' he kept saying, 'and that good jacket.'

'Did you see anyone about the grounds of Green Pond Hall?'

'Some fella up to no good, d'you mean?'

'I meant anyone at all.'

'We didn't have sight nor sound of no one.'

There might have been marks of car tyres on the drive in from the Forby Road or on the track that ran around the lower bank of the pond, the constant rain had turned these surfaces to mud, but any tracks there were had been obliterated by the heavy tyres of Mid-Sussex Waterways' mechanical digger.

Milvey simply couldn't remember if there had been any tyremarks on the track. They had the other man in and asked him, but he couldn't remember either.

'Fifty quid,' said Milvey, 'and that good jacket. Just chucked away.'

'Let me have your address, will you, Mr Milvey? I'll very likely want to talk to you again. Home or business?'

'They're one and the same. I operate from home, don't I?' He said this as if it were a fact he would have expected Wexford to know, and adding his address, used the same patient, mildly surprised tone. 'Twenty-seven Alverbury Road, Kingsmarkham.'

'Are you telling me you live next door but one to Mr Williams?'

Milvey's expression, though bland and innocent, had become a little uncomfortable. 'I reckoned you knew.'

'No, I didn't know.' Vaguely now Wexford recalled reading a planning application made to the local authority for permission to erect a garage – more a hangar really – large enough to house a JCB in the garden of 27 Alverbury Road. The area being strictly residential, the application had naturally been rejected. 'You must know Mr Williams then?'

'Pass the time of day,' said Milvey. 'The wife has a chat with Mrs Williams. My girl's in the same class at school with their Sara.'

245

'Mr Williams is missing,' said Wexford flatly. 'He's been missing from home for the past month or more.'

'Is that right?' Milvey didn't look surprised but he didn't say he knew either. 'Fifty quid in notes,' he said, 'and a jacket worth three times that.'

Wexford let him go.

'It has to be coincidence,' Burden said.

'Does it, Mike? It would be a hell of a coincidence, wouldn't it? Williams disappears because he's done something or someone's done something to him. His overnight bag is dumped in a pond and who should find it but the guy who lives two doors down the street from him? I haven't read any John Buchan for – well, it must be forty-five years. But I can remember in one of his books the hero's car breaks down and the house he calls at for help just happens to be the home of the master anarchist. A bit later on the hit man who's sent to get him turns out to be a burglar he's recently successfully defended in court. Now that's fiction and strictly for persons below fifteen, I'd say. But this that you call coincidence is comparable to those. Have you had any coincidences of that magnitude in your life?'

'Both my grandmothers were called Mary Brown.'

'Were they really?' Wexford was temporarily distracted. 'You never told me that before. And did they come from the same part of the country?'

'One from Sussex and one from Hertfordshire. I bet you the odds against that happening are a lot longer than against Milvey finding Williams's bag. You look at it and you'll see it's not that much of a coincidence. If it had been buried, say, or stuck in a hollow tree and Milvey had found it, that would be something else. But it was in a pond and Milvey's in the pond-dragging business. Once it got in the pond and the pond was due to be dragged – which whoever put it there wouldn't know, of course – the chances would be that Milvey *would* find it. You want to look at it like that.'

Wexford knew there was more to it than that; he couldn't dismiss it in the easy way Burden did. Milvey's behaviour had been a shade odd anyway and Wexford was sure he hadn't told all he knew.

'How long do you think the bag's been in the pond?'

It was on the floor between them, deposited on sheets of

newspaper, its contents, which Wexford had already examined, now replaced.

'Since the night he went, I suppose, or the next day.'

Wexford didn't go along with that either but he let it pass for the time being. As well as the brown suede blouson there was a raincoat in the bag, a trendy version of a Burberry, the fifty pounds, a toothbrush, tube of toothpaste and disposable razor wrapped up in a pair of underpants, a bottle of Monsieur Rochas cologne and a pair of brand-new socks with the label still on them. The underpants were a young man's Homs, pale blue and white, the socks dark brown, an expensive brand made of silk.

It was the kind of packing a man would do for an overnight stay somewhere, not for three nights, and the pants and socks and cologne seemed to indicate a night not spent alone. Or had there been more articles in the bag which had been removed? This could surely only have been done to prevent identification of the bag's owner. In that case why leave the donor card in the blouson pocket? 'I would like to help someone to live after my death', it stated somewhat naively in scarlet and white, and on the reverse side Rodney Williams had requested that in the event of his death any part of his body which might be required should be used in the treatment of others. Underneath this was his signature and the date a year past. The next of kin to contact was given, as might have been expected, as Joy Williams with the Alverbury Road phone number.

Men's natures were a mass of contradictions, there was no consistency, and yet Wexford marvelled a little that a husband and father could deliberately and ruthlessly deceive his wife over his income and pursue a course of skinflint meanness to her and his children yet want to donate his body for transplants. It would cost him nothing though, he would be dead after all. Was he dead?

'We're going to have to start looking for him. I mean really looking. Search the grounds of Green Pond Hall for a start.'

Burden had been pacing the office. He had taken to doing this lately and his restless pacing had a stressful effect on anyone he happened to be with, though he himself hardly seemed aware of what was going on. Twice he had been to the window, twice back to the door, pausing once to perch briefly on the edge of the desk. Now he had reached the window again where he stopped, turned and stared at Wexford in irritable incredulity.

'Search for *him*? Surely it's plain he's simply done a bunk to escape the consequences of whatever it is he's done.'

'All right, Mike. Maybe. But in that case what *has* he done? Nothing at Sevensmith Harding. He's as clean as a whistle there. What else could he have done? It's just possible he could be involved in some fraud that hasn't yet come to light but there's a strong case against that one. He got out. The only reason for that would be that discovery of the fraud was imminent. In that case why hasn't that discovery been made?'

Burden shrugged. 'Who knows? But it may just be a piece of luck for Williams that it hasn't been.'

'Why hasn't he come back then? If the outcome of this fraud has blown over why doesn't he come home? He hasn't left the country unless he's gone on a false passport. And why bother with a false passport when he'd got one of his own and no one started missing him till three days after he'd gone?'

'Doesn't it occur to you that leaving one's clothes on the river bank is the oldest disappearing trick in the world?'

'On the beach, I think you mean, not on the shores of a pond where the water's so shallow that to commit suicide you'd have to lie on your face and hold your breath. Besides, that bag has been in the pond only a couple of days at most. If it had been there since Williams went it'd be rotting by now, it'd stink. We'll sent it over to the lab and see what they say but we can see what they'll say with our own eyes and smell it with our own noses.'

'Williams is dead. This bag of his tells me he is. If he had put it into the pond for the purpose of making us think he was dead he'd have done so immediately after he left. And the contents would have been different. More identification, for instance, no scent and powder blue knickers. And I don't think the money would have been in it. He would have needed that money, he would have needed all the money he could lay his hands on. There's no reason to think he could easily spare fifty pounds – whatever he's done he hasn't robbed a bank.'

'He's dead and, letter and phone call notwithstanding, he was dead within an hour or two of when his family last saw him.'

Next day the searching of Green Pond Hall grounds began. The grounds comprised eight acres, part woodland, part decayed overgrown formal gardens, part stables and paddock. Sergeant Martin led the search with three men and Wexford himself went down there to have a look at the dragged pond and view the terrain. It was still raining. It had been raining yesterday and the day before and for part of every day for three weeks. The weather people were saying it would be the wettest May since records began. The track was a morass, the colour and texture of melted chocolate into which a giant fork had furrowed. There were other ways of getting down to the pond but only if you went on foot.

At three he had a date at Stowerton Royal Infirmary. Colin Budd had been placed in intensive care but only for the night. By morning he was sufficiently recovered to be transferred to a side room off the men's surgical ward. The stab wounds he had received were more than superficial, one having penetrated to a depth of three inches, but by a miracle almost none of the five had endangered heart or lungs.

A thick white dressing covered his upper chest, over which a stripped pyjama jacket had been loosely wrapped. The pyjama jacket was an extra large and Wexford estimated Budd's chest measurement at thirty-four inches. He was a very thin, bony, almost cadaverous young man, white-faced and with black, longish hair. He seemed to know exactly what Wexford would want to know about him and quickly and nervously repeated his name and age, gave his occupation as motor mechanic and his address a Kingsmarkham one where he lived with his parents.

'Tell me what happened.'

'This girl stuck a knife in my chest.'

'Now, Mr Budd, you know better than that. I want a detailed account, everything you can remember, starting with what you were doing waiting for a bus in the middle of nowhere.'

Budd had a querulous voice that always sounded mildly

249

indignant. He was one of those who believes the world owes him elaborate considerations as well as a living.

'That's got nothing to do with it,' he said.

'I'll be the judge of that. I don't suppose you were doing anything to be ashamed of. And if you were what you tell me will be between you and me.'

'I don't know what you're getting at!'

'Just tell me where you'd been last evening, Mr Budd.'

'I was at snooker,' Budd said sullenly.

What a fool! He'd made it sound at least as if he was having it away with a friend's wife in one of the isolated cottages on the hillside.

'A snooker club?'

'It's on Tuesday evenings. In Pomfret, a room at the back of the White Horse. It's over at ten and I reckoned on walking home.' Budd shifted his body, wincing a bit, pulling himself up in the bed. 'But the rain started coming down harder, I was getting soaked. I looked at my watch and saw the ten-forty bus'd be along in ten minutes and I was nearly at the stop by then.'

'I'd have expected a motor mechanic to have his own transport.'

'My car was in a crunch-up. It's in dock having a new wing. I wasn't doing no more than twenty-five when this woman came out of a side turning . . .'

Wexford cut that one short. 'So you reached the bus stop, the bus shelter. What happened?'

Budd looked at him and away. 'There was this girl already there, sitting on the seat. I sat down next to her.'

The bus shelter was well known to Wexford. It was about ten feet long, the seat or bench inside two feet shorter.

'Next to her?' he asked. 'Or at the other end of the seat?'

'Next to her. Does it matter?'

Wexford thought perhaps it did. In England at any rate, for good or ill, for the improving of social life or its worsening, a man of honourable intent who goes to sit on a public bench where a woman is already sitting will do so as far away from her as possible. A woman will probably do this too if a woman or man is already sitting there, and a man will do it if another man is there.

'Did you know her? Had you ever seen her before?'

250

Budd shook his head.

'You spoke to her?'

'Only to say it was raining.'

She knew that already, Wexford thought. He looked hard at Budd. Budd said, 'I said it was a pity we were having such a bad May, it made the winter longer, something like that. She pulled a knife out of her bag and lunged it at me.'

'Just like that? You didn't say anything else to her?'

'I've told you what I said.'

'She was mad, was she? A girl who stabs men because they tell her it's raining?'

'All I said was that normally at this time I'd have had my vehicle and I could have given her a lift.'

'In other words, you were trying to pick her up?'

'All right, what if I was? I didn't touch her. I didn't do anything to frighten her. That was all I said, that I could have given her a lift home. She pulled out this knife and stabbed at me four or five times and I cried out or screamed or something and she ran off.'

'Would you know her again?'

'You bet I would.'

'Describe her to me.'

Budd made the mess of that Wexford thought he would. He didn't know whether she was tall or short, plump or thin, because he only saw her sitting down and he thought she had a raincoat on. A thin raincoat that was a sort of pale colour. Her hair was fair, he did know that, though she had a hat on or a scarf. Bits of blonde hair showed under it. Her face was just an ordinary face, not what you'd call pretty. Wexford began to wonder what had attracted Budd to her in the first place. The mere facts that she was female and young? About twenty, said Budd. Well, maybe twenty-five or six. Pressed to be more precise, he said she could have been any age between eighteen and thirty, he wasn't good on ages, she was quite young though.

'Can you think of anything else about her?'

A nurse had come in and was hovering. Wexford knew what she was about to say, he could have written the script for her — 'Now I think that's quite enough. It's time for Mr Budd to have his rest . . .' She approached the bed, unhooked Budd's chart and began reading it with the enthusiastic concentration of a scholar who has just found the key to Linear B or some such.

'She had this sack with her. She grabbed it before she ran off.'

'What sort of sack?'

'The plastic kind they give you for your dustbin. A black one. She picked it up and stuck it over her shoulder and ran off.'

'I think that's quite enough for now,' said the nurse, diverging slightly from Wexford's text.

He got up. It was an extraordinary picture Budd's story had created and one which appealed to his imagination. The dark wet night, the knife flashing purposefully, even frenziedly, the girl running into the rain with a sack slung over her shoulder. It was like an illustration in a fairy book of Andrew Lang, elusive, sinister and other-worldly.

6

What had Burden meant when he said this amniocentesis had discovered something to worry Jenny? Wexford found himself brooding on that. Once or twice he had woken in the night and the question had come into his mind. Sitting in the car, being driven to Myringham, he saw a woman on the pavement with a Down's Syndrome child and the question was back, presenting itself again.

He hadn't liked to pursue it with Burden. This wasn't the sort of thing you asked a prospective father about. What small defect was there a father wouldn't mind about but a mother would? It was grotesque, ridiculous, there was nothing. Any defect would be a tragedy. His mind ranged over partial deafness, a heart murmur, palate or lip deformities — the test couldn't have shown those anyway. An extra chromosome? This was an area where he found himself floundering in ignorance. He thought of his own children, perfect, always healthy, giving him no trouble really, and his heart warmed towards his girls.

This reminded him that he had the National Theatre's programme brochure for the summer season in his pocket. Sheila was with the company and this would be the first season she had top lead roles. Hence the disengagement from further work on *Runway*. He got out the programme and looked at it. Dora had asked him to decide which days they should go to London and see the three productions Sheila was in. For obvious reasons it always had to be he who made those kind of decisions.

The new Stoppard, Ibsen's *Little Eyolf*, Shelley's *The Cenci*. Wexford had heard of *Little Eyolf* but he had never

253

seen it or read it, and as for *The Cenci*, he had to confess to himself that he hadn't known Shelley had written any plays. But there it was: 'Percy Bysshe Shelley' and the piece described as a tragedy in five acts. Wexford was making tentative marks on the programme for a Friday in July and two Saturdays in August when Donaldson, his driver, drew into the kerb outside Sevensmith Harding.

Miles Gardner had been watching for him and came rushing out with an umbrella. It made Wexford feel like royalty. They splashed across the pavement to the mahogany doors.

Kenneth Risby, the chief accountant, told him Rodney Williams's salary had been paid into the account Williams had with the Pomfret branch of the Anglian-Victoria Bank. From that account then, it would seem, Williams had each month transferred £500 into the joint account he had with Joy. Risby had been with the company for fifteen years and said he could recall no other arrangement being made for Williams, either recently or in the days when he was a sales rep. His salary had always gone to the Pomfret bank, never to Kingsmarkham.

'We've heard nothing,' Miles Gardner said. 'Whatever he meant by the PS to that letter he hasn't been in touch.'

'Williams didn't write that letter,' Wexford reminded him.

Gardner nodded unhappily.

'The first time we talked about this business,' Wexford said, 'you told me someone phoned here saying she was Mrs Williams and that her husband was ill and wouldn't be coming in. Would that have been on Friday, April the sixteenth?'

'Well, yes, I suppose it would.'

'Who took the call?'

'It must have been one of our telephonists. They're part-timers. I can't remember whether it was Anna or Michelle. The phone call came before I got in, you see. That is, before nine-thirty.'

'Williams had a secretary, I suppose?'

'Christine Lomond. He shared her with our assistant sales director. Would you like to talk to her?'

'Not yet. Maybe not today. It's Anna or Michelle I want. But which one do I want?'

'Michelle, I expect,' said Gardner. 'They tend to swop shifts a bit but it's usually Michelle on mornings.'

It had been, that Friday, and it was today. Michelle was a very young, very pretty girl with a vividly made-up face. The room where the switchboard was, not much more than a cupboard, was stamped with her personality (or perhaps Anna's) and there was a blue cineraria in a pot, a stack of magazines, a pile of knitting that had reached the bulky stage, and on the table in front of her, hurriedly placed face downwards, the latest diet paperback.

It was clear that Michelle had already discussed that phone call exhaustively. Perhaps with Anna or with Christine Lomond. Williams's disappearance would have been the talk of the office.

'I get in at nine,' she said. 'That's when the phone calls really start. But the funny thing was there weren't any that morning till Mrs Williams phoned at about twenty past.'

'You mean till someone phoned who *called* herself Mrs Williams.'

The girl looked at him. She shook her head quite vehemently. 'It was Mrs Williams. She said, "This is Joy Williams."'

Wexford let it go for the time being.

'What exactly did she say?'

' "My husband Mr Williams won't be coming in today.' And then she sort of hesitated and said, "That's Mr Rodney Williams, I mean, the marketing manager." I said there was no one else in yet and she said that didn't matter but to give Christine the message he'd got flu and wouldn't be in.'

Whoever it was, it hadn't been Joy. At that time Joy didn't know her husband was Sevensmith Harding's marketing manager. Wexford had thanked Michelle and was turning away, diverting his mind to the matter of the firm's stock of typewriters, when he stopped.

'What makes you so sure the woman you spoke to was Mrs Joy Williams?'

'It just was. I know it was.'

'No, let me correct that. You know it was a woman who *said* she was Mrs Joy Williams. She had never phoned here before, had she, so you couldn't have recognized her voice?'

'No, but she phoned here afterwards.'

'What do you mean, afterwards?'

'About three weeks later.' The girl spoke with exaggerated patience now, as if to a very confused or simple minded person. 'Mrs Joy Williams phoned here three weeks after her husband left.'

Of course. Wexford remembered that call. It was he who had advised Joy to make it.

'I put her through to Mr Gardner,' Michelle said. 'I was a bit embarrassed, to be perfectly honest. But I know it was the same voice, really I do. It was the same voice as the woman who phoned that Friday morning, it was Mrs Williams.'

He picked up the girl at the roundabout where the second exit is the start of the Kingsmarkham bypass. She was standing on the grass verge at the side of the roundabout, holding up a piece of cardboard with 'Myringham' printed on it. Brian Wheatley pulled in to the first exit, the Kingsmarkham town-centre road, and the girl got into the passenger seat. Then, for some unclear reason, perhaps because he had already pulled out of the roundabout and it would not have been easy to get back into the traffic, Wheatley decided to continue through the town instead of on the bypass. This wasn't such a bad idea anyway, the anomaly being that the bypass which had been built to ease the passage of traffic past the town was often more crowded than the old route.

Wheatley was driving home from London where he worked three days a week. It was about six in the evening and of course broad daylight. He had moved to Myringham only two weeks before and was still unfamiliar with the byways and back-doubles of the area. The girl didn't speak a word. She had no baggage with her, only a handbag with a shoulder strap. Wheatley drove through Kingsmarkham, along the High Street, and became confused by the sign-posting. Instead of keeping straight on he began to think he should have taken a left-hand turn some half a mile back. He therefore – on what he admitted was a lonely and secluded stretch of road – pulled into a lay-by and consulted his road map.

His intention to do this, he said, he announced plainly to

256

the girl. After he had stopped and switched off the engine he was obliged to reach obliquely across her in order to open the glove compartment where the map was. He was aware of the girl giving a gasp of fright or anger, and then of a sharp pain, more like a burn than a cut, in his right hand.

He never even saw the knife. The girl jumped out of the car, slamming the door behind her, and ran not along the road but onto a footpath that separated a field of wheat from a wood. Blood was flowing from a deep cut in the base of Wheatley's thumb. He tied up his hand as best he could with his handkerchief but shock and a feeling of faintness made it impossible for him to continue his journey for some minutes. Eventually he looked at his map, found himself nearer home than he had thought, and was able to drive there in about a quarter of an hour. The general practitioner with whom he had registered the week before was still holding his surgery. Wheatley's wife drove him there and the cut in his hand was stitched, Wheatley telling the doctor he had been carving meat and had inadvertently pressed his hand against the point of the carving knife. Whether or not the doctor believed this was another matter. At any rate he had made no particular comment. Wheatley himself had wanted to tell the truth, though this would have meant police involvement. It was his wife who had dissuaded him on the grounds that if the police were called the conclusion they would reach would be that Wheatley had first made some sort of assault on the girl.

This was the story Wheatley told Wexford three days later. His wife didn't know he had changed his mind. He had come to the police, he said, because he felt more and more indignant that this girl, whom he hadn't touched, whom he had scarcely spoken to except to say he was going to stop and look at his map, should make an unprovoked attack on him and get away with it.

'Can you describe her?'

Wexford waited resignedly for the kind of useless description furnished by Colin Budd. He was surprised. In many ways Wheatley did not seem to know his way around but he was observant and perceptive.

'She was tall for a woman, about five feet eight or nine. Young, eighteen or nineteen. Brown hair or lightish hair, shoulder-length, sunglasses though it wasn't sunny, fair skin – I noticed she had very white hands. Jeans and a blouse, I think, and a cardigan. The bag was some dark colour, black or navy blue.'

'Did she give you the impression she lived in Myringham? That she was going home?'

'She didn't give me any sort of impression. When she got into the car she said thanks – just the one word "thanks", otherwise she didn't speak. I said to her that I thought I'd drive through the town instead of the bypass and she didn't answer. Later on I said I'd stop and look at the map and she didn't answer that either, but when I reached across her – I didn't touch her, I could swear to that – she gave a sort of gasp. Those were the only sounds she made, "thanks" and a gasp.'

The same girl as attacked Budd, one would suppose. But if Wheatley were to be believed, while there was some very slight justification for the attack on Budd, there was none for this second stabbing. Could the girl possibly have thought that the hand which reached across to open the glove compartment intended instead to take hold of her by the left shoulder? Or lower itself onto her knee? There was something ridiculous about these assaults, and yet two meant that they were not ridiculous at all but serious. Next time there could be a fatality.

Or had there been one already?

The manager of the Pomfret branch of the Anglian-Victoria Bank bore an extraordinary resemblance to Adolf Hitler. This was not only in the small square moustache and the lock of dark hair half covering Mr Skinner's forehead. The face was the same face, rather handsome, with large chin and heavy nose and small thick-lidded eyes. But all that would have passed unnoticed without the moustache and the lock of hair, so that it was impossible to avoid the uncomfortable conclusion that Mr Skinner was doing it on purpose. He knew whom he looked like and enhanced the resemblance. Wexford could only attribute one motive to a bank manager who wants to look like Hitler – a desire to intimidate his clients.

258

His manner, however, was warm, friendly and charming. All those, and implacable too. He could not consider either letting Wexford look into Rodney Williams's bank accounts or disclose any information about their contents.

'Did you say accounts plural?' said Wexford.

'Yes. Mr Williams has two current accounts here – and now I've probably said more than I should.'

'Two current accounts in the name of Rodney Williams?'

Skinner was standing up with his head slightly on one side, looking like Hitler waiting for Franco's train at Hendaye. 'I said two current accounts, Chief Inspector. We'll let it go at that, shall we?'

One for his salary to be paid into, Wexford thought as he was driven away, and the other for what? His Kingsmarkham household expenses were drawn from the Kingsmarkham account which he fed with £500 a month from Pomfret account A. Then what of account B?His wife didn't know of the existence of account A anyway. It alone was sufficient to keep his resources secret from her. Why did he need a third current bank account?

They were searching for him now on the open land, partly wooded, that lay between Kingsmarkham and Forby. But so far, since the discovery of the bag in Green Pond, nothing further had come to light. He's dead, Wexford thought, he must be.

Burden had been at Pomfret, talking to the Harmer family, Joy Williams's sister, brother-in-law and niece. John Harmer was a pharmacist with a chemist's shop in the High Street.

'They say Joy was with them that evening,' Burden said, 'but I wouldn't put that much credence on what they say. Not that they're intentionally lying – they can't remember. It was seven weeks ago. Besides, Joy often goes over there in the evenings. More or less to sit in front of their television instead of her own, I gather. But I suppose she's lonely, she wants company. Mrs Harmer says she was definitely there that evening, Harmer says it must be if his wife says so and the girl doesn't know. You can't expect a teenage girl to take much notice of when her aunt comes.'

Wexford told him what he had learned from the telephonist at Sevensmith Harding. 'Of course, the girl may be mistaken about the voices or she may have persuaded herself they were the same voice in order to get more drama out of the situation. But it's more than possible that the woman who phoned Sevensmith Harding the day after Williams left to say he was ill and the woman who phoned three weeks later to inquire as to his whereabouts are one and the same. And we know the second time was Joy. Now Joy was very keen to have me look for her husband when he first disappeared, but later on much less so – indeed, she was obstructive. That first time I talked to her she said nothing about having gone out herself that evening. That was only mentioned the second time. Joy is devoted to her son Kevin. Her daughter is nothing to her, her son everything . . . What on earth's the matter?'

Burden's face had set and he had gone rather pale. He had taken a hard grip on the arms of his chair. 'Nothing. Go on.'

'Well, then – her son always phones on Thursday evenings and that particular Thursday was the first one he had been back at college. Wouldn't a devoted mother have wanted to know all those things mothers worry about in such circumstances? Did he have a good journey? Was his room all right? Had he settled in? But this devoted mother doesn't wait in for his call. She goes out – not to some important engagement, some function booked months ahead, but to watch television at her sister's. What does all this suggest to you?'

Having struggled successfully to overcome whatever it was that had upset him, Burden forced a laugh. 'You sound like Sherlock Holmes talking to Watson.' Since his second marriage he occasionally read books, a change in him Wexford couldn't get used to.

'No,' he said, 'more "a man of the solid Sussex breed – a breed which covers much good sense under a heavy silent exterior".'

'I wouldn't say "silent". Was that from Sherlock Holmes?'

Wexford nodded. 'So what do you make of it?' he said more colloquially.

'That Joy is somehow in cahoots with her husband. There's a conspiracy going on. What for and why I wouldn't pretend to know but it's got something to do with giving everyone the impression Williams is dead. He left that evening and she went out later to meet him away from the house. Whatever they were planning was done away from the house

260

because it had to be concealed from the daughter Sara as much as from anyone else. Next morning Joy rang Sevensmith Harding to say her husband was ill. Of course, it's nonsense to say she didn't know that he was their marketing manager and the extent of his income. Next he or she typed that letter on a *hired* typewriter. She probably did that, not knowing what he called Gardner and making the mistake of addressing him as 'Mr Gardner'. The abandoned car, the dumped bag of clothes were all part of a plan to make us think him dead. But the increased police attention frightened Joy, she wanted things to go more at her pace. Hence the obstructiveness. I said I didn't know why but it could be an insurance fiddle, couldn't it?'

'Without a body, Mike? With no more proof of death than a dumped travelling bag? And if you wanted people to think you were dead, aren't there half a dozen simpler and more convincing ways of doing it?'

'You feel the same as me then? You don't think he's dead?'

'I know he's dead,' said Wexford.

Next day he was proved right.

It looked like a grave. It was in the shape of a grave, as clearly demarcated as if a slab of stone lay upon it, though Edwin Fitzgerald did not at first see this. In spite of its shape he would have passed it by as a mere curiosity, a whim of nature. It was the dog Shep who drew his attention to it.

Edwin Fitzgerald was a retired policeman who had been a dog handler. He lived in Pomfret and had a job as a part-time security guard at a factory complex on Stowerton's industrial estate. The dog Shep was not a trained dog in the sense of being police-trained – as a 'sniffer', for instance. Fitzgerald had bought him after his last dog died – a wonderful dog that one, more intelligent than any human being, a dog that understood every word he said. Shep could only follow humbly in that dog's footsteps and was often the subject of unfavourable comparisons. He didn't understand every word Fitzgerald said, or at any rate behaved as if he didn't.

On this particular morning in June, a dry one, the first really fine morning of the summer, Shep disregarded all Fitzgerald's words, ignored the repeated 'Leave it, sir' and 'Do as you're told' and continued his frenetic digging in the corner of what his master saw as a patch of weeds. He dug like a dog possessed. Indeed, Fitzgerald informed him that he was a devil, that he didn't know what had got into him. He shouted (which a good dog handler should never do) and he shook his fist until he saw what Shep had unearthed and then he stopped.

The dog had dug up a foot.

Fitzgerald had been a policeman, which had the double advantage of having taught him not to be sickened by such a discovery and not to disturb anything in its vicinity. He attached Shep's lead to his collar and pulled the dog away. This took some doing as Shep was a big young German Shepherd intent on worrying at the protruding thing for some hours if possible.

As far as Fitzgerald could see, now he had got the dog clear, the foot was still attached to a limb and the limb probably to a trunk. It was inside a sodden, blackened, slimy shoe caked with mud, and about the ankle clung a bundling of muddy wet cloth, once the hem of a trouser leg. Shep had dug it out from one of the corners of this curious little plot of ground. All around, on this edge of the meadow, grew tall grass ready to be cut for hay, high enough to hide the dog when he plunged in among it, but the rectangle – seven feet by three? – which Shep had found in there and had dug into was covered closely and in a neat rather horticultural way with fresh green plants. Weeds they were, but weeds attractive enough to be called plants, red campion, clover, speedwell, and they covered the oblong patch as precisely as if they had been sown there in a seed bed.

The grass which surrounded it, gone to seed, bearing light feathery seed heads of brown and greyish-cream and silvery-gold, hid it from the sight of anyone who kept to the foot-path. It took a dog to plunge in there and find the grave. A day or two of sunshine, Fitzgerald thought, and the farmer would have cut the hay, cut those weeds too without a thought. Shep was a good dog after all, even if he didn't understand every word Fitzgerald said.

He retraced his steps to the branch of the lane that led to Myfleet and hurried down the hill to his bungalow where he phoned the police.

7

From the Pomfret road a narrow lane winds its way up into the hills and to the verge of the forest. All down the hedges here grows the wayfarer's tree with its flat creamy bracts of blossom, and beneath, edging the meadows like a fringe of lace, the whiter, finer, more delicate cow parsley. There are houses, Edwin Fitzgerald's among them, approached by paths, cart tracks or even smaller narrower lanes, but the lane gives the impression of leading directly to the obelisk on the hill.

It is like downland up here, the trees ceasing until the forest of conifers begins over there to the east, chalk showing in outcroppings and heather on the chalk. And all the way the obelisk looming larger, a needle of granite with its point a tetragon. The road never reaches it. A quarter of a mile this side it swerves, turns east and divides, one fork making for Myfleet, the other for Pomfret, and soon there are meadows again and the heath is past. It was in one of these meadows, close to the overhang of the forest, traversed by a footpath leading from the road to Myfleet, that the discovery had been made. Over to the west the obelisk stabbed the blue sky, catching a shred of cloud on its point.

The grave was in a triangle formed by the wood, the lane and the footpath, in a slightly more than right-angled corner of the field. It was near enough to the forest for the air to smell resinous. The soil was light and sandy with an admixture of pine needles.

'Easy enough to dig,' said Wexford to Burden. 'Almost anyone not decrepit could dig a grave like that in half an hour. Digging it deep enough would have taken a little longer.'

They were viewing the terrain, the distance of the grave from the road and the footpath, while Sir Hilary Tremlett, the pathologist, stood by with the scene-of-crimes officer to supervise the careful unearthing. Sir Hilary had happened to be at Stowerton when Fitzgerald's call came in. By a piece of luck he had just arrived at the infirmary to perform a postmortem. It was not yet ten o'clock, a morning of pearly sunshine, the blue sky dotted with innumerable puffs of tiny white cloud. But every man there, the short portly august pathologist included, had a raincoat on. It had rained daily for so many weeks that no one was going to take the risk of going without; no one anyway could yet believe his own eyes.

'The rain made the weeds grow like that,' said Wexford. 'You can see what happened. It's rather interesting. All the ground here had grass growing on it, then a patch was dug to receive *that*. It was covered up again with overturned earth, the weed seeds came and rain, seemingly endless rain, and what grew up on that fertile patch and that patch only were broad-leaved plants. If it had been a dry spring there would have been more grass and it would all have been much less green.'

'And the ground harder. If the ground hadn't been soft and moist the dog might not have persisted with its digging.'

'The mistake was in not digging the grave deep enough. It makes you wonder why he or she or they didn't. Laziness? Lack of time? Lack of light? The six-foot rule is a good one because things of this kind do tend to work to the surface.'

'If that's so,' said Dr Crocker, coming up to them, 'why is it they always have to dig so far down to find ancient cities and temples and so forth?'

'Don't ask me,' said Wexford. 'Ask the dog. He's the archaeologist. Mind you, we don't have any lava in Sussex.'

They approached a little nearer to where Detectives Archbold and Bennett were carrying out their delicate spadework. It was apparent now that the corpse of the man that lay in the earth had been neither wrapped nor covered before it was buried. The earth didn't besmear it as a heavier clayey soil might have done. It was emerging relatively clean, soak-

265

ing wet, darkly stained, giving off the awful reek that was familiar to every man there, the sweetish, fishy, breath-catching, gaseous stench of decomposing flesh. That was what the dog had smelt and liked and wanted more of.

'I often think,' said Wexford to the doctor, 'that we haven't much in common with dogs.'

'No, it's at times like this you know what you've always suspected, that they're not almost human at all.'

The face was pale, stained, bloated, the pale parts the colour of a dead fish's belly. Wexford, not squeamish at all, hardened by the years, decided not to look at the face again until he had to. The big domed forehead, bigger and more domed because the hair had fallen from it, looked like a great mottled stone or lump of fungus. It was that forehead which made him pretty sure this must be Rodney Williams. Of course, he wasn't going to commit himself at this stage but he'd have been surprised if it wasn't Williams.

Sir Hilary, squatting down now, bent closer. Murdoch, the scene-of-crimes officer, was beginning to take measurements, make calculations. He called the photographer over but Sir Hilary held up a delaying hand.

Wexford wondered how he could stand that stink right up against his face. He seemed rather to enjoy it, the whole thing, the corpse, the atmosphere, the horror, the squalor. Pathologists did, and just as well really. It wouldn't do if they shied away from it.

The body was subjected to a long and careful scrutiny. Sir Hilary looked at it closely from all angles. He came very close to touching but he did not quite touch. His fingers were plump, clean, the colour of a slice of roast pork. He stood up, nodded to Murdoch and the photographer, smiled at Wexford.

'I could have a poke-about at that after lunch,' he said. He always spoke of his autopsies as 'having a poke-about'. 'Not much doing today. Any ideas who it might be?'

'I think I have, Sir Hilary.'

'I'm glad to hear it. Saves a lot of hassle. We'll smarten him up a bit before his nearest and dearest come for a private view.'

Joy Williams, Wexford thought. No, she shouldn't be subjected to that. He felt the warmth of the mounting sun kind and soft on his face. He turned his back and looked across the sweep of meadows to the Pomfret road, green hay gold-brushed, dark green hedgerows stitched in like tapestry, sheep on a hillside. All he could see was that face and a wife looking at it. This horrid image doth unfix my hair and make my seated heart knock at my ribs . . .

It occurred to him that the nearest point on the main road to this place was the bus stop where Colin Budd had been attacked. Did that mean anything? The lane that passed within yards of the burial place met the road almost opposite the bus stop. The brother-in-law might do the identification instead. John Something, the chemist. John Harmer.

He seemed a sensible man. Younger than Williams by five or six years, he was one of those tailored people, a neat, well-made, smallish man with regular features and short, crisply wavy hair. He had closed up his dispensary and left the shop in the care of his wife.

Having taken a deep breath, he looked at the body. He looked at the face, his symmetrical features controlled in blankness. He wasn't going to show anything, not he, no shock, disgust, pity. You could almost hear his mother's voice saying to a small curly-haired boy: Be a man, John. Don't cry. Be a man.

Harmer remembered and was a man. But he might have said with Macduff that he must also feel it like a man, for his face gradually paled until it became as sickly greenish white as the corpse's. His stomach, not his will, had betrayed him. Or threatened to. He came out into the air, into the sunshine, away from charnel-house corpse rot, and smelt the summer noonday, and the bile receded. He nodded to Wexford, he nodded rather more and longer than was necessary.

'Is that your brother-in-law, Rodney Williams?'

'Yes.'

'You are quite certain of that?'

'I'm certain.'

Wexford had thought of asking him to be the bearer of the news to Joy but he had quickly seen Harmer wouldn't be a suitable, let alone a sympathetic, messenger. He went

267

himself, walking to Alverbury Road, thinking as he walked. There wasn't much he personally could do until the pathologist's report came and the lab had been over Williams's clothes. With distaste he recalled the bloodied mass of cloth that had wrapped the wounds. He felt glad now he had had the lab go over that car so carefully and at a time when it looked as if Williams might have been guilty of some misdemeanour and have done a moonlight flit.

Those crumbs of plaster in the boot could be vital evidence. At first he had supposed they derived from some routine of Williams's work. But Gardner had told him there was never a question of Williams having handled the stuff he sold. More likely the truth was that those plaster crumbs had been caught up in the folds of that bloodstained cloth and the body itself had been in the boot of the car . . .

In the front garden of 31 Alverbury Road someone had mown the bit of lawn and cut the privet hedge. It looked as if both these tasks had been performed with the same pair of blunt shears. Rodney Williams had been in one respect domestically adequate – he had kept his garden trim.

Sara opened the front door to him. He hadn't expected her to be there and he was a little taken aback. He would have preferred breaking the news to her mother alone. The school term wasn't yet over but A-levels were and with those examinations behind her there was perhaps nothing for her to go to school for.

She had on a white tee-shirt, pure unrelieved white, short-sleeved and showing felt-tipped pen drawings on her arms and hands, the snake again in green, a butterfly with a baby face, a raven woman with aggressive breasts and erect wings, somehow obscene on those smooth golden arms, childish and rounded.

'Is your mother in, Sara?'

She nodded. Had the tone of his voice told her? She looked sideways at him, fearfully, as they went down the short passage to the kitchen door.

Joy Williams anticipated nothing. On the table at which she was sitting were the remains of lunch for two. She looked up with a mildly disagreeable inquiring glance. They had been eating fish fingers with baked beans – an infelicitous mixture, Wexford thought. He could tell the constituents of their lunch by the quantity of it Sara had left on the plate. Joy had been reading a women's magazine of the royalty-sycophantic-crocheted-tea-cosy kind which was propped against a bottle of soy sauce, pathetic import surely of Sara's. What does a daughter do for her mother in a situation such as this? Go to her and put an arm round her shoulders? At least stand behind her chair? Sara went to the sink, stood with her back to them, looking out of the window above it at the grass and the fence and the meagre little apple trees.

Wexford told Joy her husband had been found. Her husband's body. More than that he couldn't tell her, he knew no more. The girl's shoulders twitched. Mrs Williams leaned forward across the table and put her hand heavily over her mouth. She sat that way for a moment or two. The whistling kettle on the stove began to screech. Sara turned round, turned the gas off, looked at her mother with her mouth twisted up as if she had toothache.

'D'you want a coffee?' Joy said to Wexford.

He shook his head. Sara made the coffee, instant in two mugs, one with a big 'S' on it and the other with the head of the Princess of Wales. Joy put sugar into hers, one spoonful, then after reflection, another.

'Shall I have to see him?'

'Your brother-in-law has already made the identification.'

'John?'

'Have you any other brothers-in-law, Mrs Williams?'

'Rod's got a brother in Bath. "Had", I should say. I mean he's still alive as far as I know and Rod's not, is he?'

'Oh, Mum,' said Sara. 'For God's sake.'

'You shut your mouth, you little cow!'

Joy Williams screamed it at her. She didn't utter any more words but she went on screaming, drumming her fists on the table so that the mug bounced off and broke and coffee went all over the strip of coconut matting on the floor. Joy screamed until Sara slapped her face – the doctor already, the cool head in an emergency. Wexford knew better than to do it himself. Once he'd slapped a hysterical woman's face and later been threatened with an action for assault.

'Who can we get hold of to be with her?' he asked. Mrs Milvey? He thought of Dora and dismissed the thought.

'She hasn't any friends. I expect my Auntie Hope will come.'

Mrs Harmer that would be. Hope and Joy. My God, he thought. Although the girl was sitting beside her mother now, holding her hand, while Joy leaned back spent, her head hanging over the back of the kitchen chair, the tears silently rolling out of her eyes, he could see that it was all Sara could do to control her repugnance. She was almost shaking with it. The need to be parted, the one from the other, was mutual. Sara, no doubt, couldn't wait for those exam results, the confirmation of St Biddulph's acceptance of her, for October and the start of term. It couldn't come fast enough for her.

'I'll stay with Mum,' she said, and there was stoicism in the way she said it. 'I'll give her a pill. She's got Valium. I'll give her a couple of Valium and find something nice for her on the TV.'

The ever ready panacea.

It was too late for lunch now. He and Burden might have something in the office, get a sandwich sent down from the canteen. He had said he'd see the press at 2.30. Well, young Varney of the local paper who was a stringer for the nationals . . .

There was a van on the police station forecourt marked TV South and a camera crew getting out of it.

'They've been up at the forest getting shots of the grave and Fitzgerald and the dog,' Burden said, 'and they want you next.'

'Good. I'll be able to put out an appeal for anyone who may have seen that car parked.' A less encouraging thought struck Wexford. 'They won't want to make me up, will they?' He had never been on television before.

Burden looked at him morosely, lifting his shoulders in a shrug of total indifference to any eventuality.

'It's not the end of the world if they do, is it?'

There was no time like the present, even a present that would end in ten minutes with his first ever TV appearance.

'What's happened to end your world, Mike?'

Burden immediately looked away. He mumbled something which Wexford couldn't hear and had to ask him to repeat.

'I said that I supposed I should tell you what the trouble is.'

'Yes. I want to know.' Looking at Burden, Wexford noticed for the first time grey hairs among the fair ones. 'There's something wrong with the baby, isn't there?'

'That's right.' Burden's voice sounded very dry. 'In Jenny's opinion, mind you. Not in mine.' He gave a bark of laughter. 'It's a girl.'

'*What*?'

Wexford's phone went. He picked up the receiver. TV South, the *Kingsmarkham Courier* and two other reporters were downstairs waiting for him. Burden had already gone, closing the door quietly behind him.

271

8

She was laying the table with their wedding present glass and silver. The lace cloth had been bought in Venice where they went for the first holiday after their honeymoon. Domesticity had delighted her when, as soon as she knew she was pregnant, she gave up teaching. It was the novelty, of course, being at home all day, playing house. Since then she had grown indifferent, she had grown indifferent to everything. Except to the child, and that she hated.

Sometimes, walking about the house after Mike had gone to work, pushing the vacuum cleaner or tidying up, the tears fell out of her eyes and streamed down her face. She cried because she couldn't believe that she who had longed and longed for a baby could hate the one inside her. All this she had told to the psychiatrist at their second session. She had listened to her in almost total silence. Once she said, 'Why do you say that?' and once 'Go on', but otherwise she simply listened with a kind interested look on her face.

Mike had suggested the psychiatrist. She had been so surprised because Mike usually scoffed at psychiatry that she said yes without even protesting. It was somewhere to go anyway, something different to do from sitting at home brooding about the future and her marriage and the unwanted child. And inevitably crying, of course, when she remembered as she always did what life used to be – when the days seemed too short, when she was teaching history to sixth formers at Haldon Finch, playing the violin in an orchestra, taking an advanced art appreciation course.

Jenny despised herself but that changed nothing. Her self-pity sickened her.

272

The sound of his key in the door – time-honoured heart stopper, test of love sustained – did nothing for her beyond bringing a little dread of the evening in front of them. He came into the room and kissed her. He still did that.

'How did you get on with the shrink?'

She resented the haste he was in. He wanted her cured, she felt, so that life could get back to normal again. 'What do you expect? A miracle in two easy lessons?'

She sat down. That always made her feel a little less bad because the bulge was no longer so apparent. And, thank God, the child was still, not rolling about and kicking.

'Don't let him give you drugs.'

'It's a woman.'

She wanted to scream with laughter. The irony of it! She was a teacher and this other woman was a psychiatrist and Mike's daughter Pat was very nearly qualified as a dentist, yet here she was reacting like a no-account junior wife in a harem. Because the baby was a girl.

He gave her a drink, orange juice and Perrier. He had a whisky, a large one, and in a minute he would have another. Not long ago he hadn't needed to drink when he got home. She looked at him, wishing she could bring herself to touch his arm or take his hand. An apathy as strong as energy held her back.

'Mike,' she said, and said for the hundredth time, 'I can't help it, I wish I could. I have tried.'

'So you say. I don't understand it. It's beyond my under-standing.'

In a low voice, looking down, she said, 'It's beyond mine.' The child began to move, with flutters only at first, then came a hearty kick right under her lower ribs, giving her a rush of heartburn. She cried out, 'I wish to God I'd never had the thing done. I wish I'd never let them do it. They shouldn't have told me. Why did I let them? If I'd been ignorant I'd have gone on being happy, I'd have had the baby and I wouldn't have minded what it was, I'd have been pleased with any healthy baby. I didn't even specially want a son, or I didn't know I did. I didn't mind what it was, but now I know what it is I can't bear it. I can't go through all this and all through having it and the work and the pain and

273

the trouble and a lifetime of being with it, having it with me, for a *girl*!'

He had heard it all before. It seemed to him that she said it every night. This was what he came home to. With slight variations, with modifications and changed turns of phrase, that was what she said to him on and on every evening. Until she grew exhausted or wept or slumped spent in her chair, until she went away to bed – earlier and earlier as the week's passed. In vain he had asked why this prejudice against girls, she who was a feminist, a supporter of the women's movement, who expressed a preference for her friends' small girls over their small sons, who got on better with her step-daughter than her stepson, who professed to prefer teaching girls to boys.

She didn't know why, only that it was so. Her pregnancy, so long desired, at first so ecstatically accepted, had driven her mad. The worst of it was that he was coming to hate the unborn child himself and to wish it had never been conceived.

The wine bar was dark and cool. The restoration of an old house in Kingsmarkham's Queen Street had revealed and then opened up its cavernous cellars. The proprietor had resisted the temptations of roof beams, medieval pastiches, flintlocks and copper warming pans and simply painted the broad squat arches white, tiled the floor and furnished the place with tables and chairs in dark-stained pine.

Wexford and Burden had taken to lunching at the Old Cellar a couple of times a week. It had the virtue of being warm on cold days and cool on hot ones like this. The food was quiche and salad, smoked mackerel, coleslaw, pork pie, quiche, quiche and more quiche.

'What did they serve in these places before quiche caught on? I mean, there was a time not long ago when an English-man could say he'd never heard of quiche.'

'He's always eaten it,' said Wexford. 'He called it cheese and onion flan.'

He had the morning papers with him. The *Kingsmarkham Courier* was a weekly and wouldn't be out till Friday. The national dailies had given no more than a paragraph to the discovery of Rodney Williams's body and had left out all the background details he was sure Varney had passed on to them. The *Daily Telegraph* merely stated that the body of a man had been found in a shallow grave and later identified as Rodney John Williams, a salesman from Kingsmarkham in Sussex. Nothing about Joy, his children, his job at Sevensmith Harding or the fact that he had been missing for two months. True, they had put him, Wexford, on TV but only on the regional bit that came after the news and then only forty-five seconds of the half-hour-long film they'd made.

The corpses of middle-aged men weren't news as women's were or children's. Women were always news. Perhaps they would cease to be when the day came that they got their equality as well as their rights. An interesting speculation and one which reminded him . . .

'You were going to tell me but we were interrupted.'

'It's not that she's anti-girls usually,' Burden said. 'For God's sake, she's a feminist. I mean, it's not some stupid I-must-have-an-heir thing or every-woman's-got-to-have-a-son-to-prove-herself. In fact I think she secretly thinks women are better than men – I mean cleverer and more versatile, all that. She says she doesn't understand it herself. She says she had no feelings about the child's sex one way or the other, but when they told her, when she knew, she was – well, dismayed. That was at first. It's got worse. It's not just dismay now, it's hatred.'

'Why doesn't she want a girl?' Wexford remembered certain sentiments expressed by his daughter Sylvia, mother of two sons. 'Is it that she feels women have a raw deal and she doesn't want to be responsible for bringing another into the world?' By way of apology for this crassness, he added, 'I have heard that view put.'

'She doesn't know. She says that ever since the world began sons have been preferred over daughters and now it's become part of race memory, what she calls the collective unconscious.'

'What Jung called it.'

Burden hesitated and then passed over that one. 'She's mad, you know. Pregnancy has driven her mad. Oh, don't look at me like that. I've given up caring about being disloyal.

I've given up damn well caring, if you must know. Do you know what she says? She says she can't contemplate a future with a daughter she doesn't want. She says she can't imagine living for twenty years, say, with someone she hates before it's born. What's my life going to be like with that going on?'

'At the risk of uttering an old cliché, I'd say she'll feel differently when the baby's born.'

'Oh, she will? You can be sure of that? She'll love it when it's put into her arms? Shall I tell you what else she says? That she never wants to see it. We're to put it up for adoption immediately without either of us seeing it. I told you she was mad.'

All this made Wexford feel like a drink. But he couldn't start drinking at lunchtime with all he'd got ahead of him. Burden wasn't going to drink either. Judging by the look of him some mornings, he saved that up for when he got home. They paid the bill and climbed up the stone steps out of the Old Cellar into a bright June sunshine that made them blink.

'She's seeing a psychiatrist. I pin my faith to that. Me of all people! I sometimes wonder what I've come to, saying things like that.'

Sir Hilary Tremlett's report of the results of the post-mortem had come. To decipher the obscurer bits for Wexford, Dr Crocker came into the office as Burden was departing. They nearly passed each other in the doorway, Burden long-faced, monosyllabic. The doctor laughed.

'Mike's having a difficult pregnancy.'

Wexford wasn't going to enlighten him. The other chair had been pushed under the desk. He shoved it out with his toe.

'He says here he found three hundred and twenty milligrammes of cyclobarbitone in the stomach and other organs. What's cyclobarbitone?'

'It's an intermediate-acting barbiturate – that means it has about eight hours duration of effect – a hypnotic drug, a sleeping pill if you like. The proprietary brand name would be Phanodorm, I expect. Two hundred milligrammes is the dose. But three hundred and twenty wouldn't kill him. It sounds as if he took two tablets of two hundred each.'

'It didn't kill him, though, did it? He died of stab wounds.'

Wexford looked up to see the doctor looking at him. They were both thinking the same thing. They were both thinking about Colin Budd and Brian Wheatley.

'What actually killed him was a wound that pierced the carotid.'

'Did it now? The blood must have spouted like a fountain.'

'There were seven other wounds in the neck and chest and back. A lot of stuff here's about fixed and mobile underlying tissues.' Wexford handed the pages across the desk, retaining one. 'I'm more interested in the estimate he makes of the proportions of the knife. A large kitchen knife with a dagger point, it would seem to have been.'

'I see he suggests death occurred six to eight weeks ago. What d'you reckon? He took two sleeping pills and someone did him in while he was away in the land of nod? If it happened as you seem to think soon after he left his house at six that evening, why would he take sleeping pills at that hour?'

'He might have taken them,' said Wexford thoughtfully, 'in mistake for something else. Hypertension pills, for instance. He had high blood pressure.'

While the doctor was reading Wexford picked up the phone and asked the telephonist to get him Wheatley's number. Wheatley had said he worked in London on only three days a week so there was a chance he might be at home now. He was.

'I didn't think you showed much interest,' he said in an injured way.

That one Wexford wasn't going to answer. It was true anyway. They hadn't shown all that much interest in a man getting his hand scratched by a girl hitchkiker. Things had taken on a different aspect since then.

'You gave me a detailed description of the girl who attacked you, Mr Wheatley. The fact that you're a good observer makes me think you may have observed more. Will you think about that, please, and try and remember every-thing that happened? Principally, give us some more infor-mation about what the girl looked like, her voice and so on. We'd like to come and see you.'

Mollified, Wheatley said he'd give it some thought and tell

277

them everything he could remember and how about some time that evening?

The doctor said, 'It couldn't have happened inside a car, you know, Reg. There'd have been too much blood.'

'Perhaps in the open air?'

'And tied his neck up in a Marks and Spencer's floral-printed teatowel?'

'It doesn't say that there!'

'I happened to notice it when the poor devil was resurrected. We've got one like it at home.'

The phone rang. The telephonist said, 'Mr Wexford, there's a Mrs Williams here wanting to talk to someone about Mr Rodney Williams.'

Joy, he thought. Well.

'Mrs Joy Williams?'

'Mrs Wendy Williams.'

'Have someone bring her up here, will you?'

The sister-in-law? The wife of the brother in Bath? When you don't know what to do next, Raymond Chandler advised writers of his sort of fiction, have a man come in with a gun. In a real-life murder case, thought Wexford, what better surprise visitor than the mysterious Wife of Bath?

He looked up as Burden re-entered the room. Burden had been going through the clothes found on Williams's body: navy blue briefs – very different from the white underwear in the cupboard in Alverbury Road – brown socks, fawn cavalry-twill slacks, blue, brown and cream striped shirt, dark blue St Laurent sweater. The back pocket of the slacks had contained a cheque book for one of the accounts with the Anglian-Victoria at Pomfret (R. W. Williams, private account), and a wallet containing one fiver, three £1 notes and two credit cards, Visa and American Express. No car keys, no house keys.

'He probably kept his house key on the same ring as his car keys,' Burden said. 'It's what I do.'

'At any rate, we'll get at that bank account now. The doctor here says there was a teatowel wrapped round his neck. To staunch the blood presumably.'

There came a knock at the door. Bennett came into the room with a young woman, not anyone's idea of a Wife of Bath.

278

'Mrs Wendy Williams, sir.'

She looked about twenty-five. She was a pretty girl with a delicate nervous face and fair curly hair. Wexford asked her to sit down, the doctor having sprung to his feet. She slid into the chair, gripping the arms of it, and jumped as Crocker passed behind her on his way to the door. Burden closed the door behind him and stood there.

'What did you want to see me about, Mrs Williams?'

She didn't answer. She had fixed him with a penetrating stare and her tongue came in and out, moistening her lips.

'I take it you're Rodney Williams's sister-in-law? Is that right?'

She moved her body back a little, hands still tight on the chair arms. 'What do you mean, his sister-in-law?' She didn't wait for a reply. 'Look, I . . . I don't know how to say this. I've been so . . . I've been nearly out of my mind.' Mounting hysteria made her voice ragged. 'I saw in the paper . . . a little bit in the paper and . . . Is that, that *person* they found . . . ? Is that my husband?'

9

It was seldom he could give people reassuring news. He was tempted to say no, of course not. The body has been identified. She was holding on to the arms of the chair, rubbing her fingers up and down the wood.

'What is your husband's name, Mrs Williams?'

'Rodney John Williams. He's forty-eight.' She spoke in short jerky phrases, not waiting for the questions. 'Six feet tall. He's fair going grey. He's a salesman. It said in the paper a salesman.'

Burden stared, then looked down. She swallowed, made an effort against panic, an effort that concentrated on tensing her muscles.

'Could you . . . please, I have a photo here.'

Her hands, unlocked from the chair, refused to obey her when first she tried to open her bag. The photograph she handed to Wexford fluttered, she was shaking so. He looked at it, unbelieving.

It was Rodney Williams all right, high domed forehead, crack of a mouth parted in a broad smile. It was a more recent picture than the one Joy had and showed Williams in swimming trunks (flabby hairless chest, spindleshanks, a bit knock-kneed) with this girl in a black bikini and another girl, also bikini'd but no more than twelve years old. Wexford's eyes returned to the unmistakable face of Williams, to the head you somehow wanted to slap a fringed wig on and so transform it.

She was waiting, watching him. He nodded. She brought a fluttery hand up to her chest, to her heart perhaps, froze for a moment in this tragic pose. Then her eyelids fell and she sagged sideways in the chair.

Afterwards he was to think of it as having been beautifully done but at the time he saw it only as a genuine faint. Burden held her shoulders, bringing her face down onto her knees. Picking up the phone, Wexford asked for a policewoman to come up, Polly Davies or Marion Bayliss, anyone who was around. And someone send a pot of strong tea and don't forget the sugar basin.

Wendy Williams came out of her faint, sat up and pressed her face into her hands.

'You are the wife of Rodney John Williams and you live in Liskeard Avenue, Pomfret?'

She drank the tea sugarless and very hot, at first with her eyes closed. When she opened her eyes and they met his he noticed they were the very clear pale blue of flax flowers. She nodded slowly.

'How long have you been married, Mrs Williams?'

'Sixteen years. We had our sixteenth wedding anniversary in March.'

He could hardly believe it. Her skin had the clear bloom of an adolescent's, her hair was baby-soft and the curl in it looked natural. She saw his incredulity and in spite of her emotion was flattered, a little buoyed up. He could tell she was the sort of woman to whom compliments, even unspoken ones, were food and drink. They nourished her. A faint, tremulous smile appeared. He looked again at the photographs.

'My daughter Veronica,' she said. 'I got married very young. I was only sixteen. That picture was taken three or four years back.'

A bigamist he had been, then. Not a common or garden wayward husband with a girlfriend living in the next town, not a married man with a sequence of pricey mistresses, but your good old-fashioned true blue bigamist. There was no doubt in Wexford's mind that Wendy Williams had as good-looking a marriage certificate as Joy's and if hers happened not to be valid she would be the last to know it.

That, then, was why he had taken no change of clothes

281

with him. He had those things in his other home. And more than that, much more. Wexford now saw the point of those bank accounts: one for his salary to be paid into and two joint accounts to be fed from it, one for each household, R. W. Williams and J. Williams; R. W. Williams and W. Williams. There had been no need to assume a different name on his second marriage – Williams was common enough to make that unnecessary. He had been like a Moslem who keeps strictly to Islamic law and maintains his wives in separate and distinct dwellings. The difference here was that the wives didn't know of each other's existence.

That Williams had had another wife, what one might call in fact a chief wife, was something this girl was going to have to be told. And Joy was going to have to be told about her.

'Can you tell me when you last saw Mr Williams?' Not calling him 'your husband' any more was the beginning of breaking the news.

'About two months ago. Just after Easter.'

This wasn't the time to ask her to account for that eight week gap. He told her he would come and see her at home that evening. Polly Davies would look after her and see she got home safely.

Something had at last happened to distract Burden temporarily from his private troubles. His expression was as curious and as alerted as a little boy's.

'What did he do at Christmas?' he said. 'Easter? What about holidays?'

'No doubt we shall find out. Other bigamists have handled it. He probably had a Bunbury as well.'

'A *what*?'

'A nonexistent friend or relative to provide him with alibis. My guess is Williams's Bunbury was an old mother.'

'Did he have an old mother?'

'God knows. Creating one from his imagination wouldn't have been beyond his capacity, I'm sure. You know what they say, a mother is the invention of necessity.'

Burden winced. 'That night he left Alverbury Road, d'you think he went to his other home?'

'I think he set off meaning to go there. Whether he reached it is another matter.'

Fascinated by Williams's family arrangements, Burden said, 'While Joy thought he was travelling for Sevensmith Harding in Ipswich he was with Wendy and while he was with Joy Wendy thought he was where?'

'I don't suppose she knew he worked for Sevensmith Harding. He probably told her a total lie about what he did.'

'You'd think he'd have got their names muddled – I mean called Wendy Joy and Joy Wendy.'

'There speaks the innocent monogamist,' said Wexford, casting up his eyes. 'How do you think married men with girlfriends manage? Wife and all get called "darling".'

Burden shook his head as if even speculating about it was too much for him. 'Do you reckon it was one of them killed him?'

'Carried his body and stuck it in that grave? Williams weighed a good fifteen stone or two hundred and ten pounds or ninety something kilos or whatever we're supposed to say these days.'

'It might have been Wendy made that phone call.'

'You reckon her voice sounds like Joy's?'

Burden was obliged to admit that it didn't. Joy's was monotonous, accent-free, uninflected; Wendy's girlish, rather fluting, with a faint lisp. Wexford was talking about voices, about the rather unattractive but nevertheless memorable quality of Joy's voice when his phone rang again.

'Another young lady to see me,' he said to Burden, putting the receiver back.

'Bluebeard's third wife?' it was the first attempt at a joke he had made in two months.

Wexford appreciated that. 'Let's say a fan, rather. Someone who saw me on the telly.'

'Look, why don't I take Martin and get on over to Wheatley? Then I'll be able to come to Wendy's with you tonight.'

'OK, and we'll take Polly along.'

The girl walked into his room in a breeze of confidence. She was seventeen or eighteen and her name was Eve Freeborn. Apposite names of the Lady Dedlock-Ernest Pontifex-Obadiah Slope kind that Victorian novelists used are in real life less uncommon than is generally supposed. That Eve Freeborn was aptly named Wexford came quickly to understand. She might have been dressed and cast for the role of

Spirit of Freedom in a pageant. Her hair was cropped short and dyed purple in parts. She wore stretch jeans, a check shirt and thongs.

The story she told Wexford, sitting with legs wide apart, hands linked, forearms making a bridge from the chair arms to rest her chin on, was delivered in a brisk and articulate way. Eve was still at school, had come there straight from school. President of the debating society no doubt, he thought. As she turned her hands outwards, thumbs on her jaw, he noticed the felt-tipped pen drawing on her wrist, a raven with a woman's head, and then as she moved her arm the shirtsleeve covered it.

'I realized it was my duty as a citizen to come to you. I delayed just long enough to discuss the matter with my boyfriend. He's at the same school as me – Haldon Finch. In a way he's involved, you see. We have the sort of relationship where we believe in total openness.'

Wexford gave her an encouraging smile.

'My boyfriend lives in Arnold Road, Myringham. It's a single-storey house, number forty-three.' Opposite Graham Gee who had reported the presence of poor old Greta, Wexford thought. 'His mother and father live there too,' said Eve in a tone that implied enormous condescension and generosity on the part of the boyfriend in allowing his parents to live in their own house. 'The point is – and you may not believe this but it's the honest truth, I promise you – they don't like him having me to stay the night with him. I mean, not me personally, you could understand that if they didn't like me, but any girl. So what we do is I come round after he's gone to bed and get in the window.'

Wexford didn't gape at her. He merely felt like doing this. He couldn't resist asking, 'Why doesn't he come to you?'

'I share a room with my sister. Anyway, I was telling you. I went round to his place around ten that Thursday night. There wasn't all that much space to park and when I was reversing I went into the car behind. I just bashed the wing of it a bit, not much, it wouldn't have had to have a new wing or anything, but I did think it was my duty to take responsibility and not just leave it, so I . . .'

'Just a moment. This was the night of April the fifteenth?'

'Right. It was my boyfriend's birthday.'

284

And a charming present he must have had, Wexford thought.

'What was this car you went into?'

'A dark blue Ford Granada. It was the car you asked about on TV. I wrote a note and put it on the windscreen, under a wiper. Just with my name and address on and phone number. But it blew away or got lost or something because the car was still there a long while after that and the driver never got in touch with me.'

At ten that night. Greta the Granada had been there at ten but how long had it been there?

'Just as a matter of curiosity, whose car were you driving?'

'My own,' she said, surprised.

'You have your own car?'

'My mother's technically. But it comes to the same thing.'

No doubt it did. They were amazing, these young people. And the most amazing thing about them was that they had no idea previous generations had not behaved as they did. People got old, of course, became dull and staid, they knew that, but in their day surely teenage girls had slept with their boyfriends, appropriated their parents' cars, stayed out all night, dyed their hair all colours of the spectrum.

He thanked her for her help and as she got up he saw the little drawing or tattoo again. He realized that he didn't know which of the local schools Sara Williams attended. And there remained the as yet unknown quantity, Veronica Williams . . .

'Do you know a girl of your own age called Sara Williams? Is she perhaps at school with you?'

He was positive she hadn't made the connection before, was making it now for the first time. 'Do you mean Sara is the daughter of this man who was murdered?'

'Yes. You go to the same school?'

'No, we don't,' she said carefully, 'but I know her.'

Wheatley lived on an estate of new houses on the Pomfret side of Myringham. They had been built, Burden recalled, by a company so anxious to sell their houses that 100 percent mortgages had been guaranteed with them and a promise given to buy a house back for its purchase price if after two years the occupier were dissatisfied. The place had a raw look, oddly cold in the June sunshine. Wheatley's pregnant wife came to the door. A child of about three, a girl, was behind her, holding on to her skirt. Burden registered the fact of the pregnancy and the sex of the child with his heightened sensitivity to such matters and then he thought that his wife's pregnancy might have affected Wheatley's attitude to the girl he picked up. For instance, he might be sexually frustrated. Burden knew all about that. Wheatley too might have exaggerated the purity of his attitude towards the girl because he dared not risk the possibility of his pregnant wife finding out he was capable of putting his hand on other women's knees – or, in this instance no doubt, on other women's breasts.

The third bedroom of this very small house had been turned into a study or office for Wheatley. He was on the phone but rang off within seconds of Burden's and Martin's arrival. Yes, he had remembered some more about the girl. He was sure he could give them a more detailed description. There was no question of his remembering more of what the girl had said to him because she hadn't said any more. 'Thanks' and a gasp had been the only sounds that had come from her.

'I told you she was tall for a woman, at least five feet nine. Still in her teens, I'm sure. She had dark brown shoulder-length hair with a fringe, very fair skin and very white hands. I think I can remember a ring, not a wedding or engagement ring or anything, but one of those big silver rings they wear. I wouldn't call her pretty, not a bit.' Was that a sop to the wife who had come quietly into the room, carrying the little girl? 'Sunglasses, a dark leather shoulder bag. She had blue denim jeans on and a grey cardigan. She was thin – really skinny, I mean.' Another matrimonial sop. 'And underneath the cardigan she had a tee-shirt on. It was a white tee-shirt with a crazy picture on it – some sort of bird with a woman's head.'

'You didn't mention that before, Mr Wheatley.'

'I didn't mention the ring before or what colour her clothes were. You asked me to think about it and I thought about it and that's what I remember. You can take it or leave it. A white tee-shirt with a bird on it with a woman's face.'

*

'I don't believe it!'

She stared at Wexford, her mouth open in an appalled sort of way, her eyelids moving. She brought her hands up and scrabbled at her neck.

'I don't believe it!' Now there was defiance in her tone. Then, by changing one word, she showed him she accepted, she understood that what he had told her was true. 'I *won't* believe it!'

Polly Davies was with him, sitting there like a good chaperone, silent but attentive. She glanced at Wexford, got a nod from him.

'I'm afraid it's true, Mrs Williams.'

'I don't – I don't have a right to be called that, do I?'

'Of course you do. Your name doesn't depend on a marriage certificate.' Wexford thought of Eve Freeborn. There was a world between her and Wendy Williams, though a mere fourteen years, less than a generation, separated them. Would Eve know such a thing as a marriage certificate existed?

'Mrs Williams,' said stalwart Polly, 'why don't you and I go and make some coffee? We'd all like coffee, I'm sure. Mr Wexford will want to ask you some questions but I know he'd like you to have time to get over the shock of this.'

She nodded and got up awkwardly as if her bones were stiff. A glazed look had come across her face. She walked like a sleepwalker and no one now would have mistaken her for a twenty-five-year-old.

Burden shrugged silently as the door closed behind them and subsided into one of his typical morose reveries. Wexford had a look round the room they were sitting in. The house was newer than the Williams home in Kingsmarkham, a small 'town house' with an integral garage, built probably in the late 1960s. Wendy was a thorough meticulous and perhaps fanatical housekeeper. This was a through room with a dining area and it had very recently been redecorated in gleaming white with an undertone of palest pink. One of the colours in the Sevensmith Harding 'Ice Cream' range? The carpet was deep strawberry pink, some of the furniture mahogany, some white canework, cushions in various shades of pink and red. It was tasteful, it was a far cry from the stereotyped shabbiness of Joy's home, but somehow it was also uncomfortable, as if everything had been placed there – hanging baskets, little tables, red Venetian glass – for effect rather than for use.

He remembered that a young girl also lived here. There were no signs of her. But what sign did he expect or would he recognize if he saw it? She had been twelve in the picture . . .

'My daughter is sixteen now,' Wendy said when the coffee was brought. A slightly defiant note came into her voice as she added, 'She was sixteen three weeks ago.'

Her gaze fell. He did some calculations, remembering what she had said about her wedding anniversary taking place in March. So Williams had 'married' her three months before the child was born. He had had to wait until she reached the legal age for marriage.

'Where were you married, Mrs Williams?'

'Myringham Registry Office. My mother wanted us to have a church wedding but – well, for obvious reasons . . .'

Wexford could imagine one very obvious reason if she had been six months pregnant. The nerve of Williams, a married man, 'marrying' this child, as she had been, a mere dozen miles from his home town! The wedding to Joy, Dora had told him, had been at St Peter's, Kingsmarkham, the bride in white slipper satin . . .

Wendy was thrusting a paper at him. He saw it was her marriage certificate.

In the Registration District of Myringham, at the Registry Office, Rodney John Williams, aged thirty-two. In some respects, at any rate, he had been honest. Though he could hardly have distorted those facts. They had been on his birth certificate. A Bath address, his brother's probably, his occupation sales representative. Wendy Ann Rees, aged sixteen, Pelham Street, Myringham, shop assistant. The witnesses had been Norman Rees and Brenda Rees, parents presumably, or brother and sister-in-law.

He handed it back to her. She looked at it herself and her tongue flicked out to moisten her lips. For a moment, from the way she was holding it, he thought she was going to tear the certificate across. But she replaced it in its envelope and laid the envelope on the low white melamine table that was close up against the arm of her chair.

She pressed her knees together and folded her hands in

288

her lap. Her legs were very good with elongated slim ankles. To come to the police station she had worn a grey flannel suit with a white blouse. He had a feeling she was a woman who attached importance to being suitably dressed. The suit was changed now for a cotton dress. She was the type who would 'save' her clothes, not sit about in a straight skirt or risk a spot on white silk. In her sad wistful look youth had come back into her face.

'Mrs Williams,' he began, 'I'm sure you won't mind telling me how it was you weren't alarmed when your husband was away for so long.'

She did mind. She was reluctant. Patience, simply waiting quietly, succeeded with her where pressing the point might not have.

'Rodney and I . . .' She paused. It was always 'Rodney' with her, Wexford noted, never 'Rod'. 'We – we quarrelled. Well, we had a very serious quarrel. That must have been a few days after Easter. Rodney spent Easter with his mother in Bath. He always spent Christmas and Easter with her. He was an only child, you see, and she's been in an old people's home for years and years.'

Wexford carefully avoided looking at Burden. Wendy said, reminded by her own explanation, 'Has she been . . . ? I mean, has anyone *told* her?'

Enigmatically, Wexford said that had been taken care of. 'Go on please, Mrs Williams.'

'We quarrelled,' she went on. 'It was a very private thing we quarrelled about. I'll keep that to myself if you don't mind. I said to him that – well, I said that if he – if *it* didn't stop, if he didn't promise me faithfully that never – well, I said I'd take Veronica away and he'd never see us again. I – I struck him, I was so angry, so distressed, I can't tell you – well, he was angry too. He denied it, of course, and then he said I needn't trouble about leaving him because he'd leave me. He said he couldn't stand my nagging any more.' She lifted her head and looked Wexford straight in the eye. 'I did nag him, I'll be honest about it. I couldn't bear it, never seeing him, his always being away. We'd never had a single Christmas together. I always had to go to my parents. We hardly ever had a holiday. I used to *beg* him . . .' Her voice faltered and Wexford understood that realization was dawning. She was beginning to see what the real reason was for those absences. 'Anyway,' she said, making an effort at control, 'he – he calmed down after a while and I suppose I did too. He was going away again and he was due back on the Thursday – the fifteenth, that is. I was still very sore and upset but I said goodbye to him and that I'd see him on Thursday and he said maybe I would and maybe he'd never come back, so you see, I – when he didn't come back I thought he'd left me.'

It wasn't a completely convincing explanation. He tried to put himself in her shoes. He tried to think how he would have felt years ago when he and Dora were young if they'd had a row and she, going away to visit her sister, say, had told him maybe she wouldn't come back. Probably such a thing had actually happened. It did happen in marriages, even in excellent ones. But if she hadn't come back on the appointed day, if she'd been a couple of hours late even, he'd have started going out of his mind with worry. Of course, much depended on the seriousness of the quarrel and on the reasons for it.

'Tell me what happened that Thursday.'

'In the evening, do you mean?'

'When he didn't come.'

'I was at work. Thursday's our late night. I didn't tell you, did I? I'm manageress of the fashion floor at Jickie's.'

He was surprised. Somehow he had taken it for granted she didn't work. 'In Myringham?' he asked. 'Or the Kingsmarkham branch?'

'Oh, Kingsmarkham. In the Precinct.'

Jickie's was Kingsmarkham's biggest department store and the largest area of the Kingsbrook Shopping Precinct was given over to it. Doubtless Rodney Williams had taken care never to accompany Joy when she went shopping there for a jumper or a pair of tights on a Saturday afternoon. Had he risked walking arm in arm down Kingsmarkham High Street during shopping hours? With his son or daughter in the car, had he risked parking in the precinct car park? It was a tightrope he had walked and no doubt, for such is the nature of people like him, he had enjoyed walking it, but he had fallen off at last. Because of the tightrope or for some entirely different reason?

290

'We stay open till eight on Thursdays but I can never get away till nine and it takes me a quarter of an hour to get home. When I did get back Veronica was here but Rodney hadn't come. I thought there was still a chance he might come but he didn't and then I knew. Or I thought I knew. I thought he'd left me.'

'And in all the weeks that followed,' Burden put it, 'you weren't anxious? You didn't wonder what could happen to you and your daughter if he didn't come back?'

'I'd be all right financially without him. I've always had to work and now I'm doing quite well.' There was a note of self-esteem in the little soft voice now. Inside the white and pink and fair curls and underneath the lisp and diffidence, Wexford thought there might be a core of steel. 'We had a ninety per cent mortgage on this house and up till five years ago it was all Rodney could do to keep us. He got promotion then and things were easier but I kept on working. I needed a life of my own too, he was away so much.'

'Promotion?' hazarded Wexford, feeling his way.

'It's quite a small company and they haven't been doing too well lately – bathroom fittings and furniture, that sort of thing. Rodney was made sales manager for this locality.'

Polly Davies picked up the tray and took it away into the kitchen. Wexford thought how easy it was to imagine Rodney Williams – or his idea of Rodney Williams – in his other home but next to impossible to imagine him here. Seated at that glass-topped dining table, for instance, with its bowl of pink and red roses or in one of those pink chintz armchairs. He had been a big coarse man and everything here had a daintiness like a pink shell or the inside of a rose.

'I have to know what you quarrelled about, Mrs Williams.'

Her tone became prissy, very genteel. 'It has nothing whatsoever to do with Rodney's death.'

'How do you know?'

She looked at him as if this were unfair persecution.

'How could it be? He got killed because he picked up someone hitching a lift and they killed him. Something like that . . . It's always happening.'

'That's an interesting guess but it's only a guess, isn't it? You've no evidence for it and there's plenty of evidence against it. The car being returned to Myringham, for instance. A phone call was made to your husband's employers and a letter of resignation sent to them. Do you think that phone call was made by some homicidal hitchhiker?'

She sat rigid, keeping her eyes obstinately averted. Polly came back.

'Are you all right, Mrs Williams?'

A nod. An indrawn breath and a sigh.

'What did you quarrel about?'

'I could refuse to tell you.'

'You could. But why take a stand like that when what you tell us will be treated in the strictest confidence? Ask yourself if it's so awful that we won't have heard it before. And don't you think that if you don't tell us we may come to think it is something worse than it really was?'

She sat silent. She wore an expression like someone who expects at any moment to see something nasty and shocking on television. It was an anticlimax when she said almost in a whisper, 'There was another girl.'

'You mean your husband had a woman friend he'd been seeing?'

' "Seeing",' she said, 'I like that expression – "seeing". Yes, he'd been seeing a woman friend. That's one way of putting it.'

'How would you put it?'

'Oh, like that. The way you do. What else does one say? Something crude, I suppose.' The repressive lid suddenly jumped and let out a dribble of resentment, of bitterness. 'I thought no one else but me would ever matter to him. I look young, don't I? I'm pretty enough, I don't look my age. People say I look eighteen. What was the matter with him that he . . . ? Yes, we quarrelled about that. About a girl. I wanted him to promise me it would never happen again.'

'He refused?'

'Oh, he promised. I didn't believe him. I thought it would start up again when he got the chance. I couldn't stand it, I didn't want him if he was going to do that. I was glad when he didn't come back. Don't you see? I was *glad*.'

'I'll have to have this girl's name.'

Quick as a flash: 'I don't know her name.'

'Come now, Mrs Williams.'

292

'I don't know it. He wouldn't tell me. Just a girl. What does it matter?'

She had said too much already, she was thinking. He could read that, plain in her face, the look in her eyes of being appalled at her own indiscretion. At that moment, before he could say any more, the door opened and a young girl came in. Just before this happened there had been a sound downstairs and footsteps on the stairs – the living room was on the middle floor – but it had all taken place very quickly, within a few seconds. And now, without warning, the girl was here among them.

What first struck Wexford was that although she was not so tall and her hair was shorter she looked exactly like Sara Williams. They might have been twins.

10

Her hair was the same pale fudge colour, not curly but not quite straight either, the tips just touching her shoulders. Brown eyes, ellipse eyebrows, small straight nose, fine white skin sprinkled with freckles. Rodney Williams's high domed forehead and his small narrow mouth. But instead of jeans she wore a summer dress with white tights and white sandals. She stood in the doorway looking surprised at the sight of them, a little more than just startled.

Wendy Williams was taken aback.

In a flustered way she said, 'This is my daughter Veronica,' and to the girl, 'you're home early.'

'Not much. It's after nine.'

The voice was her mother's, soft and slightly affected but without the lisp. It was quite unlike Sara's abrupt uninflected tones. Recovering poise Wendy said to her, 'These are police officers. They'll only be a few minutes.' She lied fluently, 'It's to do with trouble at the shop. You won't mind leaving us alone for a bit, will you, darling?'

'I'm going to have a bath anyway.'

Closing the door with the sort of precision her mother might use, she went off up the spiral staircase that was the core of this house.

'I don't know why she's so offhand with me lately. This past year . . .'

Wexford said, 'You haven't told her?'

'I haven't seen her. She always goes to her friend's straight from school on a Tuesday. Or so she says, she's so secretive . . .'

'Which school, Mrs Williams?'

294

'Haldon Finch Comprehensive. I'll tell her about her father after you've gone. I suppose I shall have to tell her what he was – a bigamist, with another wife somewhere. It won't be easy. I don't know if you appreciate that.'

Wexford, when interrogating, would allow any amount of digression but never total distraction. Those he questioned were obliged to come back to the point sooner or later. It was hard on them for often they believed they had escaped. The leash had snapped and freedom was surely there for the taking, but the hand always came down and snatched up the broken end.

'We were talking about this woman friend your husband had. He may have gone to her on the night he died.'

'I don't know any more about her!'

Fear had come into her voice now. It was what many would have called caution or apprehensiveness but it was really fear.

'You called her a girl. You implied a young girl.'

A panicky jerky rapid way of speaking – 'A young single girl, very young, that's all I know. I told you, I don't know any more!'

Wexford recalled the overtures Williams had once made to Sylvia. When Sylvia was fifteen. Was it something like that that Wendy had implied when she asked so pathetically if she didn't still look young? That she at thirty-two to his forty-eight might not be young enough for him?

'Do you mean she's young enough to live at home with her parents?'

A nod, painful and perplexed.

'What else do you know of her, Mrs Williams?'

'Nothing. I don't know any more. Do you think I wanted him to talk to me about her?'

That was reasonable enough. At first he thought she was lying when she said she was ignorant of the girl's name. Now he was less sure. How often had he heard people say, 'If my husband (my wife) were unfaithful to me I wouldn't want to know', and when they were forced to know, 'I don't want to hear anything about it'? The knives of jealousy are honed on details.

The question he sensed she would hate but which must be asked he had saved till last.

'How did you know it was happening at all? How did you know of her existence?'

He had been wrong. She didn't mind. She didn't mind because her answer was a lie that she had been rehearsing in her mind, silently and busily while they talked, waiting for the past half-hour for the question to come.

'I had an anonymous letter.'

Eventually he would get at the truth. It could wait.

'Now, Mrs Williams, your daughter . . .'

'What about her?' Very quick and defensive.

'I shall want to talk to Veronica.'

'Oh no, not that. Please.'

'When you have told her and she has had a day or two to get over the shock.'

'But why?'

'Her father has been murdered. He was due to come here and she was here, alone here. It's possible he did come and she was the last person to see him alive.'

'He didn't come here. She would have told me.'

'We'll see, Mrs Williams. We shall also want to look over this house, particularly at any of your husband's personal property.'

'We keep coming back to these young girls,' Burden said.

'And to ravens with women's faces.'

'That too. Budd and Wheatley were both attacked by a young girl – not very seriously, either of them, but they were attacked and the assault was with a knife. Rodney Williams liked young girls – I mean, he seems especially to have liked them very young – and he had a very young girlfriend. He died as the result of a knife attack, he was stabbed to death. Now Wheatley says the girl who attacked him was wearing a white tee-shirt with a design on it of a sort of bird with a woman's head . . . '

'And Sara Williams,' said Wexford, 'possesses just such a tee-shirt and has a poster with a similar motif on her bed-room wall.'

'Does she? You're kidding.'

'No. It's true. And Eve Freeborn has a raven with a woman's head tattooed or drawn on her left wrist, and since the sun came out, Mike, and women aren't bundling themselves up in cardigans and jackets I've seen no less than five girls around Kingsmarkham and Pomfret wearing white tee-shirts with ravens with women's faces on them. How about that?'

'God, and I thought we were really getting somewhere. It's like that bit in Ali Baba and the Forty Thieves when the woman says he'll know the right oil jar because it'll have a cross on it and when he gets there someone's put crosses on all the oil jars.'

'You've been reading again. Or going to pantomimes. It looks to me as if these raven-harpy pictures are the motif or symbol of some sort of society or cult. Latter-day anarchists or some sort of spurious freedom fighters.'

'Animal Rights?' said Burden doubtfully.

'It could be, I suppose. The implication being that the animal – or in this case bird – has the feelings and rights of a human being? The poster Sara Williams has in her bedroom has some letters on it as well as the picture. An acronym, I think, a, r, r, i, a, Arria.'

'Animal Rights something or other?'

'There was a woman called Arria, in Roman history, I seem to remember. I'll try and find out. If it's animal rights, Mike, you would expect its members to make their attacks on people who in their view were being cruel to animals. Factory farmers, for instance, or masters of foxhounds. I don't suppose Wheatley keeps calves chained up in boxes in his back garden, does he? We'll ask Sara. But first I want to leave her and Joy to get over the shock of Williams having another wife and another child.'

'You've told them?'

'Yes. It was the money aspect that seemed to mean most to Joy. She had been deprived in order that he could maintain another household. She gave that bitter laugh of hers. If I'd had to live with that laugh it would have got horribly on my nerves.'

'How's Martin getting on with his typewriter inquiries?'

Wexford threw the report across the desk. It was no Sevensmith Harding machine that had been used to type Williams's letter of resignation. All the typewriters in use in the Myringham office were of the sophisticated electronic kind. Neither of the Williams households contained a typewriter of any sort. The Harmers had a typewriter in the two-storey flat over the shop where they lived and both Hope Harmer and her daughter Paulette used it. It was a small Olivetti, an electric machine.

'His new young lady typed that letter,' Burden said. 'Find her and we find the typewriter.'

'Find her and it won't matter whether we find the typewriter or not.'

Sergeant Martin had also been to Bath.

There, it seemed, Rodney Williams had had his origins. On an estate of houses some few miles outside the city, in a house very like the one Rodney had bought for his second bride, lived his brother Howard. It was Howard's address that appeared on Wendy's marriage certificate.

His parents had also once lived in Bath but his father had died when he was a child and his mother when Rodney was twenty-seven. That dead mother Rodney in his calculating way had used to his advantage. No doubt he had told Wendy that old Mrs Williams disapproved of his marriage to a young girl, would never wish to meet her, but the good son would be obliged to pay the occasional duty visit . . .

The brother seemed honest and straightforward. There was very little contact between him and Rodney. Years ago, fifteen or sixteen at least, some of Rodney's mail had been sent to his address by mistake. He had simply sent it on. Communications from the registrar at the time of the marriage to Wendy, Wexford thought. Howard Williams was also a salesman and on 15 April he had been in Ireland on business for his firm.

Joy hadn't told him of his brother's death. He had seen it in the papers and seemed to have reacted with calm indifference.

Wendy Williams's home was on the outskirts of Pomfret and a mile from the Harmers' shop. Had the relative nearness of his in-laws to his second and bigamous home worried Williams? Had he only agreed to buy a house there to placate Wendy or gratify some wish of hers? Or did he see this sort of risk as just part of the tightrope walk?

Between the estate and the nucleus of the town, that which not long ago *was* the town, lay the sports grounds of the

Haldon Finch Comprehensive School, playing fields, tennis courts, fives courts, running track. The Haldon Finch, though new and an example of the new education with its two thousand pupils of both sexes housed in no less than six buildings, was as much 'into' games as any public school of the past. You might get ten O-levels but you were nothing if you weren't good at games.

At 5.30 in the afternoon twelve girls were playing tennis on the courts adjacent to Procter Road.

'It must be a match with another school,' Burden said. 'They start after school's finished.'

He and Wexford were in the car, on their way to see Veronica Williams. Donaldson had taken a short cut, or at least a traffic-avoiding cut, and they had found themselves amid this complex of sports fields.

'We'll get out and watch for a minute or two.'

Burden got out, though demurring.

'It makes me feel funny standing about watching girls. I mean, you ask yourself – *they* ask *them*selves – what sort of blokes would do that?'

'What would you think if you saw two middle-aged women watching young men playing squash?'

Burden looked sideways at him.

'Well, nothing, would I? I mean, I'd think they were their mothers or just women who liked watching sport.'

'Exactly. Doesn't that tell you something? Two things? One is that, whatever the women's movement says, there is a fundamental difference between men and women in their attitude to sex, and the other that this is an area in which women might claim – if it's occurred to them – to be superior to us.'

'It's changing though, you have to admit. Look at all those clubs up north where men do strips for women audiences.'

'The attitude is still different. Men go to strip shows and gawp in a sort of seething silence.'

'Don't women?'

'Apparently women laugh,' said Wexford.

One of the tennis players was Eve Freeborn. He spotted her from the purple slick in her hair. Her partner was a thin dark girl, their opponents a big heavily built blonde and another thin dark girl, this one wearing glasses. This four was on the court nearest to the road. Wexford could see enough of the other two courts and the other four couples only to be sure that Sara Williams was not among them. Sara didn't attend the Haldon Finch, of course – that would have been too great a risk even for Rodney Williams – but if this was a match six of the girls must come from another school. Seated on the three umpire chairs were three young women who had the look of games teachers.

He was aware at once that no one was playing very well. Had the standard deteriorated since the days when he had watched Sylvia and Sheila playing tennis? No, it wasn't that. It was television. These days you saw tennis played on TV. Top championships week after week, it seemed, here or in Europe or in America, and it spoiled you for the real thing, the local article. A pity really. It made you irritated at how often they missed the ball. Eve Freeborn had a good hard service. She would have served aces – only they were always on the wrong side of the line. Her opponent in the glasses was the worst player of the twelve, slow on her feet with a weak service and a way of scooping the ball up into the air, making it easy prey for Eve's slamming racket.

'Two match points,' said Burden, who had been attending more closely to the progress of the set.

Eve served a double fault. One match point. She served again, weakly, and the blonde shot it back like an arrow down the tramlines. The umpire announced deuce. Eve served another double fault.

'Van out,' said Wexford.

'My God, but that shows your age. That's what they said at tennis parties in the thirties.'

The umpire corrected him by saying crisply that the score was 'advantage Kingsmarkham'. So it was Kingsmarkham High who were the visitors here, once a grammar school, now private and fee-paying, no longer state-aided.

Kingsmarkham won the game. They changed ends, the girls paused by the umpire's chair and wiped faces and arms, drank Coke out of cans. Eve was standing only a few yards from Wexford. The little flame-coloured badge he had till now seen only as an orange spot near the neckline of her white tee-shirt showed itself at closer quarters to be a badge. He could make out spread wings on it and the letters ARRIA.

Eve didn't or wouldn't look at him. Perhaps he wasn't recognizable out of his office, in shirt-sleeves. He peered more closely. The umpire got down from her chair and came to the wire fence. She was a stocky, muscular young woman with a cross face and flashing eyes. In a voice full of crushed ice she said, 'Was there something you wanted?'

Wexford inhibited all the possible replies, improper, provocative, even mildly lecherous, that sprang to mind. He was a policeman. Anyway, Burden got in first with the flasher's classic caught-before-the-act answer.

'We were just looking.'

'Well, perhaps you'd like to get on with whatever you're supposed to be doing.'

'Move along, Mike,' said Wexford.

They went quickly to the car. The games mistress glared after them.

'Do they still call them that?'

'Call them what? Games mistresses?' Burden was silent for a moment. Then he said, screwing up his face, 'I'll tell you when my new daughter's eleven. If she gets to exist. If she gets to be eleven. If she and I are together when she does.'

'It's not as bad as that.'

'No? Maybe not. Maybe it's she and I that'll be together and not Jenny and I.'

Things must be bad with Burden for him to burst out with that in Donaldson's hearing. Not that Donaldson would say a word. But he would hear and he would think. Wexford said nothing. He watched Burden's face close up, the eyes grow dull and the mouth purse, the frown that was hardly ever absent re-establish itself in a deep double ridge. The car drew away. He looked behind him and saw Eve leaping to achieve her best volley of the match.

'Veronica was supposed to be playing in a tennis match,' said Wendy Williams, 'but of course she was too upset. She hasn't been to school today and I had to take the day off. I had to tell her her father had another wife and family. It was bad enough telling her he was dead.'

The second Mrs Williams, whom Wexford had at first thought of as rather sweet and gentle, he now saw had other

301

sides to her nature, among them a rather unpleasant habit of laying the blame for her misfortunes on whomsoever else might be present.

'I told her everything and at first she wouldn't speak and then she became very distressed.' The soft little voice trickled round the phrases. The eyes opened wide and wistful, like a Pears Soap child seeing distant angels. Wexford had the disturbing thought that perhaps she had cultivated all this because Williams had fancied little girls. 'You'll be gentle with her, won't you? You'll remember she's only sixteen? And it's not just that she's lost her father, it's worse than that.'

No question here of being sent up to the girl's bedroom. Veronica would come down. And Wendy would be there. He supposed Veronica must have been the missing tennis player for whom the dark girl not wearing glasses had substituted. While he was speculating Veronica came in, walking diffidently, a dead look still on her face. She had been crying but that was a long while ago now. Her eyes were dry and the lids pale, but a puffiness remained. Nevertheless she had dressed herself carefully for this encounter, as had her mother. Such things, which would have been lost on many men, never escaped Wexford. Wendy was in a black cotton dress with big sleeves that was a little too becoming to qualify as true mourning and Veronica in a pink pleated skirt, sweat shirt with a gold V on it and pink and white running shoes. Probably Wendy got their clothes from Jickie's at a discount.

'This is Chief Inspector Wexford and Inspector Burden, darling. They want to ask you one or two questions. Nothing difficult or complicated. They know what a bad shock you've had. And I shall be here all the time.'

For God's sake, she's not ten, Wexford thought. The girl's dull staring look disconcerted him.

'I'm sorry about your dad, Veronica,' he began. 'I know you're feeling unhappy and you'd probably like to be left alone. But your mother's told you what's happened. Your father isn't simply dead. He was killed. And we have to find out who killed him, don't we?' A not unfamiliar doubt assailed him. Did they? *Cui bono?* Who would be satisfied, avenged, recompensed? He was a policeman and it wasn't for him to think such thoughts. Not a hint of them was in

302

his tone. He looked at the girl and wondered what had been going on in her mind all those weeks her father was missing. Had she believed, like her mother, that he was with another woman? Or had she accepted his absence as she must have accepted all his other absences when he was allegedly away travelling for his firm or paying filial visits in Bath? She was no longer looked at him but down at the floor, her head drooping like a tired flower on a stalk.

'Do you think we could go back to April the fifteenth?' he said. 'It was a Thursday. Your mother expected your father home that evening but she had to stay on late at work. You were here though, weren't you?'

The 'yes' came very quietly. He might not have understood it for what it was if she hadn't nodded as well.

'What did you do? You came home from school when – at four?' He too was talking to her as if she were ten, but something in her attitude, her bowed head, feet crossed, hands in lap, seemed to invite it. Again that nod, the head lifted a little to make it. 'And then what happened? What sort of time did you expect your father to come?'

She murmured that she didn't know.

'We never knew what time to expect him,' Wendy said. 'We never knew. It might have been any time.'

'And did he come?' said Wexford.

'Of course he didn't! I've told you.'

'Please, Mrs Williams, let Veronica answer.'

The girl was shy, nervous, perhaps also unhappy. She was certainly in shock still. But suddenly she made an effort. It was as if she saw that there was no help for it, she was going to have to talk, she might as well get it over. Sara's tortoiseshell brown eyes looked in his and Sara's Primavera lips parted with a quiver.

'I had tea. Well, a Coke and some stuff Mummy left me in the fridge.' Yes, Wendy for all her own youth was the kind of woman who would be smotheringly protective, even to the extent of preparing meals in advance for a sixteen-year-old as if she were an invalid. Veronica said, 'I'd asked my friend round – the one whose place I was at when you came before – but she rang up and said she couldn't come. She said I could go to her.'

'But you wanted to wait in for your father?'

303

She was no Sara, no Eve Freeborn. She turned her head and looked to her mother for help. It came, as no doubt it always did.

'Veronica had no need to wait in for Rodney. I've told you, we never really thought he'd come at all.'

' "We", Mrs Williams?'

'Well, I don't really know what Veronica thought. I hadn't said anything to her then about the possibility of our splitting up. I was waiting to see what would happen. But the point is Veronica had no need to wait in for him and I wouldn't have . . . well, she's got her own life to lead.'

What had she been going to say when she broke off and made that extraordinary statement about this little creature's obviously nonexistent independence?

'You went out then?'

'I went to my friend's. I didn't stop there long. We played records. I wanted her to come out for a coffee but she couldn't, she was baby-sitting with her brother. She's got a brother who's only two. That was why she couldn't come over to me.'

'So you went back home. What time?'

'I didn't go straight home. I had a coffee on my own at Castor's. I got home about nine and Mummy came in ten minutes after.'

'You must have been disappointed your father wasn't there.'

'I don't know,' she said. 'I didn't think about it,' and surprisingly, for this wasn't really at issue, 'I don't mind being alone. I like it.'

'Well, my goodness,' said Wendy, not letting that one pass, 'you're never left alone if I can help it. You needn't talk as if you'd been neglected.'

Wexford asked the name of the friend and was told it was Nicola Tennyson and given an address that was between here and the town centre. No objection was put up by Wendy to their examining such of his personal property as Rodney Williams had in this house. It left Wexford with the feeling that this was because she rather wanted them to see over her house, its cleanliness, its elegant appointments and the evidence of her skill as housekeeper.

Here, at any rate, was the rest of Williams's wardrobe. It

was interesting to observe how he had kept his more stylish and 'in' clothes for this household. Jeans hung in the gilt-decorated white built-in cupboard, Westerner shirts, a denim suit and another in a fashionably crumpled stone-coloured linen mixture. There were two pairs of half-boots and a pair of beige kid moccasins. And the underwear was designed for a younger man than the part-time occupant of 31 Alverbury Road.

'He was two different men,' Wexford said.

'Perhaps three.'

'We shall see. At any rate he was two, one middle-aged, set in his ways, bored maybe, taking his family for granted, the other young still, even swinging – take a look at these underpants – making the grade with a young wife, living up to this little bandbox.'

Wexford looked around him at the room, thinking of Alverbury Road. There were duvets on the beds here, blinds at the windows, a white cane chair suspended from the ceiling, its seat piled with green, blue and white silk cushions. And the bed was a six-foot-wide king-size.

'He probably called it the playpen,' said Burden pulling a face.

'Once,' said Wexford.

In this house Williams had had no desk, only a drawer in the gilt-handled white melamine chest of drawers. This had been Wendy's house, no doubt about it, the sanctum where Wendy held sway. Girlish, fragile, soft-voiced though she might be, she had made this place her own, feminine and exclusive – exclusive in a way of Rodney Williams. He had been there on sufferance, Wexford sensed, his presence depending on his good behaviour. And yet his behaviour had not been very good even from the first. There had always been the travelling, the Bunbury of a mother, the long absences. So Wendy had made a home full of flowers and colours and silk cushions in which he was allotted small corners as if – unconsciously, he was sure it was unconsciously – she knew the day would come when it would be for herself and her daughter alone. Wexford looked inside the drawer but it told him little. It was full of the kind of papers he would have expected.

305

Except for Williams's driving licence with the Alverbury Road address.

'He was taking a risk leaving that about,' said Burden.

'Taking risks was his life. He took them all the time. He enjoyed the high wire. Anyway, suspicious wives read letters not driving licences.'

There were bills in the drawer, the counterfoils from credit-card chits, an American Express monthly account. Which address had that gone to? Yes, this one. It fitted somehow. Visa and Access were the workaday cards, American Express more cosmopolitan, more for the playboy. No doubt it was Wendy who paid the services' bills from the joint account. There was none in the drawer, only a rates demand, a television rental account book, an estimate from Godwin and Sculp, builders, of Pomfret, dated 30 March, for painting the living room, and an invoice from the same firm (stamped *Paid*) for renewal of a bathroom cistern. Under this lot lay Rodney's joint account cheque book, a paying-in book for the joint account, and a small glass bottle, half full of tablets, labelled 'Mandaret'.

On this the top floor of the house were two more bedrooms and a bathroom. Veronica's room was neat as a pin, white with a good deal of broderie anglaise about it and owing much to those magazine articles prevalent in Wendy's own childhood on how to make a dream bedroom for your daughter. No doubt poor Wendy had never had a dream bedroom of her own, Wexford thought, and he sensed that her youth had been nearer to that of Sara. No posters here, no home-made mobiles and no books either. It was designed for a girl who would do nothing in it but sit in the window seat looking pensive and wearing white socks.

The spiral staircase, a contraption of hideous discomfort and danger to all but the most agile, went through the middle of the house like a screw in a press. Down on the ground floor was a shower room, a separate lavatory, the third door on that side opening into the integral garage, and at the end of the passage a room the width of the house that opened through french windows onto patio and garden roughly the size of a large dining table. The room, that might have been for dining in or a study for Rodney Williams if he had been allowed one, was plainly devoted to Wendy's interests. She

306

had a sewing machine in it and a knitting machine, an ironing board set up with two irons on it, one dry and one steam, and there were clothes everywhere, neatly hung or draped, sheathed in plastic bags.

Mother and daughter were still sitting upstairs at the glass-topped table. Wendy had taken up some sewing, a handkerchief or possibly a traycloth into which she was inserting tiny stitches, her little finger crooked in the way it used to be said was vulgar to hold a teacup. Veronica nibbled at dry roasted peanuts out of a foil packet. The dry kind it would be, the other sort tending to leave grease spots. They were both as tense as compressed springs, waiting for the police to go and leave them alone.

'Have you heard of a society or club called ARRIA?' Wexford said to Veronica.

The spring didn't leap free of its bonds. There was no shock. Veronica merely nodded. She didn't screw up the empty peanut packet but flattened it and began folding it very carefully, first into halves, then quarters.

'At school?'

She looked up. 'Some of the girls in the sixth and seventh years belong to it.'

'But you don't?'

'You have to be over sixteen.'

'Why girls?' he said. 'Haldon Finch is co-ed. Don't any boys belong?'

She was a normal teenager really. Underneath the prissy looks, the shyness, the Mummy's girl air, she was one of them. The look she gave him seethed with their scorn for the cretinous incomprehension evinced by adults.

'Well, it's all women, isn't it? It's for women. They're – what d'you call it? – feminists, militant feminists.'

'Then I hope you'll keep clear of it, Veronica,' Wendy said very quickly and sharply for her. 'I hope you'll have nothing to do with it. If there's anything I really hate it's women's lib. Liberation! I'm liberated and look where it's got me. I just hope you'll do better than I have when the time comes and find a man who'll really support you and look after you, a nice good man who'll – who'll *cherish* you.' Her lips trembled with emotion. She laid down her sewing. 'I wasn't enough of a woman for Rodney,' she said as if the girl

307

wasn't there. 'I wasn't enough of a girl. I got too hard and independent and – and *mature*, I know I did.' A heroic effort was made to keep the tears in, the break out of the voice, and a victory was won. 'You just remember that, Veronica, when your turn comes.'

Sergeant Martin was handling the complaint though, as he told Wexford, he hadn't much to go on. Nor had any harm been done – yet.

'A Ms Caroline Peters who's a physical education instructor at the Haldon Finch Comprehensive,' Martin said. 'Miz not Miss. She got very stroppy, sir, when I called her Miss. I called her an instructress too and had a job getting my tongue round it but that wasn't right either. She says two men were hanging about watching the girls playing a tennis match. Acting in a suspicious manner, she says. Came in a car which was parked for the express purpose of them getting out to watch. Voyeurs she called them. Afterwards she asked the girls if any of them knew the men but they denied all knowledge.'

Thank you Miss Freeborn, thought Wexford.

'Leave it, Martin. Forget it. We've better things to do.'

'Leave it altogether, sir?'

'I'll handle it.' A note to the woman or a phone call explaining all, he supposed. She had a right to that. She was a good conscientious teacher acting in a responsible manner. He mustn't laugh – except later perhaps with Burden.

There had been much food for thought picked up on his visits to Liskeard Avenue. And there had been something to make him wonder, something that was neither a piece of information nor the germ of an idea but entirely negative.

Wasn't it extraordinary that during those visits, those long talks, and during his initial interview with her, Wendy Williams had shown not the slightest interest in Rodney's other family? She had asked not a single question about the wife she had supplanted but not replaced, nor about the children who were siblings by half-blood of her own Veronica. Because she was inhibited by intense jealousy? Or for some other reason more germane to this inquiry?

11

Kevin Williams looked more like his mother than his father. He wouldn't have been recognizable as Veronica's half-brother. The genetic hand-down which was so distinctive a feature in Sara and Veronica had missed him and his forehead was narrow with the hair growing low on it. His manner was laconic, casual, indifferent.

Wexford, who had Martin with him, had interrupted what seemed to be a family conclave. For once the television was off, sight and sound. Joy Williams introduced no one but her son and his introduction she made proudly and with abnormal enthusiasm. Wexford was left to deduce that the woman and the girl who sat side by side on the yellow sofa must be Hope Harmer and her daughter Paulette.

Mrs Harmer, though plumper, fairer and better cared for than her sister, looked too much like her for her identity to be in doubt. She was a pretty woman and even in the present crisis she looked pleased with life. But the girl – to use an expression favoured by Wexford's grandsons – was 'something else again'. She was beautiful with a beauty that made Sara and Veronica merely pretty young girls. She reminded Wexford of a picture he had once seen, Rossetti's portrait of Mrs William Morris. This girl was dark and her face had the same dark glow as the face in the picture, her features the same symmetry and her large dark eyes the same otherworldly soulfulness. When he asked her if she was who he thought she was she raised those dark grey dreaming eyes and nodded, then returned to what she had been looking at, a magazine that seemed entirely devoted to hairstyles.

Kevin's term had ended the day before and he had come

straight home. Not to stay, though, he made clear to Wexford when they were alone in the stark dining room. He owed it to his mother to stay a few days, but next week he intended to stick to the plan he had made months before of going down to Cornwall to stay with a friend and later he would be camping in France. He seemed astonished when Wexford asked him for the address of the Cornish friend.

'We'd rather you didn't leave the country at present.'

'You can't keep me here. My father's death has nothing to do with me.'

'Tell me what you did on the evening of Thursday, April the fifteenth.'

'Was that when he died?' The casual manner had grown sullen. He was his mother in truculent mood all over again.

'I'll ask the questions, Kevin.'

It wasn't said roughly, but nevertheless the boy looked as if no one had spoken like that to him before. His low forehead creased and his mouth pouted.

'I only asked. He was my father.'

In his tone, that of contrived, badly acted sentiment, Wexford suddenly understood that no one in this household had cared a damn for Rodney Williams. And they hadn't in the other household either. People didn't care for him for long. In this area he had, at any rate, got his deserts.

'What happened that evening? What did you do?'

'Phoned home, I suppose,' he said, careless again. 'I always do on Thursdays or my mother goes bananas.'

'You phone from college?'

'No, the phones are always out of order or it's a hassle finding one that's free.' Kevin seemed to have decided he might as well give in to Wexford's questioning if not with a good grace. 'I go out to phone. Well, two or three of us do. To a pub. I phone home and transfer the charge.'

'You'll remember that Thursday if I tell you it was the first Thursday after you got back to college from the Easter vacation.'

The boy thought about it, seeming to concentrate. Wexford had no doubt he had known perfectly well all along.

'Yeah, I do remember. I phoned home around eight, eight-thirty – I don't reckon you want to know to the minute, do you? My mother was out. I talked to Sara.'

'That must have surprised you, your mother being out when you phoned.'

'Yeah, it was unusual. She thinks the sun shines out of my arse, as you've maybe noticed.' He jerked his shoulders in an exaggerated shrug. 'Unusual,' he said, 'but not unknown.'

More indignation came when Wexford asked for the names of Kevin's companions on the trip to the pub where the phone was. But it was hot air, pointless obstructiveness. The names were forthcoming after some expostulation.

'How did you get on with your father?'

'There was no communication. We didn't talk. The usual sort of situation, right?'

'And your father and Sara?'

The reply came sharply. It was incredible. It was exactly the reply a boy of Kevin's age might have made a hundred years before – or, according to literature, might have made.

'You can leave my sister out of this!'

Wexford tried not to laugh. 'I will for now.'

He found Joy and her sister questioning Martin in depth about Wendy Williams. The girls, the two cousins, had gone. Martin was answering in monosyllables and he looked relieved when Wexford came in. Joy broke off at once and, having seen he was alone, said, 'Where's my son?' as if Wexford might have arrested him and already stowed him away in a police car.

This would be his first encounter with Miles Gardner since the discovery of Rodney Williams's body. He and Burden waited for him in the managing director's office. The panelled room was dim and shadowy in spite of the bright day outside. A copper pot filled with Russell lupins stood on the window-sill. Wexford picked up the desk photograph of Gardner's family and looked at it dubiously.

'I suppose I'm sensitized to adolescent girls,' he said. 'I see them everywhere.'

'Just remember what the games mistress said.'

'I don't think I'm in danger, though they're a very pretty lot we're in contact with. One can almost see Williams's point of view.'

'He was just a dirty old lecher,' said Burden, apparently forgetting Williams had been a mere three years his senior. 'The primrose way to the everlasting bonfire.'

Gardner came in, apologizing for having kept them waiting. He began on some insincere-sounding expressions of sorrow at Williams's demise which Wexford listened to patiently and then cut short.

'If you're free for lunch we might all go over to the Old Flag.'

But this was something Gardner, regretfully, couldn't manage. 'I've promised to give my daughter lunch, my youngest one, Jane. She's got the day off school to go for an interview at the university here. A bit of an ordeal, she's a nervous kid, so I bribed her with the offer of a slap-up lunch.'

The University of the South was situated at Myringham. Another eighteen-year-old then . . .

'She should get a place,' Gardner said, and with a kind of rueful pride, 'There go our holidays abroad for the next three years.'

Wexford said he would like to talk to Christine Lomond, and in the room that had been Williams's if possible. Gardner took him there himself, up in the small slow lift. There were two desks and two typewriters, a Sierra 3400 and an Olympia ES 100. But this place was 'clean' as far as typewriters went. Martin had seen to that. The girl who came in was fresh-paint glossy in a suit of geranium-red linen, dark green cotton blouse, green glass rhomboid hanging on a chain and on her left wrist a watch with a red and green strap. Her hair had been touched with what his daughter Sylvia assured him were called 'low lights', though Wexford couldn't quite believe this and thought she must have been having him on. Christine Lomond's fingernails were the brilliant carmine of the latest Sevenshine front-door shade Pillarbox ('A rich true red without a hint of blue, a robust high gloss that stands up ideally to wind and weather'). They scuttled over the filing cabinet like so many red beetles.

Wexford had asked her to see what she could find him as samples of Williams's own typing, any report, assessment, rough notes even, he might have brought to the office with him. She said she was sure anything of that sort would have been handwritten, and it was two or three handwritten sheets that she produced for him, and then several more which she told him had probably been typed on the Olympia machine but using a different daisywheel, thus altering the typeface. Wexford was particularly interested because there seemed to him to be a flaw in the apex of the capital A.

The experiment, however, showed nothing but his own ignorance of typewriters or at any rate of recent technological advances made in typewriters. The red-tipped white fingers whipped a sheet of paper into the machine, switched it on, switched it off, whipped out the daisywheel, inserted another, and rapidly produced a facsimile of the first four lines of Williams's sales forecast for the first three months of the year.

'It's getting a bit ragged,' Christine Lomond said. 'We need a new wheel,' and she pulled the damaged one out and dropped it into the wastepaper basket.

'Where do you live, Miss Lomond?'

'Here. In Myringham. Why?' She had a rather abrupt manner, of the kind that is usually called 'crisp'.

'Did you like Mr Williams?'

She was silent. She seemed affronted, having anticipated perhaps nothing more than an investigation of papers and machines. How old was she? Twenty-six? Twenty-seven? She could be a good deal less than that. The heavy make-up and elaborate hairstyle aged her.

'Well, Miss Lomond?'

'Yes, I liked him. Well, I liked him all right. I didn't think about liking or disliking him.'

'Would you think back, please, and give me some idea of what you were doing on the evening of April the fifteenth?'

'I can't possibly remember that far back!'

Her eyelids flapped. They were a gleaming laminated sea blue ('Delicate turquoise with a hint of silver, ideal for that special ceiling, alcove or display cabinet').

'Try and pinpoint it,' said Burden, 'by thinking of what you were doing next day. That was the morning someone phoned to say Mr Williams was ill and wouldn't be in. Does that help?'

'I expect I was at home on my own.'

She didn't sound defensive, guilty, afraid. She sounded

sullen, as if the clothes and the make-up, the 'grooming' had not been effective.

'Do you live on your own or with someone?'

Surely the most innocent of questions. She pounced on it as surely as if those red nails had seized and clutched.

'I certainly do not live with someone! I was at home on my own watching the TV.'

Another one. What had they done in the old days before the cathode conquest? He ought to be able to remember pre-television alibis but he couldn't. I was reading, sewing, putting up shelves, fishing, listening to the radio, out for a walk, in the pub, at the pictures? Maybe.

Unwillingly, even grudgingly, she gave them her address. She admitted to possessing a typewriter, an old Smith Corona, though not a portable, and insisted it was in her parents' house in Tonbridge and she had never had it with her in the Myringham bedsit.

Downstairs in the reception area they encountered a young girl undressing. Or so to Wexford's astonished eyes it at first appeared. She was talking to the telephonist (Anna today) and in the act of pulling a cotton dress off over her head. Long slim legs in white tights, pale blue pumps with curly heels, and yes, a skirt which dropped to its former just-above-the-knee length when the garment, evidently a middy blouse, was off. Underneath it was a white tee-shirt. Her back was to Wexford. She kicked off the blue pumps, sending one flying across the room and leaving no doubt in the mind of an observer that this was a cathartic shedding of a hateful costume after an ordeal was over.

'Jane,' said Anna in a warning tone, 'there are some . . .'

She spun round. On the front of the tee-shirt were printed the letters ARRIA.

The first thing that struck Wexford about the house in Down Road, Kingsmarkham, was that there was no question of any of its occupants being obliged to share a bedroom. It was a very large, castellated, turreted, balconied Edwardian pile. Most houses like it had been converted into flats but not this one. A single family inhabited it and its (at least) eight bedrooms. Yet Eve Freeborn had given him the reason

314

for going to her boyfriend in Myringham instead of his coming to her that she shared a bedroom with her sister. Perhaps she hadn't a sister either. He would soon see.

At first he thought the girl who opened the front door to him *was* Eve. After all, the fact that this one had green hair meant nothing. They changed their hair colour these days as fast as they used to change their lipstick. A second look told him they weren't even identical twins. Twins, yes, fraternal twins with the same build of body and the same eyes. That was all. God knew what colour their hair really was. They had probably forgotten themselves.

The house smelt faintly of marijuana. An unmistakable smell that was like woodsmoke blended with sweet cologne.

'Eve?' Eve's sister said with incredulity. 'You want to see Eve?'

'Is that so difficult?'

'I don't know really . . .'

He had shown her his warrant card. After all, she was a young girl and it was evening. She shouldn't admit unidentified men into the house. But she was looking at it as if it were a warrant for her arrest. He felt impatient.

'Perhaps I should fill in a form or produce a sponsor.'

'Oh, no, come in. I'm sorry. It's just that . . .'

She had an irritating way of leaving her sentences unfinished. He followed her into the hall, darkly panelled like the offices of Sevensmith Harding, and up a big elegant winding staircase with a gallery at the top. The marijuana smell was fainter but it was still there. What astonished him about the house was the aura of the sixties that pervaded it. On the wall here was a poster (albeit a glazed and framed poster) of John Lennon seated at a white grand piano. A vase stood on a side table filled with dried grasses and shabby peacock's tail feathers. And hanging up as an ornament, not because it had been left there by chance, was an antique red silk dress embroidered with gold, its red and its gold tattered and shredded by time and moths. He said, 'Are your parents at home?'

'They've got a flat in London. They're there half the time.'

Impossible to tell if she minded or was glad. Those parents need not be more than forty themselves, he thought, and

Mother might be less. Eve's twin said, 'Perhaps you'd better wait here. I'll just see if . . .'

All the bedroom doors were open. Only they weren't bedrooms, not exactly. Each one, as far as he could see, had the look rather of a bedsit, with chairs and tables and floor cushions and a couch or divan with an Indian bedspread flung artlessly over it, posters on the walls and postcards pinned up higgledy-piggledy. He sat down to wait in a rocking chair that had its rockers painted red, black and white and a dirty lace veil draped over its back, and wondered how to explain this mysterious house.

Then he understood. It wasn't the girls who were living in the past, who were twenty years out of date, or purposely living in an anachronism. Those parents had been young in the sixties, had revelled probably in that new inspiring freedom, and now the spirit of the sixties, the flavour, the mores would never leave them. Not the girls but the parents were the marijuana users. He would have to do something about that . . .

How long was she going to keep him waiting?

He got up and went out into the passage. There was no one about. But from somewhere he could hear the sound of female voices – a sound that was not in the least like the twittering of birds, strong earnest talk rather than a murmuration. A staircase led to the attic floor but it wasn't from up there that the voices came.

There was a burst of laughter, some sporadic clapping. He walked down the passage towards the sound, came out into another smaller, squarer landing, a map of the heavens painted on its ceiling by a trained but unsure hand. An amateur astrologer who had been to art school, he thought, which brought the sixties once more to mind. As he stood there, doubtful of the wisdom of bursting into a room full of women, the door opened and two girls came out. They stopped in the doorway, looking at him in astonishment. One was unknown to him, the other was Caroline Peters, physical training instructor.

Before anyone spoke Eve Freeborn came out of the room, shouldering her way past the two who blocked the doorway. She was once more in the pelvis-crusher jeans but this time with a purple satin blouse to match her hair. Caroline Peters, on the other hand, was dressed exactly like a boy – or like boys used to dress before punk apparel came to stay: blue jeans, brown leather jacket, half-boots; no make-up, hair cropped in a crewcut.

'Sorry,' Eve said. 'Have you been waiting long?'

'*They* kept *us* waiting,' said Caroline Peters with the maximum venom, 'for four thousand years.'

She had recognized him and wasn't pleased. Or had he been recognized for what he was in addition to being a policeman – a man? Wexford had never before personally encountered the kind of militant feminist who advocates total separatism. Enlightenment broke upon him.

'Have I by any chance interrupted a meeting of ARRIA?'

'It's over,' said Eve. 'It's just over.'

'We wouldn't have permitted interruption.'

Wexford looked at Caroline Peters. 'Don't go yet, please. I'd like to talk to you too.'

She lifted her shoulders, went back into the room. Eve waved a hand at the other girl, a pretty, sharp-faced redhead.

'This is Nicky.'

Inside the room, another, larger, bedsit hung with striped bedspreads on ceilings and walls like a Bedouin tent, half a dozen more girls were standing about or preparing to leave. Sara Williams was there and her cousin Paulette, the two of them talking to Jane Gardner, and all of them wearing ARRIA tee-shirts. A black girl, thin and elegant as a model, sat crosslegged on a floor cushion.

Eve said to the company, 'I don't remember what he's called,' as if it hardly mattered, 'but he's a policeman.' She pointed at one girl after another: 'Jane, Sara, Paulette, Donella, Helen, Elaine, and Amy, my sister, you've met.'

Caroline Peters pushed her hands into the pockets of her leather jacket.

'What is it you want?'

'I'd like to know more about ARRIA for a start.'

'For a *start* it was *started* by me and a like-minded woman, a classical scholar now at Oxford.' She paused. 'Arria Paeta,' she said, 'was a Roman matron, the wife of Caecina Paetus. Of course she was obliged to take his name.' Wexford could tell she was one of those fanatics who never miss a trick. 'Ancient Rome was known for its gross oppression and exploitation of women.' Teacher-like, she waited for his comments.

They came – perhaps to her surprise. 'The Emperor Claudius,' said Wexford who had done his homework, 'ordered Paetus to commit suicide but he proved too cowardly, so his wife took the sword and plunging it into her own heart, said, "See Paetus, it does not hurt . . ." '

'You've been reading Graves!'

'No. *Smith's Classical Dictionary*.' The girl called Nicky laughed. 'But I don't know what the letters stand for,' he said.

'Action for the Radical Reform of Intersexual Attitudes.'

'A case of making the nym fit the acronym? Or is it a deliberate obscuration?'

'Perhaps it is.'

'How many schools are involved?'

It was Eve who answered him. 'Kingsmarkham High, Haldon Finch, St Catherine's . . .' but Caroline Peters interrupted her.

'I teach at Haldon Finch. ARRIA had its inception just over a year ago at St Catherine's. We admitted as members only those women over sixteen, those in fact in the sixth and seventh years. I'm glad to say it had an immediate appeal – how could an organization designed expressly for women, designed to give men no quarter – be otherwise?' She turned on him a glacial look of distaste and it gave him a most unpleasant feeling. He didn't belong to a minority, there was no way he could be categorized into a minority, yet the sensation she gave him was of doing so and of an oppressed one at that. 'Our very well-organized propaganda machine,' she said, 'spread the good news through the other schools in the area and we soon had considerable cells at Pomfret College of Further Education and Kingsmarkham High.' The good news, he thought, the 'gospel' no less. She astonished him by saying, 'We now have a membership of just over five hundred women.'

He suppressed the whistle he wanted to give. What must the local population of seventeen- and eighteen-year-old girls be? All of them, including those who had left school, could surely hardly amount to more than a couple of thousand and that meant 25 per cent in ARRIA. Why, they could almost start a revolution!

'All right, you've got badges, you've had tee-shirts printed, you hold meetings, but what do you *do*?'

Caroline Peters answered readily. 'Basically, have as little contact with men as possible. Defy men by intellectual and also by physical means.'

He pricked up his ears at that. She wasn't carrying a bag but she had pockets. Most of the other girls had bags. He hadn't got a warrant and, almost more to the point, hadn't a woman with him to carry out a search.

'We have a constitution and manifesto,' she said. 'I expect there's a copy about and I see no objection to your having one. Would you women agree to that?' There was a murmur of assent, some of it amused. 'But I must point out that our aim isn't to meet men on equal terms. It isn't to come to a truce or compromise with them nor to reach that uneasy détente which in past revolutions has sometimes come into being between a proletariat and a bourgeoisie. As Marx said in another context: Philosophers have tried to explain the world. The point surely is to change it. Good night, everyone.' She went out of the room, closing the door with a somewhat sinister quietness behind her.

Silence. The black girl, Donella, cast up her eyes, rolling sloe-brown pupils in moon-white whites. Eve said, 'By physical means, she only meant self-defence stuff. It's compulsory when you join to take a self-defence course, karate or judo or tai chi or whatever.'

'Personally,' said Donella, 'I think that's one of the things that attracts people – the sport, you know.'

'You may have noticed, there've been three times as many evening courses in martial arts started since ARRIA began. That's in response to increased demand, that's ARRIA.'

Nicky had spoken with pride, not aggressively. She made a swift chopping movement with one arm. Wexford, a large man over six feet tall, felt relieved he wasn't on the receiving end of that blow. It was true about the judo and karate courses, he had remarked on it himself to Burden, pleased that women were at last taking steps to defend themselves against the muggings and rapes which in the past few years had so disproportionately increased.

'All right,' he said, 'that's for self-defence. How about aggression? I don't suppose anyone's going to admit to carrying an offensive weapon?'

Nobody was. They didn't look scared or guilty or even alert. He fancied he saw wariness in one or two faces.

'I'll give you a copy of the constitution,' Eve said. 'There's nothing private about it. Everyone's welcome to know what we do, men as well as women. Do you have daughters?'

'They're a lot older than you.'

She looked at him in a not unkindly way, assessing. 'Well, they would be, wouldn't they? You can't be too old for ARRIA, though.'

The constitution was typed and photocopied. He noted that there were no flaws in the apexes of the capital As or the ascenders of the lower-case ts. It went into his pocket to be read at leisure. Sara Williams, he observed, was watching his every movement. The big fair girl called Helen he now realized had been Eve's partner in the tennis match. He said to Eve, 'If everyone is in fact going I'd like to talk to you alone for five minutes.'

The brisk policeman's tone replacing the one of easy jocularity seemed to jolt her. She pushed fingers through the purple crest of hair.

'OK, if that's the way you want it. Everybody out, right?' She gave a hiccuping giggle. 'Home, women!'

Amy said, 'Well, I think I'll just . . .' and drifted vaguely towards the door.

They all began to take their leave in ways peculiar to young girls, whether feminists or reactionaries. Helen and Donella closed in upon each other with a tight bear hug which ended in giggles and heads subsiding on each other's shoulders. Sara wrapped her arms round herself and moved across the floor with vague dancing steps. Jane humped her bag, filled with ARRIA constitution sheets, as if it weighed a ton, making agony faces. Nicky was lost in a dream that seemed to turn her into a sleepwalker so that she neither paused in her exit nor spoke but merely raised a languid flapping hand in farewell as she passed through the doorway.

Alone with Eve, Wexford said, 'You've been telling me lies.'

'I have not!'

320

'Why did you tell me your boyfriend couldn't come here because you had to share a bedroom with your sister? This is an enormous house and as far as I can see your parents mostly aren't here anyway. But you told me lack of space – and you implied lack of privacy – stopped him coming here.'

'Well,' she said, a sly look in her eyes, 'I can explain that. You'll see the answer in our constitution actually. Rule 4.'

He pulled the constitution out of his pocket. Here it was, Rule 4. 'Women' – not ARRIA members, he saw, but always 'women' as if the society contained the world's entire female population – 'Women shall avoid the company of men wherever possible but should their presence be required for sexual, biological, business or career purposes, it is expedient and desirable for women to go to them rather than permit them to come to us.'

'But why?'

'Caroline and Edwina – she's the classical one who's at Oxford – they said it smacked of the sultan visiting his harem. You've got to think it through, you know. When you do you can see what they mean.'

'So that's why you went to your boyfriend in Arnold Road? You required his presence for sexual or even biological purposes?'

'Isn't that why women usually require men?'

'There are other ways of putting it. More aesthetic ways, I'd say. Maybe more civilized.'

'Oh, *civilized*. Men made civilization and it's not up to much, is it? It's no big deal.'

He left it. 'Did you know Sara Williams was the daughter of the murdered man whose car you saw in Arnold Road?'

'Not then I didn't. I do now. Look, I only know her through ARRIA and I didn't know her father. For all I knew, she mightn't have had a father.'

He accepted that. 'Miss Peters didn't tell me much about this society of yours, did she? Only that it's a wildfire movement, it's caught on in all the local schools. How about the – what shall I call it? – esoteric stuff? How do you join? Do you pay a subscription? Is there any sort of ritual – like freemasons, say?'

'We don't need money,' she said, 'so there's no sub. Where would they get it from anyway? Most of our members are still at school. They'd have to get it from their fathers and that's out. See Rule 6 on dependence. The only thing that costs us is the photocopying, only it doesn't because Nicky does it on her dad's Xerox in the night, when he's asleep.'

There was an irony there but Wexford didn't point it out. 'Anyone can join?'

'Any woman over sixteen who's not married. Obviously a married woman has already capitulated. Anyway, it wouldn't be possible for her to keep to the rules.'

'That would let my daughters out.'

She ignored him. 'I'm a founder member. When we started there was a lot of really wayout stuff going on. Edwina wanted initiation ceremonies, sort of baptisms of fire if you can imagine.'

'What sort?'

He was deeply curious. At the same time he was afraid she would soon realize she was spending too much time unnecessarily in the society of a man. She considered his question in thoughtful silence. She was not a pretty girl. But perhaps this didn't matter in these days when beauty was no longer at a premium. She had one of those chinless faces, long-nosed, full-lipped, but with creamy delicate skin. A frown creased, or rather crumpled, her forehead. Creasing was for older people. Eve's frown was like the bunching of a piece of cream velvet.

'Some of the others went along with her ideas,' she said. 'I mean, she was a radical feminist. For instance, she used to say we couldn't make revolution on Marxist principles on account of Marx having been a man. She said sexuality was politics and the only way to get freedom was for all women to be lesbians. Any hetero behaviour was collaborating with the enemy. Even Caroline Peters never went as far as that.'

'You were going to tell me about initiation.'

Eve seemed reluctant to reach the subject. 'They actually formed a splinter group over it. Sara, the one whose father was murdered, she was one of them and Nicky Anerley was another. One of the things they objected to was being educated along with the other sex. They wanted schools and colleges run by women and with women teachers. Of course, it would be best, it's the ideal if you know what I mean, but it's a bit fantastic.'

322

'Particularly as it's only in very recent years that women have gained admission to certain men's colleges, notably at Oxford.'

'That's beside the point. This would be a question of getting the men out altogether. Edwina and the rest of them who were at mixed schools wanted to go on strike until they agreed not to admit boys. But Caroline wouldn't have that. I suppose she was afraid of losing her job.'

'And that's what caused the rift in the party?'

'Well, partly. This was all last summer and autumn. It more or less stopped when Edwina went up to Oxford in October and the others drifted back. I may as well tell you. It was all a sort of fantasy anyway. Edwina said in order to prove herself a true feminist a woman ought to kill a man.' Eve looked at him warily. 'I don't mean everyone who joined ARRIA was to have to kill a man to get to be a member. The idea was for groups of three or four to get together and . . .

'But that's not an initiation ceremony really, is it? I could tell you about some of those if you want.'

12

With inscrutable face Jenny Burden sat reading ARRIA's manifesto. She was past the stage now of prettifying disguises of her pregnancy. It was beyond disguise and her condition didn't flatter her. Younger than her years though she had always looked, she now appeared too old to be having a baby. Her face was not so much lined as lacking in its former firmness, caverns hollowed out under the eyes and chin muscles sagging. She had no lap now so she held the flimsy sheets against a book propped up on the table in front of her.

But Wexford could tell by Burden's pleased expression that he was content to see his wife making even this small effort to escape from the apathy that had settled on her as the psychotherapy she was having progressed. No longer in revolt, no longer violent in her hatred of the child, she had become resigned. She waited in hopeless passivity. When Wexford arrived she had taken his hand, put up her face for a kiss, inquired in a limbo voice after Dora and the girls. And he had thought: when the baby is born she could go completely mad, enter a schizophrenic world and pass the rest of her life in hospital. She wouldn't be the first to whom such a thing had happened.

Still, now she was reading ARRIA's constitution, and apparently reading every word with care. Wexford wouldn't talk about the Williams case in her presence and Burden knew that. Suddenly she began reading aloud.

'Rule 6: With certain limited exceptions, no woman shall be financially dependent on a man. Then they list the exceptions. Rule 7: All women shall take a course in some martial art or self-defence technique. Rule 8: All women shall carry a permitted weapon for self-defence, i.e. ammonia spray, pin, penknife, pepper shaker, etc. Rule 9: No member shall marry, participate in the bourgeois concept of becoming 'engaged' or share accommodation with a man in a cohabiting situation. Rule 10 . . . Do you want Rule 10?'

'Oh, I have read it,' Wexford said. 'It is heresy!'

She didn't recognize the quotation. 'You're bound to think that way, aren't you? Perhaps I should have read all this before I met you, Mike.'

He took the blow with a physical flinch.

'ARRIA didn't exist then. It was around earlier this year before I gave up work, though. I always wanted to get hold of their manifesto but no one would even talk to me about it. I was a married woman, you see.'

'I suppose I was lucky to get it,' Wexford conceded.

Burden was making an effort to recover from the pain she had given him. 'I want to hear Rule 10.'

'All right. Rule 10: Women wishing to reproduce should select the potential father for his physique, health, height, etc., and ensure impregnation in a rape or near-rape construct.'

'In a *what*? What the hell does it mean?'

Wexford said, 'Margaret Mead says men of the Arapesh fear rape by women just as women in other cultures fear rape by men.'

'The mind boggles.' By this, Wexford knew, Burden meant he would dearly have loved to inquire further into the mechanics and techniques but was hampered by inhibition. 'The trouble is surely that most of this was written by lesbians like Edwina Klein and Caroline Peters. It doesn't seem to cater for women who actually *love* men – and those are surely in the vast majority.'

Jenny looked coldly at her husband. 'In the sort of explanation bit that comes after the rules it says the authors realize woman may feel affection for men and even – I quote – "what is termed sexual love" but it is necessary that something must be given up for the cause. Other women in the past have denied themselves this indulgence and been amply compensated. It goes on: "After all, what does this so-called 'love' amount to when a woman sets it against its concomitants: gross exploitation, pornography, degradation, career prohibition or curtailment, rape, father-daughter incest and the still-persisting double standard?" '

'It doesn't seem to bear much relation to our own home lives, does it?' said Burden.

Jenny had tears in her eyes, Wexford saw. They shone there, unshed. 'Revolutionaries are always extreme,' she said. 'Look at the Terror of 1793, look at Stalinism. If they're not, if they compromise with liberalism, all their principles fizzle out and you're back with the status quo. Isn't that what's happened to the broader women's liberation movement?'

The men looked at her with varying expression of doubt and dismay. Burden had gone rather pale.

'If these girls,' said Jenny, 'can accomplish just a fraction of what they're setting out to do, if they can begin to make people see what "inequitable arbitration" really amounts to, perhaps – perhaps I shan't so much mind my daughter being born.'

This time she didn't break down into tears. 'I know you want to talk. I'll leave you.' She turned to her husband, kissed his forehead, carried herself clumsily to the door. There was no dignity there and no beauty because the child that made her heavy was unwanted ... Burden put out one finger to touch the ARRIA manifesto like someone steeling himself to make contact with something he has a phobia about.

'I feel it threatens me, all this. I'm frightened of it.'

'It's good that you're honest enough to admit it.'

'Do you really think there's anything in this killing a man stuff?'

He had done so at first. It had seemed the obvious answer and for a moment or two the only possible answer. At that point his whole tone towards Eve had changed. He had been dancing lightly with her and then, suddenly, the music stopped and he seized hold of her. That was what it was like. Of course, he had frightened her with his quick rough questions ...

'But nobody ever did it! It was a fantasy – like group sex or something. Like an orgy. You think about what it would be like, you fantasize, but you don't *do* it.'

326

'Many do.'

'Well, OK, that wasn't a very good comparison. The point is fantasy doesn't become reality, the two don't mix.'

'Don't they? Isn't that what a psychopath is? Someone who confuses fantasy with reality?'

She had insisted, with the panic of someone who realizes she has said too much, that Edwina Klein's idea had been hers alone, even the splinter group had opposed it. Knives next. He had gone on to ask her what was meant by 'permitted weapons'. Did this category include knives? Not *real* knives, she said, and she had looked at him as a child might, round-eyed, afraid of something it doesn't understand.

'It's tempting,' he said to Burden, 'to think of a group of those ARRIA girls grabbing hold of poor old Williams like the Maenads with Orpheus and doing him in on the Lesbian shore.'

Burden looked at him, mystified. 'Shall we have a beer?' he said.

'Good idea.'

> ' "Malt does more than Milton can
> To justify the ways of God to man". '

'You're right there,' Burden said feelingly.

He came back with two cans and two tankards on a tray. Poor chap, Wexford thought, he's had enough. And how curious it was that all these dramatic things happened to Burden, who was such an ordinary, unimaginative, salt-of-the-earth person. The prototype surely of Kafka's man to whom who, though he shut himself up in his room, hid himself, lay low, life nevertheless came in and rolled in ecstasy at his feet. Whereas for him, Wexford, nothing much came along to disturb his private peace. Thank God for it!

'Just the same,' he said, 'we're going to have our work cut out checking out every one of ARRIA's members. There are said to be five hundred of them, remember.'

'The girl who stabbed Budd may not be the same girl who stabbed Wheatley who may not be the same girl as the one that killed Williams, but on the other hand they may be one and the same.'

'Right,' said Wexford. 'But don't let's talk of the "one" that killed Williams. No girl on her own could have carried

327

his body into that car and then carried it out again and buried him.'

'The way I see it, we have to think of it along these lines. On the one hand we have the radical feminists of whom we know (a) that the notion of killing a man was at any rate considered by them and (b) that they are required by their own rules to carry offensive weapons. We also know that Wheatley certainly and Budd probably were stabbed by ARRIA members. We've been told too that Williams, pursuing his well-known tastes, had a very young girl-friend. Now is this girlfriend a member of ARRIA?'

'Whatever the ARRIA rules may say,' said Wexford, 'we know members do have to do with the opposite sex. Look at Eve climbing in through her boyfriend's window. She hasn't made the supreme sacrifice of giving up men. And if you want to kill a man what better way of doing it than in what ARRIA would probably call a libido-emotional construct – in other words a love affair?'

Burden finished the last of his beer. In the next room Jenny had put a record on, Ravel's *Pavane on a Dead Infanta*. 'Who said that about malt and Milton?'

'Houseman. His life was ruined by an unrequited love.'

'Blimey. Why ravens?'

'In ARRIA's logo, d'you mean? They're predatory birds, aren't they? No, I suppose not. Harsh-tongued? I really don't know, Mike. At any rate, they're not soft and submissive. The collective noun for them is an "unkindness". An Unkindness of Ravens. Appropriate, wouldn't you say? In their attitude to the opposite sex anyway. They stab at us with knives rather than beaks.'

'Not without provocation, of course.'

'That's true. Budd on his own admission tried to get fresh with the girl who attacked him. He may have got fresher than he says. Wheatley says he didn't get fresh at all but I'm not inclined to believe him. They made passes and got themselves stabbed. Makes you wonder what Williams did, doesn't it?'

As Wexford walked home he thought about what he had had to do as a result of his visit to the Freeborns' house.

Sergeant Martin and Detective Bennett had paid a follow-up call and this morning Charles Freeborn, the girls' father, had appeared at Kingsmarkham Magistrates' Court charged with possessing cannabis and with permitting cannabis to be smoked upon his premises. Bennett, who detected the stuff in a positively cat-and-mouse way – or cat-and-catmint way – had begun a methodical search of the big overgrown garden, starting at the conservatory, following the crazy-paving path through a copse of unpruned dusty shrubs. This path curved all round the perimeter of the garden, winding its way between ghosts of flowerbeds where a few attenuated cultivated plants thrust their heads through a matting of bindweed, ground elder and thistles. A gate in the fence at the garden's foot afforded a shortcut into a path to the High Street. Bennett had been wondering if he was getting obsessional imagining *Cannabis sativa*, which requires sunlight and space, might even flourish here when he suddenly came upon the only tended flowerbed in the whole half acre.

He was nearly back at the house again, the stifling, shadow-spreading trees behind him. A neat rectangular clearing had been made in the shaggy grass here, the soil well watered, weeded, and the bed bordered with bricks. Martin had declared the vigorous young plants to be seedling tomatoes but Bennett knew better. Infra-red light is essential to the Indian hemp if its effect when ingested is to be the characteristically hallucinogenic one, and these plants were basking in it, for their bed was in the only part of the garden to enjoy day-long uninterrupted sunshine.

Wexford pondered, not for the first time, on the ethics of going into someone's house for a check and a chat, while there detecting a forbidden drug and immediately, scarcely with a qualm, taking steps to prosecute the offender. One's host *in absentia*, so to speak. Of course he was right, *it* was right. He was a policeman and that came first. That must always come first or chaos would come instead . . .

By the time the schools broke up towards the end of July Wexford's men had vetted and cleared something like 50 per cent of the ARRIA membership. Tracking them down was the difficulty, for Caroline Peters denied the existence of a list of members. Why should a list be needed when there was no subscription, and dates and venues of meetings were passed on by grassroots?

Paulette Harmer, Williams's niece, a sixth-form-college student, was cleared. She had been out with her boyfriend, to whom she would become engaged at Christmas – thereby abrogating ARRIA membership? – on the evenings Budd and Wheatley were stabbed, and at home with her parents and her aunt Joy on 15 April. Eve Freeborn, before going to her boyfriend in Arnold Road, had spent the evening at home with her parents and her sister. This alibi also accounted for Amy. Neither could be cleared of the Budd and Wheatley stabbings. Nor could Caroline Peters who, however, had been at a meeting in London on the evening of the 15th. The redheaded Nicky turned out to be Nicola Anerley and not the Nicola Tennyson who was Veronica Williams's friend. She had been at a party on 15 April, Helen Blake's eighteenth party, which had also been attended by another twelve members of ARRIA, all of whom Wexford was able to discount as far as the murder of Williams was concerned.

Jane Gardner he questioned himself. She was the right age, pretty and lively, an active member of ARRIA. He owed it to the cordial relationship he had had with her father to go himself and not send Bennett, say, or Archbold.

Miles was at home, had made a point evidently of being at home. He was affronted and preparing to be bitterly offended. He and his tall wife were in the drawing room (walls of Sevenstar Chinese yellow, black carpet, *famille jaune* porcelain) and Wexford was shown in by the cleaning lady masquerading as a maid. They spoke to him, he thought, in the aghast tones of parents asking a headmaster why he intends to expel their daughter from his school. Pamela Gardner called him 'Mr Wexford' though it had been 'Reg' in the past. Since she had no means of summoning the cleaning lady except by shouting, she went to fetch Jane herself.

'This is so entirely unnecessary,' Gardner said in a hard voice.

Wexford said it was routine and felt like a cop in an ancient Cyril Hare detective story.

The girl came in smiling and perfectly at ease. Then he had to ask the parents to go. They did but with a very ill

330

grace. At first Pamela Gardner pretended she didn't understand what he meant. Light dawned, then came incredulity, lastly disgusted acceptance. She took her husband's arm as if the very cornerstones of their home life had been threatened.

'Did you get a university place? Wexford asked Jane as soon as they were alone.

'Oh, yes, thanks. We met before, didn't we? At Dad's office? I never thought I would actually. I'd even enrolled at secretarial college in London just in case. My school doesn't have a commercial department.'

There came back to him a recollection of this girl changing her clothes in full view of the street. In 'Dad's office'. And when she had turned round to see him looking at her she hadn't turned a hair.

'Did you know Rodney Williams, Jane?'

'I'd met him. At the office. Dad introduced us. He had a lot of charm, you know.' She smiled, reminiscently, a bit sadly. 'He could make you feel you were the only person there worth talking to.'

It struck Wexford that this was the first person he had spoken to with a good word to say for Rodney Williams. She spoiled it a little.

'I expect he was like that with all girls of my age.'

Was she an enthusiastic member of ARRIA? Had she been in the splinter group? Did she carry a weapon? Where had she been when Budd was stabbed, when Wheatley was stabbed, when Williams was killed? Yes to the first and second questions, an indignant no, wide-eyed and law-abiding, to the third. A baby-sitting alibi for 15 April, a visit to her newly married sister for a Budd alibi, no memory of what she had been doing on the evening of the Wheatley stabbing. Apropos of none of this, surprising her with what seemed inconsequential, he said, 'Which schools do have commercial departments?'

'Haldon Finch, Sewingbury Sixth Form.' She gave him an earnest look. 'Dad's really upset that you suspect me.'

'There's no question of that. This is routine.'

'Well . . .' Suddenly she was the good daughter, dutiful, compliant, obedient. 'He and Mummy are dead against you taking my fingerprints.'

'You' presumably implied the Mid-Sussex Constabulary

or did she think he had come armed with pads and gadgets? The cleaning lady showed him out, her apron changed for rather smart dungarees. There was no sign of Miles or Pamela. Donaldson drove him back to Kingsmarkham and dropped him outside his own house. Dora, dressed up, was on the phone to Sylvia.

He passed close by her and touched her cheek with his lips. She responded to the kiss, mouthed something about getting a move on, went on talking to Sylvia. He went upstairs, changed into what he called his best suit, grey like the others but the latest and least shabby. When he retired he would never wear a suit again – not even to the theatre.

In the train he told Dora about the Gardners and said he had a feeling they wouldn't be asked to any more garden parties. She said that didn't matter, did it? she didn't care. And he shouldn't care either, he should relax, especially tonight.

'I wish I'd read the play.'

'You haven't had time.'

'You can always make time for things you want to do,' he said.

As it was he didn't even know what *The Cenci* was about and of its history only that it had for a long time been banned from the English stage. He and Dora, on holiday in Italy, had seen Guido Reni's portrait of Beatrice Cenci in the Galleria Nazionale in Rome, though he wouldn't have connected that with the play but for Sheila's saying it would be reproduced in the programme. It would have been a good idea to have read the play – or to have read Moravia's *Beatrice Cenci*, a novel that might be more entertaining.

The play threatened at first not to entertain at all. Shelley, Wexford thought to himself while aware he was no informed critic, wasn't Shakespeare. And wasn't he, in writing this sort of five-act tragedy in blank verse, some two hundred years out of date? Then Sheila came on, not looking like the portrait but with a small cap on her golden hair and dressed in white and grey, and he forgot everything, even the play, in his consuming pride in her. She had a peculiar quality in her acting, which critics as well as he had remarked on, of bringing clarity to obscure or periphrastic lines, so that her entrances always seemed to let light in upon the arcane. It

332

was so now, it continued to be so ... He saw and understood. The plot and purpose of the play began to unfold themselves for him and Shelley's style ceased to be an anachronism.

The effect on Dora was less happy.

She whispered to Wexford while they were having a glass of wine during the interval, 'There's more to it than I can see, I know that. It's not just that they can't stand the old man's harshness any longer, is it? I mean, why did Sheila come tearing in screaming about her eyes being full of blood?'

'Her father raped her.' Wexford realized what he had said and corrected himself. 'Count Cenci raped his daughter Beatrice.'

'I see. Oh yes, I do see. It's not made very clear, is it?'

'I imagine Shelley couldn't afford to spell it out. As it was, it must have been the incest theme that got the play banned.'

While waiting for the curtain to go up on Act Four he read the essay on the historical facts on which the play was based which had been written for the programme by an eminent historian. Beatrice, her stepmother and her brother had been put to death for the murder of Count Cenci. They really had. It had all happened. Guido had painted the portrait while Beatrice was in prison. Later they had tortured her to extract a confession.

It wasn't the kind of piece, he decided, that one would ever want to see again or read or remember a line from. When it was over they went backstage. They always did. Sheila, though in jeans and sweater now, still had a mask of gleaming white paint on her face and her hair top-knotted for execution as when she had cried:

> '... Here, Mother, tie
> My girdle for me ... My Lord,
> We are quite ready. Well, 'tis very well.'

Going home, Dora fell asleep in the train. Wexford found his mind occupied with the prosaic subject of typewriters.

It was the caretaker of the Haldon Finch Comprehensive School, primed by a phone call from the County Education

Department, who showed them round. Wexford had been inside the school before, years ago when the nucleus of these buildings had been the old county high school. Incorporated into it now were the buildings next door, a former clinic and health centre, as well as a vast new assembly hall and the glass, concrete and blue-slate complex of classrooms, music room and concert hall, with the sports centre a gilt-roofed rotunda that the sun set ablaze.

'It reminds me,' Wexford said to Burden, 'of a picture I once saw of the Golden Temple at Amritsar.'

But the commercial department had no new building to house it. It was pushed away into three rear classrooms at the top of the old high school, as if the education authority had half-heartedly accepted the recent remark of a government minister that shorthand and typing were no part of education and should not be taught in schools. Wexford followed Burden and the caretaker up a remarkable (and remarkably battered) Art Deco marble staircase and along a wide vaulted passage. The caretaker unlocked and opened the double doors into the commercial department. These too were Art Deco, with parabolas and leaves in green ironwork on their frosted glass. The old high school had been built in 1930 and the classrooms inside looked as if they had received no more than one coat of paint since then. They were shabby, typically green and cream, with a view of rooftops and a brick well full of dustbins.

It was in the farthest room that the typewriters were. Wexford asked himself what he had expected. The latest in word processors? Obviously here the country's resources were mainly devoted to science and sport. Nor presumably would ARRIA encourage its members towards a secretarial career. There was not an electric typewriter among the machines and some of them looked older than the building itself. Burden, walking between the tables, had a piece of paper in his hand, probably with the faults of the typewriter they were looking for written on it. As if he couldn't remember without that! A break in the head of the uppercase A and the ascender of the lower-case t, a comma with a smudged head.

He felt a small flicker of excitement when he spotted the first of the Remington 315s.

334

'Can you type?'

'Enough to test these,' said Burden and impressed Wexford by getting to work and using all his fingers.

Nothing wrong with the A, the t and the comma on the first one. Burden slipped his paper into the roller of the second. The capital A wasn't all it might have been but neither was the B or the D or a lot of others. The lower-case faces and the comma seemed unflawed. He tried the third machine, the caretaker watching with the fascinated awe of one who expects the litmus paper to turn not red but all the colours of the spectrum. This typewriter, however, seemed without faults. It produced the best-looking copy so far. There was only one more. Burden slipped his paper in and this time, instead of 'Now is the time of All good men to come to the Aid of the party', typed 'A thousand ages in Thy sight are like an evening gone'. If he had been a Freudian, Wexford thought, he would have wanted to know why. Perhaps it was just done to astonish the caretaker. Anyway, whatever the reason, this wasn't the machine Rodney Williams's letter of resignation had been typed on.

'That's it then.'

'Show my four samples to the experts. We could be wrong.'

'We're not wrong. These are all the typewriters the school has?'

'Apart from them as has gone away to be serviced.'

'Now he tells me,' said Wexford.

'There's always some go away in the summer holidays. It's never the lot of them. They go in, like, rotation.'

'Do you know how many have gone and where?'

The caretaker didn't know the answer to either question. No more than, say, five, he thought. He had never heard the name of any firm which might be servicing the machines or seen a van arrive to take them away.

'We must be thankful,' Wexford said as they came out of the school, 'that at least it's an old manual portable we're looking for and not one of the modern kind with a golfball or daisywheel.'

'A what or a *what*?'

'Let's say with a detachable typeface that our perpetrator could simply have taken out and thrown away.'

School might have broken up but sport went on. Half a dozen boys in shorts and tee-shirts were running laps round the biggest playing field and on the tennis courts a doubles game and a singles were in progress. The umpire seats were empty but Caroline Peters was there in the role of coach, and as they approached the wire fencing Wexford saw that what he had supposed to be a singles match was in fact instructor and instructed, the pupil here being Veronica Williams.

The four doubles players were Eve and Amy Freeborn, Helen Blake and another girl he had never seen before. So there were actually seventeen- and eighteen-year-olds in this corner of Sussex he had never seen before? He was beginning to think he knew them all by sight and usually by name too. He and Burden went over to the fence and watched, as they had done that previous time. Caroline Peters glared but didn't come over to admonish. She knew who they were now.

It was clear from the first that Veronica was streets ahead of the other players, though two years younger than any of them. She was the best tennis player Wexford had ever seen on a local court. This time the discrepancy between what he saw on TV and what he saw at home did not seem quite so wide. She was a strong, lithe, fast player with a hard accurate backhand and a powerful smashing action. When Caroline Peters made her serve her service was as hard as Eve's but the balls struck the court well inside the line.

The doubles players changed ends. Eve looked in Wexford's direction and then ostentatiously away. Loyalty to the father he had had charged with possessing cannabis, he supposed. He had been getting a lot of stick of that kind lately. All part of a policeman's lot, no doubt. Veronica returned Caroline Peter's lob with a hard transverse drive which Caroline ran for but couldn't reach. It was a mystery, Wexford thought, where somebody got that kind of talent from. You couldn't imagine that finicking Wendy playing any sort of game or even walking more than half a mile, while Rodney Williams had been out of condition for years. Did the other Williams family play games? There had been a tennis racket up on Sara's bedroom wall, he remembered. Of course, the probable answer was that any healthy young girl keen on tennis could be coached to the standard of Veronica Williams. She was already sixteen. It was already too late for her to begin competing in anything much more significant than inter-school matches.

The girl whose face and name he didn't know served a double fault. One more of those and the set would be lost. She served one more of those and threw her racket down in the kind of petulance she wouldn't have known about if she hadn't watched Wimbledon on TV. Wexford and Burden walked back to the car.

'Have we got anything on the fingerprints found in Williams's car yet?' Burden asked.

'They took about sixty prints,' Wexford said, 'all made by nine people. By far the greater proportion were made by one man and they've more or less established that man was Williams.'

'I don't suppose his fingers were in very good shape after being in the ground for nine weeks.'

'Exactly. They matched the car ones to prints in his bedroom – well, bedrooms – of course. The other prints were made by two unknown men, and may well belong to whoever began the dismantling of Greta, by Joy, Wendy, Sara, Veronica, and two more women or girls who might be friends of the wives and daughters – or who might not. The steering wheel had been wiped.'

'Much what you would expect really,' said Burden.

Nicola Tennyson, Veronica's friend, was thrilled to have her fingerprints taken. She was unable to remember much about 15 April. Certain it was that she had been babysitting her brother that evening and Veronica had come in, but she couldn't remember times. Veronica and she were often in each other's homes, she said.

One of the two unidentified sets of fingerprints on Greta turned out to be hers.

13

Wheatley said that the woman who stabbed him had been more than commonly tall. Budd said that because he had only seen her sitting down he couldn't tell her height. That wasn't strictly true. He had seen her running off with the sack over her shoulder. The sack was the only thing he could really remember, that and the fact she had blonde hair. The girl who attacked Wheatley had 'brown or lightish' hair. She was eighteen or nineteen. Budd thought his assailant was twenty. Or twenty-five or-six. Or any age between eighteen and thirty.

In each case their wounds had been made with the blade of a large penknife. Not necessarily the same penknife, though. Not necessarily the same woman. Wexford asked himself what had been in the sack. He didn't think Budd had invented the sack. Budd wasn't endowed with enough imagination for that. There had been a sack all right, a black plastic dustbin liner. What had she been carrying it for and why?

It had been pouring with rain. Those plastic sacks were very good for keeping things dry. Keeping what dry? The bus stop was the nearest one to the place where they'd found Rodney Williams's body. But he had been dead six weeks by the night Budd was attacked. Wendy Williams wasn't particularly tall but she was blonde and she looked much younger than she was. To Budd she might seem in her early twenties.

She had begun a fortnight of her annual holiday. Wexford

338

thought to himself that she might be spending the major part of it at Kingsmarkham Police Station. He went with the car to fetch her.

Veronica was in the raspberry-ice-cream living room, seated at the glass-topped table, turning the pages of *Vogue*. He thought she looked like a teenage girl in a French film of the sixties. He hadn't seen many French films of the sixties but nevertheless the impression was there in Veronica's band-box look, the beautifully cut, newly washed, pageboy hair, the clothes – primrose pinafore dress, starched white blouse, blue bootlace tie, white ankle socks, sky-blue sandals – that were just a little too young for her, the expression on her face that was 99 per cent innocence and 1 per cent calculation.

'I saw you playing tennis the other day.'

'Yes, I saw you too.'

Why the wary look suddenly, the shade of unease across that naivety?

'You're very good.'

She knew that already, she didn't need to be told. A polite smile and then back to *Vogue*. Wendy Williams came down the spiral staircase, walking slowly, giving him a voyeur's look if he had wanted it of shapely legs in very fine pale tights all the way up to a glimpsed border of cream lace. He wasn't looking, but out of the corner of his eye he saw her hold her skirt down as if he had been.

She had dressed up. Women these days didn't bother with fancy dressing except for special occasions, except when it was fun. That was general, not just the ARRIA view of things. For going down the cop shop, Wexford thought, you went in the jeans and shirt you wore around the house. But this was something that hadn't yet got through to Wendy Williams and maybe never would. She probably didn't pos-sess a pair of jeans. And Veronica's would be the designer kind with Vidal Sassoon or Gloria Vanderbilt on the back-side. Wendy had a pretty cotton dress on, the kind that needs a lot or ironing, a wide black patent belt to show she still had an adolescent waist and red wedge-heeled shoes that pinched where they touched.

The car filled with her perfume. Estée Lauder's White Linen, decided Wexford, who was good on scent. He made up his mind to take her up to his office, not into one of the interviewing rooms.

'You haven't told me much about this girlfriend of your husband's, Mrs Williams,' he said when they were there.

'I've told you all I know. I've told you it was a very young girl and that's all I know.'

'I don't think so,' he said. 'There's more if you search your memory.'

A secretive look was closing up her face. Why? Why should she want to conceal this girl's identity from him?

'I wish I'd never mentioned any girl to you!' Exasperated. The tone of a mother to a child who keeps nagging her about a treat she had promised him.

'You had an anonymous letter, you said.'

She hesitated. She opened her mouth to begin an explanation. He cut her short.

'You didn't keep it though. You burned it.'

'How did you know?'

'Mrs Williams, let me tell you what I do know. First, it's only in books that people burn anonymous letters. In real life they may not care much for them, they may even recoil from them in disgust, but they don't burn them. Most people don't have fires any more, for one thing. Where would you burn something?'

She didn't say anything. A sullen crushed look made her almost ugly.

'People who get anonymous letters may not like looking at them. Usually they put them away in a drawer in case or until we want to see them. Or there's the dustbin. You read somewhere that the requisite thing to do with an anonymous letter was burn it, didn't you? In a detective story probably. The truth is you never received one.'

'All right, I didn't.'

'Hasn't anyone ever told you you mustn't tell lies to the police?'

He hadn't spoken harshly. His tone was almost bantering. It was mockery, even as mild as this, she couldn't stand. She flushed and her mouth set mulishly.

'I didn't tell lies. There was a girl.' Perhaps she could see he wasn't going to say anything for a moment or two. 'He was perverted about young girls, that's what it amounted to

340

and it ruined my life.' Her voice rose, edgy and plaintive. 'I thought he was in love with me when we first met. I thought he loved me but now I know he just fancied me because I was young. And when Veronica was coming he had to marry me. Well, *marry*. It's easy to marry, isn't it? You can do it over and over again.

'I never had any life, I never had any youth. Do you know something? I'm thirty-two and I've never so much as been taken out to dinner in a decent restaurant by a man. I've ' never been abroad. I've never had a thing to wear that didn't come discount from Jickie's. I never even had an engagement ring!'

He asked her how she knew of the girl's existence. Just at this point Marion came in with coffee on a tray, three unprepossessing cheese sandwiches and three custard-cream biscuits. Wendy looked at the sandwiches and shook her head in a shuddery genteel sort of way.

He repeated the question.

'Rodney confessed.'

'Just like that? Out of the blue? You didn't suspect anything but he confessed to you he had a young girlfriend?'

'I told you.'

'Why did he confess? Was he intending to leave you for her? As in fact you thought he had done?'

That made her laugh in the way someone does who has knowledge of a secret you will never guess. He persisted and she looked exasperated, answering that she had told him already. She ate nothing, he ate a sandwich, leaving the rest for Marion, who had a hearty appetite. Afterwards, he thought, Wendy Williams would probably tell people she was kept at the police station for hours and not given a thing to eat or drink.

He asked her once more about 15 April. The evening. What time had she left Jickie's to drive home to Pomfret? all the staff at Jickie's had been questioned by Martin and Bennett and Archbold. They had forgotten. Why should they remember that particular evening? One of the girls on the fashion-floor pay desk said that if Mrs Williams hadn't actually left the building before nine, that would have been very late for her. On Thursdays she usually left as soon after eight as possible and had been known to leave at 7.30.

341

Wendy insisted she left at nine. She stuck to that. He left it. He said there was something he had to ask her. Seeing that her husband consistently neglected her and for two months she believed he had finally left her, had she formed a friendship with any other man?

'It would be a natural and normal thing to you. You're a very young woman still. You said yourself that you felt life and youth had been denied you.'

'Are you suggesting I was having a – a relationship with someone?'

'It would be very understandable.'

'I think that's disgusting! That's really immoral. I've got my daughter to think of, haven't I? I've got Veronica to set an example to. Just because Rodney behaved in that horrible way, that's no reason for me to do the same. Let me tell you, I've always been absolutely faithful. I've never looked at another man, it would never have entered my head.'

He was beginning to know her and her protests. He said not another word on that one but thought the more. It was afternoon now and Burden would be setting in motion their prearranged plan. It might not work, of course – and if it did what would it show or prove? He didn't even know if he expected it to work.

In the meantime he questioned her about her life, her feelings, her reactions. Still she hadn't said a word about the other Williams family. She was prepared to acknowledge Rodney Williams had married her bigamously while ignoring the existence of his first or true wife. You would have expected her natural curiosity to get the better of her. Was she rising above such human failings? That was a possible explanation.

'Mrs Joy Williams,' he said deliberately, 'has a son and daughter. Her daughter and Veronica are very much alike. Do you have any feelings about these people?' He was aware he sounded like a psychotherapist, though any interrogating policeman was one of those. But nevertheless he made a slight correction. 'Aren't you interested in knowing something about them?'

'No.' Once more she had flushed. She looked mulish. 'Why should I be? They're nothing to me. Rodney can't have cared much for them.'

'Why do you say that?'

She made a little gesture with her hands to indicate that the answer was obvious. Wexford said that was enough for today and he'd organize a car to take her home. They went down in the lift, timing it perfectly, for as the lift came to a stop and the doors opened Burden came walking across the black and white checkerboard floor towards it with Joy Williams beside him. Wexford spoke to Burden for the sake of stopping and saying something. The two women stood there, Joy staring at Wendy, Wendy contemplating the wall ahead of her as if it were the most fascinating example of interior decor since the cave paintings of Trois Frères.

They presented a contrast, pathetic and grotesque. It was almost too marked to be quite real. They were like a cartoon for an old-fashioned advertisement, the wife who doesn't use the face cream, floor polish, deodorant, stock cubes, and the wife who does. Joy had a cardigan on over a cotton dress with half its hem coming down. All her shoes had a curious way of looking like carpet slippers though they weren't. Wendy swayed a little on her high heels, craning her neck and putting on a winsome look. Wexford smelt a gush of White Linen from her, perhaps because she was sweating. The irony was that both these women had been rejected.

Burden and Joy went into the lift. The doors closed.

'Do you know who that woman was?'

'What woman?' said Wendy.

'I'm not talking about Detective Bayliss. The woman who has just gone up in the lift with Inspector Burden.'

She raised her eyebrows, moved her shoulders.

'That was Mrs Joy Williams.'

'His wife?'

'Yes,' said Wexford.

'She looked about sixty.'

Upstairs Burden was asking Joy about the phone call, the letter of resignation. Why had she gone out on the evening of 15 April instead of remaining at home to await her son's phone call?

'I can't be always at his beck and call,' she said, her voice full of bitterness. 'It's all one to him whether I'm there or not. He's his father all over again – indifferent. I've done everything for him, worshipped the ground he walked on.

343

Might as well not have bothered. Do you know where he is now? In Cornwall. On holiday. That's all it means to him that his mother's a widow.'

It could just be true. It could just be that she had at last seen the results of spoiling a son. A quarrel, Burden thought, the day before Kevin returned to university. He could hear the things that would have been said – all right, just wait till next time you want something; you phone, my lad, but don't count on me being here . . . Yet there had been no sign since then of adoration flagging.

'Do you know who that woman was with Chief Inspector Wexford?'

'I can guess.' The harsh clattering laugh. 'Cheap little tart. I don't admire his taste.'

He asked her if Sara had a boyfriend. Incredibly, she said she didn't know. It was plain she didn't care. Hatred came into her eyes when her daughter's name was mentioned.

'And after all I've done for her,' said Joy as if their discussion had been on the subject of the host of services she had performed for Sara and the girl's ingratitude. Burden had her driven home. He felt as if he had been brought up against a wall, the solid brick an inch from his face.

Carol Milvey was not a member of ARRIA but she was eighteen years old and lived next door but one to Joy Williams. And it was her father, the boss of Mid-Sussex Waterways, who had found Rodney Williams's travelling bag in Green Pond, a coincidence which had never been explained. Sergeant Martin saw her. The interview was a brief one, for Carol Milvey had been ill in bed with tonsillitis on 15 April and had taken two days off school.

A further ten members of ARRIA were cleared, both for 15 April and the evening on which Brian Wheatley had been stabbed in the hand. It was August now and people were beginning to go away on holiday, ARRIA members surely included. The Anerley family and their daughter, the red-headed Nicola, had been in France since the end of the school term and were not expected back until 12 August. On this date too Pomfret Office Equipment Ltd were due to reopen after two weeks' holiday closure, a southern version of North

Country wakes weeks, as Wexford remarked. If the type-writers missing from Haldon Finch were serviced in the neighbourhood it was with Pomfret Office Equipment they had to be. No other firm of typewriter engineers admitted to knowledge of their whereabouts.

The commerce department at Sewingbury Sixth Form college had been checked out. They had microcomputers, ACT Apricots, as well as four dedicated word processors, and their typewriters were ten highly sophisticated Brother machines. Kingsmarkham High School had one typewriter only in the building and that in the school secretary's office.

Kevin Williams came back from Cornwall and left again with six like-minded students to camp in the Channel Islands. The Harmers with Paulette's boyfriend went to North Wales for a week, leaving an Indian pharmacist and his wife, both highly qualified but jobless, in charge of shop and dispensary. Sara went nowhere. Sara stayed at home, awaiting no doubt the A-level results due the second or third week of the month, after the degree results and before the O-levels.

'I can't help wondering if there'll still be A-levels when this new baby of ours grows up,' said Burden. Nowadays he talked gingerly and awkwardly about the coming child but as if its birth were a certainty and its future more or less assured. 'I'll be an old man by the time she wants to go to university. Well, I'll be in my sixties. I'll be retired. Do you remember filling in those grant forms? Getting one's employer to vouch for one's earnings and all that? Still, by then they'll do it all on a computer, I suppose, a kind of twenty-first-century Apricot.'

'Or an Apple,' said Wexford. 'Why do computer makers call their wares after fruit? There must be some unexpected Freudian explanation.' A glazed look of boredom blanked Burden's face. 'Talking of unexpected explanations.' Wexford said quickly, 'do you realize there's one aspect of this case we've given no thought to? Motive. Motive has scarcely been mentioned.'

Burden looked as if he were going to say that the police need not concern themselves with motive, that perpetrators in any case often stated motives that seemed thin or incredible. But he didn't say that. He said hesitantly, 'Aren't we concluding Williams was killed in what ARRIA would call self-defence?'

'Surely the difficulty there is that if we assume – which we are doing – that the woman or girl who made the phone call and wrote the letter was Williams's girlfriend, why should she need to defend herself against him? Budd and Wheatley were attacked because they made sexual advances. But this girl, being his girlfriend, presumably welcomed his sexual advances.'

Burden said in his prudish way, 'That might depend on their nature.'

'You mean they were sadistic or he wanted to wear one of her nightdresses? We've no evidence Williams was funny in that way. And aren't you forgetting something? It looks as if this murder was somewhat premeditated. Williams was given a sleeping drug before he was stabbed. I don't see my way to accepting a theory that one day Williams suggested to his girlfriend that they have sex in this new naughty way, whereupon she substitutes a sedative for his blood-pressure pill and when he's asleep stabs him eight times with a French cook's knife.'

'Then what motive do you suggest?'

'I don't. I can't see a girlfriend killing him to be rid of him because surely all she had to do was give him the out, tell him to go back to his wife or wives. And although a girl could have killed him on her own, she couldn't have disposed of his body on her own. A girl with a jealous husband or boyfriend? ARRIA members don't have husbands. ARRIA members aren't supposed to get sufficiently involved with men for a triangular jealousy situation to arise. But is she an ARRIA member? Does she exist?'

'If one could only read the book of fate,' said Burden, unaware that he was quoting and no longer thinking about the Williams case anyway.

'If this were seen,' said Wexford, 'the happiest youth, viewing his progress through, would shut the book and sit him down and die . . .'

He went home to fetch Dora and the two of them went to see Sheila in *Little Eyolf* at the Olivier.

346

14

Pomfret Office Equipment Ltd was open for business by 9.30 on the morning of 12 August. It was a shopfront with a big storage shed behind. The business was run by two men called Ovington, father and son. Edgar Ovington, the father, acknowledged at once that his firm serviced typewriters for the Haldon Finch Comprehensive School. The machines were usually attended to during the long summer holiday. His son had fetched the Haldon Finch machines the day before term ended, 26 July.

Wexford and Burden followed him into the shed at the back. It was full of typewriters, manuals, electric and electronic machines. They stretched away, rows of them ranked on slatted shelves, all labelled with tie-on luggage labels. Ovington pointed out the Haldon Finch typewriters, three on the lower shelf, two on the upper. The label on each said: H. Finch. Three portable Remington 315s, two Adler Gabrielle 5000s. Burden gave Ovington a condensed explanation of why they were looking for a particular typewriter and what made it particular. He asked for a sheet of paper. Ovington broke open a packet of 70-gramme white bond and peeled off two sheets from the top.

A flaw in the upper-case A, the ascender of the lower-case t and the head of the comma smudged. Burden slipped a sheet of paper into the roller of the first machine and typed a few lines from 'O God Our Help in Ages Past', the only hymn he knew by heart. No flaws. No flaws in the second machine either.

'You haven't put a new typeface on any of these machines?' Wexford asked.

'I haven't so much as touched them yet,' said Ovington.

Burden tried the third Remington. It was perfect, a better face than the others had, its need of servicing apparent only in the tendency of one or two of the keys to stick.

'These were the only typewriters fetched from the Haldon Finch Comprehensive School?'

'That's right. I label everything the minute it comes in to be on the safe side.'

'Yes, I see. So there's no possibility one of these machines could accidentally have been returned to a private customer?'

'It wouldn't go to a private customer if it was labelled Haldon Finch, would it?' said Ovington truculently.

He was a dour, prickly, suspicious man, always on the lookout for slurs anyone might cast on his ability or efficiency. Burden's request to try out any other Remington 315s there might be among the two hundred or so machines in the shed started him arguing and might have held them up but for the arrival, smiling and anxious to please, of the son, James Ovington. He was a tall, big-built young man with a toothy smile and a head as bald as an egg.

'Help yourselves. Be my guest.' The big white teeth glared as the lips stretched. 'Would you like me to have a sample of typing done from every machine here?' He meant it too, there was no sarcasm.

'We'll do it,' said Burden. 'And it's only the 315s we're interested in.'

Two more stood on the shelves besides the three he had tested. 'Sufficient is Thine Arm alone,' he typed, 'And our defence is sure'. Nothing wrong with that one. 'The busy tribes of flesh and blood. With all their cares and fears, Are carried downward by the flood, And lost in following years.' No flaws.

'Thanks for your help,' said Wexford.

James Ovington said it was his pleasure and smiled so widely that his dragon-seed teeth threatened to spill out. His father scowled.

'It's going to be in a ditch somewhere or a pond,' said Burden.

'Not in Green Pond, anyway. Or Milvey would have found it.' Wexford was reminded again of the as yet unexplained coincidence. The connecting link between Milvey and

348

Rodney Williams wasn't Carol Milvey, for Carol Milvey had been ill with tonsillitis on the evening of Williams's death. So what was it? Connecting link there must be. Wexford refused to believe that it was by pure chance that Milvey had discovered his neighbour's overnight bag in Green Pond.

And coincidence became remarkable beyond any possible rational explanation, entering the realms of magic or fantasy, when a call came in from Milvey himself next day to say he had found not the typewriter but a long kitchen knife, a French cook's knife, in a small ornamental pond on the Green Pond Hall estate.

The three ponds in the old water garden, now a wilderness, had been silted up with soil and fine sand washed down by springs from Cheriton Forest. Wexford's men had cleaned out those ponds during their search of the estate but since that time a further silting-up had taken place. The prospective trout farmer had called Mid-Sussex Waterways in once more to attempt to find a solution to the problem of the clogged water course.

Had the knife been placed there since the police search? Or had it been washed down from a hiding-place upstream? It was a large knife, the handle of ivory-coloured plastic six inches long, the blade nine inches, a right-angled triangle with the hypotenuse the cutting edge. It had a sharp and vicious-looking point. There were traces of grey mud in the rivet sockets of the handle but not a streak or pinpoint of rust anywhere. Wexford had the knife sent to Forensics at Stowerton. The Milvey link was still a mystery to him. He confronted Milvey across his desk, at a loss for what to ask him next. The wild thought entered his head that Milvey and Joy Williams might have been lovers. It was too wild – not fat dull Milvey and draggle-tailed Joy. And if Milvey were involved in Williams's death, why should he produce the weapon?

He found himself reduced to saying, 'You do see, don't you, Mr Milvey, that this situation and your position in it is a very mystifying one. The man who lives next door but one to you is murdered. You find first the bag he had with him when he disappeared, then a knife that in all probability is the murder weapon.'

'Somebody,' said Milvey who didn't seem to see the point, 'had to find them sooner or later.'

'The population of Kingsmarkham is somewhere in the area of seventy-eight thousand souls.'

Milvey stared at him with bull-headed stupidity. At last he said with truculence, 'Next time I find something I reckon will help the police with their inquiries I'll keep quiet about it.'

While Forensics were testing the knife against Williams's wound measurements Sergeant Martin with Bennett and Archbold made inquiries as to its provenance. They listed thirty-nine shops and stores in the area where similar knives were sold. Only Jickie's however, stocked that particular brand of French cook's knife.

'Wendy Williams may work there,' Wexford said, 'but everyone shops there. We do. You do. Martin's asking the staff in the hardware department if they can remember anyone recently buying a French cook's knife. You know how far that'll get us. Besides, they've stocked the things for the past five years. There's no reason to believe the knife was bought specifically to kill Williams. In fact, the chances are it wasn't.'

'Yes, we're still at square one,' Burden said.

'You're being faint-hearted. Come and spend an afternoon among the typewriters. I've a hunch I want to put to the test.'

Ovington senior was on his own. He tried at first to fob them off with pleas of pressure of work. Wexford suggested gently that this might be construed as obstructing the police in the course of their inquiries. Ovington, grumbling under his breath, led them once more into the shed at the back of the shop.

· Walking between the rows, Wexford examined the labels tied to the machines.

'You always used this method of labelling?'

'What's wrong with it?'

'I didn't say there was anything wrong with it. I don't think it's very clear, that's all. For instance, what does "P

350

and L" stand for?' He pointed to the labels on a pair of Smith Corona SX 400s.

'Porter and Lamb on the estate,' said Ovington gruffly. He meant the industrial estate at Stowerton.

'And TML?'

'Tube Manipulators Limited.'

'And you know absolutely what those initials – I might say codes – mean when you're returning machines? You know that "P and L" stands for Porter and Lamb and not, for instance, for Payne and Lovell, the hardware people in the High Street here?'

'We don't do any work for Payne and Lovell.' Ovington looked astonished.

'I think you understand me though. With this system of labelling mistakes could be made. I'll come to the point. "H. Finch" is rather a rough and ready way of indicating the Haldon Finch Comprehensive School.'

'It serves its purpose.'

'Suppose you had a customer called Henry Finch. What would stop his machine getting mixed up with the Haldon Finch ones?'

'We don't have a customer called Henry Finch, that's what.'

Burden said sharply, 'D'you have any customers called Finch?'

'We might have.'

It was the curious reply, or a version of it, Wexford had so often heard witnesses give in court when they did not want to commit themselves to a positive 'yes'. 'I might have', 'I may have done'. Ovington, in his greasy old suit, open-necked shirt, his chin pulled back into his neck and his lips thrust forward, looked shifty, guilty, suspected and suspicious, truculent for the mere sake of truculence.

'I'd like you to check, please.'

'Not Henry,' said Ovington. 'Definitely not. A lady. Not an H at all.'

'You're wasting my time, Mr Ovington.'

He was enjoying it, with sly malice. 'We did some repairs on a Remington for her a while back. Not a 315 though.' At last, scratching his head, 'I could look in the book.'

'This could be it,' Wexford said when he and Burden were

351

alone for a moment. 'They could have got mixed up and sent the wrong one back.'

'Wouldn't she have noticed?'

'She might not be a regular typist. She might not have used the machine since its return.'

He began looking at labels on all the typewriters on the lower shelf on the left-hand side. P and L, E. Ten (what could that mean?), TML, HBSS, H. Finch, J. St G, M. Br . . . Ovington came back with a ledger.

'Miss J. Finch, 22 Bodmin Road, Pomfret. She collected the machine herself on July the twenty-sixth.' He slammed the book shut as if he had just proved or disproved something to his triumphant satisfaction.

July 26. The day the Haldon Finch machines were collected and brought here, Wexford thought. Did all this mean anything or nothing? Were the girlfriend and the girlfriend's typewriter after all sitting pretty somewhere in London or Brighton?

Neither he nor Burden knew where Bodmin Road was.

'You know something?' Burden said. 'Wendy Williams lives in Liskeard Avenue and Liskeard's a place in Cornwall. Bodmin's the county town of Cornwall. It may be just round the corner.'

'We'll look it up as soon as we get back.'

It was just round the corner. Liskeard Avenue, Falmouth Road, Truro Road, with Bodmin Road running crossways to connect them all.

'She was practically a neighbour of his,' Burden said, sounding almost excited. 'An ARRIA member, I bet you. Here she is on the Electoral Register. Finch, Joan B.'

'Wait a minute, Mike. Are we saying – are we assuming rather – that a Haldon Finch typewriter was collected by her in error or that it's her own typewriter she has, that this is the machine we're looking for, and we've stumbled upon her not by deduction but by pure luck?'

'What does that matter?' Burden said simply.

Twenty-two Bodmin Road was a small purpose-built block of four flats. According to the doorbells, J. B. Finch lived on the first floor. However, she was not at home either in the afternoon or at their two further calls at seven and eight in the evening. Wexford had been home an hour when a call came through to him to say a fourth man had been stabbed, this time in the upper arm, not a serious wound, though there had been considerable loss of blood.

The difference was that this time his cries were heard by two policemen sitting in a patrol car in a lay-by on the Kingsmarkham bypass. It was after sunset, the beginning of dusk. They had found the victim of the attack lying half across a public footpath, bleeding from a wound near his shoulder. While they were bending over him a girl came out from among the trees of the woodland on the north side of the path, announced her name as Edwina Klein and handed them a penknife from which she had wiped most of the blood.

15

ARRIA expected a show. Its members were in Kingsmark-ham Magistrates' Court in force. Wexford had never seen the small wood-walled area that passed for a public gallery so full. Caroline Peters was there and Sara Williams, redhaired Nicola Anerley, Jane Gardner and the Freeborn twins, Helen Blake and Donella the black girl, the tennis player who wore glasses and the tennis player who did not.

It was to be a test case, of course. Wexford had guessed all of it pretty well before he talked to Edwina Klein. She had not exactly been an *agent provocateur*. It was a terrible world we lived in if a woman who chose to walk alone along a field path at dusk could be called that. But the truth was that Edwina had set out to walk there, and to do so evening after evening since she came down from Oxford at the end of June, in the expectation of being attacked. She had been frank and open with him, hiding nothing, admitting, for instance, that it was she who while home for a weekend had been Wheatley's assailant. For this reason he had decided not to oppose bail. She would talk freely to him again, she had promised and, with a faith that would have set the Chief Constable's hair standing on end, he believed her.

With Caroline Peters a founder member of ARRIA, she was a thin straight girl of medium height, fiercely intelligent, a pioneer and martyr. She was dressed entirely in black, black trousers, black roll-neck sweater, her hair invisible under a tightly tied black scarf. A raven of a woman, the only colour about her the tiny orange ARRIA badge pinned on near her left shoulder.

What did the girls in the public gallery expect? Something

354

like the trial of Joan of Arc, Wexford supposed. All were ignorant of magistrates' court procedure, all looked disbelieving when in five minutes it was all over and Edwina committed for trial to the crown court. The charge was unlawful wounding. She was released on bail in her own surety of £1000 and for a similar sum in that of an elderly woman, her great-aunt, not old enough to have been a suffragette but looking as if she might regret having missed the chance.

The ARRIA contingent filed out, muttering indignantly to each other. Helen Blake and Amy Freeborn picked up the orange banner with a woman-raven on it that they had been obliged to leave outside. The others fell in behind them and what had been a group became a march. 'We shall overcome,' they sang, 'we shall overcome some day.' They marched behind the banner up to the police station forecourt and across it and out into the High Street.

Joan Finch was sixty-five years old, perhaps more. Wexford wasn't surprised. There must be a few women called Joan under fifty, and even fifty years ago Joan was becoming an old-fashioned name. It was Burden who had built so much on the chance of her being the girl they were looking for.

She took them into the poky little den, designed for surely no more than luggage storage, where she worked, and showed them the typewriter, a big manual Remington at least as old as herself. Fingers today would flinch at that iron forest of keys that took so much muscle power to fell it.

As Ovington had told them, she had collected it from Pomfret Office Equipment on 26 July. There was no doubt at all that it was hers. It had been her mother's before her and seemed as much of a family heirloom as any clock or piece of china.

Of sole significance to Wexford and Burden was the fact that it wasn't a Remington 315 portable machine. This was something Miss Finch seemed unable to grasp. She insisted on sitting down at the typewriter and producing for them a half page of men coming to the aid of the party and quick brown foxes. The Ovingtons had done a good job. There wasn't a flaw or an irregularity to be seen.

355

They had lunch at the little bow-fronted wine bar two doors away. Pamela Gardner was at a corner table lunching with a woman friend. She looked through Wexford with a contemptuous stare. Her daughter had bounced along that morning, singing as heartily as anyone and a good deal more loudly, waving to him as if they were old friends. Edwina Klein was coming to the police station at 2.30 to talk to him. It was no part of the conditions of her bail that she should do this but he felt sure she wouldn't fail him. Burden said, 'Only three weeks to go now.' He was talking of the coming baby. 'They say it'll be on time. They don't really know though.'

'There's more they don't know than they ever let on.'

Burden picked at his quiche. 'She had the heartburn at the beginning and I'm getting it now.' He was pale, bilious-looking.

'We'll see if the Harmers can supply you with an indigestion remedy.'

The Pre-Raphaelite head of Paulette could be seen through the window of the dispensary where she was evidently helping her father. It was Hope Harmer who served Burden. She seemed discomfited by their visit, unable perhaps to realize that policemen too have private lives and are as liable to bodily ills as anyone else.

'Did you have a good holiday?' Wexford asked her.

'Oh yes, thank you, very nice. Very quiet,' she added as people do when describing their Christmas celebrations as if to admit to liveliness and merriment were to deny respectability. 'All good things come to an end though, don't they? We could have stayed away another week only my daughter's expecting her A-level results. They're due any day.'

Sara Williams must also be on tenterhooks then . . . 'Another would-be doctor in the family?'

'No, no. Paulette's hoping to follow in her Daddy's footsteps.'

She was all bright placatory smiles, accompanying them to the door when they left like an old-fashioned shopkeeper. Wexford walked into the police station just before 2.30. Edwina Klein was waiting for him, shown upstairs to his room, and he felt relief at the sight of her in spite of his

356

confidence that she would keep her word. With her, seated in the other visitor's chair, like a chaperone, was the aunt.

Wexford was surprised. He had seen Edwina as the very epitome of independence, of self-reliance.

'I happen to be a solicitor as well as an aunt.'

'Very well,' said Wexford, 'but this won't be an interrogation, just a talk about various aspects of this case.'

'That's what they all say,' said the aunt whose name was Pearl Kaufmann. In appearance she was rather like Virginia Woolf in her latter days, tallish, thin, long-faced, long-nosed, with a full mouth. She wore a navy blue silk dress, mid-calf length, and clumpy white sandals that made her feet look large.

Edwina was still in the black she had worn in court but with the roll-necked sweater changed for a sleeveless black tee-shirt that was better suited to the heat of the day. The ARRIA badge had been transferred to this. Edwina had sunglasses on which turned her face into an expressionless mask.

'He treated me exactly as if I was a prostitute,' she had said to him of Wheatley at that earlier conversation. The black glasses hadn't covered her eyes then. They had been bright with eagerness, with earnestness, with the zeal of youth. 'Not that there's anything wrong with being a prostitute. That's OK, that's fine if that's where you're at. It's just the way men *assume* . . .'

'Only some men.'

'A lot. He didn't even talk to me. I tried to talk to him. I asked him where he worked and where he lived. When I asked him where he lived he gave a strange sort of laugh as if I'd said something *wrong*.'

'Why did you ask him for a lift? To provoke exactly the sort of situation that arose?'

'No, I didn't. Not that time. I admit I did last night but it was different with the man in the car. I'd had a lift from London to Kingsmarkham and the guy couldn't take me any farther.' She seemed to consider. 'It was because of what happened in the car that I decided to try walking in the forest and see.'

'You'd better tell me what happened in the car, hadn't you?'

'He pulled into a lay-by. He did talk then. He said, "Come

on, we'll go in the wood". I didn't know what he meant, I really didn't. Do you know what he thought? He thought I wanted paying first. He said, "Will ten pounds do?" And then he touched me.' Edwina Klein laid her right hand on her left breast. 'He touched me like I'm doing now. Like it was a tap or a switch. He didn't try to put his arms round me or kiss me or anything. It was just offering to pay and feeling the switch. I took out my knife and stuck it in his hand.'

There had been no aunt present when she talked to him then and no black circles to take the character from her face. Her manner now was more subdued, less indignant. Her experience of the court had perhaps chastened her. She waited almost meekly for him to begin questioning her. Miss Kaufmann sat looking at Wexford's wall map with simulated interest.

'Have you stabbed any other men?' he said abruptly, knowing the remark would be objected to.

Edwina shook her head.

'We won't mind about that, Mr Wexford.' It seemed highly suitable to the aunt's manner and appearance that she should use this obsolete Victorian phrase. She elucidated with something more contemporary. 'We'll forget you said that.'

'As you please,' said Wexford. 'When the police use *agents provocateurs* – as, for example, in the case of a policewoman sitting in a cinema where a member of the audience is suspected of assaulting women – the public, particularly the public of your sort of persuasion, gets up in arms. There's an outcry when a young policeman deliberately uses a public lavatory frequented by homosexuals. In other words, it's not all right for them to do this in the interests of justice but it's all right for you to in the mere interest of a principle. There's rather a crude name for what you did and were, isn't there?'

He had been too mealy-mouthed, too gentlemanly, he quickly saw.

'A pricktease,' she said flatly. The aunt didn't move an eyelid. 'I didn't do that. I didn't do anything but go for a walk in a wood. I wasn't provocatively dressed.' Scorn came into her voice now and she lifted up her head. 'I wouldn't be! I had jeans on and a jacket. I never wear make-up, not ever. The only thing I did to provoke anyone was *be* there and be a woman.'

'I think my niece is saying,' said Miss Kaufmann dryly, 'that it isn't possible to be a woman in certain places with impunity. She was out to prove this and she did prove it.'

He let it go. He left it. He felt the force of what the two women said and he knew it was true, and that this was an instance of a policeman knowing that the opposing argument is sounder than his own but of having to stick to his own just the same. That all women who intended to go about by themselves at night should learn self-defence techniques seemed to him the best answer. The alternative was that men's natures should change and that was something which might slowly happen over centuries but not in years or even decades. He wrote busy nothings on the sheet of paper in front of him to fill thirty seconds of time and keep them temporarily silent. At last he lifted his head and looked at Edwina Klein. For some reason, perhaps because his eyes were naked, she took off her glasses. Immediately she looked earnest again and very young.

'You know the Williams family, I think?'

She was prepared for this. Somehow she knew that this was what she was really there for. Her answer surprised him.

'Which Williams family? There are two, aren't there?'

'There may be two hundred in this neighbourhood for all I know,' he said sharply. 'It's a common name. I'm talking about the Williams family that live in Alverbury Road, Kingsmarkham. The girl is called Sara. She was in court this morning. I think you know her.'

She nodded. 'We were at school together. She's a year younger than I am.'

'Did you know Rodney Williams, the dead man?'

She was very quick to reply. Miss Kaufmann looked up as if warningly. 'Him and Mrs Williams, yes. Sara and I used to do ballet together.' She smiled. 'Believe it or not.' Miss Kaufmann cast up her eyes as if she could hardly believe it. 'They'd come for Sara or one of them would. I remember him because he was the only father who ever came. Sometimes he'd come and sit through the whole class.'

Watching pubescent girls in little tutus, thought Wexford, or more likely leotards these days.

'You asked me which family I meant,' he said.

'I slightly know the other one.' She lifted her shoulders. 'Veronica Williams looks exactly like Sara.'

He felt a tightening of nerves. She might be a link between the two families. She was the only person he had yet talked to who knew – or admitted to knowing – both sets of Williamses.

'You were aware that they were half-sisters then? You knew Williams was their father?'

'No. Oh no. I suppose I thought – well, I didn't think about it. I honestly don't know, really. Perhaps that they might be cousins?'

'When did you last see Rodney Williams?'

'Years ago.' She was becoming nervous, frightened. It meant nothing, it was evidence only of her realization that she had been brought her to face one sort of ordeal and, that over, was being subjected to another of an unexpected kind. 'I haven't seen him for years.'

'Then how do you know Veronica?'

No dramatic *crise de nerfs* and no hesitation either. 'I played tennis against her. When I was at school.'

'She's three years younger than you.'

'OK. Sure. She was a sort of child prodigy. She was in Haldon Finch's first six when she was under fourteen.'

It was all reasonable, more than plausible. She had been in Oxford the night Rodney Williams died, having gone up early, a week before her term began. She had told him so last evening and told him, in grave and careful detail, whom to check this with. Bennett was in Oxford checking now but Wexford had little doubt Edwina hadn't lied to him.

'You knew both families,' he said now, 'but you didn't know, so to speak, they were one family? You didn't know Rodney Williams was the father of Veronica as well as of Sara and Kevin?'

'Kevin? I've never even heard of him before.'

'Sara's older brother.' He decided to be entirely frank with her. Miss Kaufmann sat watching him, an acid twist to her mouth. 'They didn't know of the existence of the others,' he said. 'The Pomfret family didn't know of the existence of the Kingsmarkham family and the Kingsmarkham family didn't know of the existence of the Pomfret family until quite a

360

while after Rodney Williams was dead. So if you knew, that must mean you also knew Rodney Williams was a bigamist or at least a married man maintaining two households. And if you knew that how did you know it?'

'I didn't.'

The cool negative disappointed him. He had felt on the brink of a breakthrough. But she qualified it.

'I didn't know. I said they looked alike, I'd noticed that, and I remember once saying to my aunt that they must be cousins.' Edwina looked at Miss Kaufmann and Miss Kaufmann nodded in a rapid impatient way. 'I didn't know either of them well,' Edwina said. 'You've got to remember that. I'd never spoken more than a few words to Veronica. And Mrs Williams, that's the real wife, I've seen her about but she's forgotten who I am or something, and as far as the other one goes I was just a customer.'

He had nothing else to ask her. She had stabbed Brian Wheatley and Peter John Hyde, her assailant in the wood, but he was certain she hadn't killed Williams. If a woman had done that she would have needed a second to help her.

'That's all then, thank you, Miss Klein.'

She got up and walked slowly and gracefully to the door, holding herself erect but with her head slightly bowed. They had the same figure, the same walk, this aunt and niece, though fifty years separated them. What would become of Edwina Klein now? It was inevitable she would be found guilty. Would her college have her back? Or was her whole future spoiled? Had she blown it for the sake of a lost cause? At the door, just before he opened it for her, she said, 'There's one thing. You said the Pomfret Williamses and the Kingsmarkham Williamses didn't know about each other. For the sake of setting the record straight, that's not right.'

The excitement was back, drying his throat. 'What do you mean?'

'What I say. They did know about each other.'

He took his hand from the door and leaned against it like someone barring egress. But Edwina Klein stood there willingly, looking a little puzzled, the aunt bored but patient.

'How do you know that?'

'Because I've seen them together,' she said.

361

Relief ran over him like sweat. He felt cool and lightheaded with it. She was aware now that she had told him something revelatory, unguessed at, and her face, close to his, was full of alert inquiry.

'Whom did you see together?' he asked her.

'Those two women. I saw them in the Precinct Café in Kingsmarkham having coffee together.'

'When? Can you remember when?'

If it were a week ago or even a month ago it meant nothing.

'Last Christmas, I think. It must have been Christmas or Easter for me to have been home. The only weekend I've been home was when *Wheatley* gave me that lift.' Edwina put infinite scorn into the pronunciation of his name. 'It wasn't then and it wasn't Easter. I know it can't have been because there was snow on the ground.'

'Snow fell,' said Miss Kaufmann, helpful now her niece was not directly threatened, 'during the first week of January.'

'It must have been then,' said Edwina.

She smiled, as if pleased to have been of help at last. He knew she hadn't lied.

16

As Wexford opened the gate of 31 Alverbury Road the postman was coming down the path, a wad of mail fastened with a rubber band in his left hand. None of it apparently was for 29 and his next call was at Milvey's, two doors down. Watching him, Wexford suddenly understood how Milvey came into the case. There was no coincidence at all, it was all simple and logical, only he had been putting the cart before the horse...

He rang the bell. As he did so St Peter's clock struck nine. It was Sara who opened the door and so quickly he knew she must have been standing directly behind it. She was holding a paper.

'Two As and a B,' she said, and smiled with gratification.

She had spoken as if the sole purpose of his call had been to hear about her A-level results. Before she closed the door she must have seen the police car outside with Donaldson at the wheel and Marion Bayliss in the back.

'Congratulations,' Wexford said. 'Where's your mother?'

She didn't answer. She might not have heard for all the notice she took.

'St Biddulph's told me they'd take me with three Bs or two Bs and an A, so this is rather better.'

Frenetic excitement was in the girl's eyes, an excitement that was manic and all the more disconcerting for being under such tight control. He had seen her as a Botticelli girl, mild-faced, tranquil, with a spring-like innocence. Primavera should not tremble with triumph nor Venus's eyes glitter.

'I'm going to phone my cousin Paulette, find out how she did.'

363

To crow a little? Or to be kind? Joy Williams came out from the kitchen, dressed as he had never seen her before. He hadn't told her but perhaps she had guessed she would be meeting Wendy again. Or Wendy herself had told her the evening before? He was prepared for that. He rather hoped they realized he knew of their prior acquaintance. Joy wore a clean, tidy skirt and blouse. She had washed her hair and smudged lipstick on her mouth, in the uncertain slapdash way women do who seldom wear it and somehow feel ashamed to do so. Probably she always dresses up when she and Wendy meet, he thought. There would be rivalry there even if they were allied in a common hatred of Williams. Besides, an alliance would not mean they actually *liked* each other . . .

Sara could be heard on the phone. 'Have they come? Well?'

Not much of a bedside manner. He imagined her talking in that hectoring way to a patient. A hard, neurotic little go-getter, he thought her, without an atom of concern for the mother whom the police suspected of murdering her father.

'That's not bad though, is it?' she was saying. 'It's not as if you need As or even Bs.'

Patronizing. Somewhat lofty. The pharmacist, of course, was the poor man's doctor, or the doctor for the faint-hearted. 'I'll ask the chemist to give me something for my throat.' Or my head, back, cystitis, bleeding, lump in the breast . . . He took Joy out and closed the front door behind them.

Sergeant Martin and Polly Davies brought Wendy in. The evening before she had been in tears of vexation at missing a day's work but that she could have refused to come – that the police were still in a position only to ask and persuade – seemed no more to have occurred to her than to Joy. They were not blessed with lawyers for aunts. The senior wife – the Sultana Valideh – was already seated in the interview room when Wendy was brought in, the expressionless face averted, the dark brown animal eyes staring past her at the window.

Wendy wore a printed smock dress, Kate Greenaway-like,

in a Laura Ashley print, at the neck and wrists frills tied with bows. She had white tights on and white shoes. While the sergeant and Polly stood by (Polly told Wexford later) Wendy had taken her daughter Veronica in her arms and hugged her in a highly emotional way, bringing a fresh rush of tears. Veronica had looked very taken aback. But Wendy had pressed her close to her, stroking her hair, almost as if she expected never to see her again. And Polly, who was a reader of romantic period fiction, said it was like Marie Antoinette setting off in the tumbril.

'Farewell, my children, for ever! I am going to your father.'

Now all that remained as evidence of this scene was the swollen pinkness of Wendy's face. She gave Wexford a piteous look. She would have preferred Burden to interrogate her, she found him more sympathetic than this elderly, hard, sardonic man, but Burden wasn't there. He was in Alverbury Road in conversation with Mrs Milvey.

Wexford said, and he seemed to be addressing either or both of them, 'Which of you first found out the other existed?'

It was Wendy who answered. Her voice was even more fretful than usual. 'I don't understand what you mean.'

'I'll put it another way. When did you first discover Rodney Williams had a wife? And you, Mrs Williams, when did you find out your husband had "married" again?' He put very audible inverted commas round that past principle. 'Well?' he said. 'I know you haven't been truthful with me. I know you knew each other. The question is when did you first know?'

'I never knew she existed till you told me.' Joy spoke in her weary lifeless way. 'When you told me my husband was a bigamist on top of all the rest.'

'All what "rest", Mrs Williams?'

'Lying to me about his job for a start.'

Wendy murmured something.

'I'm sorry, Mrs Williams, I didn't catch that.'

'I said, "having other women". I meant that's what the rest was, having other women.'

'He never had other women,' said Joy. She was responding to Wendy's prompting but she wasn't speaking to her. It was

365

Wexford she was addressing. 'He had *her* but he never had others.'

'Let her delude herself if she wants,' said Wendy to no one in particular, lifting her shoulders and smiling very faintly.

'When did you first meet her, Mrs Williams?' Wexford was finding it a shade awkward, their both sharing the name. He got up and came round the table to address the words specifically to Wendy. Joy burst out, 'You've no business to call her that! She's no right to that name. She's Miss Whatever-she-used-to-be. You call her that!'

'The manners of a fishwife,' said Wendy. 'She's as common as dirt. No wonder he came to me.'

'Nasty little bitch! Look at her, dressed up like a kid!'

They're staging it, Wexford thought, they must be. It's all set up for my benefit, rehearsed as like as not. He called the two women quietly to order.

William Milvey was at home that day. The offices of Mid-Sussex Waterways were in his house and he was awaiting the visit of the VAT inspector. That was who he thought Burden was and for some moments they talked at cross-purposes, having one of those conversations so amusing to hearers and so frustrating to the participants.

Their hearer in this case was Mrs Milvey, a big-built lady, very ready with her laughter. She laughed merrily at their discomfiture. But Burden's troubles were quickly over. After that all went smoothly and it turned out to be as Wexford had supposed.

'The wife's a director of our company just as much as me,' Milvey said importantly. 'And naturally she knows the ins and outs of the business equally to what I do.'

'I have to know where he's going to be every day in case there's phone calls,' said Mrs Milvey, who was less pompous than her husband. 'The fifteenth of April? I'll have a look in the book, shall I, Bill?'

At this point the VAT inspector did arrive, a man in his early twenties by the look of him, carrying a briefcase. Milvey seemed reluctant to absent himself from the more interesting (and perhaps less alarming) examination but he was obliged to go. He took the VAT man into his office and closed the door. Mrs Milvey smiled comfortably at Burden.

'From Easter right up till the end of April they was working up Myringham way, she said, referring to the ledger she was holding. 'They never started on Green Pond till a month later.'

'Are you sure?'

'Positive. No doubt about it. It's down here in black and white. Green Pond, May the thirty-first. Besides, I remember it all now. Bill had a job lined up for the end of May, a big drainage job over to Sewingbury, and the chap cancelled at the last minute. But as luck would have it, this trout farm chap at Green Pond had been given his name and he rung up and said could he drag the pond? Well, Bill happened to be free on account of the cancellation. Must have given the trout farm fella a bit of a surprise, him saying yes, I'll start prompt on Monday.'

The office door opened again and Milvey put a hand out for his book. His wife gave it to him.

'Did you tell anyone?'

'I expect so. There was no secret about it, it was open and above board. You like to have a bit of news to tell folks, don't you? Now you're wanting to know if I told my neighbour Mrs Williams, aren't you?'

'Did you?'

'I never knew a thing about her husband then, mind you. I met her going down to the shops. Bill was getting the van out. I said something like, Monday he'll be doing a job at Green Pond Hall. There's going to be a trout farm, did you know? Something like that.'

'But you definitely told her your husband would be dragging the pond on Monday, May the thirty-first?'

'I couldn't see it would do any harm, could I?'

Had it? Wexford hadn't been entirely correct in his supposition, which was that Mrs Milvey had told Joy the pond had already been dragged or was not to be dragged until a much later date. But this gave a different – and incomprehensible – look to thing. If Joy had known Green Pond was to be dragged on the following Monday, the pond into which she had dumped her husband's travelling bag, wouldn't she have retrieved it during the weekend? The alternative possibility was that she had hidden it elsewhere and only put it in Green Pond when *she knew it was to be immediately dragged*. Why should she do such a thing, why behave so absurdly?

This was a hunch of Wexford's that had gone awry. Burden was on his way to put the second one to the test. They seemed no nearer, as far as he could see and in spite of Edwina Klein's revelation, to breaking the case. Next week he would probably start his paternity leave . . .

Bald-headed James Ovington, the son, was alone in charge of Pomfret Office Equipment. His ingratiating smile was as broad as ever. Burden noticed a new mannerism, a nervous way he had of rubbing his hands together. At any rate, the dour and obstructive father was nowhere around.

'Now can I help? Tell me what I can do.'

'You have a method of labelling your machines here,' said Burden. 'Not exactly a code, a kind of speedwriting. Last time we were here we noticed one labelled "E. Ten". I wondered what that stood for. It wasn't a Remington 315, of course, we'd have pounced on it if it had been. This is a kind of shot in the dark and I daresay I'm not making myself too clear.'

'It's clear enough you want to know what "E. Ten" stands for and that's easy.' Nevertheless, he hesitated and Burden wondered why a shade of unease seemed to cross his face.

'Eric Tennyson,' Ovington said. 'That's who it is, that's who "E. Ten" stands for.'

Second time lucky . . . 'I don't suppose you know if he has a daughter called Nicola?'

'Well, I do know as a matter of fact. The answer's yes.'

Veronica Williams's friend, her home the house to which Veronica regularly went on Tuesdays. But the typewriter labelled 'E. Ten' wasn't a Remington 315. Unless . . .

'An Olivetti,' said Ovington. 'They've got another machine. I don't rightly remember what. She types stuff for people, I mean does it for a living.' The uneasy look was back again. 'I may as well tell you,' he said as if about to make a confession of something that for a long while had weighed heavily on him. 'They're friends of mine. I knew I ought to tell you last time you were here.'

368

'But why shouldn't they be friends of yours, Mr Ovington?'

'Well . . . They're friends of Mrs Williams too. I mean the Mrs Williams whose husband got killed, the one you're making inquiries about. I mean that's where I met her, in their house.'

'Are you trying to tell me something, Mr Ovington?'

This fresh smile, a forced straining of the muscles, turned his face into a gargoyle. He rubbed his hands briskly, then clasped them behind his back to prevent a repetition of the gesture. Light from the shallow overhead lamps in the shed shone with a yellow gleam on the hairless head. Why were the heads of bald men compared to eggs? Ovington's head more than anything resembled a polished pebble.

'What is it you're saying, Mr Ovington?'

'I've been getting friendly with her. With Mrs Williams. There was nothing wrong, I don't mean that. I met her at Eric's and we'd have a drink sometimes, go for a walk, that sort of thing. When it looked as if that husband of hers had finally – well, when it looked as if he'd gone for good, I – I hoped things could get more serious.' He spoke jerkily, floundering, hopelessly unable to handle the situation he had got himself into. 'There was nothing *wrong*. I'd like to repeat that.'

Burden thought irrelevantly that Wendy Williams must be attracted by bald men, first Rodney with his exaggerated forehead, naked as an apple, then this pebble-head.

'But I thought,' Ovington said earnestly, 'that it would be wrong of me – disloyal, you know – to deny the relationship at this juncture, sort of deserting the sinking ship when you hear the cock crowing, if you get my meaning.'

More or less Burden did get it. He thought of the joy Wexford would have in that gloriously mixed metaphor. Now for the Tennysons. Half an hour later he was in their house on the Haldon Finch side of Pomfret, being told by Mrs Tennyson that her daughter was camping in Scotland till the end of the month but could she help him?

Her husband had fetched the repaired and serviced Olivetti from Pomfret Office Equipment three days before. Yes, she had her small portable for use when the other one was away

369

for its annual overhaul. She showed it to him: a Remington 315.

Burden stuck the sheet of paper she gave him into the roller. 'A thousand ages in They sight, Are like an evening gone . . .' A flaw in the apex of the capital A, the ascender of the lower-case t, the head of the comma . . .

'I'd never seen her in my life till you had us meet here.'

That was Wendy. Joy said nothing.

'I put it to you that you'd known each other for a long time. I suggest it was like this: Mrs Joy Williams came into Jickie's as a customer one day and in conversation you discovered the link between you. This happened a year ago. You've been in touch with each other ever since.'

Joy gave one of her cold rattling laughs that had something in it of the cackle of a game bird.

'If I'd known about her why should I pretend I didn't?' said Wendy.

Joy answered. She didn't exactly address Wendy, she hadn't yet done that except to abuse her, but she made her first statement not inimical to the other Mrs Williams.

'If her and me knew each other he thinks we might have murdered Rod.'

'I'm more likely to have murdered *her*,' said Wendy in a lofty voice. She looked down and noticed a ladder in her pale milk-coloured tights. It crept up the outside of her right leg like a millipede. Joy noticed it too. She fixed her eyes on the slowly mounting run and her mouth moved. It was nearly a smile.

Wexford said, looking at Joy, 'Someone phoned Sevensmith Harding on Friday, April the sixteenth, to say Rodney Williams was ill and wouldn't be coming to work. The girl who took the call isn't in much doubt that it was your voice, Mrs Williams.'

'She doesn't know my voice. How could she, whoever she is? Aren't you forgetting, I didn't know Rod worked there?'

The door opened and Burden put his head round. Wendy was licking her finger and dabbing at the ladder with her wet fingertip, dabbing as it happened in vain, for the ladder quite suddenly crept another half-inch. It was this which might have occasioned Joy's rattle laugh. Wexford got up and went out of the room, leaving the two women with the two women detectives.

Burden had sent his typing sample to the forensics lab. He told Wexford the substance of his interview with Mrs Tennyson. She had typed no letter of resignation herself and no one had asked her to do such a thing. Wendy Williams she had known for years, though her acquaintance with Rodney had been slight. Their daughters were the same age, were at school together, were 'best friends'.

'Could Wendy have typed it?' Wexford asked him. 'I mean, could she have had access to this machine? If this killing was premeditated, and it looks as if it was, she could have typed that letter days or even weeks before.'

'The Tennyson woman shuts herself up in a room she uses as an office and types for three or four hours a day. As a regular thing she uses the Olivetti and the Remington isn't even kept in there. It's usually in a cupboard in the hall unless the husband Eric wants it or the daughter Nicola uses it to type a school essay. Apparently, they're allowed to do that at the Haldon Finch. Could you credit it?'

'It seems a sensible and harmless practice,' said Wexford. 'Was Wendy ever alone in that house?'

'Early in April she came to call for Veronica, take her home or something. It was dark or late or she was passing. Anyway, the two girls were still out and Mrs Tennyson was typing something. She left Wendy alone for at most ten minutes, she says, until she finished off what she was doing.'

'Wendy would have to know the machine was there. She would have to have paper. But I agree it goes a long way to answering the question of how and where the letter was typed. As to typewriters, what better than to use one that was normally kept shut up in a cupboard? It was by the merest luck that we got on to it.' He listened while Burden told him about Ovington. 'Is that a motive, Mike? We keep coming back to that, the lack of motive. But if Wendy wanted to marry Ovington . . .'

'Who did Joy want to marry?'

'Yes, OK, I see your point. If they did it they did it together and Joy wouldn't be likely to help murder Rodney so that Wendy could marry someone else.' Wexford brought his fist to his forehead and drummed against it. 'I'm a fool! There's no motive. If Wendy knew about Joy she also knew she wasn't married to Rodney, so there was no legal bar to her marrying someone else . . . What about the knife, the weapon we're never going to prove *was* the weapon beyond a doubt? It could have been Joy's or Wendy's.'

'Wendy works at Jickie's and Jickie's stock those knives.'

'Wendy works there but the whole neighbourhood shops there.' Wexford thought for a moment. 'Among the stuff we found in Rodney Williams's bedroom in Liskeard Avenue,' he said, 'was an estimate from a firm of decorators for painting Wendy's living room. When we saw that room it had obviously been painted very recently. By that firm? By another? By Wendy herself? I think we ought to find out, don't you?'

Burden looked at him. They were both thinking that Rodney Williams had been stabbed to death. One of the knife thrusts had pierced the carotid. 'Yes, I do,' he said.

The day was very warm and close, a heavy, sultry, almost sunless day of the kind that only comes as August wanes. For the few moments he and Burden were in his office, the window open and the half-closed blinds swaying slightly in a hint of breeze, he had kept his jacket off. Now he put it on again and went back downstairs to the interview room where the two women were.

17

A picture of Joy and Wendy leaving Kingsmarkham Police Station was on most front pages of the national press next day. The more sensational of the newspapers managed to give the impression that they were not leaving but entering and that readers would not be too wide of the mark in concluding they had never left. Joy had her hand up over her face, Wendy looked piteously into the cameras, a distraught waif in her little-girl smock. The ladder in her tights was cruelly evident. Burden stood by, cool and rather aloof in a newish suit.

'You look young and handsome,' said Jenny at the breakfast table. 'You look so thin!' She shifted her huge weight, pushing back her chair.

'It's the worry.'

'I expect it is, poor Mike.' She put up her arms and hugged him. It was now only possible for her to do this while sitting down. He held her and thought, It may still be all right, we may still survive.

He went out before nine into a morning that was anything but fresh, a grey, sultry, sticky day. The sky was a flat, very pale grey with the sun a puddle of white glowing through it. This was the kind of day, he thought, that only England knows. Fifty of them can compose a summer.

How many builders and decorators were there in Pomfret? In Kingsmarkham? Not just the established firms but the one-man bands, the man who works in his spare time for money in the back pocket? With luck the Pomfret Williamses had availed themselves of the services of the firm who sent Rodney the estimate.

373

He didn't go to the police station first, so he was not present when Hope Harmer phoned to say her daughter was missing, had not been home all night or reappeared that morning.

John Harmer was in his dispensary and business was as usual. That is, when customers wanted soap or disposable razors instead of a prescription made up he came out and served them. He refused to believe anything had happened to his daughter. She was a grown woman well able to take care of herself as her prowess at that judo stuff evinced. Her absence probably had something to do with this women's movement nonsense.

Paulette's mother had come to work but only perhaps because of the pressures put on her by her husband. It was from there that she had phoned, the culminating act of a scene between them, Wexford guessed. She was in a piteous state. Hope Harmer was a woman whom it suited only to be happy. She was easily content and in contentment her plump, fair good looks bloomed. Unease affected her as it does an animal, drawing her face, freezing her features, mysteriously making bright hair lank and placid eyes stark with fear.

Wexford had Martin with him, the two of them top brass for the mere matter of a missing girl – but circumstances alter cases.

'My husband says what do I expect when I let her go out with her boyfriend at all hours and stay the night at his place. But they all do it these days and you can't be different. Besides they're engaged and I always say if you really love each other . . .'

She was talking for the sake of talking but her voice faltered. She began twisting her hands.

'Did Paulette go out with her fiancé last night?'

'No, he's in Birmingham. He had to go to Birmingham for his firm.'

Not for the first time Wexford marvelled at how illogical human thinking can be.

'But she did go out? Where did she go?'

'I don't know. She didn't say. She just went out at about seven.'

Martin said, 'You didn't want to know where she was going?'

'Want to know! Of course I wanted to know. If I had my way I'd know where she was every minute of the day and night. I mean I didn't ask her, I'd forced myself to that. When she was younger her father used to say: I want to know where you're going and who with but once you're eighteen you're legally grown-up and you can do what you like. Well, she's eighteen and she remembered that and my husband remembers it and he stops me asking and Paulette wouldn't answer anyway.'

The poor woman was wretchedly caught between husband and daughter, and bullied, doubtless, by both – or had she been happy to have decision-making taken out of her hands?

'Tell me what happened later on. Of course you didn't wait up for her?'

'I would have. I knew Richard was in Birmingham, you see. John said he wasn't having me get in a hysterical state. He took a sleeping pill and he made me take one.'

Presumably sedatives were unlimitedly on tap *chez* Harmer . . .

'This morning I – well, I left her bedroom door open before I went to sleep. That way – if it was shut, you see, I'd know she'd come in. I – I had to make myself open my own bedroom door and look. Her door was still open, it was such a shock, I . . . Well, I went to look, in case she'd come in and left her door but, of course, she hadn't. John still wasn't alarmed. Somehow I couldn't make him see that if Richard was in Birmingham Paulette couldn't have been with him . . .'

Mrs Harmer burst into raging tears. Instead of falling forward onto her arms to cry she lay back, let her head hang back and wailed. Martin went into the dispensary and fetched John Harmer. He came in looking cross and harassed. The noise his wife was making had the effect of causing him to put his hands over his ears in the manner that does nothing to block out sound but indicates that the sound is in some way distasteful or irritating.

375

'She'd better have a Valium. That'll help her pull herself together.'

'What she had better do, Mr Harmer,' said Wexford, 'is get off home. And you had better take her. Never mind the shop.'

Godwin and Sculp had not done Wendy Williams's decorating but they knew who had – a man who had once worked for them, who had left to set up in business on his own and who undercut them, Burden was told, at every opportunity. Running Leslie Kitman to earth was less simple. He had no wife and his mother was no Mrs Milvey to have his precise location at her fingertips. She gave Burden five possible addresses at which her son might be found: a farmhouse between Pomfret and Myfleet, a block of flats in Queen Street, Kingsmarkham, a cottage in Pomfret, and two houses on new estates outside Stowerton. Kitman was at none of them but the second Stowerton household told Burden he might just be lucky and find him in – Liskeard Avenue.

And it was there, three houses away from Wendy Williams's, that Burden discovered Kitman on top of a ladder. The house was like Wendy's, grey bricks and white weatherboard and picture windows. Kitman was painting a top-floor window frame. When Burden, standing at the foot of the ladder, shouted up who he was, Kitman launched immediately into a catalogue of reasons for not renewing his car tax. Burden hadn't even noticed his car, still less that the tax disc showed an expiry date of the end of June. At last, though, Kitman was made to understand and he came quickly down the ladder, his brush dripping white paint onto the lawn beneath.

The evening before Wendy Williams had spent in bed where she had retired, worn out, as soon as she returned from the police station. Veronica had brought her tea and bread and butter. It was all she ever seemed to fancy when upset. Joy Williams had also been at home with her daughter. At any rate they had been in the same house, Sara in her room as usual, Joy watching television and intermittently struggling

376

to complete the form of application for a grant that would take Sara through medical school. And although it was a Thursday evening there had been no phone call from Kevin who extended this courtesy to his mother only when he was at college and not while junketing around holiday resorts.

These were the alibis Wexford was given by his two principal suspects. Richard Cobb came back from Birmingham in the course of the afternoon and furnished Wexford with a very detailed and apparently satisfactory account of where he had been the night before. Police in Birmingham would help with a check on that. By six Paulette hadn't come home and Wexford knew she never would, he felt in his bones she wouldn't.

The day was sultry and overcast. For hours the thunder had been growling and rumbling and gradually a wind had risen, a dry gusty wind that did nothing to lower the temperature. It still remained hot and stuffy. Wexford and Burden sat in Wexford's office. A search for Paulette hadn't begun yet. Where would one search?

'The lines I'm thinking along,' said Wexford, 'are that Paulette Harmer procured the Phanodorm with which Rodney Williams was sedated. She was in a position to do that, she could easily have done it. I'm wondering if she lost her nerve and told someone – well, Joy – she was going to admit it before we found out.'

'Of course, there's another possibility . . .' Burden left the suggestion suspended.

Wexford looked abstractedly out of the window. It was time to go home but he had no inclination to go. The weather, the atmosphere, the late day, hung heavy with expectation. The thunder, of course, was a threat in itself, a sign of imminent storm, yet it seemed to contain some kind of emotional menace as well, as of looming tragedy.

'Tell me about Kitman,' Wexford said. 'In detail.' Burden had already given him an outline of his talk with the painter.

'He started doing that job for Wendy on April the fourteenth. There was paper on the walls, he said, and he had a job stripping it off. He was doing it all through the fourteenth and the fifteenth and he still hadn't finished by the time he knocked off on the fifteenth.'

'Should have used Sevensmith Harding's Sevenstarker,

shouldn't he?' said Wexford and quoting, ' "The slick, sheer, clean way to strip your walls". '

'Maybe he did. He says the room was still furnished but he had covered the pieces of furniture up with his own dustsheets. When he came back in the morning – the morning of Friday the sixteenth, that is – some of the sheets were off and folded up. But that was also on the morning of the fifteenth and other mornings, I gather. Wendy and Veronica were to some extent still living in that room.'

'Did he notice anything else that Friday morning?'

'A stain on the wall is what we want, isn't it? A great bloodstain? And blood all over his dustsheets? There wasn't anything like that or if there was he didn't notice or can't remember. The walls were splashed and marked and patchy anyway, you can imagine. And on the sixteenth he covered up whatever might have been there by putting his first coat of paint on. Sevenstar emulsion, no doubt. One thing he did notice, though, and I didn't ask him about this, he volunteered it. Apparently it's been vaguely preying on his mind ever since. One of the dustsheets wasn't his.'

'*What?*'

'Yes. I thought that'd make you sit up. He has a few dustsheets he takes about with him. Some of them are old bed sheets and there are a couple of curtains and a candlewick bedspread too. Well, according to him, when he left on the fifteenth all seven of his sheets were covering the furniture and part of the carpet. Next morning he came in to find that three of the sheets had been taken off the furniture and were folded up on the floor. He thought nothing much of it but later he noticed that one of the folded sheets wasn't his. It was newer than his and in better condition.'

'Did he ask Wendy about it?'

'He says he did. On the Saturday. She told him she knew nothing about it. And what did it matter to him, after all? He had the right number of dustsheets. You don't go to the police because someone has taken one of your dustsheets and substituted another. But he wondered about it, he says. It niggled him is the way he puts it. Are we going to have those two women back?'

'Of course we are.'

It was Friday, the last Friday in the month. ARRIA met

on the last Friday of the month, Wexford thought. No, the last Thursday. It was two months ago yesterday that he had gone to the Freeborns' house and interrupted a meeting.

He picked up the phone and spoke to John Harmer. Paulette's father was anxious now, no longer calm and scathing. He said his wife was asleep. Heavily sedated, Wexford guessed.

'The place is crawling with police,' said Harmer.

Wexford replied dryly, 'I know.'

He thought it an unfortunate way of describing the initial search he had mounted in the environs of the Harmers' home. The man's breathing at the other end of the line was audible. His voice had been rough and shaky. If insulting the police helped him, well . . .

'I can't tell you I don't think this a serious cause for concern, Mr Harmer. I'm very sorry. I think you should prepare yourself for bad news. Perhaps it would be best to say nothing to your wife as yet.'

'I'm not likely to wake her up and tell her you think her only child's dead, am I?'

Wexford said a polite goodbye and rang off. Harmer's rudeness gratified him a little. It was more than excusable in the circumstances and at least it showed Harmer wasn't the unfeeling husband he had thought him. Tomorrow morning they would widen the search for Paulette. By then he might have some idea of where and how to widen it.

A few drops of rain struck the windows, needles on the glass. The thunder thudded and cracked over Myringham way. Martin and Marion Bayliss brought the two Mrs Williamses in and Wexford went down to the interview room to confront them. Wendy in her Jickie's suit, hair freshly set – in Jickie's hairdressing department? – was in tears, dabbing at her eyes with a pink tissue. Joy had never looked so down at heel, broken sandals on her bare feet, a button missing from her button-through creased cotton dress, a scarf tied round her head. She looked like a refugee, such as have passed in streams across Europe at frequent times in modern history. Her face was grey and drawn.

Burden came in and sat beside him. The room had got so dark they had to have the light on. Still it wasn't really raining. When no one attempted to comfort Wendy and no offers of cups of tea were made she stopped crying. Rather defiantly, she produced the box of pink tissues from her bag and set it on the table in front of her.

'Was Paulette Harmer the girl your husband was seeing?'

Wexford addressed the question to both women. It was awkward. It seemed to treat polygamy as a legal state. Joy gave a dry cackle, more than usually scornful. Wendy said she didn't know who Paulette Harmer was, she had never heard of her.

'Who was it then?'

'He didn't have a young girlfriend,' said Joy. 'He didn't have any girl.' She nodded at Wendy. 'Unless you count her. And that's not the word I'd use for her.'

Wendy sniffed and pulled a tissue out of the box.

'Well, Mrs Williams?' Wexford said to her.

'I told you, I don't know.'

'On the contrary, you told me you knew there was one. This very young girl living around here with her parents – you never heard of her, she doesn't exist?'

Wendy looked at Joy. Their eyes met. For the first time Wexford thought he sensed a rapport between them. Then Wendy turned sharply away and shook her head violently.

'Rodney Williams was attracted by young girls,' Wexford said. 'You're an example yourself, Mrs Williams. How old were you when you and he met? Fifteen? Is that why you invented a young girlfriend for him? You knew it was in his nature?'

'I didn't invent it.'

He was suddenly aware of a change taking in place in Joy. She was shaking with emotion. Her hands held the table edge. Rain had begun to patter on the windows. Burden got up and closed the fanlight. Joy leaned forward.

'Has Sara been talking to you?' she said.

It was on the tip of his tongue to say he would ask the questions. But he didn't say it. He felt his way. 'It's possible.'

'The little bitch!'

How was it he sensed that the two women were at last united by some common bond? And that bond wasn't the dead man. The noise of the rain was intense now, a crashing cloudburst. He thought, they did know each other. The Klein girl was telling me the truth. They were close in a conspiracy and they're back in it again, the acting is over . . . He turned to Joy and it was as if his approaching, ultimately fixed gaze lit the fuse.

She spoke in a raucous throaty voice.

'You may as well have it. It wasn't young girls he was attracted to, not *any* young girls. It was his own daughter.'

18

It happened, it wasn't even uncommon. Lately it had been the modish subject for the pop sociology paperback. Yet that father-daughter incest might be a motivating factor in this case had not crossed Wexford's mind. Afterwards he was to ask himself *why* it hadn't crossed his mind, knowing his mind and the way it worked, but now in the interview room with the two women across the table from him he could only recall *The Cenci* and Beatrice – his own daughter playing Beatrice – running onto the stage crying:

'O World! O life! O day! O misery!'

That should have told him. Wendy had covered her face with her hands. Joy stared at him, her lips sucked in. A bead of saliva had appeared at the left corner of her mouth. She put her hand out for one of Wendy's tissues, tentatively, cautiously, watching Wendy, like an old dog approaching the food bowl but uncertain as to what the young dog will do. Wendy took her hands down. She didn't speak. She gave the tissue box a little push in Joy's direction. Burden sat, wearing his stony, contemptuous look.

Wexford was framing a question. Before he could utter it Joy spoke.

'She came and told me. Her own mother! His own wife! She said he'd come into her bedroom in the middle of the night. He said he was cold, he never seemed to get warm since we'd slept in twin beds. That's what he said to her. He said she could make him warm. Why didn't she scream out? Why didn't she run away? He got into bed with her and did it to her. I'm not going to repeat the word she used, they all

382

use it for *that*. It was while I was asleep. I was asleep and he was doing that with his own daughter.'

She laughed. The sound was drier than ever with more of a rattle in it but it was a laugh. She looked at Wendy and directed the laugh at her. And, Wexford thought, she may have been in cahoots with her, she may have told her all this before in womanly confidence, in sisters-under-the-skin conspiracy, but she enjoys telling it now – in our presence, a public triumphant putdown.

Like the therapist to whom he had compared himself, he would let her talk without interruptions, without breaking in to question. If she would talk. The pause endured. Wendy looked away and at the screen of water, curiously claustrophobic, the rain was making down the panes. She had pushed her fingers so hard into the skin of her face that they left pink pressure marks. Without prompting, Joy went on.

'She waited till he'd gone to work and then she told me. I was ironing her a blouse for school.' Insult had been thus added to injury, she implied. The father's rape would have been less offensive to the mother if the news had been imparted to her while she was ironing a shirt for Kevin. 'She burst right out with it. There wasn't a question of being tactful, mind, of – well, breaking it gently. He was only my husband. It was only my husband she was telling me about being unfaithful to me.' The laugh came again, but a ghost of it this time. 'I wouldn't listen to her. I said, don't tell me, I don't want to hear. I put my hands over my ears.'

A rejecting gesture not unknown in the Harmer-Williams families, Wexford thought. He nodded at Joy, feeling it was necessary to give some sign.

'I put my hands over my ears,' she said again. 'She started shouting at me. Didn't I care? Wasn't I upset? I answered her then. I said of course I was upset. No mother wants to hear her daughter's like that, does she? I said to her, You spread that about and you'll split us up, your father'll go to prison and what are people going to think of me? What's Kevin going to say to them at college?'

Burden said quietly, 'What did you mean by that, Mrs Williams, your daughter was "like that"?'

'It's obvious, isn't it? I'm not saying he wasn't weak.' A

383

glance for Wendy and a quick withdrawal of the eyes. 'Well, we know he was. But he'd never have done that without . . .'

She stopped and looked at Wexford. He remembered when he had first talked to Sara and her mother had sent him up to her bedroom saying she wouldn't object – 'Rather the reverse if I know her.'

'Encouragement?' he said flatly.

She nodded impatiently. 'Putting her arm round him, trying to get his attention. She wasn't *ten*. I said to her, you're not ten any more. Sitting on his knee – what did you expect? Now the least you can do is keep quiet about it, I said, think of my feelings for a change.'

'When did all this happen?'

'It was before Christmas. I know it was because I remember saying that she'd picked a fine time, hadn't she, just when we were all going to be together for Christmas.'

Wendy, whose face had been impassive, winced slightly. Had she realized at last where and how Rodney Williams spent his Christmases? It was soon after that, probably in the first week of January, Wexford recalled, that Edwina Klein had seen the two women together.

'Did you tell anyone?' Burden asked.

'Of course I didn't. I wasn't going to broadcast it.'

He turned on Wendy. 'When did she tell you? Or should I say warn you?'

Wendy had looked shocked by none of this. Not even surprised. But she shook her head. 'She never did.'

'Come on, Wendy . . .' Wexford had solved the names problem at last. 'Joy found out you existed, sought you out especially to tell you what Rodney was really like. To tell you, in fact, to have a care to your own daughter.'

'Tell her?' said Joy. 'Why should I care?'

'Wendy,' Wexford said more gently, almost insinuatingly, 'you're not going to tell us you didn't know about Rodney and his daughter Sara. You're not going to make believe what we heard just now was all news to you. You couldn't have looked less surprised than if I told you it was raining. Joy came into Jickie's, didn't she, and told you who she was? I'll make a guess at the week before Christmas. How did she know who you were? She'd seen Veronica in the street and

384

spotted the resemblance to Sara – a likeness no one could mistake . . .'

That they were surprised now, both of them, he couldn't doubt. He had been wrong there then. Never mind. There were other ways – following Rodney, seeing him and Wendy together, a host of ways.

'You met at Jickie's, went on to meet again after Christmas. No doubt there were many meetings . . .'

Wendy jumped up, eyes full of tears, grabbing a handful of tissues.

'I want to talk to you alone! Just you and me quite alone!'

'Surely,' said Wexford.

He got up. Burden didn't wait for them to leave the room before starting on Joy with his questions. When did she first suspect Rodney had a second home? Did she ever ask him? Joy was laughing at this second suggestion when Wexford closed the door. He took Wendy upstairs to his own office. The rain had abated, was now merely trickling, slipping, spilling, down the washed gleaming glass. Twilight hadn't yet begun and the sky was a clear grey, light from cloud-coated sunshine. Wendy stumbled a little going into the room. He thought it might be unwise to touch her, even to the extent of steadying her. She held on to the door frame and shot him a look of grievance.

In the chair he held out for her she sat down gingerly, treating herself as if she had become fragile. She had turned into a convalescent, tentatively putting out feelers to the world. Her shoulders she was keeping permanently lifted.

'What did you want to say to me, Wendy?' He had dropped the 'Mrs Williams' altogether now.

She whispered it, sustaining the invalid image, a broken woman, wan-faced, such as might fittingly inhabit the Castle of Petrella and be called Lucretia.

'The same as what she said.'

'I'm sorry, Wendy. You must make yourself plainer than that.'

'It was the same for us. The same as what she said. Or – well, it would have been. I mean, he would have done but he went away and got himself killed.'

Light penetrated. 'You mean Rodney also made advances

385

to Veronica? Only, if I interpret what you're saying correctly, it was merely advances?'

She nodded, tears splashing now, wads of tissues held to her eyes like swabs.

'Before Joy warned you or afterwards?'

A shrugging, then a shaking, of the whole body. Make-up scrubbed off with that cheapest and most readily available cleanser, tears. Wendy presented to Wexford a youthful, naked, desperate face.

'He had been a little more attentive to her, had he, than we in our society expect of a father to a teenage daughter? Did she tell you or did you see? Kissed her and said it was good to be alone with her and you out of the way?'

She jumped up. 'Yes, yes, yes!' she shouted.

'So on April the fifteenth, although you didn't think there was much chance of Rodney coming back, you encouraged your daughter to go out so as not to be alone with him? You told her not to run the risk of being alone with him but to stay out until you came home?'

Guilt was heavy on her face now, driving away indignation. He felt she was on the brink of a confession.

'Or did you send her out so that *you* could be alone with Rodney – you and Joy?'

The air was sharply clear, the rain past, the sky two shades of blue, a dark clean azure and the smoky blue of massed cloud. Nine o'clock and growing dark. Water lay in glassy pools, reflecting the sky. There was an unaccustomed coolness, almost a nip in the temperature. Before morning there would be more rain. Wexford could see it in the clarity and smell it in the atmosphere. He walked from the police station and kept on walking, just to get away from the enclosing four walls, the stuffiness, the millions of uttered words, the weariness of lies.

People used to tell him when they needed an alibi – now they cited television – that they had been for a walk. They didn't know where, just for a walk. He hadn't believed them. Everyone knew where they had been on a walk. Now he thought he might not be able to say where he had been tonight. His progress was aimless, though not slow, a fairly brisk marching in the fresh cold air, a thinking walk to dwell on what had passed.

So inconclusively. So unsuccessfully. He had wrung those two women, turned the handle and ground them through the rollers. Joy had laughed and Wendy had wept. He had kept on repeating over and over to himself: Edwina Klein saw them together. Why should she lie? Why should she invent? He had to let them go at last. Wendy was near collapse – or feigning it beautifully.

It was clear, the whole case, Burden said. A motive had at last emerged. Joy killed out of bitterness and jealousy, Wendy out of fear Rodney would serve Veronica the same way as he had served Sara. An unfortunate verb in the circumstances, but perhaps not inept . . . A conspiracy laid just after Christmas, brooded over through the early spring, hatched out in April. Murder in the room that would be decorated tomorrow. Staunch the blood with Kitman's dustsheet, realize too late what you have used.

It must have happened that way, there was no other. Perhaps they hadn't intended to kill, only confront him jointly, threaten and shock. But the French cook's knife had been handy, lying on the table maybe. That didn't explain drugging him with Phanodorm. The knife Milvey had found? Its blade matched with the width and depth of the wounds. So would a thousand knives.

He was in Down Road, under the dripping lime trees. Perhaps, all along, he had known he was making his way here. The big old houses, houses that could justly be called 'piles', seemed sunken tonight in dark, still, sodden foliage. A dark green perfume arose from grass and leaf and rain-bathed flowers. Somewhere nearby a spoilt dog, left alone for the evening, vented its complaints in little bitter whimpering wails. Wexford opened the gate to the Freeborns' house. Lights were on, one upstairs and one down. The dustmen had been that morning, long before the rain started, and left the scattering of litter they didn't bother to remove from places where the occupants failed to tip lavishly. A sodden sheet of paper, pasted by rain onto the gravel, bore the ARRIA logo and a lot of printing it was too dark to read.

Both twins came to the door. He approved their caution. Once more they were alone in the house, left to their own

387

devices, the switched-on parents far away at some veteran hippies' haunt. Both had pale blue hair tonight, pink stuff on their eyelids, otherwise the nearly identical faces were bare. And identical on both faces was dismay at the sight of him. Eve spoke.

'Do you want to come in?'

'Yes, please.' The house no longer smelt of marijuana. That was one thing he had achieved, a dubious success. The girls seemed not to know where to take him. They stood in the hall. 'There was a meeting of ARRIA last night,' he said. 'Where was it? Here?'

'They're mostly held here,' said Amy.

'And it was here last night?'

'Yes.'

He pushed open a door and switched a light on. It was a huge living room, floor cushions making islands on parquet that hadn't been polished for two decades, a divan with thrown over it something that might have had its origin in Peru, the only chair a wicker hemisphere hanging from the ceiling. French windows, uncurtained, gave onto what seemed an impenetrable wood.

He sat in the hanging chair, refusing to be alarmed by its immediate swinging motion.

'Who was at the meeting?'

They exchanged glances, looked at him. 'The usual crowd,' said Amy, and conversationally, 'It's always the same lot that turn up, isn't it?'

The names he ran through got a nod at every pause. 'Caroline Peters? Nicola Anerley? Jane Gardner? Paulette Harmer?' Eve nodded. She nodded in the same way as she had at the other names. 'Edwina Klein?'

There must have been a note of doubt in his voice.

'Yes, Edwina was here. Why not?'

'Why not indeed. And why not Sara Williams, come to that?'

'Sara didn't come,' said Amy. 'She had to stay home with her mother.'

So John Harmer hadn't been so far out when he suggested his daughter's disappearance had something to do with this 'women's movement nonsense'.

'What time did the meeting end?'

'About ten,' said Amy. 'Just about ten.' She had forgiven them if her sister never would. She had altogether put off that distant manner. 'Someone told me today that Paulette didn't go home all night and . . .' She left the sentence hovering.

'You never told me,' Eve said sharply.

'I forgot.' Amy turned her eyes back on Wexford. 'She was a bit late. She didn't say why. Edwina brought her aunt – not to join, just to see what went on, though she's eligible of course, never having married. It was good seeing someone old who'd had principles and stuck to them.'

'I have fought the good fight,' said Wexford. 'I have run a straight race. I have kept the faith.'

'That's right. That was exactly it. How did you know?'

He didn't answer her. The Authorized Version was unknown to them, lost to their generation as to the one before, a dusty tome of theology, in every way a closed book.

'Was Paulette alone when she left?'

'The meeting was upstairs.' Eve was chilly and unbending but she had spoken. 'We didn't see people out. They went downstairs and let themselves out. Paulette left with Edwina and her aunt.'

'They may have left together,' said Amy, 'but they didn't go off together. I looked out of the window and saw Edwina and her aunt getting into the aunt's car and Paulette wasn't with them.'

'What's out there?' Wexford said abruptly. He pointed at the long windows beyond which was visible only a mass of foliage.

'The conservatory.'

Amy opened the doors, swung them open and put her hand to a switch. Unconventional the Freeborn family might be; they were not feckless. The old domed conservatory, its upper panes of stained glass, claret and green in an Art Nouveau design of tulips, was full of dark green leafy plants, some of which looked subtropical, all demanding ample water and getting it. It must cost a fortune to heat in winter, Wexford thought, coming closer, entering the conservatory and spotting an orchid or two, the velvety mauve trumpet of a *brunfelsia*.

Eve, without being asked, flooded the garden beyond with

389

light. Touching another switch brought on arc lamps, one on the conservatory roof, another in the branches of an enormous ilex. The garden, so-called, hardly deserved flood-lighting. It was a wilderness of unmown grass, wild roses, brambles, the occasional hundred-year-old tree. And it was huge, the kind of garden whose owners might justly say they were never overlooked. Shrubs that appeared dense black at this hour made an encircling irregular wall round its peri-meter.

'We don't any of us go in it much,' said Amy. 'Except as a shortcut to the High Street. And when it's muddy or whatever . . .' Another sentence was left hanging. She went on vaguely, 'Dad's keen on the conservatory. It's him that grows the plants.'

The *Cannabis sativa*, thought Wexford, but hardly in here. You need infra-red light for that and plenty of it. He opened the door into the garden, a glass door of slender green and white panels. The cold damp air breathed water in suspen-sion at him. He noticed a path among the grass, pieces of crazy paving let into what had once been turf, was now wet hay. The girls weren't coming with him. Eve wound her arms round her body, hugging herself against the cold. Amy breathed on the glass and with her fingertip began drawing a raven with a woman's face. Wexford went down the path. The arc lamps reached no further than thirty feet or so. He took his torch out of his pocket and switched it on.

The path led to the gate in the far fence, he thought. That was what Amy meant by a shortcut to the High Street. First it wound through a copse of dark shrubs, laurels, rhododen-drons, all glistening and dripping with water. He was curi-ously reminded of walking in a cemetery. Cemeteries were like this, untended often, places of ornamental shrubs, funereal trees, like this without flowers, unlike this with gravestones.

He came upon the fence and the gate quite suddenly, almost bumping into the gate which was in a break in the untrimmed hedge that followed the line of the close-board-ing. From here the backs of other big houses could just be seen, two of them with yellow rectangles on black that were lights in their windows. The light didn't reach here and no moon had appeared. The path curved its way all round the garden. He followed its ellipse, returning on the right-hand side. Bamboo here, half dead most of it, a mass of canes. Then something prickly that caught at his raincoat. He pulled and heard the tearing sound. Turn the torch on it to see what had happened . . .

Turn the torch into the midst of this circle of briar roses, brambles with wicked thorns – onto an outflung arm, a buried face, a logo and an acronym, red on white cotton – ARRIA and the raven-woman.

It was more like a cemetery here than he had supposed . . .

19

The scene-of-crimes officer. Dr Crocker. Sir Hilary Tremlett fetched out of his bed and wearing a camelhair coat over pyjama top and grey slacks. Burden as neat and cool as at mid-morning. And the rain coming down in summer tempests. They had to rig a sort of tent up over the body.

She had been strangled. With a piece of string or cord perhaps. Wexford himself could see that without reference to Dr Crocker or Sir Hilary. The photographer's flash going off made him blink. He didn't want to look at her any more. It sickened him, though not with physical nausea, he was far beyond that. No pharmacology degree now, no marriage to Richard Cobb, no full flowering of that strange beauty that had been both sultry and remote.

The girls worried him, Eve and Amy, alone in that house with a young girl, a contemporary, dead in the garden. Marion Bayliss had tried to reach their parents but they were at none of the phone numbers the twins could produce. Neighbours shunned the Freeborns. With the families immediately next door they weren't even on speaking terms. Eve thought of Caroline Peters and it was she who came to the house in Down Road and stayed for the rest of the night. Wexford crawled into bed at around three. There was a note for him from Dora which he read but did not mark or inwardly digest: 'A man called Ovington keeps phoning for you.' She was deeply asleep and in sleep she looked young. He lay down beside her and the last thing he remembered before sleeping himself was laying his hand on her still-slender waist.

'She'd been dead about twenty-four hours,' said Crocker, 'which is about what you thought, isn't it?'

When you don't get enough sleep, Wexford thought, it's not so much tired that you feel as weak. Though perhaps they were the same thing. 'Strangled with what?' he asked. 'Wire? Cord? String? Electric cable?'

'Because it's easily obtainable and pretty well impossible to break I'd guess the kind of nylon cord you use for hanging pictures. And where were your suspects – ' Crocker looked at his watch ' – thirty-six hours ago?'

'At home with their daughters, they say.'

Wexford began going through the statement Burden had taken from Leslie Kitman, the painter. A description of the missing dustsheet was gone into in some detail. Useless now, of course. It was four months since that dustsheet, concealed in a plastic bag, had been removed by the council's refuse collectors. And the knife as likely as not with it. Somehow he couldn't believe in Milvey's knife, he couldn't take two Milvey coincidences . . .

The walls had been stained and pitted, Kitman said. He couldn't remember if the stains had looked any different on the morning of 16 April from the afternoon of 15 April. Some of the holes, he thought, might have been filled in by someone else. He had made good some of the cracks and holes with filler which, when it dried, left white patches. On 16 April and the morning of the 17th he had lined the walls with wood-chip paper and on the Monday following begun painting over the paper.

Was he going to have those women in again? One of them had killed the girl the night before last. To keep her from confirming their guilt in the matter of the Phanodorm. Only one of them or both? Joy could easily have known where she would be and that she left by the shortcut to the High Street where she would catch the Pomfret bus.

Burden was late. But then he too had been up and on the go since early yesterday morning, finally getting to bed even later than Wexford. To be up after midnight, thought Wexford, is to be up betimes. He had always liked that, only no one knew what 'betimes' meant any more, which rather spoiled the wit of it. Thinking of going to bed reminded him of Dora's note and he was about to pick up the phone and get hold of Ovington when Burden walked in.

He didn't look tired, just about ten years older and a stone thinner. He was wearing his stone-coloured suit with a shirt the same shade and a rust tie with narrow chocolate lines on it. Might be going to a wedding, thought Wexford, all he needed was a clove carnation.

'Jenny's started,' he said. 'I took her to the infirmary this morning at eight. There's not going to be anything doing much yet awhile but they wanted her in promptly.'

'You'd better start your leave as from now.'

'Thanks. I thought you'd say that. I must say these babies do pick their moments. Couldn't she have waited a week? She's going to be Mary, by the way.'

'After your grandmothers, no doubt.'

But the coincidence he had related to Wexford had slipped Burden's memory. 'Do you know that never crossed my mind? Perhaps Mary Brown Burden then?'

'Forget it,' said Wexford. 'It sounds like an American revivalist preacher. Keep in touch, won't you, Mike?'

Later in the day, with luck, the pathologist's report on Paulette Harmer would come and also perhaps something from Forensics on the murder weapon. He had Martin go to a magistrate and swear out a warrant to search the Williams home in Liskeard Avenue, and he wasn't anticipating any difficulties in getting it. In the meantime he had himself driven to the other Williams home. He didn't feel up to walking, whatever Crocker might advise.

Sara was mowing the front grass with one of those small electric mowers that cut by means of a line wound on a spool and are principally intended for trimming edges. As he got out of the car the motor whined and stopped cutting and the girl, crimson with bad temper, up-ended the flimsy machine and began tugging furiously at the line. He heard a hissed repetition of the word Joy disliked so much that she had used of her father's assault.

'Fuck, fuck, fuck, fuck!'

'If you do that with the current switched on,' Wexford said, 'one day you're going to cut your hand off.'

She cooled as rapidly as she had become incensed.

'I know. I've promised myself I'll always switch it off

before I fiddle with it. But these god-damned things never work for long.' She pulled prongs out of a socket to oblige him and smiled. An ARRIA tee-shirt today, identical to the one on dead Paulette. 'This is the fourth of these spools we've had this summer. Do you want to see my mother?'

And yet she couldn't know about Paulette. He remembered her thinly veiled boasting to her cousin on the phone and he didn't think she would much care. Nor would she much care when her mother was arrested for the murder. But perhaps it was natural for victims of incest not to care much about anything. He felt a wrench of pity for her.

'I want to talk to you first.'

The garage, now there was no car to occupy it, had become a toolshed and repository for rather battered garden furniture. Sara indicated a deckchair to Wexford. For her part she sat down on an upturned oil drum and set about struggling with the stubborn spool. This looked as if it might go the way of its fellows, three of which lay on a shelf next to a dozen half-used Sevenstar paint tins. He supposed she was busying herself so as not to have to look at him while he talked to her about her father.

At his first mention of incest, a tactful broaching of what her mother had told him, she didn't flush but turned gradually whiter. Her skin, always pale, grew milk-like. And he noticed a phenomenon, perhaps peculiar to her. The fine gold down on her forearms erected itself.

He asked her gently when it had first happened. She kept her head bent, with her right hand attempting to rotate the spool while with her left forefinger and thumb she tugged at the slippery red line.

'November,' she said, confirming his own ideas. 'November the fifth.' She looked up and down again quickly. 'There were only two times. I saw to that.'

'You threatened him?'

She hesitated. 'Only with the police.'

'Why didn't you tell your brother? Or did you? I have a feeling you and your brother are close.'

'Yes, we are. In spite of everything.' She didn't say in spite of what but he thought he knew. 'I *couldn't* tell him.' Like a different girl speaking, her face turned away, 'I was ashamed.'

And she hates her mother, so it was a pleasure to tell *her*? She gave a final tug and the line came through, far too much of it, yards of loosely-coiled scarlet flex.

Kevin was indoors, having unexpectedly arrived that morning by means of some comfortless and inefficient transport. He was lying spent, exhausted, dirty and unkempt, on the yellow sofa, his booted feet up on one of its arms. Joy had answered Wexford's knock with refreshments for Kevin in her hands, a trayful of sandwiches, coffee, something in a carton that was ice cream or yogurt. Wexford shut the door on him, hustled Joy into the kitchen. She was dressed exactly as she had been the day before, even to the headscarf – had she tied it on to run to the shops for Kevin-provender? – and gave the impression of having never taken her clothes off, of sleeping in them. He told her, quite blandly, about Paulette, but she knew. John Harmer had phoned her while Sara was in the garden. Or that was the explanation she gave Wexford for knowing. He said he would want her later at the police station, she and Wendy. He would send a car for her.

'What's my son going to do about his evening meal?'

'Give me a tin opener,' said Wexford, 'and I'll teach him how to use it.'

She didn't observe the irony. She said she supposed he could have something out of a tin for once. At least she didn't suggest his sister might cook for him, which was an improvement (if that was the way you looked at things) on twenty years ago.

The next stop was Liskeard Avenue, Pomfret. Martin had got his warrant and was there with Archbold and two uniformed men, PC Palmer and PC Allison, Kingsmarkham's only black policeman. A tearful Wendy was trying to persuade them it wouldn't be necessary to strip the paper off her living-room walls.

At the glass table sat Veronica. Evidently she had been at work on the hem of a white garment that lay in front of her but had laid down her needle when the policemen arrived. Wexford thought of the girl in the nursery rhyme who sat on a cushion and sewed a fine seam, feeding on strawberries, sugar and cream. It must have been her dress which suggested it to him with its pattern of small wild strawberries and

396

green leaves on a creamy ground. Tights again, dark blue this time, white pumps. Another thing that made those girls look alike was the way neither of their faces showed their feelings. They were the faintly melancholy, faintly smug, nearly always impassive faces of madonnas in Florentine paintings.

Wexford's daughter Sylvia had a cat which uttered soundless mews, going through the mouth-stretching motion of mewing only. Veronica's 'hello' reminded him of that cat, a greeting for a lip-reader, not even as audible as a whisper. Wendy renewed her appeals as he came in, now making them to him only.

'I'm sorry, Wendy. I understand your feelings. We'll have the room redecorated for you.' Or for someone, he thought but didn't say aloud. 'And there'll be as little mess as possible.'

And it really was Sevensmith Harding's Sevenstarker they intended to use for the job, four large cans of it, each labelled in red italic script that this was the slick, sheer, clean way to strip your walls. Wexford found himself hoping this wasn't too gross an exaggeration.

'But what for?' Wendy kept saying, at the same time, curiously enough, picking up ornaments and pushing them into a wall cupboard, loading a tray.

'That I'm not at liberty to say,' said Wexford, falling back on one of the stock answers of officialese. 'But there's plenty of time. Please clear the room yourself if you want to.'

In silence Veronica picked up her sewing. She threaded her needle, using a small device manufactured for that purpose, and slipped a pink thimble onto her forefinger.

'She's doing the hem of her tennis dress. She's playing in the women's singles final at the club this afternoon.' Wendy spoke in tragic tones, only slightly modified by a faint proud stress on the word 'club'.

Kingsmarkham Tennis Club, presumably, or even Mid-Sussex. 'We shan't stop her,' Wexford said.

'You'll upset her.' She drew him into the kitchen, through the already open doorway. 'You're not going to say anything to her about you-know-what? I mean you're not going to go into it?'

'I'm not a social worker,' he said.

397

'Nothing actually happened anyway. I saw to it nothing happened.'

Impossible, though, not to see Rodney Williams, hitherto no more than liar and con-man, as some sort of monster. To make a sexual assault on one daughter was heinous enough, but almost immediately to have designs on her younger half-sister?

'Of course, you wouldn't have suspected anything *might* happen if Joy hadn't warned you.'

'How many times do I have to tell you I never saw the woman till you – introduced us?'

'Something you haven't told me is how you knew Rodney made sexual advances to Veronica. He didn't tell you but you knew. Veronica was the young girl living at home with her family you led us a wild goose chase about, wasn't she?' He closed the door between the rooms and leaned against it.

Wendy nodded, not looking at him.

'How did you know, Wendy? Did you see something? Did you notice something in his behaviour when he thought you weren't looking? Was that after or before Joy warned you?'

She mumbled, 'I didn't see anything. Veronica told me.'

'*Veronica*? That innocent child in there who's more like twelve than sixteen? That child you've very obviously sheltered from every exposure to life? She interpreted her father's affectionate kisses, his arm around her, his compliments, as sexual advances?'

A nod. Then a series of vehement nods.

'And yet you say "nothing actually happened". By that I take it you mean there was no more than a kiss and a touch and a compliment. But she – *she* – saw this as an incestuous approach?'

Wendy's response was characteristic. She burst into tears. Wexford pushed up a stool for her to sit on and found a box of tissues, never a difficult task in that house. He returned to the living room where the carpet was now covered with sheets and from which Veronica had disappeared. Allison was daubing the walls with Sevenstarker, Palmer already at work with a metal stripping tool. The hunch he had about what was under that paper was probably crazy, but besides that it was just possible an analysis of old plaster might show traces of Rodney's blood. And might not. Anyway, it was work for Leslie Kitman. He could come in next week and put it all back again at the expense of the Mid-Sussex Constabulary.

The rain had started again. That would put paid to Veronica's match in the afternoon as neither the Kingsmarkham Tennis Club nor the Mid-Sussex County at Myringham had covered courts. Wexford, back in his office though it was Saturday, noted the time. Twelve-thirty. Getting on for three hours since Mike had been in and announced the imminence of his new daughter. Well, it was too soon yet to expect much, early days.

Something kept nagging at the back of his mind, something Wendy had said. About the tennis match, he thought it was. But she hadn't said anything except that Veronica would be playing that afternoon. Why did he have this curious feeling then that in what she said lay the whole answer to this case? He often had feelings like that about some small thing when a case was about to break, and the small thing always turned out to be vital and his hunch seldom wrong. The difficulty was that he didn't know what he had a hunch about.

All the available men he had were either at Wendy's taking her room apart or else, the far greater number of them, conducting a house-to-house in Down Road and interrogating every girl who had been at the ARRIA meeting. A mood of loneliness and isolation enclosed him. Dora had gone to London and to stay the night with Sheila in Hampstead. His elder grandson Robin would be nine today, his birthday party due to begin three hours from now. Crocker played golf all day on Saturdays. Wexford would have liked to sleep but he found it hard to sleep in the daytime. What the hell was it Wendy had said? What *was* it? Tremlett was probably still at work on that poor girl's body . . . She had got Phanodorm for Joy and threatened to tell that she had. Well, not threatened, warned rather that she would have to, she would be scared not to. Joy had given Rodney the Phanodorm, substituting it for his blood-pressure pills, and it took just the time of a drive to Pomfret to act. Follow him by bus to Wendy's. He's asleep when you get there and you look at

399

him and remember what he's done to you by way of what he's done to your daughter. Married another woman too, like a bloody sheikh. And the other wife goes along with you, though you hate her. It's her daughter at risk now since you told her where his tastes lie. Why let him ever wake up again? If there's a mess she says the room's going to be decorated tomorrow. And if you hide the body for long enough . . .

In the morning phone the office, say he's ill, disguising your voice a bit. She'll type his letter of resignation for you, she's got access to a typewriter in a friend's house that no one's going to trace. You're both in it equally, you and she, the two wives of Rodney Williams, for better for worse, till death parts you. She stabbed him too, though you gave him the sleeping pill. You and she together carried the body down that crackpot spiral staircase, through the doorway into the integral garage. Laid him in the car with his travelling bag. She drove because you never learned, but you did most of the grave digging. Soiling your hands never bothered you the way it did her. Two wives, in it together equally, and whom murder has joined let no man put asunder.

Wexford had got himself under Joy's skin and he very nearly finished this internal monologue with one of her awful laughs. The chances were Burden wouldn't phone before evening. And then surely he'd phone him at home. He drove to the Old Cellar and had himself a slice of quiche, broccoli and mushroom, a pleasant novelty, one small glass of Frascati to go with it – it was Saturday, after all, though with nothing to celebrate – and then back again to the estate where the streets were named for Cornish towns, Bodmin, Truro, Falmouth, Liskeard. A cold grey rain fell steadily. They were back to the weather they had had between Rodney Williams's disappearance and the discovery of his body.

In Wendy's living room considerable progress had been made. Three walls were more or less stripped. It wasn't what Wexford would have called slick, sheer and clean but it wasn't bad. Martin had got hold of someone from Forensics, a shaggy girl in navy all-in-ones, who nevertheless had the air of an expert and was painstakingly scraping samples of brownish plaster off the walls.

Wendy was downstairs in her sewing-ironing-laundry

400

room or whatever, cutting patterns out of magazines. For therapy, no doubt. Veronica was with her, Miss Muffet on a velvet pouffe. No match for her today as he had predicted. He suddenly remembered his threat to send a car for Joy 'later' and the crisis over Kevin's dinner this had precipitated. Well, it would have to be much later . . . Or tomorrow. Or every day on and for ever. No, he mustn't think that way.

Wendy had changed her dress for a linen suit. Perhaps she had been going to watch her daughter play, for Veronica, as though not resigned to the cancellation until the last moment, was in her tennis whites, pleated miniskirt – who could imagine her in shorts? – and a top almost too well finished to be called a tee-shirt.

'I suppose they'll postpone it till Monday night,' said Wendy in a high rather mad voice, 'and that means half the spectators won't come.'

Down the spiral staircase came the expert with her case of samples, the scraper in her hand.

'I think I'm going to be sick,' whispered Veronica.

Her mother was all care, all solicitude, jumping up, hastening her to the ground-floor bathroom.

Wexford went back upstairs. Archbold had gone. The expert had gone. Martin was drinking tea from a flask and the other two Coke from cans while they waited for the Sevenstarker on the fourth wall to do its stuff. Wexford felt something very near a qualm. The room, which had been a shell-pink sanctuary, was a nasty mess. A shambles, Martin called it, but a shambles, meaning a slaughter house, was just what Wexford thought it had been used for, the reason for this destruction. Suppose he was wrong? Suppose the killing of Rodney Williams had taken place elsewhere?

Too late now.

The police's loss would be Kitman's gain. It is the business of the thinking man, he paraphrased, to give employment to the artisan.

'Let me have one of those, will you?' he said to Martin, pointing to the scrapers. The white patches of plaster among the brown were the areas Wendy herself had filled before Kitman began papering.

It wouldn't budge the white plaster.

'Want me to have a go, sir?' Allison produced what Wexford thought might be a cold chisel.

'We'll all have a go.'

It made Allison's day. He had never before distinguished himself in any way since joining the force two years before. Sometimes he thought – and his wife – that they had only taken him on because he was black and not because he was suitable or any good. They were inverted race snobs. For weeks everyone had bent over backwards to treat him with more kindness, courtesy and consideration than they would show, for instance, to a millionaire grandfather on his death-bed. That had worn off after a while. He was a bit lonely too in Kingsmarkham where only his wife, his kids and two other families were West Indian like him. But today paid for all that. It was what made him in his own eyes an officer of the law.

'Sir, I think I've found . . .' he began.

Wexford was there beside him like a shot. Under his eyes Allison dug in carefully, thanking his stars he'd remembered to put his gloves on. The object was stuck in the fissure wrapped up in newspaper, plastered over. He chipped and dug and then put his hand to it, looking at Wexford, and Wexford nodded.

The knife didn't clatter out. It was unveiled as reverently as if it were a piece of cut glass. They all looked at it lying there on its wrappings, clean as a whistle and polished bright as a long prism in a chandelier.

20

Wexford had them with him all day Sunday and Monday morning's papers said an arrest was imminent. But Wexford wanted the two women, not just one, Joy as well as Wendy. Charging Wendy with Rodney Williams's murder was an obvious act. The knife buried in her living-room wall had a blade which exactly matched the knife wounds on the body and it was wrapped in part of the *Daily Mail* of 15 April. Still, he wanted Joy as well and Joy had no apparent connection with the crime. The only evidence he had was a witness who claimed to have seen the two women together and a voice on the phone that was probably hers.

Joy also had an alibi. Wendy didn't. All day long nails were going into Wendy's coffin, or at least the shades of the prison house were closing about her. Until Ovington came. That is, until Ovington's second visit.

Alone in the house, eating a junk food supper, Wexford got a call from Burden late on Saturday evening. Jenny's labour hadn't exactly been a false alarm but it had gradually subsided during the day. They were keeping her in, though, and considering some method of induction . . .

'You wanted her to wait a week,' said Wexford nastily. 'You'd better come back to work.'

He phoned Ovington first thing in the morning. Never mind about Sunday and all that. By the time Ovington arrived at the police station he and Sergeant Martin and Polly Davies had Joy and Wendy in an interview room, the demented refugee and the broken doll. The curious thing was they had come closer to each other. In appearance that is. There had been a sort of blending, and he thought of

403

Kipling's hedgehog and tortoise, combining to make an armadillo. Joy and Wendy hadn't gone that far, but anxiety and harassment had done their work on the younger woman and the older had smartened herself up, perhaps because her son was back. At any rate the headscarf was gone and she had proper shoes on. But Wendy's make-up was stale, she had hairs all over the shoulders of her black cotton dress and the ladder that sprang in her tights didn't fidget her.

He left them to go and talk to Ovington. Smiling as usual, absurdly ingratiating, he could hardly have persuaded even the most gullible to believe him, certainly not a hard-headed policeman.

'She was with you on April the fifteenth?' Wexford said. 'She came to your place after work for a drink? Why hasn't she so much as mentioned this to me?'

'She doesn't want anyone to know she was seeing me while her husband was still alive.'

That was in character. Wifely virtue was one of the aspects of the image Wendy liked to present. That didn't mean Ovington's story was true. Ovington was trying it on, a kind, stupid man with a misplaced idea of duty. Absently Wexford thanked him for coming. Then, as he was going back to the Williams wives, it occurred to him Ovington might have been in it with Wendy instead of Wendy with Joy. In that case who had made the phone call?

Wendy was crying. She said she was cold. It was true that the weather had turned very cold for the time of year but she should have been prepared for that, sacrificed vanity and brought a coat. He thought of all the places in the world and all the policemen in them where Wendy would have been allowed to shiver, where the temperature would have been lowered if possible, a little hypothermia encouraged. You couldn't call it torture, cooling someone into admissions . . .

'Get her something to put on,' he said to Polly.

He took them through the incest again and he got more stories full of holes. Joy hadn't believed Rodney would do that, yet she insisted Sara had led him on, insisted too that he would have gone to prison if she had breathed a word. Wendy now said Veronica had told her Rodney had started coming into her bedroom to kiss her good night and it wasn't

404

'nice'. That, said Joy, forgetting her former statement, was just how it had begun with Sara. Polly came back into the room with a grey knitted garment, something from Marks and Spencer's range for old ladies – God knows where she found it – which Wendy put on with a show of reluctance.

Sandwiches were brought in to them at lunchtime, one lot corned beef, the other egg and cress. Not exactly the Sunday joint, two veg and Yorkshire pudding. By that time Wexford had taken them through 15 April and was getting on to last Thursday night. Wendy had forgotten her coat but not her box of tissues, shades of peach this time. She sat snivelling into handfuls of them.

Just before three Joy broke at last. She started to howl like a dog. She rocked back and forth in her chair, howling and drumming her fists on the table. Wexford stopped the proceedings and sent for a cup of tea. He took Wendy into the interview room next door and asked her about Ovington. Rather to his surprise she agreed without much reluctance that she had been in Ovington's flat on 15 April from about 7.45 until about 9.15. Why hadn't she said so before? She gave the reason Ovington had given for her. They had hatched this up together, Wexford thought.

'I thought I might as well tell you,' she said with an aplomb that almost staggered him. 'I didn't before because you've all got minds capable of anything. But there's been so much real dirt dug up I don't think my innocent little friendship amounts to much.'

What did any of it weigh against that knife in the wall?

Late in the afternoon Burden walked in, looking a hundred years old.

'For God's sake,' said Wexford. 'I wasn't serious.'

The truth was Burden didn't know how otherwise to pass the time. He started on Joy, trying to break her alibi. But the tea had done wonders for her. She stuck to her story about watching television at the Harmers' and after half an hour of that had the brainwave that might have struck her days ago. She didn't have to talk at all if she didn't want to. Nobody had charged her with anything.

Unfortunately, by this time Wendy was back in the room with her and heard what she said.

Through her tears she smiled quite amicably at Joy. 'Good idea. I'm not talking either then. Pity I didn't think of it before.'

Joy uttered one last sentence. 'It was me thought of it, not you.'

United in silence, they stared at Wexford. Why not charge them both? With murdering Rodney Williams and, if he couldn't make that stick, with murdering Paulette Harmer? Special court in the morning, a remand in custody . . . Archbold came in and said there were three people to see him. He left the silent women with Burden and Martin and went down in the lift.

James Ovington was sitting there with his taciturn father and an elderly woman he introduced as his mother. Somehow Wexford had never thought of Ovington *père* as having a wife but, of course, he would have; James Ovington must have come from somewhere. He only looked like a waxwork. More so than ever this afternoon, his complexion fresher, his cheeks pinker, his smile flashing.

'My parents want to tell you something.'

That was one way of putting it. They didn't look as if they had any desire beyond that of going home again. Wexford asked them to go up to the first floor with him to his office but Mrs Ovington said she'd rather not, thank you, as if any suggestion of going upstairs in the company of men was indecent. They compromised with an interview room. Mrs Ovington looked disparagingly about her, evidently thinking it wasn't very cosy. James Ovington said, 'What were you going to tell the chief inspector, Dad?'

Nothing apparently.

'Now you know you were willing to come here and tell him.'

'Not willing,' said Ovington senior. 'If I must I must. That's what I said.'

'Is this something about Mrs Wendy Williams, Mr Ovington?' prompted Wexford.

Very slowly and grudgingly Ovington said, 'I saw her.'

'We both did,' said Mrs Ovington, suddenly brave. 'We both saw her.'

Wexford decided patience was the only thing. 'You saw her, yes. When was this?

James opened his mouth to speak, wisely shut it again. His father pondered, at last said, 'She's got a car. She'd parked it outside the shop on the yellow line. That don't matter after half six. We never saw her go in.'

Silence fell and endured. Wexford had to prompt.

'Go in where?'

'My son's place, of course. What else are we talking about? He's got the bottom flat and we've got the top, haven't we?'

'Up four flights,' said his wife. 'Wear the old ones out first, that's what it is.'

'We saw her come out,' said Ovington. 'Out of our front window. Round a quarter past nine. Tripped over and nearly fell in them heels. That's how Mother come to see her. I said, Here, Mother, look at this, them heels'll have her over.'

'It was April the fifteenth!' said James, unable to contain himself any longer.

'I don't know about that.' His father shook his head. 'But it was the first Thursday after Easter.'

That night he went to bed early and slept for nine hours. He didn't let himself think about the two women, Joy with no evidence against her, Wendy exonerated by the Ovingtons. They had been sent home with the warning that he would very likely want them back again on Monday morning. Old Ovington hadn't been lying but still his story didn't militate against the possibility that while Joy had done the deed in Wendy's house Wendy had later met her in time to help her dispose of the body, the clothes and the car.

In the morning he awoke clear-headed and calm. Immediately he remembered what it was Wendy had said to him. It had been when she told him Veronica was to play in a tennis singles final. The significance was in what it reminded him of, and now he remembered that too and as he did so everything began to fall gently and smoothly into place, so that he felt like one recalling and then using the combination of a safe until the door slowly swings open.

'But what a fool I've been,' he said aloud.

'Have you, darling?'

'If I'd got on to it sooner maybe that poor girl wouldn't have died.'

'Come on,' said Dora. 'You're not God.'

The phone was ringing as he left the house. It was Burden but Wexford wasn't there to answer it and Dora spoke to him.

A report on the postmortem, rushed through by Sir Hilary Tremlett, was awaiting Wexford. He went through it with Crocker beside him. Strangling had been with a fine powerful cord and whatever this was had left a red staining in the deep indentation it had made around the victim's neck.

'The nylon line from the spool of an electric edge trimmer,' said Wexford.

Crocker looked at him. 'That's a bit esoteric.'

'I don't think so. Joy Williams has three such spools in her garage and one of them, unless I'm much mistaken, will be empty.'

'Are you going to go there and check that?'

'Not just at the moment. Maybe later. Do you think it wrong to encourage a child to inform against its immediate family?'

'Like what happens in totalitarian societies, d'you mean? Or what I suppose happens. Extremists always believe the means are justified by the end. It depends what you mean by immediate family too, I mean, against a parent is a bit grim. That sticks in one's throat.'

'Drugging a man and stabbing him and burying the knife in a wall sticks in one's throat too.' Wexford picked up the phone and put it down again. 'I've got two women to arrest,' he said, 'and the way things are I'll never make the charges stand up. When do the schools go back?'

Crocker looked a little startled at this apparent *non sequitur*. 'The state schools – that is, the older kids – sometime this week.'

'I'd better do it today if I'm to catch her without her mother.' He lifted the phone again, this time asked for an outside line. It rang for so long he began to think she must be out. Then at last Veronica Williams's soft, rather high voice answered, giving the number in all its ten digits. Wexford spoke her name, 'Veronica?' then said, 'This is Chief Inspector Wexford of Kingsmarkham CID.'

'Oh, hello, yes.' Was she afraid or did she always answer the phone in this cautious breathless way?

'Just one or two things to check with you, Veronica. First, what time is your match tonight and where is it?'

'Kingsmarkham Tennis Club,' she said. 'It's at six.' She gathered some courage. 'Why?'

Wexford was too old a hand to answer that. 'After that's over I'd like to talk to you. Not you and your mother, just you alone. All right? I think you have quite a lot of things you'd like to tell me, haven't you?'

The silence was so heavy he thought he'd gone too far. But no. And it was better than he had hoped. 'I have got things to tell you. There are things I've *got* to tell you.' He thought he heard a sob but she might only have been clearing her throat.

'All right then. When you've finished your match come straight here. D'you know where it is?' He gave her directions. 'About ten minutes' walk from the club. I'll have a car to send you home in.'

She said, 'I'll have to tell my mother.'

'By all means tell your mother. Tell anyone you like.' Did he sound too eager? 'But make sure your mother knows I want to see you alone.'

The enormity of what he was doing hit him as he put the phone down. Could anything justify it? She was a sixteen-year-old girl with vital information for him. The last teenage girl with vital information for him had been strangled before she could impart it. Was he sending her to the same death as Paulette Harmer? If Burden had been there he would have told him everything but with the doctor he had reservations.

'You're not going round there, then?' Crocker said, a little mystified as much by Wexford's expression as by the cryptic phone conversation.

'That's the last thing I must do.'

Later, when the doctor had gone, Wexford thought, I hope I have the nerve to stick it out. Pity it's so many hours off. But the advantage of an evening match was that afterwards it would be dark . . . Advantage! She would be phoning her mother now at Jickie's to tell her, he thought, and somehow – hopefully – persuading Wendy not to come with her. He would have that girl watched every step of the way.

The phone rang.

He picked it up and the telephonist said she had a Miss Veronica Williams for him. What a little madam she was giving her name as 'Miss!'

'I could come and see you now,' the childish voice said. 'That might be easier. Then I wouldn't have to upset Mummy. I mean I wouldn't have to tell her I don't want her with me.'

He braced himself. He hardened his heart. 'I'm too busy to see you before this evening, Veronica. And I'd like you to tell your mother, please. Tell her now.'

If she called back, he thought, he'd relent and let her come. He wouldn't be able to hold out. Would she recognize Martin? Archbold? Palmer? Certainly she'd know Allison. But would it matter if she did recognize them? He'd be there himself anyway. There was no way he was going to let her take that ten-minute walk in the half-dark from the club down a lane off the Pomfret Road to the police station, especially in the case of her following his directions and taking the footpath across one and a half fields.

The phone rang again. That's it, he thought. I can't keep it up. I'll go round there and she'll tell me and that'll be evidence enough . . . He picked up the receiver.

'Inspector Burden for you, Mr Wexford.'

Burden's voice sounded strange, not really like his voice at all.

'It's all over. Mother and baby are doing fine. Jenny had a Caesarean at nine this morning.'

'Congratulations. That's great, Mike. Give my love to Jenny, won't you? You'd better tell me what Mary weighed so that I can tell Dora.'

'Eight pounds nine ounces, but it's not going to be Mary. We're changing just one letter in the name.'

Wexford didn't feel up to guessing. Jenny's persuaded him into something fancy against his better judgement, he thought.

'Mark, actually,' said Burden. 'I'll see you later. Cheers for now.'

21

A woman had once been found murdered on that very footpath.* They would all have that in their minds, even Palmer
and Archbold who hadn't been there at the time, who had
probably still been at school. As Veronica Williams still was.
Had she ever heard of the murder? Did people still talk about
it?

That woman had lived in Forest Road, the last street in the
area to bear the postal address Kingsmarkham. The Pomfret
boundary begins there, though it is open country all the
way to Pomfret in one direction and nearly all the way to
Kingsmarkham Police Station in the other. The tennis club,
however, is not in Forest Road but in Cheriton Lane which
runs more or less parallel to it on the Kingsmarkham side.
Smallish meadows enclosed by hedges cover the few acres
between the club and the town, and the footpath runs alongside one of these hedges, at one point skirting a little copse.
It emerges into the High Street fifty yards north of the police
station and on the opposite side.

Wexford had Martin and Palmer in a car in Cheriton Lane,
would station himself and Archbold in the copse, Loring
among the spectators at the match, Bennett to start walking
from the High Street end, Allison to follow her at a discreet
distance.

'One black man'll look very like another to her, sir,' Allison had said. 'That mightn't be so in a city but it/is out
here.'

'Don't tell me Inspector Burden and I look alike to you.'

* See *A Sleeping Life*.

'No, sir, but that's a question of age, isn't it?'

Which puts me firmly in my place, thought Wexford. Burden was in his office, sitting beside him, anxious to take part in the protection-of-Veronica exercise. Can't keep away from the place for more than five minutes, Wexford had grumbled at him. At least Burden had supplied a diversion in the lull of the long afternoon.

'I don't understand how they could make a mistake over the sex like that. God knows I don't know much about it, but if a man has an XY chromosome formula and a woman XX surely they must always have it from embryo to old age?'

'It's not that. It's like this. In an amniocentesis they extract cells from the amniotic fluid the foetus is in. But occasionally they make a mistake and once in about ten thousand times they take cells from the mother not the child. And even then they aren't always going to know their error. Because if the child does happen to be a girl . . . In this case, though, I gather someone's head is going to roll.'

'It caused a lot of unnecessary misery.'

'Misery, yes,' said Burden, 'but maybe not unnecessary. Jenny says it's taught her a lot about herself. It's taught her she's not what you might call a natural feminist and now she has to approach feminism not from an emotional stand-point but from what is – well, right and just. We didn't know, either of us, what a lot of deep-rooted old-fashioned prejudices we had. Because I felt it too, you know, I also wanted a son though I never said. It's taught us how much we've concealed from the other when we thought we were frank and open. All this has been – well, not far from – what does Jenny call it? – Guided Confrontation Therapy.'

With difficulty Wexford kept a straight face. 'So long as now you've got a son you don't wish it was a girl.' He said 'you' but he meant Jenny whom he thought the kind of woman for whom the unattainable grass might always be the greener.

'Of course not!' Burden exclaimed, looking very sour. 'After all, as Jenny says, what does it really matter so long as it's healthy and has all its fingers and toes?'

This was a cliché Wexford didn't feel he could compete with. Now Burden was here how would he feel about taking part in the Veronica watch? Not much, said Burden, he had to be back at the hospital. Then Wexford thought it might start raining. If it rained the match would be cancelled and in all probability Veronica would simply take the bus to the police station from Pomfret.

But the sky lightened round about 5.30. He wondered what those two women were thinking. How had they reacted to being left all day to their own devices? Unless the match was over in two straight sets Veronica could hardly expect to leave the club before seven. Should he fill in the time by seeing what he could get out of Kevin Williams? But he didn't really want to get anything out of him. He knew it all already. Why not simply go and watch the match?

It hadn't occurred to him to ask himself – or anyone else for that matter – if the tournaments of the Kingsmarkham Tennis Club were or were not open to the public. And it wasn't until he walked through the doors of the clubhouse that the question came into his mind. But a hearty elderly man with the air of a retired Air Force officer who said he was the secretary welcomed him with open arms. They loved spectators. If only they could get more spectators. It provided such encouragement for the players.

He had already spotted Martin and Archbold sitting in the car a discreet distance from the gates. Now if Veronica saw him, as it was most likely she would do, his best course would be to leave. Then, later, she wouldn't fail to follow. The great thing was not to give her a chance to speak to him. Therefore, to the bar, a refuge which was also the last place to which a sixteen-year-old competitor was likely to retreat before a match. The secretary, seeing him headed in that direction, trotted up to say that as a non-member he wasn't allowed to purchase a drink but if he would permit a drink to be bought *for* him . . . ? Wexford accepted.

The bar was semicircular, with a long curved window offering a view of three of the club's nine hard courts. Wexford had a half of lager, the club like most places of its kind being unable to provide any sort of draught beer or 'real ale'. The secretary talked rather monotonously, first about the bad public behaviour of certain international tennis stars, then their own disappointment at Saturday's rain and the enforced cancellation of this singles final. There would have been more spectators on a Saturday, he said sadly. In fact, nine people had actually come along – he had counted – but had had to be turned away. Of course, they were most unlikely to come back tonight. Wexford had the impression that if any of them had turned up the secretary would have bought them drinks too.

It got to six, to ten past. She's not going to come, Wexford thought. Then an umpire arrived and climbed up into the high seat. Five canvas chairs and a wooden bench had been arranged for a possible audience. It looked as if they would remain empty but after a while two elderly women with white cardigans over their tennis dresses came and sat down and at the same time, approaching by the path that led from the farther group of six courts, Loring sauntered up. In sound English fashion the women sat in the canvas chairs on the left-hand end of the row and Loring at the extreme right-hand end of the bench. Colin Budd should have been so wise.

Veronica and a taller, older, altogether bigger girl appeared outside the court and let themselves in by the gate.

'Well, best get out there and give them some moral support,' said the secretary, rubbing his hands together.

It was certainly cold. A gust of wind whipped across the court, tearing at Veronica's short pleated skirt. In classic style they began with a knock-up.

'I don't think I will,' said Wexford. 'D'you mind if I watch from in here?'

The secretary was terribly disappointed. He gave him a look of injured reproach.

'You mustn't buy any drinks, you do know that, don't you? And you're not to serve him, mind, Priscilla.'

Loring, his jacket collar turned up, was smoking a cigarette. The secretary appeared, running up to the two women, and sat beside them. The knock-up, in which Veronica had had the best of it, was over and the match began.

Dark would come early because the day had been so dull. Wexford wondered if the light would hold long enough for the match to be played to the finish. Veronica, whose service

414

it was, won the first game to love but had a tougher time when her opponent came to serve.

'You can have a drink if you like,' said Priscilla. 'I work it like this. I give it to you for free and next time a member buys me a drink I'll charge yours up to him. I'm a total abstainer actually but I don't let on to this lot.'

Wexford laughed. 'Better not, thanks all the same.'

'Suit yourself.' She came over and stood beside him and watched.

Three games all. It looked as if it would go on and on and then quite quickly it was all over, Veronica having won her own two service games and broken her opponent's.

'She's a little cracker, that kid,' said Priscilla. 'Strong as a horse. She's got arms like whipcord.'

It was twenty to seven and the edge of dusk. Veronica won the first two games but the other girl was fighting back for all she was worth. Perhaps she had never played against Veronica before. At any rate, it had taken her all this time to find her weakness but she had found it at last. Veronica couldn't handle long swift diagonal drives to her forehand, though backhand presented her with no problems. It was half a dozen of those forehand drives that won her opponent the next game and the next and the next two until she was leading 4–2. The light had grown bluish but the white lines on the court were still clearly visible, seeming to glow with twilight luminosity.

And then it was as if Veronica mastered the craft of dealing with those hard cross-court strokes. Or, curiously, as if some inspiration came to her from an external source. Certainly it was not that she had spotted him or had recognized Loring, whom she had never previously seen. But a charge of power came to her, a gift of virtuosity she had not known before. She had never before played like this, Wexford was sure of it. For a brief quarter of an hour she played as if she were on the centre court at Wimbledon and was there not by a fluke but by a hard-won right.

Her opponent couldn't withstand it. In that quarter hour she gained only four points. Veronica won the set by 6 games to 4 and thus secured the match. She threw her racket into the air, caught it neatly, ran to the net and shook hands with her opponent. Wexford said good night to Priscilla and left the way he had come, having watched the players go into the pavilion where the changing rooms were. Loring was still sitting on the bench.

Allison he spotted as soon as the footpath entered the field. He was lying very still in the long grass by the hedge and mostly covered by it. But Wexford saw him without giving any sign that he had done so. He was pretty sure Veronica wouldn't. The path wound on parallel to the hedge, then began to skirt the copse.

The false dusk hung still, suspended between light and dark. If it had been much darker no prudent young girl would have dared walk this way. Veronica Williams, of course, in spite of the impression she gave, was not a prudent young girl.

The air was still and damp and the grass moist underfoot. Wexford made his way along the path, under the high hedge, certain as he had been all along that Veronica's assailant would wait for her in the copse. Archbold had been there since 5.30 to be on the safe side. It was too late now for Wexford to join him without taking the risk of being seen. As it was, by staying to watch the match, he was taking a chance of spoiling the whole plan. Ahead of him a maple tree in the hedge spread its branches in a cone shape, the lowest ones almost touching the ground. He lifted them, stood against its trunk and waited.

By now it was 7.30 and he had begun to wonder if she would come at all. Though members had been thin on the ground there might have been some plan to fête her in the clubhouse. Hardly with drinks though. And she would have got out of it, she needed to see him as much as he her. Then he remembered she was her mother's daughter; it would take her longer than most girls to change her clothes, do her hair. She might even have a shower. Wendy was the sort of woman who would get a dying person out of bed to change the sheets before the doctor comes.

He stood under his tree in the silent dusk which was growing misty. Occasionally it was possible to hear in the distance a heavy vehicle on the Kingsmarkham to Pomfret road. Nothing else. No birds sang at this season and this hour. He could see the path about ten yards behind only and perhaps fifty yards ahead and it seemed to him then the emptiest footway he had ever contemplated. Allison would get rheumatism lying there on the damp ground, the cold seeping into his bones. Archbold, wrapped in his padded jacket, had probably fallen asleep . . .

She appeared quite suddenly. But how else could she have come but noiselessly and walking quite fast? She didn't look afraid though. Wexford saw her face quite clearly for a moment. Her expression was – yes, innocent. Innocent and trusting. She had no knowledge that there was anything to fear. If Sara, her half-sister, was a Florentine madonna, she was a Medici page, her small face grave and wistful in its gold-brown frame of bobbed hair and fringe. She wore her pink cotton jeans, beautifully pressed by Mother, her pink and white running shoes, a powder blue and white striped anorak that hung open over a white fluffy pullover, and she was carrying her tennis racket in a blue case. Wexford took all this in as she passed him, walking quickly.

He didn't dare come out. She might look back. Instead he dropped down into the field at the other side of the hedge. There had been a crop growing here, wheat or barley, but the grain had been cut and all that remained was a stubble that looked grey in this light. He ran along the hedge side, some few feet above the footpath. A long way ahead now he could just see the top of her head bobbing along. She had reached the corner of the copse.

There was a barbed-wire entanglement here that threatened to bar his passage, the spaces between the wires too narrow to squeeze through, the top wire too high to sling a leg over without terrible detriment to trousers. There was nothing for it but to retrace steps, pass through the hedge and clamber up the bank onto the footpath. She was too far away to see him even if she did look back. He jumped down, rounded the bend in the path, but now, though the copse was in full view, he couldn't see her at all.

His heart was in his mouth then. If she had met her assailant and gone into the wood, if Archbold truly had gone to sleep . . . He left the path and plunged into the copse. It was dark and dry in there, a million needles underfoot from the firs and larches. He ran through the trees and met Archbold head on.

'There's no one here, sir. I haven't seen a soul in three hours.'

'Except her,' said Wexford breathlessly.

'She just walked past. She's on her own, heading for the High Street.'

He came out of the wood on the Kingsmarkham side, Archbold behind him. She was nowhere to be seen, the hedges too high, the foliage on the trees too thick and masking. And then he forgot discretion and catching a murderer and ran along the path in pursuit of her, afraid for her and for himself. A moment before he had been praying Bennett wouldn't appear, walking from the Kingsmarkham end, and spoil it all. Now he hoped he would.

There was one more field and that low-lying, the path passing diagonally across it and then running beside a hedge at right angles to the road. No sign of Bennett. Because he had seen her? Or seen her attacker? Would he be capable of that in this fast-fading light? The meadow was grey and the hedges black and the air had the density of fallen cloud. Through the mist you could just see a light or two from cars on the Pomfret road, behind that an irregular cluster of pale lights that was probably the police station.

She was nowhere. The meadow was empty. There was a movement just discernible on the far side of it, where the path met the hedge. She had crossed the diagonal and come to the last hundred yards, her pale clothes catching what light there was so that she gleamed like a night moth. And like a night moth fluttered along against the dark foliage.

Wexford and Palmer didn't take the diagonal. They dared not risk being seen. They kept to the boundary hedge, though there was no path here, and Palmer, who was thirty, outran Wexford who felt that he had never run so hard in his life. All the time he could see the pale fluttering moth moving down there, homing on the stile that would bring her to the wide grass verge of the Pomfret road.

She never reached it. The fluttering stopped and there was something else down there with her at the bottom of the field where the dead elms stood, their roots a mass of underbrush, of brambles and nettles and fuzzy wild clematis. The something or someone else had come out of that and barred her way. He thought he heard a cry but he couldn't be sure.

418

At any rate it was no scream but a thin shriek of – perhaps surprise. He cut the corner, running hell for leather, his heart pounding fit to burst, running the way no man of close on sixty should run.

And Archbold got there only just first. It was strange that the knife should catch a gleam on it even in this near darkness. Wexford saw the gleam and then saw it drop to the ground. Archbold was holding Veronica who had turned her face into his chest and was clinging to his coat. He went up to the other himself. She made no attempt to run. She clasped her hands and hung her head so that he couldn't see her face.

In that moment Bennett materialized, so to speak. He came out of the dark, running. Sara Williams looked up then with an expression of faint dull surprise.

'Take them both,' said Wexford. 'They'll be charged with the wilful murder of Rodney Williams.'

22

'It was they, not their mothers, who knew each other,' Wexford said. 'Edwina Klein told me but I misinterpreted what she said. "Those two women knew each other", she said to me. "I saw them together". I took her to mean Joy and Wendy. Joy and Wendy were women and Sara and Veronica were girls. Except that to a militant feminist founder member of ARRIA all females are women. Just as they are,' he added, 'to organizers of sports events. It's the women's singles even if both players are fifteen.'

Burden and the doctor said nothing. They were all sitting in Burden's grass widower's house, drinking Burden's grass widower's instant coffee. It was over. A special court for one and a special juvenile court for the other and the two girls had been committed for trial. Afterwards the press had caught Wexford, a camera crew springing out of their van with the agility of the SAS, and once again he would be on television. Looking a hundred years old, he thought, after being up half the night talking to Sara Williams. People would phone in suggesting it was time he retired.

'They met at a tennis match, of course. The second time I met Sara I noticed she had a tennis racket up on her bedroom wall. She wasn't anywhere near Veronica's standard, not in the high school's first or second six. She just scraped into their reserve. Still, one day she was called on to play and she met Veronica as her opponent. What happened then? I don't know and she hasn't told me. I'd guess that one of the other girls there commented that they looked alike and seeing they had the same surname, were they cousins? It was up to one of them to probe further and one of them

420

did. Sara, probably. After that it wouldn't have been hard to find out, would it? "Look, I've got a photo, this is my mum and dad . . ." '

'Something of a shattering experience, wouldn't you say?' said the doctor.

'Also I think an exciting one.'

'That's a superficial way of looking at it,' said Burden. 'I'd almost say unfeeling. Both those girls were lonely, Veronica sheltered and smothered, Sara neglected, no one's favourite. Wouldn't it have been both shattering and immensely *comforting* to find a sister?'

The sensitivity which had developed in Burden late in life always brought Wexford a kind of affectionate amusement. It was so often misdirected. It resembled in a way those good intentions with which hell is paved.

He picked his words carefully. They were strong words but his tone was hesitant.

'Sara Williams doesn't have normal feelings of affection, need for love, loneliness. I think she would be labelled a psychopath. She wants attention and she wants to impress. Also she wants her own way. I imagine that what she got from her half-sister was principally admiration. Sara has an excellent brain. Intellectually, she's streets ahead of Veronica. She's a strong, powerful, amoral, unfeeling solipsist with an appalling temper.'

Crocker's eyebrows went up. 'You're talking about an eighteen-year-old who was raped by her own father.'

Wexford didn't respond. He was thinking about what the girl had said to him, presiding at the table in the interview room with Marion Bayliss at one end, himself opposite and Martin facing Marion. But Sara Williams had presided, holding her head high, describing her feelings and actions without a notion of defending herself.

'My sister looks just like me. I used to feel she was another aspect of me, the weaker, pretty, feminine part, if you like. I wanted ultimately to be rid of that part.'

Solipsism, according to the Oxford dictionary, is the view or theory that self is the only object of real knowledge or the only real thing existent.

'Why didn't you tell your parents you and Veronica had met?'

421

'Why should I?'

Her cool answers took the breath away.

'It would have been the natural thing to confront your father with what you had found out.'

She was honest in her way. 'I liked having the secret. I enjoyed knowing what he thought I didn't know.'

'So that you could hold it over him?'

'Perhaps,' she said indifferently, bored when the discussion was not totally centred on herself.

Was that what she had had to threaten him with in the matter of the incest? Was that how she had stopped it?

'You prevented Veronica from telling her mother?'

'She did what I told her.'

It was uttered the way a trainer speaks of an obedient dog. The trainer takes the obedience for granted, so effective are his personality and technique, so unthinkable would an alternative reaction be. Wexford thought Crocker and Burden would have had to hear and see Sara to appreciate all this. He couldn't even attempt to put it across to them. 'The two girls met quite often,' he went on. 'Sara even went to Veronica's home when Wendy was at work. Veronica came to admire her extravagantly. She followed her, she would have obeyed her in anything.'

'Would have?'

'Did. Psychiatrists call what overtook them *folie à deux*, a kind of madness that overtakes two people only when they are together and through the influence of each on the other. But in all such cases you'll always find one party who is easily led and one who is dominant.' Wexford digressed a little before returning to the point. 'Looking back, I don't think Sara Williams has ever addressed a sentence to me that didn't begin with "I" or wasn't about herself.'

He went on, 'The coming and going between the Williams homes led to a pooling of information. For instance, Sara had believed her father was a sales rep with Sevensmith Harding for the Ipswich area. Veronica thought he was a rep with a bathroom fittings company. They took steps to find out the truth and did. It's over a year now since they found out what Rodney really did, what his position was, and discovered – via some research into marketing managers' earnings on Sara's part – what his actual salary was.

422

'Sara also warned Veronica of their father's – proclivities. That, of course, is how Wendy came to fear an incest attempt. Not because she witnessed anything herself or because Veronica put two and two together from a kiss and a cuddle but because Sara told Veronica what to expect and Veronica passed it on without disclosing her source. One way and another Sara made Veronica into a very frightened girl. A very bewildered and confused girl. Think of her situation. First she discovers her father has a legal wife and a grown-up family, next that he could never have in fact married her mother and she must be illegitimate. Necessarily, therefore, he's deceitful and a liar. He doesn't even have the job he says he has. Worst of all, he has raped his other daughter and will certainly have the same designs on her. No wonder she was frightened.

'Telling Wendy her fears of a sexual attack had the effect only of causing trouble between her mother and father. Did Wendy accuse Rodney and Rodney hotly deny it? Almost certainly. The quarrel was at any rate bad enough to make Wendy believe Rodney would leave her but fear that if he didn't Veronica would be in danger. So we see that the reason she didn't want Veronica to stay in on the evening of April the fifteenth was that if Rodney did come back she would be alone with her father – and this would be the first time she would be alone with him after the disclosure was made.

'But Veronica had another confidante and friend now, apart from her mother. She had Sara. And Sara absolutely justified the faith she put in her. Sara had a good idea for diverting Rodney's attention from his daughter, diverting his attention from everything, in fact. Substitute sleeping pills for his blood-pressure tablets. It was something that could only be done once though and in an emergency.

'Now on April the fifteenth, however much their mothers may have been in ignorance, Sara and Veronica knew that when Rodney left Alverbury Road he would drive straight to Liskeard Avenue. So Sara herself made the exchange of tablets, two only remaining in the container. Don't forget we found an empty Mandaret container in Alverbury Road and a half-full one in Liskeard Avenue. Rodney took his two Mandaret as he thought, leaving the container in his bedroom, and drove to Pomfret. No doubt he began to feel drowsy on the way.'

'But these were Phanodorm, supplied by Paulette Harmer?' said the doctor.

'I suppose they were supplied by her. It seems most likely. But Paulette didn't die because she illicitly provided a sleeping drug. She died because the turn events were taking made her concentrate her mind on the evening of April the fifteenth, made her remember in fact what had really happened. What she remembered was her mother speaking to her aunt Joy on the phone that evening and making some remark about being glad Kevin had settled in back at college. And she was going to tell us because she knew from the papers and television and her parents' conversation how strong was the suspicion against her aunt. She knew very well her aunt had been at home that evening, in at eight to receive Kevin's phone call and still in at eight forty-five to receive her mother's.'

The girl should have been strewing flowers or rising from the waves in a cockleshell. The face was bland, innocent and somehow secretive. Even now there was a tiny self-satisfied smile. Her hair was scraped back tight from that high forehead but wisps had come free and lay in gold tendrils on the white skin.

'I got a phone call from Veronica. It was just to tell me he'd gone to sleep like I said he would. I said I'd come over.'

He had interrupted her to ask why.

'I just thought I would. I wasn't going to get a chance like that again, was I?'

He stopped himself asking her what she meant. Her eyes seemed to enlarge, her face grow blanker.

'I saw him sleeping there and I thought, I've got him in my power. I thought of the power he had over *me*. I started to get angry, really angry.'

'And Veronica?'

'I didn't think about Veronica. I suppose she was there. Well, I know she was. I said to her, "We could kill him and stop all of it". I told her to get me a knife. I wasn't serious then, it was fantasy. I was angry and I was excited – high like when you've had a drink.'

Folie à deux. Was Veronica excited too? He wouldn't get much about another's feelings out of this girl.

'I took the knife out of her hands and took off the cardboard guard that was on it. I went up to my father who was lying on the settee and I started playing around, waving the knife over him, pretending to stick it in him. I could tell he was sound asleep. I was making Veronica laugh because I was doing all this stuff and he was just oblivious of it. I don't remember what made me stop playing. I was so excited and high I don't remember. But that's how it was. One minute it was fantasy and the next it was for real.'

She looked down at the table at Marion and then the other way at Martin. It was as if she were gathering the attention of her audience. Once more her eyes met Wexford's in a steady gaze.

'I raised the knife and stuck it in his neck, right in hard with both hands. I'd made him wake up then and make noises, so I stabbed him a few more times to stop the blood spraying like that. I'm going to be a doctor so I knew the blood would stop when he was dead . . .'

It took Wexford, hardened as he was, a moment or two to collect words.

'Did Veronica stab him?'

'I gave her the knife and told her to have a go. I'd made a big wound in his neck and she stuck it in there and then she went off and was sick.'

'Completely mad,' said Burden. 'Bonkers.'

'Perhaps. I'm not sure. Let's not get into defining psychosis.'

'What happened next?' said the doctor.

'The room was covered for the most part in dustsheets. Rodney had come in half asleep, climbed the stairs and lain down on the settee which had a dustsheet over one end. The end, incidentally, where he laid his head. It was this sheet, the property of Leslie Kitman, which received most of the blood. Some went on an area of wall from which the paper had been stripped that day. Sara washed the wall and wrapped Rodney's head up in the dustsheet. Veronica, recovered and very much under orders from Sara, washed the knife and then had the idea of plastering it into the wall. This was the first weird too-clever thing the girls did. There were others. There were fissures in the walls needing to be filled in and in the garage was a packet of filler. Also in the garage was Rodney's car, Greta the Granada, which Sara, though not Veronica, was able to drive. They rolled up the dustsheet and wrapped two of Wendy's Marks and Spencer's teacloths round Rodney's neck. Having cleaned up the room, they carried Rodney down the spiral staircase, through the door from the hall into the garage and put him into the boot of the car. On their way out in the car they deposited the dustsheet in the dustbin. It was about seven-thirty.'

'Then,' said Burden, 'how did Kevin manage to speak to his sister when he phoned Alverbury Road at eight o'clock?'

'He didn't. He spoke to his mother. And, of course, he and Joy were both well aware it was his mother he had spoken to. They lied to protect Sara. Oh, I know Joy hasn't much affection for Sara but she was her daughter. Once she began to think about it she saw that Sara might have had something to do with Rodney's disappearance. At first she genuinely thought he had left her and she got me in to advise her. But then things changed. I think I know why. On my advice, she phoned Sevensmith Harding and they told her *she* had spoken to them on Friday, April the sixteenth, to explain Rodney was ill. Now Joy no doubt at first thought this a mere mistake but they had been so sure it was her voice. Joy knew someone whose voice sounded very like hers – her own daughter.

'Don't forget that she knew how Sara felt towards her father on account of the incest. She also knew Sara had been out of the house for hours on the evening of April the fifteenth. So she told us and got Kevin to agree – no difficulty there, he distrusts the police and is close to his sister – that it was she who had gone out and Sara who had been at home to take the phone call. Was there collusion with Sara? I doubt it. There was no real communication between her and her mother. My guess is Joy said it might be wiser to arrange things this way and Sara agreed with just a nod and a "yes" probably.'

426

'You're painting a picture of a self-sacrificing maternal type,' said the doctor, 'which doesn't at all accord with our concept of Joy Williams. Rather like the old story of the mother pelican tearing at its own breast to feed its young – and just as much of a myth.'

'No. Joy quite rightly believed there was no real risk in it for her. She thought it impossible we could arrest the wrong person. Her trust must have been sorely put to the test these past few days.'

Always happier on circumstantial details, Burden said, 'So the two girls took Williams's body up to Cheriton Forest and dug a grave for him with his own snow shovel?'

'A shallow grave because, having killed him, Sara didn't want it to be too long before the body was discovered. She wanted a couple of weeks to pass only, rightly believing that this was the sort of time which would be just about right to blur the evidence. In fact, things didn't go her way and it was two months before the body was found.

'I turned over and over in my mind the complication of the Milvey coincidence. But now it has come out quite clearly. There is no coincidence. Sara and Veronica hid Rodney's travelling bag – in the forest probably – hoping it would be found within, say, the next few days. But as it happened, no one found it. Then one day Mrs Milvey happened to say to Joy in Sara's hearing that Milvey would be at Green Pond next day, dragging the pool. Sara retrieved the bag and dumped it in the pool in time for Milvey to find it next day.'

'But why did she want the body found? What difference could it make to her?'

'I'll come to that later.'

'I don't see why go to all the trouble of phoning Sevensmith Harding and forging a letter to delay discovery, and then later try to accelerate it. Incidentally, I take it it was Sara who made the phone call? Her voice is very like Joy's.'

'She made the phone call and Veronica typed the letter. At her friend Nicola Tennyson's house, on Nicola's mother's typewriter.

'They buried the body, hid the travelling bag, and Sara drove Veronica back to Pomfret to be sure she got home before Wendy did. That was at about nine. Wendy, of course,

427

didn't get home until nine thirty, being out doing some mild courting with James Ovington. Sara drove to Myringham and dumped the car in Arnold Road where no more than half an hour later it was seen and indeed bumped into by Eve Freeborn. If Sara had been a bit later and Eve a bit earlier those two members of ARRIA would have encountered each other and made our task a lot easier. But by the time Eve came Sara was on the bus for home.

'In the morning she shut herself in the living room and made the phone call before she went to school. Of necessity it was a very early call and she was lucky there was someone there to receive it. And that, I think, accounts for all the circumstances of the murder of Rodney Williams.'

Burden picked up the tray.

'Does anyone want more coffee?'

Neither did. Wexford said it was nearly beer time, wasn't it? The doctor frowned at him and he deliberately looked away, out into Burden's bright, neat garden, the flower borders like chintzy dress material, the lawn a bit of green baize. The sunshine was making Jenny's yellow chrysanthemums nearly too bright to look at. Burden opened the french windows.

'The sad thing,' said Crocker, 'is that all this is going to make it next to impossible for Sara Williams to make a career in medicine.'

Burden looked at him. He said sarcastically, 'Oh, surely St Biddulph's will overlook a little matter like stabbing her father to death with a carving knife.'

'You don't think it justification then, and more than justification, for a girl to make a murderous assault on the father who has raped her and shows signs of meting out the same treatment to her younger half-sister? Don't you think any judge or jury would see this as an extentuating circumstance?'

It was Wexford who answered him. 'Yes, I do.'

'Right, then there's not going to be any question of years of imprisonment, is there? She'll never have the dubious distinction of being a GP like your humble servant here, but at least there won't be punishment in the accepted sense.'

'I wouldn't be too sure of that.'

428

'On account of the planning and the covering of tracks, do you mean?'

'She killed Paulette Harmer,' Burden said.

'She did indeed but that wasn't what I meant. You see, Rodney Williams never committed incest with his elder daughter. He never showed signs of committing incest with his younger daughter. And I very much doubt if he ever sexually assaulted anyone, even in the broadest meaning of that term.'

23

Crocker had caught on quickly. Wexford left it to him to explain. The doctor began outlining Freud's 'seduction theory' as expressed in the famous paper of 1896.

Thirteen women patients of Freud claimed paternal seduction. Freud believed them, built on this evidence a theory, later abandoned it, realizing he had been too gullible. Instead, he concluded that little girls are prone to fantasize that their fathers have made love to them, from which developed his stress on childhood fantasy and ultimately his postulation of the Oedipus Complex.

'You're saying it was all fantasy on Sara's part?' Burden said. 'She's not exactly a *little* girl.'

'Nor were Freud's patients little girls by the time they came to him.'

Wexford said, 'I think Sara had a daughter's fantasy about her father. When she was older she read Freud. She read books on incest too – they're all there in her bedroom. There's a mention of father-daughter incest in the ARRIA constitution. Did she read that too or did she write it? At any rate, *in her mind* she was heavily involved with her father, far more involved with him than he was with her.'

'How do you know the seduction didn't really take place? Men do commit incest with their daughters. I mean, how could Freud have known one of those thirteen wasn't fantasizing but telling the truth?'

'I can't answer that,' Wexford said, 'but I can tell you it never happened to Sara. She isn't the kind of girl to whom it happens. She isn't ignorant or obtuse or cowed or dependent. This seduction, or apparent seduction, followed a

430

classic pattern as laid down in the books. The girl doesn't struggle or fight or scream. She doesn't want to make a disturbance. At the first opportunity she tells her mother and mother reacts with rage, reproaches, accusations of the girl's provocative behaviour. Now Joy, as we might expect, fitted beautifully into the classic pattern. But Sara? If it had really happened wouldn't Sara, a leading member of ARRIA, a militant feminist, have fought and screamed? She was very handy with a knife, wasn't she? And she's the last person to care about making a disturbance in a household, either emotional or physical. As for telling her mother – Sara tell her mother? There's been no real communication between them for years. She despises her mother. If she'd told anyone it would have been her brother Kevin. No, there was no seduction, for if there had been she would have kept the experience secret to use against her father, not come running with it to Joy.

'It was Sara who stabbed Colin Budd, of course. It happened, if you remember, the night before Milvey started dragging Green Pond. Sara retrieved the bag after dark, went up to the forest to do it and put the bag inside a plastic sack. When Budd came along she was waiting to catch the bus that would take her to the other end of Kingsmarkham, near enough to the Forby road and Green Pond Hall. The last thing she wanted was Budd taking an interest in her. Besides, she had indoctrinated herself to be always on the watch for sexist approaches. What was she doing but going about her private business? And this man has to treat her as if her primary function in this world was to be an object for his diversion and entertainment. No doubt she also lost her nerve. She stabbed him with a penknife.'

'If it was all fantasy,' said Burden, reverting to the analysis of Sara Williams's character, 'why did she warn Veronica? Why warn her of something that would never happen?'

'You're supposing fantasy is something "made up", so therefore something the fantasizer herself doesn't believe in?'

'Well, does she? Did Sara convince herself.'

'Yes and no. She's admitted to me nothing ever happened. On the other hand, I wouldn't be surprised if tomorrow

431

she says it did and believes it herself. Having this secret to communicate, this awful and horrifying secret, must have much increased her ascendancy over Veronica. It enhanced her power. Veronica was very frightened of her, you see, full of admiration, awe almost, but even before the killing of Rodney becoming unnerved by the whole set-up.'

Wendy had been sent for and for once had been calm, sensible, steady. He had considered the atmosphere of his office more relaxing than one of those stark interview rooms. Marion and Polly were seated side by side and Veronica a little apart from everyone until Wexford came in. Little Miss Muffet and the great spider who sat down beside her. Only there was no frightening her away. It would be a long time now before Veronica Williams could get away.

She was very pale. Her hair, he noticed, was a couple of inches longer than when he had first seen her, six inches longer than the crop of the beach photograph. Had she been growing it in imitation of her idol and model Sara? He had asked her when she first met her half-sister.

'It was September.' Her voice was so soft he had to ask her to repeat it. 'September – a year ago,' she said.

'And you met how often after that? Once a week? More?'

Very quietly, 'More.'

He extracted from her the information that they constantly spoke on the phone. It was like a game sometimes, Sara phoning and saying she would be in Liskeard Avenue in five minutes, she phoning Sara to say if Sara was careful not to be seen she could come and watch Rodney and Wendy watching *her* play tennis.

'It stopped being a game, though, didn't it? On April the fifteenth it stopped?'

She nodded and her body convulsed in an involuntary shiver. Wendy said, 'Why did you always do everything she said? Why did you tell her everything?'

How could she answer that?

'You told her you were coming here to confess your part in it, didn't you, Veronica?' Wexford spoke very gently.

Her eyes went to Wendy. 'I thought the police would arrest my mother.'

A small spark of triumph on Wendy's doleful face. In

these unbelievable circumstances her years of devotion were rewarded . . .

Wexford surfaced from his reverie to see Burden depositing three beer cans in front of them from a tray laden with the kind of junk food he lived on while Jenny was away.

'Wake up!'

'Sorry.'

'Look, if there was no incest and therefore no renewed assault from Rodney to be feared, if there was no threat to Veronica, what was the motive for killing him? All through this case we could never come up with any sort of solid motive. Or are you saying a psychopath doesn't need a motive – at any rate not a motive understood by normal people?'

Wexford said slowly, 'I've suggested to you that there was a good deal of calculation in Sara's behaviour, some of it of an apparently incomprehensible kind. Her original conceal- ment of the body, for instance, and later her anxiety for it to be found. I've also made it clear – rather to your joint disapproval, I think – that I don't feel much sympathy towards Sara. And this is because I feel she had no justifi- cation for what she did.

'She had a motive all right, and as calculated and cold- blooded a motive as any poisoner polishing off an old relation for his money.'

'But Rodney didn't have any money to leave, did he?' Burden objected.

'Not so's you'd notice, though the manager of the Anglian- Victoria has shown me how a nice little bit was accumulating in the account from which the two joint accounts were fed. Enough, anyway, for him to recommend that Rodney put it into investments. Still, it wasn't for a possible inheritance that Sara killed him, though money was her motive.'

'Not a cash gain though, I think,' said the doctor.

Wexford turned to Burden. 'You raised this very subject not long ago, Mike. That was when you thought you were going to have a daughter – and that's relevant too. You talked about her going to university and applying for govern- ment grants. Do you remember?'

'I suppose so. I don't see where the relevance comes in.'

'Sara wants to be a doctor,' said Wexford. 'Well, *wanted*

433

to be, I should say. It was a driving ambition with her. And increasingly hard though this is becoming, she knew she had the ability to get into medical school. Her parents, however, discouraged her. And it must have looked to her at that stage as if this was a classic case of opposition to daughter's ambitions simply because she was a daughter and not a son, because in fact she was a woman. On Joy's part it probably was. Very likely she wouldn't have cared for Sara to achieve greater success and have a more prestigious profession than Kevin.

'At first this parental opposition didn't much worry Sara. I'm speaking, of course, about this time last year. Sara remembered her brother getting a place at Keele and the form of application for a grant coming from Sussex County Council Education Committee to her father. At the time she didn't take much notice. Certainly she didn't see the completed form. But she knew that the greater the parental income the smaller the grant would be and that with the form there came a form of certificate of parental employment the parent's employer had to complete detailing his gross salary, overtime, bonus or commissions and his taxable emoluments. Now, Mike, you'll recall that certificate in your own case and sending it to the Mid-Sussex Constabulary when you applied for grants for John and Pat?'

Burden nodded. 'I'm beginning to see the light here.'

'Twelve months ago Sara met Veronica. Gradually, when the shock of that encounter began to recede, when it provided the solution to certain unexplained anomalies, shall we say, Sara saw the cold reality for what it was. Her father might talk about not wanting his daughter to be a doctor for aesthetic reasons, for reasons of suitability, she would get married and her education be wasted, et cetera. He might talk that way but the reason behind the talk was very different. Finding that he had lied both to her mother and Veronica's about what his position and his earnings were, she had taken steps to discover what he did and what he earned. Now she understood. If he filled in the grant application form for her he would have to declare to the Sussex County Council that his income was not £10,000 a year but two and a half times that, and there would be no way he could deceive the authority as he had deceived her mother because his employers, Sevensmith Harding, would have to complete the certificate of parental income from employment.

'Now according to the grants department's contribution scales, a parent earning £10,000 per annum would have to contribute to medical school costs only something in the region of £470 but a parent earning £25,000 a sum of nearly £2000. Rodney had two homes and two families, he was already paying out this sort of sum for Kevin at Keele – remember he had to tell the grants department the truth, whatever he told his wives – and Sara could see the way the wind was blowing. She could see there was no way he would part with £2000 a year for her benefit. And when she asked him point blank if he would fill in the form when it came he told her he wouldn't – she would never make a doctor and he was doing her a kindness in not encouraging her.'

'What a bastard,' said Crocker.

Wexford shrugged. 'The mistake is ours when we deceive ourselves about parent-child relationships. When we keep up the belief that all parents love their children and want what's best for them.'

'Surely, though, if Sara had talked about this at school or discussed it with some sympathetic officer at the grants department, a way could have been found for her to get a grant, bypassing Rodney? There must be many cases where a parent withholds consent and won't complete a grant application.'

'Probably. But Sara is only eighteen. And remember that to have done what you suggest she would have to reveal that her father was a liar and a cheat, that he deceived her mother, that he was a bigamist. And how long would all this take? Would it mean her waiting a year? And what of her place at St Biddulph's, a teaching hospital where places are like gold dust and where they keep a reserve list bursting with applicants dying to be accepted? What she decided on instead was, first, persuasion and if that failed, blackmail.'

'She told him that if he didn't consent to fill in the form she'd tell Joy about Wendy and get Veronica to tell Wendy about Joy?'

'She was *going* to tell him that. She had a bit of time though. She hadn't even sat her A-levels. The grant form wouldn't come till July. And she also had the incest. Of course, it had never taken place but Joy thought it had, Veronica was scared stiff it had. If all else failed she might be able to use it as another weapon in the blackmail stockpile. That was why she was pleased to see how effective her warnings had been in Veronica's case. Veronica was beginning to be afraid of the affectionate attention Rodney paid her. Veronica didn't want to be alone with him and if she had to be she wanted him disarmed and immobilized. Sara saw to that with the Phanodorm, and increased Veronica's fear by the seriousness of taking such a step.

'But how much simpler, after all, to kill him! And there he was, lying asleep, the potential destroyer of her future. Kill him now, in this room which will soon be made pure and immaculate, cleansed of all signs of violent death. Rid the world of him, seize your opportunity. And perhaps it would also be a heroic act. Hadn't there almost been a clause in the ARRIA constitution demanding a man's death as qualification for entry? Veronica will help because Veronica also hates him now and is mortally afraid of him ...

'But suppose they never find the body? Suppose the weeks go by and July comes and August and with them the grant application and you can't fill in the section that says "Father, if deceased the fact should be stated ..." because only you and Veronica know he is deceased? You have finished your A-levels and the time is going by – the moment has come to take steps for that body to be found without more delay.'

'You might say,' said Crocker, 'that the murder was both coolly premeditated and carried out on an impulse.'

'You might. Because of what Sara is, a highly complex personality, this was all kinds of a murder. A ritualistic killing – remember that Veronica was required to stab him too. A revenge killing – Sara had more than half-convinced herself and wholly convinced Veronica of the reality of the incest. When she stabbed Rodney she was a woman out of classical myth, she was Beatrice Cenci. It was an *experimental* killing, a kind of vivisection, carried out by Sara the scientist, to see if it would work, to see if it could be done. It was murder from disgust, from disillusionment. Rodney, whom she had once worshipped, was just a squalid bigamist with another daughter, a copy of herself, he loved as much as or more than he had ever loved her. But above all, in spite

436

of all those other factors, it was murder for gain, carried out so that she might satisfy her ambition at all costs. All in all, I don't think that's the sort of person I'd care to have as my family physician, still less performing surgery on me and mine. So perhaps Rodney was right when he told Sara she was an unsuitable candidate for medical school. Who knows? Perhaps it wasn't simply meanness with him, he wasn't quite the bastard you make out. Perhaps he sensed in that daughter of his, without ever examining his conclusions, traits in her character that were abnormal, that were destructive, and it was to these he referred when he said she would never make a doctor.'

Wexford got up.

'I shall call it a day,' he said. 'I shall go to the wife of my bosom the same as I ought to go.'

Burden began tidying the room, putting things on a tray. 'And tomorrow the wife of my bosom comes home to me.' He looked pleased, satisfied, hopeful, as if there had been no five months' long disruption of his happiness. 'One of her old pupils at Haldon Finch went in to see her and the baby. An ARRIA member. She told Jenny the raven bit means they're cleaning up the carrion men have left behind in the world. We did wonder.'

'Ah,' Wexford paused in the doorway. 'Something I nearly forgot to tell you. About Williams's young girlfriend . . .'

They looked at him. 'Williams didn't have a young girlfriend,' Burden said.

'Of course he did. She had nothing to do with his death, nothing to do with this case, so she hardly concerned us. But a man like Williams – it was in his nature, inevitable. Both his wives knew it, they sensed it. Probably he's always had a young girlfriend, a succession of them.

'This one – hers were the other set of prints on the car. No wonder she said her dad didn't want me to take them. They met at Sevensmith Harding, of course. In the office.'

'Jane Gardner . . .'

'That's who he had his date with on April the fifteenth in Myringham. Join her for her baby-sitting, then spend the night together at the Cheriton Forest Hotel. Why else did he have a bag with him with a single change of underwear and a toothbrush and toothpaste? But the sleeping pills overcame

437

him as he was driving through Pomfret, and instead of going on to meet Jane he was just able to make it to his own house. What she thought was that he'd stood her up. Then, when he disappeared, that he'd gone off with another woman. I had a word with her this morning and she admitted it – no more need to conceal it now we'd made an arrest.'

'What put you on to her?'

'I don't know. Guesswork. She was the only person I ever spoke to who had a good word for Rodney Williams.'

Wexford let himself out, closing Burden's blue front door behind him.

The Veiled One

For Simon

I would like to thank Leonie Van Ness for an idea which she suggested to me in Ottawa and which contributed to the plot of this novel – Ruth Rendell

1

The woman was lying dead on the floor when he came in. She was already dead and covered up from head to toe but Wexford only knew that afterwards, not at the time. He looked back and realized the chances he had missed but it was useless doing that – he hadn't known and that was all. He had been preoccupied, thinking of an assortment of things: his wife's birthday present that was in the bag he carried, modern architecture, yesterday's gale which had blown down his garden fence, this car park that he was entering from the descending lift.

Even the lift was not as other lifts elsewhere, being of rattling grey metal undecorated except for graffiti. Irregular printing from whose letters the red paint had dripped like trails of blood, informed him that someone called Steph was 'a diesel dyke'. He wondered what that meant, wondered too where he could look it up. The lift was going down. Into the bowels of the earth, he thought, and there was something intestine-like about this place with its winding passages and its strictly one-way direction. Perhaps, though, it was better to excavate for this purpose than to erect above the ground, especially as any extraneous building would inevitably have been in the style of the shopping centre itself – ramparts, perhaps, or the walls of a city, some quaint attempt at a reconstruction of the Middle Ages.

He had just come from the Barringdean Centre, the new shopping complex built to look like a castle. That was the style modern planners thought suitable on the outskirts of an ancient Sussex town where nothing genuinely medieval remained. Perhaps that was why. Anyway the centre looked less like a real castle than a toy one, the kind you have to assemble from a hundred plastic bits and pieces. Shaped like a capital 'I', it had four towers on the ends and a row of turrets along its length. Looking back at it, he half-expected bowmen to appear in the Gothic windows and arrows to fly.

But inside all was of the late twentieth century, only to be expressed in eighties words – amenities, facilities, enclaves and approaches. A great fountain played in the central concourse, its waterspouts almost reaching but not quite touching the pendent chandelier of shards of frosted glass. Wexford had entered at this point by the automatic doors and approach from the glass covered way. He had gone up the escalator where a breath of spray stung his fingers on the hand-rail, realized at the top that the shop he sought must be downstairs after all – was not Suzanne the hairdresser who also sold wigs and leotards, or Linen That Shows or Laceworks – and went down again by the escalator to the Mandala. This was a set-piece in the area at the other end with potted plants in concentric circles – brown chrysanthemums, yellow chrysanthemums, white poinsettias and those plants with cherry-like orange fruit that are really a kind of potato. The crowds were thinning out; it was getting on for six when the centre closed up. Shop assistants were weary and growing impatient and even the flowers looked tired.

A Tesco superstore filled the whole crosspiece of the 'I' on both floors at this end, British Home Stores the other. Between them was Boots the Chemist with W. H. Smith facing it, the Mandala in between. Down a side passage that led from the main above-ground car park, children still played on a fat zebra made of black and white leather, a hi-tech climbing frame, a dragon on wheels. Wexford found the shop where Dora, a week ago, had pointed out to him in the window a sweater she liked. Addresses it was called, with a chocolate shop next to it and a wool and craft place Knits 'n' Kits on the other side. Wexford was not a man to hesitate or deliberate over a matter like this. Besides, Demeter the health-food shop opposite was already closing and the jewellers next to it were lowering the fancy gilt latticework bars inside the window. He went into Addresses and bought the sweater, the transaction taking four minutes.

By now shoppers were being hustled out, even Grub 'n' Grains the café having someone suspiciously like a bouncer on its door. And the lights were dimming, the leaping spouts of the fountain slowing . . . subsiding, until the ruffled surface of the pool into which it played became glasslike. Wexford sat down on one of the wrought-iron benches that were ranged along the aisle. He let the crowd make its way out through the various arteries that led from this central column and then he too left by the automatic doors into the covered way.

A great exodus of cars from the above-ground car parks was under way. At the far end he looked back. Flags flew from all the turrets along the centre's spine, red and yellow triangular pennants which had fluttered all day in the tail-end of the gale but drooped now in the stillness of a dark, misty evening. Slits of light still showed in the narrow pointed-topped Gothic windows. Wexford found himself alone here at the entrance to the underground car park, the only evidence of those hordes of shoppers being their abandoned trolleys. Hundreds of these jostled each other in higgledy-piggledy fashion, and would no doubt remain here till morning. A notice informed their users that the police took a serious view of those who allowed a shopping trolley to obstruct the roadway. Not for the first time, Wexford reflected that the police had more important things to do – though how much more important he was only to realize later.

The planners had decreed that this car park must be subterranean. He came into the lift and the stairs by way of a metal door whose clanging reverberations could still be heard as the lift descended. Wexford heard its echoes and at the same time feet pounding up the stairs, the feet of someone running hard; that was something else he remembered later. Down here it was always cold, always imbued with an acrid chemical smell as of metal filings awash in oil. Wexford stepped out of the lift at the second of four levels and came into the wide aisle between the avenue of pillars. Most of the cars were gone by now and in their absence the place seemed more desolate, uglier, more of a denial. Of course it was foolish and fanciful to think like this – a denial of what, for instance? The car park merely served a purpose, filled a need in the most practical utilitarian way. What would he have had instead? White paint? Murals? Tiles on the wall depicting some episode of local history? That would have been almost worse. It was irrational that the place reminded him of a picture it did not in the least resemble – John Martin's illustration of 'Pandemonium' for *Paradise Lost*.

His car was parked at this end. He didn't have to walk the length of the place – under the low concrete ceiling, between the squat uprights, into the wells of shadow – but merely cross over the bays along the left-hand wall. There was an echo down here and the sound of his footsteps rang back at him. If his powers of observation, in general so sharp, were less acute than usual, at least he noticed the numbers of cars that remained and their makes and colours. He saw the three between him and the middle of the car park where one ramp came up and another went down: one on the left, a red Metro, and diagonally opposite it on the right, parked side by side, a silver Escort and a dark blue Lancia. The woman's body lay between these two, closer to the Escort, concealed by a shroud of dirty brown velvet which made it look like a heap of rags.

Or so they told him afterwards. At the time he saw only the cars, the colours of their bodywork not entirely drained by the cold strip lights but muted, made pale. He lifted the boot-lid and put inside it the dark blue bag with 'Addresses' stamped on it in gold. As he closed it a car went by him, a red car going rather too fast. There were more red cars than any other colour, he had read somewhere. Motorists are aggressive and red is the colour of aggression. He got into the car, started it and looked at the clock. This was something he always did quite naturally, looked at the clock when he started the ignition. Seven minutes past six. He put the automatic shift into drive and began the climb out of the earth's bowels.

On each level the way out wound round half the floorspace at the opposite end from where the lift and stairs were, wound round anticlockwise and turned right up the ramp to the next level. He passed the three cars – the two on the left first, then the red Metro. Of course he didn't look to the right where the woman's body was. Why should he? His exit route took him round the loop, on to the straight on the

444

other side. Not a car remained here; the bays were empty. He climbed up to the first level, looped round and out into the night. There might have been cars remaining on that level, but he hadn't noticed and he could only remember the red Vauxhall Cavalier with a girl in the driving-seat facing him as he came up the ramp. She pulled out and followed him, impatient to be off and exceed the speed limit. Teenage girls at the wheels of cars were worse then the boys these days, Burden said. Wexford emerged into the open air, up the ramp. Most of the shoppers were gone; it was ten past six, they closed the centre at six and only the last stragglers remained, moving towards cars in the above-ground parking areas. The girl overtook him as soon as she could.

Wexford had pulled in and slowed to allow her to do so and it was then that he saw the woman emerge from the glass-covered way. He observed her because she was the only person to approach the car park and because she wasn't hurrying but walking in a controlled, measured fashion threading her way between the trolleys, fending off with her foot one that rattled into her path. She was a small, slender, upright woman in coat and hat carrying two bags of shopping, both red Tesco carriers. The metal door clanged behind her and he drove on across the wide nearly empty car-less space where the mist hung as a glaucous clouding of the air, out of the exit gates and half a mile on into Castle Street and the town. The traffic lights in the High Street outside the Olive and Dove turned red as he approached. The hand-brake on, he looked down at the evening paper he had bought before he drove to the centre but so far had not even glanced at. His own daughter's famous face looked back at him, affording him only a mild jolt. Pictures of Sheila in the papers weren't unusual. Seldom, however, were they accompanied by revelations of this sort. There was another photograph beside the portrait; Wexford looked at that one too and with lips pursed drew in a long breath. The lights slipped through amber into green.

The Barringdean Shopping Centre was on the outskirts of Kingsmarkham but nevertheless within the town. It had been built on the site of the old bus station when the new bus

445

station was put up on the site of the old maltings. Everyone went shopping there and the retailers in the High Street suffered. By day it was a hive of bees buzzing in and swarming out, but at night the centre was left to its fate – two break-ins during it first year of life. Apart from the security men and store detectives within the centre itself, there was a caretaker who called himself the supervisor and who patrolled the grounds or, more usually, sat in a small concrete office next door to the car-park lift-shaft, reading the *Star* and listening to tapes of *Les Misérables* and *Edwin Drood*. At six-fifteen each evening David Sedgeman performed his last duty of the day as Barringdean Shopping Centre supervisor. He put the trolleys into some sort of order, slotting one inside another to form long articulated carriages, and closed the gates of the pedestrian entrance in Pomeroy Road, fastened the bolts and attached the padlock. These gates were of steel mesh in steel frames and the fence was eight feet high. Then Sedgeman went off home. If anyone remained about the grounds, they had to leave by the traffic exit.

The residents of Pomeroy Road had benefited from the removal of the bus station. It was quieter now that no buses turned in and departed from six in the morning until midnight. Instead there were all the shoppers coming and going, but soon after six they had all left. On the opposite side of the street short terraces of Victorian houses alternated with small blocks of flats. Directly facing the gates, in one of these houses, Archie Greaves lived with his daughter and son-in-law. He spent a large part of his days sitting in the downstairs bay window watching the people; it was far more entertaining for him now than in the bus station era. He watched the people go into the phone box just outside the gates on the right-hand side and some of them must have seen him watching them, for more than once he had been approached, accosted by a tap on the window and asked for change for the phone. He watched the shoppers arrive and the shoppers leave; it amused him to make a mental note of arrivals and check on their departure. He recognized certain regulars and because he was a lonely man – his daughter and her husband out all day – thought of them almost as his friends.

This evening was misty. It had got dark very early and by six was black as midnight, the mist very apparent where lights caught it and made a greenish shimmer. The gutters of Pomeroy Road were clogged with fallen leaves, the plane trees almost bare. Beyond the open gates lamps lit the car parks that were fast emptying and in the shopping centre building itself, where the turrets were silhouetted black like the teeth of a saw against the streaked cloudy purple of the sky, the lights were beginning to dim. Before many more minutes had passed by, they would all have gone out.

Pedestrians had been coming out sporadically ever since Archie first went to sit there at four o'clock. His breath clouded the glass and he rubbed it with his jacket sleeve, taking his arm away in time to see someone running out of the gates. A young man it was – a boy to him – empty handed, going as if all the devils in hell were after him. Or store detectives, Archie thought doubtfully. Once he had seen a woman running with people pursuing her and he guessed she had been shoplifting. This boy he had never seen before; he was a stranger to him and he passed out of sight under the plane trees into the misty dark.

Archie hadn't put a light on because he could see better sitting in darkness. An old-fashioned electric fire made a glow in the room behind him. No one was pursuing the boy – perhaps he had only been in a hurry. The people who were leaving at a more leisurely pace had looked at him without much curiosity and, like Archie, expected to see retribution coming. But the darkness absorbed them as well. He saw a car come up out of the mouth of the underground park and then another. The lights that illuminated the shopping centre turrets went out. Then Archie saw David Sedgeman appear from behind the angle of the concrete wall with the padlock keys in his hand. Because of the mist and because Archie hadn't put his light on, Sedgeman had to peer to see the pale blur of the old man's face and then he nodded and raised his hand. Archie gave him a salute. Sedgeman closed the gates, looped the chain through the steel mesh, fastened and locked the padlock. Then he shot both bolts, one at the bottom and another a foot above his head. Before he went back, he gave Archie another wave.

This was the signal for Archie to get moving. He got up and went to the kitchen where he made himself a mug of tea with a tea-bag and took two chocolate chip cookies out of the biscuit tin. No potatoes to peel tonight because his daughter and her husband would be out at a friend's son's engagement party. There would be no cooked supper for Archie, but at his age he preferred little snacks of tea and biscuits and bits of chocolate anyway. Back in the front room he put the television on, though he had missed most of the six o'clock news and the bit he got was all about the trial of terrorists and some actress damaging Ministry of Defence property. He didn't turn it off but just turned down the sound and switched on the central light. Archie had read somewhere that watching television in the dark turns you blind eventually.

The light was also on in the phone box now. It came on at six-thirty when the box hadn't been vandalized and the lamp smashed as sometimes happened. Archie sat on the window once more, one eye watching the street and another the screen, hoping something more cheerful would come on soon. By now the shopping centre was in darkness, though two lamps were still alight in the open air car parks. A middle-aged man, one of the neighbours, came long with his dog which lifted its leg against the red metal door of the call box. Archie felt like banging on the window but knew it would do no good. Dog and owner went off into the mist while Archie drank his tea, ate the second biscuit and wondered whether he should get himself a third or wait an hour. Weather forecast now; he couldn't hear it, but he could see by all those little clouds and whirly lines that it was going to be a mixture as before.

Outside was silence, darkness, mist which moved and cleared and rolled sluggishly back, which the lights – half-obscured by plane-tree branches – turned to a watery, acid-green phosphorescence. The darkness was deep in the tarmac desert, nothing visible but two islanded spots of light and now these also went out . . . one, two . . . leaving blackness that met a dark grey but luminous sky. Only the lamps of Pomeroy Street and a ray or so from the mouth of the underground car park faintly lit the area behind the gates. And into this a little woman walked from behind the concrete wall, having perhaps come from the car-park lift, Archie thought. She walked a few yards in one direction to stare into the blackness, then she turned and gazed towards the

448

gates and him. She seemed to be looking to see if there was anyone about, or looking for someone or something. There was anger, repressed and contained, revealed in the slow deliberate way she moved – he could tell that even in the dark.

She might have a car in there and be unable to get it started. There was nothing he could do and now she had gone again, the wall cutting her off from his view. Archie switched off the television, for he could stand no more of what had appeared silently on the screen – starving Africans with pot-bellied dying babies, more of those people that he in his impotence and penury could not aid. He looked back at the empty stillness outside. Fetching the third biscuit might be postponed for an hour or so. He had to find ways to fill up his evening, for he couldn't very well go to bed until nine which was more than two hours away. The chances were that nothing more would happen out there until eight next morning when the shopping centre opened, nothing at all except cars passing and maybe a couple of people coming to use the phone box. He was thinking this, reflecting on it, when the woman appeared again, walking now in the stalking single-minded fashion of a cat homing on it pray.

When she came up to the gates, she got hold of them as if expecting they would open, as if the padlock would fall apart and the bolts slide back. Archie got to his feet and leaned forward on the window sill. The woman was much too short to reach the top bolt; she seemed now to have realized that the padlock was fastened and the key gone, and she began to rattle the gates. Her eyes were not on him but on the phone box, which was only a few yards from her but tantalizingly outside those gates.

She shook the gates more and more violently and they clanged and rattled. Anyone could see it was useless doing that because of the bolts and the padlock, and Archie began to wonder, because of the sudden and violent change in her demeanour, if she wasn't quite all there, if she were a bit mad . . . crazy. His reaction to anything like that would usually be to ignore it, to shut his eyes or go away. But it was the phone box she wanted; all this frenzy was on account of not being able to reach the phone box. There were always the neighbours – let someone else attend to it, someone

younger and stronger. Only no one ever did. Archie sometimes thought a person could be murdered in Pomeroy Street
in full view, in broad daylight, and no one would do anything. The woman was shouting now – well, screaming. She
was stamping her feet and shaking the gates and roaring at
the top of her voice, yelling things Archie couldn't make out
but which he heard all right when he had put his cap on and
his raincoat round his shoulders and was making his way
out on to the pavement.

'The police! The police! I've got to get the police! I've got
to phone. I've got to get the police?'

Archie crossed the road. He said, 'Making all that fuss
won't help. You calm down now. What's the matter with
you?'

'I've got to phone the police! There's someone dead in
there. I've got to phone the police – there's a woman and
they've tried to cut her head off!'

Archie went cold all over; his throat came up and he tasted
tea and chocolate. He thought, my heart, I'm too old for
this. He said feebly, 'Stop shaking those gates. Now, come
on, you stop it! I can't let you out.'

'I want the police,' she shrieked and fell to lean heavily
against the gates, hanging there with her fingers pushed
through the wire mesh. The final clang reverberated and died
away, as she sobbed harshly against the cold metal.

'I can go and phone them,' Archie said and he went back
indoors, leaving her sagged there, still, her hands hooked on
the wire like someone shot while trying to escape.

2

The phone rang while he was in the middle of going through it all with Dora. Supper had been eaten without enthusiasm and the bag containing Dora's birthday sweater lay unregarded on the seat of the chair. He had turned the evening paper front-page downwards but – unable to resist the horrid fascination of it – picked it up again.

'Mind you, I knew things weren't going well with her and Andrew,' Dora said.

'Knowing one's daughter's marriage is going through a bad patch is a far cry from reading in the paper that she's getting a divorce.'

'I think you mind about that more than about her coming up in court.'

Wexford made himself look coolly at the newspaper. The lead story was the trial of three men who had tried to blow up the Israeli Embassy and there was something too about a by-election, but the page was Sheila's. There were two photographs. The top picture showed a wire fence – not unlike the fence that surrounded the shopping complex he had recently left, only this one was topped with coils of razor wire. The modern world, he sometimes thought, was full of wire fences. The one in the picture had been mutilated and a flap hung loose from the centre of it, leaving a gaping hole through which a waste of mud could be seen with a hangar-like edifice in the middle of it. From the darkish background in the other photograph his daughter's lovely face looked out, wide-eyed, apprehensive, to a father's eye, aghast at the headlong rush of events. Wisps of pale curly hair escaped from under her woolly cap. The headlines said only 'Sheila

Cuts the Wire'; the story beneath told the rest of it, giving among all the painful details of arrest and magistrates' court appearance the surely gratuitous information that the actress currently appearing in the television serialization of *Lady Audley's Secret* was seeking a divorce from her husband, businessman Andrew Thorverton.

'I would have liked to be told, I suppose,' Wexford said. 'About the divorce, I mean. I wouldn't expect her to tell us she was going to chop up the fence around a nuclear bomber base. We'd have tried to stop her.'

'We'd have tried to stop her getting a divorce.'

It was then that the phone rang. Since Sheila had been released on bail, pending a later court appearance, Wexford thought it must be her at the other end. He was already hearing her voice in his head, the breathy self-reproach as she tried to persuade her parents she didn't know how the paper had got that report about her divorce . . . she was overcome . . . she was flabbergasted . . . it was all beyond her. And as for the wire-cutting . . .

Not Sheila though. Inspector Michael Burden.

'Mike?'

The voice was cool and a bit curt, anxiety underlying it, but he nearly always sounded like that. 'There's a dead women in the shopping centre car park, the underground one. I haven't seen her yet, but there's no chance it's anything but murder.'

'I was there myself,' Wexford said wonderingly. 'I only left a couple of hours ago.'

'That's OK. Nobody thinks you did it.'

Burden had got a lot sharper since his second marriage. Time was when such a rejoinder would never have entered his head.

'I'll come over. Who's there now?'

'Me – or I will be in five minutes. Archbold. Prentiss.' Prentiss was the Scene-of-Crimes man, Archbold a young DC. 'Sumner-Quist. Sir Hilary's away on his hols.'

In November? Well, people went away at any old time these days. Wexford rather liked the eminent and occasionally outrageous pathologist, Sir Hilary Tremlett, finding Dr Basil Sumner-Quist less congenial.

'There's no identification problem,' said Burden. 'We

452

know who she is. Her name's Gwen Robson, Mrs. Late fifties. Address up at Highlands. A woman called Sanders found her and got hold of someone in Pomeroy Street who phoned us.'

It was five-past eight. 'I may be a long time,' Wexford said to Dora. 'At any rate I won't be back soon.'

'I'm wondering if I ought to phone Sheila.'

'Let her phone us,' said Sheila's father, hardening his heart. He picked up the bag with Dora's present in it and hid it at the back of the hall cupboard. The birthday wasn't until tomorrow anyway.

The car-park entrance was blocked with police cars. Lights had appeared from somewhere, the place blazed with light. Someone had shot the linked shopping trolleys across the parking area to clear a space and trolleys stood about everywhere but at a distance, like a watching crowd of robots. The gates in the fence at the pedestrian entrance in Pomeroy Street stood wide open. Wexford pushed trolleys aside, spinning them out of his way, squeezed between the cars, opened the lift door and tried to summon the lift. It didn't come, so he walked down the two levels. The three cars were still there – the red Metro, silver Escort and dark blue Lancia – but the blue one had been backed out of its parking slot up against the wall and reversed into the middle of the aisle, no doubt to allow room for pathologist, Scene-of-Crimes officer and photographer to scrutinize the body that lay close up against the offside of the silver Escort. Wexford hesitated a moment, then walked towards the group of people and the thing on the concrete floor.

Burden got to his feet as Wexford approached and Archbold, who had old-fashioned manners, nodded and said, 'Sir!' Sumner-Quist didn't bother to look round. The fact that he happened at that moment to move his shoulder so that the dead woman's face and neck were revealed was, Wexford thought, purely fortuitous. The face bore the unmistakable signs of someone who has met her death by strangulation. It was bluish, bloated, horrified, and the mark on her neck of whatever was responsible for her asphyxiation was so deep that it had more the appearance of a circular cut, as if the blade of a knife had been run round throat and nape. Blazing lights in a place usually feebly lit showed up all the horror of her and her surroundings – stained and discoloured concrete, dirty metal, litter sprawling across the floor.

The dead woman wore a brown tweed coat with fur collar and her hat of brown fawn checked tweed with narrow brim was still on her grey curly hair. Apparently small and slight, she had stick-like legs in brown tights or stockings and on her feet brown lace-up low-heeled walking shoes. Wedding and engagement rings were on her left hand.

'The Escort's her car,' Burden said. 'She had the keys to it in her hand when she was killed. Or that's the way it looks, the keys were under the body. There are two bags of groceries in the boot. It looks as if she put the bags in the boot, closed the boot-lid, came round to unlock the driver's door and then someone attacked her from behind.'

'Attacked her with what?'

'A thin length of cord, maybe. Like in thuggee.' Burden's general knowledge as well as sharpness of intellect had been enhanced by marriage. But it was the birth of his son, twenty years after his first family, that had made him abandon the smart suits he had formerly favoured for wear even on occasions like this one. Jeans were what the inspector had on this evening, though jeans which rather oddly bore knife creases and contrasted not altogether happily with his camel-hair jacket.

'More like wire than a cord,' Wexford said.

The remark had an electric effect on Dr Sumner-Quist who jumped up and spoke to Wexford as if they were in a drawing room, not a car park, as if there were no body on the floor and this were a social occasion, a cocktail party maybe: 'Talking of wire, isn't that frightfully pretty TV girl who's all over the paper this evening your daughter?'

Wexford didn't like to imagine what effect the epithet 'TV girl' would have had on Sheila. He nodded.

'I thought so. I said to my wife it was so, unlikely as it seemed. OK, I've done all I can here. If the man with the camera's done his stuff, you can move her as far as I'm concerned. Myself, I think it's a pity these people don't go cutting the wire in Russia.'

Wexford made no reply to this. 'How long has she been dead?'

'You want miracles, don't you? You think I can tell you

454

that after five minutes' dekko? Well, she was a goner by six, I reckon. That do you?'

And he had been there at seven minutes past . . . He lifted up the grubby brown velvet curtain that lay in a heap a few inches from the dead woman's feet. 'What's this?'

'It was covering the body, sir,' Archbold said.

'Covering it as might be a blanket, do you mean? Or right over the head and feet?'

'One foot was sticking out and the woman who found her pulled it back a bit to see the face.'

'Yes – who was it found her?'

'A Mrs Dorothy Sanders. That's her car over there, the red one. She found the body, but it was a man called Greaves in Pomeroy Street phoned us. Davidson's talking to him now. He found Mrs Sanders screaming and shaking the gates fit to break them down. She went raving mad because the phone box is outside the gates and she couldn't get out. Diana Pettit took a statement from her and drove her home.'

Still holding the curtain. Wexford tried the boot-lid of the red Metro. There was shopping inside that too, food in two red Tesco carriers and a clear plastic bag full of hanks of grey knitting-wool done up with string like a parcel. He looked up at the sound of the lift, an echo from it or reverberation or something; you could always hear it. The door to the lift had opened and a man appeared. He was walking very diffidently and hesitantly towards them and when his eyes met Wexford's he stopped altogether. Archbold went up to him and said something. He was a young man with a pale heavy face and dark moustache and he was dressed in a way which while quite suitable for a man of Wexford's own age, looked incongruous on someone of – what? Twenty-one? Twenty-two? The V-necked grey pullover, striped tie and gray flannel trousers reminded Wexford of a school uniform.

'I've come for the car,' he said.

'One of these cars is yours?'

'The red one, the Metro. It's my mother's. My mother said to come over and bring it back.'

His eyes went fearfully to where the body lay, the body that was now entirely covered by a sheet. It lay unattended – pathologist, photographer and policeman having all moved away towards the central aisle or the exits. Wexford noted that awe-stricken glance, the quick withdrawing of the eyes and jerk of the head. He said, 'Can I have your name, sir?'

'Sanders, Clifford Sanders.'

Burden asked,'Are you some relation of Mrs Dorothy Sanders?'

'Her son.'

'I'll come back with you,' Wexford said. 'I'll follow you; I'd like to talk to your mother.' He let Clifford Sanders, walking edgily, pass out of earshot and then said to Burden, 'Mrs Robson's next-of-kin . . . ?'

'There's a husband, but he hasn't been told. He'll have to make a formal indentification. I thought of going over there now.'

'Do we know who that blue Lancia belongs to?'

Burden shook his head. 'It's a bit odd, that. Only shoppers use the car park – I mean, who else would want to? And the centre's been closed over two hours. If it belongs to the killer, why didn't he or she drive it away? When I first saw it I thought maybe it wouldn't start, but we had to move it and it started first time.'

'Better have the owner traced,' said Wexford. 'My God, Mike, I was in here, I saw the three cars, I drove past her.'

'Did you see anyone else?'

'I don't know, I'll have to think.'

Going down in the lift, he thought. He remembered the pounding footsteps descending, the girl in the red Vauxhall following him, the half-dozen people in the above-ground parking areas, the mist that was visible and obscuring but really hid nothing. He remembered the woman carrying the two bags coming from the covered way, strolling, languidly kicking the trolley aside. But that was at ten-past six and the murder had already taken place by then . . . He got into the car beside Archbold. Clifford Sanders in the red Metro was waiting a few yards along the roadway while a uniformed officer – someone new that Wexford didn't recognize – trundled the scattered trolleys out of their path.

The little red car led them along the High Street in the Stowerton direction and turned into the Forby Road. Archbold seemed to know where Sanders lived, in a remote spot down a lane that turned off about half a mile beyond the house and parkland called 'Sundays'. In fact it was less then three miles outside Kingsmarkham, but the lane was narrow and very dark and Clifford Sanders drove even more slowly than the winding obscurity warranted. Thick, dark, leafless hedges rose high on either side. Occasionally a pulling-in place revealed itself, showing at least that passing would be possible if they met another vehicle. Wexford couldn't remember even having been down there before, he doubted if it led anywhere except perhaps finally to the gates of a farm.

The sky was quite black, moonless, starless. The lane seemed to wind in a series of unneccessary loops. There were no hills for it to circumvent and the river to flow in the opposite direction. No longer were any pinpoints of light visible in the surrounding countryside. All was darkness but for the area immediately ahead, illuminated by their own headlights, and the twin bright points glowing red on the rear of the Metro.

But now Clifford Sanders' left-hand indicator was winking. Plainly, he was a kind of driver who would signal his intention to turn a hundred yards before the turning. A few seconds elapsed. There were no lights ahead, only a break in the hedge. Then the Metro turned in and Archbold followed, guided by the red tail-lights. With a kind of amused impatience Wexford thought how they might be in some Hitchcock movie, for he could just make out the house – a house which probably looked a lot less disagreeable by daylight but was now almost ridiculously grim and forbidding. Behind two windows only a pallid light showed. There was no other light either by the front door or about the garden. Wexford's eyes grew accustomed to the darkness and he saw that the house was biggish, on three floors, with eight windows here in the front and a slab of a front door. A low light of steps without rails led up to it and there was neither porch nor canopy. But the whole façade was hung, covered, clothed in ivy. As far as he could see it was ivy, at any rate it was evergreen leaves, a dense blanket of them, through which the two pale windows peered like eyes in an animal's shaggy face.

A garden surrounded the house – grass and wilted foliage at any rate, extending at the back to a wooden fence. Beyond that only darkness, fields and woods, and over the low hill the invisible town which might as well have been a hundred miles away.

Clifford Sanders went up to the front door. The bell was a very old-fashioned kind which you rang by turning the handle back and forth, but he had a key and unlocked this door, though when Wexford started to follow him he said in his flat chilly tone, 'Just a minute, please.'

Mother, evidently, had to be warned; he disappeared and after a moment or two she came out to them. Wexford's first thought was how small she was, tiny and thin; his second that this was the woman he had seen entering the underground car park as he had left it. Within moments then she had found the body that he had missed. Her face was very pale, as near a white face as you could find, very lined and powdered even whiter, a young girl's scarlet lipstick unbecomingly coating her mouth. She was dressed in a brown tweed skirt, beige jumper, bedroom slippers. Did her recent discovery account for the curious smell of her? She smelt of disinfectant, the apparent combination of lime and thymol which hospitals reek of.

'You can come in,' she said, 'I've been expecting you.'

Inside, the place was bleak and cavernous; carpets and central heating were not luxuries that Mrs Sanders went in for. The hall floor was quarry-tiled, in the living room they walked on wood-grain linoleum and a couple of sparse rugs. There was scarcely an ornament to be seen – no pictures, only a large mirror in a heavy mahogany frame. Clifford Sanders had seated himself on a very old, shabby horsehair sofa in front of the fire of logs. He now wore on his feet only grey socks; his shoes were set in the hearth on a folded sheet of newspaper. Mrs Sanders pointed out – actually pointed with an extended finger – precisely where they were to sit: the armchair for Wexford, the other section of the sofa for Archbold. She seemed to have some notion of rank and what was due to it.

'I'd like you to tell me about your experience in the Barringdean Centre car park this evening, Mrs Sanders,' Wexford began. He forced himself to shift his eyes from the newspaper on which his daughter's face looked out at him

458

from between the pair of black lace-up brogues. 'Tell me what happened from the time you came into the car park.'

Her voice was slow and flat like her son's, but there was something metallic about it too, almost as if throat and palate were composed of some inorganic hard material. 'There isn't anything to tell. I came up with my shopping to get my car. I saw something lying on the ground and went over to look and it was . . . I expect you know what it was.'

'Did you touch it?'

'I pulled back the bit of rag that was over it, yes.'

Clifford Sanders was watching his mother, his eyes still and blank. He seemed not so much relaxed as sagging from despair, his hands hanging down between his parted legs.

'What time was this, Mrs Sanders?' Wexford had noted the digital watch she wore.

'Exactly twelve minutes past six.' To account for her leaving the shopping precinct so late, she gave an account of a contretemps with a fishmonger, speaking in the measured level way – too measured. Wexford, who had been wondering what her tone reminded him of, now recalled electronic voices issuing from machines. 'I came up there at twelve minutes past six – and if you want to know how I can be sure of the time, the answer is I'm *always* sure of the time.'

He nodded. Digital watches were designed for people like her who, prior to their arrival on the scene, had to make approximate guesses as to what time was doing between ten-past six and six-fifteen. Yet most of them were speedy people, always in a hurry, restless, unrelaxed. This woman seemed one of those rare creatures who are constantly aware of time without being tempted to race against it.

She spoke softly to her son. 'Did you lock the garage doors?'

He nodded. 'I always do.'

'Nobody always does anything. Anybody can forget.'

'I didn't forget.' He got up. 'I'm going into the other room to watch TV.'

She was a pointer, Wexford saw, a finger-post. Now the finger pointed into the hearth. 'Don't forget your shoes.'

Clifford Sanders padded away with his shoes in his hand and Wexford said to Dorothy Sanders, 'What were you doing between twelve minutes past six and six forty-five when you managed to attract the attention of Mr Greaves in Queen Street?' He had registered very precisely the time of the phone call Greaves made to Kingsmarkham police station: fourteen minutes to seven. 'That's half an hour between the time you found the body and the time you got down to the gate and . . . called out.'

She wasn't disconcerted. 'It was a shock. I had my shock to get over and then when I got down there I couldn't make anyone hear.'

He recalled Archbold's account, albeit at third hand. She had been screaming and raving inside those gates, shaking them 'fit to break them down' because the phone box was on the other side. Now the woman looked at him coldly and calmly. One would have said no emotion ever disturbed her equilibrium or altered the tone of the mechanical voice.

'How many cars did you see parked at that time on the second level?'

Without hesitation she said, 'Three, including mine.'

She wasn't lying; perhaps she hadn't been lying at all. He recalled how when he had passed through the second level there had been four cars parked there. One had pulled out, the one driven by the impatient young girl, and followed him fretfully. That had been at eight or nine minutes past six . . .

'Did you see anyone? Anyone at all?'

'Not a soul.'

She would be a widow, Wexford thought, nearly pensionable, without any sort of job, dependent in many ways and certainly financially dependent on this son who no doubt lived not far away. Later on, he reflected that he couldn't have been more wrong.

A wave of disinfectant smell hit him and she must have seen him sniffing.

'Coming in contact with that corpse,' she said, looking at him with steady, unblinking eyes, 'I had to scrub my hands with antiseptic.'

It was years since he had heard anyone use the word corpse. As he got up to go, she crossed the window and began to draw the curtains. The place smelt like an operating theatre. The better to observe Clifford's arrival with the car, Wexford supposed, the curtains – of brown rep, not velvet – had been left drawn back. He watched her pull them

460

together, giving each an impatient tug. Attached to the top of the door into the room was one of those extendable brass rails made to accomodate a draught-excluding curtain. No curtain, however, hung from it.

Wexford decided the time was not ripe to ask the question that came to his lips.

It had fallen many times to Michael Burden's lot to be the bearer of bad tidings of a particular kind, to break the news of a spouse's death. He, whose own first wife had died prematurely, flinched from this task. And it was one thing having to tell someone, for instance, that his wife had died in a road accident; quite another that her murdered body had been found. No one knew better than Burden that the majority of those who are murdered have been done to death by a near relative. The chances are that a murdered wife has been murdered by her husband.

It was only a few moments before Wexford's arrival that he had looked inside the dead woman's handbag. After the first photographs had been taken and the dirty brown velvet curtain lifted from the body, her handbag had been revealed lying under her, half concealed by her thigh. More photographs were taken, Sumner-Quist came and at last he was able to free the bag from where it lay and, holding it in gloved hands, undo the clasp and look inside. It was a standard cache of documents: driving licence, credit cards, dry-cleaning bill, two letters still in their envelopes. Her name and address presented themselves to him before he had even noted the other contents of the bag – chequebook, purse, pressed powder, packet of tissues, ballpoint pen and two safety-pins. Gwen P. Robson, 23 Hastings Road, Highlands, Kingsmarkham KM10 2NW. One of the envelopes was addressed to her as Mrs G. P. Robson, the other to Mr and Mrs R. Robson.

It might not be a shock to Robson; part of Burden's job was to observe whether it was a shock or not. He silently framed the words he would use as the car climbed the long hill that led up to the Highlands estate. All this had been countryside when Burden first came to Kingsmarkham, heathy hillsides crowned with woods, and from the top of

461

this incline by day you had been able to see the ancient landmark called Barringdean Ring. It was very dark tonight, the horizon defined only by an occasional point of light, and the circle of oaks was invisible. Nearer at hand Highlands was cosily lit. This was the way Gwen Robson had no doubt intended to come home, driving the silver Escort, entering Eastbourne Avenue and soon turning left into Hastings Road.

Burden had been there only once before, though the estate had been put up by the local authority some seven years ago. Street trees and garden trees had grown up and matured: the first newness of the houses had worn off and they looked less as if built from playbox bricks by a giant's child. Smallish blocks of flats no more than three storeys high, alternated with terraced or semi-detached houses, and opposite the block in which No. 23 was located stood a row of tiny bungalows designed as housing for the elderly. Not too far a cry from the old almshouses, thought Burden, whose wife had made him a lot more socially conscious than he used to be. On the doorstep of the Robson's house stood a rack made for holding milkbottles; it was of red plastic-covered wire, surmounted by a plastic doll in a white coat with 'Thank you, Mr Milkman' in red letters under it and a clip to hold a note in its outstretched hand. This absurd object made Burden feel worse, indicative as it was of domestic cheerfulness. He looked at DC Davidson and Davidson looked at him and then he rang the bell.

The door was answered very quickly. Anxious people fly to doors, to phones. Their anxiety, of course, may not be brought about by the obvious cause.

'Mr Robson?'

'Yes. Who are you?'

'Police officers, Mr Robson.' Burden showed his warrant card. How to soften this? How to ease it? He could hardly say there was nothing to be alarmed about. 'I am afraid we have very serious news. May we come in?'

He was a smallish, owl-face man, rather overweight; Burden noticed that he used a stick even to bring him this short distance. 'Not my wife?' he said.

Burden nodded. He nodded firmly, his eyes on Robson. 'Let's go in.'

462

But Robson, though they were in the hall now, stood his ground. He leant on his stick. 'The car? A car accident?'

'No, Mr Robson, it wasn't a car accident.' The bad part was that this could all be fake, all acting. He might have been rehearsing it for the past hour. 'If we could go into your . . .'

'Is she – is she gone?'

The old euphemism. Burden repeated it. 'Yes, she's gone.' and he added. 'She's dead, Mr Robson.'

Burden turned and walked through the open doorway into the well-lit, warm, over-furnished living room. A fire of gas flames licking beautifully simulated smokeless fuel looked more real than the real thing. The television was on, but more indicative of Robson's recent tension was the clock patience game laid out on a small appropriately round marquetry table in front of the armchair with its indented seat and crumpled pink silk cusions. Only a murderer who was also a genius would have dreamt up that one, Burden thought.

Robson had turned very pale. His thin-lipped mouth trembled. Still upright but leaning heavily on the stick, he was shaking his head in a vague, uncomprehending way. 'Dead? Gwen?'

'Sit down, Mr Robson. Take it easy.'

'Would you like a drink, sir?' DC Davidson asked.

'We don't drink in this house.'

'I meant water.' Davidson went off and came back with water in a glass.

'Tell me what happened.' Robson was seated now, no longer looking at Burden, his eyes in the circle of playing cards. Absently he took a minute sip of the water.

'You must prepare yourself for a shock, Mr Robson.'

'I've had a shock.'

'Yes, I know.' Burden shifted his gaze and found himself looking at the framed photograph on the mantel-shelf of a very good-looking girl who rather resembled Sheila Wexford. A daughter? 'Your wife was killed, Mr Robson. There is no way I can make this easier to hear. She was murdered and her body was found in the Barringdean Shopping Centre car park.'

Burden wouldn't have been surprised if he had screamed,

463

if he had howled like a dog. They came upon all sorts in their job. But Robson didn't scream; he merely stared with frozen face. A long time passed, a relatively long time, perhaps nearly a minute. He stared and passed his tongue over the thin lips, then he began mumbling very rapidly.

'We were married very young; we'd been married forty years. No children, we never had chick nor child, but that brings you closer; you're closer to each other without them. She was the most devoted wife a man ever had; she'd have done anything for me, she'd have laid down her life for me.' Great tears welled out of his eyes and flowed down his face. He sobbed and wept without covering his face, sitting upright and holding the stick with both hands, crying as most men only cried when they were very young children.

3

'It looks as if she was garroted.'

Sumner-Quist's voice sounded pleasurably excited as if he had rung up to impart a piece of gossip: that the Chief Constable had run off with someone else's wife, for instance.

'Did you hear me? I said she was garroted.'

'Yes, I heard,' Wexford said. 'Good of you to tell me.'

'I thought you might go for a tasty little titbit like that before I let you have the full report.'

Extraordinary ideas some people have about one's tastes, Wexford thought. He tried to assemble in his mind what he knew about garroting. 'What was it done with?'

'A garrote,' Sumner-Quist chuckled cheerfully. 'Search me what kind. Home-made, no doubt. That's your problem.' Still laughing, he told Wexford that Mrs Robson had met her death after five-thirty and before six and had not been sexually assaulted. 'Merely garroted,' he said.

'It used to be a method of execution,' Wexford said when Burden came into the office. 'An iron collar was attached to a post and the victim's neck placed inside. The mind boggles a bit when you start thinking how they *got* the victim's neck inside. Then the collar was tightened until asphyxiation occurred. Did you know this method of capital punishment was still in use in Spain as late as the 1960s?'

'And we thought it was only bull-fighting they went in for.'

'There was also a more primitive implement consisting of a length of wire with wooden handles.'

Burden sat on the edge of Wexford's rosewood desk. 'Haven't I read somewhere that if you were up for burning

465

by the Inquisition the executioner would garrote you for a small fee before the flames got under way?'

'I expect that was where the wire-with-wooden-handles type came into its own.'

He wondered digressively if Burden's jeans were the kind called 'designer'. They were rather narrow at the ankle and matched the inspector's socks that were probably of a 'denim blue' shade. Unconscious of this rather puzzled scrutiny, Burden said, 'Is Sumner-Quist saying that's what was used on Gwen Robson?'

'He doesn't know, he just says "a garrote". But it had to have been something of that kind. And the murderer has to have had it with him or her, ready-made, all prepared – which when you come to think of it, Mike, is pretty strange. It argues unquestionably premeditated murder, yet in a situation where no one could have forecast the prevailing conditions. The car park might have been full of people, for instance. Unless our perpetrator carries a garrote about with him as you or I might carry a pen . . . I don't think we can say much more about that until we get the full forensic report. In the meantime, what's the sum total of our knowledge of Gwen Robson?'

She was fifty-eight years old, childless, a former home help in the employment of Kingsmarkham Borough Council but now retired. Her husband was Ralph Robson, also a former Borough Council employee, retired two years before from the Housing Department. Mrs Robson had been married at eighteen and she and her husband had lived first with his parents at their home in Stowerton, later on in a rented flat and then a rented cottage. Their names high on the borough housing list, they had been allocated one of the new houses at Highlands as soon as they were built. Neither was yet eligible for the state retirement pension, but Robson derived a pension from the local authority on which they had contrived to live in reasonable comfort. For instance, they had managed to run the two-year-old Escort. As a general rule they took an annual holiday in Spain and had been prevented from doing so this year only by Ralph Robson's arthritis, which was seriously affecting his right hip.

All this had been learned both from Ralph Robson himself

and from his niece Lesley Arbel, the original of the photograph that had so much reminded Burden of Sheila Wexford.

'This niece – she doesn't live with them, does she?'

'She lives in London, Burden said, 'but she spent a lot of time down here with them. More like a daughter than a niece, I gather, and an unusually devoted daughter at that. Or that's how it appears. She's staying with Robson now – came as soon as he told her what had happened to his wife.'

According to Robson, his wife had been in the habit of doing their weekly shopping every Thursday afternoon. Up until six months ago he had always gone with her, but his arthritis had made this impossible. On the previous Thursday, two days before, she had gone out in their car just before four-thirty. He had never seen her again. And where had he been himself between four-thirty and seven? At home alone in Hastings Road, watching television, making himself tea. Much the same as Archie Greaves, Wexford thought, whom he had been to see earlier that morning.

A policeman's dream of a witness, the old man was. The narrowness of his life, the confined span of his interests made him into a camera and tape device for the perfect recording of incidents in his little world. Unfortunately, there had not been much for him to observe: the shoppers leaving, the lights dwindling and going out, Sedgeman closing and locking the gates.

'There was this young chap running,' he said to Wexford. 'It was just on six, a minute or two after. There were a lot of people leaving, mostly ladies with their shopping, and he came running from round the back of that wall.'

Wexford followed his gaze out of the window. The wall in question was the side of the underground car-park entrance beside which stood a small crowd of ghoulish onlookers. There was nothing to see, but they waited in hope. The gates stood open, an empty food package rolled about the tarmac propelled by gusts of wind. The pennants on the turrets streamed in the wind, taut and fluttering. I was there, Wexford thought, almost with a groan, I came out of there at ten-past six and saw – nothing. Well, nothing but the Sanders woman.

467

'I reckoned he was in trouble,' Archie Greaves said. 'I reckoned he'd done something he shouldn't and been spotted and they was after him.' The man was so old that his face as well as the skin of his hands was discoloured with the liver spots that are called 'grave marks'. He was thin with age, his knitted cardigan and flannel trousers baggy on a bony, tremulous body. But the pale blue eyes, pink-rimmed, could see like those of someone half his age. 'He was just a boy with one of them woolly hats on his head and a zip-up jacket and he was running like a bat out of hell.'

'But there was in fact no one after him?'

'Not as I could see. Maybe they got fed up and turned back, knowing as they wouldn't catch him.'

And then he had seen Dorothy Sanders who was later to scream and rattle the gates, walking up and down searching the car parks for something or someone, her anger contained but her affronted indignation vibrating as later a demented terror was to stream from her, making Archie Greaves shiver and shake and fear for his heart.

An incident room had been set up in Kingsmarkham Police Station on Thursday night to receive calls from anyone who might have been in the Barringdean Shopping Centre underground car park between five and six-thirty. The local television station had broadcast an immediate appeal for possible witnesses to come forward and Wexford had managed to get a nationwide appeal on that night's ten o'clock news going out on the network. Calls started coming in at once – before the number to call had even disappeared from the screen, Sergeant Martin said – but of these the great majority were well-meant but misleading, or ill-meant and misleading, or were deliberate attempts to deceive. A call came from a young woman called Sarah Cussons who identified herself as the driver of the Vauxhall Cavalier which had followed Wexford's out of the car park, and another from a man beside whose car Gwen Robson had parked her red Metro. He had seen her drive in and was able to give her time of arrival at the centre as about twenty to five.

Throughout Thursday night the calls continued to come in, many of them from drivers of cars parked on all the levels who had seen nothing untoward. They were interviewed just the same. Early on Friday morning came a call on behalf of the owner of the blue Lancia. Mrs Helen Brook, nine months pregnant, had gone into labour while in the health-food shop in the shopping centre at about five on the previous evening. An ambulance had been called and she had been taken to the maternity wing of Stowerton Royal Infirmary.

None of the obviously genuine and well-intentioned callers was able to describe anyone else they had seen while parking or fetching their cars, though plenty of fantastic descriptions came in from those jokers who enjoy teasing the police. Two assistants from the Barringdean Centre shops phoned in to say they had served Gwen Robson, one just before five and the other, Linda Naseem – a checkout assistant at the Tesco supermarket – half an hour later. But by that time two of Wexford's officers were at the shopping centre questioning all the shop-workers, and Archbold had interviewed the man in charge of the fish counter in the Tesco superstore who confirmed he had had a row with a woman answering Dorothy Sanders' description 'at around six when they were closing up'. All that did was confirm her time of coming into the car park which Wexford could confirm himself.

That same morning Ralph Robson made a formal identification of his wife's body; the neck had been discreetly covered during this ordeal. He hobbled in on his stick, looked at the horror-stricken face from which some of the blue colour had faded, nodded, said, 'Yes,' but didn't cry this time. Wexford had not seen him on that occasion, hadn't yet seen him. He had interviewed David Sedgeman, the car park supervisor, himself. The man should have been a valuable witness, yet he seemed to have seen nothing or to have registered nothing he had seen. He could recall waving to Archie Greaves because he did this every evening, and for the same reason could recall locking the gates. But his memory offered him no worried woman or running man, no fast-driven car or suspicious escaper. Everything had been normal, he said in his dull way. He had locked the gates and gone home just as he always did, collecting his own car from where he always left it in a bay in one of the open-air parking areas.

The November air felt raw and the sky was a leaden grey.

A reddish sun hung over the roof-tops, not very high in the sky but as high as it would get. Burden had on a padded jacket, a pale grey Killy, warm as toast and turning him from a thin man into a stout one. His wife was away, staying with her mother who was convalescent after an operation, and that disturbed Burden, making him jumpy and insecure. He would spend tonight with her and their little son in his mother-in-law's house outside Myringham, but what he really wanted was his own family back home with him in his own house. His face took on a look both irritable and cynical as Wexford spoke.

'Did Robson strike you,' Wexford said in the car, 'as the sort of man who would sit himself down and with deliberation fashion a wire implement with a handle at each end for the express purpose of garroting his wife?'

'Now you're asking. I don't know what sort of a man that would be. He had no car, remember, his wife had the car. The centre's a mile away from Highlands . . .'

'I know. Is the arthritic hip genuine?'

'Even if it isn't, he had no car. He could have walked, or there's the bus. But if he wanted to murder his wife, why not do it at home like most of them do?'

Wexford couldn't keep from laughing at this insouciant acceptance of domestic homicide. 'Maybe he did, we don't know yet. We don't know if she died in that car park or the body was only dumped there. We don't even know if she drove the car.'

'You mean Robson himself may have?'

'Let's see,' said Wexford.

They arrived at Highlands and Lesley Arbel opened the front door to them. She didn't remind Wexford of his own daughter; to him she bore no resemblence to Sheila. He saw only a pretty girl who struck him at once as being exceptionally well-dressed, indeed almost absurdly well-dressed for a weekend of mourning in the country with one's recently bereaved uncle. She introduced herself, explained that she had not waited until the prearranged time for her visit but had come on Friday morning.

'My uncle's upstairs,' she said. 'He's lying down. The doctor came and said he was to get as much rest as he could.'

'That's all right, Miss Arbel. We'd like to talk to you too.'

'Me? But I don't know anything about it. I was in London.'

'You know about your aunt. You can tell us something of what sort of a person she was, better than your uncle can.'

She said in a rather pernickety way. 'That's right, he's my real uncle. I mean, my mother was his sister; she was my aunt because she married him.'

Wexford nodded, aware that his impatience showed. Mentally he cautioned himself against deciding too soon that a witness was irredeemably stupid. She took them into the Robsons' brightly furnished living room where a conflict of textile patterns dazzled Wexford — flowers on the carpet, flowers of a more formal design on the curtains, trees and fruits on the wallpaper, a rug with a sunburst pattern. The flames of a gas fire licked indestructible coals. The girl sat down and her own face smiled over her shoulder out of a silver frame. His question astonished her.

'These curtain, are they new?'

'Pardon?'

'Let me rephrase it. Were there ever different curtains at these windows?'

'I think Auntie Gwen once had red curtain, yes. Why do you want to know?'

Wexford made no answer but watched her while Burden asked about the telephone call her uncle had made to her on Thursday evening. Her clothes were remarkable, somehow evoking the unreal elegance of actresses in Hollywood comedies of the thirties, as sleek and as unsuitable for the wear and tear of living. A bunch of gold chains that looked too heavy for comfort hung against her cream silk shirt between the lapels of the coffee-coloured silk jacket. Crimson-nailed hands lay in her lap and she lifted one to her face, touching her cheek as she replied to his questions.

'You intended coming down for the weekend of Saturday as you often did?'

She nodded.

'But your uncle phoned you himself on Thursday evening and told you what had happened?'

'He phoned me on Thursday, on Thursday night. I wanted to come then, but he wouldn't have that. He had one of the neighbours, a Mrs Whitton, with him so I thought he'd be all right.' She looked from one to the other of them. 'You said you wanted me to talk about Auntie Gwen.'

'In a moment, Miss Arbel,' Burden said. 'Would you mind telling me what you were doing yourself on Thursday afternoon?'

'What do you want to know for?' She was more than astounded; her manner was affronted as if she had encountered insolence. Her long elegant legs, the feet encased in high-heeled cream leather pumps, drew close together, were pressed together. 'Why ever do you want to know that?'

Perhaps it was pure innocence.

Burden said blandly, 'Routine questions, Miss Arbel. In a murder enquiry, it's necessary to know people's whereabouts.' He attempted to help her along. 'I expect you were at work, weren't you?'

'I went home early on Thursday, I wasn't very well. Don't you want me to tell you about Auntie Gwen?'

'In a moment. You went home early because you weren't well. You had a cold, did you?'

A vacuous stare was turned on Burden, but perhaps not entirely vacuous for it seemed to contain an element of earnestness. 'It was my PMT, wasn't it?' she said as if she were famous for this disorder. as if all the world was aware of it. Wexford doubted if Burden even knew what those initials stood for, and now the girl seemed equally dubious. Frowning, she leaned towards Burden. 'I always have PMT and there's not a thing they can do about it.'

At this point the door opened and Ralph Robson came in, leaning on his stick. He had a dressing gown on, but with a shirt and pair of slacks underneath it. 'I heard voices.' His flat but beaky face was turned on Wexford with a puzzled look.

'Chief Inspector Wexford, Kingsmarkham CID.'

'Pleased to meet you,' Robson said, sounding anything but pleased. 'You coming here has saved me a phone call. Maybe one of you can tell me what's become of the shopping?'

'The shopping, Mr Robson?'

'The shopping Gwen got on Thursday, as was in the boot of the blessed car presumably. I can see I can't have the car back yet awhile, but the shopping's a different story. There's meat in those bags, there's a loaf and butter and I don't

472

know what else. I don't say I'm poor, but I'm not so rolling in money as I can just let that lot go, right?'

Self-preservation or a tenacity for life overcame grief. Wexford knew this, but it never ceased mildly to surprise him just the same. It might be that this man felt no grief; it might be that he was responsible for his wife's death, but it might only be that he had ceased to feel much emotion for anyone or anything. That sometimes happened to people as they aged and Wexford had noticed it dispassionately but with an inner shiver. Yet Burden said he had wept when first told.

'We'll get it back to you later today,' was all Wexford said.

He had carefully gone over the contents of the shopping bag himself before having the perishable items placed in one of the police canteen fridges. There had been nothing among them to excite much interest: mostly food, but things from the chemist as well – toothpaste and talcum powder – and from the British Home Stores four light-bulbs; all of these contained in a BHS bag, indicating perhaps that she had stopped there first. Mrs Robson's handbag, which would also soon be returned and which Burden had first looked into in the car park, contained her purse with twenty-two pounds in it, plus some small change and a chequebook from the Trustee Savings Bank. The credit cards were a Visa and the card which the Barringdean Shopping Centre supplied for its patrons. Her handkerchief and the two folded tissues were unused. The letters which had provided the police with her identity and address were from a sister in Leeds and the other – scarcely a letter in any sense – an invitation to a Christmas fashion show at the shop where Wexford had bought Dora's sweater.

'Are you missing a brown velvet curtain, Mr Robson?'

'Me? No. What do you mean?'

'A curtain which might have been kept in the boot of your car for the purpose, say, of covering up the windscreen in frosty weather?'

'I use newspaper for that.'

Lesley Arbel said suddenly, 'Could you eat a bit of lunch, Uncle? A little something light?'

473

He had sat down and was leaning forward in the chair, pressing one hand on his thigh in what seemed genuine pain, his face twisted with it. 'There's nothing I fancy, dear.'

'But you're not still having those pills, are you? The ones that upset your tummy?'

'Doctor took me off the blessed things. There's some they don't suit, he said; they can give you ulcers.'

'You've got arthritis, have you, Mr Robson?'

He nodded. 'You listen,' he said, 'and you can hear the hip joint grind.' To Robson's evident agony there came a shift of bone in socket and Wexford did hear it, heard with dismay an unhuman ratchet-like sound. 'It's a bit of bad luck for me that I'm allergic to the painkillers. Got to grin and bear it. I'm in line for one of those replacement ops, but there's a waiting list round here of up to three years. God knows what sort of a state I'll be in three years. It'd be a different story if I could have it done private.'

This was no news to Wexford, that hip replacements could be carried out almost at once if the patient were prepared to pay but that the waiting time for National Health Service surgery might be very protracted. The unfairness of this was not lost on him, but he was more intent on trying to assess the genuineness of Robson's disability. He turned his eyes towards the girl and she looked at him artlessly, her face a beautiful blank.

'Where do you work, Miss Arbel?'

'*Kim* magazine.'

'Could you give me the address, please, and your own address in London too? Do you live alone or share?'

'I share with two other girls.' She sounded peevish, muttering the north-west London address. '*Kim*'s office is at Orangetree House in the Waterloo Road.'

Wexford had only once seen the magazine when Dora had bought it for the sake of some mail-order bargain it featured. A semi-glossy weekly, it had seemed aimed at a not very youthful market but at the same time making little provision for women past forty or so. The issue Wexford had seen had carried articles he thought dreary but which the magazine itself vaunted as controversial and lively, under such headings as: 'Is it OK to be a Lesbian?' and 'Your Daughter Your Own Clone?'

'Could you eat some scrambled egg, Uncle, and a little thin bread and butter?'

Robson shrugged, then nodded. Burden began speaking to him of Mrs Whitton, the neighbour who had come to sit with him before Lesley Arbel arrived. Had he seen anyone, spoken on the phone to anyone, while his wife was out?

Lesley got up, said, 'Well, if you'll just excuse me . . .'

While Robson told Burden about the Hastings Road neighbours, speaking in a wretched halting monotone and separating virtually every sentence from the next with a phrase to the effect that Gwen had known them all better than he did, Wexford left the room. He found Lesley Arbel standing in front of an electric stove, a printed tea-towel rather than an apron tied round her waist to protect the coffee silk skirt. Two eggs reposed in a bowl, a beater beside them, but instead of preparing her uncle's lunch she was examining her face in a handbag mirror and painting something on to it with a small, fat brush.

As soon as she saw Wexford she put brush and mirror away with extreme haste, as if this rapid manoeuvre would somehow render the prior activity invisible. She broke open the eggs, not very skilfully, got a piece of shell into the bowl and had to pick it out with a long red nail.

'Why would anyone want to murder your aunt, Miss Arbel?'

She didn't answer him for a moment, but reached up into a cabinet for a plate and put a cruet on to the tray she had laid with a cloth. Her voice when it came was nervous and irritable. 'It was some crazy person, wasn't it? There's never any reason for murders, not these days. The ones you read about in the papers, they're all people who say they don't know why they did it or they've forgotten or had a blackout or whatever. The one who killed her will have been like that. I mean, who would have wanted to kill her for a reason? There wasn't any reason.' She turned away from him and started beating the eggs.

'Everybody liked her?' he said. 'She wouldn't have had enemies?'

In her left hand she held the pan in which butter was smoking too strongly, in her other the bowl with the egg mixture. But instead of pouring one into the other, she stood

475

with the two vessels poised. 'It's a laugh really, hearing you talk like that. Or it would be if it wasn't such a tragedy. She was a wonderful, lovely lady – don't you understand that? Hasn't anyone told you? Look at Uncle Ralph, he's heart-broken, isn't he? He worshipped her and she worshipped him. They were just a lovely couple, like young lovers right up to when this happened. And this'll be the death of him, I can promise you that – this'll be the end of him. He's aged about twenty years since yesterday.'

She swung round, tipped the eggs into the pan and began rapidly cooking them. Wexford had the curious feeling that for all the apparent sincerity of her words what she was really trying to do was impress him with a kind of caring competent maturity – an ambition that went wrong when she seemed to realize that though the eggs were cooked she had forgotten about the bread and butter. Rather harassed by now, she cut doorsteps of bread and covered them with wedges of butter chipped from the refrigerated block. He opened doors for her, feeling something very near pity without exactly knowing what he pitied her *for*. The apron improvised from a tea towel fell off as she teetered into the living room on her stilt heels. But even so, as she passed the small wall mirror which hung between kitchen and living-room doorways, she was unable to resist a glance into it. Balanced on her pointed toes, holding the tray, flustered, she nevertheless took the opportunity of a narcissistic peep at her own face . . .

Robson was lying back in his armchair and had to be jolted out of his half-daze. This his niece did not only by propping him up with a cushion behind him and plumping the tray down on his lap, but also with the rough and some-how shocking, 'He asked me if Gwen had enemies! Can you credit it?'

Dull, bewildered eyes were lifted. Incredibly came the mumble, 'He's only doing his job, dear.'

'Gwen,' she said, and sentimentally, 'Gwen that was like a mother to me.' Suddenly her manner sharpened. 'Mind you, she wasn't soft. She had principles, very high principles, didn't she, Uncle? And she knew how to speak her mind. She didn't like that couple living together, the ones next-door-but-one, whatever they're called, the people that run a business from home. I said times had changed from when she got married, but it didn't make any difference. I mean, everyone does that now, I said. But she wouldn't have it, would she, Uncle?'

They were all looking at her, Robson as well. She seemed to realize how animated her manner had been for one so recently bereaved and she flushed. Not much real love there, Burden thought, and said, 'Now we'd like to take a look round the house. Is that OK?'

She would have argued but Robson, having eaten almost nothing, pushing away his plate, nodded and waved one hand in an odd gesture of assent. Wexford wouldn't have bothered with the house; there was nothing relevant to Mrs Robson's life or death he expected to find. He was already half-adhering to the girl's view, that some badly disturbed person had killed Gwen Robson for no better reason than that she was there and a woman, unprepared and frail enough. However, he made his way into the bedroom she had shared with Robson and saw everywhere signs of domestic harmony. The bed was unmade. On an impulse aimed at no particular enlightening discovery, Wexford lifted up the flatter and less rumpled of the pillows and found underneath it Mrs Robson's nightdress just as it must have been folded and tucked away by her on Thursday morning . . .

A framed photograph showed her as she had once been, her hair dark and plentiful, mouth widely smiling, plumper than now. She was seated and her husband was looking over her shoulder, perhaps to give an illusion of the greater height he had not possessed. The books on her bedside cabinet were two novels of Catherine Cookson, on his the latest Robert Ludlum. On the dressing table a small container of Yardley 'Chique' perfume stood between his hairbrush and a pincushion in which were pinned three brooches. A surprising number of pictures covered the walls: more framed photographs of the two of them, a framed collage of postcards, sentimental mementoes of their own holidays, cat and dog pictures perhaps cut from calendars, a cottage in the flowery garden embroidered by someone – perhaps Gwen Robson herself.

The curtains in the room were as floral as this picture. In spite of her sober style of dressing, she had liked bright colours – pinks and blues and yellows. She might have worn brown, but she would not have furnished her house with it. A neatly stacked pile of *Kim* magazines occupied half the top of a long stool and on top of these lay last night's evening paper. Did that mean that the night after his wife had been murdered Robson had taken the evening paper up with him for his bedtime reading? Well, why not? Life must go on. And no doubt he had been given sleeping pills, had needed something to read while waiting for the drug to take effect. Wexford just glanced at the lead story and the photograph of the barrister Edmund Hope, as handsome and striking-looking as any of the Arab bombers he was prosecuting, then he turned away to study the view.

Beyond the window the Highlands estate presented a panorama of itself she must often have seen while standing here: Hastings Road where the house was, Eastbourne Road leading down to the town, Battle Hill mounting to the crown of the estate, pantiled roofs deliberately placed at odd angles to one another to give the illusion of some little hillside town in Spain or Portugal – coniferous trees bluish, dark green and golden-green because conifers are cheap and grow swiftly, winding gravel paths and concrete paths, windows dressed in Austrian blinds, looped-up festoons and frills, one solitary resident only to be seen: an elderly, very stout woman in long skirt and multi-coloured jacket who was breaking into pieces the end of a loaf of bread and putting them on to a bird-table in a garden diagonally opposite. The house she returned to was the first of those past the row of old people's sheltered housing. She looked back once at where Mrs Robson had lived, as anyone must look who lived here or came into this street. That was human nature. Her eyes met Wexford's and she immediately looked away. It was rather as Lesley Arbel had quickly put away her mirror and brush, as if this would negate the past act.

Wexford said, 'We may as well go. We'll give Mrs Sanders a ring and get her down to the station.'

'You wouldn't prefer to go to her?'

'No, I'd prefer to give her a bit of trouble,' said Wexford.

4

It was spread out on the table in the interview room – a curtain that had once been handsome, of a rich thick-piled tobacco-brown velvet, lined and weighted at the two corners of its lower hem. But splashed the centre of it was a large dark stain, a stain which might have been blood but which Wexford had already ascertained was not. Other stains had since been super-added; there was certainly an impression that the original splashings had ruined the curtain as a curtain, and that since the occurrence which had led to them any further damage to the velvet had been of no account.

Dorothy Sanders looked at it. Her eyes flicked and as she looked back at Wexford he noticed for the first time that they were of a curious pale fawn colour.

'That's the curtain that used to hang up on my door.' And then, after a long blank stare at Wexford had elicited no particular reaction, 'It's still got the hooks in it.'

He continued to stand and watch her, his face expressing nothing, but now he gave a small reflective nod. Burden was frowning.

'Where did you get it?' she said. 'What's it doing here?'

'It was covering Mrs Robson's body,' Burden said. 'Don't you remember?'

The change in her was electric. She jumped back, retracting arms and hands as if it were offal or slime her fingers had touched. Her face flushed darkly, her lips sucked in. She put a hand to her mouth – a characteristic gesture, he thought – and then flung the hand away, aware of what it had been in contact with. He had a glimpse then of how this slow, deliberate woman could become a screaming demented crea-

479

ture, and for the first time he understood that the old man called Archie Greaves might not have been exaggerating.

'You've touched it before, Mrs Sanders,' he said. 'You pulled it back to look at her face.'

She shuddered, her arms stretched out and shaking as if she could shake off her hands and so get rid of them.

'Come and sit down, Mrs Sanders.'

'I want to wash my hands. Where can I go and wash my hands?'

Wexford didn't want her to run away, but as he picked up the phone DC Marian Bayliss tapped on the door and came in. She began on a routine question and he nodded assent and said, 'Would you take Mrs Sanders to the ladies' loo, please?'

Dorothy Sanders was brought back after about five minutes, calm again, stony-faced and with more red lipstick on her mouth. He could smell the police station liquid soap ten feet away.

'Have you any suggestions, Mrs Sanders, as to how your curtain came to be covering Mrs Robson's body?'

'I didn't put it there. The last time I saw it was in a ...' she hesitated, went on more carefully, '... a room in my house. Folded up. In the attic, they call them attics. My son may have gone up there; he may have wanted it for something, though he'd no business ... without me saying he could.' A grim look cramped her features.

This hadn't occurred to Wexford as a possibility before, but it did now. 'Does your son live with you, Mrs Sanders?'

'Of course he lives with me.' She spoke as if, though it were possible there were some very few grown-up children who through general viciousness or perhaps being orphans lived apart from their parents, such situations were rare enough to provoke incredulity and even disgust. She spoke as if Wexford were a depraved ignoramus to suppose otherwise. 'Of course he lives with me. Where did you think he lived?'

'Are you sure this curtain was in a room in your house? It couldn't have been in the boot of your car?'

She was no fool. At least, she was sharp enough.

'Not unless he put it there.' The identity of 'he' was evident enough. She thought, reasoned, nodded her head. This was

480

not one of those women, Wexford thought with a kind of grim amusement, who even at the cost of their own lives would protect a child, criminal or otherwise – the kind who hid a wanted son or lied when questioned as to his whereabouts, who regarded a son not so much as an extension of herself, but as a precious superior. 'I expect he did put it there,' she now said. 'I'd sent through my catalogue for a proper nylon cover for the car. Nylon or fibreglass or one of those things.' Mail order she meant, Wexford decided. 'I'd sent for it a good two months ago, but they take their time, these people. I expect he couldn't wait.'

'She looked up at him, making him perform one of those about-turns in his assessment of human nature. For moment he felt he knew nothing; people and their ways were as much a mystery as ever they had been. She looked human at least, she spoke in a human way. 'He's not like me he hasn't got much patience. He can't help it. I expect he thought he'd just take that curtain and use it when we had a cold spell. You can't be kept waiting about for ever, can you?' She looked down at her watch, drawn to this recorder of time's passage by her references to its delays. Her wrist was like a bundle of wires, thinly insulated.

Burden had been pacing up and down. He said, 'It's your car but your son uses it?'

'It's my car,' she said. 'I bought it and paid for it and I'm the registered owner. But he has to go to work, doesn't he? I let him use it to go to work and then if I want to go shopping, he can take me and pick me up. He's got to have transport.'

'What does your son do, Mrs Sanders?'

She was one of those who expect their private arrangements to be intimately known by others, to need no elucidation, yet who show affront when those others reveal a knowledge gained by sensitivity or intuition. 'He's a teacher, isn't he?'

'You tell me,' Burden said.

She curled her nostrils in disgust. 'He teaches in a school for children who can't pass their exams without extra coaching.'

A crammer's, Wexford thought. Probably Munster's in Kingsmarkham High Street. It surprised him a little and yet

481

– why not? Clifford Sanders, he thought in the light of his new knowledge, would be one of those who lived at home while they attended university, going to and fro by bus. It would be interesting to find out if he was right there.

'Part-time,' she said, and astonished them both by saying in the same level, indifferent tone, 'He's inadequate in some ways.'

'What's wrong with him? Is he ill?'

Her old harshly censorious manner was back. 'They call it ill nowadays. When I was young, they called it lacking character.' A dark flush moved into her cheeks, mottling them. She was dressed in green today, a dark dull green, though her shoes and gloves were black. When the blush faded, the dull seaweed green seemed to show up the pallor of her skin. 'That's where he was, wasn't he, when he was supposed to be coming for me in the car park? He'd been to this psychiatrist. They call them psychotherapists; they don't have any qualifications.'

'Mrs Sanders, are you telling me that your son was in the Barringdean Centre car park when you were?'

Emotions warred behind the blush, the succeeding pallor, the muffling screen of green and black. She had not meant to let that out. Protecting her son was not as unknown to her as Wexford had at first believed: he could even see that in an intense, self-disgusted, incredulous way she loved her son, but perhaps she had not been able to resist that dig at a profession she disapproved of. She spoke with extreme care now, the pace of the voice electronically slowed to make understanding easier.

'He should have been there but he was not. He had come in, the car was there, but he . . .' she paused, breathing deeply, '. . . was not.'

An abrupt halting explanation followed. At first, when she saw the car and a body, she had thought it was Clifford lying there dead. She couldn't see the body because it was covered up and believing it to be Clifford, she pulled back the brown velvet covering. It wasn't Clifford, but it had been a great shock just the same. She had had to sit in her car and rest, recover herself. Clifford had been going to pick her

up as he always did on Thursdays, always. It was an unvary-
ing arrangement, though the school time might vary. She
looked at her watch as she said this. Clifford brought her to
the shopping centre, went to his session with the psychotherapist, returned to pick her up. She didn't drive. This Thursday they had arranged for him to be in the car park on the
second level by six-fifteen. On her arrival she had had her
hair done at Suzanne's on the upper floor of the centre –
another inflexible arrangement – shopped, come back to the
car park at twelve minutes past six.

After the shock of finding the body, after she had recovered
somewhat – Wexford found this frailty of hers rather hard
to believe in – she had gone up to look for Clifford. She had
walked about looking for him, a statement that was confirmed by Archie Greaves. At last she had gone to the pedestrian gates . . .

'I broke down,' she said, giving each word equal monotonous weight.

'Where was your son, then? No, you needn't answer that,
Mrs Sanders. You tell him we're interested and we'll have a
talk with him later. We'll all take a break and he can do
some thinking. How's that?'

She moved towards the door. Someone would drive her
home. Her manner had in it something of the sleepwalker,
or as if almost everything she thought and felt – perhaps
momentous or amazing things – she kept veiled. She was so
thin and wiry you would expect her to be a brisk woman,
Wexford thought, but she was as languid as some slippery,
rotund sea creature. Burden said as soon as she had gone,
'Is she saying he's potty?'

'I should think that depends on how strict you are and – '
Wexford looked up at Burden with a half-smile, 'how out
of date. Apparently he can hold down a job and drive a car
and carry on a normal conversation. Is that what you mean?'

'You know it isn't. He sounds very much like a candidate
for Lesley Arbel's psychopath role to me.'

' "The outstanding feature is emotional immaturity in its
broadest and most comprehensive sense. These people are
impulsive, feckless, unwilling to accept the results of experience and unable to profit by them . . ." ' Wexford faltered
for a moment, then went on, ' " . . . sometimes prodigal of

483

effort but utterly lacking in persistence, plausible but insincere, demanding but indifferent to appeals, dependable only in their constant unreliability, faithful only to infidelity, rootless, unstable, rebellious and unhappy".'

Burden gaped a bit. 'Did you make that up?'

'Of course I didn't. It's David Stafford-Clark's definition of a psychopath – or part of it. I learned it by heart because I thought it might come in useful, but I can't say it ever has.' Wexford grinned. 'I liked the prose too.'

The expression on Burden's face rather indicated that he didn't know what prose was. 'I think it's very useful. It's good. I like that bit about dependable in their constant unreliability.'

'Oxymoron.'

'Is that another mental disease?' When Wexford only shook his head, Burden said, 'That bit you quoted – is it in a book? Can I get it?'

'I'll lend you my copy. I expect it's out of print; it must be twenty years since I read it. But you can't apply that to Clifford Sanders, you know. You've hardly talked to him.'

'That can be remedied,' said Burden grimly.

It was dark as Wexford drove along the street where he lived and approached his own house. A car was parked on his garage drive, Sheila's Porsche. He felt a tiny dip of the heart and immediately reproached himself. He loved his daughters dearly and Sheila was his favourite, but for once he wouldn't be elated to see her. A quiet evening was what he had looked forward to; it might be the last for a long time, for he had no faith in Burden's forecast of the straightforwardness of this case. And now it would be given over not only to talk, but talk on serious matters.

Irritation of a different kind succeeded this initial flash of dismay. She had parked her car on the garage drive because she supposed him to be home already, even supposed this to be his day off as it should have been, and expected his car to be inside the garage. Now he would have to leave it out in the street. Unburdening her heart to her mother would have taken priority over everything. He could imagine her

484

saying every ten minutes or so how she must rush out and move the car before darling Pop got home . . .

Thinking like that cheered him, made him smile to himself, hearing with his mind's ear her enchanting, slightly breathless voice. He would say nothing, he resolved, of the wire-cutting, the reports of her coming divorce; he would utter no word of reproach, certainly no intimation of disappointment or upset, would cast on her no grave looks. He touched the Porsche lightly on its long, gleaming, nearly horizontal rear window as he passed it. Did she go to demonstrations in that? Well, it was only a small Porsche and black at that . . . Would she come and kiss his cheek or would she hang back? There was no knowing. He went in the back way, into the hall from the kitchen, hung up his coat, hearing her voice from the living room – hearing the voice of Beatrice Cenci, Antigone, Nora Helmer and now Lady Audley – falter and fall silent. He went into the room and immediately she was rushing to him and in his arms.

Over her shoulder he saw the small satirical smile on Dora's face. He hugged Sheila and as she relaxed, distanced her with his arms stretched and said, 'Are you OK?'

'Well, I don't know,' she giggled. 'Not really. I'm not really OK. I'm in an awful mess. And Mother's being very sniffy. Mother's being horrible, actually.'

Her rueful smile showed him this was only half-meant. Foolish this was, he knew it every time, but when he looked at her like this he could never help admiring afresh the beautiful, fair, sensitive face that would with luck defy time, the long, pale, soft hair, the eyes as clear as a child's and as blue, but not a child's. There was no wedding ring on her left hand, but often she wore no rings, just as she nearly always kept her fancy clothes for public or publicity appearances. The jeans she wore were shabby compared with Burden's. She had on a blue sweater of a similar shade and a string of wooden beads.

'Now you're home, darling,' said Dora, 'we can all have a drink. I'm sure I need it. In fact . . .' she looked from one to the other with a certain tact, with a knowledge that they might care for two minutes alone together, '. . . I'll get it.'

Sheila fell back into the chair she had jumped out of.

'Aren't you going to ask me why? Why, why, why everything?'

'No.'

'You have a blind faith in the rightness of everything I do?'

'You know I don't.' He was tempted to say of the husband she had left, 'I liked Andrew,' but he didn't say it. 'What are we talking about, anyway? Which of your sensational acts?'

'Oh, Pop, I had to cut the wire. It wasn't done hysterically or without thinking or for publicity or in defiance or anything. I *had* to do it. I've been psyching myself up to it for ever so long. People take notice of what I do, you see. I don't just mean *me*, I mean anyone in my position. They kind of say, "If Sheila Wexford does it there must be some meaning to it, there must be a point if a famous person like her does it".'

'What happened?' He was genuinely curious.

'I bought a pair of wire-cutters in a DIY place in Covent Garden. There were ten of us, all members of PANDA – Players Anti-Nuclear Direct Action – only I was the only well-known one. We went to a place in Northamptonshire called Lossington and we went in three cars, mine and two others. It's an RAF station where they have obsolete bombers. The importance of the place doesn't matter, you see, it's the gesture . . .'

'Of course I see,' he said a little impatiently.

'There was this bleak plain with a couple of concrete huts and some hangars and grass all round and mud and a wire fence gone rusty – miles of it, and high enough not to lose tennis balls if you were playing inside. Well, we all stood up against the wire and each of us cut a bit and a great flap of wire came down, then we went to the nearest town and the police station and walked in and told them what we'd done and . . .'

Dora came in with their drinks on a tray – beer for Wexford, wine for herself and her daughter. Having heard the last words, she said, 'You might have given a little more thought to your father.'

'Oh, Pop, the first idea was for us to cut the wire at RAF Myringford, but I stood out against that because of you,

486

because it was on your patch. I did think of you. But I had to do it, I *had* to – can't you understand?'

His temper for an instant got the better of him. 'You're not Antigone, however much you may have played her. You're not Bunyan. Don't keep saying you *had* to do it. Do you really believe your cutting the wire round an obsolete bomber station or whatever is going to lead to a total ban on nuclear arms? I don't like them, you know, I don't believe anyone likes them; I'm afraid of them. When you and Sylvia were little I used to be – oppressed with fear for you. And if they've kept the peace for forty-five years, that doesn't mean a thing; it certainly doesn't mean they'll keep it for ninety. But I know better than to suppose this kind of thing is going to affect government.'

'What else can we do?' she said simply. 'I often think I don't believe that either, but what else can we do? They all think that banning Cruise missiles solves everything, but they're getting rid of less than ten per cent of the world's arsenal. The alternative is apathy, is pretending everything's solved.'

'You mean that "for evil to triumph",' Wexford said, ' "it is only necessary for good men to do nothing"?'

But Dora followed sharply with, 'Or do you mean that between the early warning and the bomb going off you'll have ten minutes in which to congratulate yourself on not being an ostrich?'

Sheila sat up, was silent for a while. It was as if what her mother said had not touched her, had gone unheard. Then she said very quietly, 'If you're a human being, you have to be against nuclear weapons. It's a . . . a sort of definition. Like . . . like mammals suckle their young and insects have six legs. The definition of a human being is one who hates and fears and wants to be rid of nuclear weapons. Because they're the evil, they're the modern equivalent of the devil, of Antichrist – they are all we'll ever know of hell.'

After that, as he remarked to Dora while Sheila made a mysterious secret phone call, there didn't seem any more to be said. Or not for the present. Dora sighed. 'She says Andrew's right wing and only interested in capitalism and he doesn't have an inner life.'

'Presumably she knew that before she married him,' Wexford said.

'She isn't in love any more and that always makes a difference.'

'It's not so much a depraved society that we live in as an idealistic one. People expect to remain in love with their partners all their lives or else break up and start again. Are you still in love with me?'

'Oh, darling, you know I love you very much, I'm devoted to you, I'd be lost without you, I –'

'Exactly,' said her husband, laughing, and he went outside to get himself another beer.

Nothing had been said about Sheila staying the night. She had arrived at four and in the usual course of things would have started back for London at about nine. It was less than an hour's drive. But the phone call she had made changed her mind, or so it seemed. She came back into the room looking pleased, looking happier than she had since Wexford arrived home, and announced that if they didn't mind – this with the self-confidence of the always-beloved child to whom parents' 'minding' was unknown – she would stay until tomorrow, she might even stay until after lunch tomorrow.

'Mother's the only person I know who still cooks roast beef and Yorkshire pudding for Sunday lunch.'

Wexford thought that asking her where she was living now could hardly be construed as interference, but he resisted saying how much he had liked the house in Hampstead.

'I had to move out, didn't I? I couldn't go on living in Downshire Hill, in Andrew's house that he'd paid for, and turn him out. Someone told him it was worth two million.' She sat down on the floor, hugging her knees. 'I can't cope with that kind of money. I've got this flat in Bloomsbury, Coram Fields, and it's OK, it's really quite grand.' She flashed a smile at her father. 'You'll like it.'

Dora had the *Radio Times* on her lap. 'Nearly time for Lady Audley. I don't want to miss it, so if you don't like watching yourself I'll have to send you to bed.'

'Oh, Mother. Do you really imagine I haven't seen it? I don't mind watching it again with you, but of course I saw a preview. Look, I must rush outside though and move my car so that Pop can put his in. No, I'll move mine, and put his in. It doesn't matter if I miss the beginning of – '

'I'll move the cars,' Wexford interposed. 'We've got five minutes. Keys, please, Sheila.'

She fished them out of her jeans pocket. His car was a little wide for the garage and he had made his offer less out of altruism than for fear of getting the new Montego scraped. Dora switched on the television. The wind had dropped and the night was dark and quiet, rather misty, each streetlamp a yellow blur. Between his garden and the empty site next door that had never been built on, the fence was sagging, in places laid flat on the flowerbed where the wind had felled it. The last few leaves on the cherry tree in his front lawn had been shrivelled by early frost and still clung to the nearly bare branches. Leaves lay everywhere, dark and wet, a blackened coating on path and pavement. Someone had found a child's Fair Isle glove on this mat of leaves and laid it on top of the low wall. The street was deserted. In a bay window opposite, between dark evergreen shrubs standing like sentries, between open curtains, he saw the blue glow of a screen suddenly flooded with colour and his daughter's face filling it in close-up.

Sheila hadn't locked the Porsche. Wexford opened the door and got into the driving-seat. It was an irony that his much cheaper and less prestigious car had automatic transmission, while this one had a manual gearbox. Presumably Sheila preferred it that way. The Montego had been his for only six months and it was the first automatic car he had ever possessed, but even so he was coming as near to forgetting about letting in clutches and shifting handles. So much so that when he switched on the ignition he failed to notice she had left the car in bottom gear. It jumped – being a powerful sports car it bounded like a spirited horse – and stalled. Wexford grinned to himself. So much for his conviction that he was the more careful driver. Another two inches and the Porsche would have hit his garage doors.

He moved the gear lever into neutral and switched on the engine once more. His foot on the clutch pedal, he was moving the lever into reverse when he became aware of a feeling of unparalleled strangeness, an unaccountable sen-

489

sation of being more than usually alert and alive. It was as if he were young again, a young man with the vigour and carefree nature of youth. Some strengthening elixir seemed to surge through his veins. On this damp, dark night when he was tired at the end of a long hard day, he was visited with a renewal of youth and power, a springiness in muscle and nerves like a young athlete's.

All this was momentary. It came in a flash that was also a piercing ray of enlightenment. Did he hear anything? The ticking mechanism as of a clock – or was that imagination, some vibration in his brain? The thrusting gear slid into the reverse position, made contact, and without knowing why, without a pause for reasoning, he flung open the car door and precipitated himself with all his force horizontally out as the roar came behind him, the earthquake, the loudest most violent explosion he had ever known.

It happened simultaneously, all of it – the bomb going off, the leap from the doomed car, the fierce blinding pain as he struck his head on something cold and upright and hard as iron . . .

5

After Dorothy Sanders had been driven home, Burden meant to go to the Irelands' house at Myringford. But he would be too late now to see his son put to bed, too late to enjoy (as Wexford, quoting, had once expressed it) '. . . those attractions by no means unusual in children of two or three years old; an imperfect articulation, an earnest desire of having his own way, many cunning tricks and a great deal of noise.' His wife didn't expect him until later and the house would be full of visiting relatives.

Instead, after a lapse of ten minutes or so and without giving any warning of his intention, he followed Dorothy Sanders. Something in her son's appearance and manner told him this wasn't the kind of young man who went out on Saturday nights. And indeed it was Clifford himself who opened the door to him. His was a shut-in face, mask-like and inexpressive, with a pudginess about the features. He spoke lifelessly, showing no apparent surprise at another visit from a policeman. Burden was rather curiously reminded of a dog owned by a former neighbour of his. The owner had been inordinately proud of its submission, its total obedience, the subservience with which it had responded to his severe training. And one day, without warning, without any apparent prior change in its character, it had savaged a child.

Clifford, however, seemed to have the right idea and was leading Burden into that back room to which, on the inspector's previous visit with Wexford, he had retreated to watch television, when his mother opened the living-room door and said in her slow harsh voice to come in, as there could be

491

nothing the policeman had to say to her son which she couldn't hear.

'I'll have a word with Mr Sanders on his own for the time being, if you don't mind,' Burden said.

'I do mind.' She was rude in a way that wasn't even defiant; it was uncompromising, straight rudeness, with a straight look into her interlocutor's eye. 'There's no reason why I shouldn't be there. This is my house and he'll need me to get his facts straight.'

Clifford neither blushed nor turned pale; he did not even wince. He simply stared ahead of him as if thinking of something deeply sad. Long, long ago Burden had learned that you do not let the public get the better of you. Lawyers, yes, inevitably sometimes, but not the untrained public.

'In that case, I'll ask you to accompany me to the police station, Mr Sanders.'

'He won't go. He's not well, he's got a cold.'

'That's unfortunate, but you leave me no choice. I've my car here, Mr Sanders. If you'd like to get your coat on? It's a nasty damp night.'

She yielded, going back into the room she had come from and slamming the door with calculation, not from temper. Burden resisted the hackneyed maxim that bullies give way if you stand up to them, but he had found nevertheless that it was usually true. Would Clifford profit by his example? Probably not. It had gone too far with him; he needed help of a more expert kind. And it was of this that Burden first asked him when they were seated in the bleak dining room, furnished only with table, hard upright chairs and television set. On one wall hung a mirror, on another a large dark and very bad painting in oils of a sailing vessel on a rough sea.

'Yes, I go to Serge Olson. It's a sort of Jungian therapy he does. Do you want his address?'

Burden nodded, noted it down. 'May I ask why you go to . . . Dr Olson, is it?'

Clifford, who showed no signs of the cold his mother claimed for him, was looking at the mirror but not into it. Burden would have sworn he was not seeing his own reflection. 'I need help,' he said.

Something about the rigidity of his figure, his stillness and the dullness of his eyes stopped Burden pursuing this. Instead

492

he asked if Clifford had been to the psychotherapist on Thursday afternoon and what time he had left.

'It's an hour I go for, five till six. My mother told me you knew I was in the car park – I mean, that I put the car there.'

'Yes. Why didn't you tell us that at first?'

He shifted his eyes, not to Burden's face but to the middle of his chest. And when he answered Burden recognized the phraseology, the manner of speech, as that which people in therapy – no matter how inhibited, reserved, disturbed – inevitably pick up. He had heard it before. 'I felt threatened.'

'By what?'

'I'd like to talk to Serge now. If I'd had some sort of warning I'd have tried to make an appointment with him and talk it through with him.'

'I'm afraid you're going to have to make do with me, Mr Sanders.'

Burden was apprehensive for a moment that he was to be confronted with total silence against which even an experienced detective can do little. Sounds from Mrs Sanders could now be heard. She was in the kitchen, moving about, making an unnecessary noise by putting crockery down heavily and banging instead of closing cupboard doors. Whatever she was doing it seemed to be contrived to disturb. He winced at the sound of something breaking as it fell from her hands on to a stone floor. And then he heard another sound – he had got up to stand by the window – and this was far distant, the dull roar of an explosion. He stood quite still, his ear to the glass, listening to the reverberations die away. But he thought no more of it once Clifford began to speak.

'I'll try and tell you what happened. I should have told you before, but I felt threatened. I feel threatened now, but I'd be worse if I didn't tell you. I left Serge's place and I drove to the car park to pick up my mother. I saw there was a dead person lying there before I parked the car. I went to look at it – when I had parked the car, I mean – because I meant to call the police. You could see the person had been killed; that was the first thing you could see.'

'What time was this?'

He shrugged. 'Oh, evening. Early evening. My mother wanted me there at a quarter-past six. I think it was before that; it must have been, because she wasn't there and she's never late.'

'Why didn't you call the police, Mr Sanders?'

He looked at the picture on the wall, then at the dark shiny window. Burden saw his reflection in it, impassive, one would have said devoid of feeling.

'I thought it was my mother.'

Burden turned his eyes from the reflected image in the dark glass. 'You what?'

With patience, in a heavy, almost sorrowful way, Clifford repeated what he had said. 'I thought it was my mother.'

And she had thought it was her son. What was the matter with the pair of them that each expected to find the other dead? 'You thought Mrs Robson was your mother?' There was a slight resemblance between the two women, Burden thought wonderingly – that is, to a stranger there might be. Both were of an age, thin, grey-haired, dressed in the same kind of clothes of the same sort of colour . . . but to a son?

'I knew it wasn't really my mother. Well, after the first shock I knew. I can't explain what I felt. I could tell Serge, but I don't think you would understand. First I thought it was my mother, then I knew it wasn't and then I thought someone was doing it to . . . to mock me. I thought they had put it there to get at me. No, not quite that. I said I couldn't explain. I can only say it made me panic. I thought this was an awful trick they were persecuting me with, but I knew it couldn't be. I knew both things at the same time. I was very confused – you don't understand, do you?'

'I can't say I do, Mr Sanders. But go on.'

'I said I panicked. My "shadow" had taken me over completely. I had to get out of there, but I couldn't just leave it lying there like that. Other people would see it like I had.' Dark colour had come into his face now and he held his hands clasped tightly. 'I had an old curtain in the boot of the car I'd used to cover the windscreen in cold weather. I covered it up with that.' Suddenly he shut his eyes, screwing them up as if to drive away the sight, to blind himself. 'It wasn't covered, you understand, when I found it, not when I found it. I covered it up and then I went away, I ran away. I left the car and ran out of the car park. Someone was in the lift, so I ran up the stairs. I went home, I ran out into the street at the back and then home.'

'It didn't occur to you then that you'd meant to phone the police.'

The eyes opened and he expelled his breath. Burden repeated his question and Clifford said, with a tinge of exasperation now, 'What did it matter? Someone would phone them, I knew that. It didn't have to be me.'

'You went out by the pedestrian gates, I suppose.' Burden remembered Archie Greaves' evidence, the running 'boy' he had taken for a scared shoplifter. And he remembered what Wexford had said about the sound of feet pounding down the car park stairs. That had been Wexford in the lift. 'Did you run all the way home? It's getting on for three miles.'

'Of course I did.' The voice held a tinge of contempt.

Burden left it. 'Did you know Mrs Robson?'

The blank look was back, the colour returned to normal – a clay pallor. Clifford had never once smiled; it was hard to imagine what his smile would be like. 'Who's Mrs Robson?' he said.

'Come now, Mr Sanders. You know better than that. Mrs Robson is the woman who was killed.'

'I told you I thought it was my mother.'

'Yes, but when you realized it couldn't be?'

He looked Burden in the eyes for the first time. 'I didn't think any more.' It was a devastating remark. 'I told you, I didn't think, I panicked.'

'What did you mean just now by your "shadow"?'

Was it a pitying look Clifford Sanders gave him? 'It's the negative side of personality, isn't it? It's the sum of the bad characteristics in us we want to hide.'

Not at all satisfied with what he had been told, finding the whole of this man's behaviour and much of his talk incomprehensible and even sinister, Burden resolved just the same to pursue it no further until the next day. It was at this point, though, that his determination began to take shape, a decision to get to the bottom of Clifford's disturbed mind and whatever motives had their source there. His behaviour was immensely suspicious; and more than that – disingenuous. The man was trying to make him, Burden, look a fool; he thought himself the possessor of an intellect superior to a policeman's. Burden was familiar with this attitude and the reaction it produced in himself – the chip on his shoulder, as Wexford called it – but he could not be persuaded that it was unjustified.

In the living room now, he talked to a rigid and sullen Dorothy Sanders, getting nowhere in his attempts to discover if Mrs Robson had been known to the family. Clifford brought in a basket of coal, fed a fire which did little to raise the temperature in the room, went away and returned with soap-smelling hands. Both mother and son insisted Mrs Robson had been unknown to them, but Burden had the curious feeling that though Dorothy Sanders' ignorance was genuine, her son was lying, or at least evading the truth for some obscure reason of his own. On the other hand, Clifford might have killed without motivation, or without the kind of motivation that would be understandable to a rational man. For instance, suppose he had not found a dead body and thought it was his mother's but had seen a woman who had suggested to him his mother in her worst aspects and for this reason had himself killed her?

After leaving them, Burden drove further down the narrow road which he now remembered – though there was nothing to show it – was called Ash Lane. The Sanders' house therefore was very likely Ash Farm. But as this passed through his mind and as he was thinking that they seemed to have no neighbours, he came to a bungalow set a little way back from the road which proclaimed itself as Ash Farm Lodge on a rustic board attached to wrought-iron gates. This he could see in his headlights. The bungalow itself was in darkness but as he paused, the engine running and the headlights beam undipped, a light came on in the house and a man appeared at the window.

Burden reversed and began turning the car, a lengthy process in that narrow defile. When he was once more pointing in the direction of Kingsmarkham he glanced to his right and with a start – more a jolt than an actual shock – he saw that the man had come outside and was standing on the doorstep looking at the car, his hand clutching the collar of a cowed-looking retriever. By now the whole place – with the two barns and tall silo behind it, plainly the present farmhouse – blazed with light. Burden drove off. He wouldn't have been surprised to hear a shotgun let off behind him, or to see the dog frenziedly pursuing the car. But nothing happened, there was only darkness and silence and an owl calling.

The news about Wexford reached Burden in a peculiarly horrible way. It was due to his own haste and keenness, he afterwards realized, behaving like some young ambitious copper instead of enjoying his day of rest. Of course, the point was that it would hardly have been a day of rest with Jenny's demanding mother and the Ireland aunts, and Jenny running up; and down stairs. Even if he had glanced at the Sunday paper before he left Myringford, he would only have read commentaries on the latest dramatic developments in the Israeli Embassy trial; there would have been nothing in it about the car bomb. The explosion had happened too late in the evening for that. And because the house was full of guests, no one had looked at television on Saturday night.

He phoned Ralph Robson before he left, but it was Lesley Arbel who answered, who agreed to his coming though telling him she couldn't think why as they had absolutely nothing more to tell him. Driving up the hill to Highlands, he told himself it was a pointless interview he had ahead of him, as the obvious thing was to wait until the next day and consult the Social Services department of Kingsmarkham Council. They might keep no records of those for whom their past home helps had worked, but they were more likely to put forward ideas and suggestions than Ralph Robson was.

The invalidism his niece fostered still kept the widower in his dressing gown. He seemed to have aged even in this short time, to hobble more painfully and be more bent. He sat by the gas fire with on his lap a little circular tray fancifully printed with wild birds in improbable colours, on which reposed a cup of tea and a plate of sugar-frosted biscuits. Burden had hardly been taken into the room by the girl – who this morning was dressed in a pink silk outfit, a kind of trouser suit with sarong top and harem pants, and very high-heeled pink shoes – when there came a ring at the doorbell and another visitor arrived. Lesley Arbel had no scruples about showing in the newcomer, though he must have been aware that Burden expected a private interview with her uncle. It was the neighbour opposite he and Wexford had seen from the window who had called, a Mrs Jago as far as Burden could gather from the mumbled introduction Robson made.

The reason for the visit seemed to be the usual one at a time of bereavement. She had come to see if there was anything she could do – any shopping, for instance, that she could get on the following day when Lesley Arbel had gone. Burden wasn't much interested in her, noticing only that she was a large stout woman, puffily overweight, dark and florid, and with a strong accent that suggested Central Europe to him. At least she seemed to have the tact or the good sense to realize Burden wanted privacy, and she left again as soon as Robson had said he would take up her offer and would she mind coming in again on the following morning?

The front door had scarcely closed and Lesley Arbel passed the hall mirror with an inevitable glance into it, when Robson said, 'It's time they did something for us. It's their turn, the lot of them. When you consider what my wife did for everyone in this blessed street, never spared herself, nothing was too much trouble. She'd only to hear someone was a bit under the weather and she'd be round seeing what she could do. Especially the old folks. I reckon she did more good on her own than all those so-called social services people. Isn't that right, Lesley?'

'She did a lot more good than my agony aunt,' Lesley said. 'Well, she was a sort of agony aunt herself, wasn't she? I used to call her that – joking, of course.'

Mystified, Burden echoed her words. 'Your agony aunt?'

'People brought her their troubles, didn't they?' It was Robson who answered for her. 'She works,' he said in a rather proud way, 'for the agony aunt on the magazine. For *Kim*. It's the problem page – you know, all those letters from readers about their troubles that the agony aunt answers. Lesley's her assistant.'

'Secretary, Uncle.'

'A bit more than a blessed secretary to my way of thinking. More a right hand. I thought you knew all that,' he said to Burden.

498

'No,' Burden shook his head. 'No, I didn't know. Your aunt – I mean your real aunt, Mrs Robson – I understand she'd been a council home help. Can you remember the names of some of the people she worked for?'

He addressed this question as much to Robson as his niece and Robson immediately took exception to it. 'Home helps don't work for people. They don't have employers, they have clients. They're more civil servants really.'

With an effort at patience Burden accepted this. He had to listen while Robson made out a case for his wife's having carried out her civil servant's function in the home of (it sounded like) every elderly, sick or deprived person in greater Kingsmarkham. Individual names, though, he couldn't recall. He enumerated the tasks his wife and performed gratuitously for the neighbours, and by association this recalled shopping to him and from here the two bags of groceries which the police still retained. With a slightly scathing edge to his voice, he said, 'I suppose you'll say you've got too much on your plates with last night's trouble to worry about a minor matter like that.'

'Last night's trouble?'

'The car bomb. One of your blokes got blown up, didn't he?'

Lesley Arbel said, 'The one that was here with you – or that's how I understood it from the TV. I'm sure it was his name they said.'

Practice at not showing one's feelings comes in useful. And it is true that shock stuns. Burden remembered now the dull and distant explosion he had heard on the previous evening while standing up against the french windows in the Sanders' dining room. Some sense of dignity, some knowledge that it would be wrong and a matter for later regret to do so, stopped him enquiring any more from Robson and his niece. But he was numbed with shock too, getting up almost mechanically, making routine remarks, the replies to which he found afterwards that he had totally forgotten. He was aware too – and this he did remember – of their faces looking at him curiously and with a mild, perhaps only imagined, malice.

Robson said something more about his groceries, something about wanting them before he gave his neighbour Mrs

Jago a shopping list, and then Burden had made his escape, was keeping himself from running to his car until the door had closed on Lesley Arbel's pink silk and high heels. He ran then.

Wexford's house was about as far from Highlands as it was possible to be, yet still be situated in Kingsmarkham. It wasn't wasting time, it was to calm himself, to make him a safer driver, that he went first into the phone box at the foot of the hill only to find it vandalized and the lead pulled from the wall. The second phone box he tried was the kind which, along with its fellows in the railway-station entrance, could only be operated with a Telecom card. Burden got back into the car, the palms of his hands damp and sliding on the steering wheel. He turned into Wexford's street with the feeling that he hadn't really breathed for five minutes; he seemed to have been holding his breath until his throat closed up. Yet all the time he was clinging to the hope that Robson and his niece might somehow be mistaken. Now he 'found the difference' as Wexford could have quoted him, 'between the expection of an unpleasant event, however certain the mind may be told to consider it, and certainty, itself.'

The sight of Wexford's house came as a second shock, and one not dulled by the first.

The garage was no longer there. The room over the garage was no longer there. The whole area between what remained of Wexford's house – the basic three-bedroomed structure – and the open ground next door was a heap of rubble, bits of car body, branches and twigs, shreds of fabric, twisted metal, broken glass. The side of the house from which the garage and the room above it had been torn was open to the weather – fortunately this morning mild and dry – and no attempt had yet been made to shroud in tarpaulins the gaping rooms in one of which a bed could be seen, in the other a picture hanging crooked on blue wallpaper. Burden sat in his car with the window down and stared at it. He stared in horror at the devastation and at the garden now revealed beyond, where fruit trees held leafless boughs against a tranquil pale blue sky.

In the middle of the front lawn the stout cherry tree still retained its branches – even, incredibly, some of its frostbitten leaves. And the lavender hedge which Wexford had

500

so frequently in the past weeks promised to trim back as soon as he had the time was mostly still there, while looking as if the passage through it of a heavy missile had crushed some of it to the ground. The front wall was still there and undamaged, a child's woollen glove lying on one of the piers; Burden couldn't imagine how it came to be there. He looked back again at the wreck of the house, at what seemed to him only half or less of a house remaining. Then, slowly, he got out of the car and walked towards the front door, though he knew there could be no one living there now. If either of them survived, there could be no one there now . . .

He found himself numbed where he stood, paralysed and quite unable to think how next to act, when a man came out of the house next door, the house Wexford called next door though it was separated from his by a narrow open space that no one had ever been able to decide was large enough for a building site.

He said to Burden, 'How is he? Is he..?'

'I know nothing. I didn't even know . . .'

It was as if the street had been watching for him, took him necessarily for the bringer of news. A woman came out from opposite, a couple with a small child from further down on the same side.

The man next door said, 'He was in the car, his daughter's car. Sheila, you know. It was a hell of a bang, like the bombs in the war. I can just remember the war. My wife and I, we came out and there was smoke and you couldn't see a thing. I said to phone the police first thing and I did, but someone else had done it already. The ambulance got here like a shot. I must hand it to them, they didn't waste time. But we couldn't see what happened, only that they took someone away on a stretcher and then it was on the late-night news on telly about Mr Wexford and a car bomb, but they didn't know much, they couldn't tell you much.'

'He was lying on the lawn there,' said the woman with the child. 'He was lying there unconscious.'

'He was blown out of the car,' said her husband. 'It was the most amazing thing. We were watching Sheila in her serial and we heard this terrific bang and it was here, it was her car . . .'

501

'Where are they now, Sheila and her mother?' Burden asked.

'Someone said they went to the other daughter, wherever she lives.'

Burden said no more. Shaking his head, aware that he held one hand pressed against it as if it ached, he went back to his car and started the engine.

6

His dream was of cherry trees, notably the one George Washington was said to have chopped down and then been unable to tell a lie about when questioned by his father. A white cherry though, presumably that was, like the ones he had seen in a picture somewhere that were planted along the shores of the Potomac. Because of Washington's particular affinity with cherry trees? It must be. Probably those pink double cherries whose flowers looked as if made from crêpe paper weren't invented then. The one in his garden had been given him a year after he moved into the house by his father-in-law and he had never liked its papery blossoms and unnatural weeping branches. though he had liked his father-in-law very much. The tree was pretty for one week of the year, around the end of April . . .

He wasn't dreaming any more; this was more in the nature of a reverie. In some cherry-growing areas they put scarecrows in the trees, and in others sewed together sheets of netting large enough to protect the fruit from birds. Not that his tree was the kind that ever bore fruit but was sterile, those bright fluffy blossoms falling and leaving not a trace behind. He was aware now of a dull ache in his head above the forehead, a pain unaccountably associated with cherry trees. And yet not unaccountably . . . no. He opened his eyes, said to anyone who might be there, though for all he knew no one was, 'Did I hit my head on the cherry tree?'

'Yes, darling.'

Dora was sitting at his bedside and round the two of them the curtains were drawn. He tried to sit up but she shook her head, putting out her hand.

503

'What time is it?'

'About eleven. About eleven on Sunday morning.' She read what was passing through his mind. 'You haven't been unconscious all this time; you came round in the ambulance on the way here. You've been asleep.'

'I don't seem to remember anything except hitting my head on the cherry tree. Oh, and taking a sort of flying leap for some unknown reason . . . maybe from the front doorstep? I can't think why.'

'There was a bomb,' she said, 'underneath the car. It wasn't our car, it was Sheila's. Something you did set it off – I mean, whoever had driven it would have set it off.'

Wexford digested that. He couldn't remember; he wondered if he ever would. Dora and Sheila had been watching television and he came into the front garden for something and leapt into the darkness as a man who flies in a dream might, but the tree was in his way . . . Dora, though, was saying he was in a car, Sheila's car.

'I was in a car?'

'You went out to move Sheila's car and put ours away.'

'The bomb was meant for Sheila?'

She said unhappily, 'It looks like that. Well, it must have been. You mustn't distress yourself, you're supposed to rest.'

'I'm all right. I've only had a bang on the head.'

'You've got cuts and bruises all over you.'

'It was meant for Sheila,' he said. 'Oh, God, thank God I drove it. Oh, thank God! I don't remember, but I must have driven it. Am I in the Infirmary? In Stowerton?'

'Where else? The Chief Constable's downstairs and he wants to see you. And Mike's dying to see you; he thought you were dead. It was on television about you. Lots of people thought you were dead, darling.'

Wexford was silent, digesting it. He wouldn't think about Sheila at the moment and how near she had been to death, he wouldn't think of that yet. A sense of humour began creeping back.

'One thing, we shan't have to have the fence done,' he said and then he went on, 'A bomb. Yes, a bomb. Have we got any house left?'

'Well, you mustn't distress yourself. A bit more than half a house.'

504

Burden was temporarily in charge of the Robson case. It was his belief that Wexford would be off for at least a fortnight, though Wexford himself said that a day or two would do it. That was what he said to Colonel Griswold, the Chief Constable, whose sympathy was conveyed in incredulity that Wexford could remember nothing about the bomb and unreasonable anger against Burden for going away for the night without telling anyone.

'I'll make them let me go home tomorrow,' he told Burden.

'I shouldn't — not if I'd got your home to go to.'

'Yes. Dora says there's only about half of it left. I never liked that garage extension; I said it was jerry-built. No doubt that's why it fell down. I understand that people in our sort of situation usually go and live in a caravan.'

He had a large bandage round his head. Cuts on his left cheek were dressed with a white plaster. The other side of his face was turning black — before Burden's very eyes, it seemed. Sheila came in while he was still there and threw her arms round her father until he groaned in pain. And then the bomb expert from the Myringham Division of the Serious Crimes Squad came to question him and he and Sheila were obliged to leave. Now Burden, with Sumner-Quist's medical report in front of him, had to make up his mind whether it would be good for Wexford to be shown it later in the day. He would probably ask for it anyway, thus taking the power of showing it or withholding it out of Burden's hands.

In fact, there wasn't much in it Wexford didn't already know. The time of Mrs Robson's death was as firmly fixed as it ever could be at between five-thirty-five and five-fifty-five. And death had taken place on the spot where the body was found. She had died of asphyxiation as the result of a ligature being applied to her neck. Sumner-Quist went on to suggest that the ligature — he never once here used the term 'garrote' — was of wire probably in some kind of plastic coating, minute particles of such a substance having been found in the neck wound. This substance, presently being subjected to lab analysis, was most likely flexible polyvinyl chloride or polyvinyl chloride in combination with one of the polymers such as styrene acrylonitrile.

Burden winced a bit at these names, though he had a pretty good idea of the kind of stuff meant; no doubt it was much like the substance that insulated the lead on his desk lamp. It was suggested that the ligature had a handle at each end which the perpetrator must have grasped in order to secure a purchase on it and avoid cutting his or her own hands.

Gwen Robson had been a strong and healthy woman, five feet one inch tall, weight one hundred and ten pounds. Sumner-Quist estimated her age at three years less than what it had been in fact. She had never borne a child, suffered surgery of any sort. Her heart and other major organs of the body were in sound condition. She had lost her wisdom teeth and three other molars, but otherwise her teeth were present and healthy. If someone hadn't come up behind her in a car park with a garrote, thought Burden, she would very likely have lived another thirty years; she would long have outlived that arthritic, prematurely aged husband.

The Home Help Service was administered by the County Council, not the local authority, Burden soon discovered. It functioned from one of those bungalow buildings that house administrative offices in the grounds of once great private houses all over England. The great house in question was called Sundays on the Forby Road near the junction with Ash Lane. It had until recently been in private hands and, approaching it, Burden remembered the pop festival which had been held there back in the seventies and the murder of a girl during that festival. A huge sum had been spent on the purchase, causing anger among local ratepayers. But Sundays had been bought and these ugly single-storey buildings soon put up in the environs of the house. The mansion itself, though in part offices, was also available as a conference centre and for courses. Burden noted that a course in word processing was due to begin that day. His appointment was with the Home Help Supervisor, but it was her deputy who met him and began by telling him pessimistically that they could give him very little help. Their records went back only three years and Mrs Robson had been gone for two. The Deputy Supervisor could remember her, but the Supervisor herself had been in her present post less than two years. She produced for Burden a list of names, with addresses, of those men and women who had been Gwen Robson's 'clients'.

'What does a cross after a name indicate?'

'It means they've died,' she said.

506

Burden saw that there were more crosses than otherwise. On an initial glance no name or address leaped out significantly.

'What did you think of Mrs Robson?' he asked. This was Wexford's technique and although Burden did not altogether approve of it, he thought he might as well give it a go.

The reply came slowly, as if a good deal of thought and calculation was going into it. 'She was efficient and very reliable. A great one for phoning in, if you know what I mean. She'd warn you by phone if she was going to be even ten minutes late.'

Burden, irrepressibly, saw again the resemblance between the dead woman and Dorothy Sanders. Here was a new point of similarity – a shared obsession with time – but what he wanted was a meeting point, a location at which she and Clifford Sanders might have come into collision.

'I don't want to speak ill of her. That was a dreadful way to die.'

'It won't go any further,' said Burden, hope springing. 'What you say to me will be treated in confidence.'

'Well, then, she was a terrible gossip. Of course I didn't have that much to do with her, and to tell you the truth I used to avoid having much contact with her, but it seemed to me sometimes that she liked nothing better than finding out some poor old dear's private trouble or secret or whatever and spreading it round this place. Starting off always of course with that old one about it being within these four walls and she wouldn't say it to anyone else and so forth. I don't say there was any harm in it, mind, I don't say there was malice. As a matter of fact it was all done quite sympathetically, though she was a bit moralistic. You know the kind of thing – how wicked it was to have a baby without being married, how unfair on the child, and people living together not knowing the rewards of a happy marriage.'

'There doesn't seem much in that,' Burden said.

'Probably not. She was a great talker, she never stopped talking, and I don't suppose there's much in that either. I'll give her one thing, she was devoted to her husband. She was one of those women who are married to perfectly ordinary men and go about saying how wonderful they are – one in a million – and how lucky they are to have got a man like that. I don't know whether it's sincere, or if they're trying to make out they've got an exceptional marriage or what. I remember her going on in here one day about someone she knew who'd had a Premium Bond come up. If that happened to her, she said, the first thing she'd do would be to buy her husband some special kind of car – I don't know what, a Jaguar maybe – and then she'd take him on holiday to the Caribbean. Anyway, you've got your list; it's the best I can do, and I hope it's of some help.'

Burden was disappointed. He wasn't sure what he had expected – some name on the list, perhaps, to tally with that of a witness in the case or with someone he had talked to in connection with it. As it was, because he had gone so far, everyone whose name was here would have to be seen. Archbold or Davidson could do that. Among those whose names were followed by a cross Burden noted that of a man who had lived in the sheltered housing at Highlands opposite the Robsons' own home: Eric Swallow, 12 Berry Close, Highlands. But what could that signify? The only difference between Eric Swallow and the others was that he was a 'client' who happened to have lived on the other side of the street from his home help.

The alibi of Clifford Sanders was the next important question of Burden's day. He saw from his notes that Clifford had told him he had left the psychotherapist Serge Olson at six p.m. Queen Street, where Olson had his premises in the flat over the hairdressers, was metered and except on Saturday mornings there were usually meters available. Burden, due to see Olson at half-past noon, stood in Queen Street observing that now, late on a Monday morning, three of the twelve meters were vacant. Clifford could easily have been in his car and away by two minutes past six if he left Olson at six. The worst of the Kingsmarkham rush hour traffic would have been over by then and he could have got into the Barringdean Shopping Centre car park with ease by ten-past six. But there was no way, if he was telling the truth, that he could have been there before five minutes to six.

Briefly calling in at the police station, Burden had phoned Stowerton Royal Infirmary to be told that Wexford was 'satisfactory and comfortable', a formula that conveys to the nervous caller the imminence of death. Burden had wasted

508

no more time on the Infirmary, but phoned Dora at her elder daughter's. They had said that if Wexford continued to make good progress he could leave the hospital on Thursday. Wexford said he was going out tomorrow. Bomb experts were at the house, sifting through rubble and until they were finished nothing could be done about clearing up the mess. Burden was early for his appointment and he walked up and down looking in the windows of the newly refurbished Midland Bank, the shoe boutique and the toy-shop, but thinking about the bomb and wondering if it had really been meant for Sheila. Why would anyone want to blow up Sheila? Because she had cut the wire round a Ministry of Defence air base?

Burden strongly disapproved of the Campaign for Nuclear Disarmament and Greenpeace and Friends of the Earth and 'all those people'. This was one of the few issues on which he and his wife disagreed, or on which his wife had not won him over to her point of view. He thought they were all cranks and anarchists, either misguided or in the pay of the Russians. But it was quite feasible that other cranks, equally if not more reprehensible, might try to blow them up. Such a thing had been attempted – and indeed had succeeded – in the case of the Greenpeace vessel in the South Pacific. On the other hand, suppose some enemy of Wexford's – even if it were not too far-fetched, someone involved in the Robson case – knew that when Sheila stayed with him he was always in the habit of moving her car in order to put his own away? Whether or not this was true Burden was unsure but he thought it likely, knowing his chief. It had a been dark, misty evening. Would it have been possible to creep unseen across the wasteland and fasten that bomb to the underside of the Porsche? Burden found he knew very little about bombs.

The hairdressers was called Pelage which Wexford, who had looked it up out of curiosity, said was a collective noun for the fur, hair or pelt of a mammal. It had been open only six months and the interior décor was very hi-tech, resembling nothing so much as the inside of a computer. But the building in which it was housed was as ancient as anything in this part of Kingsmarkham High Street and the narrow steep staircase up which Burden made his way was a good hundred and fifty years old. By the look of the wormholes in the treads, it wouldn't endure much longer. If the woman descending hadn't been as thin as Burden they would have had difficulty in passing one another, for neither had been prepared to retreat. At the top a door was slightly ajar. There was no bell, so Burden pushed open the door and walked in, calling out, 'Hallo!'

He was in an ante-room, unfurnished but for floor cushions and something folded up to large suitcase size which reminded him of a mobile bench he had once borrowed for pasting wallpaper on, but was more likely to be a massage table. The ceiling was painted rather ineptly with signs of the zodiac and on the walls hung strange posters – one of a pair of boots with no legs in them but with distinctly separate toes and toenails, which Wexford could have told him was from a Magritte painting, and another of cats in cloaks and boots riding white horses. Burden remembered what Clifford Sanders had told him about his feelings and thought that this was what he felt here; he felt threatened.

A door at the opposite end of the room opened and a man came out in a very unhurried way. He stood just outside the door with his arms folded. He was a short man and extremely thickset without being fat; great breadth of shoulder and width of hip and thigh were not matched by a big belly. His hair – 'pelage', Burden could not help thinking – was dark and curly, long and thick as a woman's growing low over his forehead, linked by brown curly sideburns to his round bushy beard which itself was linked to a dense and rather more gingery moustache. Very little face showed, no more than a surprisingly fine-pointed nose, thin lips and a pair of dark eyes like those of a fierce animal.

On the phone Burden had given his full name, but Olson extended his hand and said, 'Come in here, Michael – or is it Mike?'

Burden had an old-fashioned and (his wife said) ridiculous antipathy to being called by his christian name except by friends. But he was aware too of how foolish it made him look to stand on his dignity with a contemporary, so he merely shrugged and followed Olson into . . . what? A consulting room? A therapy room? There was a couch and it was so much like the famous one in the Freud museum in London that Burden and Jenny had been to, even to the scattered oriental rugs, that he was sure a deliberate attempt at duplication had been made. Apart from the couch the room was cluttered with cheap ugly furniture and hung with posters, including an anti-nuclear one which pictured a devastated globe and above it a quote from Einstein: 'The unleashed power of the atom has changed everything except our modes of thinking and thus we drift towards unparalleled catastrophe'. This obscurely reminded Burden of Wexford and recalled to him with how much more of an open mind his chief would have approached this man . . . yet, how could you, at his age, conquer your prejudices?

Olson had sat down at the head of the couch, no doubt a customary position for him. He gazed at Burden in silence, again probably a habitual pose.

Burden began, 'I understand Mr Clifford Sanders is a patient of yours, Dr Olson.'

'A client, yes.' There it was again, that word. Patients, customers, guests – all in his contemporary world had become clients. 'And I'm not a doctor,' Olson went on.

This immediately recalled to Burden indignant articles he had read about purveyors of various forms of psychiatry being permitted to practise without medical degrees. 'But you have some sort of qualification?'

'A psychology degree; Olson spoke with a kind of calm economy. It was as if he would attempt to justify nothing, explain nothing; there he was, to be taken or left. Such a manner always gives an impression of transparent honesty and therefore made Burden suspicious. It was time for Olson to ask him precisely what it was that Burden wanted to see him about – they always did ask at this point – but Olson didn't ask, he merely sat. He sat and looked at Burden with a calm, mild almost compassionate interest.

'I am sure you have your own code of professional conduct,' Burden said, 'so I won't – at any rate, at this stage – ask you to divulge anything you may have diagnosed in Mr Sanders' . . . personality.' He frankly thought he was being magnanimous and rather resented Olson's faint smile and inclination of the head. 'It's a more practical matter I'm concerned with – the times of Mr Sanders' last appointment with you, in fact. Now as I understand it, he had a five o'clock appointment for a one-hour session and left you at six?'

'No,' said Olson.

'No? That isn't so?'

Shifting his gaze with what seemed perfect control, Olson turned his eyes on to the grey and cratered globe and the Einstein prediction. 'Clifford,' he said, 'comes at five as a general rule, but sometimes I've had to ask him to change and I did that last Thursday. I was giving a lecture in London at seven-thirty and I wanted to allow myself more time.'

'Do you mean to say Mr Sanders didn't come to you last Thursday?'

Olson was perhaps a man who would always smile indulgently at needless consternation. His smile was slight and a little sad. 'He came. I asked him to come half an hour earlier and in fact he came about twenty minutes earlier. And he left me at five-thirty.'

'Do you mean five-thirty, Mr Olson? Or with time for various parting remarks and fresh appointments and so on, would that be nearer twenty to six, say?'

Olson took off his watch, laid it on the table beside him and, indicating it, said, 'At five-thirty I pick up my watch and tell the client – in this case, Clifford – that time's up and I'll see him next week. There are no parting remarks.'

Jenny, Burden's wife, had been in analysis during her pregnancy. Had it been like this? Burden realized he had never exactly asked her. If you lay on that couch – did you? or wasn't it for lying on? – if you talked to this man, then, and opened your heart and spoke of your inmost secrets, he would be like an enormous impersonal ear . . . Burden, without liking or trusting him, suddenly understood that this of course was what was required.

'So Clifford Sanders left here at five-thirty sharp?'

Olson nodded indifferently; there was no question of Burden's disbelieving him. He said, 'You went to London? Where were you . . . lecturing?'

'I left here at six and walked to the station to get the six-seventeen train that arrives at Victoria at ten-past seven. My talk was on projection-making factors and I gave it before an audience of MAPT – that is, the Metropolitan Association

of Psychotherapists – at the Association's premises in Pim-
lico. I went there by taxi.'

The man seemed to have perfect assurance. Burden looked
closely at him and said, 'Can you think of any reason, Mr
Olson, why Clifford Sanders should have told us that his
appointment with you was from five until six and that he
left here at six?'

He's going to tell me he was threatened, Burden thought.
He's going to talk about threats and defensiveness and pro-
jection. Instead, Olson got up and, moving to a very untidy
desk which had perhaps once been a kitchen table, slowly
turned the pages of an appointment book. He seemed to be
examining some particular entry with care. Then he glanced
at his watch and some inner reflection made him smile. He
closed the book and still standing up, turned to face Burden.

'You may not know this, Michael. You may never have
considered what a powerful figure time is in the human
psyche. It might not be too presumptuous to suggest he could
be another Jungian archetype in the collective unconscious.
Certainly for some he can be an aspect of the Shadow.'

Burden stared at him with a failure of understanding as
deep as disgust.

'Let's call him Time with a capital T.' said Olson. 'He has
been depicted as a god in a chariot with wings and even been
given a personification as Old Father Time – I expect you've
come across that. Some people seem to be enslaved by time,
by this old man with a skull for a face and a scythe in his
hand, by this god in the winged chariot hurrying by behind
them. They are his servants and they become very worried
– very anguished, indeed – if they are not there, all present
and correct, to bow down to him and do his bidding. But
there are others, Michael, who hate time. They fear him and
because this dread is so great and so omnipresent, they have
no recourse but to drive him back into the unconscious. He
is too frightening and so they banish him. The result of
course is a total lack of knowledge of him, a world in which
he is absent. His hours and half-hours for them to pass
uncounted. These are the people – and we all know them –
who can never get up in the morning and at night are always
astonished that it should be three or four by the time they
get to bed. To be on time for a date entails for them an

513

almost superhuman effort. Their friends get to know this and invite them to come half an hour earlier than the party begins. As for a memory of time – to ask them to have any kind of accurate record is almost an act of violence.'

Burden blinked a little. He had seized on a point though.

'Are you telling me that these regular five o'clock appointments with Clifford Sanders were in fact made for four-thirty?'

Olson nodded, smiling.

'But I thought you said he had the five p.m. appointment?'

'I said that he *comes* at five; that isn't quite the same thing.'

'So last Thursday when you phoned him you must have asked him to come at four?'

'And he came about ten minutes late. That is, as I said, he came at about four-forty.' A genuinely good-humoured smile now broke across Olson's face. 'You're thinking I'm dishonest with my poor clients, aren't you, Michael? I'm pandering to their neurosis in a way perhaps that robs them of their basic human dignity – is that it? But I have to live, too, you see, and I have to recognize Time as a figure in my life. I can't afford to waste half an hour of him any more than one of his most abject slaves.'

Neither can I, thought Burden, getting up to take his leave. To his dismay, as he showed him out Olson laid an almost affectionate arm across his shoulder.

'You won't resent a lesson, I'm sure, Mike.'

Burden looked at him, then at the couch, and recovered some of his aplomb. He said with an edge of sarcasm, 'I expect it makes a change for you to talk.'

At first Olson, frowned, then his face cleared. 'That's for the Freudians, the silent listening therapist. I talk quite a lot; I help them along.' He had the happy man's simple unclouded smile.

It looks very much as if it was intended for your daughter, the Serious Crimes Squad man from Myringham said. You say your daughter hadn't given you any prior warning of her intention to visit you? She hadn't given me any prior warning, Wexford said. I don't know about my wife, I didn't ask.

You'll have to ask my wife. We have asked her, Mr Wexford, and no – your daughter's visit was a complete surprise to her.

What made the bomb go off?

You were about to back the car, weren't you? You were going to back it out of the garage drive in order to put your own car in, your wife says. We think it was activated by the reverse gear – triggered off by putting the gear into reverse. You see, your daughter says she never had the Porsche in reverse between getting into it outside her London flat and arriving at your home about an hour and a half later. And one can see, sir, that there would have been no occasion for her to use the reverse gear.

The bomber wasn't bothered, you can see that. It didn't bother him whether the bomb went off five minutes after she started and outside the Great Ormond Street Hospital for Sick Children, for instance, or down here on Sunday afternoon when she was backing out to go off home. It was all the same to him as long as she was in the driving-seat.

As long as she was in the driving-seat . . . Wexford lay in bed thinking about it. They got him up at four and made him have his tea with a lot of other men seated round a table in the middle of the ward. Some bomber had tried to kill Sheila and had failed – but he wouldn't stop, would he, because he had failed once? He would try again and again. It might be because of her anti-nuclear activities, but on the other hand it might not. Freaks and oddballs, were envious of the famous the successful, the beautiful. There were even people who equated actors with the parts they played and who were capable of seeing Sheila as Lady Audley, a bigamist and murderess. For that she must be punished, for her beauty and her success and her lack of morals; for acting a treacherous wife and for being one . . .

How was he going to live and go about his daily work with that ever-present fear of an assassin stalking Sheila? The newspapers were full of it; he had three daily papers lying on his bed, all of them speculating with a kind of merry cynicism as to what particular terrorists might have it in for Sheila. How was he going to stand all that?

Sylvia came after she had fetched her son Robin from his choir practice and then Burden came at evening visiting, full

515

of the Robson medical report, his theories about Clifford Sanders as perpetrator, Gwen Robson as arch-gossip and ferreter out of secrets in the home help sorority and a curious interview he had had with a psychiatrist.

'This stuff about some people being unpunctual – because that's really what it amounts to – doesn't really effect the issue. Sumner-Quist gives the latest time at which Mrs Robson could have been killed as five to six. Clifford could easily have got there before five to six. Without hurrying he could have got there by a quarter to.'

Wexford made an effort. 'Intending to meet Mrs Robson there? You're saying it was premeditated? Because to keep in with your theory he certainly couldn't have encountered her by chance. He wouldn't have gone to that dreary car park to sit there for half an hour and wait for his mother. Or are you saying he was so lost to time that he didn't know whether it was a quarter to or half-past?'

'Not me,' said Burden, 'Olson the shrink. Anyway, I don't go along with that. I think Clifford has a perfectly normal attitude to time when he wants to have. And why shouldn't it have been premeditated? I don't believe Clifford thought or imagined or fancied or however you like to put it that Gwen Robson was his mother. Anyone would have to be a total banana truck to do that. And if he wanted to kill his mother, he could do that at home. No, the motive is likely to be a good deal more practical than that, as motives usually are.' He looked defiantly at Wexford, waiting for argument, and when none came went on, 'Suppose Gwen Robson was blackmailing him? Suppose she found out some secret about him and was holding it over him?'

'Like what?' said Wexford, and even to Burden his voice sounded weary and uninterested.

'He could be queer – I mean, gay – and afraid of Mum finding out. I mean, that's just a possibility since you ask.'

'But you haven't established any sort of link between them, have you? There's no evidence they knew each other. It's the kind of situation in which a son would only know a woman of her age if she were a friend of his mother's – and she wasn't. It's not as if Clifford has ever been in the market for a home help; he's not a housebound octogenarian or some

516

bedridden invalid. And while Mrs Robson *may* have been a blackmailer, have you any actual evidence that she was?'

'I will have,' Burden said confidently. 'Inquest in the morning. I'll give you a complete run-down on what's happened tomorrow.'

But Wexford seemed no longer to be following what he said – to be distracted by some action of his neighbour in the next bed, and then by the arrival of a nurse with a drugs trolley – and Burden, looking at him with slightly exasperated sympathy, thought how true it was that patients in hospital rapidly lose all interest in the outside world. The ward and its inmates, what they had for lunch and what sister said, these things are their microcosm.

The inquest opened and was adjourned, as Burden had expected. It could hardly have been otherwise. Evidence was taken from Dr Sumner-Quist, who was again making very free with the term 'garrote'. And a lab expert was able to treat the coroner to some very abstruse stuff about polymers and long-chain linear polyesters and a substance called polyethylene terephthalate. It was all by way of discovering what the wire of the garrote had been coated in and Burden wasn't much wiser when the expert had finished, though he gathered it all amounted to grey plastic.

Robson was not in court. There was no reason for him to have attended. Clifford Sanders and his mother were both there; Clifford due for a drubbing from the coroner, Burden thought, for his curious action in covering up the body and running away. But the first witness of all was Dorothy Sanders, who went into the box with deliberate self-assured deportment – having dressed herself, no doubt by chance, in clothes very like those found on the dead woman, even to the lacy brown stockings.

The man who had evidently come with them and who now sat beside Clifford he recognized as the farmer he had seen in Ash Lane, and who had come out on to the doorstep with his dog to stare after Burden's departing car.

517

7

Houses without women – Burden could always recognize them. It was not that such places were particularly dirty or uncared-for, but rather that the absence of a woman's hand showed in an asymmetry, a placing of objects in bizarre ways, clumsy makeshifts. The kitchen of Ash Farm Lodge – a large kitchen, since the bungalow had obviously been pur-pose-built for a farmer – was like that: the table littered with account books and pamphlets, a pair of boots standing on a magazine on top of the oven, a dishcloth spread out to dry on the back of a Windsor chair, a twelve-bore shotgun suspended from what was originally a saucepan rack.

The man Burden had seen in court said his name was Roy Carroll. He looked about fifty, perhaps more. His hands were particularly large, red and calloused, and the skin of his face was a darkly-veined red. The dog lay curled up not in a basket but a large drawer. Burden had the feeling that before it dared wake up it would have to indicate in some canine way a request for permission to do so.

Carroll was brusque and uncouth. He had admitted Burden to the house in a grudging fashion and his replies to questions were hardly fulsome, a 'Yes' and a 'No' and a 'Yes' and other grunted monosyllables. He knew 'Dodo' Sanders, he knew Clifford Sanders; he had lived in this house since it was built. When was that? Twenty-one years ago.

'Dodo?' Burden queried.

'That's what they called her, her husband and that. His mum. Dodo they called her, that's what I call her.'

'You're friends?'

'What does that mean? I know her, I've done odd jobs for her.'

Burden asked him if he was married.

'Never you mind that,' Carroll said. 'I'm not now.'

Gwen Robson? He had never heard of her until her death was on television. He had never had a home help in the house. Where was he on the previous Thursday afternoon? Carroll looked incredulous at being asked. Out shooting, he said, getting a rabbit for the pot. This time of the year he was out shooting most days at dusk. Burden noticed something that was interesting but surely of no importance. The magazine the boots stood on was a copy of *Kim*, the last kind of reading matter to associate with a man of Carroll's sort. It brought to mind the poster in Olson's room, the one with the boots that had five toenailed toes but no legs in them, and unaccountably he shuddered.

A weekday morning and Clifford very likely at work. Burden phoned Munster's, the school which ran crash courses for A levels, and asked to speak to Mr Sanders. He wasn't even sure Clifford worked there, but it turned out to have been an intelligent guess. Mr Sanders was teaching. Could they take a message? Wexford would have treated this more delicately, Burden knew that, but he didn't see why he should be tender towards the feelings of someone who was probably a layabout and certainly a liar, who was very probably homosexual, who had mixed-up feelings of confusion between his mother and dead women and was a psychopath anyway. He asked the woman who answered the phone to give Clifford Sanders a message that Detective Inspector Burden had called and would like him to come to the police station and ask for him as soon as his class was finished.

In the meantime, he made an application for a warrant to search the Sanders' house in the expectation of finding something in the nature of a garrote somewhere. Of course he could simply have asked Mrs Sanders' permission to search, most people don't refuse this request, but he felt she would. While he was waiting for Clifford he suddenly remembered Robson's shopping bags, so he summoned DC Davidson to find them, locate their contents and have the lot taken round to Highlands. The bags were red Tesco carriers and Burden had had intensive enquiries made at the Tesco store in the Barringdean Shopping Centre. Dressed in brown clothes similar to those worn by Mrs Robson, Marian Bayliss had retraced her possible steps through the centre. One of the checkout assistants remembered her passing through on the previous Thursday and put the time at about five-thirty. Burden began re-reading DC Archbold's report.

Linda Naseem knew Mrs Robson by sight, indeed knew her well enough to comment on the weather and ask after her husband. Gwen Robson was a regular shopper in the store and almost always came in on a Thursday afternoon, but what most interested Burden about this evidence was that Linda Naseem claimed to have seen Mrs Robson in conversation with a girl. This encounter, she said, took place immediately after Mrs Robson had paid and received her change, and when she was standing at the end of the check-out counter putting the goods she had bought into a carrier.

Describe the girl? She had been attending to her next customer and she hadn't taken much notice. Indeed, she hadn't seen the girl's face at all, only her back and the back of her head. She had been wearing a beret or some sort of hat. When Mrs Robson finished packing her bag, she and this girl went off together. At least, they went off. Linda Naseem couldn't absolutely say they went together.

Clifford came to the police station about half an hour after Burden had made his phone call; Munster's School was only about two hundred yards down the High Street. Burden's own office was rather a pleasant, comfortable place where any visitor might have felt he was paying a social call, so Burden didn't take him in there but into one of the interview rooms at the back on the ground floor. The walls were bare, painted the colour of scrambled eggs, and the floor was of grey vinyl tiles. Burden motioned Clifford into one of the grey metal chairs and himself sat down opposite him at the plastic-topped yellow table.

Almost without preamble, he began, 'You told me you didn't know Mrs Robson. That wasn't true, was it?'

Clifford looked truculent to Burden, his dull face sullen. He wasn't showing any obvious symptoms of fear as he spoke in his slow, monotonous voice. 'I didn't know her.'

There was a point in any interrogation or enquiry when Burden simply changed from using a suspect's surname and title to his or her first name. Wexford asked permission before he did this, but Burden never did. Using people's surnames and titles, in his opinion, was very tied up with feeling respect for them. This was why he needed to be called 'Mr' himself. He would have said he reached a stage when he lost respect for the person he was questioning and therefore pushed them a few rungs down the ladder of his esteem. If we had a language – where you could tutoyer and vouvoyer, said Wexford, you'd start thouing them.

'Now, Clifford, I'll be honest with you. Frankly, I don't yet know where you met her or how you knew her, but I know you did. Why not tell me and save me the trouble of finding out?'

'But I didn't know her.'

'When you say that, you're not helping yourself or deceiving me. All you're doing is wasting time.'

Clifford repeated doggedly now, 'I did not know Mrs Robson.' He laid his hands on the table and contemplated them. The nails were closely bitten, Burden noticed for the first time, this gave them the look of a child's hands, pink and pudgy.

'All right, I can wait. You'll tell me in your own good time.'

Did he really take that phrase literally or is he sending me up? Burden wondered. Not a gleam of humour showed on the round blank face when Clifford said, 'I don't have my own good time.'

A change of subject and Burden said, 'You must have been in that car park well before six. Mr Olson has told me you left him not at six but at five-thirty. You must have been there by five-forty-five at the latest. Would you like to know when Mrs Robson died? It was between five-thirty-five and five-fifty-five.'

'I don't know what time I got there,' Clifford said, speaking very slowly. 'It's no use asking me about times. I don't wear a watch, perhaps you've noticed.' He raised his arms in what Burden saw as an effeminate gesture, exposing plump white wrists. 'I don't think I went straight to the car park. I sat in the car and thought about what I'd been saying to

521

Serge. We'd been talking about my mother; hardly anyone calls my mother by her first name any more, not now, but when they did they called her Dodo. It's short for Dorothy, of course.'

Burden said nothing, perplexed as to whether he was being teased or whether Clifford generally talked to strangers like this.

'Dodos are large flightless birds, now extinct. They were all killed by Portuguese sailors on Mauritius. My mother isn't a bit like that. Serge and I talked about a man's anima being shaped by his mother and my mother having a negative influence on me. That can express itself in the man having irritable depressed moods, and when I was sitting in the car I thought about that and went back over it all. I like to do that sometimes. The car was on a meter and there was ten minutes to run. And I got out and fed the meter some more.'

'So you do take note of time sometimes, Clifford?'

He looked up and turned on Burden a troubled gaze. 'Why are you asking me questions? What do you suspect me of?'

'Suppose I said you went straight to the shopping centre, Clifford. Isn't that what you did? You parked the car in the car park and then you went in to the shopping centre and ran into Mrs Robson, didn't you?'

'I've told you the truth. I sat in the car in Queen Street. You ought to tell me what you suspect me of doing.'

'Perhaps you'd better go and sit in your car and think about that one,' said Burden, and he let him go.

Such mock naïvety angered him. Dodos, indeed, flightless birds! What was an anima anyway, or come to that a negative influence? Grown men didn't naturally behave and talk like children, not men who were teachers and had been to universities. He was suspicious of the childlike stare, the puzzled ingenuousness. If Clifford was sending him up, he would be made to regret it. In the morning they would search that house. Burden couldn't help thinking how satisfying it would be to have the case all wrapped up before Wexford was back at work.

Sheila, Wexford discovered on being driven from hospital to his other daughter's house, was staying at the Olive and

522

Dove, Kingsmarkham's principal hostelry. There was no room for her as well at Sylvia's, where her parents now occupied the only spare room.

'Anyway, I expect she feels it's easier to have her boyfriend there.'

There was rivalry between the two sisters of a never-quite-expressed kind. Sylvia cloaked her envy under the complacency of a happily married mother of sons. If she would have liked what her sister had – success, fame, the adoration of a good many people, lovers past and in the future – her covetousness was never explicit. But comments were made; a virtue was made of necessity. There was a tendency to talk about fame and money not bringing happiness and show-business people seldom having stable relationships. Married at eighteen, Sylvia would perhaps have liked at least a memory of lovers and the consciousness of something attempted, something done. Sheila, more open about her views, frankly said how nice it must be to have no worries, no fear of the future, reading in a leisurely way for an Open University degree, to be dependent on a loving husband. She meant she would have liked children, Wexford sometimes thought. Sylvia was waiting for him to ask for enlightenment, but he kept his enquiry to himself until she had gone to fetch the boys from school.

'I know there's someone,' Dora said. 'She was phoning someone she called Ned just before you went out and set that bomb off.'

'Thanks very much,' said Wexford. 'You make it sound as if I put a match to a fuse.'

'You know what I mean. When she comes over this evening, we can ask her about him.'

'I wouldn't ask her,' said Wexford.

But Sheila phoned to say she wasn't coming, that she was postponing her visit to her father until the following morning. Something had come up.

'Come down, I should say,' Sylvia said. 'Come down on the London train. I suppose he's an actor or a Friend of the Earth or both.'

' "Those who find ugly meanings in beautiful things",' said her father austerely, ' "are corrupt without being charming." ' He returned to the copy of *Kim* magazine he had found lying about.

Sylvia had told him she took it occasionally and had supplied the little defensive explanation people in Jane Austen's day thought they had to give for reading novels. It was something to pass the time; you could pick it up and put it down; some of the stories were of a really high standard. Wexford liked the name of the magazine which seemed to him very avant-garde and appealing, for he confessed to himself that a part of him still lived in a world of *Home Knits* and *Modern Mother*. He turned to the page of enquiries from worried readers.

The 'agony aunt' Lesley worked for was a woman of the name, or alias, of Sandra Dale. At the head of the page was a photograph of her, a plump, middle-aged woman with fair curly hair and a sympathetic expression. Two of the letters were featured in bold-face type. One didn't appear at all, only the answer to it: 'T.M., Basingstoke: Practices like this may seem fun and I can understand they please your boyfriend, but is it worth risking your whole future sexual happiness? One day when you are married or in a permanent relationship, you may bitterly regret habits you can't break but which are keeping you from true fulfilment.'

Wexford wondered if the purpose of this sort of thing was simply the titillation of readers. It would be a very strong-minded or deeply inhibited *Kim* reader who didn't speculate as to the nature of T.M.'s unbreakable habits. Very likely it was Robson's niece who had typed all these replies, having taken them down at Sandra Dale's dictation.

'There's a piece in there about Sheila,' Sylvia said, 'and some quite nice photos from the TV series.'

He turned to look at pictures of Sheila in a white ball-gown, in her Victorian lady's black street dress and bonnet. The last instalment of *Lady Audley's Secret* was showing that evening; it would be repeated on Saturday, but who knew where they would be on Saturday? Neil wanted to watch a programme about finance on another channel and his elder son Robin was trying to persuade his mother to let him stay up and see Auntie Sheila. Rather surprisingly, Sylvia came down on her mother's side and in favour of watching this final episode. Had Neil forgotten they wouldn't be able to see the repeat because they were going out to dinner on Saturday night?

Neil lost and Robin lost. The little boy had come down for the third time in his pyjamas and was standing wistfully in the doorway. Wexford suddenly knew he wasn't going to be able to watch; he had re-read the novel while Sheila was rehearsing for the television adaptation, and he knew very well what was to happen to Lady Audley tonight: she was to be cast into the continental insane asylum. The way he felt, he would be unable to bear seeing Sheila even acting that stuff, to see her manhandled and screaming . . .

His head ached and he was tired. He got up and took the little boy's hand and said he was going to bed, too, so he would come up with Robin. The introductory music, melancholy-sweet, followed them softly up the stairs and then someone closed the door.

It was a dangerous feeling, this excitement born of hunting down a quarry – or born, rather, of creating a quarry fit to be hunted. Burden knew he was doing this and that it would be wise to pause and take stock. He did pause, briefly, and reminded himself how important it was not to tailor facts to fit a theory. On the other hand, he was growing very sure that Clifford Sanders was guilty of this crime. All he must be careful to do was to avoid pushing witnesses. Guide them, yes, but not give them enthusiastic shoves. In a frame of mind he told himself was cool and unbiased, he went very early in the morning to Highlands. There he got a surprise; as he turned into Hastings Road, he saw Lesley Arbel come out of Robson's house and approach his car, the silver Escort which was parked at the kerb. Burden pulled up behind the Escort.

'Not back at work, Miss Arbel?' he asked.

She was dressed with extreme severe formality in a black suit, white tie-necked blouse, black transparent seamed stockings and very high-heeled black patent shoes. With her glistening chestnut-coloured hair and painted eggshell face, she reminded Burden of one of those 'grown-up' dolls little girls have for birthday presents and which come with their own fashionable wardrobe.

525

'I'm not at work this week. I'm doing a course in word processors.'

'Ah,' said Burden. 'That would be the one at Sundays.'

'The Sundays Conference Centre, yes. The company have given me two weeks off to take the course and it happened to be very convenient to stay with Uncle.' She put a hand in a sleek black glove on the car door, remembered something. 'Uncle's got a bone to pick with you. Those bags of stuff you sent over, he said the piece of beef had gone off. It smelt disgusting, he said. I never saw it – he'd wrapped it up and put it in the bin before I ever got home.'

Taken aback, Burden had no rejoinder, but at that moment another car drew up and parked on the opposite side of the street. The woman called Mrs Jago came down to her front gate as a little girl of about three and a young woman got out of the car; there appeared to be another, bigger child sitting in the passenger seat. The visitor, though thin as a reed, was sufficiently like Mrs Jago as to leave no doubt this was a daughter. A mass of dark curly hair, rather resembling Serge Olson's but longer and glossier, covered half her back. The child, who also had long curly hair, ran to her grandmother and was taken up in her arms, where she clung to the massive bosom like a limpet to a domed, shiny, seaweed-clothed rock.

Ralph Robson was a long time coming to the front door. Burden could hear his stick making muffled thuds on the carpet. By the time the door opened, the two little girls and their mother had once more driven off. Robson was more owl-like than ever this morning, his nose apparently beakier, his mouth pursed, his eyes round and cross. A sports jacket of brindled brown tweed enhanced the effect and the hand on the stick gripped like a bird's claw round a twig. Burden was prepared for an exchange of courtesies, but Robson plunged straight into the bone-picking of which Lesley Arbel had forewarned him: he wanted compensation, he wanted reimbursement to the amount of four pounds fifty-two which was the price of the piece of spoiled sirloin.

Burden told him to put it all in writing and where to send his complaint. As soon as Robson had switched off that particular diatribe, he got on to the subject of his hip. The pain had intensified since his wife's death, it was ten times as bad as it had been a week ago and he could hear the joint grinding when he so much as shifted his position in a chair. Of course he was having to move about a lot more now that his wife was gone, she had saved him all that. There were areas in this country, he said, where you could get a hip replacement on the National Health Service in a matter of weeks. And he had heard that if you lived elsewhere they could transfer you to one of those places, but his doctor wouldn't have that – his doctor had said it couldn't be done. He had got himself to the surgery the day before, and that was what the doctor had said. It would have been different, he was sure, if he had had his wife to speak up for him.

'Gwen would have got things moving. Gwen would have told him what's what. If she'd known they could get me into some hospital on the other side of the country, she'd never have rested until she got some sense out of him. What's the use of talking now she's gone? I'm stuck with this for years maybe, until I can't stick another blessed day of it and take an overdose.'

It crossed Burden's mind that Robson was rather more than naturally obsessive about his arthritic hip. On the other hand, if you had a thing like that perhaps it would tend to exclude everything else from your existence. That physical pain might even distract you from the mental pain of losing your wife. Intent on not leading Robson (as the judges say), he asked him, once they were seated in front of the realistic blue flames, if he could remember any comments his wife might have made about her past 'clients'. Robson, as expected, immediately said it was a long time ago. Burden pressed him, which only had the effect of making him return to the subject of his hip and Gwen's remarks on what had brought it about and why he should have had arthritis when she didn't. This time Burden said he thought Robson was being obstructive and presumably he did not want his wife's killer found.

'You've no business talking to me like that,' Robson said, thumping his stick on the floor and wincing.

'Then cast your mind back and try to remember what your wife said to you about these people. She was a talkative woman, I'm told; she was interested in people. You're not going to tell me she'd come home at lunchtime or in the evening and not say a word to you about the old people she'd been working for? What, she never came back and said old Mrs So-and-So kept all her money in a stocking under the bed, or old Mr Whatever had a lady-friend? Nothing like that, ever?'

Burden need not have worried about leading Robson. These examples, far from stimulating him to invention or recall, seemed to provoke a truculent bewilderment. 'She never said about any old lady keeping money under the bed.'

'All right, Mr Robson,' Burden said, keeping his temper with difficulty, 'what did she talk about?'

An effort was made, as of a disused engine sparking into life with rusty wheels turning. 'There was that old boy over the road – Gwen was very good to him. She went on popping in there day after day long after she stopped working for the council. A daughter couldn't have done more.'

Eric Swallow of 12, Berry Close, Highlands, Burden thought, nodding encouragingly at Robson.

'Mrs Goodrich – that was the name. She wasn't so old, but she was crippled with one of those things they just give letters to, MS or MT or something. She'd been a lovely woman, a concert pianist Gwen said. She said she'd got some beautiful furniture in her place – valuable pieces, Gwen thought, worth a fair bit.'

Julia Goodrich of Paston Avenue, since moved from the district.

'I can't remember the rest of them; there was dozens and I can't remember them by name. I mean, there was one as told Gwen she'd had three kids by three different fathers and not married to any of them. That really upset Gwen. And there was an old boy as hadn't nothing but his pension, and used to give Gwen five-pound notes just for cutting his blessed toenails. She gave him a lot of her time, she'd be a good hour with him . . .'

'Someone gave your wife five pounds to cut his toenails?' Burden was intrigued and imagined Wexford's reaction to this bizarre picture. Was some sexual titillation or even satisfaction involved? Surely there must have been.

'There was nothing wrong in it,' Robson said, on the defensive at once. 'He just took his socks off and sat there and she did his nails with clippers. He never touched her, she wasn't that sort. His feet were spotless, she said, clean as a baby's. And there was someone else – I can't remember names – as she gave a regular bath to. He was getting over some illness; he wasn't old, but he couldn't stand the district nurses bathing him and he said Gwen was a gentle as his own nanny when he was a little kid.'

Don't lead him, Burden said to himself. You must take your chance.

'Wait a minute, I've thought of a name: an old spinster called Miss Mac-something.'

'Miss McPhail,' said Burden, thinking this justified. Robson didn't seem interested in how he knew; like a lot of people, he took a degree of omniscience in the police for granted. They only asked questions to catch you out or for their own amusement. 'Miss McPhail of Forest Park.'

'That's her. She was wealthy, had a big house that was going to rack and ruin for want of looking after, and a blessed great garden. This young boy used to come in and do a bit to the garden in his college holidays. She wanted Gwen to come and work full-time for her. No thanks, Gwen said, I've got a husband to see to. I'll give you a hundred pounds a week, she said, and this was four years ago. You're joking, Gwen said, but she said no, that's what she'd give her to be her full-time cook and companion . . . and I reckon Gwen was tempted, only I put my foot down.'

Robson shifted his weight in the armchair and this time Burden thought he heard the hip joint grind. He heard something and saw Robson's face contort. Then Robson said, 'Is that all, then? Got enough, have you?'

Burden didn't answer but got up to go. Miss McPhail was dead now, he reflected as he was leaving, hers was one of the names on the list with cross after it. Passing his own home, he went in to use the phone and check up on Wexford's recovery, then continued to Ash Farm where a search had been in progress for the past two hours. Clifford wasn't there. Burden hadn't expected him to be, but Dorothy Sanders was waiting for him, her face tragic with woe, her eyes staring.

'They said two hours was the maximum. They said two hours at the outside, and they started at nine.'

'It's only ten-past eleven, Mrs Sanders,' said Burden, who should have known better.

'Why do people say these things and not stick to them?'

'They won't be long now. They'll put everything back as they found it; we do make a point of that.'

He made his way upstairs to Davidson and Archbold on the first floor. Archbold pointed up the narrow flight of stairs which led to the top storey and said the rooms up there were stuffed with old furniture – rubbish, junk, the accumulation of years. Going through all that had delayed them. Burden decided to investigate outside, where Diana Pettit had gone to search the garage and a kind of toolshed attached to the rear fence. He made his way along the passage that must lead to a kitchen and a back way out. Dorothy Sanders had her face pressed against the window, watching the search. Her back was rigid and her arms flexed and she was perfectly still, reacting to his arrival with not the faintest twitch of her body. Burden went out by the back door.

Beyond the Ash Farm ground – you could hardly call it a garden – farmland, drowned in rain, stretched away in all directions. There was no other house in sight. A hill shaped like a camels' hump cut off the view of Kingsmarkham and heavy clouds rested on the ridge of it.

Diana looked round when Burden came in and said, 'There's nothing here, sir.'

'That depends on what you're looking for, Diana. I suppose you've been told what you're looking for?'

'A garrote, though I'm not very sure what that is.'

Burden put his hands into the box of tools. It was one of those metal boxes divided into sections on two levels, in which the upper drawers can be drawn outwards by a kind of concertina motion. He picked out two objects, saying, 'These could answer the purpose very well.'

530

8

Diana Pettit and DS Martin both told Burden these were the kinds of things to be found in every toolbox in every garden shed. You might as well find a hammer or screwdriver in such a place and call it an offensive weapon. Everybody had a spool of plastic-covered wire and a great many people a garden line for making straight edges. Burden said he didn't; he had never even seen a garden line before. Was DC Pettit sure that's what it was?

Two metal pegs, ring-headed, were linked buy a length of twine. The twine was merely knotted on to the pegs and a piece of the plastic wire might well have temporarily replaced it, thus making a serviceable garrote. He took the things away, getting Diana to give Dorothy Sanders a receipt for them. The wire went to the lab for analysis and comparison with the particles of plastic found in Gwen Robson's neck wound. With a similar length of plastic wire which he had been out to buy tied to the iron pegs, Burden shut himself up in his office and practised garroting first the angled lamp and then one of the legs of his desk. Neither was the right size for a human neck.

Next morning Linda Naseem, who had Wednesdays off, was back on her checkout. Burden went to talk to her himself. It was exactly a week today since Gwen Robson had come in here, having parked her car underground on the second level, and walked under the glazed covered way to the Barringdean Shopping Centre, arriving inside at about four-forty. The next three-quarters of an hour were easily accounted for: a little window-gazing and the purchase of two items from Boots where an assistant remembered her.

531

The toothpaste and talcum powder had been in one of the carriers with the groceries and the light-bulbs from British Home Stores. No one remembered her in there, but that was to be expected. She had probably entered Tesco at about ten-past five, taken a trolley or perhaps only a basket and begun walking round the store picking out items from her list. Clifford Sanders at that time had certainly still been with Olson. Burden saw that he was putting Gwen Robson's visit to the store too early; it was far more likely that she had not gone into Tesco until twenty-past five. That way she wouldn't have reached the checkout until five-thirty-five or maybe a little later.

There were five girls on the Tesco checkouts. Burden was looking for an Indian and three of the girls appeared to be of vaguely Indian origin. He went up to one of them and she pointed down the line to where a small, slight girl of ethereal fairness, white-skinned and flaxen-haired, was changing the spool in her till. As he approached her, he noticed her wedding ring. Of course she was called Naseem because she was married to a Moslem from the East or Middle East. Burden reprimanded himself for jumping to conclusions as he knew Wexford would have admonished him. It was inexcusable in someone of his experience.

She took him into a side room or office marked 'Private' on the door.

'You knew Mrs Robson by sight, I think?' he began.

She nodded, looking slightly apprehensive.

'What time did you say she passed through your checkout last Thursday?'

She hesitated. 'I know I did tell the other policeman five-fifteen, but I've thought about it since and it could have been later. I remember looking at my watch and seeing twenty to six and thinking good, only half an hour to go. We close at six, but they're still going through after that.'

'How much later?' Burden asked.

'Pardon?'

'How long after you had seen Mrs Robson did you look at your watch and see five-forty?'

'I don't know. It's ever so hard to say, isn't it? Ten minutes?'

Ten minutes or five minutes, thought Burden, or even two

minutes. He asked her about the girl she had seen Mrs Robson talking to – was she quite sure it was a girl?'

'Pardon,' she said again.

'If you only saw the back of this person, who was in any case wearing a hat and presumably a coat or jacket as well, how did you know it was a girl and not a boy – a man, that is?'

She said slowly, as if reorganizing impressions and conclusions, 'Well, I just sort of knew – I mean I think it was. Oh, yes, of course it was. She had a hat on – a beret, I think.'

'It could have been a man, couldn't it, Mrs Naseem?'

'That just wasn't the impression I got,' said Linda Naseem.

Burden didn't ask her any more. Looking back on the interview, he felt he had been in the role of counsel who breaks down a witness's evidence by subtle questioning, leaving the jury to draw very firm conclusions from her uncertain replies. There had been no jury in Tesco's, but if there had been he had no doubt its members would have been thoroughly convinced of this fact: that on the previous Thursday Gwen Robson had been seen in the store talking to a young man at twenty minutes to six. He wandered back into the wide gallery of the lower level and stood in the Mandala concourse. It was all red and white poinsettias today and some sort of dark blue flower. Why these signs of patriotism on November 26? Probably those were simply the flowers the florist had most of.

Burden had a look in Boots, paused to examine the window of Knits 'n' Kits which today was full of tapestry canvases printed with dog and cat faces, glanced across at Demeter with its display of water filters and air ionizers. None of the assistants in any of these shops remembered seeing Gwen Robson. The fountain was playing, shooting up its jets of water to splash the lowest prisms of the chandelier. Burden went out through the main car-park exit, from the dry warmth and air freshener smell of the place into a cutting wind.

How long was he going to have to wait for a result from the lab? Several days probably. A phone call to Wexford's daughter's home obtained the engaged signal. Burden took his improvised garrote out of the desk drawer and practised flexing his hands round the pegs. One possibly got a better purchase by putting one's fingers through the rings and gripping the handles that way. He needed something more closely resembling a human neck than the desk leg. Into his mind's eye came an urn-shaped plant-pot container made of white polystyrene cunningly contrived to look like marble. DC Polly Davies had left it behind, with instructions as to the proper care of the cyclamen it contained, when she took her maternity leave and it had ended up in Wexford's office, the cyclamen long perished. The stem of that urn would be just about the right size and with a similar flexibility.

Still holding his garrote, Burden went up in the lift and along the corridor. The office door was slightly ajar and he pushed it open and went in. Wexford was sitting behind the desk, hunched up, wrapped in his old tweed overcoat. His head was plastered up and the bruises on his face had turned a sickly yellow-green. The small grey eyes that turned on Burden and his improvised weapon had a glassy look, atypically apprehensive, but his opening remark wasn't uncharacteristic.

'So it was you all along.'

Burden grinned. 'I've made this up and I was going to try it out on your plant-pot. Don't look like that; it's quite a reasonable idea.'

'If you say so, Mike.'

'What are you doing here, anyway? You're supposed to be off till the end of the week.'

'This is the end of the week.' Wexford said, shifting in his seat and flexing bruised hands. 'I've been reading all this stuff.' Every report made on the case so far had been sent up and lay on the desk in front of him. Burden, who loved reporting every interview in detail and even recording his own thoughts, had typed screeds. 'There are some quite interesting bits. I like Mrs Robson getting five quid for cutting the old boy's toenails.'

'I thought you would.'

'It makes me wonder how much of that sort of thing there was. This bath business, for instance. It's a fascinating line of enquiry.' Burden raised an eyebrow. Not quite certain what Wexford meant and somewhat repelled by the image, he picked the mock-marble urn off the windowsill and set about strangling it with his garrote. Wexford watched him speculatively. 'There are a lot of things I'd like to know which no one seems to have bothered with much,' he said. 'Lesley Arbel, for instance. Where was she last Thursday afternoon? We don't seem to know, though we do know that Gwen Robson was seen talking to a girl at five-thirty.'

'That was a man and it was five-forty,' said Burden, pulling on his handles, feeling the polystyrene crack and split, the wire digging into the spongy white flesh-like substance.

'I see. It would be a help to know why she was always down here and what she found so compelling about that not very exciting couple.' Wexford had picked up the only photograph they had of Gwen Robson – the snapshot, much blown-up, which the *Kingsmarkham Courier* had used. ' "One of those characteristic British faces",' he quoted, ' "that once seen are never remembered".'

'Those Sanderses say they don't remember her; both of them say they never saw her before. But I just know Clifford knew her, I feel it in my bones.'

'For God's sake give over doing that, Mike. I'm not squeamish, but it turns me up. Her home help visits are another interesting thing. You note how she never seems to have spent much time with those who had little or nothing to give. I wonder what old Mr Swallow had on offer, the one who lived opposite. Did she cut his toenails too – and did she perhaps have some particularly erotic technique with the scissors?'

'It's rather disgusting, isn't it?'

Wexford grinned, lifted his shoulders.

'Is it important?' Burden put the garrote into his pocket and came to sit on the edge of the rosewood desk. When Wexford made no reply to this but only sat there looking bemused, he said, 'You don't look well, you know. I doubt if you should be here.'

'I'm going to have a quiet day,' Wexford told him. 'I'm going to see how many cups of tea I can drink between two and five this afternoon.' Enlightening Burden, he added, 'it seems to me we haven't chatted up Robson's neighbours nearly enough.'

But he went on sitting there after Burden had gone. If he hadn't put out his hand to the radiator and felt it almost too hot to handle he could have sworn the central heating had gone wrong. Without the comfort of his old overcoat, he would have been freezing. Sheila was back in London; he hadn't wanted her to go, but of course he hadn't said a word. What he would have liked was to shut her up somewhere for ever and stand guard over the door. But she had gone back to London in a rented car, back to the flat by Coram Fields that those people – whoever they were, those bombers, terrorists, fanatics – very well knew she occupied. Sylvia had the radio on most of the day, so Wexford got to hear every news bulletin, and every time he braced himself to hear the sentence that would start, 'An explosion . . .' That was why he had come back to work so soon really.

Bomb experts from Scotland Yard had come down to talk to him and the Myringham man had been back. Wexford had wanted to know what they were doing to protect Sheila and they had given him plenty of sturdy reassurance, only he wasn't reassured. He knew he wouldn't have felt so frightened if Sheila had been living with her husband, though that was illogical enough. If anyone had told him he would actually be glad to hear that his daughter was living with a man while married to someone else, he wouldn't have believed them. But that was how he felt now. It would comfort him to know that Sheila had that man Ned, whoever he might be, around night and day. What would comfort him most, of course, was what his son-in-law Neil advocated.

'Get her to stop doing acts of criminal damage. Take away her wire-cutters, or better still get her to make a public statement of guilt and her intention not to do it again.'

Surprisingly, it was Dora who countered, 'Would you have much respect for her if she did a thing like that?'

'Being alive's more important than respect, I should say.'

'Of course she won't do that,' Wexford had said. He was almost cross. 'She can't deny her principles, can she? She doesn't think she's guilty; she thinks the law's wrong – the law itself is guilty, if you like.'

Sylvia looked askance. 'Rather a strange commentary from a policeman, surely, Dad?'

He hadn't said any more. Apart from finding some way out of this anxiety, of making Sheila safe, he wanted more than anything to avoid a flaming row with Sylvia and Neil. The Chief Constable had said something to him on the phone yesterday about the loan of a police house until his own was repaired – well, largely rebuilt, and at the pace at which builders worked nowadays that would be a year hence.

At any rate it was peaceful here. It was quiet and the cold he felt wasn't real. He had to 'struggle against a great tendency to lowness', as he put it to himself, and he went up to the canteen to get some lunch. Working his way through hot soup, hamburger and chips, comforting if not healthy food, he faced the prospect of getting into a car again and driving it. Neil had brought him to work and dropped him outside the gates. Donaldson, his driver, would take him up to Highlands. But sooner or later he was going to have to overcome the great barrier of inhibition that reared up between him and the driving-seat and the wheel of a car. He would have to conquer the paralysis he felt would descend upon his left hand as it tried to close over a gear shift, even in his case an automatic shift. Last night he had relived in a dream the explosion he thought he had no memory of, but had said nothing about it to anyone, not even Dora.

Patterns of life had changed subtly but radically during the years since Wexford had first become a policeman interviewing witnesses. In those early days all the men were out at work and all the women at home. Split-shift working, the advance in women's education and freedom, self-employment and of course unemployment had changed all that. He was not much surprised, at the first house where he called after leaving the car and Donaldson, to be admitted by a young man with a baby in his arms and a child of about three clinging to the legs of his jeans.

This was John Whitton, student and father of two, whose wife was a systems analyst in a full-time job. It was she who had spent time with Ralph Robson while he awaited the arrival of his niece. The house inside had that curious faint smell which all who have themselves been parents recognize – that of a compound of milk, infants' digestive processes, ammonia and talcum powder. This young parent had lived next door but one to Gwen Robson for three years since his marriage when the local authority had allocated him and his wife a house at Highlands, but he assured Wexford that their

537

acquaintance had been slight. Knowing her to be a council home help and with a reputation for philanthropy (his own word), they had once ventured to ask her if she would baby-sit for them.

'Our regular sitter had let us down and it was a special occasion. As a matter of fact it was our third wedding anniversary, and Rosemary was expecting this one any day. We knew it would be months before we got out in the evening again. I asked Mrs Robson and it wasn't that she wouldn't do it; it was the amount she wanted paying. We couldn't run to that, living on one salary; we couldn't give her three pounds an hour. It wasn't as if Scott ever wakes in the evening – it would have been twelve quid for just sitting about watching telly.'

It was a long shot but Wexford thought he might as well try it, and he asked John Whitton about the previous Thursday. Had he seen Ralph Robson during the course of the afternoon, preferably after four-thirty? But Whitton shook his head. He had been at home, for his wife had the car that day, but it was a busy time for him with the children's tea to get and both of them to be bathed. He couldn't even recall having seen Gwen Robson go out.

Next door, between the Whittons and Ralph Robson, lived the couple Mrs Robson had so disapproved of, Trevor Morrison and Nicola Resnick. They were both in the house from which they ran a mail-order secondhand-book business which Wexford guessed was of a rather precarious kind. Here the first of that anticipated tea was offered, though of the herbal sort – crimson liquid with a floral-labelled bag loating in it. Wexford accepted a coarse, dark brown crunchy biscuit. Nicola Resnick, though young and liberated-looking in jeans and boots and Guernsey, turned out as much of a gossip as ever her grandmother could have been.

'She tried to get that old boy opposite to make his will in her favour. He used to tell everybody about the money he'd got in the bank. He was about a hundred, wasn't he, Trev?'

'He was eighty-eight when he died,' Trevor Morrison said.

'Yes, well, ancient. You see, he was always whingeing about not being able to manage, especially his fuel bills in the winter. And he liked to use his phone. He'd got this daughter in Ireland or somewhere and he liked to phone her;

no good waiting for her to phone him, he used to say. Well, I said to him you ought to apply for supplementary benefit. Why not? You've got a right to it and I believe in getting what you're entitled to. These old people are proud but it's just pointless, that sort of pride. You work all your life, you've got a right to anything the state will let you have. But it wasn't that with him. It's no good me applying, he said to me, I've got money in the bank and I'll have to tell them; I've got more than three thousand in the Trustee Savings Bank and when I let on about that, no way are they giving me benefit. And it was true.'

'This is Mr Eric Swallow we're talking about?' Wexford asked, making a valiant effort to drink his hibiscus tea.

'Old Eric, yes. I don't think I ever knew his other name, did you, Trev? Anyway, he used to tell everyone about this three thousand in the bank; he used to boast about it. And I heard him say his daughter was counting on getting that but she mustn't think it was automatic; it was his money to do as he liked with. Mind you, he was whingeing about her at the time, he hadn't had a word from her for weeks.'

'What was this about a will?'

'It must have been a year ago or more – at least that. She'd just given up being a home help, but she was in and out over the road every day. I was sitting here working on our catalogue and Trev was here too when she came to the door and asked if we would witness some document old Eric had got. It was quite a surprise – I mean, I'd hardly spoken to her before that and she'd ignore me if she saw me in the street. She said he had to sign this form and he needed two witnesses. And then do you know what she said? That we'd be better not being married, not being connected with each other! I was amazed. Well, I thought maybe it was something to do with this supplementary benefit and I was going to go, but Trevor asked Gwen what it was and all she said was it was nothing we need worry about, just a form. Well, naturally, that wasn't good enough for Trev and he said we had to know what we were signing before we went over there, and then she said it was Eric's will.'

'And that put me off quite a bit, as you can imagine,' said Trevor. 'It smelt, if you know what I mean.'

'That's absolutely right, it smelt. Anyway, I just said we

were a bit busy and to count us out. Gwen said that was OK; she'd soon find someone and anyway her niece would be down the next night. I expect you know that niece, don't you, the one that looks like she was modelling clothes?'

It was all interesting enough, and would have been useful if Gwen Robson had been suspected of murder and Eric Swallow and any of these other old people her victims. But it was she who had been the victim. Wexford asked his question about Ralph Robson's movements and Nicola Resnick was able to tell him that she had heard sounds from next door late on Thursday afternoon. The wall between the houses was thin and you could hear the click of lights being switched on and off, the thump-thump of Robson's stick and of course the television.

How could she particularly remember last Thursday?

Robson had had the children's programme *Blue Peter* on, she told him. That began at five-past five and was followed by a health programme about trace elements as food supplements. Nicola Resnick was interested in that and she had switched on her own set though Robson had his so loud she need scarcely have bothered.

Thursday afternoon once more, a week since the killing. Seven days ago Clifford Sanders had entered Queen Street from the High Street in his mother's car and parked it on the left-hand side on a meter, inserting into the slot, if he were to be believed, the forty pence that would ensure him one hour's parking. But it was already twenty minutes to five when he arrived, so that when he left Olson ten minutes on the meter still remained to run. And he had sat out those ten minutes, brooding on the things he had talked about to Olson, all that Dodo rubbish. Not that Burden believed that for a moment.

He went into all the shops on both sides of this part of Queen Street, the grocer's, a fishmonger, a fruiterer, a wine-shop, two cheap clothes boutiques and Pelage the hair-dressers. No one remembered seeing Clifford Sanders sitting in a car on the meter outside Pelage. The difficulty was that the red Metro was regularly parked on one of those meters on a Thursday afternoon, so it was hard to sort out when it

540

had been there and when it hadn't, and when Clifford had been seen sitting in it and when he had not. One of the stylists at Pelage was very definite about having sometimes seen him sitting in the car in the driving-seat, just sitting there as if lost in thought, not reading or looking out of the window or anything.

From the cover of the wine supermarket window, Burden watched Clifford arrive at ten minutes to five. There was no meter free and he drove as far as where Castle Street cut across, then turned and came slowly back. By now someone was pulling out so Clifford waited, moved the Metro into the space, got out of the car and locked it. The day was damp and very cold and he wore a grey tweed overcoat and grey knitted hat pulled down well over his ears. From a distance, Burden had to admit, he looked not so much like a girl as an old woman. He put a couple of coins into the meter, which must still have had time to run from the previous insertion. Then he came quite slowly across the road as if he had all the time in the world instead of being, as was in fact the case, nearly twenty-five minutes late for his appointment. Burden felt a sneaking admiration for Serge Olson's technique in deliberately naming a time for this client half an hour in advance of the five o'clock when he knew he would arrive.

After Clifford had disappeared into the entrance at the side of Pelage, Burden went off along Castle Street to have a cautionary word with a jeweller he suspected of being a fence. Then into a call box to phone his wife and say he might be late but not very late – say around eight-thirty. A cup of tea and a cake in the Queen's Café and it was two minutes to six when he came back down Queen Street. An icy rain had begun to fall and the dark was the darkness of midnight, though brightly illuminated here by dripping, fuzzy yellow and white lights that turned the pavements a gleaming dirty gold and silver. Snowflakes started appearing among the silvery rods of rain.

Clifford came out of Olson's door at two minutes past six. He wasn't hurrying, but he was moving a good deal faster than when he had arrived. Burden sheltered from the rain and Clifford's view in the doorway of the greengrocer's; they were closing up and people kept pushing past him to carry in trays of chicory and aubergines. Clifford got into the car without even glancing at the meter; he started up and was away as the hands of Burden's watch moved to five-past six.

Wexford had read and heard about people seeing on some-one else's arm the brand mark of the concentration camps, but he had not had that experience himself; and he didn't have it now – Dita Jago on this cold afternoon having her arms covered by a woolly garment that was itself a work of art: a knitted tapestry of greens and purples, rich reds and jewel blues. But when he glanced enquiringly at the great pile of manuscript which lay on the table in this strange cluttered room, the perhaps orderly muddle of notebooks and loose leaves, scrawled-on envelopes and works of reference, she had nodded to him.

'My great work,' she said. A smile made the remark a modest one. 'My memoirs of Oswiecim.'

'Auschwitz?' he said.

She nodded and, lifting up the topmost sheet of manuscript, turned it over so that only a blank side showed.

9

The room was of the same size and shape as the one in which he had talked to Robson and his niece; as the room Trevor Morrison and Nicola Resnick used as their office; as John Whitton's nursery. It was on the other side of the street and faced the opposite way, but the main difference from all those others lay in its rich clutter, the abundance of curious interesting things, the piles of books and papers and the adornment of its walls which was like nothing Wexford had ever seen before.

Unless you looked out of the window – seeing the trim little roadway, the trees in the pavement grass plots, the semi-detached houses – you might have believed yourself anywhere but on a local authority housing estate outside an English country town. What the walls were papered or painted with it was impossible to say, for they were covered all over with hangings which to Wexford had at first looked like lavish and elaborate embroideries but which, on examining them more closely, he saw to be knitted. Dora's efforts at what has been called 'the common art', resulting in jumpers for grandsons, at least told him that much. But this knitting was in all colours of the spectrum, those colours subtly matched and contrasted, creating abstract designs of immense complexity as well as pictures that in the execution of their strong primitive imagery reminded him of the paintings of Rousseau. In one a tiger crept through a jungle of green fronds and dark fruit-laden branches: in another a girl in a sarong walked with peacocks. The biggest, which covered the whole of one wall and had evidently been constructed in panels, was Chinese rather than tropical and showed a green landscape with little temples on the summits of hills and a herd of deer browsing between the woodland and the lake.

She was smiling at his wonderment. He only knew she was the creator of all this by the piece of work now in progress, another jungle picture taking shape from a circular needle, which lay on a round table beside Venetian glass animals and painted porcelain eggs. She had completed perhaps half of it.

'You're a busy woman, Mrs Jago,' he observed.

'I like to keep occupied.' Her accent was a rather unfamiliar guttural, Polish perhaps or Czech, but the English itself was grammatically and syntactically flawless. 'I have been writing my book for two years now and it's nearly done. God only knows if anyone will ever publish such a book, but I wrote it for my own satisfaction, to get it all down on paper. And it's true what they say.' She smiled at him again. 'Get it down, write it out and it's no longer such a terrible thing to remember. It doesn't cure but it helps.'

'The writer is the only free man, as someone said.'

'Whoever that someone was knew what he was talking about.'

She sat down facing him and picked up her knitting. Supplied with hibiscus tea by Nicola Resnick and Earl Grey by a Miss Margaret Anderson – who claimed never to have spoken to Mrs Robson or heard of her until she was dead – Wexford was rather relieved that Mrs Jago offered him no refreshment. Her fingers worked skilfully, moving with assurance a complex mass of coloured threads, selecting one, taking two or three stitches with it, abandoning this first shade and joining in another. Plump and tapering these fingers were, the wedding ring cutting deeply into the flesh. She was a mountain of a woman, yet somehow neither gross nor ungainly, her legs shapely with fine ankles and small feet in tiny black pumps. Remains of a gipsyish beauty showed in her full, pink-cheeked face. Her eyes were black, bright and in their cobweb wrinkles like jewels in a fibrous nest. Hair that was still dark was drawn back with combs into a large glossy bun.

'You came in and offered to do some shopping for Mr

Robson,' he began. 'That makes me think you must have known them fairly well.'

She looked up at him and the fingers were momentarily stilled. 'I didn't know them at all. I wouldn't be far wrong if I said that was only the second time I'd ever spoken to him except to say good morning.'

Wexford was disappointed. His hopes of this woman, though quite unjustifiable, had been high. Something about her made him feel she was essentially truthful.

'He was a neighbour,' she said. 'He'd lost his wife. She had been killed in a horrible way and it was the least I could do.' She remembered his name, though she had only briefly seen his warrant card. 'It was no trouble to me, Mr Wexford. I'm no Good Samaritan. My daughter takes me shopping or does it for me.'

'You may not have known him but you knew her, didn't you?'

She came to the end of her row, turned the linked needles. 'Hardly. Will you believe me if I tell you that was the first time I'd ever been in their house? Let me tell you something. I don't want you to waste your time on someone who can tell you very little. When I came out of the camp, they put me in a hospital the army ran. There was a man there, a soldier who was a ward orderly, and he fell in love with me. God knows why, for I was a skeleton and my hair had all fallen out.' She smiled. 'You wouldn't think that to see me now, would you? And I used to long and long to put on weight like they said I must. Well, this man – Corporal Jago, Arthur Jago – he married me and made me an English-woman.' She pointed to the pile of manuscript. 'It is all in the book!' Her knitting resumed, she said, 'But though I have tried I have never become very English, Mr Wexford. I have never quite learned to get on with the English way of always pretending everything in the garden is lovely. Do you under-stand what I mean? Everything in the garden is *not* lovely. There is a snake in the bush and worms under the stones and half the plants are poisonous . . .'

He smiled at the image she created.

'For example, Mr Robson – that poor man – he will say that what is to be will be; perhaps it is all for the best, life must go on. And Miss Anderson down the street who found a man who wanted to marry her at last when she was sixty years old . . . when he died a week before the wedding, what does she say? Maybe it was too late, maybe they'd both have regretted it. I cannot do with this.'

'But these are the tenets of survival, Mrs Jago.'

'Perhaps. But I cannot see that you survive any less if first you cry and rage and show your feelings. At least, it isn't my way and I am not comfortable with it.'

Wexford, who would have been quite happy to continue with this exploration of English emotion or lack of it, nevertheless thought it was time to move on. Weariness had come to take hold of him and his headache was back, a tight band wound around above the eyes. It was a piece of luck, sheer serendipity, that made him speak the name of the old man who had lived a few houses away in Berry Close.

'Eric Swallow,' he said. 'Did you have the same slight acquaintance with him?'

'I know who you mean,' she said, laying the knitting in her lap. 'That was rather amusing, but nothing to do with poor Mrs Robson being killed. I mean it couldn't be anything, really.'

'All right. But if it's amusing I'd like to hear it. There's little enough in this business to make us laugh.'

'The poor old man was dying. That isn't funny, of course. If I were English I would say maybe it was a merciful release, wouldn't I?'

'Was it?'

'Well, he was very old, nearly ninety. He had a daughter but she was in Ireland and she wasn't young, naturally. Mrs Robson used to do a lot for him; I mean, after she stopped being a home help and getting paid for it, she still went in there nearly every day. In the end when he got so that he couldn't get out of bed, they took him away and he died in the hospital . . .'

Wexford had had his eyes on the great landscape tapestry, but the sound of a car door slamming made him turn his head and then almost immediately the doorbell rang. Mrs Jago got up, excused herself and went out into the hall with a surprisingly light, springy tread. Voices could be heard, the clamorous treble of children. Then the front door closed again and Mrs Jago came back with two little girls: the younger of them, though too big to be carried, was in her arms; the other, who looked about five or six and who wore a school uniform of navy coat, yellow and navy scarf and felt hat with stripey band, walking by her side.

'These are my granddaughters, Melanie and Hannah Quincy. They live in Down Road, but sometimes their mummy brings them to me for an hour or two and we have a nice tea, don't we, girls?' The children said nothing, appearing shy. Dita Jago put Hannah down. 'Tea is all ready and we shall have it at five sharp. You can tell me when it is three minutes to five, Melanie; Mummy says you can tell the time now.'

Hannah went immediately to the table where the painted eggs and glass animals were. And though the older child had a book to read and had opened it, she was keeping a sharp cautionary eye on her sister's handling of the fragile things. Wexford, from personal experience, knew only too well the advantages and the pitfalls of that particular relationship, the stresses created in infancy that lasted a lifetime.

Dita Jago was placidly knitting once more. 'I was telling you about old Mr Swallow. Well, one afternoon – a Thursday I think it was, a year ago or a bit more – the front-door bell rang and there was Mrs Robson. She wanted me to come into Mr Swallow's with her and be a witness to something. In fact, she wanted two people and she'd seen my daughter's car outside, so she knew Nina was here. I found out afterwards that she had already been to a couple who live on the other side. He's called Morrison, I don't know her name, but anyway for some reason they wouldn't do it.

'As I've said, I don't suppose I'd ever spoken more than two words to her and she'd never met Nina. I had to introduce them. But that didn't stop her asking us both to go down there and witness this form.'

'Hannah, I'm going to be very cross if you break that little horse,' said Melanie.

A struggle ensued as the elder granddaughter did her best to prise from her sister's fingers a blue glass animal. Hannah stamped her foot.

'Grandma is going to be very unhappy if you break it. Grandma will cry.'

'No, she won't.'

547

'Give it to me, please, Hannah. Now do as you're told.'

'Hannah will cry! Hannah will scream!'

Shades of Sylvia and Sheila . . . Dita Jago intervened, drawing the younger child – who was by now carrying out her threat – on to her lap. Melanie looked mutinous, frowning darkly.

'Birds in their little nests should agree,' Mrs Jago said, not without irony, Wexford thought. She stroked the little girl's mane of dark curly hair. 'We thought it was something to do with the money he wanted to get from the what-do-you-call-it? DH-something – the supplementary benefit. There are always forms, aren't there? Anyway, we went down to Mr Swallow's with her and when we got there we found him asleep in bed. Mrs Robson was a little bit put out. My daughter said what was this form and had he already signed it? Well, you could see Mrs Robson didn't want to say. She said she'd wake Mr Swallow up; it was important and he'd want her to wake him.'

Hannah, her crying over, placed one thumb in her mouth and opening the other fist, showed her sister the blue glass horse, clenching her hand as soon as Melanie made a pounce for it.

Melanie turned away loftily. 'Five minutes to five, Grandma,' she said.

'All right. I said to tell me when it was three minutes to. Anyway, the piece of paper we had to sign was lying there on the table face-downwards. I mean we thought that's what it was and we were right. Nina just picked it up and took one look – and what do you think it was?'

Wexford had a pretty good idea, but he decided not to steal Mrs Jago's thunder and merely shrugged.

'It was a will, made out on a will form. Nina didn't get to read it because Mrs Robson snatched it away, but we could guess what was on it. It would have been leaving his money to Mrs Robson. Three thousand pounds, he used to boast he had; everyone here knew that. And she was after it – she liked money, there was no doubt about that. Well, we both shied away like anything. We told each other afterwards no way, absolutely not. Suppose that daughter had brought it up in court and we'd had to go there and say we'd signed it?'

'What was Mrs Robson's reaction to that?'

'Three minutes to five, Grandma,' Melanie said.

'I'm coming, darling. She didn't like it, but what could she do? I couldn't help having a laugh when we were outside. I heard later she went trying other people down the street, but she never struck lucky; she couldn't get anyone but her niece. It was only a few days after that they took Mr Swallow away and when he died there wasn't a will and his daughter got his money – being his real heir, you see, as was quite right. Now I must keep my promise to these children.'

Mrs Jago put the child on the floor and the knitting on the table and got up. 'You will stay for tea? We have Grandma's version of *sachertorte*.'

Wexford thanked her but shook his head. He had told Donaldson to come back for him at five and he thought of the deep pleasure of leaning back in the car and closing his eyes. Hannah had crept quietly to the table and replaced the little horse amongst the other animals with precision, with perfectly coordinated delicate fingers, her eyes all the while on her sister, her lips not quite smiling. It reminded him of Sheila playing all those years ago with a china ornament which Sylvia (though no one else) had forbidden her to touch. And Sheila had teased like this little one, peeping over a defiant shoulder with the faintest Gioconda smile.

'Of course, to do her justice she didn't want money for herself,' Dita Jago's voice interrupted his reverie. 'It was for him, it would have been all for him.' It was just as he was leaving, when they were out in the hall, that she said, 'Don't you want to know where I was last Thursday evening?'

He smiled. 'Tell me.'

'My daughter always goes shopping on Thursday afternoons and usually she takes me. But last week she dropped me off at the public library in the High Street and left the girls with me. She picked us up again at five-thirty.'

Why had she insisted on telling him that? he wondered. Perhaps merely to avoid a repetition of his visit. Or was he imagining things that the tone of her voice gave no hint of – reacting in a confused, almost fuddled, way because of the huge weariness which had overtaken him? Passing a wall mirror in the hall as he made his way out, he caught sight of his discoloured face, the bruised muzzle of a prize-fighter recovering from a bout, and turned quickly away. He was no narcissist, no lover of his own image.

The front door closed on him. Her grandchildren's demands had cut short any parting pleasantries Mrs Jago might have made. It was just before five, for her clock had been fast, and Wexford waited for the car with the anxiety of a disabled pensioner expecting an ambulance. He had to lower himself into a sitting position on the low wall, feeling his bruised body creak. Going back to work had not been a wise idea, yet it hadn't seemed like work, more a matter of paying social calls. Mike ought to be left to himself to handle this case; he was quite capable of doing so. Someone like Serge Olson would say that he, Wexford, was at fault – only probably he wouldn't use a word like 'fault' – in being unable to delegate, in refusing to yield authority to the younger man. It was very likely a sign of insecurity, fear of seeing Mike usurp his place, even his job. Psychology, he thought, and not for the first time, often just wasn't true.

Cars passed. With a strong inner shudder, an actual shrinking, he tried to contemplate what it would be like to sit at the wheel again, start the ignition, move the shift into gear. That, of course, he wouldn't quite have to do, just manipulate from 'park' to 'drive'. But the notion of putting his hand to that lever brought a darkness before his eyes and made him hear a sound he had no recollection of hearing: the roar of the bomb. He closed his eyes, opening them to see Donaldson draw up at the kerb.

A hunch he couldn't quite believe in – it all seemed behaviour of the crassest, most unfeeling kind – led Burden to assume that Clifford Sanders was heading for the Barringdean car park. He couldn't follow him: he hadn't a car immediately to hand and, making his way there on foot, he told himself he was wasting his time. No one would do that. No one would return to the scene of so horrific a crime precisely seven days to the hour later, and there go through the same prescribed ritual. With, that is, one notable exception . . .

He entered the shopping complex by the pedestrian entrance where, a week before, Dodo Sanders had stood rattling the gates and screaming for help. But first he went into the underground car park, descending to the second level in the lift. At least Clifford hadn't parked the car on precisely the spot where it had been the week before, but perhaps he had not done so only because that particular space and those next to it and opposite were already occupied. This time the Sanders' car was at the extreme opposite end to the lift and the stairs. It was empty which meant, presumably, that Clifford was somewhere in the shopping centre.

As he had been in the previous week, thought Burden, looking at his watch by the light of the glaring greenish strip-lights. Six-twenty-two, but he, of course, had walked here and taken some time to locate the car. Clifford's appointment had been at his normal time, five o'clock, so today his date to pick up his mother would be later. Six-thirty perhaps? With the centre closing at six and usually emptied by six-fifteen, would she be prepared to wait for him? But as he was speculating along these lines, watching the last cars backed out and driven away, he heard the clang of the descending lift. Clifford and his mother came out of it and Burden watched them walk towards their car, Clifford carrying two Tesco bags and a wicker basket. Burden thought he could easily be taken for a girl from the back; it was something to do with his plump hips and the rather short steps he took. He caught up with them as Clifford was lifting the boot-lid of the Metro.

Mrs Sanders turned and cast upon him a basilisk look. She was hatless, her hair set in a rather bouffant, cloudy way which didn't suit her. The red lipstick glistened in the pale face. He had wondered what that particular colour of skin reminded him of and now he knew: raw fish, a translucent, faintly pinkish white. She was perfectly calm and her voice was cold.

'I wish I'd never told anyone about finding that dead body. I wish I'd kept quiet.' Burden had an inkling then of the icy authority she exercised over her son and had no doubt exercised since he was an infant. There was an awful precision in that tone and it was backed by a great storehouse of nervous energy. 'I'm not usually a fool. I should have had the sense to stay out of it; I should have followed his example.'

551

'What example was that, Mrs Sanders?' Burden asked.

Her attention was on the time by her digital watch and that indicated on the clock in the Metro which she bent down to look at. Abstractedly, she said, 'He ran away, didn't he?'

'You tell me. I've got a very good idea what it was he did, and running away was only a small part of it.' While Clifford unlocked the driver's door, he said, 'You won't mind giving me a lift, will you? We can take your mother home first and then you and I will have another talk at the police station.'

Clifford didn't say anything. The only sign that he had heard was when he reached inside to release the lock on the passenger door. And on the way back to Ash Lane no one said a word. Half the carriageway of this end of the Forby Road was undergoing repairs, temporary traffic lights had been installed and a long queue of cars waited. Dodo Sanders, sitting in the front next to Clifford, pulled down her glove and lifted up her coat cuff to look at her digital watch. Why it should have been important to her to know the precise time they had left the car park and the precise time they began queueing at the lights, Burden couldn't guess. Perhaps, though, that wasn't the purpose of all this watch-gazing. It might be that she simply wanted to know the time, that all day long, every day, every five minutes, she had to know the time.

She spoke as Clifford drew up by the kerb. 'I can take the things in. There's no need to come with me.'

But he got out of the car, removed the bags from the boot and carried them up to the front door. He unlocked the door and stood back for her to pass in ahead of him. Burden understood it all. She was one of those people who say things like that but don't mean them. She was the sort who would say, 'Don't worry about me, I'll be all right on my own', or 'Don't bother to write me a thank-you letter', and then create hell when she got left alone or when no letter came. His mother-in-law was a bit like that, though Mrs Sanders was a thousand times worse.

Clifford got back into the driving-seat and Burden stayed where he was, in the back. He didn't care whether they talked or not; they would talk at the station. The driving was done with the slow care, the superfluous signals and excessive braking habitual to Clifford. He broke the silence as they turned in to find the last remaining parking space.

'What is it you suspect me of?'

Burden felt a reluctance to answer questions of that kind. They seemed to bring him down to Clifford's level of ingenuousness and simplicity. Simple-mindedness expressed it better, perhaps. 'Let's leave that until we're inside, shall we?' he suggested.

He called up Diana Pettit and together they shepherded Clifford into that grey-tiled interview room. It was dark now, of course, had been dark for two hours, and the lights in this room were as grim and uncompromising as those in the Barringdean Centre car park, but much brighter. The central heating was on in here, though, just as it was all over the building. Police officers just as much as those they interviewed, as Burden had once told someone without irony, were often obliged to sit there for hours. The immediate warmth, a much greater heat than he enjoyed in his own home, made Clifford ask to take off his hat and coat. He was one who would ask permission before he did almost anything; no doubt asking for leave had been a requirement of right conduct dinned into him from his earliest years. He sat down and looked from Diana to Burden and Burden back to Diana, like a puzzled new boy whom school rules bewilder.

'I'd like you to tell me what you're accusing me of.'

'I'm not accusing you of anything yet,' Burden said.

'What you suspect me of, then.'

'Don't you know, Clifford? Haven't you got a clue? What do you think it is – helping yourself out of the collection in church?'

'I don't go to church.' He essayed a faint smile and it was the first Burden had ever seen him give. The smile seemed contrived with difficulty as if a mechanical process had to be set in motion, a series of button-pressing and lever-pulling only half-remembered. It irritated Burden.

'Perhaps you stole a car then. Or nicked a lady's handbag.'

'I'm sorry. I don't know what you're getting at.'

Burden said abruptly. 'Have you any objection if I record this interview? Tape it, I mean?'

'Would it make any difference if I had?'

553

'Certainly it would. This isn't a police state.'

'Do as you like,' Clifford said indifferently and he watched Diana begin recording. 'You were going to tell me what I'm supposed to have done.'

'Let me tell you what I think happened. I think you met Mrs Robson inside the shopping centre, in Tesco's. You hadn't seen her for quite a while, but you knew her and she knew you – and she knew something about you you'd like kept secret. I wonder what it was. I don't know yet, I honestly don't know, but you'll tell me. I hope you'll tell me tonight.'

Clifford said in an uneven voice, 'When I first saw Mrs Robson, she was dead. I never saw her before in my life.'

'What you saw, Clifford, was your opportunity. You and she were alone and you very much wanted her out of the way . . .'

He had to remind himself that this was a man, not a boy, not a teenager. And not simple-minded, not retarded. He was a teacher; he had a university degree. The blank, soft face looked even more spongy, but a spark showed in each dull eye. Clifford's voice squeaked. Fear or guilt or God-knows-what had done something to the vocal cords, leaving him with a eunuch's soprano.

'You don't mean you think I'd kill someone? Me? Is that what you mean?'

Not wanting to fall in with this play-acting, this vanity – for what else would explain it? – that made a man believe he could do as he pleased without fear of discovery, Burden said drily, 'He's cottoned on at last.'

Next moment he was on his feet and Diana too, stepping back from the table. Clifford had leapt up, face and lips white as if in genuine shock, his hands grasping the table edge and shaking it, vibrating it as his mother had shaken the wire gates.

'Me? Kill someone? You're mad! You're all crazy! Why've you picked on me? I never knew you meant that with all your questions, I never dreamed . . . I thought I was just a witness. Me kill someone? People like *me* don't kill people!'

'What kind do then, Clifford?' Burden spoke calmly as he lowered himself once more into his chair. 'Some say everyone's capable of murder.'

He met the other man's round staring eyes. A dew of sweat

had appeared all over the putty-like skin, the pudgy features, and a drop trickled down his upper lip between the two wings of the moustache. Burden felt for him an impatient contempt. He wasn't even a good actor. It would be interesting to hear how all that would play back, that stuff about killing people. He'd play it to Wexford, see what he thought.

'Sit down, Cliff,' he said, his growing contempt making him accord the man less than the dignity of his unabridged Christian name. 'We're going to have a long talk.'

Exhausted when the car dropped him at Sylvia's, Wexford would have liked a home of his own to recover in, the sole companionship of his own wife. He had to settle for a drink, the whisky Dr Crocker strictly forbade. Someone had brought in an evening paper; a story on the front page was about a man who had all day been 'helping the police with their enquiries into the Kingsmarkham bomb outrage'. There was no picture and of course no name or description, nothing to make even tentatively possible the identification of this man who had wanted Sheila dead, who had conceived for her that particular brand of cold, impersonal, political hatred.

The boys were watching television, Sylvia trying to write an essay on the psychological abuse of the elderly.

'I know all about that,' Wexford said. 'Would you like to interview me?'

'You're not elderly, Dad.'

'I feel it.'

Dora came and sat beside him. 'I've been to look at our house,' she said. 'The builders have been in and weather-proofed it. At least the rain can't get in. Oh, and the Chief Constable phoned, something about a house we can have if we like. We do like, don't we, Reg?'

A leap of the heart before he started feeling ungrateful to Sylvia. 'Did he say where it is?'

'Up at Highlands, I think. I'm almost sure he said Highlands.'

10

Remorse was perhaps too strong a word; it was distaste tempered with a hint of shame that Burden felt throughout that weekend. He said to himself, and he even said it to his wife who was home again with their son, that this was what the job was about, this was police work.

'The end justifies the means, Mike?' she said.

'It's the merest idealism to deny that. Every day in everything we do, it's implicit even if we don't come out and say it. When we were going through that bad patch with Mark and we decided the only way was to let him cry, that two nights of that would cure him, we were saying the end justifies the means.'

He took the child on his lap and Jenny smiled.

'Don't teach it to him though, will you?'

He spared himself half an hour to play with Mark and eat his lunch and then he was back at the police station in that interview room, confronting Clifford Sanders once more. But on the way the task behind him and the task ahead goaded him, made him wrinkle up his nose at the nastiness of it. How far removed from torture was it, after all? Clifford had to sit there in that comfortless room, left alone for part of the time for as much as an hour, food brought to him on trays by an indifferent police constable. And it would not have been quite so bad if Clifford had been tougher, less like a child. He looked like a big child, a kind of fined-down Billy Bunter. A stoicism had succeeded his bewilderment, an air of being a brave boy and sticking it out a little longer. But here Burden told himself he was being a fool. The man was a man, educated, neurotic perhaps but sane, simply lacking character and strength of mind. And look what he had done. The facts spoke for themselves. Clifford had been in the shopping centre, had been seen with Mrs Robson, had a garrote in his possession, had run away.

Was it likely that he had found the body, covered it up because it looked like his mother and then fled? Nobody behaved like that outside the pages of popular psychiatry. All that stuff which Serge Olson no doubt dispensed – about neurotics choosing girlfriends because they were looking for a mother, or employers as father-figures, or being put off sex because you'd seen your mother in her underwear – that was strictly for the books and the couch as far as Burden was concerned. And he was a fool to let himself feel a sneaking pity for Clifford Sanders. The man had meant to kill Mrs Robson and had succeeded. Hadn't he gone specifically to meet her armed with a garrote?

Probably his self-doubt was due solely to his failure so far to find the link between Clifford and Gwen Robson. He knew there must be a link and once he had found it, he would no longer be a prey to this unprofessional and certainly unfamiliar guilt. Facing Clifford again, with Archbold there to assist in this renewed interrogation and the tape recorder on, Burden reminded himself that the police had interviewed Sutcliffe the 'Yorkshire Ripper' nine times before he was arrested. And in the intervening time Sutcliffe had murdered his final victim. It would be a fine thing if Clifford Sanders were to kill again because he, Burden, had been squeamish.

He lowered himself slowly into the chair. Clifford, who had been gnawing at a fingernail, snatched his hand from his mouth as if he suddenly recalled nail-biting was something he must not do.

Burden began, 'Has your mother ever been ill, Clifford?'

An uncomprehending look. 'What do you mean?'

'Was she ever ill so that she had to stay in bed? When she needed someone to look after her?'

'She had what-do-you-call-it once. Like a kind of rash, but it aches.'

'He means shingles,' Archbold said.

'That's right, shingles. She had that once.'

'Did a home help come in to look after her, Clifford?'

557

But this approach led nowhere. Dodo Sanders had been confined to bed for no more than a few hours throughout the whole of Clifford's life. Burden abandoned this line of enquiry and carefully took Clifford through the sequence of events from the time he left Olson until he ran from the car park out of the pedestrian gates. Clifford got in a hopeless muddle with the times, saying he had got to the centre at five-thirty, later changing it to ten-past six. Burden knew he was lying. Everything was going according to his expectations and the only surprising thing which happened was when Clifford corrected him over the use of his name.

'Why have you stopped calling me Cliff? You can call me that if you like, I don't mind. I like it.'

Awaiting him in his office was a lab report on that spool of plastic-covered wire. There was a great deal of technical detail – Burden found himself back among the polymers – but the plain fact easily sorted out was that the shreds of substance found in Mrs Robson's neck wound were quite different from the stuff coating the wire in Clifford Sanders' tool-box. Well, he had been wrong. That might only mean, of course, that Clifford had disposed of the wire he used for his garrote – thrown it in the river or, more safely, stuck it in his own or someone else's dustbin. In the meantime Clifford could sweat for a day or two. Wexford was his immediate concern, Dr Crocker had strictly forbidden the Chief Inspector to return to work at the office and to see him Burden had to drive up to Sylvia's house.

'At any rate I shall be on the spot,' Wexford said. 'I'm going to be living up at Highlands. How about that?'

Burden grinned. 'That's right. There are two or three police houses. When are you moving in?'

'Don't know yet,' Wexford said, glancing through the paperwork Burden had brought him. 'I don't think the person – a useful genderless word – that the checkout girl saw talking to Mrs Robson was Clifford Sanders at all. I think maybe it was Lesley Arbel. But I'll tell you where I agree with you – when you say Mrs Robson was a blackmailer. I think so too.'

Burden nodded eagerly. He was always disproportionately pleased when Wexford approved some suggestion of his.

'She liked money,' he said. 'She was near enough prepared to do anything for money. Look at all that stuff you told me about the old man's will. She was running up and down the street searching for witnesses to a will under which she was to be the sole beneficiary. We may laugh about her bathing someone and cutting some other old man's toenails, but weren't those normally distasteful tasks undertaken for a very inflated payment? There's probably more of that sort of thing we haven't yet uncovered.'

'Mrs Jago says she did what she did all for her husband. There's an implication that this makes it all right, exonerates her. I imagine that was precisely the way Gwen Robson saw it herself.'

'Why did Ralph Robson specifically need money anyway?' Burden asked. 'Has anyone queried that one? I mean, if I said I needed money I'd really mean Jenny and Mark and me, my family. And you'd mean you and Dora, surely?'

Wexford shrugged. 'We've looked at her bank account at the TSB. She had rather a lot in it; I mean more than one would have expected. Robson has his own personal account and they've no joint savings. But Gwen Robson had something over sixteen hundred pounds and that could be the fruits of blackmail. Your idea is that Gwen Robson had evidence Clifford had done something reprehensible and was blackmailing him?'

Burden nodded. 'Something like that. And the worm finally turned. Clifford's pretty worm-like in most respects, I'd say, so why not in that one too?'

'What could Clifford have done? It would surely have to be an earlier murder. Nobody cares much about sexual irregularities these days.'

Burden's face indicated that he did. 'Gwen Robson cared about them.'

'Yes, but you can't imagine that the cramming school would – or Dodo Sanders, come to that. It would be hard to assign any sort of moral convictions to her. She strikes me as a person who has never heard of ethics, still less ever thought she needed views about them.'

Burden wasn't interested. 'I'll find out what it was,' he

559

said. 'I'm working on it.' He studied Wexford's face: the bruises that were fading, the cut that might or might not leave a permanent scar. 'They had to let that chap go, the one they thought was your bomber. It was on the news this morning.'

Wexford nodded. He had had a phone call about it and a long talk had ensued, culminating in a request to take part in a conference at Scotland Yard. Dr Crocker had sanctioned this with the utmost reluctance and there was no way he would have agreed had he known Wexford intended to drive there. When Burden had gone, Wexford wrapped himself up, adding a scarf of Robin's that was hanging in the hall in case Dora or Sylvia should come home early and see him. His car was on the garage drive and he noticed for the first time – no one had told him – how scarred the bodywork was by chips of flying glass. He got into the driving-seat, feeling that this was unfamiliar, a strange thing to be doing, an act he hadn't performed for a long time.

Closing the door, he thought he would just rest for a moment or two, sit there holding the ignition key. Now if this were a thriller, he thought, a television drama maybe, and he an unimportant character or even a villain, he would put the key in and turn it and the car would blow up. He tried to laugh at that but couldn't, which was absurd, because he had no memory of the explosion and the bangs he thought he heard were not memory but the invention of his imagination. Go on, jump, he said, pushing himself along the plank, easing to the edge of the springboard. He took a breath, pushed the key in, turned it. Nothing happened; the engine didn't even start. Well, why would it? Dora had left it in 'drive'. He moved the automatic shift before he realized what he was doing, the terrible step that was going to be his crossing point.

Because there was nothing now but to go on, he turned the ignition key.

Burden was walking down the High Street, occasionally looking into shop windows already decorated for Christmas, when he saw Serge Olson coming towards him. The psycho-

560

therapist wore a check tweed jacket, its collar of mock fur turned up against the sharp east wind.

He greeted Burden as if they were old friends. 'Hallo, Mike, good to see you. How are you?'

Taken aback, Burden said he was fine and Serge Olson asked if he was making much progress. This wasn't a question Burden was accustomed to being asked by those he thought of as the public and he couldn't help thinking it a shade impertinent. But he made a non-committal, vaguely optimistic reply and then Olson surprised him very much by announcing that it was too cold to stand about and why didn't they go into the Queen's Café for a cup of tea? Burden realized at once that Olson must have something he at least thought important to tell him. Why else would he make such a suggestion? For all his use of Burden's Christian name, the two men had met only once before and then strictly on a policeman-and-witness basis.

But when they were seated at a table, instead of imparting secrets of the consulting room, Olson began to talk only of the recent Arab bombers' trial, the huge sentences meted out to the three guilty men and the threat made by some allied terrorist organization to 'get' the prosecuting counsel. Burden was at last moved to ask what it was in particular that Olson had wanted to talk to him about.

The fierce bright animal eyes gleamed. There was an incongruity here, for Olson's voice was always calm and leisurely and his manner placid. 'Talk to you about, Mike?'

'Well, you know, asking me in here for a cup of tea, I thought there must be some specific thing . . .'

Olson shook his head gently. 'Perhaps I might say Clifford Sanders could be a killer in certain circumstances? Or that his manner was very odd when he left me that evening? Or that men of twenty-three who live at home with their mothers must be psychotic by definition? No, I wasn't going to say any of those things. I was cold and I fancied some good hot tea I didn't have to brew up myself.'

Unwilling to let it go at that, Burden said, 'You really mean you weren't going to say any of that?' Olson's head shook more rapidly. 'Surely it is odd a man living with his mother, even if she's a widow. Mrs Sanders isn't what one would call old.'

561

Olson said nearly incomprehensibly, 'Have you ever heard of the Fallacy of Enkekalymmenos?'

'The what?'

'It means "the veiled one" and it goes something like this. "Can you recognize your mother?" "Yes". "Can you recognize this veiled one?" "No". "This veiled one is your mother. Hence you can recognize your mother and not recognize her".'

There was something veiled about Mrs Sanders. Her own face was a kind of veil, thought Burden, surprised by his own imagination. But in a brusque policeman-like way he said, 'What's that got to do with Clifford?'

'It's got something to do with all of us and our parents, and with knowing and unknowing. Over the entrance to the oracle at Delphi were the words "Know thyself" and I'm talking about a very long time ago. In the two or three thousand years since then, have we heeded that advice?' Olson smiled and, leaving a moment for his words to sink in, added, 'She's not a widow either.'

'She's not?' This was firmer, better charted terrain. Burden checked his sigh of relief. 'Clifford's father's still living, then?'

'She and her husband were divorced years ago when Clifford was a child. Charles Sanders' people were farmers and that house had been in his family for generations. He was living there with his parents when he married. Putting it bluntly, his wife Dorothy was the family servant who came in daily to clean for them. It's not known what the parents thought about that. Obviously Clifford doesn't know. You needn't look like that, Mike, I'm not being a snob. It's not her menial status that set me wondering so much as – let's say her unattractive personality. I suppose she was good-looking and in my job I've learned that in nine cases out of ten that's enough. Five years later, he left them and he gave up the house to his wife and son.'

'What about the grandparents?' Burden asked.

Olson, who had eaten two elaborate iced cakes and a slice of fruit loaf, began brushing crumbs out of his beard with a green and yellow paper napkin. 'Clifford remembers them, but only just. He and his mother had his grandmother living with them when the father left. The grandfather had just died. There wasn't much money, and Charles Sanders doesn't

562

seem to have supported them. It was a hard, lonely sort of life. I've never been to the house, but I imagine it's a bit grim and remote. She went out cleaning, did a bit of dressmaking and I'll give her credit where it's due; she insisted on Clifford's going to university – the University of the South, that is, at Myringham – though he had to live at home and take jobs in the holidays. I don't doubt she was lonely and fancied she needed him with her.'

Burden got up to pay. He felt curiously grateful that after his earlier incomprehensible remarks, Olson had managed to avoid jargon and Greek words and talk like anyone else. But something amongst what the psychotherapist had said touched a chord in his mind, set a vibration twanging.

'I invited you,' Olson said, 'but if you'll guarantee the ratepayers will foot the bill I'll give in gracefully.'

'What was that you said about Clifford taking holiday jobs?'

'The usual sort of thing, Mike, only even that kind of job is harder to come by these days. Unskilled labour, a bit of gardening, shop work.'

'Gardening?' Burden said.

'I believe he did have one job like that. He told me about it at some length – largely because he hated it, I suspect. He's not keen on an outdoor life and nor am I for that matter.'

There wasn't a chance, Burden thought. You didn't get your wishes coming true like that . . . 'You don't remember the name, I suppose?'

'No, I don't. But it was an old spinster woman in a big house in Forest Park.'

11

Waiting in reception, Wexford felt the guilt that comes from disobeying a doctor's orders. It was really a fear of being found out, of Dora or Crocker or Burden discovering that he hadn't gone straight to Scotland Yard. In fact, he probably wouldn't have phoned this woman, have come here, if he hadn't been buoyed up by his own success at starting that car, at driving that car, at eventually driving himself to the station in it. Better to think of this as his reason than his anxiety over the slow progress which was being made on the case. Curious looks were no longer levelled at his face; the discoloration had nearly gone. The cut was one he might have made while shaving – if he had been drunk, for instance, or all his life up to now had worn a beard. The Bomb Squad people, when he presented himself, would hardly believe he had been the victim of an explosion. But first there was this alibi to check and some curiosity, perhaps pointlessly aroused, to satisfy.

The brighter coloured of the two receptionists, the one with orange curls, kept assuring him that Sandra Dale wouldn't keep him a moment, then no more than one minute, finally that she was on her way. Meanwhile Wexford contemplated *Kim* covers pinned up on the carpeted walls, photographs recording various *Kim* functions, a framed certificate or diploma commemorating the award to *Kim* of something or other. Someone touched him lightly on the shoulder.

'Mr Wexford?' He started easily but she didn't seem to notice. She was a young girl, not in the least like the picture in the magazine. 'I'm Rosie Unwin,' she said, 'Sandra Dale's assistant. Would you like to come this way, please? I'm sorry to have kept you.'

They went down passages and up in a lift and then up a flight of stairs and along another passage. At least it wasn't open plan, one of those office complexes where it is impossible to shut oneself away. Rosie Unwin opened a door at the end of the corridor and Wexford saw a woman seated at a desk who was scarcely more like her own photograph than her assistant was. She got up and put out her hand.

'Sandra Dale.' She hesitated. 'It really is my name.'

'Good morning, Miss Dale.'

The photograph was purposely designed to make her look older, plumper, more motherly – or 'auntly'. Wexford didn't think this woman was much over thirty; to him she seemed a young girl, slender, long-legged, with a broad-browed round face and soft blonde hair. The picture made her into someone to be trusted, confided in, someone wise whose advice one could rely on. She asked him to sit down, herself retreating once more behind her desk. The other girl came into the room after him and stood looking not altogether confidently at a visual display unit where amber-coloured letters and geometric figures danced.

'Lesley's not here,' Sandra Dale said, 'but perhaps you knew that? She's away doing a course in working those things and I'm left to manage as best I can.'

'It's you I want to talk to,' Wexford said, 'and perhaps Miss Unwin too.'

The office was large and extremely untidy, though perhaps there was method underlying the apparent disorder. Letters lay all over Rosie Unwin's desk, face-upwards, and Wexford wondered if they could be of the kind he had read in Sylvia's copy of *Kim* but decided not. He wasn't able to read any of them and those he could see were nearly all handwritten. Another pile filled Sandra Dale's in-tray. She read his mind – or rather, misread it.

'We average about two hundred letters a week.'

He nodded. There was a little library of works of reference and two shelves of books: a medical dictionary and an encyclopaedia of alternative medicine, a dictionary of psychology, Eric Berne's *A Layman's Guide to Psychiatry and Psychoan-*

alysis. Rosie Unwin pressed a key and the screen emptied of its dancing figures.

'Would you like coffee?' Wexford had accepted before she added, 'It'll be instant and it comes in Styrofoam.'

He said to Sandra Dale. 'You'll have heard about the woman who was murdered in Kingsmarkham – you know she was Lesley Arbel's aunt?'

'I haven't seen Lesley since it happened. I know about it of course. Lesley's been very brave, I think – very gallant, carrying on with the course – considering Mrs Robson was more like a mother to her.'

'Didn't she have a mother of her own?'

She looked sideways at him, not slyly but perhaps rather mysteriously. 'You'll say she was only my secretary, but I know a lot about her. We all know a lot about each other in here. Sometimes I think the way we work is a bit like a kind of ongoing encounter group. It must be the effect of our ... our clients.' There it was, that word again. 'Their problems – they bring things up in our own lives, I guess. Lesley wouldn't mind my telling you that her mother abandoned her when she was twelve and her aunt and uncle just took her over. She was already at boarding school so they didn't adopt her, but she was almost as much their daughter as if they had.' The phone on her desk whistled and she picked up the receiver, murmured into it, 'Yes, yes ... right,' and said to Wexford, 'Excuse me just one moment. Rosie will be with you right away.'

But for a few minutes he was left alone. Curiosity that had nothing much to do with the case in hand impelled him to read the topmost letter on Rosie Unwin's desk. He didn't even have to get out of his chair, only lean to one side. Eyesight lengthens as age comes on and Wexford thought his had become about as long as anyone's could. Holding a book at arm's length was no longer any use to him. His arms were too short.

'Dear Sandra Dale,' he read, 'I know this is awful and horrible and I am disgusted with myself, but I can't pretend about it any longer. The fact is that I am experiencing very powerful sexual feelings towards my own teenage son. I think I am in love with him. All the time I struggle against

566

these feelings of which I assure you I am deeply ashamed, but just the same . . .'

He had to stop and sit up straight again as Rosie Unwin came in with the coffee, but not before he had noticed that there was an address on the letter and it was signed. Strange. He had somehow assumed most letters would be anonymous.

'About point nought-nought-one per cent,' she said when he spoke these thoughts aloud. 'And most people send us a stamped addressed envelope too.'

'How do you make your selection? The ones you decide to print, I mean?'

'We don't pick the most bizarre,' she said. 'That one you were reading, that wasn't typical. You *were* reading it, weren't you? Everyone who comes in here reads the letters; they can't resist it.'

'Well, I admit I was. You wouldn't print that, though?'

'Probably not. That's for Sandra to decide, and then if there's any query it would be the editor's decision – I mean the editor of *Kim*.'

'Like going to higher court,' Wexford murmured.

'Sandra picks out those she thinks will have the widest appeal or impact – let's say common problems, the most human if you like. We'd only print the reply to that one from the woman who fancies her own son. We'd say, "To W. D., Wiltshire," and then write our reply. I mean we do draw the line. Can you believe it, we had a letter last week from someone asking us what the protein content of semen was . . . it's about somewhere.'

Wexford was saved from replying by the return of Sandra Dale. He waited until she was seated again, then asked her, 'So you last saw Lesley when? On Thursday November 19?'

'That's right. She didn't come in on the Friday, she phoned in and told me about her aunt, though I knew then, mind you: I recognized the name. And on the Monday – Monday the twenty-third, that is – she started the computer course. It was a bit of luck, if you can call it luck in the circumstances, that the course happened to be in the same town where her uncle lives.'

'She left here on Thursday afternoon, did she? What time would that have been – five? Five-thirty?'

Sandra Dale looked surprised. 'No, no, she took the afternoon off. I thought you knew.'

Wexford smiled neutrally.

'She finished at one. It was something about having to go down to Kingsmarkham to register for the course. She'd filled in one of the forms wrongly, something like that; she tried to phone the place, but their phone was out of order. Well, according to her it was. I'll be frank with you: I wasn't terribly pleased. I mean, I'd got to do without my secretary for a fortnight as it was, and all for the sake of doing our page on a word processor instead of a typewriter which had always suited us perfectly well.'

Wexford thanked her. This was not at all what he had expected to hear. He had hoped only to pick up from the agony aunt's department some useful pointers to Lesley Arbel's character. Instead he had been handed a smashed alibi.

Rosie Unwin said as he was leaving, 'I hope you won't mind my asking, but are you any relation to Sheila Wexford?'

He was always being asked that, so he ought not to have experienced that clutch at the heart. 'Why do you ask?' he responded rather too quickly.

She was taken aback. 'Only that I admire her very much. I mean, I think she's beautiful and a great actress.'

Not that she had heard something awful on the news, or been told of Sheila's fatal injuries . . . death . . . on breakfast television . . .

'She's my daughter,' he said.

They liked him now, they were all over him. He should have told them the minute he came in, he thought. He waited for one of them – the younger, surely – to tell him as most people sooner or later did that Sheila didn't look much like him, inferring really not so much lack of resemblance as the discrepancy between her beauty and his . . . well, lack of it. But they were tactful. They didn't say anything about wire-cutting either. He went off through the labyrinthine building with Rosie escorting him, talking of Sheila all the way, then they were taking his identification disc from him and signing him out. In half an hour's time he had an appointment at Scotland Yard for another session with the Bomb Squad, and he thought he might as well walk at least part of the distance.

So he made his way across Waterloo Bridge, beneath which the river lay sluggish as oil and above him not only the sun but the sky itself was invisible.

It was three days since he had last seen Clifford Sanders and in that time Burden's enquiries had confirmed most satisfactorily that he had indeed worked as a gardener for Miss Elizabeth McPhail at Forest House, Forest Park, Kingsmarkham. Her neighbours remembered him and one of them also remembered Gwen Robson's visits. What he would have liked was to have found someone who had seen them together, talking to each other. Perhaps this was a lot to expect. Beyond a doubt, Gwen Robson had received her offer of employment as Miss McPhail's full-time housekeeper four years ago. Clifford was twenty-three and four years previously would have been a year into his university course. Burden considered his strategy. Clifford would be at work now, at Munster's; he worked all day on Tuesdays until five. He would be tired when he got home and it would do no harm for him to find Burden there waiting for him, anxious for another talk either there in the back of beyond or down at the police station once more.

Davidson drove the two of them down the long lane that went past Sundays Park. At ten to five it was already dark and pockets of fog made very slow, cautious driving essential. The ivy-clad façade of the house loomed up out of the misty dark, looking alive, looking like a gigantic square bush or a surrealist nightmare of a tree. All the leaves hung limp and gleaming, dewed with water-drops. The car headlamps alone showed him the dark glistening mass, for not a light was showing amongst the coat of foliage. What did Dorothy Sanders do there all day – her son having taken the car and no bus stop nearer than Forby or Kingsmarkham, both at least two miles distant? Once a week Clifford took her to the Barringdean Shopping Centre, had his hour-long session with Olson, went to pick up his mother. What friends did she have, if any? How well did she really know Carroll the farmer? Each, it would seem, had been deserted by a partner; they were not far removed from each other in age . . .

The door opened and she was standing there. 'You back again? My son's not here.'

Burden remembered what Wexford had said about it being hard to associate her with ethics, with any moral sense. He was aware of something else, too, something he would never have thought of himself as sufficiently sensitive to feel – a coldness emanating from her. It was hard to think of her as having a normal body temperature, warm blood. And as he reflected these things, the whole passing rapidly through his mind as he stood on the doorstep, he felt also how very much he would hate to have to touch her, as if her living flesh would feel like rigor mortis.

She would think it was the icy air that made him shiver. He said, 'We'd like a few words with you, Mrs Sanders.'

'Shut the door, then, or the fog will get in.' She spoke of the fog as if it were some sort of elemental or ghost, always waiting outside for a chance unwise invitation.

Her face was thickly and whitely powdered, the lips painted a waxy red, her head tied up tightly in a brown-patterned scarf so that no hair showed. She was dressed in her favourite brown, jumper and skirt, ribbed tights, flat tan-coloured shoes. Following her into the living room, Burden noticed how thin and upright she was – her hips narrow, her back flat – so that it was something of a shock to see her frontal aspect reflected in the big mahogany-framed mirror, her stringy neck and the deep lines on her forehead. It was cold in there and, whatever she had said about keeping the fog out, it seemed already to have penetrated. A damp chill touched Burden's skin, the only heat in the room concentrated in the few feet around the coal fire. He glanced at the empty mantelpiece of dark grey flecked marble, the chest of drawers and cabinet in a rather dull dark wood, their surfaces equally bare.

'May we sit down?' She nodded. 'Your son worked as a gardener for a Miss McPhail of Forest Park, I believe. That would have been while he was at university?'

She detected criticism Burden had not meant to imply. 'He was a grown man. Men should work. I couldn't keep him; the grant he got didn't cover everything.'

Burden said simply, 'Mrs Robson worked as a home help for Miss McPhail.'

The words were hardly out of his mouth before he realized Dodo Sanders was going to do it again. Once more she was going to register incomprehension at the name of Robson. Robson? Who's Mrs Robson? Oh, that woman, that one who was murdered, the one whose body I found, that one. Oh yes, of course. She said none of these things but she looked them all, nodding when Burden reminded her is if recollection had come tardily.

'He didn't know her,' she said evenly in her robot's mechanical voice.

'If you didn't know her, or know she worked there, how can you know that?'

She showed no sign of awareness at having betrayed herself or her son. 'She was in the house and he was in the garden; you said that. She wouldn't go into the garden and he wouldn't go into the house. Why would he? It was a big garden.'

Burden left it and allowed a silence to fall before saying, 'Have you ever let the upstairs rooms in this house?' He asked because the idea of the furniture up there intrigued him in an awesome kind of way. He remembered Diana Pettit talking about all that furniture impeding them in their search.

'Why do you ask?' The robot was talking again, its microchip tone giving each word equal weight.

'Frankly, Mrs Sanders, the place is barely furnished down here and cluttered upstairs – or so I understand.'

'You're welcome to look at it if you want.' It was a cordial turn of phrase she used, but not uttered in a cordial way. So might the wolf in Red Riding Hood have said that its teeth were all the better to eat you with. The dome-like bluish eyelids half closed once more, the head went back and Dodo Sanders said, 'My son is coming now.'

Light from the Metro turning in at the gates trickled across the ceiling and down the walls. The woman didn't speak again; she seemed to be listening, to be straining in fact to hear something. There came the distant sound of a wooden door closing, a bolt being shot. Visibly she relaxed, sinking a little from the waist. Clifford's key in the lock was succeeded by the sound of Clifford's feet being vigorously wiped. He must have known by the presence of the car that Burden

571

was here and he didn't hurry; he even pushed the door open very slowly. He entered the room, looked at Burden and Davidson without giving any sign of recognition, without speaking, and walked towards the single empty chair like someone under hypnosis.

But before he had sat down his mother did an astonishing thing. She spoke Clifford's name, just the bare Christian name, and when he turned to look slowly in her direction she leaned her head to one side and lifted her cheek. He moved towards her, bent down and planted an obedient kiss on the floury white skin.

'Can we have a talk, Cliff?' Burden found himself speaking with undue heartiness, as he might have done to a boy of ten or so who has had a fright, who requires jollying along. 'I'd like to talk to you about Miss McPhail. But first we're going upstairs to take a look round the attics.'

Clifford's head turned, his eyes rested momentarily on his mother and moved away. It wasn't exactly a glance requesting permission, more a look of incredulity that such a step might be allowed, had apparently already been sanctioned. Dodo Sanders got to her feet and they went upstairs – all four of them went. It had been a farmhouse once, so the first flight of stairs was handsome and wide, the second which led to the attics narrow and too steep to climb without grasping at banisters. At the top Burden saw closed doors all around him, smelt a cold mustiness, the smell of neglect, and an uncomfortable memory of past dreams came to him – of secrets and things hidden in lofts, of a hand coming out of a cupboard and a disembodied smiling face. But he wasn't imaginative as Wexford was. He put his hand up to a wall switch and a light of low wattage came on; then he opened the first door.

Mother and son stood behind him, Davidson behind them. The room was crammed with furniture and pictures and ornaments, but these were not arranged in any sort of order and the framed paintings were all stacked against walls. Pieces of china and books lay on the seats of chairs, cushions in a heap in the corner. None of it looked valuable, certainly not antique or even of curiosity value but dating from the twenties and thirties, a few pieces older and with turned legs and piecrust edges. Downstairs everything was clean and any

572

assessment of Dodo Sanders' character must have included her housewifely qualities, but up here there had been no sweeping and dusting. No vacuum cleaner had been lugged up the narrow stairs. Cobwebs hung from the ceilings and gathered in the corners in fly-filled traps. Because this was in the country, in a quiet place not much frequented by motor vehicles, the dust was not thick and flocculant, but dust there was: a thin, soft powdering on every surface.

The next room was the same, except that there were two bedsteads in there and two flock mattresses and feather-beds, bundles of pink satin eiderdowns and counterpanes tied up with string, sausage-shaped bolsters covered in ticking, rolled blankets, home-made wool rugs in geometric patterns and home-made rag rugs in concentric circles of faded colours. And there were more pictures, but this time they were photographs in gilt frames.

Burden took a few steps inside this room, picked up one of the photographs and looked at it. A tall man in tweed suit and trilby hat; a woman also wearing a hat, her dress shawl-collared and with a long flared skirt; a boy between them in a school cap, short trousers, knee socks, the group redolent of the mid-thirties. Man and boy closely resembled each other; it might have been Clifford's face he was looking at, the same pudginess, the same thick lips and even the same moustache, the same inexpressive eyes. But there was something in those people that Clifford lacked, an air in all of them of . . . what? Superiority was to put it too strongly. A consciousness of social position and social duties? Still carrying the framed picture, Burden looked into the other two attics while Davidson and Clifford and his mother silently followed him. Here was more furniture, more rolled-up rugs and watercolours mounted on gold paper framed in gilt, more books and china animals, but gilded pink Lloyd Loom chairs as well and a Susie Cooper teaset tumbled on a pile of cushions embroidered with flower gardens and country cottages. It was all rather dirty and shabby and practically valueless, but none of it was sinister or suggestive of the supernatural, none of it was the stuff nightmares are made of.

What had happened? Why was it all up here? He asked himself this as they descended. It wasn't as if the furnishings downstairs were superior to this or newer; nor that there was so much furniture downstairs that the surplus had found its way up here. Indeed, it was inadequate and Burden had come to the conclusion that mother and son must eat their meals from plates on their laps. He could imagine them with TV dinners or dehydrated messes, bought to save trouble. What he couldn't picture was this woman cooking the sort of food anyone would want to eat.

'Those are my grandparents and my father,' Clifford said, putting out his hand for the photograph.

Dorothy Sanders issued an order to him as if he were a schoolboy like the one in the picture. 'Take it upstairs, Clifford; put it back where it's kept.' Burden would have been more astonished to witness a protest on Clifford's part, a hesitation even, than to see what in fact happened – automatic obedience as he went immediately up to the attics.

'I'd like you to tell me a bit about your relationship with Mrs Robson, Cliff,' Burden said when they were all downstairs once more.

'His name's Clifford. It was my name . . . and he doesn't have relationships,' his mother said.

'I'll rephrase that. Tell me about when you first met her and what you talked about. It was at Miss McPhail's, wasn't it?'

Dorothy Sanders had withdrawn down the passage towards the kitchen regions. Clifford looked rather blankly at Burden and said he had once done gardening for Miss McPhail. He too seemed to have forgotten who Mrs Robson was; Burden reminded him and asked him if he ever went inside the Forest Park house – to have a cup of tea or coffee for instance, or to bring flowers in.

'There was a cleaning lady used to give me tea, yes.'

'That was Mrs Robson, wasn't it?'

'No, it wasn't. I don't remember her name; I never heard her name. It wasn't Mrs Robson.'

His mother came back and Clifford looked at her, childlike, as if for help. She had been washing her hands and reeked of disinfectant. To rid herself of contamination from all that furniture, or from that of the two policemen?

She said, 'I've already told you she was in the house and

574

he was in the garden. I've told you he didn't know her. You people don't seem to understand plain English.'

'All right, Mrs Sanders, you've made your point,' Burden said. He wasted no more time on her and looked away. 'I'd like you to come back to the police station with me, Clifford. We can get a clearer picture of things there.'

Clifford went with them in his docile way and they drove back to town. He sat at the table in the interview room and looked across it first at Burden and then at DC Marian Bayliss. His eyes went back to Burden, then were lowered towards the tiny geometric pattern on the tabletop. In a low voice, not much more than a mumble, he said, 'You're accusing me of murdering someone. It's incredible, I still can't accept what's happening to me.'

Much of the skill of a policeman in interrogation lies in knowing what to ignore as well as what to seize on. Burden said quietly, 'Tell me what happened when you first got to the shopping centre and met Mrs Robson.'

'I've already told you,' Clifford said. 'I didn't meet her, I saw her dead body. I've told you over and over. I drove down into the car park on to the second level and I was going to park the car when I saw this person lying there, this dead person.'

'How did you know she was dead?' Marian asked.

Clifford leaned forward on his elbows, holding on to his temples. 'Her face was blue, she wasn't breathing. You're beginning to make me feel what happened isn't true, that it wasn't that way. You're changing the truth with all this until I don't know any more what happened and what didn't. Maybe I did know her and I forgot. Maybe I'm mad and I killed her and forgot. Is that what you want me to say?'

'I want you to tell me the truth, Clifford.'

'I've told you the truth,' he said and then, looking away for a moment, twisting in his chair, he directed a curiously appealing gaze on Burden. His voice was the same, a fairly resonant adult male voice, but the tone was that of a child of seven. 'You used to call me Cliff. What stopped you? Was it Dodo stopped you?'

Afterwards, when he looked back, Burden thought it was at this point that he abandoned his theory of Clifford's being as sane as he and understood that he was mad.

12

Leaning over the garden gate, the new resident of Highlands surveyed the estate that would be his home for at least the next six months. It was one of those days that sometimes occur even in December, a clear sunny day of cloudless skies and a gradually falling temperature. The frost to come that night would silver all the little grass verges and turn everyone's miniature conifers into Christmas trees. On the hill behind Wexford's new home Barringdean Ring sat like a black velvet hat on a green cushion. The sky blazed silvery azure. At the bottom of Battle Lane he could see where Hastings Road turned off and make out the roof of Robson's house and the Whittons' and Dita Jago's. It was high up here, the highest point of Highlands, so that he could even see the cluster of latter-day almshouses that made up Berry Close.

The removal van, newly arrived with half the furniture from the bombed house, blocked any view he might have had of the town. Sylvia had taken the boys to school, then come with the van driver to help her mother move in. Wexford thought he would walk to work and then if he couldn't face walking home Donaldson could bring him. Dora would need their car. He went back in and said goodbye to her, looking round the bare, bleak little house, trying not to prejudice what living in these cramped quarters would be like, the neighbours and their noisy children separated from these rooms only by thin dividing walls, the strips of gardens partitioned by wire fences. More wire fences! Never mind, they were lucky to have somewhere, lucky not to have to go on living with Sylvia . . . and he reproached himself for the ungrateful thought as his kind busy daughter came in carrying a crate of his favourite books.

The air was nippy and the sunshine warm, but sun hung low on the horizon and the shadows were long. His route down into the town took him along Hastings Road and into Eastbourne Drive. There was no one about, the streets empty of people and nearly empty of cars. This was the last day of Lesley Arbel's word-processor course, but no doubt she would spend the weekend with her uncle. It was more than two weeks since Gwen Robson's death, nearly as long since someone had tried to kill Sheila. His cuts and bruises were nearly healed, his strength returning. He had several times driven his car, felt quite calm and assured at the wheel. The bomb experts kept on coming to him or getting him to go to them, pursuing their interminable questions. Try to remember. What exactly happened after you got into the car? Who are your enemies? Who are your daughter's enemies? Why did you jump out of the car? What warned you? He could recall none of it and believed those lost five minutes lost for ever. It was only in the night-time, in dreams, that he relived the explosion – or rather, instead of reliving what he couldn't remember, conjured up new versions for himself in some of which he died or Sheila died or the world itself disappeared and he hung suspended in a dark void. But last night, instead of the roar of the bomb he had heard thin reedy music and instead of Sheila's body, he had seen wheels spinning in the darkness, circles that shone and glittered and were filled with geometric patterns . . .

Striving to dispel these ideas and look at things rationally occupied his thoughts until he reached the police station. Once there, he somehow knew before he enquired that Burden had Clifford Sanders with him and Archbold in one of their interview rooms. Late in the morning Burden came out but kept Clifford there alone, sending in coffee and biscuits. Wexford couldn't tell what Clifford looked like after this continuous ordeal but Burden was haggard, his face pale and tense and his eyes exhausted.

'You were talking about the inquisition,' Wexford said. 'About executioners taking payment to garrote the condemned before they were burned at the stake.'

Burden nodded, slumped in his chair, his strained face rather ghastly in the pale, bright light from the sun.

'You said you'd read about it. Well, I've read of Inquisitors suffering as much as their victims, of the strain wearing them out and brainwashing them till they get like you. It's watching the torture that does it; you have to be a very special sort of person to be able to watch torture and not be affected by it.'

'Clifford Sanders isn't being tortured. I had doubts about that earlier on, but I don't any more. He's being put through a fairly heavy interrogation but not tortured.'

'Not physically perhaps, but I don't think you can separate mind and body like that.'

'He isn't kept awake artificially; he isn't under bright lights or kept on his feet or starved or denied a drink. He isn't even here all the time; he goes home to sleep. I'm going to send him home today, now; I've had enough for today.'

'You're wasting your time, Mike,' Wexford said mildly. 'You're wasting your time and his because he didn't do it.'

'Excuse me if I differ from you there. I differ from you most strongly.' Burden sat up revived, indignant. 'He had the motive and the means. He has strong psychopathic tendencies. Remember that book you lent me with that piece in it about psychopaths? The Stafford-Clark? "The outstanding feature is emotional instability in its broadest and most comprehensive sense . . ." Let me see, how does it go on? I haven't got your memory. ". . . prodigal of effort but utterly lacking in persistence, plausible but insincere, demanding but indifferent to appeals, dependent only in their constant unreliability . . ." '

'Mike,' Wexford interrupted him. 'You haven't got any evidence. You've trumped up what you've got to suit yourself. The single piece of evidence you do have is that he saw the body and instead of reporting it, ran away. That is absolutely all you've got. He didn't know Gwen Robson. He was a gardener in a place where she popped in sometimes in her home-help role, and he may once or twice have said hello to her. He wasn't seen talking to her in the shopping centre. He doesn't and didn't possess a garrote or anything that could be made into a garrote.'

'On the contrary, he has a hard and fast motive. I can't

578

yet prove it, but I'm convinced he committed a crime in the past which Gwen Robson discovered and started blackmailing him over. Blackmailers don't succeed for long with psychopaths.'

'What crime?'

'Murder, obviously,' Burden said on a note of triumph. 'You suggested that yourself. You said no one would care about some sex thing, it had to be murder.' His voice grew tired again as he suppressed a yawn. 'Who, I don't know, but I'm working on it. I'm probing into his past. A grandmother maybe? Even Miss McPhail herself. I'm having Clifford's past looked into for signs of any remotely possible unexplained deaths.'

'You're wasting your time. Well, not your time – ours, the public's.'

This was an accusation to which Burden was particularly sensitive. He was beginning to look angry as well as tired and his face grew pinched as it always did when he was cross. He spoke coldly. 'He met her by chance in the shopping centre, she asked for more money and after he had followed her down into the car park, he killed her by strangling her with a length of electric lead he was carrying in the boot of the car along with that curtain. This he took with him and threw away on his way home.'

'Why cover the body and run away?'

'You can't account for inconsistencies of that sort in a psychopath, though probably he thought that if he covered the body it might not be found for a rather longer time than if he left it exposed. Linda Naseem saw him talking to Mrs Robson. Archie Greaves saw him running away.'

'Mike, we know he ran away, he admits that himself. And it was a girl with a hat on that Linda Naseem saw.'

Burden got up and walked the length of the room, then came back to lean on the edge of Wexford's desk. He had the air of someone who is bracing himself to say something unpleasant in the nicest possible way. 'Look, you've had a bad shock and you're still not well. You saw what happened when you came back to work too soon. And for God's sake, I know you're worried about Sheila.'

Wexford said dryly but as pleasantly as he could, 'OK, but my mind's not affected.'

'Well, isn't it? It would be only natural to think it was – temporarily, that is. All the evidence in this case points to Clifford and, moreover, not a shred to anyone else. Only for some reason you refuse to see that, and in my opinion the reason is that you're not right yet, you're not over the shock of that bomb. Frankly, you should have stayed at home longer.'

And left it all to you, Wexford thought, saying nothing but aware of a cold anger spreading through him rather like a draught of icy water trickling down his gullet.

'I shall break Clifford on my own. It's only a matter of time. Leave it to me, I'm not asking for help – or advice, come to that. I know what I'm doing. And as for torture, that's a laugh. I haven't even approached anything the Judges' Rules would object to.'

'Maybe not,' Wexford said. 'Perhaps you should remember the last lines of that passage you like so much defining a psychopath, the bit about the ruthless and determined pursuit of gratification.'

Burden looked hard at him, looked in near-disbelief, then walked out, slamming the door resoundingly.

A quarrel with Mike was something that had never happened before. Disagreements, yes, and tough arguments. There had been the time, for instance, when Mike had lost his first wife and gone to pieces and later had that peculiar love affair – Wexford had been angry with him then and perhaps paternalistic. But they had never come to hurling abuse at each other. Of course he hadn't meant to infer that Mike was a psychopath, or had psychopathic tendencies or anything of that sort, but he had to admit it must have sounded like that. What had he meant then? As with most people in most quarrels, he had said the first hurtful, moderately clever thing that came into his head.

Some of the things Mike had said he was sure were right. In his assessment of the character of Gwen Robson he was right. She would do a great deal for money, almost anything, and what she had done had led to her death. He knew that and Burden knew it too. But he had chosen the wrong person from among her possible . . . what? Clients? Perhaps that was the best word even in this context. Clifford Sanders was not Gwen Robson's murderer.

Wexford looked out of the window and saw him being shepherded out to one of the cars. Davidson was about to drive him home. Clifford neither trudged nor shuffled, he didn't walk with his head bowed or his shoulders hunched, yet there was something of desperation in his bearing. He was like one caught in a recurring dream from which to awaken is to escape, but which will inexorably return the next night. Fanciful nonsense, Wexford told himself, but his thoughts persisted in dwelling on Burden's chosen per-petrator as Davison drove out of the forecourt and on to the road, and all that could be seen of Clifford Sanders was his solid heavy-shouldered shape through the rear window, his round cropped skull. What would he go home to? That cold, dictatorial woman, that house which was big and bare and always chilly and where, according to Burden, everything that might have made it comfortable was stored away up in the attics. Useless to ask why he stayed. He was young and fit and educated; he could leave, make a life of his own. Wexford knew that so many people are their own prisoners, jailers of themselves, that the doors which to the outside world seem to stand open they have sealed with invisible bars. They have blocked off the tunnels to freedom, pulled down the blinds to keep out the light. Clifford, if asked, would no doubt say, 'I can't leave my mother, she's done everything for me, brought me up single-handed, devoted her life to me. I can't leave her, I must do my duty.' But perhaps it was something very different he said when alone with Serge Olson.

Wexford might not have gone to Sundays that day, might have sat on his office for a long time brooding over his quarrel with Burden, but a call came through from a man called Brook, Stephen Brook. The name meant nothing, then recall came with a recollection of the blue Lancia and a woman who had gone into labour while in the shopping centre. Brook said his wife had something to tell the police and Wexford's thoughts went at once to Clifford Sanders. Suppose this woman wanted to tell him something that would put Clifford entirely beyond suspicion? She might know him. It could, with some exaggeration, be said that in a place like Kingsmarkham everyone knew everyone else. It would bring him considerable satisfaction to have Clifford exonerated and might also heal the breach between himself and Burden – without if possible Burden's losing face.

The Brooks lived at the Forby Road end of town, their home a flat in the local authority housing area of the Sundays estate. From the window of their living room Sundays Park could be seen – its hornbeam avenue, its lawns and cedars, the cars of those taking the word-processor course parked at the side of the big white house. This small room was very warm and Mrs Brook's baby lay uncovered in a wicker cradle. The Brooks' furniture consisted of two battered chairs and a table and a great many small crates and boxes, all of them covered or draped with lengths of patterned material and shawls and coloured blankets. There were posters on the walls and dried grasses in stoneware mustard jars. It had all been done at the lowest possible cost and the effect was rather charming.

Mrs Brook was all in black. Dusty black knitted draperies was the way Wexford would have described her clothes if he had had to do so. She wore wrinkled black and white striped stockings and black trainers, and a very curious contemporary madonna she looked when she lifted the baby and, unbuttoning black cardigan and black shirt, presented one round white breast to its mouth. Her husband – in jeans, shirt and zipper-jacket uniform – would have appeared more conventional if he had not dyed his spiky hair to resemble the bird of paradise flower, a tropical blue and orange. Their modulated Myringham University accents came as a slight shock, though Wexford told himself he should have known better. Both of them were about the age of Clifford Sanders, but how different a life they had made for themselves!

'I didn't tell you before,' Helen Brook said, 'because I didn't know who she was. I mean, I was in hospital having Ashtoreth and I didn't really think much about all that.'

Ashtoreth. Well, it sounded pretty and was just another goddess like Diana.

'I mean, it was all a shock really. I meant to have her at home and I was all set to do that. Squatting, you know, not

582

lying down which is so unnatural, and three of my friends were coming to perform the proper rites. The people at the hospital had been really angry at me for wanting to have her the natural way, but I knew I could prove to them my way was right. And then of course they caught me. It was almost as if they set a trap to get me into hospital, though Steve says not – they couldn't have.'

'Yeah, that's paranoia, love,' said Stephen Brook.

'Yes, I just started these labour pains – how about that? I was in Demeter and these pains just started.'

'In what?' Wexford said before he remembered this was the Barringdean Centre's health food shop. Briefly, it had sounded like some obstetrical condition.

'In Demeter,' she said again, 'getting my calendula capsules. And I sort of looked up and through the window and I saw her outside talking to this girl. And I thought I'll go out and show myself to her and I wonder what she'll think – the way she used to go on saying she hoped I'd never have children, that was all.'

'He doesn't know what you're on about, love.'

Wexford nodded his assent to this as Helen Brook shifted the child to her other breast, cupping the soft downy head in her hand. 'Saw whom?' he asked.

'That woman who got killed. Only I didn't know; I mean, I didn't know what her name was. I just knew I knew her, then when we read in the paper that she'd been a home help and where she lived I said to Steve, that's the woman who used to look after the lady next door to Mum. I was in Demeter and I recognized her, I hadn't seen her for yonks. You see, she'd heard about the way Steve and I got married and she was all peculiar about it.'

'The way you got married?'

'Well, Steve and I didn't go to a register office or a church or anything on account of our beliefs. We had a very beautiful ceremony at Stonehenge at dawn, with all our friends there. I mean, they won't let you go up into the stones like Mummy said you used to, but it was very beautiful just being able to see Stonehenge. Steve had a ring made of bone and I had a ring made of yew wood and we exchanged them, and our friend who's a musician played the sitar and everyone sang. Anyway, the council let you have a flat even if you don't get married the official way. Mum told the lady – what was she called, Gwen? – Mummy told her that, but she was still really sniffy and when she saw me that's what she said. She said I hope you don't have children, that's all. Well, that was two years ago and I hadn't seen her since and then I did see her talking to this girl outside Demeter. They went off into Tesco's together and I was going to follow them and kind of say, look, how about that? And then I had this terrific pain . . .'

She sat there, smiling blandly, the baby Ashtoreth now recumbent in her lap and subsiding into sleep. Wexford asked her to describe the girl.

'I'm not very good at describing people. I mean it's the way they are inside that counts, isn't it? She was older than me but not all that much, and she had dark hair that was quite long and she was wearing the most amazing clothes; that's what stuck in my memory, her amazing clothes.'

'Are you saying she was smartly dressed?' Wexford understood at once that he was using very outdated terms and Helen Brook looked puzzled. She leaned forward as if she had misheard. 'Her clothes were particularly elegant?' he corrected himself, and added, 'New? Beautiful? Fashionable?'

'Well, not specially new. Elegant – that might be the word. You know what I mean.'

'Was she wearing a hat?'

'A hat? No, she wasn't wearing a hat. She had lovely hair; she looked lovely.'

A young woman ought to be able to judge the style of a contemporary. What she had told him had confirmed Linda Naseem's evidence – or had it? Hats, after all, can be temporarily taken off. If this were the same girl both she and Helen Brook had seen, it meant that Gwen Robson had met her in one of the aisles of the shopping centre and presumably walked through the Tesco supermarket with her, the two of them then leaving together for the underground car park. If it was the same girl . . .

It is rare to recognize someone at the wheel of a car. Generally, it is the car we recognize, then look quickly to identify the driver. Silver Escorts attracted Wexford's attention at present, as did red Metros, and a closer look at the one approaching showed him Ralph Robson in the driving-seat. So Lesley Arbel was without transport today . . .

'Turn round,' he said to Donaldson. 'Take me to Sundays.'

When they arrived, people were coming down the steps of the Regency mansion; the course had come to an end. There were as many men as women and most of them were young. Lesley Arbel, emerging from the open double entrance doors, stood out conspicuously from the rest by her looks and her clothes. Wexford, who when he first met her had been reminded by her sleek dressing of actresses in the early days of the talking cinema, now again recollected those thirties' films. Only in them was it possible to capture such a scene, where there was no room for doubting who were extras and who the star. But because this was not a film and Lesley Arbel no confident movie queen swanning on celluloid, her appearance was a little ridiculous by contrast with all those tweed coats and anoraks and jackets over tracksuits. She even came rather awkwardly down those steps, her heels so high as to throw her off-balance.

The Kingsmarkham bus passed along the Forby Road, stopping opposite the gates and Sundays Lodge, and it was no doubt this bus she meant to catch. But her heels and the long tight black skirt restricted her steps and she was making very slow progress towards the avenue when Wexford put his head out of the car window and asked if they might give her a lift home. It was more than a surprise, it seemed a shock, and she jumped. He had a feeling that if more comfortably shod, she would have made a run for it. However she came cautiously up to the car. Wexford got out, opened the rear door for her and she got awkwardly in ahead of him, ducking her head and holding on to her small black grosgrain hat.

'I thought we might have a talk in private,' he said. 'Without your uncle, I mean.'

She was too nervous to speak and sat with her hands in her lap, staring at Donaldson's broad back. Wexford noticed that her nails — which had protruded a good half-inch from her fingertips — had been filed down and were unpainted. Donaldson began to drive slowly down the avenue, between

585

the lines of leafless hornbeams. The sun had just set and all the trees made a black tracery against a spectacular crimson sky.

Wexford said quietly, 'You didn't tell me you were in Kingsmarkham on the day your aunt was killed.'

She responded quite quickly and it was as if the question had been of no great significance. So might she have replied if a friend had reproached her for failing to make a promised phone call.

'No, I was upset and I forgot.'

'Come now, Miss Arbel. You told me you left Orangetree House early because you weren't feeling well.'

She muttered, 'I *wasn't* feeling well.'

'Your illness didn't prevent your coming to Kingsmarkham.'

'I mean I forgot it might be important where I was.'

She had been frightened, but she wasn't frightened now; this must mean he had not asked the question she feared to hear. 'It's very important where you were. I understand you came here to check that you were on this course that was to start the following Monday?' She nodded, relaxing a little, her body less rigid under the stiffly padded shoulders of her pink and black striped jacket. 'That can be verified, you know, Miss Arbel.'

'I did check up on the course.'

'You could have done that by phone, couldn't you?'

'I did try but their phones were out of order.'

'And then you went to meet your aunt in the Barringdean Centre.'

'No!' He couldn't tell if it was a cry of denial through fear of discovery or simple astonishment that such a meeting could have been suspected. 'I never saw her, I never did! Why would I go there?'

'You must tell me that. Suppose I told you that you were seen by at least one witness?'

'I'd say they were lying.'

'As you were lying when you told me you were ill on November 19 and went home early from work?'

'I wasn't lying. I thought it wasn't important just coming down here to look at a form and check up and then go back again. That's all I did. I never went near the Barringdean Centre.'

'You came and went by train?'

She gave an anxious nod, falling into his trap.

'You were very near the centre then, considering the pedestrian entrance is in the next street to Station Road. Wouldn't it be right to say you returned to the station from Sundays and, remembering your aunt would be in the Barringdean Centre at that time because she always was, you went in and met her in the central aisle?'

It was a vehement, tearful denial she made, but again Wexford had the feeling that whatever she was afraid of it was not this; it was not fear of having been seen with her aunt half an hour before her death that frightened her. And to his astonishment she suddenly exclaimed miserably, 'I'll lose my job!'

This seemed almost an irrelevancy, at least a minor matter compared with the enormity of Gwen Robson's death. He let her go, opening the door for her when the car stopped in Highlands outside her uncle's house. For a few moments he stood there, watching the house. Behind drawn curtains the lights were already on. She had gone up the path at a hobbling run and was fumbling with her key when Robson opened the door to let her in. It was closed very rapidly. Now for the long evening, Wexford thought; the making of tea and perhaps scrambled eggs, the chat about the day she had passed and he had passed, complaints about his arthritis and sympathy from her, the relief of television. What had people in that situation done before television? It was unthinkable.

Was it all out of the kindness of her heart? Was it that she had truly loved her aunt and now loved and pitied her uncle? A saint, an angel of mercy – that she must be to remain here for yet another weekend when London and her own home and friends were available to her, when there were three trains an hour to take her there. But Wexford didn't think she was an angel of mercy; she hadn't impressed him even as being particularly kind hearted. Vanity and self-absorption don't generally go with altruism – and what was the meaning of that final impassioned cry?

Dita Jago's daughter had called to collect her little girls

587

and Wexford said to Donaldson, 'You can take the car back and knock off if you like. I'll walk home from here.'

A momentary surprise crossed Donaldson's face, then he remembered where home now was. Wexford strolled across the road. The Highlands lights were not the gentle amber lamps of the street where his own house was but the harsh white kind, glass vases full of glare borne on concrete stilts. They stained the dark air with a livid fog and turned people and their clothes reptile colours, greenish and sour brown and sallow white. Melanie and Hannah – what was their name, Quincy? – looked tubercular, their lively dark eyes dulled and their red cheeks pallid. Their mother was wearing one of her own mother's brilliant knitted creations, a sweater that probably had as many colours as a Persian carpet, a skirt of thick gathered folds on which the intricate stripes, no doubt of rich and varied shades, undulated like shadows in the wind . . . only it all looked brown and grey in that light.

Nina was her name? As Wexford asked himself that, he heard Mrs Jago call her by it and Nina Quincy, having settled her children in the back of the car, went up to her mother, put her arms round her and kissed her. Strange, Wexford thought; they see each other every day . . . Mrs Jago waved as the car departed; a shawl wrapped her shoulders today, a tapestry-like square with a fringed border. It seemed to suit her monumental shape, the heavy-featured face with its load of bunched coils of hair, better than contemporary dress. She acknowledged Wexford calmly.

'You're living up here now, they tell me.'

He nodded. 'How are the memoirs?'

'I haven't been doing much writing.' She gave him that look peculiar to people who have something to confide but don't know if this is the right confidant. Should I? Shouldn't I? Will I regret it once the words are out? 'Come in a moment and have a drink.'

A chat with a neighbour on the way home. A sherry. Why not? But it wasn't sherry she gave him, far from it. A kind of schnapps probably, Wexford thought: icy-cold, sweetish and unbelievably strong. It made his eyebrows shoot up, it made him feel as if his hair stood on end.

'I needed that,' she said, though there had been no alteration in her pleasant friendly manner, no gasp of relief.

The pile of manuscript was precisely where it had been when he was last in this room, a hair lying across the top of the title page. He was sure that hair had been there last time. If Mrs Jago had not been writing she had been knitting, and the jungle landscape had grown several more inches from the long curled needle, palm trees now sprouting fronds and a sky appearing. The germ of an idea pushed a shoot into his mind.

'Did Gwen Robson know you were writing this book?'

'Mrs Robson?' It sounded like a measure, if not of her indifference to her dead neighbour, of the degree of acquaintance she had had with her in life. A remoteness was implied that Wexford found himself not quite believing in. 'She was only once in this house; I don't suppose she noticed.' Wexford thought for a moment that she was going to sneer, to add that Gwen Robson wasn't the kind to read books or be interested in them. But instead she said, in such sudden contrast as to be shocking, 'My daughter and her husband have parted. "Split up" is what they say, isn't it? I hadn't any idea of it, I hadn't any warning. Nina just came in this afternoon and said their marriage was over. My son-in-law left this morning.'

'My daughter's parted from her husband too,' Wexford said.

She said, rather sharply for her but with some justice perhaps, 'That's different, though. A famous actress, rich, with a wealthy husband, always in the public eye ...'

'Only to be expected, do you mean?'

She was too old and experienced to blush; it was more a wince she gave. 'I'm sorry, I didn't mean that. It's only that Nina's got the two girls and it's terrible for the children. And women left on their own to bring up children, they lead a miserable existence. She earns so little from her job, it's only part-time. He's leaving her the house, he'll have to support them, but – if only I could see why! I thought they were so happy.'

'Who knows what goes on in other people's marriages?' said Wexford.

Leaving her, he set off to walk up the hill. Wexford's Third

589

Law, he thought, ought to be: always live at the foot of a hill, then you'll be fresh for climbing it in the morning. It was quite a steep haul up and all the way he could see his new home ahead of him, glowering uncompromisingly from the crown of the hill. There was no garage, so his car stood outside with Sylvia's behind it and behind that another unidentifiable one that might be a neighbour's. The removal van had gone. He wasn't out of breath as he opened the gate (wooden in the wire fence) and walked up to the front door. I must be quite fit, he was thinking as he turned his key in the lock, opened the door and had his ears at once assaulted by the voice of Sylvia – shrill, cross, loud, easily penetrating these thin walls: 'You ought to think of Dad! You ought to think how you're putting his life in danger with your heroics!'

13

The other car must have been Sheila's, rented or else a replacement for the Porsche. Both sisters were standing up, glaring at each other along the length of the room. It was a very small room and they seemed almost to be shouting into each other's faces. There was a door into the hall and another door into the kitchen and as Wexford came in through one Dora entered by the other, accompanied by the two little boys.

Dora said, 'Stop it, stop shouting!'

But the boys were indifferent. They had come in to secure a pocket calculator (Robin) and a drawing block (Ben), and they proceeded to forage for these items in diminutive school briefcases, undeterred by the slanging match going on between their mother and their aunt. Their reaction would have been different if this had been parents quarrelling, Wexford thought.

He looked from one young woman to the other. 'What's going on?'

Sylvia's reply was to throw up her hands and cast herself into an armchair. Sheila – her face flushed and her hair looking wild and tangled, though this might have been by design – said, 'My case comes up on Tuesday week, in the magistrates' court. They want me to plead guilty.'

'Who's "they"?'

'Mother and Sylvia.'

'Excuse me,' Dora said. 'I didn't say I wanted you to do anything. I said you ought to think about it very seriously.'

'I have thought about it. I hardly think of anything else and I've discussed it with Ned exhaustively. I've discussed it

591

with him because he's a lawyer as much as . . . well, my boyfriend, or whatever you call it. And it isn't doing our relationship a lot of good, to tell you the truth.'

Robin and Ben gave up the search and carried their cases outside to the kitchen. Tactfully, Ben closed the door behind him.

It was as if this freed Sylvia to speak openly and she said in a hard, unsympathetic way, 'What she does is her own business. If she wants to stand up in court and say she's not guilty, that governments are guilty for breaking international law or whatever – well, she can do that. And when she gets fined and refuses to pay the fine, she can go to prison if that's what she likes.'

Wexford interrupted her. 'Is that what you're going to do, Sheila?'

'I have to,' she said shortly. 'There's no point otherwise.'

'But it's not just her,' Sylvia continued. 'It's all the rest of us she involves. Everyone knows who she is, everyone knows she's your daughter and my sister. What's that going to do for you as a police officer, having a daughter go to prison? This is a democracy and if we want to change things we've each got a vote to do it with. Why can't she use her vote and change the government like the rest of us have to?'

Sheila said tiredly, 'That's the biggest cop-out of all. If you had a hundred votes all to yourself down in this neck of the woods you couldn't change anything, not with a sitting Member with a sixteen-thousand majority.'

'And that's not the worst,' Sylvia went on, ignoring this. 'The worst is that when those people who tried to bomb her know what she thinks, when she gets up and says it in court, they're going to have another go, aren't they? They nearly got you by accident last time and maybe this time they really will. Or maybe they'll get you on purpose – or one of my children!'

Wexford sighed. 'I've been drinking schnapps with a lady of my acquaintance.' He glanced at Dora and gave her the ghost of a wink. 'I rather wish I'd got the bottle with me.' How wrong of me it is, he thought, that I love one of my children more than the other. 'I suppose you've got to do what you've got to do, as the current phrase has it,' he said to Sheila, but as he got up and made for the kitchen door –

made for the beer he trusted was in the fridge – it was Sylvia on whose shoulder he laid a caressing hand.

'Not all that current, Pop,' said Sheila.

Things calmed down. At any rate, Sylvia soon left to take her sons home and cook her husband's supper. Then Sheila and her parents went out to eat, no one yet feeling comfortable in what Dora called 'this horrid little house'. Sheila talked moodily about Ned not wanting it known that someone in his position was consorting with someone in hers, though she didn't explain what his position was and Wexford, true to his principles, wouldn't ask.

'When peace is so beautiful,' Sheila said, 'and what everyone wants, why do they treat workers for peace like criminals?'

Passing the police station on their way back from the restaurant in Pomfret, Wexford saw a light on in one of the interview rooms. Of course there was no real reason to suppose that Burden was in there with Clifford Sanders, yet he did suppose it with a chilling sense of unease. Forgetting Sheila and her troubles for a moment, he thought: I shall be embarrassed when I next see Mike, I shall feel awkward and therefore shall postpone that meeting. What am I going to do?

Burden had not meant to recall Clifford to the police station. His intention had been to call off his dogs for the duration of the weekend and let his baited creature make a partial recovery. The metaphor was his wife's, not his, and he reacted with some anger to it. He now regretted discussing the case with Jenny and wished he had stuck to the principle (never much honoured in the observance) of not taking his work home.

'I've had the same sentimental rubbish at work,' he said. He would normally have said 'from Reg', but he was too angry with Wexford even to want to think of him by his Christian name. Burden had a Victorian attitude in this area, rather in the manner of those fictional heroines who called a man William while they were engaged to him and Mr Jones after they had broken it off. 'I don't understand all this

sympathy with cold-blooded killers. People should try thinking of their victims for a change.'

'So you've said on numerous previous occasions,' said
Jenny, not very pleasantly.

That did it. That sent him back to the police station after
his dinner and Archbold to the Forby Road to fetch Clifford
again. He used the other ground floor interview room this
time, the one at the front where the window gave on to the
High Street, where the tiles were shabby black and tan (like
an ageing spaniel, said Wexford) and the table had a brown-
checked top with a metal rim.

For the first time Clifford didn't wait for Burden to begin.
In a resigned but not unhappy voice, he said, 'I knew you'd
fetch me back again today. I sensed it. That's why I didn't
start watching TV; I knew I'd only be interrupted in the
middle of a programme. My mother knew too; she's been
watching me, waiting for the doorbell to ring.'

'Your mother's been asking you about this too, has she,
Cliff?'

Again Burden reflected how much like an overgrown
schoolboy he looked. The clothes were so much the conventional wear of a correct well-ordered teenager at a grammar
school in, say, the fifties, as to seem either a mockery or a
disguise. The grey flannel trousers had turn-ups and were
well-pressed. He wore a grey shirt – so that it could be worn
two or three days without washing? – striped tie, grey hand-
knitted V-necked pullover. It was plainly hand-knitted, well
but not expertly, the hand of the imperfectly skilled evident
in the neck border and the sewing up. Somehow Burden
knew it had to be Mrs Sanders' work. He already had an
idea of her as a woman of many activities, but who did none
of them well; she would not care enough to do things well.

Clifford's face was its usual blank, revealing no emotion
even when he spoke those surely desperate sentences. He
said, 'I may as well tell you. I tell you all the truth now, I
don't hide anything, I hope you believe that. I may as well
tell you that she says I wouldn't be questioned like this day
after day, on and on, if there wasn't something in it. She
says I must be that sort of person, or you wouldn't keep
getting me down here.'

'What sort of person would that be, Cliff?'

594

'Someone who would kill a woman.'

'Your mother knows you're guilty then, does she?'

Clifford said with curious pedantry, 'You can't know something that isn't true; you can only believe it or suspect it. She says that's the sort of person I am, not that she thinks I killed anyone.' Pausing, he looked sideways at Burden in what the latter thought of as a mad way, an unbalanced way. It was a sly, crafty look. 'Perhaps I am. Perhaps I am that sort of person. How would you know till you did it?'

'You tell me, Cliff. Tell me about that sort of person.'

'He would be unhappy. He'd feel threatened by everyone. He'd want to escape from the life he had into something better, but that better would only be fantasy because he wouldn't be able to escape really. Like a rat in a cage. They do these psychological experiments; they put a piece of glass outside the open door of the cage and when the rat tries to get out it can't because it bumps into the glass. Then when they take the glass away it could really get out but it won't, because it knows it gets hurt bumping itself on the invisible thing outside.'

'Is that yourself you're describing?'

Clifford nodded. 'Talking to you has helped to show me what I am. It's done more for me than Serge can.' He looked into Burden's eyes. 'You ought to be a psychotherapist yourself.' To Burden's ears it was a slightly mad laugh that he gave. 'I thought you were stupid, but now I know you're not. You're not stupid; you've opened up places in my mind for me.'

Burden wasn't sure he knew what this meant. Like most people, he didn't like being called stupid even though the term was immediately revoked. But he had a feeling that Clifford would be even franker if they were alone and so he sent Archbold away, ostensibly to fetch coffee from the canteen. Clifford was smiling again, though there was nothing pleased in that smile, nothing happy.

'Are you taping all this?' he asked.

Burden nodded.

'Good. You've shown me what I'm capable of. It's frightening. I'm not a rat and I know I can't break the invisible wall, but I can force the person who put it there to break it.' He paused and smiled, or at any rate bared his teeth.

595

'Dodo,' he said, 'Dodo, the big bird. Only she's not, she's a little pecking bird with claws and a beak. I'll tell you something; I wake up in the night and think what I'm capable of, what I could do, and I want to sit up and scream and yell – only I can't because I'd wake her up.'

'Yes,' said Burden, 'yes.' He didn't much care for this sudden feeling he had of being in waters that were too deep for him. He had had enough too and would have liked to send Clifford home. Not very vigorously he asked, 'What are you capable of?'

But Clifford made no answer to this. Archbold came in with the coffee and at a nod from Burden left the room again. Clifford went on, 'At my age I oughtn't to need my mother. But I do. In a lot of ways, I rely on her.'

'Go on,' said Burden.

But Clifford sidetracked, saying, 'I'd like to tell you about myself. I'd like to talk about me. Is that all right?'

For the first time Burden felt . . . not fear, he would never have admitted this was fear – but apprehensiveness perhaps, a tautening of muscles, the cautionary chill of being alone with a mad person.

However, he only said, 'Go on.'

Clifford spoke dreamily. 'When I was young – I mean really young, a little boy – we lived with my father's parents. The Sanders family had lived in our house since the late seventeen-hundreds. My grandfather died and then my father's and mother's marriage came to an end. My father just walked out on us and they were divorced and we were left with my father's mother. Mother put her into an old people's home and then she moved everything out of the house that reminded her of my father and his people; she moved all the furniture and the bed linen and the china upstairs into the attics.

'We hadn't any furniture, only mattresses on the floor and two chairs and a table. All the carpets and the comfortable chairs were upstairs, locked away. We never saw anyone, we hadn't any friends. My mother didn't want to send me to school, she was going to teach me herself at home. Dodo! Imagine! She'd been a cleaner before she got married – Dodo, the maid. She hadn't any qualifications to teach me and they caught her and at last they made her send me to school.

She'd walk me into Kingsmarkham every morning and come and fetch me every afternoon. It's nearly three miles. When I grumbled about walking, do you know what she said? She said she'd push me in my old pushchair. I was six! Of course I walked after that; I didn't want the others to see me in a pushchair. There was a school bus, but I didn't know I could have gone on that: she didn't want me to, it was two years before I knew I could go on it and then I did. When she wanted to punish me she didn't hit me or anything; she shut me up in the attics with that furniture.'

'All right, Cliff,' said Burden, looking at his watch, 'that'll do for now.' He realized, when Clifford was silent and got up obediently, that he had spoken as a psychotherapist might: he had spoken in the manner of Serge Olson.

A confession was what he had expected from Clifford on the previous night. That confiding manner, that unprecedented free and open way of speaking, those discomfiting references to his mother's nickname had seemed to herald it. All the time they seemed on the brink of the final revelation, the ultimate admission, but it had not come and Clifford had digressed into that account of his early youth which was the last thing Burden wanted to hear. But one good thing had resulted; he no longer felt guilt or much unease. Jenny had been wrong and Wexford had been wrong. Clifford might be mad, might well be the psychopath Burden had designated him, but he was not being terrorized or pushed over some edge or driven to desperation. He had been almost cheerful, talkative, in command of himself, and he had seemed – odd though this was – actually to enjoy their talk and look forward to more.

It must only be a matter of time now, Burden would have liked to discuss all this with Wexford. Best of all he would have liked Wexford in on his next session with Clifford, sitting there at the table, listening and occasionally putting a question of his own Burden didn't feel like an inquisitor or torturer any more, but he did feel the responsibility, that it weighed heavily on his own shoulders.

In the morning Sheila made amends.

'Sylvia wanted me to apologize in court,' she said. 'Can

you imagine? I'm to stand there and make a public retraction and say I'm sorry to a bunch of terrorists, plead guilty and promise not to do it again.'

'She didn't mean that,' Dora put in.

'I think she did. Anyway, I'm not apologizing to anyone except you and Pop. I'm sorry I made a row in your . . . new home. Especially considering I'm kind of responsible for wrecking your old one.'

She kissed them goodbye and went off to Ned and Coram Fields. Half an hour after she had gone, Sylvia rang up to apologize for what she called 'that unnecessary scene'. Perhaps she could come over and explain what she really felt about the whole Sheila-wire-cutting situation?

'All right,' Wexford said, 'but only if you'll bring me every copy of *Kim* magazine you've got in the house.'

First of all she said she was sure she hadn't any copies; then when her father told her she was like her mother and never threw anything away, she said that she only kept them for the knitting patterns. In the afternoon she turned up with a stack too heavy to be fetched out of the car at one go and Wexford himself had to make two trips to carry them. There were more than two hundred, covering a period of something like four years. He knew that nothing except Sylvia's guilty feelings would have induced her to reveal to her father such a propensity for magazine-reading – and downmarket magazine reading at that. Dora said nothing when they were brought into the small living room, but her face registered a restrained dismay as Sylvia stacked them up into a kind of tower block between the bookcase and the television table.

Her explanation and a kind of manifesto of her views on the nuclear issue and the role of public figures in civil disobedience and non-violent direct action took a long while. Wexford listened sympathetically because he knew he would have listened to Sheila, and of course he bent over backwards to be fair to the daughter he loved less. Even thinking in those terms made him feel mean and rotten. And if she was really concerned that he might get blown up again, really worried about him and his life being in danger, he ought to go down on his knees to her in gratitude for caring that much for him. So he sat there hearing it all and nodding and agreeing or gently disagreeing, trying not to acknowledge the enormous relief, the leap of the heart when the doorbell rang and, looking out of the window, he saw Burden's car at the kerb. The odd thing was that he forgot all about being embarrassed.

Burden had Jenny with him and the little boy, Mark. If Sylvia's children had been girls – a comparable pair for instance with Melanie and Hannah Quincy – they would have immediately taken the two-year-old under their wing, talked to him and played with him with a precocious maternity. But being male they merely looked at him with bored indifference and, when adjured by Sylvia to show Mark their Lego, responded with, 'Do we *have* to?'

'I was going to ask you to come out for a drink,' Burden said, 'but Jenny says she won't have any of that sexist stuff.'

Sylvia said enthusiastically, 'Absolutely not! I quite agree.'

At the old house Wexford would have taken Burden into the dining room but there was no such place here, only a corner behind a strip of counter called a 'meals area'. But the kitchen, though small, had a table in it and two chairs which there was just room to sit in if you weren't overweight and were prepared to keep your elbows close to your sides. The big fridge dominated the room. Wexford took out two half-pint cans of Abbot.

'I'm sorry, Mike . . .' he was beginning as Burden simultaneously started to say, 'Look, I do regret saying those things yesterday . . .'

Their joint laughter was shamefaced as embarrassment gripped them.

'Oh, for Christ's sake,' Wexford said, nearly groaned it. 'Let's get it over with. I never meant you had psychopathic tendencies – I mean, would I say anything so daft?'

'No more than I meant that the accident had made you – well, lose your grip . . . or whatever it was I said. Why do we say these things? They just seem to come out before you think.'

They looked at each other, each one holding his green can of beer, each rejecting the actual use of the glasses Wexford had fetched from the cupboard. Burden was the first to break the eye contact which anyway had been only momentary. He looked down, busied himself with the can fastener and said in an uneven, hearty voice, 'Look, I want to talk to you

599

about Clifford Sanders. I want to tell you everything he's told me and hear what you think. And then I want something I don't think you'll consent to do.'

'Try me.'

'To interview him with me – sit in at one of our sessions.'

'Your what?' said Wexford.

'Sorry, I mean interrogations.'

'Tell me what he's told you.'

'I could play you the tapes.'

'Not now. Just tell me.'

'He's been going on about his childhood, about that weird mother of his. He keeps calling her Dodo and laughing. I don't want to have to think him unbalanced – that is, I don't care for the idea of him getting off on the grounds of diminished responsibility – but I reckon I have to.' And then Burden told him all that had taken place at the interview of the night before, detailing what Clifford had said.

'You don't want me there,' said Wexford. 'He'll clam up if I'm there.'

'You've changed your mind, though, haven't you? You agree with me he's guilty?'

'No, I don't, Mike. Not at all. I just see that your believing it is more reasonable than I thought it was. You've no weapon that you can trace to his hand. However you may be deceiving yourself, you've no motive, and frankly I don't think you've even got opportunity. You'll never prove it; you haven't a hope unless you get him to confess.'

'That's just what I do hope for. I'm going to have another go at him on Monday.'

When they had all gone peace descended on the little house on Battle Hill, a peace however that was not entirely silent for through the thin dividing walls could be heard neighbours' noise: light-switches clicking, inane cackles of televised laughter, children's running feet, unidentifiable crashes. Wexford sat down with the new A. N. Wilson and was absorbed in it when the phone rang.

Dora went to answer it, 'If that's anyone else wanting to come and apologize, tell them I'm quite at leisure.'

But it was Sheila. He heard Dora speak her name and

heard the deep concern and shock in her voice, then he was out of that chair at a bound.

She turned to him from the receiver. 'She's all right. She didn't want us to hear it on TV first. A letter-bomb . . .'

Wexford took the phone from her.

'It was there with the rest of my post. I don't know why, but I didn't like the look of it. The police came like a shot and they took it away and did I don't know what to it and it blew up . . . !'

She started sobbing, her words no longer comprehensible, and Wexford heard a man's voice murmuring comforting things.

14

'My grandmother Sanders had some money, but she left it all to my father,' said Clifford. 'I never saw my father again. He went away when I was five; he didn't even say goodbye to me. I can remember it all quite well. He was there when I went to bed and in the morning when I woke up he was gone. My mother just said to me that my father had left us, but that I should see him quite often – that he would come to see me and take me out. But he never did come and I never saw him again. It's no wonder my mother didn't want anything about the place to remind her of him; it's no wonder she put all his family things up there in the attics.'

Involuntarily, Burden followed his glance upwards to the cracked and rather discoloured dining-room ceiling. Beyond the french windows a thin mist hung over the wintry garden, and the hill that hid the prospect of Kingsmarkham was a grey, treeless hump. It was Sunday afternoon and at a quarter-past three already growing dark. Burden had not intended to come here – had meant, as he told Wexford, to postpone any further interrogation of Clifford until the following day. But as he was finishing his lunch Clifford had phoned.

There was no reason why he shouldn't have found Burden's home number, it was there in the telephone directory for anyone to see, but Burden was astonished to get the call, astonished and encouraged. A confession was surely imminent, an intuition he had which was very much substantiated by the low, wary tone in which Clifford spoke – as if he feared being overheard – and the sudden haste with which he rang off as soon as Burden said he would come. The suspicion was inescapable that Dodo Sanders had come into the room; another word and she would have guessed what Clifford was up to and surely tried to stop him.

It was Clifford who had admitted him to the house. His mother put her head round the door of what was perhaps some kind of washroom and stared, saying nothing. Her head was swathed in a towel, obviously because she had just washed her hair in spite of visiting the hairdresser three days before. But this brought to Burden's mind what Olson had said about the fallacy of 'the veiled one'. Of course he had not meant anything of this sort, that particular veiling surely referring to hidden aspects of personality or nature. The turbanned head ducked back and the door closed. Burden looked at Clifford, whose appearance was much as usual. He wore his school uniform clothes, no concession to the casual having been made for Sunday. Yet there was a subtle change in his manner, something indefinable that Burden couldn't put his finger on. Up until yesterday, he had come into Burden's presence grudgingly or with injured outrage or even straight fear. This afternoon Clifford had admitted him to the house not as one might a friend, not that, but at least as some visitor whose call was a necessary and inevitable evil, a tax inspector perhaps. Of course it must be remembered that he had come at Clifford's personal invitation.

A fire had been lit in the dining room and it was fairly warm. Burden was sure Clifford had done this himself. He had even drawn up two of the dining chairs to the fireplace – hard upright chairs, but the best he could offer. Burden sat down and Clifford launched at once into this resumed story of his life.

'Children don't question what they live on, where the money comes from, I mean. I was a lot older when my mother told me that my father had never paid her a penny. She tried to force him to pay her through the court, but he couldn't be found; he'd just deserted her and disappeared. And he had a private income, you know; I mean he had investments of his own, just enough to live on without working. She had to go out cleaning to keep us and then she made things, sort of cottage industry things – bits she knitted and sewed. I was nearly grown-up before I knew any of this. She never told me before. I was at school while she was working and of course I never guessed.'

Burden didn't know what questions to ask, so he said nothing. He just listened, thinking of his confession, pinning faith on that. The recorder was on the dining table; Clifford had placed it there himself.

'I owe her everything,' Clifford went on. 'She sacrificed her whole life to me, wore herself out to keep me in comfort. Serge says I needn't think of it like that, that basically we all do what we want and that was what she wanted. But I don't know. I mean I do know intellectually, I know he's right, but that doesn't do away with my guilt. I feel guilty about her all the time. For example, when I left school at eighteen I could have got a job; someone I knew at school, his father actually offered me an office job, but my mother insisted on my going to university. She always wanted the best for me. Of course I got the maximum grant, but I was still a drag on her; I wasn't earning money except for a bit I got from gardening for people like Miss McPhail. When I got to Myringham University I never lived in; I came back home every night.' Clifford shifted his eyes, looking quickly into Burden's and then away. 'She can't be left alone at night, you see. Not in this house, at any rate, and she always is in this house. She hasn't anywhere else to go, has she?' He made the astounding statement with low-key carelessness, 'She's afraid of ghosts.'

Another little shiver exacerbated Burden's discomfort and he found himself nodding, murmuring, 'Yes, yes, I see.'

It was quite dark outside now. Clifford drew the brown velvet curtains, remained standing, holding the border of one of them rather too tightly and clutching it in a fist. 'I feel guilty all the time,' he said again. 'I ought to be grateful, and I am in a sort of way. I ought to love her, but I don't.' He lowered his voice, glanced at the closed door, and then, bending towards Burden said in a near-whisper, 'I hate her!'

Burden just stared at him.

'My other grandmother died, the one called Clifford,' Clifford said, sitting down once more. He smiled in a slightly contemptuous way. 'My mother's mother, that was. My mother got her furniture and the money she had in the Post Office. It wasn't much, just enough to buy a secondhand car. We got that Metro and I learned to drive. I can learn things, I'm quite good at that. Not much good at earning my living though, and I feel guilty about that too, because there's a part of me knows that I ought to be able to pay my mother back for all she did for me. I ought to – well, buy her a flat to live in where she wouldn't be afraid of the ghosts and then I could stay on alone here, couldn't I? Actually, I think I'd like that. She'd take the glass wall with her and . . .'

The door was suddenly opened and Dodo Sanders stood there in her brown clothes, flat polished lace-up shoes, the white lined face on those trim shoulders always a shock, the scarlet mouth a clown's painted gash. A fresh turban concealed her hair which under the brown-patterned scarf was perhaps done up in curlers. She looked at her son, then slowly turned her head to fix her eyes on Burden. He tried to avoid meeting those eyes but he failed.

'You're wrong if you think he killed that woman.'

Burden thought of that machine voice on his tape, wondering if it would sound more or less metallic. 'Whatever I may think, Mrs Sanders,' he said mildly, 'I'm sure I'm not wrong.'

'It's impossible,' she said. 'I should know. My instincts would know. I know all about him.'

Clifford seemed about to bury his head in his hands, but instead he sighed and said to Burden, 'Could we talk some more tomorrow?'

Burden agreed, feeling confused and helpless.

Nothing had happened to her; she was all right. The letter had been sent to 'the occupier' and perhaps had not been meant for her or indeed anyone specific – was possibly a mere wanton arbitrary missive of destruction directed at whichever tenant of the flat might have the misfortune to open it. Wexford told himself all this as he descended Battle Hill, his umbrella up against the ferocious rain of Monday morning. But he didn't believe it. Coincidence had not that long an arm.

Next week she would appear in court to be charged, he supposed, under the Criminal Damage Act of 1971, and he repeated the charge over to himself: 'That you on Thursday, 19th November, at RAF Lossington in the County of Northamptonshire, had in your custody or under your control a pair of wire-cutters and did use them without lawful excuse to damage certain property, namely the perimeter fence belonging to the Ministry of Defence . . .' Something like that. Dora was right and Sylvia and Neil were right. She had only to make a statement in court to the effect that her action had been misguided – plead guilty, pay her fine, do no more. They would leave her alone then; they would let her live. He was tempted for a moment, seeing it briefly as such a small thing, such an easy thing to do in exchange for life and happiness, remarriage, children perhaps, a glorious career. But of course she couldn't do it. He almost laughed out loud at the idea, walking down there through the rain, and suddenly felt a lot better.

It wasn't Ralph Robson who admitted him to the house, but Dita Jago. Wexford furled his dripping umbrella and left it in the porch.

Mrs Jago said: 'We came in to see if we could get anything for him while we're out.'

Nina Quincy was sitting in that cheerful but somehow comfortless room, having taken her daughters to school, and Robson was in an armchair on the opposite side of the fireplace. He had taken up the hunched, lopsided attitude arthritic people adopt to minimize suffering, one leg stretched out, one shoulder raised. But even so his owl's face was sharp with pain. Dita Jago's daughter provided a cruel contrast to him, not only young and beautiful but blooming with beauty and health. Her face, innocent of make-up, was rosily flushed and her dark eyes bright; dark chestnut hair fell below her shoulders in a mass of waves. She had something of the appearance of a healthy Jane Morris, but Rossetti would have resisted painting anyone as fit and flourishing as she. Both women wore garments of unmistakable Jago manufacture, the younger a tunic of dark chenille patterned all over with stylized crimson and blue butterflies. In a stiff, rather formal way her mother introduced her to Wexford.

She held out her hand, said unexpectedly, 'I must tell you how I admire your daughter. We loved her in that serial. Not much like you, is she?'

It was a little meagre voice to emanate from so much rich, colourful beauty and momentarily he marvelled that someone could look so intelligent yet in a couple of sentences

606

reveal she was not. He acknowledged her comment with a small, dry shake of the head and turned to Robson.

'Your niece has gone back to London, has she?'

'She went last evening,' Robson said. 'I shall miss her; I don't know what I'll do without her.'

Dita Jago said with unexpected briskness, 'Life must go on. She's got her living to earn, she can't stay here for ever.'

'She got down to it and spring-cleaned the whole blessed house for me while she was here.'

Spring-cleaning in December? It was an activity, anyway, which Wexford had imagined must be obsolete. Hard, too, to picture the exquisitely dressed and coiffed Lesley Arbel brushing ceilings and washing paint. His raised eyebrows elicited more information from Ralph Robson.

'She said she might as well give the place a complete turn-out while she was here. Not that it needed it; Gwen kept it like a new pin, as far as I could see. But Lesley insisted; she said she didn't know when I'd get it done again and she was right there. She had all the cupboards out, and the wardrobes, went through Gwen's clothes and took them off to Oxfam. Gwen has a good winter coat – only bought it last year and I thought Lesley might have liked to keep that for herself, but maybe it wasn't smart enough for her.'

Wexford saw Nina Quincy's lips twitch, her eyes shift if not quite cast up as Robson went on, 'She even went up in the roof, but I said to leave that; I said you can't take the blessed Hoover up there. There was no need to lift up fitted carpets either. But when Lesley does a thing she does it thoroughly and the place is like a new pin, spotless. I shall miss her, I can tell you; I'll be lost without her.'

Nina Quincy got up. Her attitude, her look showed her as a woman easily and quickly bored, needing new sensations. She yawned and said, 'Shall we go if you've got that list?'

Wexford parted from the two women when they reached the gate. Again he marvelled at Mrs Jago's light, springy tread as she made for the car under the yellow and black golfing umbrella her daughter held up over them. For no reason apparent to him at that moment, he found himself thinking of Defoe who had written his *Journal of the Plague*

Year as if it were autobiography, as if he had witnessed the plague's horrors instead of being an infant at the time.

Burden was in his office, awaiting the arrival of Clifford Sanders whom Davidson had gone to fetch. Clifford had asked on the previous day if they could talk again this morning and Burden was puzzled by the request, or had been for a while after it was made. But now his hopes had rallied and his expectation of a confession was restored.

When Wexford came in he said, 'I never thought I'd see the day when the hottest suspect in a murder case started asking to help us with our enquiries.'

It was delicate ground for Wexford and he put on a look of polite interest.

'He actually wants to come here this morning. I suppose it's one way of skiving off work.'

Wexford just looked at him. 'I'll tell you an interesting thing. Lesley Arbel's been spring-cleaning Robson's house, turning out all the cupboards, been up in the roof pretending to want to vacuum-clean it, had the carpets up. What was she looking for?'

'Maybe she was just cleaning.'

'Not she. Why would she? The house was clean enough for any normal person not a fanatic already. Young girls these days aren't mad about cleaning, Mike. They don't know how to do it, or else they don't care. It would have been a different matter if she'd come down to be with Robson and found the place in a mess. Then she might have cleaned up – if she was exceptionally kind and thoughtful for her age ... which she's not. And then there's the matter of her fingernails. Her nails were long and varnished earlier last week, but when I saw her last Friday they'd been cut short. That means she either broke a nail cleaning or thought it wiser to cut her nails before the cleaning started. And I should think she was the kind of girl who would be as proud of her long red nails as any Chinese emperor's concubine.'

'Maybe she had to cut them for the computer.'

Wexford shrugged. 'No different from a typewriter keyboard, is it? She'd been typing with long nails for years probably. No, she sacrificed her nails in order to perform the supremely generous task of cleaning her uncle's house.'

'What is it you're trying to say?'

'That she wasn't cleaning, or that the cleaning was incidental or an excuse to make to Robson. She was looking for something; she was turning the house upside down, lifting up the carpets, going up in the loft in search of something. I don't know what it was, though I've got a few ideas. I don't know if she found it, but I think the search was what brought her here and kept her here so long, not devotion to Robson. And I don't think we'll see her here again very much, either because she found what she was looking for or because she realizes she isn't going to find it. And that means it isn't in the house or that it was very cleverly hidden indeed.'

Instead of asking the obvious question, Burden said, 'We haven't searched the place ourselves. Should we?'

Wexford was hesitating when the phone rang and Burden picked up the receiver. Apparently Clifford had arrived.

'I'll have to go. What was she looking for, anyway?'

'The documentary evidence on which Gwen Robson based her blackmailing activities, of course.'

'Oh, there wasn't any of that,' Burden said breezily. 'It was all hearsay, all just what she'd heard or suspected.' He didn't wait for Wexford's reply, but went off down to the interview room on the ground floor, the one done up in shades of ancient spaniel. Rain was streaming down the window, making the glass opaque. Clifford sat at the table with a styrofoam beaker of coffee in front of him, Diana Pettit on the opposite side reading the legal page of the *Independent*. She got up and Burden gave her the sideways nod that meant to leave them with the tape recorder running. Clifford half rose and put out his hand; Burden was so surprised that he had shaken it almost before he knew what he was doing.

'Can we start?' Clifford asked eagerly.

It was difficult for Burden to handle this. For the first time in his career as a policeman he had the feeling that he had been insufficiently trained or that a branch of his training had been neglected. 'What is it you want to tell me?' he asked in a voice he knew sounded tentative and unsure.

'I'm telling you about the sort of person I am. I'm talking about my feelings.' Clifford's eyes moved and to Burden's astonishment a mischievous gleam appeared in them; it was

609

so incongruous as to be shocking. He laughed gleefully. 'I'm trying to tell you what made me do it.'

'Do it?' Burden leaned forward across the table.

'Do what I do,' Clifford said blandly. 'Lead the life I do.' He laughed again. 'That was a joke. It was meant to make you think I was going to say "murder Mrs Robson". Sorry, it wasn't very funny.' Drawing a long breath, he made a throat-clearing sound. 'I am a prisoner. Did you know that?'

Burden said nothing. What was there to say?

'I am my own jailer, Dodo has seen to that. Why does she want that, you ask? Some are born to be jailers. It's for power. I am the first person she has really had in her power, you see – the only one. The others resisted, they got away. Shall I tell you how she met my father? My father was quite an upper class sort of person, you know; he had an uncle who was the High Sheriff of the county. I don't know what that really means, but it's very important. My grandfather was a gentleman farmer, he owned three hundred acres of land. It was all sold when my father was young so that they could keep on living in the style they were accustomed to. A lot of Kingsmarkham is actually built on my grandfather's land.'

Looking at him with mounting exasperation, Burden felt resentful at the stupid trick which Clifford had tried to play on him, pretending he was about to make a confession. And Clifford said, annoying him still further, 'Your own house, wherever that is, is probably on a bit of land that was my family's.'

Clifford drank his coffee, clasping the small beaker in both hands and affording Burden a close-up of his cruelly bitten nails. 'Dodo came to work for my father's parents as a cleaner. That surprises you, doesn't it? Not a maid – oh, no – but a daily cleaner they had to do the rough work. They had had maids, and a chauffeur, but that was before the war. After the war they had to make do with my mother. I don't know how she got my father to marry her. She says "love" but she would. I wasn't born till they'd been married two years, so it wasn't that. Once she was married, she wanted to own the place, to be the boss and the jailer.'

'How can you know that?' Burden found himself saying uncomfortably, for he was beginning to understand that

Olson had meant with his fallacy of recognizing and not recognizing.

Clifford seemed to underline this when he went on, 'I know my mother. My grandfather died; he was very old and he'd been ill a long time. As soon as the funeral was over, my father left us – the very next day it was, I can remember all that. I was five, you see. I can remember going to the funeral with my mother and my father and my grandmother. I had to go; there wasn't anyone to leave me with, it was before I started school. My mother wore a bright red hat with a little veil and a bright red coat. It was new and she'd never had it on before and when I saw her in it I thought that was what women wore to funerals – bright red. I thought it must be the correct thing because I'd never seen her in that colour before. When my grandmother came down, she was in black and I said to her, "Why aren't you in red, Grandma?" and Dodo laughed.

'Now I'm grown-up, I've sometimes thought it was wrong of my father to abandon his mother. I mean, it was wrong of him to go anyway, but doubly wrong really to leave his mother with Dodo. Of course I didn't think about that when I was a child. I never thought much about my grandmother and what her feelings were. My mother put her into an old people's home; it wasn't long after my father left, only a few days. She didn't say goodbye either, just went out and never came back. I asked my mother how she managed it – I mean, I asked years later when I was in my teens. Somebody had said how hard it was to get old people into those council homes. My mother told me about it, she was proud of it. She had a hired car come round – it was when minicabs first started – and told my grandmother they were going for a drive. When they got to this home, she took her in and just said to the matron or whoever it was that she was leaving her there and they'd have to look after her. Dodo doesn't mind what she says to people, you see; that's one of the things that gives her power. People say to her, "I've never been spoken to like that in my life" or "How dare you?" but it doesn't bother her; she just looks at them and says something else awful. She's got through the inhibition barrier, you see, the inhibition on being rude.'

'My grandmother lived another ten years, all the time in

611

that home and then in a geriatric ward. The social services tried to get my mother to take her back but they couldn't force her to, could they? She just refused to let them in the house. But before that, as soon as the minicab brought her back in fact, she moved all the furniture upstairs. Mr Carroll, the farmer – he and his wife were the only people I remember we ever saw. They weren't friends but they were people we knew, the only people. My mother got him to help her take all that furniture up into the attics and then when – '

'What's all this leading up to, Clifford?' Burden put in.

Clifford ignored him, or appeared to ignore him. Perhaps he responded only to what he wanted to hear. His eyes were on the window. The rain had slackened and the streaming water separated into trickling droplets between which a green-grey blur could be seen and a lowering overcast. But perhaps he saw nothing and the sense of sight was shut. Burden felt uncomfortable and his discomfort increased with every sentence Clifford spoke. All the time he was expecting some sort of climax or explosion, expecting Clifford to jump up and begin screaming. But for the present the man on the other side of the table seemed locked in an unnatural calm.

He went on in a lighter, more conversational tone, 'When I was disobedient or offended her in some way, she'd lock me up in one of those attics. Sometimes it would be the one with all the photos in and sometimes with the beds and mattresses. But I got to know I'd always be let out before it got dark. She wouldn't go up there in the dark because she's afraid of ghosts. I think the supernatural is the only thing my mother *is* afraid of. There are bits of our garden she won't go near after dark – well, in the daytime, too, come to that. I used to sit in the attic looking at all those faces.'

'Faces?' repeated Burden in a hollow tone.

'In the photos,' Clifford said patiently. He was silent for a moment and the inspiration came to Burden to do as Serge Olson did, to take off his watch and lay it on the table in front of him. Clifford's eyes flickered as he observed the movement. 'I used to study the faces of my ancestors and think to myself, all those ladies in long skirts and big hats and all those men with dogs and guns, all of them had just ended up in me, that's all they'd come to in the end – me. I'd watch the light fade till I couldn't see the faces clearly any more and when that happened I knew she'd come. When she came it would be quite slowly, taking her time, and then the door would slide open and in a nice quiet pleasant sort of way, just as if nothing had happened, she'd tell me to come down and that my tea was ready.'

Burden said wearily, picking up the watch, 'Time's up, Clifford.'

He rose obediently. 'Shall I come back this afternoon?'

'You'll hear from us.' Burden almost said, 'Don't call us, we'll call you', and then, standing alone in the room after Clifford had been taken away, asked himself with near-disbelief what he thought he was doing. Didn't he expect an admission of guilt? Wasn't that what it was all about? He went up to his own office and began looking through the reports which were the result of seemingly fruitless efforts on the part of Archbold and Marian Bayliss to find evidence of unsolved murder in Clifford's past. Both grandmothers had died natural deaths, or so it seemed. Old Mrs Sanders had died after a heart attack in the council home where her daughter-in-law had dumped her; old Mrs Clifford had been found by a neighbour dead in her bed at home. Elizabeth McPhail had died in hospital after months of incapacity caused by a stroke.

Still, he must keep on questioning him – that afternoon if necessary, and next day and the day after, every day until Clifford reached the present and finally told him in that monotonous voice that he had killed Gwen Robson.

Wexford was in the Midland Bank in Queen Street. It was four-thirty and the bank had been closed to customers for the past hour. The manager had been cooperative and answered all his questions without protest. Yes, Mr Robson had an account at the branch but no, Mrs Robson – who hadn't banked there anyway – had nothing on safe deposit. Wexford hadn't really expected it. Whatever Lesley Arbel had been searching for was hidden elsewhere – or Lesley had already found it. The manager was plainly unwilling to tell him anything about Mrs Sanders' account, also at the branch, presumably because she wasn't dead.

He came out into grey drizzle, into early dusk. The greengrocer's display looked glistening wet even though the awning was up, a sheen like dew on green leaves and citrus rind. Behind the bow window of the boutique skimpy clothes in fruit-salad colours shimmered. Into the tawny-lit warmth of the wine market Serge Olson was disappearing, passing in the doorway a man who was also known to Wexford: John Whitton, Ralph Robson's neighbour. His baby nestled fast asleep against his chest in a carrying sling; the older child, muffled to the eyes in knitted wraps and quilted nylon, grasped with a gloved hand the hem of his Barber jacket, for Whitton's arms were fully occupied with his two carrier bags of wine. He looked at Wexford without recognizing him and made for the Peugeot estate car parked at the kerb. The meter had no more than a couple of minutes to run and a traffic warden was already bearing down.

Whitton put the baby into a cot on the back seat, the wine on to the floor, and had no sooner straightened up than the crying began. The three-year-old clambered in, viewing its brother or sister with that dispassionate mild interest children often show towards a younger sibling in distress. Wexford watched because he was wondering how poor Whitton was going to extricate the car without touching the one in front or the one behind, though 'touching' was hardly the word for what had recently been done to the Peugeot; its offside headlamp had been smashed and the metal surround buckled. Nevertheless he would have turned away, knowing the dreadful irritation of being watched while one is manoeuvring a car, had Whitton — now in the driving-seat — not called out to him.

'I say, would you mind awfully telling me how near I am?'

Those people who stand in front of drivers, beckoning and holding up a warning hand — Wexford had often been exasperated by them, had long ago resolved never to join their number. It was different, though, when one was invited. The car crawled forward and he signalled to Whitton to stop when within an inch of the rear mudguard of the Mercedes in front.

'You ought to make it on the next lock,' he said as Whitton reversed.

And then Whitton did recognize him, speaking above the baby's frenetic yells: 'You came to talk to me about Mrs

Robson.' The engine stalled and he swore, made an effort, smiled. 'I shouldn't lose my cool like that. That's what happens when you do.' A thumb cocked towards the left side of the car's bonnet indicated what he meant. 'My wife had a bit of a contretemps with a parking meter here three weeks ago.'

Wexford knew Whitton was telling him this because he was a policeman, because like so many of the public he thought all policemen, whatever branch of the force they belonged to and whatever their rank, were equally preoccupied by traffic offences. In a moment he would be defending his wife lest Wexford whipped out a notebook . . .

'Mind you, she didn't so much as scratch another vehicle, which was a miracle considering the way this young fellow in a Metro got at her.'

A polite, 'Really?' and a short preamble to saying goodbye were on the tip of Wexford's tongue. Instead he said rather quickly, though knowing it was a long shot, 'When exactly was this, Mr Whitton?'

Whitton liked talking. Without being exactly garrulous, he liked a chance to talk and naturally he would, having taken over the role long assigned exclusively to women where he was locked into a daily relationship with children too young for conversation. First, however, he reached into the back of the car and picked up the baby off the back seat, its cries at once fading to whimpers. Amused, Wexford saw that he was settling down for a long, companionable talk . . . and then he wasn't amused any more, but excited.

'Three weeks ago, as I said. Well, as a matter of fact, it must have been the day Mrs Robson was killed. Yes, it was. Rosemary had the car that day and she was picking up our fruit and veg on the way home. A quarter-to-six maybe, ten-to . . . ?'

15

It was Burden's idea to have him up in his office rather than in either of the interview rooms. He couldn't stand any more of those vinyl tiles and the blank walls and the metal rim round the table. It wasn't any less warm down there than up here, but there was a sense of chill, a feeling that draughts crept in between plaster and window frame and under the unpanelled door with its corroded metal handle. So Clifford was brought upstairs and he came in as if paying a social call – smiling, hand outstretched. Burden wouldn't have been surprised if he had asked him how he was, but Clifford didn't do that.

The blinds were down and the lights were on. They were soft lights though, coming from an angled lamp on the desk, and two spots on the ceiling. Burden sat down behind the desk and Clifford in front of it, in a chair with padded seat and wooden arms which Diana Pettit pulled out for him. She was still in the room, sitting near the door, but he seemed unaware of her presence. He was wearing a different grey shirt, this one with a button-down collar, and his pullover was of a darker grey with a cable pattern but errors had been made in the knitting of the cables. Burden found himself compulsively staring at one of these flaws up near the left shoulder, where the knitter in twisting the cable had passed the rib over instead of under the work.

'I'd like you to tell me about your relations with your other grandmother,' Burden began. 'Mrs Clifford, I mean, your mother's mother. Did you see much of her?'

Instead of answering, Clifford said, 'My mother's not all bad. I've given you a bad impression of her. She's really like

616

everyone else, a mixture of bad and good, only her Shadow's very powerful. Can I tell you a story? It's a romantic story really; my grandmother Clifford told it me.'

'Go on,' encouraged Burden.

'When my mother was a little girl they lived in Forbydean, her and her mother and father. She used to go to school past Ash Farm on her bicycle and she got to know my father, who was a bit younger. Well, they played together; they got to play together whenever they could, which was mostly in the holidays because my father was away at his prep school. When she was thirteen and my father was twelve, his parents found out about the friendship and put a stop to it. You see, they thought their son was a lot too good for my mother even to play with: they said a farm labourer's daughter wasn't good enough for their son. And my father didn't put up any sort of resistance; he agreed with them, he hadn't understood before, and when my mother came round next time he wouldn't speak to her, wouldn't even look at her. And then my grandmother came out and told my mother she must go home and not come any more.'

Burden nodded abstractedly, wondering how long all this was going to take. It wasn't an unusual story for this part of the world at that period. Similar things had happened to his own contemporaries, forbidden for reasons of social snobbery to 'play in the street'.

Clifford went on, 'I'm really telling you this to show you the good side of my mother. I said it was romantic. Later on, you see, she went to work for them and they didn't recognize the little girl they'd prevented from playing with their Charles. And *he* didn't until she told him after he'd married her. I wonder what they all thought then?'

Burden was not sufficiently interested to hazard guesses. 'Did your grandmother Clifford come to see you when you were a child? Did you visit her with your mother?'

Clifford sighed. Perhaps he would have preferred to continue his speculations about the romantic story. 'I sometimes think I spent my childhood walking. I walked through my childhood, if you know what I mean. It was the only way to get anywhere. I must have walked hundreds of miles, thousands. My mother doesn't walk that fast but I was always breathless, trying to keep up with her.'

617

'You walked to your grandmother's, then?'

Clifford sighed again. 'When we went, we walked. There was the bus, but my mother wouldn't pay bus fares. We didn't go to my grandmother's very much. You have to understand that my mother doesn't like people and she didn't particularly like her mother. You see, my grandfather died very suddenly, then when my father walked out and my grandmother Sanders went into a home we were left alone with the house to ourselves. I think she liked that.' He hesitated, looked down at his bitten nails, said half-slyly, 'And she likes me, so long as I'm obedient. She moulded me into a slave and a protector. She made me like Frankenstein made the monster, to go wrong.' A small shrill laugh, which might have moderated those words, somehow made them the more terrible.

Burden looked at him with a kind of uneasy impatience. He was framing a question about Mrs Sanders' mother, a wild idea coming to him of Gwen Robson possibly having once been to her as a home help, when Clifford went on: 'Once when I wouldn't do what she wanted, she locked me in the attic with the photographs and she lost the key to the room. I don't know how she lost it – she never told me, she wouldn't – but I expect she dropped it down the plughole or it fell down a crack in the floor or something. She's accident-prone, you see, because she doesn't think about what she's doing; her mind's always on something else. So I expect that's how she lost the key. She's very strong even though she's small and she tried to break down the door by putting her shoulder to it, but she couldn't. I was inside, listening to her crashing at the door. It was winter and starting to get dark and she was frightened; I know she was frightened, I could feel her fear through the door. Maybe the ghosts were creeping up the stairs after her.'

He smiled, then laughed on a high shrill note, wrinkling up his nose as if in a mixture of pleasure and pain at the memory. 'She had to go and get help. I was scared when I heard her go away, because I thought I was going to be left there for ever. It was cold and I was only a little kid, in there in the half-dark with that old furniture and all those faces. She took the bulbs out of the sockets, you see, so that I couldn't put the light on. But that meant *she* couldn't put the light on either . . .' Another smile and rueful shake of the head. 'She went to get Mr Carroll and he came back with her and put his shoulder to the door and burst it open. I never got put in there again, because the door wouldn't lock after that. Mrs Carroll came with him and I remember what she said; she turned on my mother and said she'd a good mind to tell the prevention of cruelty to children people, but if she did they never did anything.

'Mrs Carroll went away six months ago. She ran away from her husband – with another man, my mother said. It was Dodo who had to tell Mr Carroll. She sort of hinted to him that there was this other man and then she told him straight out. I thought he was going to attack her but people don't attack her, or they never have yet. He broke down and sobbed and cried. Do you know what I thought? What I hoped? I thought, my father left my mother and now Mrs Carroll's left her husband. Suppose Mr Carroll was to marry Dodo? That would be the best escape, wouldn't it, the cleanest way to get free? I wonder if I'd be jealous, though, I wonder if I'd mind . . . ?'

He was interrupted by a tap at the door, followed by the appearance of Archbold to tell Burden that Wexford would like to see him.

'Now, do you mean?'

'He said it was urgent.'

Burden left Clifford with Diana. Perhaps it was no bad thing to take a break here. He wasn't interested in Clifford's boyhood, but he valued the mood these reminiscences seemed to bring him to, a mood of open revelation and frankness. All these stories of his youth (which was precisely how Burden saw them) would lead Clifford, though by a crazy path, to the final incriminating outburst.

Instead of taking the lift, he walked upstairs. The door to Wexford's office stood a little ajar. Wexford was nearly always to be found either behind his desk or standing at the window thinking, while apparently contemplating the High Street. But this morning he stood abstractedly looking at the plan of greater Kingsmarkham which hung on the left-hand wall. He turned his eyes as Burden came in.

'Oh, Mike . . .'

'You wanted to see me?'

'Yes. I apologize for the interruption, but perhaps you'll see it wasn't exactly an interruption, more a breaking-off. Clifford Sanders – he didn't do it, he couldn't have done. You may as well let him go.'

Hard-faced, immediate anger starting, Burden said, 'We've been through all this before.'

'No, Mike, listen. He was seen sitting in his mother's car in Queen Street at five-forty-five on November the nineteenth. A woman called Rosemary Whitton saw him; she spoke to him and he spoke to her.'

'She was trying to move her car,' Wexford said, 'and she hadn't much room, only a few inches each end to play with – '

With the sexism of the stand-up comic, but straight-faced and deadly serious, Burden interrupted him: 'Women drivers!'

'Oh, Mike, come on! Clifford was sitting in the car behind her and he had a couple of yards behind him. She asked him if he'd move and he told her to go away. "Leave me alone, go away", was what he said.'

'How does she know it was Clifford?'

'She gave me a good description. It was a red Metro. She's no fool, Mike; she's something rather high-powered, a systems analyst, though I confess I'm not sure what that is.'

'And she says it was at a quarter to six?'

'She was late, she was in a hurry. Women like her are always in a hurry – inevitably. She says she wanted to get home before the kids were put to bed at six. When she first got back into the car she looked at the clock – I always do that myself, I know what she means – and it was exactly five-forty-five. Which means it was a good few minutes after that by the time she'd had her slanging match with Clifford and crunched the headlight on a meter.'

'Is that what she did?' asked Burden ruminatively, his frown threatening a further attack on women at the wheel. 'Why didn't he tell me that?'

'Didn't notice, I daresay. She says he moved as soon as it was too late to matter.'

The woman's statement would now have to be checked,

thoroughly investigated, and until that had been done Burden's interrogation of Clifford must be suspended. He didn't go back to the interview room. The anger and frustration which might more naturally have been vented on Wexford he wanted to splash furiously over the man downstairs. He could have put through a phone call to his own office but couldn't face explaining to Clifford, so he sent Archbold back with the message to let him go, to tell him he wouldn't be needed again.

'Where would you hide something, Mike, if you were Gwen Robson?'

Smarting from his defeat, not yet fully grasping what the result of exonerating Clifford would be, Burden said sullenly, 'What sort of something?'

'Papers. A few sheets of paper.'

'Letters, do you mean?'

'I don't know.' Wexford said. 'Lesley Arbel was looking for papers, but I don't think she found them. They're not in the bank and they're not with Kingsmarkham Safe Depository Limited – I've just tried there.'

'How do you know Lesley Arbel didn't find them?'

'When I spoke to her on Friday she was worried and unhappy. If she'd found what she turned the house out for, she'd have been over the moon.'

'I'm wondering if Clifford could have killed his other grandmother, his mother's mother. He's a very strange character altogether. He has all the salient features of the psychopath . . . What are you laughing at?'

'Leave it, Mike,' Wexford said. 'Just leave it. And leave the psychiatry to Serge Olson.'

Burden was to remember that last remark when Olson phoned him on the following morning. He had thought of very little apart from Clifford Sanders during the intervening time and everything he had done had been concerned with this new alibi. He had even interviewed Rosemary Whitton himself and, unable to shake her conviction of the relevant time, had questioned the Queen Street greengrocer. If no one in Queen Street remembered Clifford in the Metro, a good many shopkeepers recalled Mrs Whitton hitting the meter post. The manager of the wine market remembered the time: it was before he closed at six, but not much before. He had turned the door sign to 'Closed' immediately he returned from inspecting the damage. Unconvinced but obliged at any rate temporarily to yield, Burden turned his attention from Clifford Sanders to Clifford Sanders' father . . . As a temporary measure at any rate. He wouldn't speak to Clifford Sanders again for a week, and in the meantime he would root out Charles Sanders and begin a new line of enquiry there. But before he could begin, Serge Olson phoned him.

'Mike, I think you should know that I've just had a call from Clifford cancelling his Thursday appointment and, incidentally, all further appointments with me. I asked him why and he said he had no further need of my particular kind of treatment. So there you are.'

Burden said rather cautiously, 'Why are you telling me, Mr Olson – Serge?'

'Well, you're subjecting him to some fairly heavy interrogation, aren't you? Look, this is delicate ground – for me, at any rate. He's my client. I am anxious not to, let's say, betray his confidence. But it's a serious matter when someone like Clifford abandons his therapy. Mike, Clifford needs his therapy. I'm not saying he necessarily needs what I can give him, but he needs help from someone.'

'Maybe,' said Burden, 'he's found another psychiatrist. You needn't worry about the possible effects of what you call heavy interrogation anyway. That's over, at any rate for the time being.'

'I'm glad to hear it, Mike, I'm very glad.'

Putting it into words, that he had given up questioning Clifford, put things into perspective. Burden suddenly realized how much he hated being closeted with Clifford and hearing all these revelations. He would have no more of it – not until, that is, he had another positive lead. His mind made up, he looked out of the window to where they were putting lights in the branches of the tree that grew on the edge of the police station forecourt. It wasn't a Christmas tree or even a conifer, come to that, but an ash whose only distinction was in its size. Burden watched the two men at work. Putting coloured lights in tree was his idea, later backed up by the Chief Constable, in the interest of promoting jollier relations with the public. Wexford's comment had been a derisive laugh. But surely you couldn't go on feeling antagonistic towards or afraid of or suspicious about a friendly body that hung fairylights in a tree in its front garden? This morning he felt neither jolly nor friendly, in the mood rather to snap at anyone who made jokes about the tree. Diana Pettit had already had the rough side of his tongue for suggesting that all the little lamps should be blue. When the phone rang again he picked up the receiver and said, 'Yes?' testily.

It was Clifford Sanders. 'Can I come and see you?'

'What about?' asked Burden.

'To talk.' No time was mentioned and Burden knew what Clifford was like about time. 'You made me finish early yesterday and I'd a lot more to say. I just wondered when we could start again.'

In my own good time, my lad, Burden thought. Next week maybe, next month. But what he said was, 'No, that's it. That's all. You can get back to work, get on with your life – OK?' He didn't wait for an answer, but put the phone down.

It rang again ten minutes later. By that time the younger and more intrepid of the two men had climbed to the top of the ladder and threaded the lead with bulbs on it through some of the highest branches. Burden thought how disastrous it would be, and what the media would make of it, if the man fell and got hurt. He spoke a milder 'Yes?' into the phone and got Clifford's voice suggesting in an eager, urgent tone that previously they had been cut off. Burden said that as far as he knew they hadn't been cut off. All that needed to be said had been said, hadn't it?

'I'd like to come and see you this afternoon if that's all right.'

'It's not all right,' Burden said, aware that he was back into an earlier mode of addressing Clifford – talking as if he were a child, but unable to do otherwise. 'I'm busy this afternoon.'

'I can come tomorrow morning then.'

'Clifford, I'm going to ring off now. OK, is that understood? We're not being cut off, I've finished, I can't discuss this any more. Goodbye.'

623

For some reason this second call disturbed Burden. It gave him a curious feeling very much like the one experienced by those who, having had little to do with the handicapped, are brought into unexpected contact with someone who lolls and drools and paws at them with spastic hands. Their recoil and gasp are unforgivable, are outrageous, and Burden felt a little ashamed of himself as he put the phone down sharply, as he stepped back, looking at the phone as if Clifford or something of Clifford actually lived inside the brown plastic instrument. What a fool! What was the matter with him? He lifted the receiver once more and gave instructions to the switchboard to put no more calls from Clifford Sanders through to him; furthermore, to monitor all calls that came.

It would be useless to search the house. Lesley Arbel had had two weeks in which to do that and she might be less experienced at searching than Wexford's officers were, but she had had more time and presumably a personal interest in what she was seeking – whatever that was. A will? Gwen Robson had had nothing to leave. Something that would incriminate a guilty, frightened person? Wexford couldn't imagine her blackmailing her own, surely loved, niece. And yet Lesley had been desperate to find those papers, if it was papers.

'I'll lose my job!' she had cried out to him.

It seemed quite inconsequential. At one moment he had been asking her why she had not told him she was in Kingsmarkham that Thursday; the next, she was bewailing her threatened job. He walked up the path to Mrs Jago's house and rang the bell. She came quickly to the door – large, smiling, light-footed. The smile looked a little forced but not, he thought, because he as a policeman was unwelcome.

'All alone today?' he asked.

'Nina doesn't work on Tuesday or go shopping. I saw her yesterday.' They were in the living room now, in the jungle of knitted flowers and trees, but the manuscript was no longer on the table. Dita Jago followed the direction of his eyes. 'I didn't want to see her today. I'd had enough, I didn't feel I could take any more.'

The miseries of a deserted wife, did she mean? The plaints

of a young woman abandoned to bring up two children on her own? He didn't enquire. He asked her where she thought Gwen Robson would have hidden whatever it was she had to hide, but as he did so he remembered how she had disclaimed all but a bare acquaintance with the dead woman. She picked up the circular needle from which the great tropical landscape hung and he saw that she had reached the sky, a blue expanse with tiny clouds. But instead of resuming her work, she sat clasping the two reinforced points of the needle in her hands. She looked at him and away.

'I knew her so little. How can I say?'

'I don't know,' he said. 'The house is the same as this one. I was thinking there might be some peculiarity, some feature of the house well known to residents but absolutely unknown to outsiders?'

'A secret panel?'

'Not exactly that.'

'Perhaps the murderer took this mysterious thing away, whatever it was. Would you like a drink?'

He shook his head rather too quickly and her eyebrows rose.

'What's become of the book?' he asked for something to say. 'You've finished it and sent it to a publisher?'

'I haven't finished it and I never will. I nearly burned it last night and then I thought – who needs emotional gestures, dramas? Just put it away in a drawer – so I did. I had such a day yesterday, it upset me so. It's a funny thing, but I'd like to tell you about it. May I? There doesn't seem to be anyone else I could tell.'

'It makes a change,' he said, 'someone wanting to tell me things.'

'I like you,' she said, and it wasn't naïve or disingenuous; it sounded simply sincere. 'I like you, but I don't really know you and you don't know me, and I doubt if we shall ever know each other much better.' A glance levelled at him seemed to ask for confirmation and he nodded. 'Maybe that's an ideal set-up for confiding.' She was silent, but her hands were still and they no longer held the needle.

'My daughter told me that she had an affair with a man – no, not an affair, not so much as that, a one-night stand, I think it's called – and she was silly enough to tell her husband about it. Not at once; she waited a long while. She should have forgotten it, put it behind her. He confessed something of his own to her, some peccadillo, and she came out with a this thing of hers and instead of being as forgiving as she was, he said that changed everything – it changed all his feelings about her.'

'Like *Tess of the d'Urbervilles*,' Wexford murmured, 'and we think times have changed. She didn't say anything of all this to you till yesterday?'

'That's right. I'd asked her if there was any hope of a reconciliation. Well, I went so far as to ask her what was the basic trouble between them. You're a parent, so you know what I mean by "went so far". They don't like questioning even when it . . . well, springs from one's real concern.'

'No,' said Wexford, 'they don't.' He considered. 'May I . . . ?' He was unusually tentative. 'Would it be possible for me . . . to read your manuscript?'

She had picked up her knitting, but now she let it fall into her lap once more. 'Why on earth. . . . ?' A sudden eagerness in her voice nearly told him he was on the wrong tack, pursuing the wrong course altogether. 'You don't know any publishers, do you?'

He did, of course. Burden's brother-in-law Amyas Ireland had become a friend over the years, but he wasn't going to encourage false hopes there. Nor to tell the whole truth at this stage. 'I'm simply curious to read it.' He observed how her attitude towards the manuscript had changed since she had taken heart from confiding in him. 'Will you let me?'

Thus it was that he found himself making his way up a hill which seemed steeper than it had the evening before, carrying what felt like ten pounds' weight of paper in one of Tesco's red plastic bags. He had planned on finishing the A. N. Wilson that evening and longed to know how it ended – but this, this was important.

It was too early yet to switch on the Christmas lights in the tree, Burden thought, only December 8. However, no one showed any signs of wanting to switch them on and to passers-by they must be invisible. The evening was dark and misty. How long was it since they had seen the sun by day or, come to that, the moon by night?

There were the usual cars on the forecourt where the lamps made everything look like an out-of-focus sepia photograph. Someone had just driven up in a Metro which could have been of any colour. It meant nothing to Burden and he took his raincoat off the hook and went down in the lift. Home early for once! His little boy would still be up, bathed and powdered, running around in pyjamas; the radio on because Jenny preferred it to television; a smell of something exotic but not too exotic, one of the few examples of foreign cuisine he liked – pesto sauce, for instance, or five spices in a stir-fry being prepared for his dinner; Jenny harassed but happy in a blue tracksuit. Burden took a yearning, sensuous delight in these things. The clutter, the pretty paraphernalia of domestic life which are the aspects of marriage many married men dislike gave him intense pleasure. He never got enough of them.

He crossed the black and white checkerboard floor of the foyer and someone got up from a chair and came over to him. It was Clifford Sanders.

Clifford said, 'I've been trying to get hold of you all the afternoon. They kept saying you were busy.'

Burden's initial reaction was to turn on Sergeant Camb who stood behind the reception counter, but as he took a step towards him he remembered he had said nothing to the sergeant, or indeed to anyone, about not admitting Clifford to the police station. It hadn't occurred to him that Clifford would actually come here. Had he the right, come to that, to exclude him? He didn't know. He didn't know if he could legally keep innocent, law-abiding members of the public out. Anger against Clifford must be kept under control.

He said stiffly, 'I was busy. I'm busy now. You must excuse me, I'm in a hurry.'

The otherwise blank, childlike, pasty face seemed to have only one expression – puzzlement. A deep bewilderment left the eyes unclouded, puckered the skin of Clifford's forehead into a concentrated frown. 'But I've got a lot to say. I've only just started; I have to talk to you.'

Not for the first time, Burden thought that if he had seen this man in the street and not known who he was, he would

627

have thought him retarded. These were deep waters, muddied and with strange things in their depths – but was it possible to be retarded not in the body or the brain but somewhere else? In the soul, the psyche? A horribly uncomfortable feeling took hold of Burden and he seemed to shrink away from the touch of his own clothes on his skin. He could no longer look into those infant's eyes, watch the working of thick, uncontrolled lips.

'I've told you, we've nothing more to say to one another.' God, he sounded like someone ending a love affair! 'You've helped us with our enquiries, thank you very much. I assure you we shan't want you again.'

With that he escaped. He would have liked to run, but dignity forbade it, that and self-respect. He was aware as he walked with deliberately measured tread towards the swing doors that Camb was watching him curiously, that Marian Bayliss who had just come in had paused to stare and that Clifford still stood in the centre of the floor, his lips moving silently and his hands held up in front of him.

Burden opened the door and, once outside, ran to his car. The red Metro he had seen come in but whose colour the yellow lamps had altered was parked beside it. Impossible to draw any conclusion but that Clifford had done this purposely.

And as Burden switched on the ignition, he saw Clifford come out. He ran up, calling 'Mike, Mike . . . !'

Burden didn't have to back. He drove straight out through the gates.

16

'He's made a transference,' Serge Olson said. 'It's a very clearly defined example of transference.'

'I don't know what that means,' Burden said.

They were in Wexford's office, the three of them. The psychotherapist's face amid surrounding and intervening bushes of hair was like that of an extremely intelligent vole peering out from a frondy sanctuary. And the bright beady eyes had their fierce animal look. Burden had expected to go to him, but Olson had said he would come to the police station as he had no clients on a Thursday morning. Throughout the previous day Clifford Sanders had pursued his course of trying to speak to Burden. None of his phone calls had been put through but Burden was told, to his considerable dismay, that fifteen had been made. And Clifford had returned to the police station in time to repeat his intercepting tactic as Burden left for home.

But it was his presence on the forecourt this morning – the red Metro parked just inside the gates and Clifford patiently seated at the wheel – which had really rattled Burden. He had had enough. No sooner was he inside than he was on the phone to Olson, and Olson had been there within fifteen minutes.

'I'll try to explain, Mike,' he said. 'Transference is the term employed by psychoanalysts to describe an emotional attitude the subject develops towards his or her analyst. It can be positive or negative, it can be love or hate. I've often experienced it with clients – though not really with Clifford.' Burden's puzzled face seemed to give him pause and he

629

looked at Wexford. 'I think you know what I mean, don't you, Reg?'

Wexford nodded. 'It's not a difficult concept. It seems natural when you think about it.'

'You mean he's got to like me? He's kind of come to depend on me?'

'Absolutely, Mike.'

Burden said almost wildly, 'But what did I do? What in God's name did I do to set something like this up? I only put him through a routine interrogation; I only questioned him the way I must have questioned thousands of suspects. No one ever did this before, they were only too glad to get shut of me and this place.'

Wexford was at the window. The red Metro was still down there, its bonnet a few inches from the trunk of the tree decorated with the lights. Clifford sat in the driving seat, not reading, not looking out of the window, just sitting with bent head.

'People are different,' Olson was saying. 'People are individuals, Mike. You can't say that because no one ever made the transference before, no one ever would. Were you particularly gentle with him? Paternal? I don't mean paternalistic. Sensitive in your approach?' The expression in those gleaming dark eyes rather indicated Olson's doubts of such a possibility.

'I don't think so. I don't know. I just listened, I let him talk; I thought I'd be more likely to get somewhere that way.'

'Ah.' Olson gave a reflective smile. 'Listening, letting the client talk – you did what the Freudians do. Maybe he prefers a Freudian therapist.'

Suddenly it began to rain. In straight glistening rods the rain bore down on the tarmac, the roofs of the parked cars, the roof of the Metro, hard enough to create immediate puddles. Wexford turned from the streaming glass with a quick, repudiating shake of the head.

'What's to be done then?' he asked.

'It's a good rule, Reg, not to yield to the subject's wishes. Part of his problem, you see, is the way in which he wants to fashion his world. But the world he makes isn't conducive to his happiness, to his adjustment. It doesn't tally with reality; it just looks easier to him. Do you understand that, Mike? If you see Clifford now, you'll be allowing him to make his world in the shape he wants and people it with the people he wants. For instance, because he's lost his own father he wants to put you in his world as his father. I'd say sure, do that, if it would be best for him, but I don't think it would be. It would deepen the transference and create even greater divergencies from reality.'

'Are you suggesting I simply have someone go out there and send him home?' asked Wexford. 'I don't know why but it seems . . . irresponsible.'

Olson got up. Taking no risks with the weather, he had arrived wrapped in yellow oilskins and these be fastened and zipped round himself once more, his sharp nose sticking out from under the canary-coloured hood.

'He's a very badly disturbed human being, Reg,' he said. 'You're right there. But you and Mike, you have to understand I'm a professional. You, Mike, were kind enough to call me "doctor" when we first met and though I'm not that, I have to have professional ethics. I can't go up to Clifford and tell him to come back to me. I can't go and tell him he's got his usual appointments at five today and mind not to be late. All I can do is go and get in that car beside him, sit there as his friend and try to persuade him to confront what he sees as his relationship with you and maybe get it into a more . . . reasonable perspective.'

They both watched from the window. The increasing torrent of rain made it difficult to see. Olson's figure looked like a bright yellow bird hopping and flapping its way to a dry nest. The Metro's door shut on him and once more the rain enclosed the car in walls of water like reeded glass.

'I suppose it's sound,' Wexford said, 'that stuff about not letting him create his own world, about not giving away to him. I must confess to feeling a bit apprehensive.'

'Of what?' Burden asked almost rudely.

A car driven recklessly, a fatal accident that was only partly accident, a handful of pills washed down with brandy, a rope slung over the beam of an outhouse . . . Wexford put none of this into words. He saw the Metro begin to back, sliding slowly through sheets of water and sending up jets

631

of spray. It turned and headed for the gates, Olson still inside.

'That's fixed him for a bit,' and Burden. 'Thank God for it! Now perhaps we can get on with some work.'

He shut the door rather too hard behind him. Wexford turned his back on the window and the rain and thought about the dreams he kept having of wheels spinning in space, of circles with squares inside them. Had they anything to do with the fact that the evening before and the evening before that he had been reading the manuscript of Dita Jago's concentration camp experiences? It was with him in the office today, Donaldson having come for him that morning in the car.

'Is it any good?' Dora had asked.

'I don't think I'd answer that question if anyone else had asked it. But "as an offering to conjugal unreserve", frankly, not much. As a writer, she makes a fine knitter.'

'Reg, that's unkind.'

'Not when it isn't heard outside these four flimsy walls. Who am I to judge, anyway? What do I know? I'm a policeman, not a publisher's reader. It's not for its style or atmosphere that I'm reading the thing.'

In her discreet way she hadn't asked why he was reading it, any more than she had asked why he always had his nose in *Kim* magazine. She knew better than that. He turned to where he had placed a marker between the sheets. It was at a point about half-way through and the young Dita Kowiak had begun work in the Auschwitz Krankenbau – the hospital – as an orderly. Wexford should have been moved by the description of emaciated patients, the administering of intracardiac injections of toxic substances, the hurling of naked corpses into trucks. Dita had survived because for a time at any rate the hospital workers were regularly fed, even if the diet of turnip soup and mouldy bread was inadequate. She told of Russian prisoners-of-war poisoned with Cyclon-B gas, the burning of five hundred corpses in the space of one hour. But instead of being affected, he felt only that he had heard all this before. She had no gift for delineating place or bringing a character to life. Her prose was wooden and repetitious and there was no impression of her own sufferings permeating the text. She might never have been there; she might have copied all this piecemeal from the concentration camp autobiographies which, after all, were legion. And perhaps she had . . .

Several times he had come to points in the narrative where pages were missing, but up till now those pages had always turned up later on. The lack of numbering made things difficult. Here, however, the narrative stopped abruptly in mid-sentence, in the middle of an anecdote about a doctor at the hospital called Dehring. Wexford carefully scrutinized all the remaining pages of the manuscript, but could find no further mention of Dehring's name. There was at least one page missing, perhaps two.

But would Dita Jago have let him take the manuscript if it contained – or conspiciously did not contain – something incriminating? It would have been easy to refuse. 'I couldn't bear to have anyone read it,' would have done the trick. Or when he asked where the manuscript was, she need only have said that she had sent it away to be typed or had even, as she threatened, burned it.

Whatever efforts Serge Olson had made, they failed to have any effect on Clifford Sanders. He made five phone calls to Kingsmarkham police station in the course of the afternoon, though none of these was actually put through to Burden. Next morning there was a letter for him, sent to his home. At the police station someone else might very likely have opened any missive that came, but here Burden naturally opened his own post. This brown envelope he had at first supposed to contain the bill for fitting a new carpet in the dining room.

Clifford addressed him as Mike. This was probably Olson's doing, Burden thought. The letter began 'Dear Mike'. The writing was a child's – or a teacher's – a round, neat, admirably legible hand, upright but with the slightest tendency to a backward slope. 'Dear Mike, I have a lot I want to say to you and I think you would be interested to hear it. I know you want me to think of you as my friend, and that is how I do think of you. In fact, I don't find it easy to confide in people, but you are an exception to this rule. We really get on well together, as I am sure you will agree.'

Here Burden laid down the letter for a moment and sighed. 'I do understand that other people, those in authority over you I mean, are doing everything in their power to stop our meeting, and I expect you feel threatened with the loss of your job. Therefore I suggest we arrange to met outside your working hours. Even employers like the police surely cannot object to their officers having their own personal friends. I will phone you tomorrow . . .' Burden noticed that he mentioned no precise hour and recalled what Olson had said about Clifford's attitude towards time. 'Please tell them you expect a call from me so that if you are out they can take a message. My idea is to call on you at your house this evening perhaps or during the weekend. With best wishes. Yours ever, Cliff.'

Burden's little boy had climbed on to his lap and he stroked his hair, held him close for a moment. Suppose his Mark should grow up into such a one? How could you tell? Clifford had looked like this once, been as endearing, inspired perhaps the same breath-catching love. Only I shan't walk out on him when he's five, thought Burden. But when he tried to summon up pity for Clifford, he failed and felt only exasperation.

'I'm taking no calls from this man,' he said when he got to the police station, 'and I'd like him to be told that no message he leaves will reach me. Right?'

After that he concentrated on the quest of the moment, finding the whereabouts of Charles Sanders. If Sanders had never paid maintenance to the wife he had deserted and she, presumably, had been too proud to ask for it, he could not be traced through the courts or social services. It wasn't an uncommon combination of names. Telephone directories and electrol registers yielded a number for Archbold, Davidson, Marian Bayliss and Diana Pettit to call on, and Archbold had run to earth a likely-sounding Charles Sanders in Manchester. Burden had plans to go up there and see him, though he wanted to get the man on the phone first, and as yet he hadn't even managed to hear the sound of his voice. Engaged signals alternated with ringing tones as if Sanders unplugged his phone between answering calls. However, he never answered Burden's.

Later in the morning when he saw the red Metro come on to the forecourt, Burden had to suppress a feeling that was not too far from panic. He was being hounded, persecuted. The anxious fears which had been building up inside him had the effect which such an accumulation sometimes does, that of heightening the powers of his imagination. He found himself envisaging a future in which Clifford Sanders dogged his footsteps, in which every time he lifted a phone receiver he heard Clifford's voice at the other end of the line, in which – worst of all – when he looked in a mirror he saw Clifford's face over his shoulder. You are a hardened, tough police officer, he told himself fiercely. Why do you let this boy shake you? Why are you rattled by it? You can keep him off, others will keep him off. Calm yourself. Ignorant as he acknowledged himself to be of the workings of the psyche, he nevertheless recognized the evidences of paranoia in Clifford's letter and now he saw them in himself. And then he recalled the precise moment when he had first recognized Clifford's madness.

A memory came to him of something he had been told by his historian wife: how going to look at the mad people in Bedlam was as popular a pastime in the late eighteenth century as safari park visiting was today. How could they? His instinct was to put himself as far from the mad as he could, to pretend they didn't exist, to build walls between them and him. Yet Clifford wasn't mad in a padded cell, straitjacket way; he was only disturbed, deprived, lonely, his thought processes somehow askew. Burden picked up the phone, arranged for Sergeant Martin to go out there and tell Clifford to leave, to tell him he was trespassing or something.

He wondered if Wexford had seen him and felt a sudden need to talk to Wexford about it, to be franker on the subject of his feelings in respect of Clifford than he had been up to now. But as he was going down, had got so far as entering the lift, he remembered that Wexford – for some mysterious reason of his own – had gone to the Barringdean Shopping Centre. Burden thought he would like a drink or even a Valium, though he hated the things and feared them. Instead he sat at his desk and briefly put his head in his hands.

The sandwich, according to the claims of Grub 'n' Grains, was 'American style', pastrami and cream cheese on rye. If he hadn't been told that it was pastrami, which he had never tasted before, Wexford would have sworn he was eating corned beef of the well-known Fray Bentos type. He had been doing a bit of crime reconstruction, mostly in his head, but the true scene of the crime seemed the right place in which to do it.

The fountain played in the left-hand concourse, its jets of spray concealing the ascending and descending escalators and the entrance to British Home Stores. But opposite him Wexford could see the several clothes shops and between them and Boots the Chemist the wools and crafts shop called Knits 'n' Kits. Next door to the café was December with its bakery adjacent, then a travel agent, then W. H. Smith. Wexford drank his tropical fruit cocktail, paid for his lunch and made his way up to Demeter.

The health foods store kept its herbal remedies on shelves immediately to the left of the window and Wexford soon found the calendula capsules. It was these which Helen Brook had been looking for when she saw Gwen Robson outside in the aisle between the shops in conversation with a very well-dressed girl. And here she had been taken with the first of those early labour pains which prevented her from going up to Mrs Robson and speaking to her. Wexford bent down, took a jar of capsules from the shelf and dropped it into his wire basket. Then he straightened up and looked out of the window. Boots the Chemist could be seen and, this side of it, the wools and crafts shop, with the Mandala – circles of chrysanthemums and cherry-fruited solanum today – cutting off sight of the entrances to Tesco. Gwen Robson had shopped in Boots, bought her toothpaste and talcum powder, paused to look at the Mandala flowers perhaps, and there encountered the girl Helen Brook had seen her speaking to. It must have been Lesley Arbel, Wexford thought, who – perhaps having time to spare before the departure of the London train – had come in here specifically to meet her aunt. He imagined a conversation, surprise expressed by Mrs Robson, a brief explanation from Lesley about the word-processing course, a promise perhaps that she would see her aunt on the following night. Or had it all been more sinister?

636

It must have been on this side of the Mandala that they had stood, for Helen Brook to have seen them. And somehow Wexford knew that if the girl were Lesley she would not have been looking at flowers but, even while talking to her aunt, would have had her eyes fixed on those shop windows to the left of her with their window displays of clothes and shoes. He looked at them himself, at the space Dora's sweater had occupied which was now filled by an extraordinary red and black frilled corselette; on to the next window which was a medley of red and black and green and white shoes and boots, to the window of Knits 'n' Kits. Here a loom with a half-completed piece of work on it – a wall-hanging or rug – predominated. He thought inescapably of Dita Jago. Did she use this shop? Making his way to the door with the basket over his arm, his thoughts miles away from herbal remedies and packets of nuts, he was jolted to attention by an indignant voice.

'Excuse me, but you haven't paid for your tablets!'

Wexford grinned. That would be a fine thing, a turn-up for the book, a detective chief inspector getting done for shoplifting. As bad as, or worse than, his daughter going to prison. But he didn't want to think about that, he wouldn't think of it. Under the resentful gaze of the shop assistant, he replaced the calendula capsules on the shelf, leaving the wire basket on the floor.

It had been there in his mind, lying under a level of consciousness, for days now . . . well weeks. Gwen Robson had been dead three weeks. It drew him to that window. Of course he had already dimly glimpsed it, half-noticing it as he came into Demeter. The pairs of knitting needles were hung in a sort of zig-zag pattern all down the right-hand side of the window, hanks of wool on the left and the loom with its half-completed achievement in between. But they weren't, strictly speaking, all pairs. Wexford went in. Better not attack the window display, he thought, not yet.

Men didn't come in here much. There were two women at the counter, one leafing through a book of patterns. Wexford found a metal stand, the kind of thing that used to be called a 'tree', with packets of needles hung all over it. He unhooked the one he wanted. Lesley Arbel might have come in here before she met her aunt. Why not? She would have known

637

the shop was here and known what she wanted. Dita Jago too, seeking only a replacement perhaps and later finding another use . . .

With a sharp tug he pulled the circular knitting needle out of its plastic pack and held it up as one might hold a divining rod, each hand clasping the thick metal pins at each end, the long wire hanging slack between and then pulled taut. Wire and pins were coated in a pale grey plastic substance. His eye caught sight of the obvious victim to experiment on – a torso in styrofoam wearing a lilac lacy jumper, with an extravagantly elongated neck on which the head was poised at an unnatural angle. Approaching it with the garrote at the ready, he was aware of a hush in the shop, then of the three pairs of eyes fixed on him and following his moves.

Hastily, he replaced the circular needle in its packet. He had found his weapon.

17

Clifford Sanders came to Burden's house at nine in the evening. It was no surprise to Burden; he had been expecting this from the moment he got home and thinking of various ways to handle it so as to avoid a confrontation. He considered getting his wife to answer the door or asking his elder son John, who had come to eat supper with them, to answer it; he thought of taking the whole family, including little Mark, out to eat. In a wild moment he even had an idea of going away for the night, booking a room in an hotel. But when the time came, he answered the door himself.

It was the first time for days that he had actually faced Clifford and spoken to him. Clifford wore a raincoat, navy blue, very like a policeman's. His face was pale, but that might have been due to the light from over head in the porch. Behind him hung a thin greenish fog. He put out his hand.

Burden didn't take it but said, 'I'm sorry you've come all this way for nothing, but I have explained I've no more questions to ask you at present.'

'Please let me talk to you.'

The foot in the door – Clifford had taken a step forward, but Burden planted himself firmly between door and architrave. 'I have to insist you understand you can give us no more help with our enquiries. It's over. Thank you for your help, but there's nothing more you can do.' Every parent knows the expression on a child's face just before it cries: the swelling of tissues, the seeming collapse of muscles, the trembling. Burden couldn't bear it, but he couldn't cope with it either. 'I'll say good night, then,' he said absurdly. 'Good night.' And stepping back, he closed the door hard.

Retreating across the hall, standing and listening, he waited for Clifford to ring the bell. He was bound to do that – or try the knocker. Nothing happened. Burden was sweating; he felt a trickle of sweat run down his forehead and one side of his nose. Mark was in bed, Jenny and John still in the dining room at the back of the house. Burden went into the living room which was in darkness, made his way stealthily to the window and looked out. The red Metro was parked at the kerb and Clifford was sitting in the driving-seat in that accustomed pose of his, the way he perhaps passed several hours of each day. Burden was still standing there watching when the phone rang. He answered it in the dark, still looking out of the window.

It was Dorothy Sanders.

Burden was obliged to recognize the voice, for she did not identify herself or ask if she were speaking to Inspector Burden. 'Are you going to arrest my son?'

In other circumstances Burden would have made some discreet and non-committal reply. Now he was beyond that. 'No, Mrs Sanders, I'm not. There's no question of that.' A mean, despicable kind of hope took hold of him that he could get this woman on his side, enlist her aid even. But he only said, 'I don't want to see him, I've no more enquiries to make of him.'

'Then why do you keep getting him down there? Why don't you leave him alone? He's never here, I never see him. His place is at home with me.'

'I quite agree,' said Burden. 'I couldn't agree more.' As he spoke the car door opened, Clifford got out and once more came up the path towards the house. The bell ringing made a searing sound in Burden's ears, almost pain. He found himself gripping the phone receiver in a wet palm as the doorbell rang again. 'He'll be back home with you in ten minutes,' he said, screwing up his nerve, feeling anger bring a fresh flood of sweat.

'I can complain to the proper authorities, you know. I can complain to the Chief Constable – and I will.' Her tone changed and she said in a slow deliberate way, pausing between the words, 'He didn't do anything to that woman. He didn't know her and he hasn't anything to tell you.'

'Then you'd better lock him up, Mrs Sanders,' Burden said

indiscreetly. He put the receiver back, heard John go to the door, a murmured exchange and then John, who had been primed, said firmly, 'Good night.'

In the dark there, Burden thought wildly of an injunction to restrain Clifford from persecuting him, of seeking out a judge in chambers, of arresting and imprisoning Clifford when he broke the order. He heard the Metro door close and listened, holding his breath, for the engine to start up. The silence seemed to endure a long time and the eventual sound of the motor turning and firing was a glorious relief. Burden didn't watch the departure of the Metro but when next he looked out of the window it was gone, the street empty, the fog thick and still and opaque as muddy water.

Returning the manuscript, he asked about the missing pages, but there were no guilty reactions and no evasions.

'I realized as soon as you'd gone,' Dita Jago said. 'I took two pages out to check something on them at the public library.' She looked at him steadily – too steadily? 'You remember I told you I was at the library on the day Mrs Robson was killed? I was checking up something about a man called Dehring.' She didn't ask if he had enjoyed reading the manuscript or what his impression was, commenting only, 'You read that far!'

While she was out of the room fetching the pages, he examined quickly the circular needle from which the great wall hanging depended. The pins at each end of the wire were of a much finer gauge than the one he had handled in the Barringdean Centre and would not have stood up to excessive pressure. But that meant nothing. Mrs Jago would have other circular needles, probably in every available size. He glanced at the sheets of paper she showed him, noting corrections made in red ballpoint. She made no comment on his interest, but as he walked down the path and glanced back he saw her watching him from the window, her expression one of benign mystification.

Ralph Robson was cleaning his car, a popular Saturday afternoon pastime at Highlands. Out here he managed without his stick, holding on to the bodywork of the car for support. Wexford said good afternoon to him and suggested that the task on which he was engaged was not perhaps the wisest activity for someone in his condition.

'Who's going to do it if I don't?' Robson said belligerently. 'Who's going to give me a helping hand? Oh, it's one thing when anything like that first happens. They're all coming round. Can I do this and can I do that? That soon cools off. Even Lesley. You wouldn't credit it, would you, but I haven't seen Lesley for a whole blessed week. She hasn't so much as phoned.'

Nor will she, Wexford thought. You've seen the last of her. She either got what she wanted or knows there's nothing in it for her.

'There's one bright spot though.' Robson winced as he straightened up from rinsing out his cloth in the bucket of water. 'I'm getting my hip done. Doctor's transferring me to another what they call health area the week after next. Sunderland. I'll be getting my replacement up in Sunderland.'

The Saab passed Wexford as he began the climb up the hill, passed him and drew into the kerb ahead. His thoughts had shifted, as they mostly did these days, from the Robson case to Sheila. She was coming to stay the night; it was years since they had seen so much of her as they had in these past few weeks, and inevitably he speculated as to why this was. Because she understood and sympathized with his anxieties for her safety? Or because she was sorry for her parents having to live in this poky, uncomfortable little house? A bit of both, maybe. She got out of the passenger side of the Saab and his heart leapt with the usual old relief.

'Pop, this is Ned.'

The man in the driving-seat was young, dark, distinguished-looking. Wexford knew at once that he had seen him somewhere before. They shook hands over the seats and Wexford got into the back of the car.

'Ned's not staying, he's on his way to Brighton. He's just going to drop me off.'

'That sounds like an early warning in case we start evincing our well-known lack of hospitality.'

Ned laughed, and there was a bit of an edge to the sound. Because Wexford had said 'early warning' which had another, quite separate, significance?

'Oh, Pop,' said Sheila, 'I didn't mean that.'

642

'At least I hope he'll stay for a cup of tea,' Dora said when they reached the house.

'Of course I will. I'd like to.'

They had rather taken it for granted that with both daughters married all this sort of thing would be over. There would be no more suitors brought home, the sight of whom aroused dismay or resignation or hope. Sylvia indeed had married so young that before Neil there had been no more than a couple of casual boyfriends. But Sheila's men had come in a constantly changing series until at last the chosen one, Andrew Thorverton, had surely put an end to this parade. Or so it had seemed to those naïve parents who, because of their age, inevitably regarded marriage – at any rate in their own family – as an institution of permanence. Was this Ned a prospective second husband? Sheila seemed to treat him in a rather cavalier fashion.

He was gone on his way to Brighton before Wexford found out his surname. She could go back on the train; he wasn't to trouble himself about her – that was Sheila's airy parting shot as she and her father stood in the flowerbed sized front garden watching him go.

'Nice car,' Wexford said tactfully.

'Well, I suppose. It's always having to have things done to it. I mean, that last weekend you were in the old house and I came down, it was in being seen to. I offered to lend him mine as a matter of fact, but considering what happened it was just as well he hired a car instead.'

They went back into the house. With the coming of early dusk the fog was returning. Wexford closed the front door on the dank chill outside. 'I've seen him somewhere, him or his picture.'

'Of course you have, Pop. His photograph was all over the papers when he was prosecuting those Arab terrorists.'

'Do you mean to say he's Edmund Hope? You're "Ned" is Edmund Hope the barrister?'

'Of course he is. I thought you knew.'

'I don't quite know how you could have thought we knew,' said Dora, 'considering you never introduced him. "This is Ned" doesn't convey much information.'

Sheila shrugged her shoulders. Her hair was tied back in a ponytail with a length of red ribbon. 'He's not "my" Ned.

We're not together any more – just friends, as they say. We actually lived together for four whole days.' Her laugh had a hint of bitterness in it. 'It's all very well these brave statements: "I don't agree with what you say, but I'd die for your right to say it". That sort of thing doesn't amount to much when it comes to the crunch. He's like the rest of you – well, not Dad – who don't want to know me if I go to jail.'

'That's not fair, Sheila. That's very unkind and unjust. I'll never not want to know you.'

'I'm sorry, Mother – not you either, then. But Ned didn't even want other people to know he knew me. And I went along with it – can you imagine?' She came up to Wexford, who had been silent and staring. 'Pop . . . ?' Her arms were on his shoulders, her face lifted up to his. She had always been uninhibited, demonstrative, a 'touching' person. 'Is this nasty house haunted? Have you seen a ghost?'

'You actually offered to lend Edmund Hope your car for the weekend while he was in the middle of prosecuting those terrorists?'

'Don't be cross, Pop. Why not?' She made a face at him, lips protruding, nose wrinkled up.

'I'm not cross. Tell me the circumstances. Tell me exactly when and how you offered to lend him the Porsche.'

Extreme surprise made her step back and hold out actressy hands in a wide sweep. 'Goodness, I'm glad I'm not one of your criminals! Well, he'd stayed the night and when he tried to start his car in the morning it wouldn't start, so I drove him to court – the Old Bailey it was. And before I dropped him I said he could borrow my car if he wanted.'

'Could anyone have heard you say it?'

'Oh, yes, I expect so. He was standing on the pavement and I called it out after him; it was a sort of afterthought. I said something like, "You can have this car for the weekend if you like", because I knew he was supposed to be staying with some friends in Wales, and he called back thanks and he'd take me up on that. Only after that I remembered I'd said I'd come down here, and I was quite glad when he rang up in the evening and said his own car would be ready in the morning.' Realization came to her quite suddenly and drained the colour from her face. The white stood out round

644

the blue irises of her eyes. 'Oh, Pop, why did I never think of that? Oh God, how awful!'

'The bomb was meant for him,' Wexford said.

'And the letter bomb too? That was during our – er, four-day honeymoon.'

'I think we'd better tell someone, don't you?' He picked up the phone, feeling an unlooked-for, absurd happiness.

The night had passed without disturbance or dreams. Burden lay awake for a long time thinking about Charles Sanders One – the Manchester one, who had eventually answered his phone and turned out to be twenty-seven years old – and Charles Sanders Two, from Portsmouth, with children of Clifford's age, a young wife and an Australian accent. But his mind was not fraught with anxieties and soon he slept heavily and uninterruptedly. The dense fog which enveloped town and countryside brought its own kind of silence, the muffled sensation less of there being no sound to hear than of deafness. Jenny was up and Mark was up on Sunday morning before he awoke to see the bedroom curtains drawn back and a fluffy whiteness pressing against the window-panes. It was the phone ringing which had awakened him and in spite of his peaceful night, the first possible caller that occurred to him was Clifford.

Jenny must have answered it on the other phone, for the ringing stopped. Burden picked up the receiver at his bedside and to his enormous relief heard Wexford's voice. It was Wexford wanting to tell him the solution to the bomb puzzle; wanting also to come round later in the day with another solution, the answer to the mystery of the weapon Gwen Robson's killer had used. Burden said nothing about Clifford or Clifford's mother's phone call. That could wait till later, till he saw Wexford – or perhaps might never need to be told.

The morning passed with no more phone calls and no more visits. There was usually considerable traffic in Tabard Road, which was a through road, but today it was quiet, the fog keeping people at home. Was it also keeping Clifford at home, or was there another reason for his absence? Burden wondered how much his mother's power and influence over

645

him would enable her, at her level of necessarily far less physical strength, to be his jailer.

The fog did not dissipate as it had on the preceding days, but seemed to thicken as afternoon came on. His sister-in-law Grace and her husband came to lunch, also Jenny's brother. Burden thought how awkward it would have been if the red Metro had arrived and Clifford presented himself once more at the front door, but nothing like that happened. His guests went at about four, when the fog darkened and the yellow gleams of streetlights faintly penetrated it. None of them lived far away and they had all come on foot. Watching the departure from the front window, he saw Amyas encounter Wexford just outside the gate. This was about as far as it was possible to see, and even so the figures of the two men seemed as if swathed in lightly swaying pennants of gauze.

'It was a huge relief,' Wexford said, taking off his coat in the hall. 'Yet when you come to think of it, what does that amount to? Aren't I really saying I'm glad it's someone else's child and not mine that's threatened? There but for the grace of God, in fact – which is only another way of saying, "I'm all right, Jack". '

'Edmund Hope may be all right too. It's likely they've found another target by this time. After all, it's more than three weeks ago.'

'Yes, and more than three weeks since Gwen Robson's death. How's this for a garrote, Mike?' Wexford drew from his pocket the circular needle he had bought at the Barringdean Centre; the pins at each end were a quarter of an inch in diameter, forming tough, strong handles to hold on to. 'You're the plastics expert,' he said. 'Would this be the right sort of stuff?'

'It's the right colour. I should say it's pretty obvious a thing like this was used. Does that necessarily make it a woman who used it?'

They went into Burden's living room, where a fire had been lighted; the blaze from it lit the room with flickering yellow. Burden put up the fireguard in case Mark came in.

'This was a premeditated crime,' Wexford said, 'only in the sense, I believe, that the perpetrator had had an idea of killing for some time and was waiting only for opportunity.

646

But I don't think he or she went into that car park with the weapon at the ready. It's more likely it had just been brought in the shop where I got this one, and that means the prospective user might have bought it or someone else purchased it *for* the prospective user. In other words, it was on a shopping list, so the purchaser could have been a man or a woman.'

'And he or she,' Burden went on, 'came up into the car park looking at it perhaps? I mean, perhaps it came loose from its packaging and the purchaser was curling it up and replacing it?'

'Or the purchaser, who wasn't the prospective user and maybe had never seen such a thing before, was fascinated by such a peculiar thing. It *is* a peculiar-looking thing, Mike. The purchaser might have just been standing there unwinding it and looking at it when Mrs Robson came along.'

A car drew up outside. Its progress sounded slow, as it would necessarily have had to be in the dense fog. Burden jumped up a bit too quickly and went to the window – not Clifford, but Burden's next-door neighbour whom he could see getting out to open his garage drive gates.

'It's not too early to draw the curtains, is it?'

'I didn't know there was any prescribed time for it,' Wexford said, eyeing him speculatively.

'It seems a pity to lose the last of the light.'

The impenetrable greyness outside made nonsense of this remark. It was now impossible to see across the street, in fact to see much beyond the pavement and kerb on this side. Burden pulled the curtains across the window and was switching on a table lamp when the phone rang. He gave a nervous start which he knew Wexford had seen.

'Hallo?'

His mother-in-law's voice and his wife's intermingled as Jenny picked up the bedroom extension. He couldn't control the little gasp of relief. Wexford said with quick intuition, 'Has Clifford Sanders been hounding you?'

Burden nodded. 'I think it's stopped though. He hasn't phoned or been here all day.'

'Been here?'

'Oh, yes. He was here last night, came to the door twice, but I do think it's over now. Anyway,' Burden lied, 'it's not important, it's not a problem. Your Mrs Jago – do you see her as . . . ?'

Instead of answering directly, Wexford said, 'Dita Jago might very well have been one of Gwen Robson's blackmailees. She had the means to kill her. Of everyone in this case, she was the most likely to have been buying a circular knitting needle in the shopping centre that afternoon. On the other hand, she says she was in the public library, the central branch in the High Street, with her grand-daughters. I jib a bit at asking those two little girls to alibi or not alibi the grandmother they're obviously fond of; I won't do it if I can avoid it, but . . .

'Anyway, the papers Lesley Arbel was looking for – and ransacked or spring-cleaned her uncle's house in the process of so doing – weren't sheets from Dita Jago's manuscript. They were photocopies of letters.'

Burden said, 'Do you mean letters Gwen Robson took or borrowed from the homes of her clients? Incriminating letters she then had copied?'

'Not quite, her niece got these letters for her. It was Lesley Arbel who made the copies to show to her aunt. Not because she thought they could be used for any criminal purpose, certainly not that, but to amuse her, I think – to entertain someone who loved gossip and took the same kind of pleasure in sexual irregularities as some of our Sunday newspapers do – gloating over matters that ostensibly they deplore.'

'Are you talking about letters to the agony aunt?'

'Of course. Lesley Arbel had easy access to them and a photocopier in the office where she worked. Some of the letters would appear in *Kim* – my God, Mike, the amount of *Kim* I've grubbed through in the past week – but most wouldn't and some, even in these days of licence, would be considered unfit for publication. And even though there's an unwritten law in the agony aunt's department that staff preserve discretion – lip service to a kind of poor woman's Official Secrets Act – it must have seemed harmless enough, what she was doing. None of it would go beyond the four walls of the house in Hastings Road . . . What is it, Mike? What's wrong?'

Burden had jumped up and stood with head lifted. 'Did you hear a car?'

Drily Wexford said, 'I hear a car every minute of my life when I'm not asleep. How do you escape it in this world?'

The door opened and Mark came in, followed by his mother. But Burden continued to stand transfixed, only holding out an absent hand to the child. Mark wasn't shy; he went up to Wexford, wanting the pencil he held in his hand, then the pad on which notes had been made, finally climbing on to Wexford's knees. Burden went to the window and parted the curtains with both hands. His knuckles had whitened and his shoulders drooped a little.

'Oh, not again?' Jenny said. 'He's not back again?'

'I'm afraid he is.' Burden turned back into the room and faced Wexford. 'Am I overreacting when I say I'm seriously thinking of applying for an injunction?'

Instead of answering directly, Wexford said, 'Let me go.' He lifted the little boy on to the floor, sacrificed pad and pencil to him. 'Don't get it on the carpet, or your Mum'll be after me.'

As he came out into the hall, the bell rang. Wexford let it ring again. Burden had joined him, was standing just behind him. The letter-box lid started flapping as fingers pushed at it and then the other hand pounded on the knocker. The fingers appeared under the opened letter-box lid and there was something about them and the smear marks they left on pale paintwork that made Burden draw in his breath with a rough hiss. Wexford crossed the hall and opened the door.

Clifford took a step back when he saw him. He was looking beyond Wexford's bulk and when he saw Burden he smiled. Wexford eyed him in a kind of stricken silence, for Clifford was covered with blood. His grey shirt and knitted pullover and the zipper-jacket he wore, his grey flannel trousers, his striped tie and grey socks and lace-up shoes – all were thick with blood, matted and plastered with it, and in places the blood was damp still, glistening still. And Clifford, smiling, stepped over the threshold into the hall with no one to impede him until the little boy came out of the living room, and Burden, sweeping him up in his arms, shouted, 'Don't let him see. For God's sake, don't let him see!'

18

The driving-seat of his mother's car which had always been a curious place of refuge for Clifford, a sanctuary and scene of unimaginable cogitations, was bloodied from his clothes. Easy to make an analogy here with wombs, but Wexford shied away from that one. Though it was dark and foggy, he had the seat of the car and the blood-encrusted steering wheel covered up before it was towed away. Now they sat in the first of a convoy of police vehicles, Clifford between him and Burden, crawling through the fog. Donaldson's headlights made two green bars of radiance that petered out into the wool-like greyness after a few feet. Behind them another driver clung to Donaldson's rear lights and a third followed, all moving at about fifteen miles an hour.

Clifford had Burden to himself now, a captive therapist, and his face wore an expression that was at the same time serene and insane. At appalling cost he had got what he wanted. He talked. He spoke uninterruptedly, sometimes lifting up his bloody hands which had smeared Burden's door with stains, the bitten nails blackened with blood, turning them over and looking at them with wondering pleasure. Already he had told Burden what he had done and – insofar as his conscious mind understood this – why he had done it. But he repeated himself as if he enjoyed the sound of his own monotonous, now measured and almost complacent voice.

'She sent me up into the attic, Mike. She thought she could shut me in like she did when I was little. I was to go up there and fetch her down a lamp. The one in the dining room had got broken, there was a fault in the connection, and she said

650

to fetch her one of the lamps that had belonged to my grandparents. But I'm cunning, Mike, I'm cleverer than she is basically, I've got a better brain. I knew she would rather sit in the dark than use anything from up there. She wouldn't use a lamp my father's mother had used.'

Burden was returning his gaze with what looked like blankness unless you knew Burden as Wexford did and then you understood it was controlled desperation.

'The truth was she wanted to keep me from seeing you. When she told me she'd phoned you to complain about our seeing each other – when she told me that, I saw red. But I didn't show my feelings, I kept everything suppressed, I didn't even answer her. I went upstairs like an obedient little boy. Of course I couldn't be sure what she was up to then; I wondered what she was at. I knew she was following me up, though, and I said to myself, why is she following me when she's asked me to fetch her something? If she's going to come up too, why couldn't she have fetched it herself?'

Forcing the words out in a voice that sounded unlike his own, Burden said, 'So what . . . what did you do, Clifford?' He had already cautioned him. It had been a bizarre ritual taking place in the hall of Burden's own house, Clifford pleasurably pointing out individual blood-stains on his jacket, his shirt, his trousers, beginning on a confession whose utterance held a childlike innocence, while Burden mouthed in that same strangled tone the words of the caution: 'You are not obliged to say anything in answer to the charge but anything you do say . . .'

Now Clifford continued in the same blithe, confiding way, 'It wasn't the attic where Mr Carroll had to break the door down. We'd never had that door mended. The photographs were in there. It was the one with the bedroom furniture.' He brought his face closer to Burden's – said in an intimate way, as to one familiar with the secrets of all hearts, 'You know what I mean.'

Donaldson braked hard as they came suddenly up against the headlights of a huge truck. It was carrying earth-moving equipment, cranes and scoops that loomed dinosaur-like out of the rolling mist. Slowly the convoy edged past it, they were beyond Sundays now, in the narrow lane that led nowhere but to the Sanders' house and the farmer's bungalow. Fog filled the channel between high hedges, hung overhead like dark fallen cloud. They weren't far from the entrance now. Donaldson crept along, stopped the car once or twice – like a dog sniffing, scenting its way to the familiar ground. And it seemed that down here in the least likely place, a low place still in the river valley, the fog had lifted a little, for a high wall of hedge was visible and a tree like a great figure with arms upraised.

Clifford hadn't once looked out of the window; Burden's face seemed the only view he required. He said conversationally, 'All those mattresses were in there, and blankets and things. I expect you remember that time I showed you. And there was a lamp there too, like she said there was. She's clever, she knows about getting her details right. But there was something she forgot. It was the wrong sort of plug, the old-fashioned sort with no earth, an old ten-amp plug with no earth. It was so absurd I could have laughed out loud, only I didn't feel like laughing then, Mike . . .'

The gap in the hedge was found and Donaldson turned in carefully. Tyres crunched on the gravel. The leafy wall of the house, a great square of dark, still, hanging foliage, reared before them. Clifford turned his head at last, gave his home an indifferent look.

'She came up behind me. She was quiet enough, but I was prepared for her. Strange, isn't it, Mike? She's a mystery, she's hidden behind a mask, and she's slow and gliding like all mysterious people. But I know her and I knew what she was going to do; it was so obvious. Her hand went down to the door handle to pull out the key and I was standing there with that old lamp in my hands –'

'Come on, Clifford,' Burden said, 'we're here.'

The air felt wet; it was just as if a cold, wet hand wiped their faces as Wexford walked up to the front door. Dr Crocker was getting our of the car behind with Prentiss, the Scene-of-Crimes man, and there was a new photographer he didn't recognize. Clifford wouldn't separate himself from Burden but stayed close to him, nearly but not quite touching him. If he had actually touched him, Burden thought he might have cried out in horror, though he would have exerted all the control he was capable of to avoid this. It was bad enough knowing some of the blood adhered to his own clothes after that nightmare car journey. He knew he would have to burn everything it had touched.

Wexford asked Clifford for the front-door key and Clifford's answer was to pull out his pockets, the pockets of his jacket and trousers. They were all quite empty. He had left his ignition key in the Metro. As to the others . . .

'I must have dropped them somewhere. I've lost them. They must be somewhere in the garden here.'

Under the wet grass, among the blackened weeds beaded with waterdrops, or on the road in the gutter outside Burden's house. Wexford made the decision quickly.

'We'll force the door. Not this one, it's too heavy. A door at the back.'

It was a slow, grim procession that made its way round the side of the house to the back regions where the rear wall and shed were just visible in the light of Archbold's and Davidson's torches, but nothing beyond. The beam of light played on a back door that looked solid enough, but was less weighty than the massive studded oak barrier whose key Clifford had lost. Davidson was the biggest of them after Wexford and he was also the youngest, but it was Burden who pushed forward and put his shoulder to the door. He had energy which must be released, some act of violence he needed to perform.

Two hard runs at it and the door went down. The crash it made set Clifford laughing; he laughed merrily as they stepped over the shattered boards, the broken glass. Olson would have said, Wexford thought, that it was more than a citadel of bricks and mortar they had broken into and laid open. The flooding of the place with light brought a kind of relief, not that a really bright illumination was possible for Mrs Sanders had been mean with the electricity. It was colder here even than outside. A little of the fog seemed to have got in as Burden recalled the woman had once warned him it would, waiting ghost-like on the threshold to slip in. The damp chill seemed to penetrate clothes and prick skin with icicles.

'Stop that laughing,' he said roughly.

His voice wiped Clifford's face clean of all amusement. It was at once grave and rueful. 'Sorry, Mike . . .'

They went upstairs, Wexford leading the way. Through

some lunatic quirk of meanness or indifference, it was impossible to turn upstairs lights on from downstairs, so that one walked out of light into a yawning darkness before a hand could reach out for a switch. The comparatively elegant staircase gave way to the steep attic flight. Wexford could see nothing at the top, only deep blackness. He put out his hand for Archbold's torch and the thin beam of light showed him a half-open door at the head of the stairs.

The light switch wasn't even on the staircase wall but up in the passage. He deliberately averted his eyes from the open door and the room until the light was on. Then he entered the room with Burden and Clifford at his heels, the others close behind. Wexford put the attic light on and then he looked.

Dorothy Sanders lay half on her back, half-sideways on one of the mattresses. A small, thin woman, composed of wire only in metaphor and fancy, she had had as much blood in her as anyone else and most of it seemed to have spilled from that fragile frame. Face and head were a mass of blood and tissue, cerebral matter and even bone chips. Her hair was lost in it, drowned in it. She lay in her own blood, dark as wine and clotted to a paste, on a mattress dyed crimson-black.

Beside the body, not flung down but set up precisely on a small round-topped beside table, was a lamp in the art nouveau style, a sculptured lily growing from its heavy metal base, its shade composed of frayed and split pleated silk. It was a forensic scientist's ideal, this lamp, from the clots of blood and bloody hair which encrusted its base to the stain which transformed its now bent silk shade from green to an almost total dark brown.

Of them all only Clifford was unused to sights such as this, but he alone among them was smiling.

It was very late. They had done everything – what Sergeant Martin insisted on calling 'the formalities'. But the idea of going to their respective homes had scarcely entered Wexford's head, still less Burden's. Burden's face had that look of a man who has seen indelible horrors. They are stamped there, those sights, but showing themselves in the staring eyes and taut skin as the skull inside the flesh reveals itself, a symbol of what has been seen and a foreshadowing of a future.

Burden couldn't rest. He stood in Wexford's office. He just stood, keeping his eyes averted from Wexford's, then bending his head and pressing his fingers to his temples.

'You had better sit down, Mike.'

'You'll be saying it wasn't my fault in a minute.'

'I'm not a psychiatrist or a philosopher. How would I know?'

Burden moved. He held his hands behind his back, came over to a chair and stood in front of it. 'If I had left him alone . . .' He didn't finish the sentence.

'Strictly speaking, it was he who wouldn't leave you alone. You had to question him in the first place; you couldn't be expected to foresee the turn things would take.'

'Well, if I hadn't . . . rejected him then, when he wanted to talk to me. It's ironical, isn't it? First he didn't want me and then I didn't want him. Reg, could I have averted this by letting him come and talk to me?'

'I wish you'd sit down. I don't know what it is you want, Mike. Do you want the hard truth or something to comfort you?'

'Of course I want the truth.'

'Then the truth probably is – and I realize it's hard to take – that when you in your own words rejected Clifford, he felt he had to do something to draw your attention to him. And the best way to draw a policeman's attention to someone is to become a murderer. Clifford, after all, isn't sane; he doesn't have sane reactions. Of course he attacked his mother to prevent her locking him in that room, but he could have achieved that without killing her. He could have over-powered her and locked her in there himself. He killed her to attract your attention.'

'I know, I see that. I realized it when we were there . . . in that room. But he was a murderer already. Why couldn't he have admitted killing Mrs Robson? That would have attracted my attention all right. Do you think – ' Burden drew in his breath, expelled it with a sigh. He was sitting down now, leaning forward and holding on to the edge of Wexford's desk with both hands. 'Do you think that's what he wanted to talk to me about when he kept on trying to see me? Do you think he wanted to confess?'

'No,' Wexford said shortly. 'No, I don't.'

He was anxious now to bring this conversation to a close. The question he was sure Burden was going to ask would be far better postponed till the morning. Burden was in a bad enough state as it was without this further addition to his guilty feelings. For this would be the ultimate guilt. Of course he would have to know tomorrow, he would have to know as soon as possible in the morning . . . before the special court sat. 'Mike, would you like a drink? I've got some whisky in the cupboard. Don't look like that, I don't tipple the stuff secretly – or even un-secretly, come to that. One of our . . . clients offered it to me as a bribe and because I thought it would be handy to have, I took it and gave him the current Tesco price for it. Six pounds forty-eight, I think it was.' He was talking for the sake of talking as, burbling on. 'I won't have one, though. Let me have the Clifford tapes, will you, and then I'm going to drive you home. I'll give you a stiff one and then take you home.'

'I don't want anything to drink. I shall feel like hell in the morning. If I could justify what I did, I'd feel better. If I could tell myself the only possible way we could have nailed this man was by waiting for him to commit another murder – giving him enough rope, so to speak. You say you don't think he wanted to confess?'

'I don't think he wanted to confess, Mike. Let's go home.'

'What time is it?'

'Nearly two.'

They closed the office door and walked down the corridor under the pale, steady, bleaching lights. Clifford was downstairs, at the back, in one of the cells. Kingsmarkham police station cells were more comfortable than most prisons, with a bit of rug on the floor, two blankets on the bunk and a blue slip on the pillow, a cubicle with loo and basin opening off the tiny room. Burden cast a backward glance in that direction as they came out of the lift. Sergeant Bray was on duty behind the desk with PC Savitt beside him, looking at something in a file. Wexford said good night but Burden said nothing.

For the first time, the Christmas lights were on in the tree.

Burden had noticed them as something unreal in the fog, a kind of mockery, as they returned from Ash Farm bringing Clifford with them. Either they were on a time clock which had failed to work, or someone had forgotten to switch them off. The reds and blues and whites came on for fifteen seconds, then the yellows and greens and pinks, then the lot, winking hard before the reds and blues and whites returned alone. By now the fog had almost lifted and the colours glimmered in a thin mist.

'Wicked waste of the taxpayers' money,' Burden growled.

'I haven't got my car,' Wexford said. 'It seems so long ago that I'd forgotten. I suppose I meant to drive you in your car.'

'I'll drive you.'

A town that slept, a town that might have been emptied of its folk that silent night – inhabitants who had fled, leaving a light on here and there.

Burden said, climbing up to Highlands, turning into Eastbourne Road, 'I still can't see how he did it – killed Gwen Robson, I mean. He must have been in that car park by a quarter to six, met her as she came in to get her car and killed her. He would have been getting out of his mother's car and she walking up to hers. That must have been the way of it – unpremeditated, a frenzied act on the spur of the moment. He'll tell us now, no doubt.'

Wexford began to say something about the grotesqueness, the incongruity, of a young man stepping out of a car and happening by chance to be holding a circular knitting needle. They passed Robson's house – dark, all the curtains drawn – and Dita Jago's where a light was on, a red glow behind drawn crimson curtains. A cat came out of the Whittons', streaked across the road. Burden braked hard as it leapt clear, on to a wall, up a tree.

'Damned things,' said Burden. 'One shouldn't brake, one shouldn't give way to one's reflexes like that. Suppose there'd been someone behind me? It was only a cat. Look, Reg, that woman Rosemary Whitton has to be wrong. I mean, it's pretty hard for me to have to face that, because it means I was irresponsible in not consenting to talk to Clifford when he wanted me to. I took her word, of course I did. But we never really confirmed it.'

Wexford sighed. 'I did.'

'What? Took her word? I know. But she was wrong. And the wine-market manager was wrong too. Rosemary Whitton must have seen Clifford ten minutes earlier and he'd gone before she hit the meter. It was a genuine mistake, but it was a mistake.'

Up Battle Hill to stop outside his gate. The house was dark; Dora had gone to bed long ago.

Wexford unclipped the seat belt. 'Wait till the morning, shall we?'

He said good night, dragged himself upstairs and fell exhausted into bed – then awoke immediately, energetically, into a prospect of sleepless hours. When they were past and he was back down there, preparing for Clifford's appearance before the magistrates, he was going to have to tell Burden the facts: that he had checked and double-checked Rosemary Whitton's statement; that he had not only checked with the wine-market manager and three occupants of flats above the wine market, but had also found the traffic warden who, arriving on the scene to examine the damaged meter, had – while talking to Rosemary Whitton – seen Clifford drive away. It had been five to six.

19

Dorothy Sanders had never been divorced; Davidson's investigation of records had established that. Nor had she needed to keep herself by the humble sewing and knitting – traditional occupations of the poor virtuous woman she had once read about in some historical romance? – which she told her son had supported them in his childhood. For during those years she had been regularly drawing on the joint bank account that was in her name and her husband's. Now that she was dead, access to that account was no longer denied to the police.

It had been fed by the interest on Charles Sanders' investments, mostly unit trusts. Over a period of eighteen years since their separation, only she had drawn on it. From the bank manager's slightly defensive manner, Wexford gathered that this perhaps curious fact had never been noticed. He was a man opposed to new technology and blamed the fault, if fault it was, on the fact that in recent years the administration of the account had been by computer. Wexford marvelled at Mrs Sanders' capacity for lying and sustained secretiveness. It made him wonder if she had ever been married to Sanders, even if Clifford was her own child, but these facts were soon established. Dorothy Clifford and Charles Sanders had been married at St Peter's, Kingsmarkham in October 1963 and Clifford born to her in February 1966.

Wexford had himself driven back to Ash Farm and he took Burden with him, insisted on it. Burden had accepted Clifford's innocence of the first crime at first with reservations and arguments, then with a deep and bitter self-reproach. It was clear to him, and this Wexford was unable

659

to deny, that the death of Dorothy Sanders had come about as the direct result of his refusal to continue the sessions with Clifford.

Burden was silent for a while. Then he said, 'I think I shall have to resign.'

'For God's sake, why?'

'If it's true that I could drive a man to murder – and it is, I did do that – I'm not fit to be a police officer. It's part of my duty to prevent crime, not provoke it.'

'So, logically, you should never have questioned Clifford in the first place. Suspecting him of the murder of Gwen Robson, you should nevertheless have ignored him because he appeared to be an unbalanced person with abnormal reactions.'

'I'm not saying that. I'm saying that having once questioned him I shouldn't have . . . well, abandoned him to his fate.'

'You should have gone on talking to him day after day, for hours on end, session after session? For how long? Weeks? Months? What about your work? Your own sanity, come to that? Am I my brother's keeper?'

Burden took that question which Wexford had meant rhetorically – which perhaps Cain had meant rhetorically – in a literal way. 'Well, yes, maybe I am. What was the answer to it, anyway? What did whoever it was – God, was it? – say?'

'Nothing,' said Wexford. 'Absolutely nothing. Come on, forget about resigning. You're not resigning, you're coming with me to the scene of the crime.'

In gloomy silence Burden sat beside him in the car. It was a passive sort of winter's day, neither cold nor mild, the sky pale grey and clotted like porridge. Sometimes the sun appeared low on the horizon, a shiny disc of plate showing through where the gruel thinned. The shop windows in the High Street were full of pre-Christmas glitter and a huge imported Christmas tree, gift from some town in Germany no one had previously heard of but which was twinned with Kingsmarkham, had been set up outside the Barringdean Centre. Burden remarked in a sour way about the amount it must cost to run that electronic digital arrangement at the Tesco end which announced alternately that here were gifts for all the family and that nine shopping days remained until Christmas.

'What are we coming here for, anyway?'

He meant to Ash Farm, down long winding Ash Lane, where the grass verges were grey with splashed mud and dead elms with peeling trunks awaited the axe. But the air was clear today and in the distance the outline of the hummocky hill that hid the town could be seen. Ivy-clad Ash Farm slid into view, its many eyes peeping from amongst the evergreen growth. Two police cars were parked in front of it and a policeman in uniform was on duty at the foot of the flight of steps.

'I hadn't thought of going inside,' Wexford said.

'You said we were visiting the scene of the crime.'

Wexford made no reply but nodded to PC Leonard who saluted him and said, 'Good afternoon, sir.' In spite of what he had seen on the previous evening he found it hard to realize that Dorothy Sanders, so strong and upright and confident, was dead, the metallic voice silenced for ever. And when he looked through the dark gleaming glass into the thinly furnished room where the ashes of a fire lay in the grate, he half-expected to see her there, moving across the uncarpeted floor, issuing her orders with a pointing finger. A ghost, that would have to be, and she had been afraid of ghosts, afraid of the dark and of letting fog enter the house . . .

With Burden following him and Donaldson, he walked round the house into the back garden. It was new to him, but Burden had been out there before on the day of the search, triumphantly discovering garrotes in the shed attached to the rear wall. A curious place to put a shed, wasn't it? In order to reach it, a considerable area of damp grass had to be crossed. Earth, whether turfed or not, is always wet in winter, even during dry spells. He felt his shoes sink into the squelchy softness.

Dorothy Sanders had paid less attention to her garden than to her house, but had nevertheless achieved out here a similar kind of barren neatness. There were few plants that looked cultivated, though it was hard to tell at this time of the year, and even fewer weeds. It looked as if Mrs Sanders – or Clifford, on her instructions – had watered the flowerbed areas with the kind of toxic stuff that destroys broad-leaved plants. It looked as if at some point during her life in this house she had set about destroying the garden as it must once have existed. The few trees had been savagely lopped, so that from the stumps of amputated branches new twigs grew out at strange angles. A faint pinkness had appeared in the sky, sign of sunset. It would be dusk very soon, then deeply dark. Nine shopping days to Christmas, seven long nights and seven short days to the Solstice. One day to Sheila's court appearance . . .

These short days, cut off in mid-afternoon, hindered his progress. Nature still had the upper hand . . . just. Or, rather, he couldn't be absolutely sure the expense of using powerful lights was warranted. He padded through the wet grass to the furthermost corner of the garden and there, up against the back fence, he could just make out in the distance the low roof of what must be Ash Farm Lodge, rising above screens of Leyland cypress.

'Would you like to introduce me to Mr Carroll?'

They drove down the lane in the sunset light, the last of the light. With a rattling cry, a cock pheasant rose out of the hedge on seldom-used cumbersome wings. There was the sound of a shot and then another.

'It's only Carroll,' said Burden. 'The way Kingsmarkham's become urbanized, we forget we live in the country some-times.'

Carroll's dog came timidly to meet them. Perhaps, though, it wasn't timid – perhaps it was shyly creeping up prepara-tory to an attack. Wexford put out his hand to the dog and a harsh voice shouted, 'Don't touch him!'

The farmer appeared with a dead hare slung round his neck, in his left hand a pair of redleg partridges he was holding by their tail feathers.

Wexford said mildly, 'Mr Carroll? Chief Inspector Wex-ford, Kingsmarkham CID. I believe you've met my colleague, Inspector Burden.'

'He was this way before, yes.'

'Can we go inside?'

'What for?' Carroll asked.

'I want to talk to you. If you'd rather we didn't go into your house, you can come back to the police station with

662

us. That will suit us just as well. It's up to you, one or the other.'

'You can come in if you want,' Carroll said.

The dog preceded them in, head down and tail between its legs. Carroll made a growling noise at it, a remarkable animal noise which might have been expected to come from the dog, not it master. This was apparently the signal for it to go into its basket which it did like a hypnotic subject, curling itself into a circle and putting its head on its paws. Carroll hung up the twelve-bore, took off his boots and put them on the now stained and corrugated magazine on the oven top which was still just recognizable as a copy of *Kim*. The hare and the birds trailed bloody heads into the sink. The table was a mass of papers, chequebook and paying-in book from the Midland Bank, a VAT ledger, crumpled invoices. Wexford knew the chances of his being asked to sit down were around a hundred to one, so he had seated himself and motioned to Burden to do the same before Carroll had got his slippers on.

'Where's your wife, Mr Carroll?' Wexford began.

'What's that to you?' He didn't sit down, he stood over them. 'It's her up the road that's dead, and her boy that's potty did it. You stick to that, you see he's put away for life; that'll keep you lot busy, not coming poking into my business.'

'Rumour has it that your wife has left you,' Wexford observed.

For a moment he thought the farmer was going to strike him. Unpleasant as that would be, it would at least provide a reason for arresting him. But Carroll, having clenched his fists and put them up, stepped back, setting his teeth. Wexford decided just the same that he might feel more at an advantage on his feet. He was a bigger man than Carroll, though older.

The kitchen was rapidly growing dark. He reached for the only switch in the room and unexpectedly bright light poured from the central blumb in its incongruous shade: pink frilled cotton in the shape of a mob-cap. There were other such touches in that grim place: a battery-operated wall clock, its face a sunflower, a calendar that pictured a kitten in a basket, the day May of this year. In the bright light Carroll blinked.

'It was about six months ago that she left, wasn't it? End of June?' If Carroll wouldn't answer, there wasn't much he could do. He changed tack a little. 'Tell me about your neighbour, Charles Sanders? Did you know him? Were you here when he was living here?'

Carroll growled. It was the same language he used when issuing commands to his dog, but succeeded by reasonably comprehensible English. 'His dad died. Day after the funeral he upped and left. What do you want to know that for?'

'You don't ask the police questions, Carroll,' said Burden. 'We ask you. Right?'

Another growl. It was almost funny.

Wexford said, 'He never came back. He never came back to see his son, he never contributed to his wife's support or his son's. He left his old mother in his wife's care and she dumped her in an old people's home. I'm being very frank with you, Mr Carroll, and I'd like you to do the same by us. It's eighteen years since Sanders left. You were newly married, newly arrived here. I don't think he left, I think he's dead. What do you think?'

'How should I know? It's no business of mine.'

'What did your wife think, Mr Carroll? She knew, didn't she? Somehow or other she found out about Sanders. Did she tell you what she knew, or did she keep it to herself? Maybe she told only one person?'

'What person?'

By that remark Wexford had meant to infer nothing that could in fact be of momentous significance to Carroll, but the farmer read into it more than was implied and his face grew red and seemed to swell. Although he made no immediate move, a change had come over him – a kind of concentration, a gathering and intensifying of power, enough to make Burden spring to his feet and push back the chair. It was that which did it. Carroll reached behind him for the gun on the wall, unhooked it and, stepping back, levelled it at them from a distance of about four feet.

'Put that down,' Wexford said. 'Don't be a fool.'

'I'm giving you one minute to get out of here.'

At least now they would be able to arrest him, Wexford thought. The farmer could look at them and keep his eye on the sunflower clock at the same time. One eye open, the dog

664

watched from his basket. This was something it understood – a gun aimed, a helpless quarry. When I double up full of shot, Wexford thought ridiculously, maybe it will come and retrieve me.

Burden said, his head cocked towards the door, 'There's Donaldson coming now,' as if he heard footsteps.

It was a trick and it worked. Carroll turned his head and Wexford's fist shot out to catch him on the jaw. The gun went off as he fell, and in that low-ceilinged bungalow room it made an enormous noise, a noise like a bomb, a noise like the bomb in his front garden which Wexford couldn't remember hearing. The farmer rolled over and the gun dropped from his hands to clatter away across the tiles. Bits of plaster dropped from the ceiling where shot had peppered it. Smoke and a stench of gunpowder and the bewildered dog looking from side to side, beginning a helpless, forbidden barking. And then Donaldson did come, pounding up the path and throwing open the back door.

'Are you OK, sir? What happened?'

'I don't know my own strength,' said Wexford. He considered poking at Carroll with his toe, but thought better of it and heaved the man up by the shoulders. Carroll groaned, his head sagging. 'I don't suppose we've got any handcuffs in the car, have we?'

'I don't think so, sir.'

'Then we must do without, but I don't think he'll give much trouble.'

Carroll was a big man and it took the three of them to get him into the car. They shut up the dog in the kitchen and Donaldson, who was fond of dogs, gave him a bowl of water and the hare.

'That's the way to undo years of training in half an hour,' he said cheerfully.

The artifacts that lay all over the surfaces in Wexford's office – in court they would have been called 'exhibits' – included Carroll's twelve-bore, a muddied copy of *Kim* magazine, a circular knitting needle, size six, and some of the contents of the dead woman's coat pockets. There was something distressing, though scarcely pathetic, about that lipstick in its shiny gilt case, the red of a fire engine. The almost white face powder with its faint iridescence had been marketed for someone young and fair, someone like Lesley Arbel. The chequebook for the joint account was in the names of C. L. Sanders and D. K. Sanders and – at least during the lifetime of this particular book it had been used only to draw sums of cash. A hundred pounds a month was what Dorothy Sanders had drawn during the past two years. It wasn't much, it was modest, but for the past two years her income had been supplemented by Clifford's earnings.

That morning Kingsmarkham magistrates had committed him for trial on a charge of murder and remanded him in custody until the trial was due. Even Burden could see now that there could be no other murder charge for him to face, that it was impossible for him to have been guilty of the death of Gwen Robson. He had seen Clifford driven away to the remand prison at Myringham before he and Wexford left for Ash Farm and had not mentioned him since. But now he came into Wexford's office and spoke abruptly.

'I felt I should have stood up before the magistrates and said I wanted to make a statement. I should have admitted my responsibility – well, my share in what that poor little guy did.'

' "Poor little guy", is it now? What's become of your much-vaunted principle of reserving pity for the victim?' Wexford was reading a letter, nodding from time to time as if what he read brought him a long-awaited satisfaction. He winced at the sounds that were coming from the depths of the building, a steady crash-crash-crash, and looked up at Burden irritably.

'I've let him down all along the line. I should have publicly admitted my part in what he did.'

'You'd make yourself a laughing-stock. Imagine what used to be called the press, and are now for some daft reason called the media, would make of that. Excuse me.' Wexford's phone was ringing and he picked up the receiver. 'Yes, yes, thank,' he said. 'You've a record of that on your computer, have you? Is it possible for me to have some sort of print-out? Yes . . . yes. Someone will come down for it before the library closes. When do you close? Six-thirty tonight? That's just about an hour. All right. Thanks for your help.'

'What's that noise?' Burden opened the door a crack the better to hear the banging. When Wexford shrugged, he asked in a tone of minimal interest, 'What was all that about?'

'A woman's alibi. And another one has just fallen neatly into place. Just a matter of clearing things up really, eliminating remote possibilities. Do you remember that gale we had in the middle of last month? It blew down the phone lines at Sundays and Ash Lane.'

'You think I'm a maundering idiot, don't you? It's all hot air and bullying with me, but underneath I'm weak and water. I was scared of Clifford, do you know that? When he came to my house, I was afraid to answer the door.'

'You did answer it though.'

'Why was I so set on it? Why did I make up my mind it had to be him when all the evidence was against it?'

'At any rate you admit that now.' Wexford sounded bored, languid. 'What can I say? Anything I say sounds like saying I told you so. Well, no, I might tell you to let it be a lesson to you. You'd like that, wouldn't you?' He got up and looked out of the window at the tree with its winking lights, the red, blue and white sequence, the yellow, green and pink sequence. The sky was dark but clear, a dome of deepening blue with stars. 'Mike, I truly think that if he hadn't killed her then, he would have killed her one day. Tomorrow or next week or next year. Murder's infectious too. Have you ever thought of that?' Clifford killed his mother because she was there and because she was restraining him and . . . to draw your attention to him. But perhaps he also killed her because the idea had been put into his head, because he knew, if you like, that it was possible to kill people. He had seen a murdered woman he thought at first was his mother. Hoped it was his mother? Maybe. But the idea was planted, wasn't it? Others could do it, so he could do it. It infected him.'

'Do you really think so?' Burden's face was desperately hopeful, the face of a man who may drown if the flung hand can find nothing stronger than a straw. 'Do you honestly think that?'

'Ask Olson, he'll tell you. Let's go home, Mike, and make a few enquiries about our prisoner on the way.'

667

The phone rang again as they reached the door and Wexford went back and picked it up. The voice at the other end was so clear that even Burden heard from three yards away, 'I have Sandra Dale on the line.'

Wexford said into the phone, 'It doesn't matter, I don't need it any longer,' and after listening for a moment, 'that doesn't surprise me. You won't find it now.'

He thanked her and said goodbye and they went downstairs. PC Savitt told them that Carroll, who had been put in the cell previously occupied by Clifford, was quiet now. Dr Crocker had seen him and offered him a sedative, which Carroll had surprisingly accepted. Before that he had threatened to break the place up, though had got no further than a regular lifting up of two of the legs of the iron bedstead prior to letting them crash on to the floor.

'Could you hear him, sir?'

'I should think they could hear him in the Barringdean Centre.'

Burden stood on the steps outside the swing doors. 'It's a funny thing the way you can do something, take a determined course of action over a length of time and be absolutely sure you're right, not have a shadow of doubt. And a week later you can look back amazed at what you did, hardly able to realize it was you who did it, and wonder if anyone like that can actually be sane. I mean, I wonder if anyone like *me* can be.'

'I'm cold,' said Wexford. 'I don't want to stand about here.'

'Yes, all right, sorry. What was that you were reading?'

Wexford got into his car. 'It was the letter Lesley Arbel was searching for and Sandra Dale has been searching for, which I have been searching for and have at last found.'

'Aren't you going to tell me what was in it?'

'No,' said Wexford and he shut the car door. Rolling down the window half-way, he said, 'I would have done but you're too late, you've missed the boat. I'll tell you in the morning.' He grinned. 'I'll tell you everything in the morning.'

And he drove away, leaving Burden standing there watching the car depart, not sure if he understood quite what 'everything' implied.

20

Burden drove the car down to the second level and parked as near as he could to where Gwen Robson's body had lain nearly a month before. Every space on the level was now full and would be all day, every day, up until Christmas and beyond during the end-of-the-year sales.

Serge Olson was the first to get out of the car. He had come into the police station just as they were leaving to enquire when and how he would be permitted to visit Clifford Sanders in the remand prison, and Wexford had invited him to go with them. An Opel Kadett and a Ford Granada were now parked where Gwen Robson's Escort and the Brooks' blue Lancia had been. A Vauxhall came nosing round looking for a space and proceeded down the ramp towards the third level. But apart from themselves there were no people. It was car world, an area of car life where bodies were cars and people their brains or moving spirits. Oil and water lay in pools, car excrement and the place smelt of car sweat.

Wexford shook himself out of fanciful imaginings and said, 'Lately we seem to have lost sight somewhat of our victim, of Gwen Robson. But if she wasn't the first to be murdered, she was at any rate the first we knew of – the first to draw our attention to this case.' Burden looked enquiringly at him, but he only shook his head.

'She brought her death on herself; she was a blackmailer. But like a lot of blackmailers she was – I won't say innocent, she was naïve. She tangled with the wrong person. And I think she justified what she was doing by the reason for which she wanted the money, which was to pay for her husband's hip replacement. If he was to have this operation on the National Health service, it was possible he would have had to wait up to three years, by which time she feared he might be totally crippled. Three or four thousand pounds would pay for the replacement to be done privately and for hospitalization. At the time of her death, she had accumulated about sixteen hundred.' Wexford's glance took in Olson and his driver. 'Let's go into the centre, shall we?'

It was one of those freak December days that are like April; all that was missing were the leaf buds on the trees. The flags on the turrets of the Barringdean building fluttered in a light breeze and the sky was milky-blue with clouds like shreds of foam. They came out of the metal lift with its graffiti into mild sunshine.

' "This castle hath a pleasant seat", ' Wexford said dryly. And if you half-closed your eyes the centre's medieval fortress look was compounded by the trolleys tumbled about the car-park entrance and across the roadway like siege-engines abandoned by their users. 'I've already discussed this with you, Mike. We know that Lesley Arbel brought her aunt photocopies of letters received by the agony aunt at *Kim*, the magazine she worked for, in disregard of the undertaking she had given when she got the job not to divulge or discuss the contents of such letters. Nevertheless, she did make photocopies of certain letters and she did show them to Gwen Robson. Now Gwen Robson, being a salacious woman, was interested in a general way in what she was shown, but she was far more deeply interested in letters coming from people who lived in this neighbourhood.'

Walking along the covered way that would bring them to the doors in the middle of the central gallery, Wexford went on, 'I don't know what gave her the idea of blackmail, but it was an idea both obvious and clever. True, she might have picked up information of a damaging kind about her clients while she was working, but it was unlikely she would have been able to acquire documentary evidence. She had tried other ways of raising money, but these ways had either ceased – the old people who paid for special indulgences had died, for example – or failed, as in the case of Eric Swallow whom she was unable to induce to make a will in her favour. Blackmail remained, the blackmail of women whose secrets they dared only divulge to a more or less anonymous oracle, an agony aunt.

'Two letters particularly interested Gwen Robson both because of their sensational content and the addresses of the women who had written them. One was from a Mrs Margaret Carroll of Ash Farm Lodge, Ash Lane, Forbydean, and the other . . . well, here we are halfway between Tesco and British Home Stores. Shall we go into the café for coffee, or a healthful veggie juice in Demeter?'

The dissenting voice was Olson's, who would have preferred the vegetable juice. But he gave away gracefully, only stipulating decaffeinated coffee.

'I believe,' Wexford went on, 'that Gwen Robson's blackmailing efforts had been successful up to a point, that is, her two women victims had been paying her for her silence over a period of weeks or months. No doubt because, poor things, they couldn't raise a lump sum. Let us come to the day in question, November 19, a Thursday and four-thirty in the afternoon, the time when more of the residents of Kingsmarkham seem to be in here than at any other. Gwen Robson arrived at four-forty, parked her car in the second level and came in most probably by the way we did, under the covered way and through the central door. Now we know what shopping she did, though not the order in which she did it, and we have no way of knowing how much window-shopping she indulged in. But we can make an intelligent guess that she started at British Home Stores where she bought her light bulbs and went on to Boots for her toothpaste and talcum powder. Let us say that brings us to five o'clock.

'Helen Brook is in Demeter next door here, buying calendula capsules. She sees Mrs Robson out of the window and at once recognizes her as the busybody home help who criticized her lifestyle and said she hoped she would never have children – this presumably because she feared they would be illegitimate. Helen Brook intends to show herself to Mrs Robson as ample proof that she is indeed about to have a child, but before she can do this she actually goes into labour, or has her first labour pain. However, she has already noticed that Mrs Robson is in conversation with a very well-dressed girl. Whom do we know that we should describe like that?

671

Lesley Arbel. The Robsons' niece Lesley Arbel, whom we know to have been in Kingsmarkham that afternoon.'

The coffee came and with it a slice of Black Forest cake for Burden. He must be eating for comfort. Not for the first time Wexford marvelled at the manifest untruth expressed by healthy eating experts: that if you give up sweet things, you soon lose your sweet tooth. He turned his eyes from the chocolate cake, the cream and the cherries, and looked at the concourse where in time for Christmas a sub-aqueous arrangement of coloured lights turned the fountain jets to red and blue and rose.

'The killer had in his or her possession, or so we have supposed,' he went on, 'a circular knitting needle of some high-numbered gauge – that is with thicker pins at each end of the wire. But suppose it was Mrs Robson herself who had it, and her killer took it from her? This is possible if in her innocence she showed it to her killer. She might have been into the wool and crafts shop immediately prior to her meeting with the well-dressed girl. Why did Lesley Arbel come in here when she knew she would see her aunt on the following day anyway? She wanted the photocopies of those letters back; she was starting to regret ever leaving them in Gwen Robson's possession.

'Lesley Arbel is a narcissist, entirely self-absorbed, interested only in her appearance and the impression she makes on others. You'll have to tell me if this is a sound description, Serge?'

'Near enough,' said Olson. 'Narcissism is extreme self-love. The soul-image is not projected and a relatively unadapted state develops. A narcissist would be suspended in an early phase of psychosexual development where the sexual object is the self. This girl, does she have friends? Boyfriends?'

'We never heard of any. The only person she seems really to have liked was her aunt. How do you account for that if they don't care for others?'

'The aunt might simply be a mirror. I mean – it's Gwen Robson you're talking about, isn't it? – if Gwen Robson was much older than she and nothing much to look at, but really admired Lesley and flattered her and showed her off, that would be the only kind of "friend" Lesley could tolerate.

Her function would be to reflect the most flattering kind of Lesley-image. A lot of girls have that kind of relationship with their mothers – and we call those good relationships!'

'I think that was it,' said Wexford. 'I think she also liked and valued her job and was very much afraid of losing it. Not only are jobs hard to come by anyway, but she feared that if she lost her job on *Kim* for this particular reason, a flagrant breach of confidence, she would in some way be blacklisted among magazines – and for all I know she was right. She wanted those letter copies back and she wanted to be sure they had not been copied in their turn.'

'Why would she kill Gwen Robson for that?' Olson asked, his frown deepening, his eyes very bright.

'She wouldn't. She didn't. It was only after she knew her aunt was dead that she became afraid about the photocopies and took the place apart trying to find them. As far as we know Gwen Robson didn't knit: there was no evidence of her knitting in the house. And I am sure Lesley Arbel didn't. Neither of them bought a circular knitting needle on the afternoon in question. Lesley, anyway, wasn't even there. It is true, as she said, that she came to Kingsmarkham, but she came for the purpose she said she did – to make certain she was properly registered for her word-processor course. According to British Telecom the phones at Sundays were out of order all that day, the cables having been damaged by wind on the previous night. Lesley was unable to get through on the phone, so down she came. All quite clear and reasonable. Far from entering the Barringdean Centre, she went straight to the station and was on a train before her aunt left home.'

Burden objected. 'But Helen What's-her-name saw her.'

'She saw a well-dressed girl, Mike. The well-dressed girl was talking to Gwen Robson out in the Mandala concourse and the time was about five. Clifford Sanders was half-way through his session with you, Serge. Where was Dita Jago? Now from the first, I was very interested in Dita Jago. She of all possible suspects possessed the weapon – or versions and repeats of the weapon: she had in her house probably half a dozen circular knitting needles in various sizes, of small and large gauge. She is a heavily-built woman, but strong and light on her feet. Suppose she was another of

Gwen Robson's blackmailees – the hold which her neighbour had over her being the fact that far from being on the receiving end, so to speak, in Auschwitz, she had in fact assisted the authorities? That afternoon we know that her daughter took her own two daughters and Dita Jago shopping, dropping her mother off at the public library and presumably leaving the two children with her. But perhaps that is only an alibi concocted by the two women. Perhaps Dita went with her daughter but instead of going into the centre, preferred to sit and wait for her inside the car in the car park.'

'Would anyone prefer sitting in that car park?'

'Someone like Dita Jago might, Mike, if she had something to knit or to read – both quite likely occupations in her case. Let us say that Gwen Robson parted from the very well-dressed girl, whoever she may be, and entered the Tesco supermarket on her own where she helped herself to a trolley and began her shopping. Now your Linda Naseem, Mike, says she saw her at about five-twenty but it might have been a bit after that. Most probably it was a little before five-thirty. Again she was observed talking to a girl, but this time only the girl's back was seen. It may have been the same girl and it may not. All we know of her was that she was a girl, was slim and wearing some kind of hat. By now, Serge, Clifford is just about taking his leave of you prior to beginning his meditations in the car in Queen Street.

'If you've finished, shall we pay the bill and take a walk? You've got chocolate icing on your chin, Mike.'

'Ratepayers?' queried Olson, eyeing the chit.

'I don't see why not.' Wexford led them out into the I-shaped gallery, crossed the wide area between the line of seats and moved towards the concentric circles of flowers: poinsettias again today, fleshy-leaved kalinchoe and the Christmas cactus with spiky vermilion blossoms.

'The Mandala,' said Olson. 'Schizophrenics and people in states of conflict dream of these things. In Sanskrit, the word means a circle. In Tibetan Buddhism, it has the significance of a ritual instrument or mantra.'

Looking at the flowers but taking in Olson's words, Wexford couldn't help seeing the instrument, also circular when so manipulated, that had killed Gwen Robson. And then he remembered his own dreams after the bomb – the circular images full of patterns, kaleidoscopic designs of extreme and severe symmetry. And there was comfort in what Olson was saying: 'Its order compensates for the disorder and confusion of the psychic state. It can be an attempt at self-healing.'

They paused outside the window and the wool and crafts shop. Today the display was of canvases for tapestry work; the hanks of wool and needles had disappeared.

'Go on, Reg,' said Olson.

'Gwen Robson talks to the girl in the hat, packs her shopping in two carrier bags and leaves the centre by the Tesco supermarket exit which brings her out some two hundred yards or so to the left of the covered way. She follows the path through the car park, probably pushing her two bags in a trolley which she abandons in the trolley park at the lift-head, then goes down in the lift to the second level. It is still full of cars, the time being no more than five-forty.

'Dita Jago, sitting in her daughter's car knitting, sees her come in and also sees her opportunity. She pulls the circular needle out from her work, leaves the car, goes up behind Gwen Robson on her light feet, and, as Gwen Robson is unlocking the door of the Escort, strangles her with this highly efficient garrote.'

'Is that really what you think happened?' asked Burden as they entered Tesco. He took a wire basket, having always in such places a uneasy feeling that to walk through without one might not be illegal but was suspect and reprehensible behaviour, likely to lead store detectives to the belief that you were up to no good. He even helped himself to a can of aerosol shoe polish. 'You really think she is our perpetrator?'

'You'll destroy the ozone layer,' Wexford said. 'You'll coat the earth in black froth – and all for the sake of shiny shoes, you narcissist. No, I don't think Dita's our perpetrator; I know she isn't. The librarian at the High Street branch of the library remembers her being there with the two little girls from somewhere around four-fifty until about five-thirty, when her daughter came back to collect her. She was checking up on facts for this book she's writing, we now know. The librarian remembers because the little girls kept asking the time; they were supposed to be reading, but they kept asking their grandmother if it was half-past five yet and then they asked other people and had to be hushed. Dita Jago took out three books and the date is on the library's computer.'

Burden took his aerosol to Linda Naseem's checkout. If she recognized him she gave no sign of it, but as they passed on he looked back and saw her chattering in whispers to the girl next to her. The main exit doors slid open to let them pass through into the sunshine. There was a seat out there, just outside, with a strip of turf dividing the centre from the biggest above-ground car park. Wexford sat down in the middle of it with Olson on his left and Burden – after examining his purchase, scrutinizing the label to see if what Wexford had said of it might be true – on his right.

Wexford said, 'We'll return to those letters. Now I knew that these particular letters would have to be out of the common run, not quite of the my-boyfriend-keeps-pressurizing-me-to-go-all-the-way genre. They were going to be the kind that even in these days *Kim* wouldn't care to print. The agony aunt's assistant gave me an example of this type when she said someone had enquired about the protein content of semen.'

'You don't mean it?' said Burden, horrified. 'You're joking.'

'I only wish I had that much imagination, Mike.' Wexford grinned. 'One thing I did understand – where the letter copies had gone. The killer took them out of Gwen Robson's handbag after the deed was done, that much seemed obvious. The killer's own letter and the other. One of the writers was Mrs Margaret Carroll, but Gwen Robson never blackmailed her; she had nothing to blackmail her about. So we come to the other.

'My daughter Sylvia brought me copies of *Kim* magazine covering four years, about two hundred copies therefore. When I read through the agony aunt's pages I wasn't looking for a letter. I was looking for an answer, only because I was hoping against hope that this would be one of those appeals considered too . . . well, what? Obscene, indecent – hardly. Too open and revealing perhaps to print. But the agony aunt's reply would be printed under a heading with enough information to give me more than a clue as to who the writer was.

'There are common initials to have and highly unusual

676

ones. I'd say mine, RW are pretty ordinary – and yours too, Mike, MB. And your wife and your elder son both with JB even more so. "JB, Kingsmarkham" wouldn't convey much, would it? But your initials, Serge, are something else; SO isn't a usual combination at all. And the combination I was looking for must be even rarer.

'Well, I found it. Take a look at this.'

He had made a copy of the relevant back page of *Kim* and he passed the original to Burden and the copy to Olson.

Burden read his aloud: ' "NQ, Sussex: I understand and sympathize with you in your dilemma. Yours is certainly a difficult and potentially tragic situation. But if there is the slightest possibility that the man you mention could be an AIDS carrier, you must see your doctor at once. Tests can be easily and quickly carried out and your mind set at rest once and for all. Feeling guilty and ashamed is pointless. Better realize that by delaying you are putting your husband, your marriage and your family life in danger. Sandra Dale." '

'Nina Quincy?' said Burden when he had finished. 'Mrs Jago's daughter?'

'The letter that was never printed was photocopied by Lesley Arbel and shown to Gwen Robson. The full name and address were on that, of course. And Gwen Robson knew at once who it was; she had met Nina Quincy in Mrs Jago's house when she was hunting for two people to witness Eric Swallow's will. She was introduced to her and noted the unusual name. Nina Quincy lives in a big house in Down Road, she had her own car. To someone like Gwen, she would appear rich and a fine potential for blackmail.

'And for a time, I believe, she paid up. She has a part-time job of her own, and the likelihood is that for some weeks she was giving a considerable part of her salary to Gwen. You must understand that she was worried sick. Picture what it must have been like. Her husband had been away abroad on business and she had gone to a party, drunk too much, spent the night with a man she afterwards discovered to be bisexual and actually living with someone dying of Aids. She was afraid to go to a doctor, especially as by the time she made her discovery her husband had been home for sometime and they had been leading a normal sex life. Or so I suppose. I haven't seen this letter because the copy of it no

677

longer exists and *Kim*, who claim to keep all letters sent to them for a three-year-period, are unable to find either this or the Carroll letter.

'On November the nineteenth, Nina Quincy – who still had not consulted her doctor or said anything of this to her husband, though the reply to the letter appeared in *Kim* last May – went as usual to the Barringdean Centre, having dropped off her mother and the two children at the library, entering here at about five to five. The first shop she went to was the wool and crafts place where she bought the first item on her mother's shopping list, a circular knitting needle gauge number eight – that is, a length of plastic-covered wire with a stout peg at each end measuring perhaps a quarter of an inch in diameter. This, or something similar, would be a purchase she had often made in the past for her mother.

'Coming out of the shop, she encountered Gwen Robson by the Mandala. It wasn't very imaginative to us to conclude that someone Helen Brook thought well-dressed would also appear well-dressed to us – at least to Mike and me, a couple of conventional coppers. Helen Brook would have turned her nose up at Lesley Arbel's pencil skirts and high heels. But Nina Quincy was dressed in just the way Helen admired: elaborate tapestry knits, a patterned beret and her hair down her back, a fringed shawl no doubt, a peasant-style skirt, jacquard socks. You see how I've worked on getting my terms right. Anyway, that's well-dressed in Ashtoreth's mother's book. What did she have to say to Gwen Robson? I think she pleaded with her to ask for no more. I think she told her that it was impossible to go on paying her at this rate – fifty pounds a week or perhaps more? And we must conclude that Gwen Robson did not relent, but said something to the effect of her need being greater than Nina's and perhaps that Nina shouldn't have done what she did if she didn't expect to pay for it. She was that sort of woman, was Gwen.

'If you've sunned yourselves enough we may as well take a look at their Christmas tree, see if it's as good as ours, then we'll go underground once more.'

'Are you going to tell us,' said Olson, 'that Nina followed her while she was shopping? That sounds grotesque.'

'Not necessarily; they may have encountered each other

678

again at the checkout. After all, whatever trouble she was in Nina did continue to lead the life of a housewife and mother; she did do her own shopping and her mother's. She had to do it and then she had her mother and her daughters to pick up at five-thirty. So, yes, we'll say the met again at the checkout and more words passed between them, only a back view of Nina and her beret being visible to Linda Naseem. But they left the Tesco separately, meeting for the third time that afternoon only when they were both in the car park.

'Those white lights look a bit stark, don't you think? I prefer our rainbow effect.'

The three of them stood underneath the Norway spruce which towered to a height of thirty feet. A notice at its foot announced that Father Christmas would be in the centre to meet children every day from Tuesday December 22. The date reminded Wexford of what today's was, one week before that, and raised into the forefront of his mind Sheila's court appearance. She would have left the court some hours ago and the waiting photographers and television cameras would have departed. By now it would be in the papers. Not for her the angry hand pushed against the lens, the averted head or coat held up like a yashmak, the veil to inhibit recognition. She would want to be seen, want the whole nation to know . . . He made one of those shifts that are much a remarkable feature of man's mental processes, as if a lever were lifted and a new picture dropped into place, or a kaleidoscope shaken. With the others following, he stepped into the shade and cold of the covered way.

'We can't tell exactly what happened next,' he said, 'but Nina Quincy – having settled matters at last, having taken action and perhaps feeling relief – had gone into her car and driven away. She picked up her mother and her children and took them home. The blackmail was over; Gwen Robson would never menace her again. She, however, had something left to do. Now that this particular threat was past, she had to go to her doctor and arrange to have that test.

'Well, eventually she did and the test was negative. She had nothing to fear and she knew her husband was an unforgiving man. Yet when he confessed to her some indiscretion of his own which he'd committed while he was in America, she was silly enough to tell him the whole story . . . and he left her.'

Beyond the open gates, across Pomeroy Road in his window sat Archie Greaves. Wexford put up his hand in a salute, though sure the old man wouldn't be able to see him, certainly wouldn't recognize him. But there was an answering wave from beyond the glass, the wave Archie would give to any friendly customer in the Barringdean Centre. They went down in the lift and stepped out at the second level. A car went round rather too fast, splashing oil from a puddle – a red car, of course.

'You didn't say anything about her taking the letter copies from Mrs Robson's bag,' said Burden.

'She didn't take them.'

'But someone – '

'Once she had made her decision, she had nothing to fear from that letter. She had already told Gwen Robson while they were in the centre that blackmail was pointless as she intended to go to her doctor and confess to her husband.'

There was a space now where the Robson Escort had been parked, and the space where the blue Lancia had been was empty too. Burden stood in the middle holding out his arms in rather a dramatic way, a foot on either side of the dividing white line. And in a voice made shrill by exasperated bewilderment, he demanded to know why it was then that Nina Quincy had done murder.

21

They stood for a while on the spot where Gwen Robson had died.

'You know, Mike,' Wexford said, 'I don't think we've considered sufficiently what a horrible crime this was. We've accepted it, not put it into perspective. Only a very few people would be capable of committing such a crime. What – approach a woman either from behind or face-to-face and garrote her with a wire? Imagine the horror of it, the helpless thrashings of the victim, her struggles ... who but one of those psychopaths you're so keen on could stand it?'

'I must say,' Olson put in, 'I wouldn't have thought a ... well, fairly sheltered ordinary middle-class sort of girl like Nina Quincy with a conventional lifestyle capable of it. But I'm not a policeman, I don't know. The affectivity might be there, but it's just that a young mother – that's the last category you'd pick on for this kind of crime. In my game, that is.'

'And in mine,' said Wexford. 'When I said that Nina Quincy felt satisfied because she had taken action, I meant only that the action she had taken was her defiance of Gwen Robson, her decision to get medical help at last. Of course she didn't kill her, though I daresay she sometimes would have liked to, which is what I think you mean. But she didn't kill her. In order to be back in the High Street and at the library by five-thirty, she must have left the Barringdean Centre by five-twenty at the latest, and we know the earliest time at which Gwen Robson could have died was five-thirty-five.'

The acrid stench of petrol made Wexford wrinkle up his nose. 'If we want to save our lungs, we'd better get back in the car,' he said. 'Before we go into the next sequence of events, perhaps we should take a look at the couple called Roy and Margaret Carroll. We already know that the writer of the other letter was Margaret Carroll – a woman with something of a social conscience, a woman who was upset when she discovered that her neighbour was in the habit of punishing her little boy by shutting him up in cold, dark attics.'

'Do you know who they are?' Burden said to Olson. 'Neighbours of Clifford and the late Dodo Sanders? Does it mean anything to you?'

'Clifford mentioned her,' Olson said carefully. 'He said she once threatened his mother with the cruelty-to-children's people.'

'That's right. She was also concerned about another aspect of the Sanders' life, though this was something she didn't begin to suspect until last summer. Strange, isn't it, how all these things erupted last summer around May and June? Her own life was none too easy, I suspect, with a husband of a kind usually called a brute – a Cold Comfort Farm kind of character, only grimly for real. He was going to have a go at us last night with a twelve-bore. Did Mike tell you?'

Olson raised his brown tufty eyebrows. 'Where is he now?'

'In custody, where I hope he'll remain for quite a while.'

'And the wife? what's happened to her?'

'She left him last summer – something else that happened then, about June, I think. The wonder was that she didn't go years ago. Well, no, I'm deceiving you and I don't want to do that. Let's say only that she seems to have left him; at any rate she disappeared. Clifford believes there was a man friend and Carroll gives the impression of believing that too. I don't. I think Margaret Carroll is dead, just as Charles Sanders is dead. A year after Roy Carroll and his wife came to live at Ash Farm Lodge, Charles Sanders died. That was why he never came back to see his little boy, why he seemed to abandon his old mother, why he contributed nothing to his son's support, why his wife was obliged to live on what she drew from their joint account – an account steadily though meagrely fed from Charles Sanders' investments – and incidentally why Mike hasn't been able to find him.

'Let's go back, shall we? We've renewed our acquaintance with the place; we can hold what we need to in our mind's eye.'

Burden reversed the car and circled slowly towards the upward ramp. 'Is that what they're doing up there at Ash Lane, searching for Charles Sanders' body?'

'Well, the remains of it, Mike. It's eighteen years past and there won't be much left. Frankly, I don't know where to begin the search for Mrs Carroll, but there are ways of help open to us.

'You see, Mrs Carroll suspected Sanders was dead when she was in her branch of the Midland Bank and saw Dorothy Sanders drawing a cheque on a joint account. She happened to stand next to her and quite innocently saw this over her shoulder. At any rate I think so; it's an intelligent enough guess. Did other others then begin to fall into place? The sudden and quite unexpected death of Charles Sanders' father? This death immediately followed by the departure of Charles? The memory soon after of secret digging? Not enough for her to come to us – or perhaps she couldn't bring herself to the enormity of such a step. It was a pity she didn't; she might be alive today if she had.'

When the car turned into the High Street something recalled Wexford's mind to Sheila and the tribulations of her day. She or someone representing her would have phoned Dora by now. What had happened to her – an account of what had happened with pictures – would be in the evening paper. It would be on the streets by now; the London evening papers were always on Kingsmarkham streets by three and it was nearly four. The sun was setting, dyeing the sky a gold that would fade to pink and darken to dusky purple. He caught sight of a newsboard with something on it about missile treaty talks and felt a ridiculous relief because Sheila's name wasn't there. As if Sheila's court appearance, Sheila's fate must as a matter of course be the lead story.

'Mike,' he said, 'put the car on one of those meters in Queen Street, will you? I have to buy a paper.'

Her face looked at him, framed in newsprint, not smiling nor laughing, no raised hand waving at cameras. She looked

683

frightened; her expression was grave and big-eyed. She was leaving the court and even without reading the caption it didn't take a policeman's knowledge to recognize where she was going and with whom. The headline he couldn't help reading, though he forced himself to postpone further elucidation until he was at home: 'Sheila Goes to Jail', the picture caption said. '*Lady Audley's Secret* star gets a week inside.'

The man behind the counter, an obliging, nothing-is-too-much-trouble Indian, smiled patiently at this apparently stupefied customer who didn't know you had to pay for an evening paper. He coughed discreetly. Wexford put two tenpence pieces on the counter and crushed the paper clumsily into his pocket.

Olson and Burden were out of the car, standing outside Pelage.

'Come up to my place,' Olson said. 'I'll make you a cup of tea.'

The steep narrow staircase was a bit like the attic stairs at Ash Farm, Burden thought. But there was something cosy, something sane for all its bizarreness, about what awaited them at the top. He remembered how it had once felt threatening and now he wondered why. What had he meant? He had become a therapist himself since then – with disastrous results. His own, sometimes timid, psyche suddenly seemed less important. Wexford, who had never been up here before, saw the poster with the globe and its ruined continents, with Einstein's ominous words, and it brought home to him Sheila's fate so that he flinched. He wondered if the others had seen, decided they hadn't and anyway, so what? Olson was using spoonfuls of powdered stuff called instant tea. Inwardly Wexford laughed at himself for minding, for caring about trivia in the midst of . . . all this. He said:

'Thanks to your tapes, Mike, I know exactly what Clifford told you. Whether those tapes could be admitted now, whether you were strictly correct to make them, doesn't matter. Clifford told you he hoped his mother and Roy Carroll might get together – might even possibly marry – and he told you how all the information about Margaret Carroll having a lover, another man in her life, came to Carroll from Dorothy Sanders. It was Dorothy Sanders, the neighbour, who was in a position to see who visited Ash

684

Farm Lodge while Carroll was out in the fields and perhaps also to see whom he went out to meet. Or so Carroll could be made to believe.

'Carroll is a jealous, possessive man. She inflamed his jealousy and terribly damaged his pride, but for her own sake she had to do it. Clifford was wrong when he guessed Carroll might be attracted by his mother or enjoyed her company; all he got from her was information about his wife's infidelity. When his wife disappeared he thought he knew why and who with, but the last thing he wanted was for the rest of the world to know. That was why he never reported her as missing when she disappeared last June. He preferred to keep her disappearance dark but if anyone suggested to him, as we did, that his wife might be somewhere living with another man, he went out of his mind with rage.'

Burden drank his tea as if it were the real stuff brewed from leaves in a hot, dry pot, as if the milk in it had come yesterday from a cow. 'So Carroll didn't kill her?'

'There was only one person in this case capable of committing these crimes, and that person is beyond our reach now. Retribution, if you like, or chance or misfortune has caught up with her. Only Dorothy Sanders could have killed a husband, depriving a child of its father and a mother of her son. Only Dorothy Sanders could have gone up to her victim and garroted her with a length of wire.

'Here's the letter Margaret Carroll wrote to *Kim* last spring,' Wexford went on, holding out the photocopy to Burden. 'I went back to Ash Farm last night and found it slipped into the back of a photograph frame in one of those attic rooms. The picture, incidentally, was of a family group I take to be Charles and his parents. I wonder why she didn't burn the letter? Because something she had done murder for must be precious? Or one day to have it to show to Clifford or Carroll if a defence was needed? We shall never know. The original would have been kept by *Kim* for two years, except that Lesley Arbel saw to that when she couldn't find the copy. She destroyed both those letters as soon as she got back after her Sundays course.'

Burden read it aloud: ' "Dear Sandra Dale, I am in a terrible dilemma and cannot decide what to do. I am so

685

worried it is stopping me from sleeping. I have good reason to believe that a neighbour of mine killed a person close to her nearly twenty years ago. The person was her husband. I won't go into what made me think this after so long, but the new evidence I got made me remember certain suspicious things happening all that time ago. Her father-in-law died too and he was a healthy strong man, not old. My husband does not like the police and would be very upset I think if I had to explain all this to them, if we had police here questioning me etc. I cannot mention names here. It has taken months to screw myself up to write this. I would appreciate your advice . . ." ' He looked at Wexford. 'Did this Sandra Dale reply?'

'Oh, yes. She didn't print the letter, of course, or the reply. She wrote back very properly advising Margaret Carroll to come to us and lose no time in doing so. But Margaret Carroll didn't – too frightened of the husband, no doubt. And by then Gwen Robson had got hold of the letter through Lesley.'

Olson put in, 'But how did she know who Margaret Carroll meant by her "neighbour"?'

'She was a Kingsmarkham woman: she knew the area and knew Mrs Carroll only had one neighbour. I daresay she remembered Clifford from the Miss McPhail days. Anyway, she took herself down to Ash Farm and asked Dorothy Sanders for money – weekly payments if she liked, she didn't mind instalments – not to tell the police about the contents of the letter. By that time she was already successfully extracting payment from Nina Quincy, stashing it away for her husband's expensive op.

'She wasn't concerned with Margaret Carroll. It wouldn't have excited her interest if she had known that Margaret Carroll had disappeared soon after Dorothy Sanders made the first payment. Besides, it was in her interest to steer clear of Mrs Carroll who, had she dreamed of what was going on, probably would have been stirred into coming to us, would have saved her own life and killed one of the geese that laid golden eggs. Dorothy Sanders made no second payment. A second payment was asked for when Gwen Robson encountered her by chance in the Barringdean Centre that

Thursday afternoon, but Dodo saw to it that it was never paid.'

Burden objected. 'But look, didn't you say you saw her come into the car park as you were leaving it at ten-past six? Gwen Robson was dead by five-to.'

'I saw her come back a second time, Mike. She had been there before.'

'She went back?' Olson said. 'When she'd committed murder? Why didn't she just leave, go home, anything?'

'She's not like other people, is she? We've already agreed on that. She didn't have their responses, their reactions, their emotions. This is what I think happened, all we'll ever know now of what did happen. First of all, it was she that Linda Naseem saw from the back talking to Gwen Robson. She had a girl's figure, we've commented on that: she looked like a girl from the back, or when you couldn't see her face and hair. Either she went with Gwen Robson into the car park – arguing perhaps, threatening even, trying to make her change her mind – or else she followed her. I lean rather towards the alternative and think she followed. You see, by then – it wasn't yet five-thirty – she hadn't finished her shopping.

'So they entered the car park more or less together. While Gwen Robson was unlocking her car Dodo went up to her and garroted her with the circular knitting needle she had bought in the centre after she had had her hair done. Remember, we know she had been in there because she had bought the grey knitting wool she placed in the boot of her car. The job done, she returned to the centre.'

'But why? If she was going to report the death to us, why not do it then? Why not pretend, as she later did, that she'd discovered the body?'

'She had her shopping to finish, Mike. She only came to the centre once a week and she wasn't going to upset her routine. There was still her fish to buy and her groceries to get. Didn't I say we aren't dealing with an ordinary normal woman here? Dodo was special, Dodo was different. She had probably killed her father-in-law, she had already killed a husband, very likely with a knitting needle garrote, and a neighbour also by the same means. Maybe she even used the garrote afterwards to knit Clifford's sweaters. Waste not, want not! She went back to get the rest of her shopping done. It was not yet a quarter to six. Possibly she thought some other car driver would see the body, for the car park at that time would still have been half-full. However, no one did. Only Clifford did, coming in at six o'clock. He thought it was his mother, he thought the body was Mother Dodo. And he did a mad thing, a typically Clifford thing. He covered it up with a curtain from the boot of the car and then he ran away, pounding down the stairs as I was coming up in the lift, bursting out through the pedestrian gates for Archie Greaves to see.

'Dodo came back at ten-past-six, so that I was permitted a sight of her emerging from the covered way, and she entered the car park as she truthfully told us at precisely twelve minutes past. One useful thing only came out of my being here, my seeing her. She was carrying two bags of shopping but not the grey knitting wool, which is how I know she had been in the car park earlier. Did she expect to find a crowd there, even the police there? By the time I saw her, she must have realized that wasn't happening. Only one thing had happened – someone had covered it up. Who? A policeman? A car driver who had gone off to get help? What? One thing was clear; it wouldn't do for her just to do nothing. Her car was there but no Clifford. If he had been there perhaps they could just have driven off, taking no action. But he wasn't and she couldn't drive. Margaret Carroll wrote about her particular dilemma. Dodo's was worse. What was she to do?

'Wait. Think. What if the driver of the only other car on the second level turned up, the blue Lancia? Where was Clifford? Where was the man or woman who had covered up the body? At least she didn't realize at that time that it was her curtain which had been used – or rather a curtain from up in her attics. She went down by the stairs or in the lift, looking for Clifford, and that was the first time Archie Greaves saw her. The second time she was screaming and raving and shaking those gates. Her nerve had broken; it was all too much, the waiting and the knowing and . . . the silence.'

Olson nodded. He offered more tea, not seeming to notice the haste with which it was refused, then pushed his hands

688

through the dense bush of curly hair. 'I suppose there was no real motive for those early murders? She was a true psychopath? Because if we're looking for self-interest, it was surely in her interest to keep her husband alive?'

'Oh, there was a motive,' said Wexford. 'Revenge.'

'Revenge for what?'

'Mike can tell you the story. He knows it, Clifford told him. Clifford thought it romantic; he couldn't see through the veil his mother wore. Her life had been dedicated to an act of revenge against the people who said she she wasn't good enough for their son, and against the son who agreed with them.

'She was a multi-murderer who killed dispassionately but who was afraid of her victims after they were dead. She disinfected herself to be rid of their contamination and was frightened of their ghosts.'

Burden and Olson had begun a discussion on paranoia, on infantilism and transference, and Wexford listened to them for a moment or two, smiling to himself as Burden said, 'We live and learn.'

'We live at any rate,' said Wexford and he left them, walking the few hundred yards back to the police station when he got into his own car under the Christmas lights which were already winking away on the ash tree. There he sat and read about Sheila, read the statement she had made, her refusal to pay the fine demanded on conviction – her brave, foolhardy, defiant declaration that she would do it all again as soon as she came out.

'The Chief Constable rang,' Dora said as he came into the house. 'Darling, he wants to see you as soon as possible; he couldn't get you at the office. I suppose it's about this place.'

I don't suppose so for a moment, said Wexford but to himself, not aloud. He knew exactly what it would be about and felt the crackle of the evening paper in his raincoat pocket. For some reason, for no reason, he gave Dora a kiss and she looked a little surprised.

'I don't suppose I'll be long,' he said, knowing he would be.

Dusk, nearly dark, a little before five. His route to Middleton where the Chief Constable lived took him along his old road. It would be the first time he had been there since the

689

bomb and he knew he had consciously avoided it, but he didn't now. The sky was jewel-blue and windows along the street were full of Christmas lights. Bracing himself for the shock of devastation, he slowed as he came to the strip of open ground, the empty site. He braked, pulled in and looked.

Three men were coming out of the gate, up to a van with ladders on its roof. He saw the contractors' board, the stack of bricks, the concrete-mixer covered up against the frost. He got out and stood looking, smiled to himself.

They had begun to rebuild his house.